LORDS OF
RUIN

ALSO BY E.M. WILLETT

GODS OF LEGEND, BOOK 1, DEAD BLOOD VOLUME I

HEIRS OF ETERNITY, BOOK 3, DEAD BLOOD VOLUME I

Lords of Ruin

Book 2
Dead Blood Volume I

E.M. Willett

Title: LORDS OF RUIN
Author: E.M. Willett
Copyright ©2025 by E.M. Willett
All rights reserved.

ISBN:
eBook ISBN: 978-1-969649-59-2
Paperback ISBN: 978-1-969649-97-4
Hardcover ISBN: 978-1-969649-96-7
Published by Pine Tree Press

www.pinetreepress.com
Printed in USA

DEDICATION

For those who stare into the dark
and refuse to look away.

CONTENTS

ACKNOWLEDGMENTS

To my younger self, for pursuing a dream. To my family, for their unwavering support. To you, dear reader, for entering the Kingdom of Vanguards.

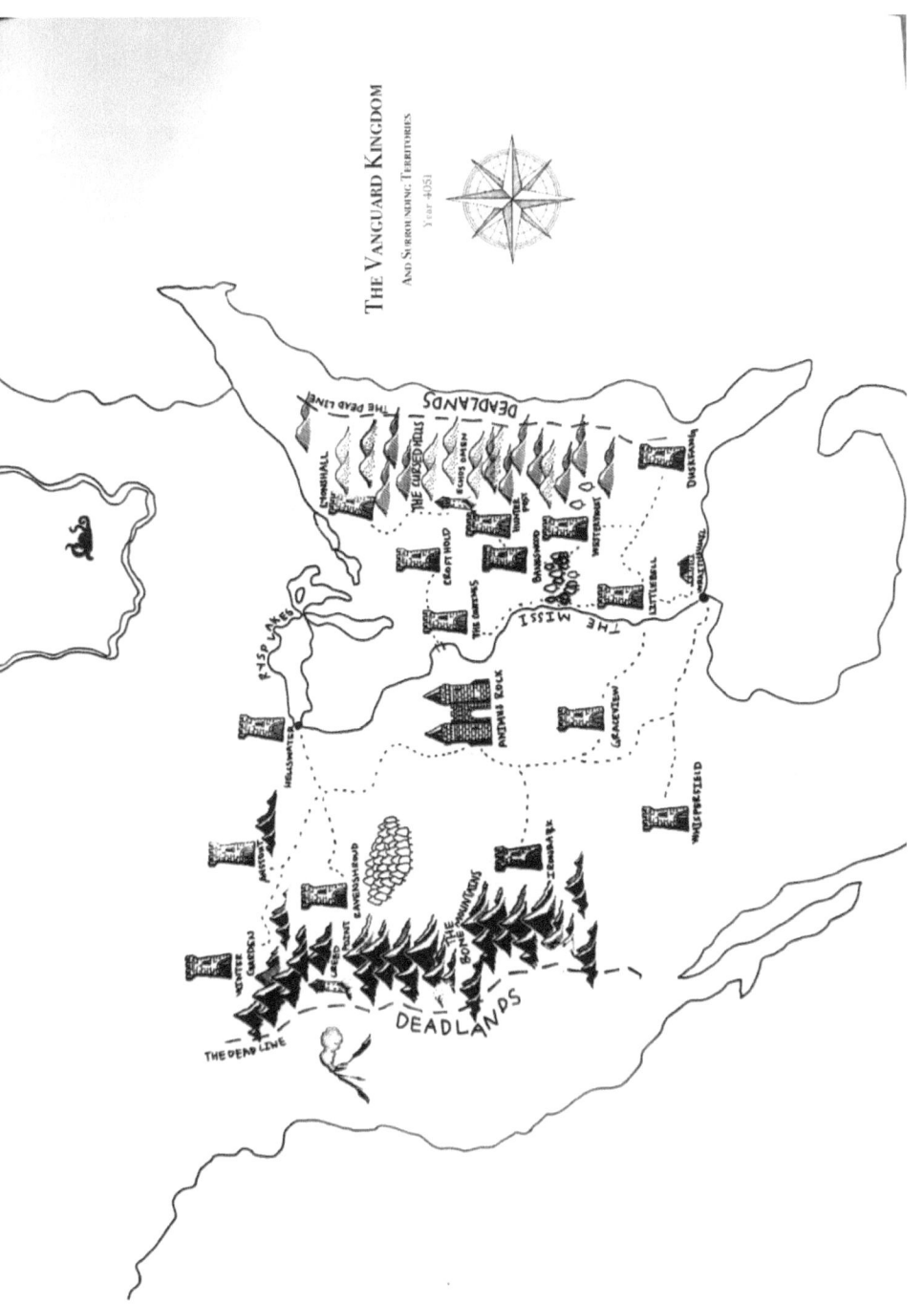

THE VANGUARD KINGDOM

AND SURROUNDING TERRITORIES

Year 4051

DEADLANDS

THE DEAD LINE

ENNISHALL

THE CURSED HILLS

KINGS BARROW

DUSKFANG

GREY HOLD

HUNTER'S REST

WINTERHEART

DARKSWORD

LITTLEHALL

FISP LANES

THE DEAD LINE

HEADSWATER

THE SHALLOWS

THE MISSI

GRACEVIEW

ARENNI ROCK

WHISPERSTEAD

WINTER GARDEN

RAVENSHEAD

THE OMINOUS

BLOOD WOODS

TIMMARK

DEADLANDS

THE DEAD LINE

TIMELINE

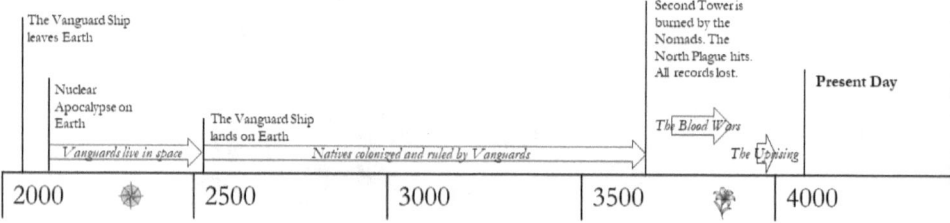

BOOK 2

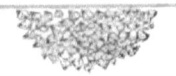

ANIMUS ROCK, EDEN

About 100 years ago...

"I don't understand why mother waited until now to send me to Animus Rock," Lilli said with an indignant huff, "as I am to be elderclaim. It doesn't seem right to keep me apart from the Kingdom that I'm meant to lead someday."

"Yes," Amos echoed absentmindedly. "Surely, Lilli," he said, "but Mother just wants what is best for you." He paused and swallowed hard. "We all do."

Lilli paused her lively gait and turned to look at her older brother, widening her turquoise blue eyes, reminiscent of a twilight sky. "How can anyone know what is best for me but me?" she asked him pointedly.

Amos blinked back at her, not having a good answer. *No one knows what's best*, he thought to himself.

Outwardly, Amos Minney shrugged.

It was nearing the end of Spring Equinox, nearly time to pack the carriages and return to Littlebell. This was the first equinox that Lilli was permitted out of their blood realm, as her eighteenth year was fast approaching. Despite their father's concerns and Amos's contesting pleas, Sia Minney demanded that her charmed daughter be sent to Animus Rock for some of the traditional Vanguard schooling. Amos agreed to bring the girl for a quarter of a moon only, to give her a taste of what she was to inherit, and to interact with the other bloodlines, under supervision, of course. Sia was staunchly New and scarred from the horrors of the Blood Wars, so she was particularly careful. But since her trusted eldest son Amos was going to be with the girl, she put her worries aside.

Amos gazed down at his comely sister where they'd paused

in Eden's maze aside white-blanketed evergreens and a snowdrift. Tiny magical flakes nestled in her pale braided hair and melted on her ebony skin. He was glad for the girl's beauty because it distracted from her genius. He was sure Lilli was much smarter than he was and although he would never admit it to himself, Amos knew deep down she would be a better leader for Littlebell's realm than he.

Still, he was stalwart in the plans he'd set into motion so many years ago.

Lilli seemed to accept Amos's non-answer and fell back into a lively pace again, nearly skipping through the banks of snow accumulating on this section of the path. She was used to her older brother's quiet ways. Her intricately patterned gown, mimicking white lilli flowers, her favorite, made a smoothing path overtop of the snow. Overhead, snow churned beneath the true sky of blinding white clouds atop of bright blue sky. Amos glanced upwards and briefly appreciated the magical secrets of his long-ago Vanguard ancestors - the ones he was intending to honor by taking back his birth right.

Amos cleared his throat. Lilli noticed with a glance over her shoulder. "I have some men to introduce you to," he said to answer her gaze. "Old companions from my time at Academy."

"Vanguards?" Lilli asked with deep curiosity. "Oldblood Vanguards?" she added, slowing her pace, creeping grin growing up both cheeks.

It made Amos's deception all the easier that his sister was intrigued by what wasn't permitted. Since childhood, if you told her she couldn't have something, the girl demanded it instantly. She always wanted what she couldn't have.

Amos nodded. "Yes," he told his little sister. "Oldblood Vanguards. Norland and Brochet."

Lilli's pale eyebrows lifted high then she squinted her brilliant almond shaped eyes. "Bin and Lucien?" she asked.

Amos nodded again. "Yes, they are old *companions* of mine," he said carefully.

"Mother would never allow it," Lilli said to Amos with a

mischievous smile. "I'm to have nothing to do with Old blood."

A third time, Amos nodded. "Yes." He paused. "But mother doesn't need to know."

Lilli's heart nearly burst from excitement and gratitude. She has always wanted to meet the other kind of Vanguards and now was her chance. "Thank you, brother!" she squealed as she leapt forward, throwing her arms around her stoic kin.

At her affectionate touch, Amos balked slightly, cringing deep down at her inherent warmth and trust.

"This way," he said in little more than a grunt after enduring the hug. The teen-years girl happily obliged and almost skipped from glee behind him, following Amos out into the Vanguard Tree field.

The enormous oak in the center of the maze towered over Lilli and Amos as they exited one of Eden's paths and walked into the flowering meadow, just recently bloomed as it was just now Springtime in the Kingdom. Overhead, the magical clouds broke and the true sky of fluffy white over top of blue was all that could be seen.

Amos headed to an outcropping of large boulders on the side of the field where his long ago sworn allies Bin Norland and Lucien Brochet stood, conferring after the previous day's Council session. Amos had not been permitted to attend, on Sia's orders. He was commanded to watch over Lilli instead.

Amos's resentment was layered so thick that, at this point, he didn't know who he was without it. Hate defined him.

"Why if it isn't *Lord* Amos," Bin said with a scathing smile and teasing inflection upon noticing Amos and Lilli approaching.

Then Bin realized instantly who the gorgeous young woman with the Minney was. She *is* real, he thought, heart dropping into his stomach with a thud. He hadn't fully believed the tale despite Brochet's assurances so many years ago. He'd heard rumors too of late, but what smart man believes rumors? Bin considered himself the type of man who needed to see and touch a thing to believe in it for himself.

Lucien Brochet stood back a bit, leaning with his accentuated white cape's shoulder against the rocks, watching Amos and Lilli approach with knowing eyes. A mischievous smile stole across his lips when they were only a few paces away. He folded his arms.

Lucien and Bin both were now nearly forty years old and their faces showed their age in wrinkled lines, mostly around their eyes.

"Lord Norland, Lord Brochet," Amos addressed each of the oldbloods as he approached with a dutiful bow of his head. "It's good to greet you."

"Aye," Bin grunted distantly, unable to take his eyes off the blue-eye, completely spellbound.

"It is good to greet you," Lucien replied customarily with impeccable diction and a slight nod.

Lilli's gaze widened as she approached. She'd heard about oldblood skin was but wasn't ready for how pale they appeared in the sunlight, particularly in comparison to her skin's coal-hue. Both men were exceedingly tall for what she was used to and both had full heads of hair, where most Littlebell native men lost theirs around the time they were that age. She felt a jolt of excitement run up and down her spine at the way they looked at her, particularly the one with the block jaw and black eyes. Lilli was used to men stumbling over themselves for her yet never had she experienced how it felt to control one so powerful. How it felt to be with another Vanguard. How forbidden. The idea was enticing. She caught the black-eyed man's gaze briefly, then bit her lip and looked away smiling.

Bin Norland blushed.

"Yes," Amos responded to Lucien's greeting curtly, "and you as well." He cleared his throat. "This here is my sister Lilli." He bit his lip to reveal a deep dimple, thrusting Lilli forward with a gentle nudge of his hand. She took a few steps then brazenly tilted her round face to gaze up at the taller men.

Lucien and Bin both had expected the girl to be meek and timid, as all Minney women were rumoured to be, but this girl was brimming intensity. Not only was she beautiful but the slight girl was extraordinarily imposing. Lilli stood with a straight back and unwavering eyes that pierced the unsuspecting oldblood men with calculated calm.

"I am Lilli Minney," the girl said with resound. "Littlebell elderclaim," she added confidently, pride bubbling in her chest.

"Is that so?" Lucien said coyly, eyes briefly flashing to glance at Amos. He looked away. "I am pleased to greet you, truly," Lucien added with feigned sincerity, an ever-present Brochet trait. "To see you with my own eyes is, well, my Lady, it is a miracle. You are as lovely as the rumors say."

"You are," Bin barked blindly without thinking. Lucien raised a sharp eyebrow his way and half frowned.

"We are to leave for Littlebell shortly," Amos said, knowingly meeting Lucien's eyes. The elderclaim ceremony was only in a handful of moons, he thought. Hardly any time for the oldblood boys to make good on their promise. "Lord Brochet," he said with emphasis and raised eyebrows. He was tired of waiting for something to happen. He had waited almost eighteen years. "A word."

Lucien nodded and pushed himself from his leaning rest aside the rocks. The pair strolled further into the center of the field, through blossoming grass, to rest underneath the Vanguard Tree as they conferred.

"Have you forgotten?" Amos asked angrily once he and Lucien Brochet were far out of Lilli's earshot. "Or do you simply want to torture me?"

Lucien raised his eyebrows slowly. "I am shocked you approach me in such a way. Afterall," he added, "we have an accord. Do you not trust?" He flashed a mischievous smile.

"But Brochet," Amos argued, "when will it happen? She is going around announcing herself as elderclaim, in front of my own face, I may add!" Amos felt his blood sizzling beneath his veins. He felt his head may burst. "It is the highest insult." He paused, nearly too dizzy from anger to speak. He'd waited patiently, feeling this way, for eighteen years. The time for action had come. "Something must be done before the ceremony," he said.

Lucien's mood fouled. "You do not command me, Minney cunt," he said in a scathing growl. "Even if I help you, if I'm kind enough to bestow elderclaim on you, you never have the right to address me in such a way. Do you not know who I am?"

"Brochet," Amos lowered his voice to a whisper. "I seek your help *because* of who you are."

At that Lucien broke again into his characteristic smile, placated for the time being. "I had spared you the details up until now, Lord Amos, thinking I was doing you a kindness. Don't twist your mind in a knot with worry. The deed will be done. Do not think I have forgotten. You know Brochet never forgets."

"I know," Amos said quickly. "It's just that…"

"You don't know," Lucien interrupted, sharp black eyebrow raising above one hazel eye. "Or else you would never have questioned me. My word eighteen years ago should have sufficed."

"Yes," Amos said, wanting to argue, yet ashamed, instead fell silent.

Lucien felt a shadow of pity for the man. He understood a bit about ambition and dreams above one's station. "I have it on good accord the girl has a favorite grove at the edge of your realm. Truth?" he tiled his head to the side, jostling his thick hair. Lucien rested his hand up against the time-weathered bark of the Vanguard tree, feeling her knots and grooves.

Amos nodded. "Yes," he said, thinking of the stories Lilli had told him about her beloved trees. She spent hours, sometimes days with them writing and singing ballads. In Littlebell, she'd gained a reputation as a talented bard. "Yet she is protected when she goes."

Lucien snorted. "By Morfit guard alone."

He was right, Amos thought, nodding slightly. How did Brochet always know *everything*? "Yes, just a Morfit Guard. But still they are well trained," Amos added, feeling a hint of defensiveness and blood pride.

Lucien chuckled, laughing in a way that made Amos feel very

small. "Not well trained compared to Westerviolet Guardsmen," he said, but Amos only shrugged.

"What is the plan then?" Amos straightened his back. "To take her from the grove?" It was hard to say the words, harder than Amos had realized it would be, although he'd fantasised about it happening over and over since her birth. He tried swallowing but a lump caught in his throat. Amos shrugged his feelings aside.

Lucien nodded. "Aye." He paused to feel crisp Spring wind rustle his hair. "It'll be as if she disappeared."

Meanwhile, Lilli was left alone with Bin. She looked up at him with wide eyes, like the child she was, never having seen any part of the Kingdom besides Littlebell. Never having been with a man. Bin gazed down at the blue-eye as if she was Emihir herself. He was awe-struck by her beauty and more-so by her command and poise.

"You're Norlandblood, huh?" Lilli asked Bin brashly, studying him as if he were a cow for the slaughter. No one had ever looked at him like that before. "You don't seem evil to me," she finally said, then flashed a deep dimpled grin. Her turquoise eyes sparkled in the bright sunlight.

Bin stood a bit straighter, yet his chest felt hot. His pale cheeks flushed. The girl's beauty was overwhelming. Her wit more-so. Everything about her ensnared him.

Despite himself, Bin Norland was in love.

ANIMUS ROCK

Present Day

Animus Rock was a massive stronghold placed along the winding Missi River, about halfway from Wraithswail to Hellswater. Sloping meadows and patchwork farmland outstretched both flat horizons, bottoming out in the Missi's river basin until lapping up against Animus Rock's fortress wall. Eight luxurious stone towers with octagon faces–atop the castle herself an octagon with eight sides–shot into the sky from the top of a high piled motte in the very center of the city. Ravens nested amongst stone statues in overwhelming multitude. The birds' bodies appeared tiny from great distance and together looked like pulsing black clouds over it all.

Sybil and Rose arrived late to the Fall Equinox Ball, a yearly celebration marking the beginning of that season's Council session. There were large balls in the fall and the spring, as well as to commemorate the Summer Solstice, with Winter Solstice reserved for Vanguard Day celebrations.

Sybil wore an intricately crafted gown in her bloodline's signature color, tight to her bust but flounced out at her waist, in mimic of the gowns of old she saw displayed in the East Tower. She'd had it custom sewn by a native brought in from Ironbark exactly for that purpose. Her hair was piled high on her head, stuck with gem pins, and the ouburous hung between her breasts. Her lips were rubbed in berry balm and her eyes, dark and biting, were unlined. Rose was in a similar dress with a much higher bodice and no flouncing. Her dress fell flatly to her well crafted boots. Her hair, like Sybil's was knotted on her head in an intricate fashion and stuck with gem pins. She felt ridiculous and uncomfortable, wishing she could let it free, but

Sybil demanded she adorn herself properly for such a formal event. Rose obliged.

When they arrived, Sybil hung back along the stone railing overlooking the large ballroom's activity. She swallowed hard, realizing her gown was entirely out of fashion. She had expected to stand out, but not so drastically. Now, the high native women of Animus Rock and most of the Vanguard women as well, oldblood or new, wore draped gowns with mostly high necks, and their hair cropped short to their chins. On their ears, endless baubles and gems hung, clanging as they turned their heads. Sybil eyed them all with distain, wishing it was an earlier time, before natives were allowed to attend such extravagant festivities. *How far we have fallen*, she thought.

Most of the newblood Vanguards hung by the large windows reaching over the ballroom, aside iron candelabras sparkling with yellow light. Most of the oldblood Vanguards gravitated towards the Tourmaline Throne–a massive block of black stone carved into a seat, where the King of the Vanguards typically rested. But that eve, Humphry Bellamine was notably absent. Sybil didn't know him. He was younger than she and only reached Academy once she was already back at Westerviolet, married to Rosen, then pregnant with Rose. But she had not heard good things about him. She did see, however, his sister Verity with her husband Herman Graves, dancing.

When Sybil had taken stock of all below her, she descended the large staircase that spilled the balcony onto the dance floor. It was as if time paused. The music even stopped. All turned to look at her, some whispering, others gasping at her arrival. She felt herself buzzing, internally screaming with glee, outwardly aloof and calm.

She greeted her old friends and was cordial to those of other bloodlines, all the while brimming with excitement. Several Norlands attempted to dance with her and she refused. Several Thornes attempted to fetch Animus wine for her and she declined. A few eligible Busk men began to approach her but she turned her nose up at them, as any respectable Vanguard woman would do. She looked for her old friend Rupert, and Hector Graves, but she did not see either.

The oldblood women fluttered around her, asking her about Westerviolet, her late husband and her plans for Council. Some newblood women, like Galla Morfit, glared at her meanly from the side of the ballroom, although she waved and smiled politely. She was still who she had always been. The center of society. In control of it all. Sybil Brochet.

While staying at Animus Rock, Rose and Sybil occupied one of eleven villas overlooking the Missi in the east of the city.

Each villa's high, arched entryway faced Animus's impressive towers on one side and the Missi on the other. Each villa was a small empire in and of itself, abuzz with life, requiring countless native hands to operate. Each structure was four stories high, constructed of yellow stone. Each was decorated differently, to suit each respective bloodline's sensibilities and style.

Inside Thorne's Villa, the ceilings were high with the walls painted thick coats of plaster in whites and creams. Gauzy curtains blew through open air doorways. The floors were polished grey stone. Inside was pristine and alluring, with unusual potted plants at every corner, yet felt inexplicably impersonal and cold. Not unlike Thorneblood. On the balcony of each level was a garden, allegedly reminiscent of Graceview herself, and from the river-facing side it appeared that an exotic forest sprouted from the murky waters of the Missi.

Sybil and Rose had a breath-taking view of the sunrise over the Confines from where they sat on the highest veranda, atop iron chairs topped with ruby cushions. The pair drank from sweating goblets and the tart lemon aroma of their homeland drink floated through the hot, late-summer air. The breeze blew ripples across the wide muddy river, cut by various fishing vessels and wide barges.

"Ice." Sybil sloshed the contents of her cool drink back and forth. "It's how you know you're somewhere of note, Rose. If they give you Winter Garden ice."

Rose nodded, sighing silently to herself. She squinted from the rising dawn, then glanced down to Ellie, snoozing at her feet.

Sybil initially forbade the dog from making the journey to Animus Rock but had a change of heart when she saw Rose's heartbroken face. Even she, for all her cold ways, couldn't take her child's only friend. Even if it was just a lowly hound. She couldn't understand the girl's connection to the animal, but she didn't have to. If the dog's presence kept Rose placated and calm, dutifully learning her lessons like an oldblood Vanguard should, then so be it, she'd thought.

"We've made it, Rose." Sybil said, taking a sip. "Nearly," she added with a wistful sigh and a quick glance to Animus Rock castle's Eighth Tower. Only the King and Queen, and their children, were allowed inside.

After Rosen's death she'd decided on a new ambition. If she couldn't have love, she wanted power. She wanted to reach the highest tower. She wanted to be Queen.

"Did you see Aftea Regnard's hair at the ball yesterday? Tousled about her face like a sand-blown hive. She went on and on and on about her daughter's delicate condition, as if everyone didn't know. Yes, they found a good earthblood to marry her to, I expected nothing less. Her being an earthblood and her reformed husband of hers can preach all they want, but mark my words, that baby is Edgar's," Sybil said in a scandalous whisper, "but, he's off at Wraithswail training. How convenient, especially for Herman."

Rose didn't respond. She hated gossip. But, oh, how her mother loved it.

"Her hair! Did you see how thin? I swear, I spotted horse mane! The scandal. Gachan Regnard's wife, balding!" Sybil laughed, taking a sip of her cold drink. "Mine doesn't look like that does it?" she asked Rose quickly, voice lowering slightly, adjusting her shiny raven mane over one shoulder.

"No. You have nice hair, Mother."

"Are you sure? You would tell me, wouldn't you?"

"Yes, Mother."

"Oh, you will never believe what happened to the Morfits! You know Lady Faye?"

Sybil blathered on as Rose pretended to listen, holding her drink, taking a slow sip, watching cawing birds with black beaks diving in search of their first meals of the day in the lazy brown Missi. Rose had never seen such strange types of fowl before, or such a large body of water. She looked upon the new scenery with wonderment.

"I heard the news last eve," Sybil said. "Both old Morfits losing it in their late years."

"That is sad," Rose replied, half listening, studying the foreign activity on the river below. She'd never seen a river before, only a mote. She imagined all how many people went up and down that river every day. Everything that lived in that river. All the animals that drank from it. How alive that river was. Part of her wished she could jump on a barge and explore it for herself. Or dive in and swim away from her mother.

"Not all!"

"Not all what?" Rose asked, concentration broken, turning to look at Sybil with a slight frown.

"Old Goodman Morfit decided to take his senile wife on a carriage ride, unaccompanied."

Rose knew it was improper for Vanguards, especially elderly ones, to travel unattended. "How far?"

"Days from Croft, I hear."

That surely sounded like something one shouldn't do. "Really?"

"He did!" Sybil said, lifting both sharp eyebrows emphatically high. "He may be the oldest in the Kingdom, after Hjalmar, and your grandfather, of course," she added. "But still, Goodman readied a cart and horse all alone. Faye is furious at the earthblood for not stopping him. Furious! Rupert more-so I'd imagine, I haven't spoken to him of it yet. He was not there last eve. I'd be surprised if they haven't already been sent to the pyre. I don't blame either of them. Those earthblood should have done something. Those earthblood should have stopped them."

"What happened?"

"Faye said they found a horse and cart missing. Searched the castle and the grounds and found no sign."

"Where'd they go?"

"No one knows," Sybil said cryptically, taking a sip from her glass as the rising sun cast her pale skin in an ethereal glow. Rose listened, concern for the old Morfits mounting despite having never met them. "They didn't leave a note nor tell an earthblood," Sybil explained. "The search went on and on. Faye said it was terrible. After four days, they were discovered in a thicket off an abandoned path, stuck in the mud. Calla was dead in the cart, like she'd starved, the invalid she was. Goodman dead next to it, as if he'd tried to go for help and fell and hit his head."

Rose gasped, face cast in gold and magenta streaks from the dawn.

"Awful," Sybil said carelessly. "How could Rupert let that happen?" she whispered, almost to herself, glancing to the side. She knew Rupert Morfit to be far more calculating. He'd never permit such an accident befall his elder. Suspicion bubbled in her chest, but she suppressed it for analysis later.

The sounds from the river played in the background as a cart barrelled and bumped over the stone road out front. Bees flew amidst the fruit trees over Rose's shoulder. Sybil snapped from her pensive lull as quickly as she'd drifted into it.

"What do you know about the Morfits?"

"You just said their castle."

"Tell me, then."

"Croft?" Rose asked, squinting her eyes from the sun.

"Say it with conviction, my sweet."

"Croft," Rose said firmly.

"Good. The proper name is Croft Hold. But close. What's their emblem?"

"I don't know."

"Think."

"Mother..."

"Try."

"I haven't learned it!"

"It's the Lady of Justice."

"What's that?"

"She's like this," Sybil demonstrated with her hand, sitting up a bit straighter in her chair, "weighing what is right and wrong. The Morfits are all about what is fair, except they change the meaning to suit their whims. Be careful about their children," she added, lowering her hands, sinking back in her iron chair. "They may be tattletales. I remember how Rupert was when we were young." Sybil took another drink, remembering the time he told the Lessonmaster that she was running in the corridors. How his eyes lit up as she was berated. That was when she decided she hated him. "Look at this great city. It's amazing what our Vanguard Ancestors did," she added gesturing up. "Do you know why it's called 'Animus Rock'?"

"No, Mother."

"It's named after the center of the mind. The *Animus*."

"Really?" Rose's eyes widened. Finally, her mother had something interesting to say.

Sybil nodded. "Oh yes," she said surely. "First built as an enormous library and the seat of power for the Ancestors. Each tower for different grand purpose. And back then, the fortress wall didn't exist."

"You mean the big one when we came in?"

"Yes, that one," she said, dark hair glinting in the rising sun as she nodded. "Back then, it was simply the castle and hailed as the center of the Kingdom and the fulcrum of all knowledge and learning left in the world. It was the second of the great bloodline castles constructed after the very first Vanguards came."

"When did they build the wall?"

"More than two hundred years ago."

"Why?"

"The Nomads."

"What happened?"

Sybil sipped her drink, furrowing her brow in a creased line briefly. "The Nomads invaded, but were no match for us," she said. "We defeated them. Yet they did considerable damage. It prompted our people to think about security. They built that monstrosity," she said and pointed at the wall. "It's overkill if you ask me, but it is impressive." She bowed her head slightly. "I will give the Ancestors that."

The Animus Rock fortress wall towered so high that it cast a shadow across the entire river and valley around, and nearly over Rose and Sybil themselves. Fortunately, the Villas were built in line with the eastern lip of the wall facing the river, bottom half fully fortified, top open in balconies looking out to the river below. Gazing to either side revealed the massive grandeur of the wall, as if it was constricting the mighty Animus Rock city from all sides, consuming whatever lie within, instead of its intended purpose of keeping things out and away.

Rose felt the sun on her face and listened to the chatter of birds, stomach knotting with pending excitement for her first day.

"Tomorrow," Sybil said, "be prepared for anything. Who knows what these children's parents have told them of you. Always remember, you are a proud Brochet. Full of honor. We are eternal. We need not stoop to their level. Never reveal your thoughts. Never let them see you sweat. Do you understand?"

"Yes, Mother," Rose said quickly, brows pinching to match her mother's expression.

"Good," Sybil sipped her drink slowly, thinking briefly about her first day of Academy so many years ago, looking out over the river. How, right after entering the lesson room, she was teased by Tamasyn Warn. The whole lesson, Sybil plotted against the girl, wanted to poison her food, or smash her stupid gem band, but then fortune favoured her. Right after the lesson, when the children were mingling in Eden, Tamasyn tripped and fell face first into the dirt. Sybil stood smugly as everyone laughed.

"I hear there are twin Warn boys around your age," Sybil said. "I'm sure they are trouble."

"Why, mother?"

"The Warns are heathens, dear. They have wild customs and barbaric, earthblood-infested traditions."

She thought about their ridiculous scars and long, scraggly hair. And, of course, their wild green eyes that looked like a Guardsman's dagger in the light and cut just as sharply when they were enraged. They would certainly be fearsome to face in a battle, Sybil thought. No wonder they earned so much coin for it.

"What's that mean?"

"The Warns have a strange tale," Sybil told Rose. "Once a storied old bloodline, they were great fighters and even held a satellite Warman training facility at Ironbark."

"Where's Ironbark?"

"West. At the edge of the Bone Mountains."

"Near Creed Point?"

"Good girl, close," Sybil praised, white-dazzling smiling. "Near it, although much further south." She gestured in that direction with her unencumbered hand, dark gown's sleeve flapping in the early breeze. "The Warns held Ironbark for the Old for years, then the Plague hit. Every single Warn, and Calvanese and Duran died during the Plague, except for Erik Warn. The youngest of the brood. He was only a boy and left alone at Ironbark, taken under the care of surviving fighters in training at the camp. These trainees rebelled from the way of the Warmen and against the Kingdom. They convinced young Erik to change his bloodline's objectives."

"How?" Rose asked.

"To be mercenaries." Rose scrunched her face. "That means they get paid to fight in wars," Sybil explained simply, at Rose's expression. "Erik Warn betrayed the Old when he married the earthblood daughter of one of the fighters who raised him. Remember what Grandfather and I told you of the Blood Wars? Erik was instrumental. He agreed to fight for the New against the Old, accepting payment from Demos and Morfit.

With Old bloodlines Duran and Calvanese dead, this gave the New a strategic position West of the river. It nearly bested us. Nearly," Sybil repeated for emphasis, taking another lemon-scented sip. "But we had the Norlands on our side. You'll meet Xoana's girl, I'm sure."

"Who's that?"

"Evia," Sybil said. "The youngest of Hadrian Norland's horde. I'd imagine she is tough. All those brothers. You'll know her by her pale skin and paler hair. She will certainly be ugly, being Xoana's," Sybil snorted, "but one cannot fault her for that. She did not choose that swine of a mother." Rose nodded and a breeze rustled her wide curls. "I hear there is a Demos this year too," Sybil added. "A girl. Malla. Like her grandmother's name, Mallia," she added, chuckling. "Poor old Antca, so jealous of her younger sister always. They were both much, much older than I, but the animosity was still palpable between the Demos girls all those years ago. It's true Antca is homely, and she shouldn't have done what she did. But still, I pity the creature. Ugly woman."

"What did she do?" Rose was having trouble following. These Vanguard stories were more confusing than any lesson she'd ever had in Westerviolet. It amazed her how her mother spoke of the interweaving threads as if they were clearly written on parchment.

Sybil took another sip of her drink, crossing her legs at the ankle. "I was quite young," she explained. "This was years ago. Antca Demos was unwed, wilting in her middle years, while her much younger sister Mallia was blooming. Antca was jealous of the attention her sister got from suitors, while Antca herself, the elder heir to the Demos fortune and bloodline, was unwed. Antca grew to despise her New family. Her mother, in particular."

"Why her mother?"

"Because her mother favored her sister," Sybil said obviously. "The girls had different earthblood fathers too. Antca's father was killed at the start of the Uprising and her mother remarried after, later giving birth to Mallia."

Rose nodded, beginning to understand.

"Antca Demos fell in line with Thorne, in fact," Sybil added scandalously. "She married Dugland Thorne against her mother's wishes. Their son is Ivor, nearly my age, just a bit older, and magistrate. No children. But, back to Antca. Her story is tragic because, on her escape from Hellswater to Graceview to be with Dugland, she murdered her own mother in spite."

"No!"

"She did," Sybil said, nodding, forcing down the sick smile she couldn't help but feel growing. Oftentimes, Sybil's emotions didn't come out correctly. She'd cry when she was happy and laugh when she felt horrified. She wasn't sure why.

"No one knows if it was out of passion or planned," she explained. "Antca stabbed her mother straight through her heart, then ran off with Dugland to Graceview in the far South where she was out of reach of retribution, since Thorne would not turn her over."

Throne was a very secretive bloodline. Hardly anything was known about them. One would call them obstinate, if not for their charm.

"The act was further catalyst for our Kingdom's political churn. Nothing is ever caused by just one thing, Rose," Sybil added, dark eyes flashing. "At Academy they may say that the Uprising began after Haulfrun Graves murdered his son's new bride, or they may say it was caused by Bin Norland's capture of Lilli Minney," she emphatically said, "or both. It's also possible it was a plot by Oliver Demos and Adrian Morfit to open lines of trade. That would surprise me least. War is good for business." She paused. "Anyway, I hear Mallia's granddaughter is just as lovely as all the Demos women are supposed to be. They are merchants and water people. Sweet talkers and swindlers. Low-bred gamblers. You should avoid the girl all together."

Demos were known to be very beautiful–in a bare type of way–unreasonably enigmatic and had addictive personalities, with a propensity for games of chance. That's largely why the best gambling was in Hellswater's realm.

Rose sighed.

"I'd avoid any Regnard children if I were you as well," Sybil added callously. "Hard to tell nowadays whether they're Old or New. They have pinched faces, brash voices, and sour dispositions. Ugly women. You can't miss them." Sybil took a sip.

The Regnard bloodline was ideologically split, therefore, the blood was muddled. This meant that the stereotypes of old applied less and less with each generation. True, in the past Regnards, particularly the women, were homely, but in the present day, that was not always the case. However, Sybil was biased. She was basing the majority of her assessment of Regnard on Xoana. And Sybil hated Xoana.

"Beware of any Thornes. You can't trust them. Beautiful, enchanting even, but avoid them. They are not worth their wiles and tricks."

The Thorne bloodline was mostly oldblood and the most mysterious of the bloodlines still living. Very little was known about them, even by the other Vanguards, and this added to their allure. It didn't hurt that they were icily attractive, usually with white blonde hair, cold stares and sharp cheekbones.

"Oh, and don't get me started on Busk! Just speaking to one may rub their stink off on you. Disgusting blood, Busk."

The Busk bloodline descended from the most lowly of Vanguards in ancient times and the other bloodlines in present day treated them like it. They were given the worst land, worst castle and, in the early days, the worst natives to experiment on. Because of that, natives from the Confines were known to be quite dull. The Busk Vanguards, whether truth or not, were thought to be as well.

"Is there anyone I can be real friends with?" Rose asked.

Sybil furrowed her brow. She took another sip. She thought to herself, *real friends do not exist.*

LITTLEBELL

A tiny bell rang overhead as Digory pushed through the yellow keyhole door, knob shaped like a pyramid, into Littlebell's Apothecary.

His eyes quickly adjusted to the low light. He sniffed the air. It was as if it had just rained, but the sun was shining outside. And indeed, petrichor-scented candles burned in two neat rows atop a wide mantel over a brick fireplace. A long examining table, lower than typical, was his focal point on entry. Refined instruments sat on a squat table aside it, also in the middle of the room. There was not a speck of dust on the surely waxed, buffed wooden floor. Far different from the Apothecary Digory was accustomed to in Westerviolet. Much neater, and cleaner. This Apothecary was kept with fastidious pride.

To his left was a fully lined wall of ancient books, arranged by color of binding, secured with ink-black geodes to hold them in place. Aside that was a wooden table covered in a pale-yellow cloth, piled with ancient books and scrolls either stacked or open and place-marked next to an assortment of parchments, a white-feathered quill, and a tiny ink vial. A four-tiered shelf loomed in the far corner like a hiding shadow. Competing vials of various sizes, shapes, colors, and opacities hung in its racks. Digory could only imagine the tinctures and potions contained within.

The air was thick and the incense hung low like fog above the slat wood floor. Digory took a deep breath and scratched his beard. He exhaled a smile while his boots kicked through the cloudy mist as he entered.

A round, old woman draped in patterned white and blue robes turned from where she stood organizing parchments and scrolls.

"What is it, child?" she asked him gently.

Digory gestured with his bandaged shoulder. "I'm injured."

Her alert expression softened. "Here, here," she shuffled over. Her skirts, covered in designs of miniature flying birds, twirled around her like white clouds against the sky in wind. She patted a wrinkled hand with many gemstone rings on the heavy examining table. It banged loudly.

"Sit."

Digory obeyed, dropping his satchel to the floor, impulsively cradling the arm of his damaged side. "What should I call you?" he asked as he studied the woman's leathered skin while she fussed with his dressings. She smelled of the earth, like fields of wheat and corn mixed with tobacco drying in an old barn's rafters. It was comforting merely being in her presence.

"I am given many names," she said, glancing up to meet his gaze briefly, "but please, Laila will do." She glanced back down at the neat bandages as she gently unravelled them.

"I've never seen eyes that color before, Lady," he said pointedly, noting her stare to match the blue in her skirts, realizing what it must mean. Realizing who she must be.

"Laila," she corrected him, smiling, dark, diaphanous skin crinkling aside her eyes and lips. She turned to fetch an implement. "Let's give this a look." She cut away the crusted cloths wrapped around Digory's shoulder and wound. They were dried and he winced as they were torn away. Digory's eyes widened as Laila poked at his wound. "You should have come sooner," her ancient voice chided.

"I came as fast as I could."

"No, no," she shook her head, intricate grey braid swaying across her back slowly. Digory shot his head up. "This happened many days ago, child." Laila met his befuddled, wide-set eyes. "Possibly a moon."

"Are you mad?" Digory broke into his brilliantly handsome smile. "It happened not two days ago!" He scratched his beard in disbelief.

She smiled warmly, poking the pink wound. "I say it's

healed."

Digory frowned as he felt it with his hand. Sure enough, tender new skin edged a caked black scab. The wound *was* healed far beyond anything possible in a day and a half. Laila continued, shuffling away from him, stitched booties sticking out beneath her sky-colored skirts.

Digory wondered silently about this strange Vanguard. Was she really who he thought she was?

"I'll apply a salve that will heal it further," Laila said over her shoulder as she headed to the far corner of the hazy room.

"I don't have coin to pay you," Digory said bluntly. Beneath the surface, his mind bubbled in thought. She couldn't be who he thought she was. And yet, her eyes told all.

As Digory pondered to himself, the entry's bell chimed. A spry young man with a deep dimple and impish brown eyes entered the cloudy chamber. He had a commanding, magnetic presence. Digory's head spun to the door and his hand jumped to hover over his hip's concealed dagger instinctually.

"Mimi," the young man said hammily, gesturing outwardly as if addressing a cheering crowd. "Don't take this man's coin."

"My Leon," Laila melted into a warm grin, thin skin pulling tight against her old cheeks and neck. Digory relaxed his hand. "What brings you to visit your old grandmother?"

If that's Leon Minney, I am right, Digory thought. *This woman is not only Vanguard. She is Littlebell's elder.*

"To ask if you'll come," Leon began. "It's the last night of 'Native's Revenge'. The people would adore it if you…"

"I have work here to do," Laila said gruffly, turning in a swish. She shuffled to the ominous shelves in the corner and picked up a series of vials filled with various tonics and herbs. She examined each vial carefully, rolling it around in her fingers, studying the various powders and liquids within, until she settled on a dusky purple mixture. Ink flower salve. It would prevent infection.

"But, Mimi," Leon pleaded, androgynous face pinching like a toddler near tears. He took a step, hand stretched outwards. "It is the pinnacle of my achiev…"

"I said," Laila interrupted again, turning in a furious huff, blue eyes gleaming, "I have work. Enough." At the stung look on Leon's face, Laila added gently, "You know my feelings, child." She paused and bit her lip as she glanced to the upper floor briefly, where those too injured or ill to move lay on cots. "I won't have you ending up like your father."

With that, Leon's huff melted. "Mimi," he said, smiling. He took a step towards her. "I am far more than my father."

Digory noted how the old woman rose her eyebrows; she was struck by the comment.

Then Laila shook her head and turned quickly, muttering something to herself as she gathered a series tiny vials filled with dire clove, yellow cane and bone violet; all in different shades of colored glass and stopped with pieces of clay. When mixed with ink flower, this assortment of herbs produced a potent healing salve rivalling blue thimbleweed poultice.

"What about you?" Leon turned, speaking to Digory directly without having glanced at him once from the time he walked in. Leon leaned towards him, dimple smiling. "You are far too beautiful for us not to have met."

Digory deep-bellied laughed, then flexed his jaw. He unconsciously leaned away. "You aren't shy, are you boy?"

Digory wasn't sure yet what to make of this newblood Vanguard. He'd heard rumors about the young man, though. Leon Minney supposedly enjoyed taboo festivities with women and men alike, as well as being a pain in his older brother's ass, more than anything else, according to Sybil.

"Not shy," Leon said, "and no boy." He held his hand up in Littlebell's customary greeting. "Leon. Leon Minney," he said. Digory watched the strange gesture wordlessly. He'd heard of Littlebell's odd customs but never witnessed them himself. Not until now. "And you are?" Leon asked.

"Rune," Digory said, lifting his right hand clumsily to match Leon's gesture, unable to properly bend his ring and pinkie finger. "Name's Rune." Digory's pride gave way to his practicality. For as silly as he felt, he knew it was in his best interest to try to fit in.

"Pleasure, Rune," Leon smiled, endeared by the foreigner's attempt at the customary Littlebell greeting. Leon eyed Digory's shirtless physique and many scars. "What brings you to my grandmother's table, Rune?"

He took striding steps to gracefully rest a hip against the examining table, not far from Digory's side.

"Helping a friend," Digory said. "His brother ran off."

"You are harbouring fugitives, is that it, Mimi?"

"We're from Baneswood," Digory offered quickly.

Leon nodded, ignoring the fact that Digory was quite puny to be a Baneswood native, assuming him to be from the Littlebell borderlands where natives between the realms mixed and tended to be smaller. He turned his head slowly then traced a finger up Digory's muscled forearm. Digory pulled back. "And what did that?" Leon pointed at the pink-healing wound in Digory's shoulder.

"Leon, leave him be," Laila said as she approached, mixing the salve. She gently applied the mixture to Digory's wound. It tingled like a creed of pin pricks against his skin, skirting the line between pleasant and painful. He swallowed hard and glanced quickly at Laila while she applied the salve.

Digory responded to Leon, "Raiders."

"You must come tonight."

Come to what, Digory wondered.

"Native's Revenge is a once in a lifetime affair," Leon went on dramatically, drawing the syllables out. In the background, Laila huffed. Leon glanced to her, frowning quickly, then smiled again while eyeing Digory.

Digory wondered what the young man had done to displease his grandmother so.

"Tell me you will be there, new friend. Beautiful stranger. I will tell just where you shall sit, and you shall be my guest after."

This was a rare opportunity to gain proximity to a newblood Vanguard and Digory wouldn't have it squandered. He looked at Laila with a wide smile and sarcastic tone. "Should I go with your grandson?"

Laila was unamused by the theatrics. Frowning, nearly muttering, she said, "Do what you wish, child. It's none of my business." She waved her hand high in the air, as if to be done with both of them.

Leon laughed in a low and throaty chuckle as he pushed himself from his lean against the table with a leap.

"What will it be, new friend?" he asked Digory, crossing his arms, colorful-patterned robes, apple red with magenta bursts, bunching at the billowy sleeves. His clothing was of significantly higher quality than most of the passers-by Digory witnessed in Littlebell so far. "I leave in five moments," he added hopefully, holding his palm out with fingers apart, glancing to his grandmother's progress dressing the wound. "Come with me if you are done here." He lowered his hand. Digory noted a heavy gemstone ring on each of his thumbs.

Rings were only worn by those of the red faction within Littlebell, and traditionally, unless Vanguard, only by men. But Digory didn't know that, much less what they symbolized, or what charms they were said to possess. The rings Leon wore hinted to his bicurious nature. And were said to make him more attractive.

"Give me two more and I will be finished with him," Laila huffed as she rewrapped Digory's wound in clean, crisp cloth bandages. "Leon," she barked, "Fetch one of your brother's tunics. I keep some in that chest over there. I won't have him leaving here like a beggar."

"Pardon me asking," Digory said, "but if you are Vanguard, why are you here?" He glanced around the tidy, smoky apothecary. "Why not in the castle?"

Leon laughed as he sifted through a chest of fabrics aside the bookshelf wall, holding up one showy garment after the other, until plucking a starched grey tunic from part-way down. The quietest one. Digory let out a slight sigh of relief. "You've never been to Littlebell, have you?"

"We live with our people," Laila interjected as Leon stood. He took several steps across the Apothecary's polished floor, then, after holding the tunic up briefly to eye that it would fit, tossed Digory the garment. Up close, the fabric was far more intricate than from a distance, edged in fine embroidered detailing of tiny ink flower bouquets. Very fine clothing indeed. Digory nodded to the doe-eyed man in thanks as Laila's ancient falsetto droned on. "Each Minney goes where they are suited. Rarely do we choose to live in the reaches of the castle. It puts us too far away. Without our people, we are nothing."

Laila Minney was a woman of the people and enjoyed being among them. While technically the elder of the realm, her eldest grandson Prihim primarily handled running it.

"Well said Mimi," Leon half hugged her with one thin arm around her sloped shoulders, then kissed her caverned forehead. "With that, I depart."

"Child," Laila shot her head up, impressively thick braid swishing across her back, "will you take something to eat? You are as thin as a pole. It isn't right."

Leon shook his pretty head, "No, no," he smiled wide. Both cheeks deeply dimpled. "I am just fine." He looked at Digory. "New friend, Rune of Baneswood, will you be my escort to the theatre this evening? You must not refuse, as I am Vanguard and..." he burst into laughter. "Just... will you come with me?"

"I don't know about escort..." Digory said, in half-seriousness, half-jest. Leon's propensity towards unspoken predilections was the talk of the Kingdom, in polite whispers, of course, although commonplace within Littlebell's realm. The concept intrigued Digory, as it was so foreign to him, although the thought of himself lying with another man turned his stomach. He'd never encountered a man who fancied men before. Such activities were obviously forbidden in Westerviolet. Punishable by death, naturally.

Leon chuckled. "It was a reach," he conceded, holding his hands out in peace. "Fine, then. As a friend?"

Digory held eye contact as Leon slipped a small tablet from his pocket into his mouth. The man smiled as he chewed, deep brown pupils growing huge. Unnervingly, he didn't once blink and never broke eyes with Digory. Digory studied the man's brown irises, like silt swirling in a river.

"Aye," he finally said, glancing away from the odd stare. Rubbing his hand unconsciously over the edge of new bandages Digory added a bit louder, "Aye, I will go with you." He couldn't miss an opportunity to learn more about the New, for Sybil, of course.

And he had to know what that pill was.

"Ay!" Leon cheered, hopping across the room. He kissed Laila on the cheek once more. "I love you Mimi," he said as he swung a thin arm around her fleshy shoulders.

"And I love you, dear Leon." She hugged him tight. "Keep this young man out of trouble," she said, pulling back. "He is not ready for your crowd."

"All respect, I can take care of myself," Digory interjected, trying not to chuckle, standing from the examining table. His etched muscles flexed beneath new crisp dressings. *These newbloods don't know the half of it*, he thought. *It is they who aren't ready for me.*

"We'll see," Leon laughed. "Let's go."

Digory pulled the grey shirt over his head quickly. It fit loosely, too long at the sleeves. "Who's is this?" he asked, examining the fine stitching, running the bumped thread and miniature beads under his finger and thumb. He rolled the tunic's sleeves in part for the length and in part to hide some of the embroidery. He didn't want to stand out. And finery didn't suit him.

"Primin's," Leon replied casually, looking up at the taller Digory. "He won't miss it. Come on."

With the chirp of a bell, Digory followed Leon out of the keyhole-shaped door and down the red and orange cobblestone streets of Littlebell.

The theatre was round with arched entryways and no windows, scented of turpentine and sawdust. It's reaching walls towered high up to vaulted rafters, painted white against dark wood. The ceiling domed at the highest point with a circular cut out directly mirroring the stage below, open to the star-filled evening sky. The stage was in the center of the structure, surrounded by semi-circle benches atop fresh cedar shavings, offering the ample audience 360-degree views of the performance. Three stories of balconies offered alternate, elevated views.

Digory sat on a low bench in the very first row closest to the stage, close enough to see a marking for direction; a small X in black soot.

It was a warm night. The air hung moist and still. Plump, furry bats flapped and dangled amongst the rafters. Crickets droned outside in symphony.

Digory sat forward, resting his elbows on wide-apart knees as he observed patrons filter into the round space, competing patterns of robed gowns, billowy tunics, and flowery trousers, laughing, talking, and arguing amongst themselves while waiting for the performance to start. Most were golden-haired and almond-eyed, with coal-dark complexions, much darker than Westerviolet natives, or the Baneswood people Digory had seen. Women with competitively intricate yet shockingly similar thick braids long down their backs. Most women had bottom lips stained tangerine, eyes lined heavy in black, and fingers tipped in red. Few here in the theatre had blue-tipped fingers. Men had short hair and clean-shaven faces. Most wore rings. The way the men and women squawked back and forth made Digory think of birds during mating season. The people gestured wildly with their hands when they spoke, or laughed, or did anything, really. And so much smiling for no reason!

Far different from the meek, understated tone of Westerviolet, Digory thought. It was raucously loud in the pitch-black theatre. It reminded him of a barnyard.

Digory leaned to a man near his age sitting immediately to his left. "Where is the curtain?"

The man sat with hands in his lap studying the tops of his square-toed boots. He popped his head up at Digory's deep voice, as if interrupted. "What?" Berry-red, dilated eyes locked on Digory's.

Digory asked in half jest, while smirking, "Aren't theatres supposed to have curtains?" That's what Sybil told him of the one she visited in Animus Rock, anyway.

The aloof man looked at him funny, as if insulted. Digory silently noted the long-ago healed scar down the man's nose, impressed into one nostril and halfway down his jowl. He wondered what this man had done to gain such a nasty mark. It wasn't long ago earned. Maybe he shouldn't have spoken to him so brazenly after all. His hand hovered over his hidden dagger.

"You've never been to the Littlebell theatre before," the man said as a statement, not a question.

Digory shook his head 'no' as the crowd groaned and moaned as performance time neared. *So much filth in one place,* he distinctly thought, squelching a sneer, glancing around. The man next to him relaxed immediately, turning to face the stage. "You will see," he said with the slightest lisp, followed by an endearing, repetitive chuckle. "You will see." The man was indeed Digory's age and nearly his stature; vascular veins snaking up hardened forearms, with thinning blonde hair speckled grey and a clean-shaven jaw.

"I'm Rune," Digory said.

The man's red eyes assessed Digory quickly, glancing him up and down briefly. "Good to greet you," he said.

Digory nodded, thankful not to make a fool of himself again, unfamiliar with Littlebell's customs. The man half shifted his weight to face him.

"I've not met you before," he observed with a squint. "Why are you here?"

"You've met everyone in Littlebell?"

"Aye. What brings you here?"

"Leon," Digory said simply.

The man turned, sitting back a bit, glancing up to the round stage. "I didn't take you for one of his."

Digory laughed, shaking his head, scratching his beard. "I'm not."

"What then?"

Digory shrugged. "Just met him."

The man's smile peeled into a curled, jesting grin. "Is that what it's called?"

"I swear it," Digory said, raising his eyebrows, shaking his head with a smile and a side glance. "I'm from Baneswood."

"I am not to judge," the man began, "but you say it is so, I believe your word." The man paused, adjusting his leather belt over an ostentatious orange, gold, and lapis floral-patterned robe, with low cut v underneath a braided toggle cloak. It seemed fine, indeed. This was likely a man of note. "If not one of Leon's, then, what brings you to Littlebell?" He turned his head slightly. "The Occident, honey or the bare? You don't strike me as one of the Faith."

The crowd around them bubbled in an excited gasp followed by an audible cheer, then a whooshing hush. Red candles laid around the perimeter of the stage, engulfed by the blackness of the theatre, indistinguishable until now, were lit by black-cloaked attendants one by one. A hooded figure appeared next to the stage to their right. He was slight-shouldered, beneath dark emerald green - black in this dim light-robes, holding matching red candles stoically.

"Later," the man whispered to Digory. "It's starting."

Both shifted to look towards the stage.

The halo of flickering candles burned in a glowing ring. A small woman appeared next to the stage holding a candle beneath her chin like the hooded figure. She had an immature face with pleading eyes and an innocent smile. She wore a sole skirt of sheer red fabric gathered at her navel, split with deep slits to her thighs, jagged and ripped at the hem, pouring down to her slight ankles like a waterfall of blood.

A series of chimes rang out from beyond the theatre's arches, harmoniously pitched with disorderly rhythm, sending the bats screeching. The cacophony was jarring; both beautiful and ominously frightening. The notes rose high in the vaulted theatre with the shrieking bats, together erupting from the circular star-filled dome.

Apart from the chiming hymn, the theatre was deathly silent.

The audience leaned forward eagerly, collectively holding its breath.

Then, the hooded figure to Digory's right lifted from the ground as if he magically took off into flight, gown flapping behind him like the wings of an angry bat. The crowd gasped, cheering oddly without sound. Instead of clapping, hands thrust upwards with elbows bent as all shook their palms back and forth while wiggling their fingers. All around the circular stage was a swirling river of silent dancing hands, nearly art by itself.

Digory glanced around in confusion, noting the unfamiliar hand movements while keeping his own hands buried deep in his lap, pressing his fingertips and thumbs together. Now he was even more uncomfortable. He just wanted to leave.

Hovering over the audience, the hooded figure rose high into the vault with cloak billowing like black smoke in his wake, illuminated from below by the halo of candles. Chimes roared in the background as figure swayed back and forth, menacingly, from above. Digory squinted, noting the series of ropes and pulleys nestled high, then turned to glance about to see the same crew who lit the candles, off-stage labouring to hoist the figure by a rope.

Then the figure threw the cloak's hood back dramatically from his hovering spot amidst the rafters. The delighted audience below erupted again in a silent, hand wiggling cheer at Leon Minney's famously dimpled face. He wore a black metal crown with sixteen points on his head, pushed down over coarse tufts of golden hair. At the silent applause, Leon beamed, smiling pridefully, then opened his hands. The discordant chimes paused briefly, then shifted to a droning, pulsing rhythm.

One hand clutching the candle, the other palm outward, Leon Minney addressed the silent crowd in an evocative song.
"All who gaze upon my face
are entitled to everlasting grace!
You heathens do not know
How far your small minds have to go.
But fear not,
for we have come

to save you from
your minds so numb.
Come, rejoice,
all who are near.
Your saviour.
Your liberator.
Your Vanguard is here!"

By the end of his first refrain, the room's mood flipped as if the hall burst into flames.

Grinning faces fell to scowling frowns. Almond eyes squinted. Hands flew up, like before, except now fingers clenched tight, pale-knuckled fisted, punching into the air, billowy patterned sleeves flailing wildly. The audience was irate. Digory shifted backwards in his seat on the bench, crossing his arms across his chest. HE smirked at the blasphemy in delight as he glanced about. *This isn't as bad as I imagined*, he thought. The half-naked woman with un-braided hair and sheer red skirts remained still aside the stage, delicate upturned face emotionless, under-lit by candlelight. Digory studied her briefly as candlelight flickered against her supple figure and innocently beautiful, nearly child-like face.

Leon raised his voice and lowered his tone, still singing in haunting melody. He pointed at the audience with a finger.

"Ignoble wretches,
every one
who fails to believe
will be undone.
We Vanguards
are here to save you.
Boorish souls.
Look to me and I will be true.
Cut your braids. Burn your boots.
Only *earthblood* will refute.
The way to piety,
to clarity, to grace
is to rub yourself clean.
You must not think

of the vile stink
of your soul."

At that the chimes abruptly ceased. Leon's melodic words reverberated about the round theatre like a gong. Incensed, the audience silently punched the air again at Leon's taunting, insulting melody. Multi-colored tunic sleeves billowed and danced.

Digory half smiled at the mocking tune, arms still crossed stoically in front of his chest, eyes upturned at the performance. He thought of how every single one of the earthblood within the round, open theatre would be cut down for such blasphemy if Tomas or Sybil had anything to do with it. For a quick moment, he imagined doing it himself. Slicing through the crowd with his blade or picking the audience off, one by one, with his crossbow.

Then, the petite woman in red was thrust unceremoniously into the rafters with surprising speed like Leon had was. This snapped Digory from his reverie, pulleys groaning under the force of robed men tugging in the background. The woman's sheer red skirts fanned out beneath her as she swayed with the undulating movement, dangling from the string. Amazingly, the candle she held stayed lit as did the one in Leon's hand despite their back and forth movements through the air. The jumping halo of flames on the stage cast coiling shadows as the woman was pulled to a daunting height. She faced Leon. Both performers swung in silence like garbed pendulums: one red, one emerald shadowed black. The audience craned their necks as they all gazed upwards in unabashed awe. Digory sceptically kicked his legs out in front of himself and crossed his arms behind his head as he lifted his eyes to glance up with the others.

The chimes changed again, this time all ceasing except a sole high-pitched tinkle, the sound stars would make if they could sing. The striking woman, bare breasts peeking through waves of hair, sheer crimson skirts, ragged at the ends, barely covering her frame, opened her mouth in the most breath-taking, complementary song.

"All who breach our noble shores,
all who eat our long-prized grain,
all who shout commanding roars
are walking,
breathing,
living
pain."

The woman's voice was warm, with raspy depth, drawing the audience in, lulling them calm. Her brow was set. It cast black shadows over ruby-red eyes that the candle she held made glow. Silent hands in the audience jumped into the air, fingers spread, wiggling violently in agreement as she went on.

"He is pestilence.

Famine.

Dread," she sang, pointing the candle at Leon with both hands.

"Vanguards lie.

Their blood is dead!"

Many in the crowd leapt to their feet including the man to Digory's left, standing with both hands high into the air, fingers spread, shaking them back and forth excitedly, calico robes bucking with his movements, dilated eyes locked on the vocal beauty above. Many had difficultly controlling themselves. Soon an audible murmur collected around the theatre.

The woman threw her candle to the stage, toppling wick over base until it crashed violently below.

When the candle landed, each candle surrounding the stage's perimeter briefly surged upwards impossibly high, as if oil had been doused on the flames. Many gasped, throwing their hands over their eyes at the shockingly painful blast of bright light in the dark, nearly un-lit theatre. A poor man to the edge of Digory's vison had a sleeve catch ablaze, luckily doused quickly by pats from nearby friends' cloaks. Watching this, Digory snickered.

Then the chimes stopped abruptly.

"I cast you down!" The woman shouted with throat-cracking emotion. Her glassy eyes pooled with tears that dripped from her cheeks.

The crowd held its' breath once more as Leon seemingly plummeted out of the rafters, as if the attendants had dropped him, free falling to the stage. His black emerald cloak flapped loudly in his wake. Many gasps and a few horrified screams cut the air. At the very last instant, the ropes held. Leon was saved, stopped just a breath from the stage. His crown fell, landing with a hollow clank, then rolled loudly until it dropped with a metallic echo, without disturbing the circle of candles. Slowly the attendants lowered Leon the rest of the way and he feigned collapse, expression dolefully pained, reaching for the woman above him.

He lay dramatically atop the black X.

"You have doomed yourself,

your family,

your town

to disrespect me,

a man of the crown!"

Leon sang like a man scorned; wrathfully, painfully inflected, pointing skyward. Pleasant face scowling. Gesturing angrily at the woman. The audience booed in response silently, with gesticulating fists. Digory was impressed by his acting.

The beauty replied in her enchanting, engulfing tone.

"Hubris alone befalls you.

How to live without the truth?

To conquer, control.

That is the lie.

You care only to pacify

and ensure you satisfy

your soul's broken ache.

Despicable snake."

All around the candle-lined stage and up three stories of balconies, dark hands with pale palms flickered with widespread fingers excitedly. Bats flapped in and out of the starry open dome. The chimes rang brusquely once more, loud and jarring, causing many to jump in their seats at the unexpected din. Digory chuckled, fully enjoying this theatre now despite himself. The woman in red opened her wide mouth again, teeth flashing as she sang her final monologue.

"I cast you out,
I cast you down.
I spit at you
and your crown.
No longer will we have you here
unless agreements you do adhere
Peace, joy, life, and love.
Alas…
Fools, each and every one.
Do not what they have done.
Wash not a metal glove."

Then the beautiful performer threw her head back. She jostled her thin hair dramatically over her shoulders, exposing her chest fully. She unfastened the ragged, blood-colored skirt, revealing a dark tuft between her thighs. The audience went up in a roar of cheering delight at her nudity. Tinkling chimes mimicked starlight once more as the woman held the sheer garment behind her, head still cocked back, face tilted up at the moon, rocking back and forth. Leon bucked and twisted beneath her. It was as if he was dying from his place on the stage.

Watching Leon, Digory was sure the man had never actually witnessed someone die.

The audience was all on their feet now, mostly faces upturned to the beauty dangling above. Her sheer red sheet was like a battle flag behind her. The rest of the audience glared and scowled at Leon. He was crumpled in a pathetic ball on the stage. Although mostly silent apart from tinkling chimes, humming crickets, and flapping bats, the theatre was quietly aroar. Everyone gestured wildly with silent wiggling claps or aggressive punching boos. Digory alone remained seated at first until the invisible pressure of the crowd was overwhelming. Despite himself, he felt compelled to join. He found himself standing with the others, shaking his palms wildly, fingers spread and wiggling. To his surprise, he was almost enjoying himself.

The chimes halted. The theatre was left gaping and soundless all the way up to the open-air dome. With little cloud cover the stars glinted elegantly above, bright white flecks flickering against the inky sky. Digory looked up at the round. It felt like the theatre had swallowed him whole, as if he peered up from the belly of a beast.

Then, without warning, the naked beauty, tears streaming down cheeks, dropped the skirt.

The audience, already all on their feet, erupted into a fury. Every manner of loud whooping, booing, and cheering imaginable, caught Digory off-guard and made him jump. The theatre pulsed with ear-cracking intensity as the silken blood skirt floated impossibly slowly to the stage, ragged edges flailing with the descent, swaying back and forth like a descending feather. It landed perfectly in the center of the stage, miraculously avoiding every flame before enveloping Leon completely.

Soon, Leon's famous profile was elegantly backlit by the halo of candles beneath the sheer blood-colored skirt.

Meanwhile, the woman dangled naked overhead with her head tilted to the stars. Slowly, with the groaning of pulleys, she was lowered down to the stage. When she began to descend, a hush fell over the audience again and all dropped to their knees. The theatre felt immediately solemn, as if in mourning. Prayer. Worship. Digory was the only fool left standing. When he realized this, glancing from side to side, he hurriedly fell to his knees, mirroring the others without a second thought.

The chimes began again in a velvety melody. The notes cascaded down like a misty rainfall. The female performer landed aside Leon atop the edge of the frayed red skirt.

The scene gave the illusion of a Vanguard Lord covered in blood with the naked dark-skinned, red-eyed beauty standing over him, victorious. It was deeply evocative imagery.

Then the woman took a deep breath and began again in heart-piercing melody, not in a song with words but in a lingering, terrifying tune of enveloping notes tinged with raw emotion. The woman's eyes glared furiously, misted with tears. All the while, she kept her head back and arms open, singing up at the open dome. The audience watched her breathlessly, many with tears in their eyes too.

Suddenly, the chimes crashed violently, then ceased, leaving the theatre in echoing silence. The gorgeous naked performer collapsed as if she'd fainted atop Leon, still beneath the sheer sheet. Each candle surrounding the stage mysteriously went out as if something sucked all the warm, stagnant air from the room. A chill descended.

The performance had obviously concluded and men and women all around Digory leapt up from their knees in a roaring cheer, both vocally and with their shimmering fingers. Digory glanced around briefly in confusion until he sighed as he placed one hand on his knee, bringing himself with a grunt to a stand. He raised his hands to match the others.

As they cheered the young man leaned over to Digory, eyes still on the stage as the performers climbed down with the help of unseen attendants.

"What are you doing after this?"

"I told you, I'm his acquaintance," Digory said with a hint of frustration, wiggling his fingers above his head mindlessly still, until he realized what he was doing and lowered them abruptly. "I'm not one of…"

The man laughed. "No, that is not my meaning."

"What then?"

"I am married and into cunt of all kinds," the man eagerly explained.

Digory was taken aback. He hadn't expected that response and was instantly intrigued, partly by the statement but more by the type of man who would lead with such a thing. Eyebrows raised, he crossed his arms and leaned one shoulder closer to the man. "How does that work, exactly?"

The man smiled, leaning closer to Digory. "I fell in love."

Rowdy patrons laughed, jested, and shouted about them, some even jostling and bumping past them, exiting the dark theatre down the narrow isles through the arched doors.

Digory chuckled politely but the hair on his neck still stood on end. His ears craned for hints of danger, but it was impossible to discern amidst the ruckus. He lowered his hand to hover over where his glass dagger was concealed. He reassured himself that he also carried his crossbow still, tucked away in the satchel that he kept at his side, slung safely over his shoulder.

"You laugh, but hear me out," the man said, speaking with his hands the whole time as everyone in Littlebell seemed to do, red eyes twinkling excitedly. "I fell in love with a woman who loves women."

"Loves women, you say?" Digory relaxed slightly. This man was merely a braggart and had pegged Digory as a man to impress. It must be due to the fine tunic.

"Aye," the man nodded. "She prefers that I bring women to our bed, from time to time," he said, slight lisp apparent.

What a hassle, Digory thought. He had partaken in affairs with two women at the same time in his younger years. It was not difficult for the handsome Guardsman to bed any maiden in Westerviolet he pleased. Yet the novelty of multiple breasts, thighs and asses quickly gave way to the annoyance of two mouths.

"That seems," he said carefully, "fortunate."

"I'm a fortunate man, it is true."

This treatment must be because I am a friend of Leon's, Digory thought. The man's glazed red eyes had undiluted over the duration of the performance and returned to their typical aperture. Digory looked him up and down. Even for the well-dressed crowd of the theatre, this man's clothes appeared lavish with fine stitching rivalling the grey embroidered Vanguard tunic Digory wore. A weighty silver-tone ring with red crystal in the center flashed from the man's right thumb.

Digory patted the man on his shoulder. "You are fortunate, then," he said as he turned to turn and exit the strange conversation.

The man smiled wide, jagged nose scar pulling taut across his chestnut skin. "That was a rare treat, you know?"

Digory turned. "Aye?"

"You surely are not from this realm," the man said in his slight lisp. At Digory's unimpressed expression, he went on. "It's the first time 'Native's Revenge' has been performed in years. Eight, in fact. Since the Lord's accident, that is."

"Lord's accident?"

"I can't believe you don't know." The man's eyes widened as he nearly jumped up and down, crouching, and then standing up tall to contain his amusement. "Giacomo," the man said.

"Minney?"

The man nodded. "Aye, yet when Lord Giacomo performed it, he really fell. The ropes failed."

"Ah," Digory said, eyebrows parting wide. He knew little of the Minney bloodline. Just that Prihim Minney sat on Council and essentially ran the realm. He didn't care to know more than that. "Dead then?"

The man shrugged. "Nearly, I gather." He placed his hands on hips and said quickly, "I'm hosting a gathering. Leon is invited. Tell him to bring you."

Digory pulsed his jaw once. What type of gathering could this be? "Who are you?" he asked carefully.

The man ignored Digory. "Tell him to bring you," he repeated casually. "Leon will know. I hope to see you later."

Without further explanation, the man turned with a swish of his braided toggle cape and disappeared into the elbowing crowd.

Digory laughed to himself at the absurdity of his evening. Ryd would never believe it, he thought. He scratched at his lengthening beard and glanced up at stars beyond the gaping circular hole in the vaulted dome above. Eventually, Leon emerged from the pulse still wearing the blackened emerald robe with the ridiculous sixteen-pointed crown atop his head. He was arm in arm with the beautiful female performer.

"Rune," Leon introduced the young woman to Digory, holding both hands out to present her, now fully clothed. She wore a diamond patterned gown, draped with wide bell sleeves.

Digory looked down at her. He'd never seen an outfit like that before. Littlebell was as ostentatious rumoured to be, he thought.

"This is Yrsa," Leon said, looking to her with clear admiration. "You should bow before her and her talent. This woman is a genius."

The beauty glanced away, kinked hair grazing her eye. She smiled coyly, obviously pleased by his praise, but didn't respond.

"You are very talented, and very beautiful," Digory said sincerely.

Yrsa was slight, child-like even, much smaller than most women in Littlebell, likely hailing from the borderlands, but her essence burned like fire. One felt warmth just standing near her.

"That's the spirit," Leon cheered, jostling his silly prop crown.

Then, Leon dropped Yrsa's hands and popped another tablet from his breast pocket. He crunched it loudly. Yrsa, noticing this, put her hand out. Leon gave her one instantly. She took the miniature pill and casually chewed it as Leon swallowed the last bits of his own.

Digory watched silently, narrowing his eyes. "I hear there's a gathering?"

Meanwhile, Leon had begun dancing in place, humming the tune from the show from earlier. He started twirling Yrsa around and around. She tried to speak and Leon would jerk the slight girl in a spinning move, causing her to slur her attempts to answer Digory's question. She giggled and laughed while trying to break free of Leon's clumsy dance.

Theatre nearly empty, Yrsa finally gathered the composure to say, "Leon let's get going."

She took a deep breath, pushing her grinning, wide-pupiled companion away as he approached her, shimmying his shoulders back and forth in another ridiculous dance. Whatever he'd taken had made him feel very good, Digory thought. Now he was even more intrigued.

Leon was almost acting as if he'd had too much ale, but he'd had none at all.

Yrsa stifled a chuckle and restrained from joining him again.

She said through a laughing smile, "Nis will not be happy if I miss too much."

Leon twirled her a final time. Then, he agreed, overly nodding, "Yes, yes, let's go. Let's go!"

Digory's deep voice cut their drugged lull. "Where are we going?"

Leon smiled, grinning with deep dimpled cheeks at Yrsa. She grinned back yet rolled her eyes at Leon's pageantry as he brazenly swung the heavy dark emerald hood of his cloak over his crown and golden locks. He lowered his eyes theatrically, as if to be menacing.

Digory looked between them, back and forth, awaiting an answer. Finally, he prodded. "Where?"

Yrsa's ruby eyes were hugely dilated. "We're going mad," she said.

Digory, nearly ready to scrap the adventure entirely, restrained himself from shouting as he lost patience.

"What the curses does that mean?" he asked through near-gritted teeth.

Leon hopped behind Yrsa and grabbed her shoulders with dainty hands, then popped his head up from behind her with a roguish grin. "We're going under Littlebell."

-

Digory followed Leon and Yrsa around several bends through the meandering roads pulsing with mainly red-fingered citizens. In the late hour, these streets were alive with music wafting from nearly every door frame. Competing yet complementary tunes with twanging strings and clinking chimes permeated the air. Throaty songs were sung in rounds. Orange cats ran hissing across the paths ahead.

A group of particularly rowdy men sloshed about ale in wide goblets singing, "The angry sky weeps blood for me / her cunt is as cold as a cunt can be!" They shouted the foreign tune back and forth at one another, right inside a passing establishment.

It sounded like something out of Baneswood.

There is certainly no shortage of revery in Littlebell, Digory thought. Next to that building was another red painted one covered in wiggling naked women beckoning from high balconies. Women and men alike stumbled into its front doors. Both sides of the cobblestone street were littered with crouched bodies wrapped in once-colorful rags, now ripped and dingy, eyes huge-pupiled and unfocused, staring at nothing. They held out cups, begging. One particularly sorry fellow with deep-set black bags beneath his pale red eyes reached out, grasping the cloth of Digory's pant leg.

"Please. Coin. Please my Lord," the man croaked.

On closer inspection, he was not much older than Digory.

With a frustrated sigh and furrowed brow, without a response or explanation, Digory kicked at the beggar, as he would any disobedient hound. He connected directly with the man's nose in a sick crack. The beggar turned away, groaning pathetically, throwing his hands up to his bloody face. He whimpered as he collapsed into a ball.

Leon turned to look at the commotion briefly, burst into a pleased chuckle, then continued to push through the crowd.

Yrsa, however, pinched her brow, but didn't respond.

After several more moments passing through the rank and lively streets of Littlebell, Leon turned down a shadowed alleyway littered with debris. It teemed with insects and rodents.

"And we're sure this is the way?" Digory asked sarcastically, stepping over a rotted carcass of an orange cat, maggots wriggling in its mouth. "This doesn't feel very festive."

Littlebell, compared to the sterile cleanliness of Westerviolet, was disgusting.

"Patience," Yrsa said.

"Listen to her," Leon added. "We're nearly there."

The trio rounded another bend to reveal a gate slightly ajar with slick steps leading down into musky darkness.

"Sewers," Digory said. "You didn't tell me that we were..."

"Patience, Rune."

Digory grumbled and fell in line as Leon pressed the gate open. Hints of laughter and music, chimes and strange instruments with plucky strings, floated up from the sewer's depths.

With dimpled smile Leon said, "We're here."

He gestured for Digory and Yrsa to follow him. The trio descended the stone staircase, musky air heavy in their lungs, deep into the belly of Littlebell.

The stairway opened into an enormous room with impressively ancient Georgian arches, age evident from patina and wear. It was dark this deep underground chamber with no windows, as was preferable to a large portion of Littlebell natives who had never been trained to be awake during the day, particularly those who had always lived in the big city. Usually, only Littlebell's farming natives could stand the sunlight.

Simple sconces with drippy candles segmented the walls, doing little for light and more for ambiance. Incense filled the air. Colorful rugs, patterned with designs to rival Littlebell's customary clothing were strewn across the floor topped with plush pillows and occasional round, very low tables. Ostentatiously dressed guests sat with crossed legs atop the pillows. Clay dishes with small red pills dotted the tables. An ethereal twangy tune segmented with clinking chimes floated about the laughing, drugged crowd. Remarkably fine tapestries were hung everywhere with regal, red-eyed figures wearing out-of-fashion feathers and gem bands, so expertly woven they appeared to move and glare at passers-by. Digory assumed them to be Minneys of days past.

At the furthest point from the stairway was an elevated platform with a pair of bare women atop large bed-like pillows. They were massaging each other's' breasts, kissing, and touching themselves on stage.

"Wow," Digory said honestly. Behind closed doors around the den, more crude acts occurred, most too taboo for even bare houses. That was part of why the Bee dens existed at all.

Yrsa smirked at Digory and met eyes with Leon knowingly. Most had his reaction upon first entering.

"She told me you preferred them," Leon sighed, eying Digory watch the oversized breasts of one particularly endowed bare woman, smiling at the crowd. The bare licked her finger then rubbed her dark nipple with it.

"Nothing personal," Digory smiled as he patted Leon on the shoulder, unable to take his eyes off the tawdry display. He had always been partial to breasts. The things he would do to that dame, he thought, if he was here on his own accord, of course.

Leon withdrew a pill from his breast pocket. He leaned closer to Digory. "The pleasures between the thighs are not what bring me here," he said in a whisper, holding the pill out in his palm. It was red like all the others in the clay dishes. On closer inspection Digory noted a tiny insect embossed on it: a bumble bee.

Curiosity pulsed in Digory's veins "What is it?" he asked, always one to try any type of ale or tonic.

He had yet to find one that he preferred over how intoxicating it felt to take a life. Many Westerviolet Guardsmen had problems with ale. Or Oblivion Tonic. Digory had problems with blood.

"No Mad Honey in Baneswood?" Leon laughed. "I thought it was there by now, despite the Dales. I should speak to Nis about that. Pity you've never tried it. What a fortunate day for you. You've come to the land of honey."

Yrsa chuckled at Leon's continual pageantry. "You're as mad as a loon, my dear," she said sweetly to him, hugging him quickly. She kissed him directly on the lips. "I will see you shortly?" She gestured to the far corner of the den. Leon nodded eagerly, flipping his hand to shoo her away.

Digory studied the little red pill still in Leon's outstretched hand as Yrsa left them. "What are you talking about?"

"This, my friend, is everything."

Digory crossed his arms sceptically, tuning out the chiming twangs of Littlebell's music. "Mad honey, you say?" He'd only heard the term spoken in regard to Ancestor worship in the old days, but most in Westerviolet considered those stories more legend than fact.

Leon leaned towards Digory. He whispered, "Calvanese."

Digory's brow popped up. "Calvanese?" That was a Vanguard name he was quite familiar with, as they were Sybil's favorite bloodline, apart from Brochet. As a girl, she adored the stories of their matriarchal ways. How easily they manipulated the men of the Kingdom in days of old. The now-extinct Calvanese women were Sybil's heroes. Digory heard all about them.

Leon nodded once, eyes shining proudly.

"What does that have to do with…" Digory gestured towards the pill.

Leon smiled. "I almost forgot," he said, then took it and chewed it with a crunch. He opened his widely dilated, bloodshot eyes and exhaled against the back of his throat as the drug's effects took hold. It was easy to build a tolerance to mad honey and Leon had, which required him to take more and more to get the same high.

"Calvanese kept the secret to the honey for centuries," he finally continued. "Now it remains at Duskfang."

Duskfang's realm was far, at the edge of the Kingdom, east and a bit south of Westerviolet, and feral after the horrors of the Plague. The castle and grounds were reported to be full of deadbloods.

"Duskfang is off limits." Digory frowned. "The Dread…"

Leon shrugged. "Nis found a way in."

"How?" Sybil had tried for years to find someone willing to take her to see the Duskfang ruins, yet all guides remotely knowledgeable of the area fully refused. It was infested with deadbloods since the Plague, without Calvanese to keep them out, or so she had been told.

"Don't know, but it's good for business. Come," Leon said eagerly, walking, "You must meet him."

"Business?"

"Yes, business," Leon said leading Digory through the crowd. He pinched the forearm of a gangly teen-years man in a yellow patterned tunic as they passed by. The man's cheeks blushed violet and Leon winked in return.

"Does the King know of this… business?"

Leon rolled his eyes, half glancing back over his shoulder at Digory. "Oh no, you aren't one of those?" He looked forward. "It's not quite *legal*, no. But what fun is?"

"What of your brother?"

"Prihim? He's at Animus. What does his opinion matter here?" Leon straightened his back a bit. "I'm the man of Littlebell."

"I hear he sits on Council. Does he know of…"

"Prihim knows what he must. This way." Leon pointed at a tapestry in the far corner, a caricature of a stern beauty with red jewels for eyes, high cheekbones, golden hair, and a thin red crown atop her head. Lady Sia Minney, one of Littlebell's legendary elders. Leon lifted the edge of the tapestry to reveal a secret wooden door hidden in plain sight. Following Leon's lead, Digory went through the door frame.

At the far end of the chamber in a high-backed chair sat the man Digory met at the theatre, instantly recognizable by the jagged scar across his nose. Two burly blond men, guards with matching dark-tone pants and tunics, stood at each side of him. Along the side of the room were plush pillows strewn with three beauties, each more stunning than the last, all naked. Yrsa sat deep in Nis's lap stroking his face and kissing his neck as he grinned and laughed, encouraging her on. He was shirtless with taut, dense muscles build up far beyond his naturally slight frame's apparent potential for strength. The man grabbed Yrsa's flank in his hand, squeezing soft, supple flesh beneath her diamond patterned gown. She squealed, biting his cheek as he laughed in a throaty chuckle.

"You?" Digory stepped forward, tone dripping accusation and confusion with a bit of respect.

The man laughed louder, from deep in his belly. He stood and Yrsa clung to him still. He grabbed her by her hips then tossed her to the side amongst the huge pillows and bare women beckoning for embrace. Once Yrsa was deep into the pillows she was absorbed, nuzzling into the downy breast of a nearby companion.

The man stood. "It's Nis," he said as he held up his hand up and did the customary Littlebell greeting. "I had to be sure you weren't Old undercover."

Digory mimicked the gesture the best he could, thankful his fumbling movements were accepted. "What now?" he asked, lowering his clumsy hand. *What irony*, he thought.

Nis pointed to the door and the guards exited the room with a flap of the tapestry. He then leaned forward, resting his weight on his elbows atop the table in front of them, speaking with his hands back and forth.

"Since Calvanese fell, all have searched for their hidden treasure, yet I alone discovered it! That's what I built my empire on. I worked with your friend here." He looked to Leon who had taken a seat in the far chair from Nis. "Luckily, he's a…" Nis paused, running his tongue over his teeth. "Freethinker."

"Aye! I like the sound of that," Leon cheered.

"Quiet," Yrsa said harshly, glaring up at her husband from where she lay in the pillows, naked, small perky breasts exposed, entangled with a larger, softer fleshed woman. While the men were talking, she'd removed her gown. It lay in a pile to her side. Yrsa casually massaged the other woman's deep burgundy nipples as the bare caressed her neck.

At Nis's questioning glance, she clarified, "Can we trust him?"

"Go back to your games," Nis spat. "My love," he added cruelly.

Yrsa pouted, half smiled, then grabbed the bare woman between her legs so quickly and violently that she painfully gasped. Yrsa kissed the woman hard and didn't break eye contact with Nis the whole time.

"That is quite a woman," Digory said. "She prefers women, except you?" Nis nodded once, hiding a smile. "Brilliant," Digory laughed, taking a seat at the long end of the table, inwardly glad he wasn't permitted to marry. What a nuisance, he thought.

"Surely," Leon laughed, glancing to Digory.

"Enough," Nis soured. He crossed his arms in front of his bare, hairless chest. "This is my wife."

Digory lowered his head. "Of course," he said.

Nis only liked the nature of his relationship discussed when he was discussing it.

"Now. I have something to show you. Something I've been working on. A new variant that will revolutionize it all."

"Brother in crime, I must hear this," Leon leapt from his seat and sauntered to Nis's side. He placed a hand on his shoulder. "Show me."

"I can do better than that," Nis said keenly, glancing at the men underneath his brow. Digory and Leon exchanged questioning glances. "I can give it to you."

Leon, a thrill-seeking man, needed no time to consider the offer. "I'm in," he said instantly.

Digory, however, was hesitant. "Do you think you should…"

"I think I should, yes!" Leon interrupted, "What is it, Nis?"

At that Nis withdrew a small clay and cob pipe and a cloth satchel from his breast pocket. It smelled like tobacco.

"I can smoke a pipe anywhere, Nis," Leon said. He went back to his seat.

"Ah ha! There, you see." Nis said while packing the pipe.

"I see nothing."

Digory's curiosity was overboiling yet he reminded himself to stay vigilant. To not be too distracted by this unusual adventure at the expense of safety. He glanced around. Music pulsed on the other side of the tapestry door guarded by hulking outlines of security. The situation was not ideal, but Digory considered his alias a good one and the risk of harm was greatly outweighed by the information he could potentially glean from this encounter, to bring to Sybil.

"You said it yourself," Nis said as he handed Digory the packed pipe. He passed it to Leon. "You can smoke a pipe anywhere."

"Yes," Leon said with a patronizing smile. "I can smoke anywhere, but I don't want to. I can't stand the stuff. The smell on my breath alone is enough to make anything beautiful flee from me quickly. And I can't have that."

Nis had a glint in his eye. "What if I told you this wasn't tobacco?"

Digory leaned forward, ever curious.

Nis pointed at him theatrically. "I have his attention. What about you, Leon?"

"What is it then?" Leon asked with wonder, finally taking the pipe from Digory. "You're telling me *this* is mad honey?"

"Yes," Nis said. "Processed correctly and with a dash of tobacco for the smell. You cannot tell the difference."

Digory only knew the stories he'd heard from Westerviolet of it, that it was utilized for Ancestral prayers. The legends said it removed one from their senses so they may hear the will of the Ancestors directly. As Digory cared not for worship, he'd never given mad honey a second thought.

"I say, try it," Nis added.

"What's it like?"

"It's safe, as long as you simply smoke it," Nis assured Digory with a chuckle. "More intense than mad ale."

"It's more than honey tablets too?" Leon asked, excitement palpably mounting, like a child gawking at sweets. His tolerance for the little red pills was so high that it took a handful to feel anything at all, and such a tendency was pricy. Although, Leon had the coin and, of course, Nis was happy to oblige his habit.

"Aye," Nis said hurriedly. "Much. "It goes to your head and chest. Your eyes," he added, smiling. "It's like you're wearing blinders, only warmer. You have to try it for yourself."

Leon furrowed his brow, then shot his head up. "Curse it," he said. "I'm in."

"Leon dear," Yrsa's soft voice cooed from beneath the gorgeous bare women. The men had almost forgotten she was there, swinging their heads when she spoke. "What of your voice, of your art?"

"My art! Yrsa this is for my art. Perhaps this is my final muse."

Yrsa rolled her eyes. "You say that each time you do anything that may be a danger to you. It's an excuse to harm yourself more, friend. You are no closer to your dreams."

"It isn't a dream; it is a vision." Leon spat at her. "It is a muse!"

"You're already high," she said disapprovingly. "Nis," Yrsa said, spinning, hair falling across her breasts, "He's too high already."

"There's no thing as too high. Relax, woman. I said, go back to your games. Interrupt again and I'll make you leave! Understand me?"

Yrsa instantly shoved the bare woman who kissed her collar bone aside. She stood, small form glorious and shamelessly nude, glaring daggers at Nis while collecting her gown from the floor, then held it crumpled in her hand.

Nis's face fell like a downpour at her reaction. His confident expression quickly washed away. "My love, I didn't mean…"

Yrsa interrupted, hair covering half of her breast. "Oh, but you did," she said calmly. Her petite stature was somehow terribly imposing. Her natural radiating warmth had flipped to icy cold.

"Don't leave," Nis pleaded up at her.

"I will do as I please," she said, turning with a spin of her hair. Then she walked across the room as nude as when she stood from the pillows. "Let me through!" Yrsa shrilly commanded the final guard. The hulking man jumped aside like a cat spooked by a mouse.

"Follow her," Nis shouted, after which one swarthy guard with curly hair nodded and jogged after her. "I cursed it," Nis muttered, shaking his head. "I cursed it."

"We've all been there."

"You haven't," Nis retorted, glancing at Leon down the rectangular table.

Leon shook his head, conceding in a dimpled grin. "Women are a certain type of mad," he admitted. "It is why I find little attraction there. Fine for playthings, nothing more."

Digory pushed the pipe to Nis. "You need it more than Leon does."

"Curse it," Nis said loudly. He beckoned for the pipe. "That's a good idea, hand it here."

They passed it over. Nis grabbed at the pipe hungrily. Using a lighting candle, he sparked the end of the pipe and the musky dark plant sizzled and cracked under the flame. Nis puffed several times. He held his lungs full of smoke before closing his eyes and exhaling a white, red-tinted cloud that smelled like damp earth, bitter moss, and tobacco. When he finally opened his eyes, his pupils grew huge – larger than they had from the pills – nearly engulfing his red irises entirely.

It looked like his eyes were swirling black.

Nis leaned back and gestured for a drink as the effects of his smokable mad honey settled upon him. He was awash in the haze. One of the almond-eyed bare women to the side of the room, coal-black skin contrasted against ice-blonde hair, sloping breasts and a soft middle, hurried to pour a goblet of Animus wine. She handed it to him before returning to the pillows. Nis took a mindless sip.

"Want to bet that has mad honey in it too?" Digory whispered to Leon.

"I'm sure it does," Leon replied, nodding. "I'd be disappointed if it didn't. I think mad honey ale is all he drinks." Mad honey ale, while bearing the name, was the weakest way to consume the drug. The effects were particularly mild and mostly made one feel drunk more quickly.

"Look how happy he looks," he added. "Makes me a bit jealous. What do you say? I'll try it if you will. I'm sure it'll make you feel better." Leon gestured at Digory's bandaged shoulder. "And besides, don't you have until morning you meet your friend?"

"So, we will stay here for eve? Is it safe?"

Leon gestured at the den's guards. "Nowhere safer in the city."

"Fair."

Meanwhile, Nis was unmoving as if made from stone apart from impossibly wide, darting eyes. A slight smile crept across his lips. He opened his mouth as if he was going to speak, then closed it and snickered about nothing, alone.

"What will it be?" Leon asked, glancing to Nis in his drugged cloud, then back to Digory. "Will you make your night in Littlebell memorable? Are you in?"

"Aye," Digory relented with a grin, hoping to escape before his turn came. He was not one to ingest toxins apart from ale while on a mission, particularly not any that incapacitated one of one's senses so significantly. He was hoping to take some with him, to partake of his own accord. Perhaps, to share with Sybil. Or possibly Ryd.

"Why not," he said, eying Nis in a bubble of hazy bliss, crumpled against his noble chair. "I'll have what he's having," Digory lied. "I'm in." He expected to be able to sneak out before his turn ever came to pass.

"Ay!" Leon cheered. "Pass it here! Pass it here," he gestured towards the pipe. With extreme effort, like he was moving through tar, Nis leaned forward and shoved the pipe towards Leon. Leon took the pipe and lit it. Mimicking Nis, Leon puffed several times before inhaling. His eyes opened wide, just as Nis's had. Then, he exhaled red-tinted smoke through his nostrils. A mischievous grin wiped across his young, dimpled face.

"Leon?" Digory asked eagerly. "Tell me what it's like."

Leon waved with extreme effort to dismiss Digory, as if dragging fingertips through mud. He paused with his hand held out in front of his face as if he'd never seen it before. He raised it up as he examined it studiously in the flickering candlelight. Nis looked on and shook his head and laughed, then laughed, and laughed more, wiping tears from his eyes as if nothing in his life had ever been so funny.

"You've both gone insane."

"Mad," Leon said slowly, then he burst into laughter again. "We've gone mad, get it?" He urged the pipe towards Digory. "Rune, try it."

Digory instantly regretted this brazen adventure. "On second thought, new friends," he said with charismatic cadence, "I will delay my sampling of your product for my next time in

Littlebell. I am on a mission and…"

Nis interrupted loudly, "You must try it." Wobbling, he brought himself to stand. The whites of his eyes were bloodshot red to match his hidden irises. He looked terrifying. As he swayed back and forth, Nis pulled a sword from a hidden sheath beneath the wooden table with a metallic twang. He placed the weapon down on point to steady himself.

"No," Digory said firmly, flexing his jaw and the muscles of his neck.

"Why won't you try it? Unless…" Nis paused, terrifying eyes darting back and forth, "Guard!" He pointed at Digory and one of the hulking blond men rushed from beyond the tapestry, holding up a club from where it had been tacked to his belt.

"Wait, hold on," Digory put his hands up, jumping from his chair, leaning with his back against cool bricks. He'd gotten himself into many predicaments but never one so potentially dire. Although he did not doubt his ability to overtake the one guard, there were more, and he feared a tussle with them would get the Gold Capes turned on him, and that would be a catastrophe he wasn't sure he could handle. Not subtly anyway. "I am a friend. I mean no…"

"I'll stop you there." Nis swayed, leaning on his sword to steady himself. "I've heard that one."

The guard moved close to Digory and held the club menacingly over him. Leon, oblivious, still stared at his hand in front of his face while giggling. Digory knew he could best them and likely escape the dens with his life, but at what cost?

"Wait!" Digory shouted.

Nis asked in a slur. "Why should I?"

"Leon! Tell him," Digory pleaded, turning to face his initial companion, but Leon was solidly in another world.

"Well?" Nis glanced to the guard about to attack.

"I'll smoke it!" Digory yelled back in more frustration than fear, not wanting a fight. With one bad arm and poor odds, he figured this was a better bet. "I'll smoke the cursed thing!"

"Hmm," Nis grunted, taking several steps backwards, placing

the simple sword with braided black leather hilt onto the table. He snatched the satchel and clumsily packed more of the tobacco-laden mad honey into the cob.

"Here," he said darkly, tilting his head towards Digory. Black shadows to pooled underneath his eyes.

Digory took it firmly, keeping eye-contact with the volatile drug lord. He rose briefly from his seat to grab the lighting candle, reaching with his long arm. He audibly took a deep breath, and, raising one sharp eyebrow, sparked the flame. Digory puffed three times on the pipe before inhaling full lungs of the vulgar, syrupy smoke. It curled in the back of his throat and seized in his chest, throwing him into a phlegmy, deep-rooted cough.

"Here, here!" Leon cheered with bloodshot eyes, swaying back and forth in a clumsy, seated dance, punching both hands upwards as he watched the exchange through his drugged haze.

Digory swallowed hard. His vision pulsed. He exhaled heavy red smoke through both his mouth and nose. He coughed.

ECHO'S OMEN SPIRE

Quentin eyed Basil Graves through the table's flames. He traced his father's backlight outline, imagining the day he would eventually command the Omen's helm of his own accord. How all eyes would follow him as he descended the Spire's stairs. How all heads would bow as he walked past the ranks of Brothers. How the keys to the Green Wing would jingle in his pocket. It was all Quentin Graves dreamed of. That, and earning his father's respect.

They sat in the Spire Hall at the highest point in the Echo's Omen fortress. It pierced gauzy clouds atop a blue-hued mountain with enormous glass all around, which allowed in sun or moonlight depending on the time of day. The Spire was wide enough to fit two hundred men within it, with space to spare. It was only accessible through three narrow staircases spiralling down at three of the four far corners of the hall, allowing three times as many men to enter and exit at the same time. There was a time, centuries ago, when the Spire was the sole military vantage point on the eastern Deadline border. That's the reason it was built. It was occupied by Vanguards of all bloodlines. But after the Plague wiped out all who resided there, it remained empty until Graves and Brochet rediscovered it during the Blood Wars decades later.

The Spire was an ideal military vantage point for the valley, giving a full view of the shorter mountain ridges to each side, and the sloping sunbloom meadow far below.

A heavy table rested in the middle of the impressive hall and a thin fireplace jutted up through the table, through the center of the room then out of the vaulted roof. This fire produced the only light in the Spire Hall apart from the deep oranges, purples, and pinks of the westward sun setting over the valley.

Basil Graves, the Brotherhood elder, was pressed up against the outer glass. He looked down below. A view of the yard, the stocks, and the mess tables. Buildings for barracks, Apothecary, and the overgrown Green Wing. He shuttered in vertigo then placed his hand to his head, wincing in pain.

Quentin leaned forward, picking at a small hole in his leather chair with his fingernails. "Headaches again, father?"

"It's nothing," Basil grumbled, steadying himself against the glass as he glanced down at the recruits. Basil was taller than average with thick once-black greying hair combed back to accentuate a sharp widow's peak, and characteristic Graves-hue skin. His oval face was deep-wrinkled with deep-set beady eyes, white-blind in left, iron-grey right.

"Why headaches?" Wolfgar whispered to Quentin.

"Watch your place, Norland," he hissed under his breath.

Yet Wolfgar Norland pressed, verdant eyes twinkling, seemingly enjoying the surly Quentin's frustration. "Come on, I just want to know."

Quentin assessed the keen young man sitting at his side. Wolfgar was more than a decade his junior with narrow-set green eyes, pasty skin, and a strong jaw. He was a near copy of Davide, *the nerve of him*, Quentin thought. He then he looked at his father. Basil was still out of earshot.

"First, boy," Quentin spat, "you are only here because your brother is a raping traitor who ruined my sister. If it weren't for him, you'd be down there with your brothers and my sons," he gestured towards the training yard. "You didn't earn this honor."

Wolfgar frowned, then flexed his square jaw. "Aye," he grunted.

Quentin smiled, pleased, and turned to look at the roaring fire cutting through the table.

"Aren't you going to tell me?" Wolfgar whispered again, more loudly this time, piercing eyes flashing.

Basil yelled from across the room, "Tell him what, son?"

He hobbled over and lowered himself into the worn chair at the head of the table.

Quentin sat forward quickly, "Father, I was..." he started, grey eyes darting back and forth.

"Quiet. Let Wolfgar speak."

Quentin sulked into his chair.

"Lord Basil," Wolfgar began.

"Basil," the old man warmly corrected.

"Basil," Wolfgar continued, Quentin scowling at his side. "Why headaches?"

"Is that all?" Basil nearly chuckled.

Wolfgar nodded.

"Why didn't you just tell him?"

Quentin held his eyes down, boring a hole in the table in front of him. He hated that Norland boy more than words could say. He imagined flaying the skin right off his body. Plucking his eyes out with his dagger. Peeling his toe nails off with his own eating implements.

"I was kicked in the head by a horse. See here." Basil gestured to a jagged white scar near his temple. "Took my cursed eye. Fuck those cursed beasts."

Wolfgar nodded, turning to Quentin, catching his gaze smugly. Quentin wanted to cut the smile off the boy's stupid bloody Norland face.

He looked away.

Then, Xavier Graves, a man who could be Basil's twin if not for being a head taller and having two good eyes entered the room, wrapped in heavy black hooded robes to match the others. Xavier, a Guildsman trained long ago during the Uprising, walked with a permanent hunch. Unlike Basil, he had a flattened bump in his nose from where it once had been broken.

"Brother," Basil gestured in the customary Brotherhood salute, "welcome."

"Brother," Xavier Graves held up his left hand, returning the salute. He shuffled to sit, choosing a seat at the table closest to Wolfgar Norland.

Quentin's mood fouled further.

Basil asked Xavier, "Have you heard from Uncle?"

"Nay, not a word," the hunched man replied. "I take it you have not either?"

He looked at Basil at the head of the table. Basil shook his head no.

"Perhaps Hector does write true. The elder fades. Strays from Grandfather's path. Hector warns us Hjalmar has gone soft. He goes so far as to say that Graves is in peril, hinting that the old man could fall completely New." Xavier paused, eyebrows raising, grey eyes widening. "I cannot believe it."

"We wrote moons ago. A response would have come by now," Basil said with spite, "if he was still loyal."

"Uncle Haj deserts us?" Xavier asked rhetorically. "No matter. If what Hector writes is true, we can take solace that there is trouble for his favorites at Animus. We won't have to lift a finger. He'll fall on his own."

"What trouble?" Basil asked.

Quentin and Wolfgar listened intently as the sun sank behind ribbons of dark clouds in swirling lilac and navy behind them. Firelight cast dancing shadows across the sharp noses and serious faces. The highest ranked Brotherhood members had met like this, at sunset, every day. It was a tradition upheld since the very beginning.

"The New Rebellion, they're calling it," Xavier said.

"The New Rebellion." Basil repeated carefully. "That's what Hector writes."

Xavier nodded, recalling the parchment he received from the Missive that morn.

"He warns it is not safe for the Old at Animus. Even for Herman. Though in favor of the crown, he is Graves in blood and name."

Wolfgar interrupted the old men's cadence. "I thought the New was peaceful?" His young voice cut the air like the light of dawn.

Quentin winced, prepared for one of Basil's characteristic outbursts, then inwardly fumed at his father's docile response to the Norland.

"That was then," Basil told him. "This is different. They want more than their ancestors. Past freedom and peace, they crave vengeance. That means blood. Hector warns we must prepare our troops for his signal."

Concern blanketed Xavier's face like a white sheet. "What is Hector's aim here?"

"His aim? It is to strike first!" Basil cried, mismatched eyes wild. "He writes that we assemble. Once a few more pieces fall into place, we will attack and take back what is ours, before they have a chance to strike."

"Brother, I caution you," Xavier said slowly, lowering his voice and brow. "This is great action for little promise."

"Hector is blood," Basil said resolutely. "That is all that matters in this world. He will not betray Graves. He will not betray the Brotherhood." He paused, squinting, listening to the fire crack. "Not like his father."

Xavier bowed, submitting to his elder's ruling. Quentin and Wolfgar briefly exchanged glances.

"I don't understand," Wolfgar said.

Basil, half-smiling, amused at the strapping lad's candor, humoured him. "What to understand? Graves is threatened. Norland too. Your blood too, boy," Basil said forcefully, pointing at him. "Our old way of life; the true way of life! It's about time the soft men of the past step aside. This is a young man's world."

"As it will be a young man's war," Xavier cautioned. "Remember brother, we are not so young."

"War, is it?" Quentin said, speaking deeper and more loudly than the others, trying to be seen as important in the discussion. "What are we up against?"

"We will prevail as we did before," Basil said dismissively, not looking at him. "As we always will. Old will always prevail."

"I fear this time could be different," Xavier said.

"Why say that?"

"The Old fights for a lost dream," Xavier replied. "The New defends against a nightmare to come."

"You Guildsmen and your riddles." Basil shook his head. "Dream, nightmare. It makes no difference. We will conquer.

We always do."

"The men are tired," Xavier cautioned. "Don't underestimate our opponents. If Regnard can fall for a second time, anything is possible."

"Regnard has fallen?" Quentin asked, anxiety obvious. "What about Lachlan?"

"I know not," Basil said.

"Hector writes that Regnard will fall," Xavier clarified for his nephew. "The grand Old Lyonshall will be no more."

Wolfgar frowned as he leaned back in his seat, crossing his arms over his chainmail.

"You know nothing?" Basil asked Wolfgar.

In stark contrast to Quentin, Wolfgar's nerves were calm. Although he was young, he had the confidence of a much older man. In that way, he was much like his father Hadrian.

"My mother is his favorite daughter," Wolfgar said. "I've heard all the stories of him but not seen the man since I was a small child. To me, Lachlan is a stranger. I know nothing."

"We need more information, my Lord." Xavier glanced at Wolfgar. "Our supply lines..." he added, then trailed off.

Lyonshall maintained vital trade routes that the Omen used frequently, mainly to gain needed ores for metalworking, but also salt, furs and grain.

Basil interrupted Xavier, loudly. "Send a convoy to Lyonshall to investigate," he barked at Quentin. "Tell them to be alert. To absorb all they can. To report back immediately."

"Aye, Father," Quentin nodded. "I'll command them to depart at dawn."

"Good," Basil cooed.

It was high praise as far as Quentin was concerned. Internally, despite his resentment, Quentin beamed.

"What of Faye Regnard and Rupert Morfit? That is an alliance made in the First," Quentin said, making the most of Basil's attention, hoping, as always, to please him.

"Lachlan nearly hunted his granddaughter down himself when he heard of the union," Basil said. "Hector tells that the pair is intent on poisoning the Capital with lies. That they are at the root of this thing, propelled by her own father."

"What lies are those? What do they preach?"

Basil began to speak but was at a loss for words, so he pointed at Xavier who removed a lengthy letter from his breast pocket. Xavier handed the letter to Basil.

"Hector writes that this New Rebellion aims to overthrow the Old Vanguards," Basil said, scanning the document with his long-nailed finger, "to destroy us as punishment for years of experimentation, torture, and war." At that, he smirked slightly before continuing. "He writes they want to give the land to the earthblood. But New Vanguards are free to do as they please despite their bloodlines' past transgressions, it seems."

"Naturally," Xavier said with a sneer.

"Hector warns us to be prepared for Dale to join the Rebellion as well," Basil went on, reading as he scanned. "Although he will do his best to see that does not occur."

"I know Baddon," Xavier said. "He will not fight for this. Not unless his people are threatened. He's nothing like his grandfather. He won't be baited."

"What of the eldest son?" Basil countered.

"Baddon has a handle on him," Xavier said surely. "He must. You know the man."

At mention of his name, all were reminded of Baddon's legendary victory in the Baneswood Games so many years ago. So much violence. So much blood. The more bloodshed he caused, the more it seemed to fuel him. A man that brutal surely had control over his own bloodline.

"What else?"

"Morfit and Regnard have allied. He writes they may have the clout to overtake the Kingdom," Basil replied, eyes still buried in the parchment. "Or, at least, they believe they do."

Morfit was a traditionally New bloodline, claiming to have been the first to end experimentation and champion equality between Vanguards and natives. A notoriously powerful bloodline that placed themselves in every other realm's affairs and had a propensity for luxury. The natives of their realm were hardworking and proud farmers. They were also known for their metalworking.

While Regnard, alternatively, was little different from Westerviolet, except instead of fields, Lyonshall natives worked in mines. Although Regnard had muddled political beliefs in recent history, it was still surprising to hear that Vanguards from those bloodlines were aligning.

"That's only if they know what they are doing," Quentin said. "Two punching arms does not make a fighting man."

Basil half nodded to Quentin. "My son makes a point."

Quentin silently beamed, glancing down not to smile outright.

"Who leads them?" Xavier asked.

"I say the son Ogo," Basil said. "I wrote to Brochet of this. Perhaps he has information to share."

"Why would you consult Tomas before me?" Xavier asked slowly.

"He is a trusted ally."

"We have no assurance that the alliance with Brochet holds. How do you know..."

Basil interrupted, "Are you angry, brother?" half-smiling at him.

"Can we trust him?" Xavier asked, forehead creased, jowls dipping in concern for his brother's cavalier ways.

Many, including Xavier, feared Basil was waning with age. Losing his sharpness. Making mistakes. But no one dared say such things. Basil would surely condemn anyone to death for even thinking of questioning his sanity. Basil was the Omen elder, after all. Within his realm, he could do as he pleased. He ruled with impunity.

Quentin frowned as Wolfgar looked from face to face. Behind him, the sun was nearly gone and stars popped out one by one, shimmering against the black sky all around them. The sunset sessions rarely lasted this long. Today, however, there was much to discuss.

"Tomas and I are old friends," Basil said.

"He's broken his word to Graves before," Xavier cautioned,

thinking of what Brochet still owed Graves.

Guy Brochet, Tomas's father, had refused to hand over his daughter Farrah under the assumption that his granddaughter, if one were to be born, would be given in her stead. But, after Guy's death, Tomas refused to give up Sybil. And then Sybil's daughter, Rose. Xavier feared, unless drastic actions were taken, the pattern would continue.

"Enough."

"But, brother…"

"Enough!" Basil growled.

Xavier sighed out of both flared nostrils, pointedly glaring at Basil like only a knowing brother could. The men locked eyes. Silence hung in the hall.

"Hector plans to use Busk," Basil broke the lull, still reading.

"Why he married Millie?"

It had always been a mystery as to why Hector Graves, a tyrant, yet rich and powerful and handsome in a chilling way, chose Millie Busk to wed. She was plain, and skittish, and quiet. Not to mention, her father Ralph was a horrid man. When they were married years ago, the Kingdom was awash with speculation. Perhaps she wasn't as plain as she seemed behind closed doors. Or perhaps, Hector preferred his wife that way, so he could do whatever he wanted to her and she would not have the capacity to stop him.

"Aye," Basil replied to Xavier, nodding, "Ralph is cursed but he does have an army. It's what Busk has always been good for."

"A blunt blade can still maim," Xavier nodded. "What of Millie's brother? Ralph's eldest?"

"The dolt who speaks like a child?" Basil scoffed. "He and his earthblood wife are solidly New, but no matter, for while Ralph is elder, the Old holds the Confines. Hector assures that we can count on their forces, as long as the old bastard is still alive," he added, dragging his finger across a line near the end of the letter.

"Hjalmar has ordered against such," Xavier said.

"Hector is ambitious," Basil countered. "He believes his

father's ways are foolish." He paused. "I agree with him."

"Hjalmar cautions against war."

"Hjalmar shows weakness." Basil glanced down then back up. "Hector sees reality. He married Millie, that ugly thing, to get near her bloodline, to gain loyalty of Busk. He says now is our time to take back the Kingdom. Hjalmar thinks we are too young and naive. I say he's jaded. We are ambitious."

"It is troublesome that as our Kingdom churns, the Brotherhood is condemned to observe it all second-hand. We are at Hector's mercy," Xavier said.

"We need someone on the inside," Quentin thought out loud.

"That is an idea," Basil grunted. "Wolfgar!" He turned to the fair-haired young man in a rush.

"But, father," Quentin stood with a scratch of his chair against stone. "I was thinking that I..."

"Nonsense," Basil interrupted cruelly. "Look at you. You are a Graves through and through. You reek of the Omen," he sneered. "We will say Wolfgar is a Thorne bastard. Your mother is a Thorne, yes?" He glanced to the young man, formulating the plot as fast as he spoke.

"Grandmothers, Lord. Both."

"Right, right. Yes, yes. Same difference. You look the part," he said, assessing Wolfgar's block jaw. A known Norland trait. "Close enough anyway. You have the Thorne green eyes and pale skin, don't you? The key is you are not Norland. They've never met you, nor your brothers at the Capital so none will know the difference," he added surely, growing more and more pleased with his mounting plan by the moment. "Let's call you Jude. Beware not to mention your true identity. You and your kin do not have the best..." he paused and half-smiled, "...reputation."

Quentin snickered. "Jude," he said under his breath.

"I wouldn't laugh if I were you," Basil told Quentin meanly. "You should hear what is said of us." Quentin sulked back down to a seat. Basil looked at Wolfgar. The charismatic man was mature beyond his years and could handle the task. "You'll leave tomorrow for Animus. Go there, say you're a bastard, half Northern earthblood, which is why you're so pale, and they won't know what to do with you. They'll bring you right to Humphry, I'm sure of it! You must remember all you hear and see, then come back here on the shortest day and tell all of what you've learned. Make it appear as if you have died so you won't be followed. You'll not speak of this to your Norland father, or brothers. Or sister. And especially not your mother. Tell your kin you are out on Omen business, if you must tell them anything at all. No more. Do you understand? The oath you owe the Brotherhood far exceeds any of father or son."

"I understand," Wolfgar said solemnly, blinking once. "If asked, who is my kin?"

Basil turned to Xavier. "What should his blood be?"

Xavier looked Wolfgar up and down, pinching his brow briefly, then raised his eyebrows apart in recognition.

"He resembles Wallace."

The room stared at Wolfgar. "You're right," Basil said. "Old loon has it coming." He flipped his wrist in dismissal. "Wallace Thorne," he said, turning to Wolfgar to answer his question. "Return by Winter solstice with all you can, then we will decide how to rid our Kingdom of this new plague. Keep ears on Regnard, Morfit, and Minney lips especially. Don't trust one of them."

"Aye, my Lord."

"It's about time our Old Plot overtakes the New once and for all. This rebellion will not stand, if Basil Graves has any say," he said loudly, shaking as he rose slowly from his seat. "For too long, the noble cause of the Ancestors has been shoved aside. No more. We will return to glory! This, my friends, will be the beginning of a long era where the Brotherhood will reign!"

Quentin beat his fist loudly on the table. "Here, here."

"Speaking of, Xavier," Basil looked at his brother, "tell of the Wing."

The Green Wing was the primary reason why Echo's Omen was reopened at all. It was rediscovered at the beginning of the

Blood Wars and the history of where it came from had died with the Plague. No one was sure how long it had been there. Rumors stated it predated the Destruction even. The Green Wing was located beneath the Spire and was the location for the majority of the Brotherhood's present-day experimentation.

Xavier's eyes darted. "I'm making progress, Basil." He swallowed hard. "Not as quickly as anticipated."

Xavier was overseeing research regarding the Deadlands, more specifically, how exactly deadbloods were able to walk there without succumbing to Dread Death. That had been Graves' aim for as long as anyone could remember, to be immune to radiation. In the present day, Gravesblood with dead blood in their veins were immune to the worst symptoms of Dread, mainly death, however contracting the illness was not pleasant. He was also attempting to perfect the Grey tonic, given to all Brotherhood members, mimicking the faint immunity that Gravesblood naturally bore to Dread. Although it came with side effects.

"Your delays are torture for me," Basil growled, taking a step towards him. "Why not?"

"Progress takes time."

"I am no child, brother," Basil spat, removing a black glass dagger from his hip, holding it to Xavier's left side. "You've had time. You try my patience. I demand results."

"Father!" Quentin chided impulsively, jumping from his chair to defend his uncle.

Basil pointed the dagger at his son. "Never speak back to me again."

"Brother," Xavier said.

Then, Basil sheathed his dagger instantly, anger washing away as quickly as it came. "Tell me of the progress you have made," he said calmly like nothing happened at all, "if you've made any."

That's how Basil was, especially as old age gripped him. His emotions were as predictable as Wraithswail weather. That is to say, not predictable at all.

Xavier exhaled loudly. "I could explain, but," he paused. "Would you like a demonstration?"

"Why not?" Basil answered with a wide, yellowed smile.

"In that case, follow me," Xavier said cryptically. "This demonstration will require a bit of an... excursion."

"Of course," Basil replied politely, half bowing his head. "After you."

The men followed each other one by one down the narrow spiral staircase in the eastern corner of the hall. There were indents into the stone for ancient iron candelabras on each side embedded deep into the mortar itself, dimly lighting the descent down dizzying flights, until they reached the main hall.

The group exited the tight stairwell by filtering out of a discrete doorway into an impressive space. Long wooden tables lined the length while commemorative armor and weapons were displayed about the walls. There was an original battle flag used during the Uprising, still spattered in blood, hung with pride. The Brotherhood emblem was front and center above the high table where Basil and his closest advisors sat at meals overseeing the common men. At the cusp of nightfall, it was empty in the hall. Xavier's slow, dragging footsteps were followed by the livelier pats of his companions. They traversed the length and exited the front archway, down three flights of stone steps, then onto the training grounds in the wake of the fortress.

"Have these recruits been assessed?" Basil said offhandedly to Quentin as they passed by beaten, naked men, chained to heavy wooden poles.

"Awaiting assessment in the morn."

"Good," Basil replied. "Do not begin without me."

"Father, you've given me full command of the..."

"Do not question me."

"But..." Quentin started, until Basil held up his hand. The younger grey-eyed man, a copy of his father, fell quiet.

After a walk across the grounds, the men reached an unceremoniously placed gate, wildly overgrown with thick ivy and leafy tendrils, situated amidst shadows in the corner of the yard. For being so important, the Green Wing was terribly unimposing. From the outside at least.

Wolfgar's eyes darted back and forth. He'd never known where the entrance to the Green Wing was. The location was kept secret from the men, even the Keys typically, to avoid anyone sticking their nose where it didn't belong.

He leaned to Quentin. "I thought this was forbidden?"

"Quiet," Quentin growled, irritated to breathe the same air as the Norland, much less speak to him. He hated Norland blood almost more than the New. Almost.

Basil stood to the side of Xavier. Both older men now hovered with backs to the gate, facing the younger men Quentin and Wolfgar.

"Do you know where we are?" Basil asked.

Wolfgar looked at Quentin, then back at Basil.

"The Green Wing," he said obviously.

"Good, good. And what do you know about it?"

"Nothing, my Lord."

"Nothing? Nothing at all? Hard to believe seeing as you've lived so much of your life within these walls."

"Aye, nothing," Wolfgar replied.

"Why is that, young Wolfgar?" Basil said, patting the overgrown building, indecently disrupting an intricate web. A striped spider scurried away quickly; angry its home had been destroyed. "Why is it that no matter who passes through these walls, this wing here holds onto her secrets?"

"I don't know, my Lord."

"What about you Quentin?" Basil turned to his son. "Do you know anything about the Wing?"

"I know it is forbidden."

"Anything else?"

"No."

"No? Surely you know some secret knowledge of it?" Quentin shook his head, yet Basil still pressed. "The Elder of the Brotherhood's own son, heir to elderclaim, does not know the secrets that it holds?"

Quentin lowered his head and shook it 'no' while Wolfgar looked on. Xavier observed with curiosity, unsure what his brother would do next. If he was anything, Basil was unpredictable.

"Do you know why neither of you know anything about it?"

The younger men shook their heads 'no' to Basil in tandem.

"Good, and it will stay that way," Basil said simply. He turned and removed a heavy skeleton key from his pocket. "I bring you here to teach you the importance of Brotherhood law. I do not tell you our secrets not because I do not wish to, rather, our law is armor. We do things the way they have always been done. It's how we survive. Only the elder and his Second have access. When I die, I will pass this to Quentin," he said, holding up the key. "If he is worthy."

Quentin reached forward to grasp it, but Basil snatched it away. "Wait your turn," Basil growled. "I am the elder now. I have done my time. You will learn our secrets when your time comes."

"If you told us now, no one would know," Quentin said, realizing his folly the instant the words came out. But he couldn't help himself.

"Laws are all that separate us from animals," Xavier added. "Break ours and you become the names they call you in the streets of the Capital. "

Quentin sighed and Wolfgar silently smirked. Quentin could feel the Norland's delight at the exchange and it was all he could do not to slit his throat right there. He reminded himself that everything he desired could come in time. He just had to wait for Basil to die.

"Prepare yourself to leave for Animus at dawn," Basil told Wolfgar. "You'll ride with the convoy to investigate Lyonshall, then break away when you reach Croft. Avoid the Morfits and head to the Rock. Understood?"

"Aye," Wolfgar nodded as he met Basil's white and grey eyes.

"I'll see to the convoy," Quentin offered eagerly, but Basil had already turned his back.

"This is where we leave you," Xavier said to Quentin and Wolfgar, standing in the chilly shadow of the Green Wing.

Basil shifted the heavy key into the rusted lock, then pushed the iron gate open with a slow creak. Musty air rushed by Quentin and Wolfgar from the darkness. The young pair watched as the old men shuffled into the doorway, dragging heavy black robes across its dirty floor. Xavier pulled the metal gate behind them with a clank.

Then, Basil and Xavier disappeared into the blackened depths of the Green Wing with cool twilight on their backs.

ANIMUS ROCK'S THIRD TOWER

The Third Tower of Animus Rock was dedicated to educating Vanguard children Old and New in the ways of the Kingdom. At the height of Vanguard prominence, prior to the Plague, the Academy educated hundreds, sometimes thousands of children at any given time. Most of which had blood powers. In the past, lessons focused less on history and more on harnessing and developing said powers—how to hone them and utilize them safely, for the good of the Kingdom.

In the modern day, officially, the children were taught the lineage and doctrine of every bloodline, primarily focused on occurrences post-Plague. Lower Academy children were given a heavy focus on memorization in addition to lessons on diplomacy and etiquette. Upper Academy children, in addition to the more gruesome details of history, were taught lessons on persuasion, silence and emotional control—how to read weakness and how to portray strength, regardless of bloodline.

Unofficially, the children were being assessed for any residual power in their blood.

"Power is not taken—it is Awakened," echoed sentiments from days long forgotten, engraved above the largest Lessonroom's high arched door.

A sturdy woman with crisp white hair stood at the head of the starkly decorated Lessonroom. It was an outrageously enormous space considering how few children filled it. It was a somber reminder of how many Vanguards were killed by the Plague.

Today, Guildswoman Rotrude was filled with purpose. She was excited to begin this session and meet the youngest group of Vanguard children. Particularly because she had never taught a Brochet before. She was wary of what to expect given the bloodline's brutal past.

Every year she learned something new about at least one of the Vanguard bloodlines, despite being educated at Hidden Den for this particular purpose. The children typically revealed talents to her that they weren't aware of themselves. That was Rotrude's true directive as Lessonmaster, hidden from the children, to identify if any possessed any interesting or particularly dangerous abilities that were missed by the Guild assessments.

It was a great honor to be chosen as Lessonmaster. She held the position in highest regard.

Rotrude understood the importance of the Lower Academy lessons. They focused on Vanguard history, to teach the children their place in the Kingdom as well as scan for the presence of any obvious abilities, although she preferred teaching the older children at Upper Academy. That was when their powers were truly tested and, if not useful to the Guild, stifled accordingly. Although all believed that only the Vanguards of the past were powerful, Rotrude knew the truth.

All who possessed Vanguard blood in the present day were innately powerful, in varying degrees, of course.

There was a time in ancient history when it was simple to predict the type of power that would present in any given Vanguard.

Dales possessed inhuman strength. Durans, invisibility and phase shifting. Bellamines, super intelligence. Brochets, longevity–typically involving regeneration, or necromancy. Beaumonts were telekinetic. Warns were able to slow time and alter perception. Graves, soul harvesting and later, immunity to Dread. Calvanese had communion with and control over spirits as well as empathetic dominion–the ability to override another's emotions and control them at will. Busk could manipulate the weather. Demos could make binding oaths. Thorne had control over plant life as well as occasionally temporal sight–the ability to glimpse into threads of possible futures. Norland possessed pulse rage–the ability to supercharge their bloodstream with violent energy, multiplying speed and strength tenfold in a berserker-like fashion. Regnards could control the earth, shifting stone, sand or metal. Morfits were dream weavers. Minney blue-eyes were known for healing and Horne had either the ability to communicate with animals or blood assimilation–the ability to gain an animal or person's strength, memories or skills through consuming their flesh.

But over centuries and centuries, as the bloodlines mixed, predictability waned. Oldblood Vanguards began to exhibit signs of madness from too much power in the blood, while Newblood Vanguards, having intermarried with natives, diluted their powers down to the point most could barely access them at all. In the present day, any given Vanguard's powers were essentially random and ranged from as powerful as a tornado to as mundane as a soft breeze, typically depending on if their blood was Old or New, and if they had been activated by trauma.

Few Vanguards possessed multiple powers while most had only one, and an innocuous one at that.

Regardless of potency, the Guild ensured that all were suppressed, including those chosen to be Guildsmen. It was what was best for the Kingdom. And Rotrude always wanted to do what was best.

Behind Rotrude, a lurching fireplace sat aside shelves stacked sparsely with ancient pre-plague books. In front of her, rows of eager young Vanguards wearing identical grey smocks stared back.

"There are many new faces," Rotrude said, warm voice echoing as she gestured outwards with both hands. "And some old."

She nodded to a pair of identical boys with copper skin, hooded emerald eyes and mops of messy, sun-highlighted hair. Characteristic Warns.

"Welcome to your first day of Academy. My name is Rotrude." She slightly bowed her head.

The modest gilded pendants hanging from her ears clinked loudly.

Rotrude was hard-looking and large for a woman, tall and imposing with broad shoulders and a square torso. Her white hair was smoothed customarily flat to her head with fish oil instead of lavender oil (as it was all she could afford) and tucked behind particularly small ears. She wore simple Tower robes in Third Purple wrapped expertly several times around her body then looped around her neck, secured at the hip with a simple copper Bellamine Griffin brooch, as was customary for all Lessonmasters.

"We'll begin with a lesson on The North Plague of 3833," she said, pacing the room, scanning eager and focused faces. "The beginning of modern history. Then, I'll allow for free time so you can get to know your new classmates," and reveal any innate abilities, she thought. "You'll be out by midday," she said to a delighted hum. The twin boys were particularly loud. "To those of you who have been here before," Rotrude eyed the twins, "it won't hurt you to hear it again. Maybe you'll catch something you missed."

The boys together rolled their eyes and laughed.

Grey light filtered in through high windowpanes and illuminated Rotrude's strong features harshly from the side and she shielded her eyes. Then she paused, stopping her gait briefly, smoothing her robes, taking in all the excitement that a new session brings.

"In 3833 a terrible plague broke out," Rotrude said dramatically, "desecrating Vanguards and natives alike."

Concern gripped the children's faces. Several furrowed their brows.

"We want to learn about the Vanguard!" one of the two boys shouted. "Yeah!" his identical copy mimicked.

"Boys, you must learn about our modern history in Lower," Rotrude turned, replying calmly. "In Upper we cover ancient history."

"Why?" they whined in unison.

"The Council ruled long ago that it is too much for your

young minds to grasp," Rotrude said patiently. "We'll learn of your history from the Nomad Conflict onward. When you are older, you'll learn of the details of your ancestors dating back over two thousand years. Once your minds can handle the…" Rotrude trailed off, upturned nose wrinkling as she thought, "…intricacies of the past," she finally said. "It's very complex." She looked at them with clay-red eyes. "One thing at a time."

The boys both sank to their stools in unison, one kicking his feet against the seat in front of him, the other biting at the skin of his nail, both wearing a scorn. They were used to far too few rules and far too much freedom, Rotrude thought. She was sure those boys experienced very little discipline, if any at all, within the walls of Ironbark.

"From now on, hands will be raised. You will announce your name when you have a question." Rotrude's tone bordered shrill. "I don't care if you've been here before or not."

One of the boys whispered something to the other, after which the second snickered loudly, causing the first boy to fall into a fit of laughter. This triggered the other children, all females, to giggle senselessly.

Disheartened that folly took hold in the very beginning of the very first lesson, Rotrude paused again, pressing her fingers to her temple. She sighed loudly. She repeated her affirmations in her head briefly until she was ready to speak.

Finally, Rotrude warned, "Boys… you understand what it means if you do not complete this session? Will you have me send the Missive to your elder?"

Eyes wide in terror, the twins sat up straight up, after which the rest of the Lessonroom quickly fell silent.

Rotrude went on.

"Due to the Plague, three of the sixteen Vanguard bloodlines went extinct: Blood Duran, Blood Horne, and Blood Calvanese," she said.

A white-blonde beauty with a diamond-shaped face and tan, nearly green-hued skin raised her hand. The girl wore a blue gem band at her neck. Rotrude already knew who she was before she called on her. She was clearly a Demos.

"Yes?" Rotrude called on her. "Your name, dear?"

"Malla," the little girl said confidently. "Demos."

"And your question?"

"They really died?" Malla asked, eyes squinted in half-fear half-awe. "All of them? What happened to their castles?"

"Yes, I mean they died," Rotrude said with a curt nod. "All of them. Duran's Whisperfield is in ruins after the beatings of constant sandstorms without anyone to maintain it. Blood Horne's Hunter Post fortress sits nearly abandoned at the edge of Baneswood and is overseen by Dale. And Blood Calvanese's temple Duskfang, in the shadow of the Cursed Hills, has been overtaken by deadbloods."

Malla raised her hand once more.

"Yes, Malla?"

"How did they die?"

Rotrude smiled. She was amused by the girl's candor, although she knew it could grow old quickly.

"Please, let me go on with the lesson," she said to the eager, frizzy-haired girl. "I will tell you. Today we'll focus on the Plague and later spend a whole day on the extinct bloodlines themselves. Patience."

Malla glanced down to her lap as the other children giggled quietly.

"Settle down, don't laugh," Rotrude chided the room. "It's good to be curious."

She glanced to Malla, who smiled slightly.

Pale grey sun broke into shards of white light as it poured through the ceiling-high windows, brightening the faces of this session's Vanguard lower class.

"To explain the whole story, I will start earlier than the Plague," Rotrude told them, pacing again, Third Tower robes lapping like purple waves in her wake. "In 3800, two hundred and fifty years ago exactly, the northern nomadic king, Emperor Amagiuaq, attacked Animus Rock. The Nomads experienced a drought that led to famine. When our Vanguard leader at the time, King Aldus Bellamine, refused to provide aid for their suffering, the Nomads invaded. There were not many casualties. The Vanguard weapons greatly bested that of their sticks and fire, but the attack was still detrimental," she said, pacing from the book-lined wall to the windows. "The Nomads burned the Grand Library. They destroyed nearly all the ancient documents and original records from the Vanguard." She paused in front of the wall of ancient books. "Here are some of the last remnants of life before," she said sombrely, gesturing at the frayed and yellowed bindings, "but it was not enough, for the Vanguard Tree herself burned and had to be replanted from a single remaining acorn, a huge blow. It meant that all records of Vanguard genealogy prior to the Nomad conflict were lost. This prompted the king at the time, Aldus the Unready—as he was later called—to build the Animus Rock fortress wall. The economic implications of this wall were enormous. They led to later conflict, all of which you will learn about in more detail in Upper Academy in years to come."

Rotrude determined all children were listening after sweeping the chamber with her eyes, then continued.

"The Nomads retreated North, defeated. Emperor Amagiuaq, not forgetting his embarrassment, plotted revenge," she said. "King Aldus died years later. He left his son Abner to inherit the throne. Make sense so far?"

Small heads around the room nodded.

"For thirty years, Emperor Amagiuaq used spies to learn all he could about the Vanguards," Rotrude explained, placing hands behind her back, walking down the center isle of children's tables with chest puffed out.

She was proud of her lofty position of Lessonmaster, and it showed. She had come so far. Unthinkably so.

"He learned of the discontent brewing and unhappiness with the King. He learned that there was a divide between the bloodlines. Emperor Amagiuaq plotted to use this fracture to his advantage."

Rotrude paused at the back of the room.

"Do you know what fracture I'm referring to?"

All turned around in their seats to look at her, engrossed with the tale.

A mousy girl with a large forehead raised her hand slowly. Malla shot hers up into the air and waved it with vigorous enthusiasm, however, Rotrude pointed at the mousy girl. The Busk. Malla sunk in her chair.

"The Old way?"

"Yes!" Rotrude clapped her hands, pleased at the Busk's engagement so early on. She was surprised that the little girl spoke at all, given what she knew of her bloodline. "And what is your name?"

The girl rose her sunken eyes slowly to meet Rotrude's. "Lucette."

"Lucette?"

"Busk," the girl whispered.

At that, the identical young boys exchanged mischievous smiles with each other, snickering. They'd never seen a Busk in person before. "Oh, how ugly! The stories were true!"

Lucette lowered her head in shame.

"Boys, quiet," Rotrude hushed a little too harshly. "She is correct."

Rotrude's heart tore for Lucette. The girl reminded her of herself at that age. Meek and without companionship.

"The fracture I refer to is the divide between Old and New. This story of the Nomad Conflict and the Plague is what leads us to where we are in politics today. It's very important to learn where you came from," she said, pacing back down the center isle to the front of the chamber once more. "It is the only way to change where you will go. You must learn from the past, children."

The little faces nodded in unison. Pleased, Rotrude took a deep breath before continuing.

"Before the Plague, the divide was only discussed in whispers and shadows. It was a much different world back then. The Kingdom followed the aims of the Vanguards. Native concerns were secondary."

A ghostly pale blonde with close-set eyes and button nose raised her hand instantly. She wore a thin gem crown with a dark purple gemstone over her forehead.

"Yes?" Rotrude turned to the pallid girl. Her lifeless hair hung flat to her shoulders like draped yarn. "What's your name?"

"Evia," the girl said confidently, as if she'd practiced many times. "Norland."

At the mention of that bloodline, Rotrude instinctively tensed, then she reminded herself internally that the girl was just a child, not at fault for the crimes of her blood.

"What's your question?" she asked Evia without discernible warmth at all.

"What's 'native' mean?" Evia asked.

Initially shocked, Rotrude looked at her sadly, white eyebrows puckering above tired eyes.

"It's another way of saying..." Rotrude began, then paused to consider her options with the delicate term. "*Earthblood,*" she finally told her in a whisper, offensive phrase biting and metallic on her tongue. Like tasting blood. It sent a shiver down her spine. "We don't use that word."

"Why not?" Evia asked with a confused expression to which the rest of the children, apart from Rose, collectively gasped.

A dark girl with a hugely intricate honey-colored braid on Evia's right stared daggers while Malla angrily frowned.

"I'll call them native people here, understood?" Rotrude said firmly, narrowing her gaze.

"But Father says..."

"I'll stop you there," Rotrude interrupted, taking three fast steps to loom over the girl. "Here in the Third Tower, you shall learn the teachings of all the Vanguards, not just your father. All bloodlines," she repeated harshly for emphasis. "This is the last time you'll tell me your bloodline has told you something different. My lesson is what we are learning. Understood?"

There's always one every year, Rotrude thought to herself.

"Yes, Lessonmaster," Evia conceded and slid down in her chair.

Rotrude collected her thoughts before continuing. She flattened her robe's pleats while calming herself externally. Although beneath her purple robes, her heart beat furiously.

"As I was saying," Rotrude finally went on, "before the Plague, the divide was hidden. Most bloodlines adhered to the Old traditions of the Vanguard. The ones who did not kept their New opinions within their realms. But discontent was brewing. A few bloodlines began to live hand-in-hand with natives. Minney, Morfit and Demos to name a few. Emperor Amagiuaq used this to his advantage. Does anyone know what he did?"

Rotrude scanned the room. There were no raised hands.

"Anyone?" she pressed, but the room stayed silent, children avoiding her eyes.

"Emperor Amagiuaq sabotaged us," she finally said. "He appealed to King Abder. He asked for diplomacy, claiming he wanted a truce. King Abder, despite nearly all counsel, welcomed the Nomads with open arms. What he didn't know was that he'd fallen right into the trap. Each one of the visiting Nomads including the Emperor Amagiuaq himself was infected with Dread Death."

Rotrude walked to and fro in the head of the Lessonroom, through the beams of bright morning light then into dark shadow.

"Does anyone know what Dread Death is?" she asked the class again, to no response. "What about you?" Rotrude glanced to Rose sitting on the right of the room, staring ahead at the tall fireplace with intensity.

She didn't understand enough about Academy to know how to act and had resolved herself to watch its happenings in silence until she did. Rose winced when she was called on.

"Me?" Rose turned her round face, dark curls bouncing around her shoulders.

"Yes, you," Rotrude answered, smiling warmly, taking the girl's quiet nature for shyness. She was so beautiful, so doll like, so innocent. She couldn't possibly be evil as her ancestors were said to be. As her bloodline was reported to be. There had to be a mistake. "What's your name?"

"Rose Brochet."

Never having taught a Brochet, Rotrude wasn't sure about

her. The Brochet bloodline was notoriously dangerous. But this small girl projected nothing but peace and poise. She couldn't be someone to fear, could she?

Do you know what Dread death is, Rose Brochet?" she asked.

Rose shook her head no.

But she did know. Grandfather had taught her about it, but she didn't want to speak.

"Any guesses?" Rotrude pressed.

"The Plague?" Rose reluctantly answered.

"Good," Rotrude said, oiled white hair glinting as she passed through a beam of light. "The North Plague was Dread Death. It's called the North Plague because it was introduced by the Nomads to the North of us."

The children nodded in understanding as Rotrude paced on.

"Dread Death comes from the irradiated Deadlands to the far east and far west of our great Kingdom. It's a horrible disease that eats the flesh and rots the mind. It's extremely contagious and can be spread from physical contact alone. Some argue that it can be contracted through the air as well, but there is no proof. Still, my Guildsmen brethren advise if you ever suspect someone has been struck with Dread you must stay far away from them. No matter the circumstance, never touch them."

The children collectively hung on Rotrude's words.

"The first symptoms of Dread are confusion, irritability, and neck pain that begin immediately," she said, imagining the specimens she was privy to during her studies at Hidden Den. "Moments later, the victim's eyes, nose, and mouth will start leaking blood. Then, hair loss will begin. The mind will deteriorate further as the deadblood madness takes hold. The skin will turn blackened grey, pussing and boiling in less than a moon. Once contracted Dread death, most don't live past that. Most, much, much less. In some, particularly natives, death comes very quickly indeed."

Evia Norland scrunched her face and put her hand up into the air.

"Yes Evia?"

"Is there a cure?"

"No, and no vaccine either," Rotrude said. "We are very vulnerable to Dread Death. The Guild works tirelessly on producing a way to defeat it, but so far, we've not developed anything. Luckily, there's not had an outbreak since the Plague."

Rotrude took a break from pacing to stand directly front and center of the chamber. She adjusted her Tower robes then stood with hands clasped behind her back.

"Hopefully," she added, "it never happens again."

Nearly tremoring in terror, little Lucette Busk raised a meek hand.

"Will we catch it?" she asked, fear palpable as if leaking from her big brown eyes.

Rotrude softened. "The only way to catch it nowadays is to have a brush with a Deadblood, and you'd have to be far into the Cursed Hills or Bone Mountains for that," she said gently, locking eyes with the girl. "We are safe here in the middle of the Kingdom," she assured.

"Why did the Nomads do it?" Malla blurted loudly.

"Remember to raise your hand, Malla." Rotrude turned quickly, ear pendants clanking, purple robes jostling. "They did it because they thought to defeat the Kingdom, it must be divided. In the ruin of the Plague, Emperor Amagiuaq planned for his forces to invade. His plan nearly worked, certainly paving the way for both the Blood Wars and The Uprising to come."

Malla began to speak, then frowned and raised her hand high.

"Yes?" Rotrude called on her more warmly this time.

"Did they invade?"

"Fortunately for the Vanguards, they didn't," Rotrude told her.

The other children listened closely.

"Not so fortunate for Emperor Amagiuaq, his plan backfired. The Nomad King sacrificed himself to infect our Kingdom, but in an ironic twist of fate, it crept back North to his own people as well. It's estimated that our Kingdom lost over ninety-five percent of its population or more in the following years, Vanguards and natives alike, however, the Nomads were hit harder than we were. Once a great force on the continent, even today, they've not built back the power they had before the Plague."

Rotrude paused briefly, allowing the message to sink in.

"It goes as a lesson," she said wisely. "Never let the pull of revenge leave you blind. Emperor Amagiuaq exacted revenge against the Kingdom at the cost of his own people. It's tragic that so many had to die for one man's prideful folly."

The children nodded together in agreement as grey morning clouds returned, casting the chamber dark like night. The large fire was all that brightened the Lessonroom.

"Although the North Plague decimated the Kingdom, thirteen Vanguard bloodlines survived to rebuild from its ashes. I'll start with your ancestor," Rotrude said, glancing at Rose, who blushed and looked down. "Rufus Brochet, born in 3810, was twenty-five years when the plague hit. He was the youngest of six brothers, all who perished with their families. Rufus survived with the assistance of Audrina Dale, the only surviving member of the Dale bloodline. She nursed him back to health. After all were dead at Westerviolet it's said Rufus ventured to nearby Baneswood in search of survivors. The charming Rufus found the fire-haired Audrina and allegedly contracted Dread death in the process of rescuing her."

Rotrude paced again through the shadowy grey-cast Lessonroom, tucking hair behind her ear with one hand, then wiping the oil from it discreetly on the side of her robes.

"Somehow, she saved him," Rotrude raised her eyebrows, speaking with drama. "Native legends say the Horned Woman interfered," to which the children collectively mumbled in question and excitement, "but no one knows for certain. What we do know is he is the only Vanguard ever reported to recover from Dreads," Rotrude said. "After the Plague was over and he was cured, Rufus married Audrina. The couple had two sons and a daughter. The eldest son inherited the name

'Brochet' and married a Green Winger. Those are her ancestors." She gestured at Rose.

A willowy girl with sharp features, upturned green eyes and blade-straight hair raised a slender hand.

"What's a Green Winger?" she asked with silvery cadence, already knowing full-well what the term meant. She simply wanted to see how this Lessonmaster responded. Grandfather had taught her to test everyone she encountered in this fashion.

"Your name?" Rotrude shot back, instantly hoping she didn't sound too harsh.

No one wanted to offend a Thorne.

"Please introduce yourself first," she added more warmly.

"Orosia."

"Bloodline?"

"Thorne."

"Welcome," Rotrude slightly bowed her head, knowing who the girl's father, and more importantly, grandfather was. "The Green Wing is a society removed on ours," she went on, "that resides in a vault."

She stopped pacing to explain, met with clouded expressions, realizing the term was confusing with no context.

"Vaults are ancient cities built by the old gods, before the Vanguard Landing, before the Destruction even, hidden underground," she clarified, to many 'ahhs' and understanding faces. "There have only ever been two vaults discovered. They are quite rare." Rotrude gestured to Rose. "Rose's ancestors, in part, hail from the vault below what is now Echo's Omen.

Rose felt everyone looking at her as she glared holes in the fireplace ahead.

"Rufus and Audrina's eldest son, Robert Brochet, born after the Plague in 3845 and his ally Humfra Graves, born in 3853, rediscovered Echo's Omen during the Blood Wars."

Rotrude nodded to the icy beauty.

"We'll cover Echo's Omen and the Blood Wars extensively other lessons, Orosia."

"Yes, Lessonmaster," the blonde said coolly. On either side of her perched near-identical copies, just smaller, mirroring her smile, beaming with matching smug pride.

Rotrude wondered what to expect from them. She studied the three girls briefly. She had never instructed Thorne children before either. She was intimidated, to say the least. They were charmed in a way even the Guild did not understand.

"I'll continue," she told the Lessonroom as a grey cloud shifted. An avalanche of light poured into the space once more.

"Plague survivors Rufus Brochet and Audrina Dale named their second son Gavin. He was given his mother's name 'Dale' to preserve her bloodline," Rotrude said. "Coincidently, he inherited the iconic Dale firehair as well. Then, the third child of Rufus and Audrina was called Rilla. Rilla Brochet was wed to her brother Gavin, to further both bloodlines and thus rekindle the Dale line. Gavin and Rilla's descendants occupy Baneswood today," she added. "After the Plague, Dale shifted New, intermarrying with natives in Baneswood while Robert Brochet's ancestors continued the tradition he started."

"Brother and sister got married?" one of the smaller copies of Orosia Thorne squealed. "Ew!"

Turning slowly, Rotrude narrowed her clay-red eyes at the precocious child. "What is your name?"

"Gracelia Thorne," the girl said hotly.

"Back then, it was not so uncommon, Gracelia," Rotrude said. "Why, if I remember the Vanguard tree correctly, you yourself are distantly Beaumont, through your famous ancestor August Norland's bride Audina. For centuries, the Beaumonts wed their own brothers and sisters. It was very common."

"Nuh, uh," the girl spat, to which Orosia elbowed her sister sharply and shot a communicative frown. Gracelia stuck her tongue out, to which Orosia turned her head sharply the other way. The whole time, the third smallest Thorne girl smirked at her bickering sisters.

"It's true Graclia," Rotrude said, nodding, crossing her arms in front of her chest. "It leads me to the next surviving bloodline."

She studied Orosia's thin-lipped scowl.

"Vladislav Beaumont, called Vlad by most, was twenty years old when the Plague hit. His younger sister Isa was fifteen. They travelled together with their parents Bernarus and Geila - married cousins - to Littlebell for the wedding of their brother Cassyon Beaumont to Anneia Minney. The Beaumonts rarely married outside of their own blood but Anneia Minney was a blue-eye. She was too tempting an alliance for the ambitious Beaumonts to refuse," Rotrude said.

It was uncomfortable for her to conceptualize the world as it was back then, for if Rotrude had been born at that time, she would still be in chains. Shaking off the unnerving realities of history, she continued to explain.

"Unfortunately, Dread Death infected the water and everyone in the wedding's attendance died except for Vlad and Isa, who arrived late," she said sombrely. "During the Plague they escaped infection by traveling the long distance back up the Missi to Winter Garden, where they wed to continue their bloodline."

Malla shot her hand into the air.

"Yes Malla?"

Streaming light from the side windows illuminated her lime green eyes glowingly bright. "Why was it so important for Beaumonts to continue their blood?" she asked.

"It wasn't just Beaumonts," Rotrude said. "Remember, Brochet and Dale married brother and sister to preserve blood at one time."

She paced to the bookshelf on the room's side. She glanced to it wistfully, mourning briefly how much of the Kingdom's knowledge was lost when the Fourth Tower burned.

"But Beaumonts were special," she said, glancing back to the children. "They believed in the ultimate purity of their own blood. That was in their creed since the beginning."

She paused, deciding whether to broach this touchy topic. There was much regarding Vanguard abilities that she was not permitted to say.

"The Beaumont bloodline is the only bloodline ever officially recorded to exhibit abilities," she finally told them.

They deserved to know some things, she thought. Besides, what she was about to tell them was essentially common knowledge.

"These abilities were present in Vlad and Isa's father, Bernarus Beaumont, born in 3780. He was the fool who nearly ended the Kingdom as we know it. He has an interesting story, in fact, although typically reserved for Upper. Would you like to hear it? It's a bit off lesson."

"Yes!" several children chimed in.

"Alright," Rotrude conceded, smiling warmly, encouraged by the collective curiosity.

She loved teaching those who wished to be taught.

"The Beaumont bloodline was particularly ambitious in their aims." Noting the hands around the room raising, she quelled them by adding, "We'll cover that and the aims of all of the other bloodlines and how they evolved over the years in much more detail in Upper, at least, what is known," to which the hands lowered.

Rotrude swept her eyes across the anticipating faces, pausing for drama, then went on.

"Bernarus could move things with his mind," she said slowly, wiggling her fingers for showy emphasis.

"With his mind?" one of the twins yelled out. "No way!" his copy whined.

"Please introduce yourself," Rotrude nearly commanded them.

She was tiring of the interruptions.

"I'm Jire," the boy on the right said. With an identical smile the one on the left chimed in, "Jole."

Most the girls watched the handsome twins closely, giggling when they smiled.

"Nice to see you again, boys," Rotrude said, sighing, hoping they weren't going to cause as much trouble as last session, wishing they'd been moved on. Although, not surprised they hadn't been, given their immaturity. Those boys were far more fit for a battlefield than a Lessonroom. "But yes, it is true," she added, nodding, gilded ear pendants clanking. "There are several accounts that survived the fire."

Jire sat back in his chair, baited, after which his twin Jole followed suit. The girls' eyes shifted back to Rotrude pacing to the other side of the chamber. She glanced at Eden's enormous, intricate maze below, outside the ceiling-height window.

"Bernarus wed his cousin Geila Beaumont. Together they had four children. But," Rotrude said, pausing dramatically, "he didn't stop there. He was seduced by the sly temptress Nicoletta Calvanese."

She realized the extent of the scandal was lost on the small children, not sure exactly why she was telling them except that she herself enjoyed the tale.

"I'll teach more about the Calvanese later, but they were a strong bloodline, maybe the strongest, dominating through the power of their femininity," Rotrude said with thoughtful warmth. "They were fascinating."

She wished she was permitted to explain more, the extent of their power, their deep tendrils in every reach of the Kingdom and beyond, then she reminded herself of her instructions from Hidden Den.

"Bernarus left his cousin-wife Geila Beaumont and went to father three daughters with Nicoletta," she continued, back on tangent. "The daughters were named Delia, Dalida, and Alina Calvanese although, unfortunately, none survived the Plague."

"None at all?" the girl with deep brown eyes and thick blonde braid halfway down her back interjected, tinny with concern.

"What's your name, dear?"

"Avina Minney," she said before bursting into a radiating smile.

The warmth off her was like hot sun in late Spring.

"Avina, it's good to greet you," Rotrude said with a nod, half bowing her head to the coal-skinned girl.

She held much respect for the Minney bloodline.

"Only one nearly survived," she replied to the question. "Delia Calvanese, Egbert Thorne's wife, was heavy with child when the North Plague hit. Egbert did what he could to get

Delia to safety. They reached Animus Rock's quarantine zone, but not after she had already contracted the disease. She died giving birth to the baby in the early North Plague stages, right outside Animus Rock's Eighth Tower. Miraculously, the baby had no signs of the disease," Rotrude said mystically. "Legend has it, Delia enacted a blessing on her offspring, Allen Thorne, in her dying moments, protecting him and all Thornes to follow." She knew she shouldn't even touch on it, yet she believed the children had a right to hear. "This is why Thornes today are considered to have charmed blood."

The three Thorne blondes beamed smugly from their seats at the rear of the chamber as the rest, murmuring, turned to glance in awe.

"The Calvanese name died with the death of his mother," Rotrude said, commanding voice bringing eyes back on her. "Throughout his lifetime, Allen Thorne used the tie to his mother's Calvanese bloodline to his advantage. But I've gotten away from myself," she said, bringing a hand to her temple briefly, leaving her perch by the window to hover over Rose's seat in the front right corner. "Let me go back to Beaumont. There is still much to learn."

She swallowed hard. This next part was difficult, yet, necessary to explain. History wasn't always pleasant, Rotrude thought.

"While Isa and Vlad were travelling to their brother Cassyon's wedding in Littlebell, before the Plague hit, August Norland kidnapped their youngest sister, Auina Beaumont."

"Why!?" Avina Minney interjected loudly, clearly distraught, voicing the emotion plastering almost all the children's faces. Only Evia Norland silently smirked as Rose Brochet glanced curiously to the side.

"In an attempt to have children with Beaumont powers," Rotrude explained grimly. "You must understand it was a very different time. A very old aim of the Norland bloodline was to intermarry between Vanguards, no matter the cost. This is your distant Thorne link to Beaumont blood, girls," Rotrude said cooly to Orosia, Gracelia and the third, smaller girl by their side.

All frowned.

Rotrude, internally smiling, continued.

"August Norland, born in 3810, abducted Auina Beaumont, born in 3815, from her family and took her back to Ravenshroud in 3834 just as the Plague began to spread. Somehow, they managed to avoid exposure to the Dread for nearly a year. Enough time for Auina to give birth to a child named Gauthier. Auina and August died during the Plague, but their son Gauthier survived to carry on the Norland bloodline."

Rotrude looked back and forth across the chamber.

"Gauthier Norland was an instrumental figure throughout the Blood Wars," Rotrude added, white hair shining in an errant beam of light. "We will learn much more about him and his children later."

She paused and exhaled slowly. The children were fidgeting and fading. She was growing weary as well.

"I know it's been a heavy lesson," she conceded in warm understanding, watching the twin Warns particularly squirm. "Only a few bloodlines left to cover," Rotrude added, to a mumbling, disembodied groan. The sun beckoned the children outside by rising higher and warmer in the sky with each passing moment.

"Garvan Busk, born in 3830," Rotrude said, "and Balthasar Graves, born in 3830 as well, were the sole survivors of the North Plague from each bloodline because they were away from home, at Animus Rock for Academy. Each only five years old at the time the Plague hit, the two grew to be quite close," she explained. "Balthasar Graves used Garvan Busk like a servant. He forced him to do his bidding."

Rotrude then remembered after she said it that there was a Busk in her class. She winced for the girl internally.

"Garvan was a nervous child it's told, who jumped at the chance to be close to the intelligent and cunning Graves. They grew up together and eventually retook their prospective realms, Anstout and the Confines, from native influence. It's presumed both sired children with natives," Rotrude said, "however," she lowered her tone ominously, "there are tales that they chose deadblood women instead."

"Oooooo!" the children erupted. A few hands jumped in the air.

"Another day," Rotrude hushed to several disappointed groans.

A lone raven landed on the outside windowsill and cawed loudly as if trying to tell the children something. Heads swung briefly to investigate the echoing ruckus, then turned back to face Rotrude, realizing it was only a bird.

"The men went on to be instrumental in the Blood Wars," she explained. "They wed their children together later, uniting the bloodlines. The Busk and Graves alliance has continued to the present day, with Hector Graves's union to Millie Busk," Rotrude added, looking to Lucette. "Millie is your Grandfather Terje's younger sister, child. Your Great Aunt."

Lucette nodded in recognition. She'd never met her aunt. Father told her that Millie was as good as dead, since she was given to Graves.

Rotrude rested her hip against the edge of the Lessonmaster's desk at the far front chamber's corner.

"Only a few more," she said to the children. "Who is left?"

"Regnard!" a tan, short girl, with hair as white as Rotrude's shouted.

"That is your bloodline?" Rotrude asked the girl sharply, already knowing the answer.

She was unable to help her lack of warmth.

"Yes," the girl replied proudly. "I'm Tiphanie Regnard."

Rotrude eyed her. "I see."

"You don't look like a Regnard," Evia said matter-of-factly, turning hotly to the girl. "You have earthblood eyes."

Tiphanie proudly yelled back, "Hey!" with a red face to match her glare.

"Girls," Rotrude chided taking bounding steps down the center aisle. She loomed threateningly over the Norland. "Evia," she said sternly, drawing the words out for emphasis, "do *not* use that word."

"Yes, Lessonmaster," Evia said obediently without blinking.

Meanwhile, Tiphanie glared daggers at her.

Rotrude swung her head back to address Tiphanie, not wanting to give Evia's outburst any more attention.

"You are correct," she said to the homely girl. "We haven't covered your bloodline."

Rotrude began after internally composing herself and walking back to stand at the chamber's head.

"Maxim Regnard, born in 3802, was twenty-eight years old when the Plague came. He survived because, at the time, he was stationed on the eastern Deadline as the Red Plume's Executioner Proxy. This was before Echo's Omen maintained primary control of the eastern Deadline, as the Brotherhood had not been founded yet. Sadly, when Maxim returned to Lyonshall, it was too late. All his kin were gone. It's presumed that he fathered a son, Uxio Regnard, with a native. Prior to that, Regnard was staunchly Old. Uxio's choices and the choices of his sons had major ramifications for our Kingdom. We'll cover that another day, but remember his name," Rotrude told them pointedly.

The children nodded.

"A few more," she offered them, noting small eyes drifting wistfully outside.

"Alden Morfit was a child when the Plague came," she continued, "and had just been sent to train as Guild. Because he was on the road to Wraithswail at the time, the disease never reached him or his caretaker. He was safely delivered to Hidden Den where he trained until he was old enough to return to Croft Hold, remaking the Morfit realm into what it is today."

As Evia Norland listened, she crossed her arms tight across her chest, glancing to Malla and Avina briefly, looking like she wanted to smack the stupid smiles off their faces. Newbloods were just like mother told her they would be. Worse. She sank into her chair.

Rotrude cleared her throat before continuing. "While at the

Guild, Alden Morfit met the only Minney bloodline survivor, Miles Minney, who had taken refuge there as well. It was then they formed an alliance. Alden vowed to protect Miles and all his Minney decedents."

The raven squawked again sharply, and several jumped at the piercing caw.

"Both are assumed to have taken natives for wives," she added, pacing to the windowsill, waving her arms to scare away the pest.

The raven flapped away, wide dark wings glinting in the sun angrily.

"On to your ancestor, Malla," Rotrude said, turning back to the class, looking to the sable beauty with frizzed blonde hair.

Malla nodded proudly. The gem at her throat sparkled. Rotrude couldn't help but momentarily note the girl's sharp beauty. She was intimidatingly gorgeous, even as a child. If only her voice didn't cut the air like an unpleasant squawk.

"Vendalin Demos, born in 3820, was the only Demosblood to survive the North Plague," Rotrude told her with the rest of the class listening closely on. "He married a native and solidified the Demos commitment to New as he rebuilt the Hellswater empire."

At that, Malla smiled. She'd heard the tales from her father, himself. Demos was a proud bloodline.

"It's your turn boys," Rotrude offered the squirming twins next.

"Yeah!" one of them cried, throwing a backwards facing hand at his copy who slapped it with the back of his own hand.

Malla, Avina, and Tiphanie each giggled as the Thorne girls judged cooly. Evia and Rose watched curiously from opposite sides of the chamber as Rotrude went on.

"Erik Warn was born 3829," she said. "He was the only Warn to survive the Plague. He was just child when his family perished and was raised by the remaining mercenaries at the Ironbark camp. Warn, once starkly Old, shifted with Erik when he married a native and sired one son. Jire, Jole," Rotrude said to the twins. "He is your distant ancestor."

"Woah," the twins said in tandem, although they'd heard the lesson before.

"Indeed," Rotrude replied raising her white eyebrows. She crossed her arms. "Does anyone have questions?"

Hands shot into the air. Rotrude called on the pensive girl with black eyes.

"Yes, Rose?"

"What about Bellamine?"

"That's right!" Rotrude said with an excited clap. "I almost forgot about King Abner the Unready, the one who invited the Nomads into the Kingdom. He died of the Plague of course. He had two sons, Degory and Danil, as well as a daughter, all who survived at Animus Rock. Their story leads directly to the beginning of the Blood Wars, but we will cover that in another lesson." She paused and took a breath. "Other questions?"

Rotrude pointed to the smallest of the pale, ice-blonde girls, presumably, the youngest Thorne sister, with a matching upturned expression.

"What is your name?" Rotrude gently asked the child, hair long to her chest, secured with a crystal band, parted far on the side and swept over one eye to match her sisters.

"Uxia," the girl said loudly.

"And what is your question, Uxia?"

"Why are there no decorations? No plants? No paintings? Nothing here?" Uxia gestured around with her hand, small face pouting. She was used to finery and expected it everywhere she went.

Presumably Graceview's castle was lavishly decorated, Rotrude thought. From what she knew of Thorneblood, she'd expect nothing less.

Rotrude paced the room. She pointed from wall to wall.

"In this Lessonroom, you mean? Animus Rock Academy was built with the purpose of filling the mind itself, not the senses. Drawings would detract from the mind's eye and sully the true creativity and ingenuity trapped in each of you. It's preached by the Guild and thus the Academy here follows suit."

"Next?" Rotrude pointed at Tiphanie Regnard, hand

stretching high in the air.

Tiphanie's voice dripped excitement. "When will we learn about *deadbloods?*"

All the other children held their breath as they awaited Rotrude's response. All had heard about the legendary monsters, in one form or another.

"In due time," she said, to which they disapprovingly sighed.

Tiphanie pointed at Evia. "Why is *she* here if she's one of them?"

"You lie!" Evia chirped, eyes narrowing in wrath. "I am not!"

"Girls!" Rotrude shouted shrilly. "Tiphanie, enough," she turned.

Her Tower robes swished. She shook a finger harshly.

"Do not spread lies."

"I do not lie!" Tiphanie said hotly. "My father told me Evia's brothers are in the Brotherhood." She pointed again at the button-nosed girl. "That makes her one of them! Traitor!" she shouted.

Evia glared, imagining slicing the girl's throat as her father had taught her how to do, if necessary. She deserved far worse, Evia thought. Earthblood never spoke to Vanguards that way. It wasn't proper.

"I said, enough!" Rotrude bellowed.

Tiphanie balked and sank back into her seat. Blood flashed in Evia's eyes.

"If we are going to learn anything together, we must learn to get along." Her gaze burned. "Do not judge each other by the sins of their blood," she chided, allowing her words to settle upon the children slowly like dust.

Fatigued from standing, she again paced to the far corner's desk, resting her hip against the side once more.

"That's enough questions for today," Rotrude told the children.

She smoothed her skirts, noticing the stain of oil from her hair on the robes with a frown. The coin it would take to get it properly clean. Coin she didn't have. She sighed. While her position was a lofty one, it was not a lucrative one. She was perpetually left wanting.

"That concludes this lesson on the North Plague of 3833," she added, deciding not to worry about the garment as she glanced up. "There is much more to learn, children, much more, but we've covered quite a bit. Later we can come back to it in more detail if you wish, but it's been a long day," she said, assessing the weary faces.

"Go to Eden and stretch your legs for a bit to reflect on what you've learned. Discuss today's lesson with your peers. Consider this part of your first day. Then, you're free to enjoy your afternoon as I ready for the Upper Academy children, due to arrive soon. Off, off you go."

She shooed the younger Vanguards with both hands.

In renewed vigour, the children laughed and whispered to each other, scurrying out of the door down the long hall and around the bend.

They spilled down the Animus Rock Third Tower's stone stairs into the strange garden below.

"My mother told me about you."

Rose looked at Evia Norland sideways.

"My mother told me about you, too."

The girls paced each other, booties sinking into sifting yellow sand blanketing the ground in this portion of Eden's looping garden maze.

Each turn of the maze was different from the last with hugely varying temperatures, precipitation, flora, and fauna to mirror the vast variants found Kingdom-wise. Every bend one took was like traveling to another realm. And no two walks through Eden were the same—it shifted, seemingly intentionally, as if it was alive.

To those unfamiliar with it, it was something out of a dream.

The towering hedged entrance to the garden's maze sported

three paths that the children had scattered down joyfully in escape of the morning's tedious lessons. Boys Jire and Jole sprinted straight ahead into a snow flurry in an impromptu game of tag. Malla and Avina gravitated towards each other and took the plush and green path to the right, followed in close pursuit by the younger and shorter Tiphanie Regnard. The Thorne girls huddled together arm in arm behind the twins while Lucette Busk faded into the shadows alone.

Rose took the path on the left, into the sand. She wanted to be away from the crowd. Evia Norland followed closely behind her.

This path led Evia and Rose into a portion of the maze devoid of moisture. The sides changed from thick leafy bushes to pointed, towering, spiky cacti. The dirt beneath their feet turned to sand. The air was drier and hotter now. Above them, the sun burned hot. The sky appeared cloudless as if the grey from earlier burnt away. A striped snake slid across the sand ahead, leaving a winding trail. It was as if they had entered the Eversands.

"I'm Evia."

"I know," Rose said. "I'm Rose."

"I know."

"What did your mother tell you about me?" Rose asked curiously, whirling her head to study the first Norland she'd ever met. The first oldblood child she'd ever met. Rose always imagined she'd be friends with other Vanguards, but this girl did not seem friendly at all. To Rose, she felt like a stone.

The girls kept pace beside each other as they walked through the maze.

Evia tucked her flat hair behind both ears, held in place by the band across her forehead. "That you're a Brochet. I can be seen with you," she said. "What'd your mother tell you about me?"

"She said you're a Norland. You have tough brothers."

Evia sighed. "That's all anyone ever knows about me," she said. "My big brothers."

"What's so special about them?"

"Mother says I'm not supposed to talk about it."

"Why not?"

"She told me not to say," Evia replied. She frowned. "But you won't tell anyone, right?"

She met Rose's black eyes, to which Rose nodded. It was as if all of Evia's apprehensions vanished magically. She was instantly at ease.

"My brothers are in the Brotherhood," Evia whispered.

"What's that?"

Evia stopped walking, stridently shocked, turning to Rose. "You mean, you don't know?" Her forehead gem caught the light in a flashing beam. "I thought everyone knew."

"Not really," Rose replied, shrugging, stopping too. "I've heard of it," she added defensively, shifting her gaze, noting the spiny body of sand scorpion briefly. "I just don't know what it is."

"Mother says it's our birth right," Evia told her in a hush. "Mother says that they do important work. Father does too," she added surely, because, to her, her father's opinion carried more weight.

"Why are you whispering?" Rose asked loudly, glancing around them, towering cacti on either side and sand in front and behind. "We're alone."

"I'm not supposed to talk about it."

"I won't tell anyone." Rose met the slightly taller girl's eyes. "What's the Brotherhood?"

She sighed, reminded of her mother's harsh teachings. "It's a secret," Evia said.

"You don't know what they do?"

Evia shook her head. "I only know it's important."

"How many brothers do you have?"

"Four," Evia said automatically, then she paused as if she'd stubbed her toe, eyes glassing and voice cracking. "I mean three."

She swallowed hard and glanced down to her sandy boots, trying her very hardest not to cry.

"Why did you say four?"

"Three," Evia said shakily.

"Why'd you say four?"

"I used to have four brothers."

"Used to?"

Sweat beaded on both girls' foreheads. Evia wiped hers as she spoke, jostling her gem crown. Rose wanted desperately to ask her what the gem was for but decided this wasn't the time. She'd remember to ask her mother of it later, she resolved.

Rose was not privy to gems or the lore associated with them. In the past, before the Plague, Vanguard women and girls typically wore a gem of their bloodline's color. Oldblood women wore gem crowns while Newblood women were partial to gem bands, worn around the neck. Men wore rings. It was said that in ancient times the gems helped the Ancestors amplify their innate powers, but in the modern day, they were simply rare family heirlooms that indicated status and high breeding. The gems had exchanged hands and bloodlines so many times, the colors did not coordinate with bloodlines any longer. Brochet was the only bloodline that, in the past, didn't typically follow the traditional fashion of wearing gem crowns or bands and instead wore gem pendants. There was only one remaining–the emerald encapsulated by the ouburous that Sybil perpetually wore around her neck.

"Davide died," Evia said sombrely, adjusting the band straight, forcing herself not to blink.

Rose's heart pricked, instantly reminded of Col.

"What happened to him?"

"Mother told me he broke the Brotherhood's rules," Evia said quietly. "That's all I know."

"The Brotherhood killed him?" Rose said wide-eyed.

A small wren chirped at them from inside of a cactus. Evia nodded.

"You don't know what happened?"

She shook her head no. "What about you?" Evia dragged her feet through the sand. "Do you have any brothers or sisters?"

"No."

"I miss my brothers," Evia said quietly to herself.

"You don't get to see them?"

Evia shook her head again.

"Why not?"

"Promise you won't tell?"

"I promise," Rose said, meeting Evia's green glassed eyes.

"I'm supposed to say they're all dead."

The right path taken by Malla, Avina, and Tiphanie evolved into an overgrown wonderland of tropical vines, exotic flowering plants and croaking frogs while the ground beneath their feet turned to sticky mud. Mosquitos bit their arms and necks. The air here was heavy and humid as thick rain clouds churned above. A bright green lizard clung to a tree, bulbed eyes going every direction, watching the children pass. Heavy rain fell sporadically. This path took them through a climate now unfamiliar to the Vanguards, but once, before the Plague, encompassed the furthermost southern, eastern point of their Kingdom, in the Duskfang realm, overseen by Calvanese. It was the city of Veastros, valuable for fur and medicine trade, presently forgotten and lost beneath jungle overgrowth.

Malia's wavy hair frizzed even larger than before. She patted it down over and over. Avina fell in line beside her as if they were old friends. Tiphanie jogged behind them to keep pace with their longer legs.

"Hey, wait up," Tiphanie shouted.

Malla and Avina sped up, ignoring her.

"Hey! I know you heard me." The girl's grating tone pierced the garden's calm. "Wait for me!"

Avina reluctantly stopped. She felt sorry for Tiphanie, reminding herself of the Teachings as she glanced backwards. Malla sighed loudly against the back of her throat and stopped as well.

"You should have gone with the Oldblood girls," Malla said hotly. Her beautiful face as pinched. She had one hand on her hip, the other tucking her frizzing hair. "There's no place for your kind here."

The much shorter Tiphanie noted both girls' judgemental stares. "What do you mean?"

"You're a Regnard," Avina said while swatting at an oversized mosquito.

"So?"

"So," Malla said, "Regnard is Oldblood. Father says you're why we lost the Uprising. I'm not to have anything to do with you."

Tiphanie was struck. She looked at Avina. Avina lowered her eyes and glanced away.

"My father isn't! And neither is my grandfather. They are against Great-Grandfather Lachlan!" Tiphanie said shrilly. "My mother is native." She pointed at her pale, ruddy face. "Look at my eyes."

Mallia exchanged a knowing glance with Avina. She looked back to Tiphanie.

"It doesn't matter," she told her. "Your Great-Grandfather Lachlan's eyes are the same, says my father. Just look at you," Malla said cruelly. Tiphanie's red eyes contrast against her pale skin and hair, like rubies laid in snow.

The sentiment knocked the wind out of her as if she'd been physically struck.

"I don't care who your mother is," Malla added, chin in the air. "You're a Regnard and I don't trust you."

"What about you?" Tiphanie asked Avina. "What do you think?"

Avina felt pity for the red-eyed Regnard yet felt stronger loyalty to her own blood.

"My father told me that your father's ideas are dangerous," she replied softly, unable to meet the girl's pleading gaze. Avina felt empathy for everything, so she had to be careful what and who she chose to care about, or else she'd be living with a perpetually broken heart.

"Why?"

"He's going against his own bloodline." Avina glanced up quickly, then back down to weighty mud on the garden's jungle floor. "Father says that always leads to war."

"We are New fighting against the Old," Tiphanie shouted. "What's wrong with that?"

"The 'New' Regnards aren't New," Mallia corrected her, placing her hand on her hip. "Not like we are."

Tiphanie stubbornly crossed arms at her own chest. She frowned. "What are we, then?"

"You're a threat. Father says New Regnard is really the New Rebellion, which is a fancy way of saying you're trying to start a war. It's greedy and foolhardy, he says."

"First you won't speak to me because you say my blood is Old, and now it's because we're not the right kind of New?" Tiphanie was flustered. "Why does it matter what my blood has done?"

"It matters," Malla said.

"But why?"

Avina's delicate brow furrowed, conflicted by empathetic pain for Tiphanie muddled with allegiance for her own blood. "I was raised here, not at Littlebell," she interjected softly, forcing herself to meet the oldblood girl's eyes. "My grandfather's bloodline is pure, but he is not elderclaim. Do you know why Lady Laila is instead. Not my grandfather or great uncle Edwarde?"

Tiphanie shook her head 'no', jostling her messy knotted hair.

Avina blinked her hooded brown eyes slowly. She told the same tale her father told her. "Because the choices from the past," she said gently. "My grandfather broke Minney tradition by marrying Warn and was cast out of Littlebell because of it. Lady Laila is a blue-eye so obviously they picked her," she added, face clouding. "It isn't fair. I should be the Lady of Littlebell, not Vera," she whined, pulsing with jealousy.

"Who's Vera?" Tiphanie asked.

"My cousin."

A shockingly green bird with orange beak and blue crown feathers cawed loudly from the garden's jungle wall to the side.

"Father says that all Vanguards are judged by their blood," Avina added, glancing to the bird, then back. "It's never fair."

Still sure her father's beliefs were true; Tiphanie scrunched her face into a displeased frown. "We should be able to change our blood," she argued. "I'm not Great-Grandfather Lachlan."

"None of us are," Malla replied, "but our blood's choices rule our lives. Like the Lessonmaster said."

"Lessonmaster said the sins of the blood don't matter!"

"Your blood is different," Malla said.

"Tell me why what my family believes is different from yours." Tiphanie felt her small heart beat fast in her chest beneath crossed arms, forehead and neck beading with sweat.

All she'd ever wanted was friends. Now was her chance to convince these girls she was worthy of friendship.

"Don't we all aim to end the Old?"

"What does your family believe?" Malla asked with a coy smile.

Tiphanie wanted to smack Malla but didn't, for she cared too much about her approval.

"Father says that we owe a debt to the Kingdom for the sins of our blood," she defended angrily. "He says our duty is to overthrow the Old since it only still reigns because of Regnard's past. Father says that there are already many supporters within the Council." Malla giggled at her, eyes as green and flashing as loudly as the parrot cawing by their side. "What is it?" Tiphanie shot at her. "What's wrong with that?"

The air charged and churned above them. Raindrops fell despite the weather that day being clear. After feeling the first drop on her skin, Malla's hands leapt to her hair self-consciously. She patted it down obsessively, each pat heightening the frizz.

"Father was right," Malla said, shaking her head, patting blonde fly-aways. She added over her grey smock's shoulder, "The New Rebellion is daft."

Avina immediately mirrored Malla's movements and fell perfectly into step aside the girl, nearly equal in size and height. Tiphanie sighed loudly to passively indicate her frustration, slogging booties through the mud, trying her best to keep up as they made their way around the looping, winding bends with soggy jungle greenery creeping in on them from every side.

Eden was massive.

"Why?" she pleaded up at Malla's striking profile.

"The key to peace is harmony, not violence," Avina chimed in. "It's why Father is at odds with Lady Lalia and Lord Prihim."

Tiphanie was unrelenting. "Why?" she whined.

"Laila and Primin are in on the Rebellion, father says." Avina glanced sympathetically to Tiphanie. "They're working with Morfitblood. He's sure it'll lead to death and suffering."

The jungle maze walls in this section of Eden were alive with insects flitting amidst rainbow blooms.

Avina glanced briefly to an orange and white butterfly as big as her face. "War should be avoided at all costs."

"A Minney would say that," Tiphanie said.

"You know nothing about me, but because I'm Minneyblood, you judge," Avina observed harshly. "You're no different from us."

Struck, Tiphanie's mouth hung agape then she jogged a few steps to catch back up.

"That's not fair," Tiphanie argued up at the taller girls. "You just said…"

Malla interrupted Tiphanie harshly, "You aren't one of us."

"But Lessonmaster said we should all get along!"

At that, Malla cackled harshly as Avina covered her mouth while giggling too.

Tiphanie hung her head.

"Don't feel bad," Malla told her insincerely. "At least you aren't one of them," she pointed at Rose and Evia appearing from around a sandy, cacti lined bend far ahead, whispering with heads close together. They looked deep in confidence.

"Their pale skin hurts my eyes," Malla teased, pulling Avina's arm into hers, warmly giggling, walking in stride. Avina's wide braid swayed against the back of her grey cloth smock.

Despite her efforts to keep up, Tiphanie fell back slightly from the pair, glaring when they locked arms. Both girls were far darker skinned than herself, Tiphanie noted silently, pursing her thin lips into a frown. She wanted to scrub her skin right off.

"I hear their brains have turned to mush," Malla said to Avina, feeding off the captive audience, Tiphanie, behind her.

"It happens when too many Vanguards marry each other," Avina replied smartly. "It's why the Old is so *evil*."

"I bet they're talking about us. I bet they're saying how ugly we are."

"You aren't ugly," Tiphanie chimed in loudly.

"I know," Malla retorted confidently, half turning head back, blonde poufy hair dusted with drops from the misty rain. "But Grandmother warned me how mean the Old girls are," she explained, turning back. "Grandmother told me everyone teased her when she was at Academy for having New blood," she said, verdant eyes blazing prideful resolve. "That is not happening to me," she added surely. "They are the ugly ones, not us."

"Yes!" Avina clapped her hands in excitement, elbow still looped with Malla's.

"Look at that stringy hair," Malla gestured ahead at the Oldbloods, still arm in arm with Avina, pacing slowly down the path, transitioning from jungle mud to more neutral, familiar wooded and grassy terrain.

"Like the Norland girl," Avina said cruelly, absorbing Malla's mean excitement, lowering her voice shamefully. "She could never make a Littlebell braid."

Tiphanie touched her own un-braided, limp hair. She tucked it behind her ears. She cast her eyes down and to the side.

"And both are so skinny! Like sticks," Malla laughed, eyes on the oldblood girls across the maze.

Tiphanie followed closely behind, skipping to keep up. She glanced down at her own thin arms and legs. She frowned silently.

Almost imperceptibly, across the central Eden meadow, one of the large boulders shifted. Slightly.

Three frosty blondes walked slowly together down Eden's middle path through a building blizzard with heads held high. They looked as if they belonged there, like icicles plucked from the frozen scenery of Winter Garden.

Orosia, Gracelia, and Uxia Thorne were near copies of each other, differing only by varying heights. All girls had an abundance of thick, straight, nearly white hair hanging lifelessly down to their waists, tucked behind clear crystal headbands like delicate crowns of ice, framing pale, narrow faces, washed out apart from their mossy, sparkling, upturned eyes. The trio was painfully thin too, like willow branches, with elongated appendages and sharp cheekbones, sallow cheeks, and long necks. Each had invisible blonde eyebrows naturally pinched in displeasure, with rosy cheeks, and dainty frowns.

"Why are there no boys?" the littlest girl whined.

She kicked a grey pebble.

The path's terrain was turning rocky, covered in a light dusting of white power, scuffed by a preceding pair of footprints. The air was thin. Wisps of white mist whipped overhead in gusts overtop heavy clouds. It smelled like snow. Brambles of berry bushes intertwined with thick pines lining either side of the garden's maze there. The air chilled considerably and the girls could see their breath before them.

"What about those boys?" the middle sister Gracelia retorted from Orosia's left, gesturing at the scuffs in the snow, reminded of Jire and Jole's handsome faces and mischievous smiles. "They are cute!"

"Quiet," tallest and eldest Orosia chided without glancing down, posture impeccable, head high. "If father heard you say something like that, about a Warn! Hush." She lowered her voice, looking angrily at Gracelia briefly then back straight ahead. "Our suitors are older. There is a plan. You'll just have to wait."

Thornes were known for wedding strategically. Every Old

bloodline and most New had hard ties to Thorne. They were like vines that crept into every crevice of the Kingdom.

Gracelia pouted, sticking her bottom lip out. She sighed hard against the back of her throat.

Either side of this portion of the maze was lined by interwoven pine trees and leafless maples covered in snow, filled with red-breasted robins and jays. The trees' branches created a canopy over the path entirely in some places. Where the trees didn't meet completely were plush bushes lining the path with hearty leaves separating this section of the maze from the next. Through a poorly placed, particularly thin bush, Gracelia watched three newblood girls pass by amidst a different setting entirely; lush, moist greenery, steaming and hot, breathing as if alive.

"Why do they get to come here?" she whined, craning to look at Orosia. "It should be for real Vanguards only!"

"Don't speak like that," Orosia scolded. "Not at Animus. Are you stupid?"

"Why not?"

Snowflakes fell upon Gracelia and Uxia's upturned faces, nearly indistinguishable against their pallid skin. Both looked to their eldest sister, always in charge. Orosia was very much like their father, Wallace Thorne.

She effortlessly exuded command.

"We must pretend to be like them," Orosia replied quickly, without patience, re-tucking hair behind both ears and her crystal crown. "You know that," she said, breath like smoke in the air.

"Why must we pretend to like earthblood?" Uxia asked in a small voice.

Orosia rolled her eyes, spinning her head to the other side to address the youngest.

"Hush, I said don't speak like that. It isn't pretending. It just isn't smart to reveal what you really think about anything, that's all. Didn't you learn anything from Grandfather Thorne?"

"Why do you always say, 'that's what Grandfather Thorne said' like you're a stupid parrot?" Gracelia retorted.

Their grandfather, Hastein Thorne, was infamous about the Kingdom. He was something akin to a Prophet believed by many to confer with the Ancestors directly. In his younger years, he produced a series of writings called 'The Teachings'. Most Vanguards, especially Newbloods, adhered to them religiously.

"Gracelia!" Orosia spun her head back the other way, smooth pale hair flying out behind her in the wake. "Stop that. Grandfather Thorne was the smartest man ever."

"Stop fighting," little Uxia cried as she kicked another grey rock.

"Don't tell me what to do!" Gracelia yelled at her sister.

"Girls!" Orosia stopped in her tracks, shouting in the quietest whisper imaginable. Between her teeth she hissed, glaring back and forth between their angelic faces, "Do not make a scene."

The smaller girls, with respect learned from fear, dutifully nodded. A snow owl interrupted the serene scene with a whooping call, hooting in rhythmic cadence on a high branch.

"We're almost at the Tree," Orosia said, "come on."

After adjusting Uxia's crystal headband straight and wiping droplets of melted snow from Gracelia's nose, Orosia gestured to her sisters to follow. She led them to the winding, snowy path's exit, into a lush green clearing.

The temperature warmed instantly as this path opened into a wide, buzzing meadow filled with white bindweed and towering sunblooms blowing in a blustery wind. It was perpetually late Summer here. Above, heavy cotton clouds parted to sunny blue sky. In the immediate middle of the huge clearing in the center of Eden's maze was an enormous tree; size and width grander than anything any of the children had ever seen. There was a cavern within the tree that the children knew better than to enter. Although even if they tried, they would not be permitted inside.

The Vanguard tree - the legendary source of Eden's magical power - towered intimidatingly over the students as they all spilled into the meadow from different directions.

The Warn twins wrestled and laughed in the dirt at the foot

of the massive trunk amidst face-size leaves and knotted roots. One's eye was already turning yellow and green at the edges. The other had a bloody nose. As they tumbled about each other one disappeared briefly, only to reappear on top of his brother. He punched him in his other eye.

Malla and Avina huddled together at the edge of the tree's shade, watching the boys, giggling a bit too loudly. Tiphanie was desperately trying to be involved, hovering aside them like a hungry dog in want of scraps, all the while being ignored.

Another boulder shifted imperceptibly.

Orosia judged the newblood girls harshly as the Thorne trio traipsed through the meadow filled with flowery grass blowing in the breeze.

"They giggle because they can't have them," she said to her younger sisters quietly, grateful for her superior breeding, intelligence and blood. "See how they blush and look away? It's like Grandfather Thorne said. All creatures want what's denied to them. It's in our nature to seek and fill empty spaces, like water spilling out of all cracks in a cup."

"Why can't they have them?" Gracelia asked, stepping high through the tall floral grass.

"You know why," Orosia told her. "They must marry earth..." she paused, taken aback briefly at how easily the term rolled off her tongue without thought. "I mean natives. It's their New way," she added with distain, nose upturned.

"Gross," Uxia said.

"Hush," Orosia chided, although proud of her sister internally. "We should introduce ourselves and be nice. Follow my lead. I have an idea," she said over her shoulder, pushing through the meadow towards the shade of the nearly 300-year-old Vanguard tree, planted right after the Nomad invasion, hair billowing like a silvery cloak behind her.

"What are you doing?" Gracelia whined, skipping to keep up. Beetles and white butterflies flitted away from her path.

"I don't want to talk to them. They look like they smell of fish oil," Uxia said from Orosia's other side.

"Girls!" Orosia scolded firmly. "Put your faces on," she

added in a quick glance from one to the other, sun glistening in their crystal headbands atop flaxen hair. "Follow me."

The younger blondes dutifully fell in line behind the eldest as they approached the group: Malla Demos, Avina Minney, and Tiphanie Regnard.

Animosity hung heavy in the breezy air.

"Hello," Orosia said politely with half a smile. She extended her slender hand, sleeves of her neatly pressed blouse beneath her smock hanging delicately from her bony wrist.

Malla crossed her arms in a huff and Avina raised her eyebrows, hands glued to her sides, confused by the foreign gesture. She'd not been taught the Oldblood greeting. Tiphanie poked her head out from behind the taller, sturdier girls, immediately impressed by the wraith-like beauties with unabashed awe. At the Newblood girls' lack of response to her offered hand, Orosia dropped it and curtsied slightly, lowering herself closer to the shorter girls' level, blinking her eyes slowly. Like matching puppets, the younger Thorne girls Gracelia and Uxia immediately mirrored their older sister, curtsying dutifully.

That movement, another traditional oldblood greeting, confused both Avina and Malla further.

Malla stood with one shoulder facing the oncoming girls. Her other shoulder was towards Avina, turned slightly as if she expected the Thornes to leave as abruptly as they arrived. She was distressed by the curtsy. Malla reached her hand out to copy the initial gesture, not wanting to be made a fool.

Orosia stood from her curtsy and took Malla's sweaty palm into her own, smugly, for the earthblood girl had played right into her trap. The girls shook briefly, after which Orosia looked down at her pale hand to reveal a new layer of grime. For all her restraint, even if she'd wanted to, she could not hide the extent of her disgust. She wrinkled her nose as she wiped her hand quickly against the cloth of her smock. It left a visible stain. Her sisters snickered.

"I... I'm sorry," Malla stuttered. "We just walked through the jungle," she added, patting down fly-aways. She glanced briefly to the lush maze's path across the meadow. "It's hot in there."

Instantly, Orosia's pleasant, welcoming smile returned strategically, hiding her discomfort with the exchange like light twinkling through an icicle.

"It's fine, it's just fine," she reassured, shaking her head to disregard Malla's apology.

Despite her chilly visage, the girl radiated calculating warmth. Like most Thornes, one couldn't help but like her, although afterwards they were not sure why.

"My hands are simply cold from the frost, is all. We've just come from Winter Garden."

Gracelia hid a snicker behind her hand. Malla breathed in gratefully, quickly locking eyes with Orosia, who slowly blinked in acknowledgement of her gratitude. A silent peace was stricken. Just as Orosia had intended.

"We've not met," Orosia seamlessly said. "We're from Graceview," she looked to each of her sisters, "but don't hold that against us."

Avina, darting doe-like eyes back and forth, laughed nervously. Tiphanie, round and sweaty face sticking out from behind her, couldn't help but smile back, entranced by the Thorne girls' dazzling smiles and polite ways, the opposite of how her father raised her to be.

Regnards were to be practical and strong, not enchanting and light.

Silent peace violated; Malla frowned.

"Why would you say that? What has Thorne done?"

"It was a joke," Orosia said flatly.

She dropped her smile, deciding she didn't like this Demos girl at all. Not even to toy with.

"Oh, right," Malla replied with brows glaring low. "It wasn't funny."

Uxia lowered her head to study a pattern she'd begun to carve with her foot in the soft dry dirt.

"I know, I just..." Orosia trailed off, then paused.

"What is it?" Avina asked.

"Well, it is a secret," Orosia baited with twinkling eyes. "I shouldn't tell you."

"Now you must," Malla commanded, falling further into Orosia's trap as wind gusted the skirts of their smocks around their knees.

A pair of songbirds chirped overhead.

Orosia leaned in, channelling the master puppeteer she was like her kin taught her to be. Thornes were notoriously manipulative. Almost as manipulative as Brochets. She lowered her voice to a whisper.

"Our father kidnapped our mother a long time ago," she said simply. "Our Regnard grandfather on our mother's side let it happen," she added, with a nearly imperceptible glance to Tiphanie. "Had it not been for that, we would have been as dark as you with an earthblood father instead of Thorne." She quickly corrected, "I mean native," but it was far too late.

Malla glared vindictive daggers and tightly crossed her arms once more. Just as Orosia had planned.

"Is that really true?" Avina looked at Gracelia and Uxia.

The younger girls nodded fiercely.

Malla pointed aggressively at Tiphanie. "She's your cousin, then?"

Tiphanie balked at the sudden attention, already red-flushed cheeks burning scarlet. She exchanged glances with the tallest beauty.

"I think so," Tiphanie said, sticking her head out from behind Avina. "We've never met though."

"Gachan is my cousin," Orosia said with resound, speaking of Tiphanie's father, "So, whatever that makes you."

She looked Tiphanie up and down. She her hardest to quell the distain she felt for all Regnards deep in her chest.

"Nice eyes," Orosia added honestly, noting Tiphanie's distinctive ruby glare.

The near-identical copies Gracelia and Uxia nodded on each side.

"Thanks," Tiphanie said quickly.

She felt an intoxicating a rush of pride for her bloodline she'd not previously known.

Mallia was shocked, unable to comprehend an oldblood could ever say such a thing. "You... like her eyes?"

"Why not?" Orosia said. "It makes her more special than you."

"What did you say!?" Malla shouted shrilly.

Demos beauty was her birth right. There were famous ballads about her kin's undeniable looks, sung throughout Hellswater. She folded her arms at her chest so tight she could hardly breathe. Avina took an unconscious step backwards and glanced away.

"You look like Demos women are supposed to look," Orosia explained, "and she looks like a normal Minney, with normal brown Minney eyes and a normal Minney braid," Orosia added, pointing at Avina. "But she's special," Orosia shifted her finger to Tiphanie, then to Malla. "You aren't."

"That is mean," Avina said.

"It's the truth," Orosia said with a dismissive shrug. "Wouldn't you rather the truth?"

Malla, arms still tight at her chest, glared like she might reply with a punch. She didn't respond.

Avina sniffled, thinking of her cousin charmed with blue eyes. The blue eyes that she deserved.

"I guess," she conceded, looking down to the side.

Tiphanie raised a grubby hand to her mouth to hide her amused smile. Orosia caught the white-haired girl's eyes briefly, blinking in recognition, then just as fast looked away. For that brief moment, for the first time in her life, Tiphanie felt special. Like she belonged.

Meanwhile, Rose Brochet and Evia Norland entered the Vanguard Tree's clearing, still deep in conversation.

The pair of oldblood girls turned away uninterested when they saw the Warn boys violently wrestling. Orosia noticed, silently noting the variance of behavior from the girls she spoke to now.

"If you really are New, despite that skin and hair," Malla said, eyeing Orosia up and down, "what do you think of them?"

She obviously meant Evia and Rose as she glanced

judgementally to the pair on the opposite side of the clearing, resting beside rather large boulder on the edge of the maze's wall. The girls leaned up against the boulder's cool shade.

"I don't know," Orosia said. "I've not met them."

"From what you've heard, then. Brochet and Norland."

"What do you think of them?"

"I... I think *they* think they're too good for us," Malla said, eyes darting. "At least you came to speak to us," she reasoned. They stay over there."

"Perhaps," Orosia said distantly.

Malla more deeply frowned.

Lucette Busk sat hugging her knees with her back pressed against the far side of the central garden's wall, woven from thick trunks with vertical black bark. The bark appeared to move like tar in the right light, with wide leaves, one side shiny and the other grey matte. Waxy ivy and creeping pale tendrils snaked the trees. Tiny sunbloom cap mushrooms clustered at the bases.

She watched the children filter into the center of the maze, one by one. She watched Malla, Avina and Tiphanie chatter under the Tree as the Warn boys rough-housed in the dirt. She watched the Thorne girls thick in plot, approaching the group of newbloods. She felt the contention of their exchange even from across the meadow. She watched Rose and Evia lost in conversation aside a boulder to her right, heads together, unsmiling and focused.

They were blithely unaware of being watched.

The clouds overhead began to darken.

It was like Lucette wasn't there at all.

Rotrude observed the children through the crystal spectacles with keen eyes. Historically, the innate magic of Eden dredged up power in even the weakest of Vanguards, particularly when at the cusp of puberty. But so far, only talk. Or perhaps these children's blood was so diluted, so far from their powerful Ancestors' blood, that none existed at all. Lately, that was a common occurrence. There hadn't been any obvious power in hundreds of years.

Rotrude reminded herself that it wasn't her station to pass judgment, only observe and record. She noted what she heard and saw in the Lower Log for this session. It would later be delivered to Hidden Den for the Masters to analyse, of course.

LITTLEBELL

Ryd continued to the Littlebell stables after parting from Digory at the white and black vase sign.

It was hot, even after the fall of night. That he was accustomed to. He was not accustomed to the noise. Westerviolet had a curfew and strictly enforced laws regarding unnecessary sound after nightfall. Littlebell was clearly the opposite. He passed through hordes of people yelling and talking and bartering left and right. Women with intense, eye-straining gowns and men with both tunics and pants or draped robes in loud, showy patterns. Women's lips were mainly unpainted here. The further north and west Ryd travelled, eyes were fiercely black-lined and more fingers blue-tipped than red. He wondered what it could all mean. Everyone in Westerviolet looked alike.

Women's braids were like that at the front gate - Ryd couldn't tell a difference - but more men here wore long braids down their backs, yet faces were still clean shaven. Far different from the common beards kept by many throughout Westerviolet. He noted wild dogs—unbred, mangy, old beasts with mostly black and white spots and visible ribs, eating from piles of garbage in narrow alleys between buildings. He momentarily felt sorry for them. He wanted to offer aide to a particularly sad looking one huddled in an alley but reminded himself of the pressing task at hand.

He had to find his brother.

There were drawings of goods on large boards hung about Artisan Alley speaking to the wares within. Each sketch was more impressive than the next depicting delicately crafted furniture, tools, and clothing, hung above each rectangular doorframe. Ryd had never imagined a market so large. Why anyone would need so many different types of clothing or furniture? If one had coin, were there not more important things to spend it on?

Anything imaginable was available for purchase. Flurries of Littlebell citizens, golden braids and dark smiling faces, darted in and out with wares in hand or satchel. Every few paces, usually right outside of a doorframe, bodies were wrapped in rags with hugely dilated eyes, begging from and being ignored by passers on the street.

The whole city pulsed like an enormous living being.

Ryd smelled it before he could see it. He smiled in reverie, glancing to his right. Down a discrete dirt road between two nondescript structures off to the side of the towering Littlebell castle was the stable. Ryd shook the reigns to urge his tired mount towards much needed sustenance and rest. There were few horses in the city of Littlebell. The path was not well travelled.

"Almost there," Ryd said gently, patting the animal. "Almost there." The horse whinnied gratefully.

Ryd dismounted after reaching the outskirts—a dusty outcropping of sand, dirt, and gravel in the wake of the castle. He took the feeble black horse by his reigns for the last several paces on foot, then entered. Ryd didn't see any men. He noted twenty well-maintained stables with brushed, calico horses. Impressive, even by Westerviolet standards. But still nothing like the stable he called home. He felt a pinch in his heart.

Ryd yelled in. "Hello?"

There was no response. Ryd walked further, assessing the barn in detail. Two familiar flanks, one bandaged, appeared in the next two stalls.

"Mabel! Chester!" Ryd cried with glee, spotting the two horses lost during the raider attack on Narrow Road.

Both appeared well taken care of. Mabel's flank was dressed from where the arrow had struck her.

"What are you doing here!?" he shouted happily at the beasts.

Both Mable and Chester's eyes lit up with recognition. They bobbed their heads and flicked their tails happily.

"Who be that?" a gruff voice barked from the shadows behind him.

Ryd whipped his head around. "Hello?"

"Who be you?" the angry voice accused.

A very short man resembling the melted stub of a candle waddled from a back room.

"I'm here seeking shelter for this steed," Ryd answered quickly. "Who are you?"

"Treave," the man grunted.

Ryd assessed his over-starched yellow tunic, black trousers that clung tightly to short legs, and a wide braided leather belt secured with a brass buckle under his ample belly.

Ryd gestured to Mabel and Chester. "Where did you get them?"

"Found," Treave answered in a grunt. "Out in the field with others." He gestured a small hand down the stall. "She be hit," he said, pointing to Mable's bandaged flank. "Why?"

He squinted his distrusting eyes. He placed his hands on his hips.

"They are mine." Ryd took a step, hoping to seem authoritative.

Treave, smirking, turned to waddle away.

"Hey!" Ryd whined. "Come back here!"

Treave paused, turning slowly in the hot and dusty stable.

"You lie," he spat. "Why I waste time?"

"I don't!"

"You have horse," Treave said, lowering his tone accusingly, pointing. "Not cared for."

"He isn't mine," Ryd tried to explain. "We were attacked by..."

"We?" Treave interrupted. "Who *we*?"

"Not this again," Ryd sighed. "I have a companion. He's injured. We were attacked," he explained. "Gone to Apothecary now."

"Why injured?"

"What the curses," Ryd spat under his breath. "I told you," he said, glaring at the ornery man, "attack."

Ryd couldn't believe, after all their travel, this unlikable squat man was his obstacle.

"Raiders. That's when I lost my horses." He pointed to Mabel and Chester. "The gold capes told me to come here!"

"Lies!" shouted Treave. "No time for lies," he said shaking round head, sweaty curls smacking against short forehead.

"I'm not lying!"

"You best be lying," Treave said ominously, shaking a finger up at Ryd. "If not lying, then large trouble," he added almost gleefully, red eyes maliciously sparkling.

Treave came from lowly beginnings. Raised on the border of Littlebell and the Confines, he was perpetually teased for his stature, lowly upbringing and lack of intelligence. Until, that is, Lady Laila took pity on him and gave him a position in Littlebell's stable. He was eternally grateful, as well as loyal, to the Minney bloodline.

Ryd was in no mood for games. He was tired and anxious to search for Col.

"What in the Kingdom are you talking about?"

Treave eyed Ryd's bare feet and tattered clothing.

"Where you be from?" he asked.

"Baneswood," Ryd said loudly, chest puffed, eyes shifting once. He cleared his throat, then said louder, "I'm from Baneswood."

"There, you see," Treave said with a triumphant smile, lips curling. "You lie."

Ryd felt a jolt of adrenaline. "I do not."

"These horses be from Westerviolet. You not trick Treave."

"How do you know?"

Treave laughed with pride. "Thought you trick Treave, did you? I know Westerviolet. The snake."

"Curses, right," Ryd sighed, remembering the Brochet emblem cast into each horseshoe. "Of course. Seems you have bested me," he said, rolling his eyes.

Treave beamed proudly. "I tell you that you not trick Treave."

"Right," Ryd replied, realizing his chances of getting his

beloved horses back were slim. "Will you keep him for the night, at least?"

He patted the tired black stallion, wide red eyes pitifully weary and drooped.

Treave put his hand out.

"What are you doing?" Ryd asked flatly.

Treave furrowed his brow, looking down at his hand, pressing it out a bit further.

"What?" Ryd asked again.

"Coin," Treave grunted.

"The guards at the gate didn't say anything about…"

"Coin!" Treave interrupted. "No coin, go."

"Please just take him. He needs water and rest. Look at him. Take pity," Ryd pleaded.

Treave waddled away from Ryd, smirking, shaking his head. He was prepared to tell Lady Laila everything about this Westerviolet snake.

"Fine! If I swear to give you coin upon my return tomorrow, will you keep him here for the night?" Ryd shouted.

Treave paused, grainy outline opaque in the dusky twilight. "You swear?"

"I swear!"

Without turning he clarified loudly, "How much coin?"

Treave figured he could wait until morn to raise the alarm. It wouldn't hurt to have a little extra coin. He wanted a new belt buckle, after all.

"I'll make it worth your time," Ryd assured anxiously, not knowing what that meant, just trying to get the man to agree. "Please."

Treave, brow low, turned towards Ryd. "Just this night?"

Ryd nodded furiously. "Just tonight."

"If no coin, I keep," he said, snatching the reigns from Ryd.

Treave planned to keep the steed regardless. He felt smug pride, knowing how clever he was being.

"Thank you. Thank you!" Ryd said, nearly stumbling over himself. "I'll be back in the morning for them." He walked over to his familiar steeds. "Hey there good girl," he said warmly to Mable's chestnut flank as she neighed, flicking her tail. "And you too buddy, hang in there," he said over the wall to Chester in the next stall.

He hoped the animals knew he didn't abandon them.

"Hmph," Treave grunted dismissively, leading the raiders' sorry horse to water.

In his mind danced visions of fists full of coins, a new buckle, and Lady Laila's warm praise.

Ryd glanced wistfully at Mable and Chester briefly, then lowered his head and walked out of the stable.

Artisan Alley ended abruptly and dumped the tempestuous, decorated crowd onto the Occident; a sprawling market that inched right up to Littlebell's docks before spreading indiscriminately down the eastern bank of the Missi. Wide barges, tactical fishing vessels and practical transport boats parked along the mud-tinted, sluggish river. The hullabaloo was backlit by the low-hanging sun, staccatoed with odd, echoing caws from small river fowl.

Ryd felt weathered cobblestones lined with grime and caked with silt from the riverbank underfoot. Sounds and smells shifted to the unfamiliar as he neared the docks and left the city proper in his wake. He'd never seen a river so large, or a market for that matter.

The Occident extended a great length along the western face of the castle, high-grown with creeping stems of spiky purple cress, allowing for one hundred parallel rows of stalls to stand perpendicular to the water. The majority were fish traders from Hellswater and Wraithswail, but Ryd also noted orange furs from Baneswood, strange spices and mushrooms from Graceview, unusual, gilded weapons from Croft Hold, metal works and stone goods from Lyonshall, clothing from Ironbark, jewellery from Winter Garden and various other oddly foreign items and delicacies, obviously from across the Kingdom, far beyond where Ryd had travelled. Or even heard of. He smiled when he passed a stall of candied lemons, as they came from Westerviolet and reminded him of home.

Many merchants, traders, and fishermen packed up stalls, barges, and tents from a long day of toil on and by the water, as others just arrived to take their places. It seemed the Occident never closed. Ryd was amazed by the flurry of chaotic activity. Not once did he see a supervisor or guard barking commands as was familiar back home. Rather, here there was no discernible pattern at all. Amazingly, all appeared to know exactly what they were doing and where they were going. It reminded him of a clump of birds, soaring together despite trees or the wind's interference.

Ryd walked slowly, sweeping his head left to right, passers-by bumping into him every so often. His nostrils pricked at the scents of ripe fish and earthy river silt.

He was pleasantly overwhelmed, trying to absorb all he could, when he heard a commotion.

"Aye!" A colossal man with a grisly beard and sun-weathered skin held a small boy up by his neck, off a side street. "Think you can steal from me?" the man taunted, shoving the poor child hard against the wall.

The boy's skinny legs thrashed below himself, helplessly searching for the ground.

"Coll?" Ryd shouted as he sprinted to the scene.

Without thinking, he shoved the larger man to the side.

"Curses!" the man groaned when Ryd pushed him.

He stumbled clumsily to the mucky ground.

The little boy dropped to his feet, blond head down, gasping for breath.

Ryd ran to the boy and put both hands on his shoulders. "I can't believe you…" he began, nearly shouting with glee, then paused when he focused on the boy's terrified, round eyes.

Although young and skin tone like Collen, the child was not his brother. Ryd let go of the stranger in gut wrenching disappointment and sulked backwards with his mouth open. He felt physically wounded. The boy sprinted off down the street and around the bend past a candlelit tavern overgrown with the same purple flowers that climbed the castle and blanketed most of Littlebell before disappearing into the twilight.

The fallen man, long-sleeved tunic with wide holes at the elbows and shoulders, front laden with putrid stains, now sullied with more dirt and filth from his push to the cobblestones, groaned from where he lay, then rolled to stand. He put one hand on each knee and, breathing heavily, leveraged himself upright. The man's untrimmed beard hung down his chest. It swayed back and forth slowly as he stood. The hair he had left on his head was patchy on the sides like a backwards crown and just as long as his beard, in similar unkempt fashion. The man's dim skin was horribly weathered. His were teeth rotten or missing. He absolutely reeked of turned fish.

Ryd was stunned and motionless as the man squared his shoulders to him.

"You shouldn't have done that," his deep voice warned.

The man, with a hulking, deadblood-like hand, cracked his neck to the left, and then the right as Ryd, jumping at each pop, eyes widening with terror, backed up. He raised his shaking hands.

The man snorted then spit phlegm as he took a step closer.

"There's nowhere to run," he said.

Ryd was positioned with his back facing a corner. There was no escape.

"I...I thought you had my brother," Ryd said timidly. "Please," he said, stepping backwards, nearly stumbling as the man loomed towards him. Ryd smelled the sharp stink wafting from his clothes, beard, and breath. It was all he could do not to gag. "I don't want trouble."

He glanced again over his shoulder, knowing it was a dead end but still hoping it wasn't.

"I think you do," the man said, taking another heavy, ominous step. His low gut jiggled. His enormous frame was backlit by the nearby tavern. "You attack Brutt, you attack the Fellowship." Another step. *Jiggle.* "You're coming with me."

"Fellowship?" Ryd asked, lowering his hands. "What's a Brutt?"

The imposing man took a third massive step then began a low throated, animalistic growl. Ryd, terrified, inched further backwards. His toes squished through rotten discarded food and old waste crammed into the far corner of the side street. His heart dropped into the pit of his stomach when his back hit cool cod.

It was a dead end.

"Don't play," Brutt said. "No exceptions."

"Exceptions to what?" Ryd asked in bewilderment. He shouted, "I'm sorry! I'm sorry I shoved you!"

Brutt stopped his approach and grunted once, throwing back his head, holding his belly with both hands as he shook in laughter. "Sorry," he said loudly to himself, shaking his head, laughing more. He wiped a tear from his eye. "Words," he finally added, righting himself. "I have not time for words."

"Please," Ryd begged.

"Sorry," Brutt smirked mockingly. He moved towards Ryd to place a hand on his shoulder.

But just as Brutt grew near, Ryd dropped to the ground and left the larger man grasping at nothing. Then, Ryd dove beneath the embrace and shot under his reach. Brutt's momentum propelled him forward and the massive man tumbled into the wall. Ryd turned to run, but Brutt spun and grabbed Ryd's trousers with unexpected speed, toppling Ryd onto the filthy ground next to him. Ryd kicked his leg, frantic for a savior or weapon. Brutt held an iron grip.

"Help!" Ryd shouted.

He opened his mouth to scream again but was interrupted by a callous blow to the side of the face by a heavy boot. Ryd's world exploded in blades of pain. He whimpered, vision pulsing, flailing to get away, but Brutt kicked him hard, again, square in the temple.

Everything faded to black.

If this is death, it rather hurts, Ryd thought.

He peeled opened his aching eyes to a musty, dim-lit den. He tried to stand and immediately realized he was restrained by both feet and hands, tied with intricate rope knots. He gagged at the mildewed rag stuffed in his mouth.

The den felt forbidden. It was rectangular with split wooden ceilings, tables and stools to match. A cyanic bar with dusky bottles in haphazard shelved rows, and watermarked mugs filled a corner. The walls were dark blue in need of another coat of paint. It was peeling and puckering to reveal wooden plank walls. An unfamiliar three-pronged, bladed weapon was hung as décor with fearsome points still tinted with long-ago dried blood. Coarse curtains, worn and dingy at the bottoms, draped from every side of the room. The curtains hid round windows, obvious only from circles of ambient light glowing behind. Mildew grew above Ryd's head on the low hung wood-planks. Mold crept out from the corners of the ceiling like rampant ivy, vibrating from heavy footsteps parading above.

It looked like the kind of place ale ballads were often sung.

Then Ryd heard noises. First a guttural shout followed by a deep-voiced cheer, then rhythmic stomping. He nervously wrenched his hands and feet but found he was expertly bound. He bit and chewed and spat at the cloth in his mouth but made no progress untying it. He only made it tighter, lodging the horrid rag further down his throat until he nearly vomited from the unpleasant taste. Fear gripped him. As more shouts and stomps rang out above, Ryd rocked himself back and forth one, two, three times until he toppled to the ground. He landed hard on his mysteriously wounded shoulder. He cried out in pain, yet his whelps were pathetically muffled by the gag.

Ryd lay on his side with his cheek pressed up against splintered ground, feeling sorry for himself. He was defeated. Now, he'd never find Col.

Then, waves of vertigo. Was he dizzy from the beating or did the ground move?

Panicked shouts cried out above his head. Different shouts than before. A frenzy of crashing footsteps followed, then more shouts, then the recognizable sound of clanking steel. Ryd felt a warm drop land on his nose. He crossed his eyes. The drop was red. Blood, he realized, was seeping through the floorboards above him.

Then, a latch on the far side of the den flung open followed by a pair of small feet descending the ladder. Ryd, strained from the floor to see his new company and noted loose black pants that met at cuffs on each of ankle, paired with a billowing black tunic, secured with a wide grey belt and a silver buckle. The slim figure wore a black, braided toggle cloak, heavy cloth to choose for the summer moons, drapery fully engulfing the rather slight frame. Ryd could not see a face. The stranger hurried to Ryd's side and untied him, first feet then hands as he grunted loudly.

"Sorry," they whispered, untying the gag last.

"Thank you," Ryd said, rubbing his wrists, under-eyes bruised. "Why'd you rescue me? Who are you?" he asked as shouts and clanks rang. Blood dripped faster from above. "Where are we?"

"No time," the cloaked saviour said, gesturing with a loose black sleeve.

They led Ryd towards the dingy curtains with pale, circular light peeping from behind them. Disorderly shouts cried out above them in a frenzy of phlegmy voices followed by heavy-booted stomps, then a loud crash like an oil lamp breaking.

Ryd dutifully followed with his head aching and shoulder throbbing, unable to think. The hooded figure grabbed one tattered curtain's edge and tore it with a loud rip from where it was nailed.

To Ryd's amazement, the snaking Missi stretched out beyond the pane. White light from the slivered moon danced on shallow ripples in the idle muddy water. The figure paused, studying the water pensively, then turned away.

They were on a barge.

Ryd was supremely bewildered.

"What's going on? Who are you?"

Without a word the hooded figure left Ryd aside the window listening to guttural dying cries above. His nostrils pricked at harsh, bitter notes of crackling cedar and stagnant smoke. Then, a creeping black cloud furled down from the latch and seeped through above floorboards.

The barge was on fire.

"Wait!" Ryd called, turning in a rush, thinking he'd been abandoned. "Who are you?" he pleaded into the shadows. "Don't leave me!"

"Hush," the figure chided angrily, returning as quickly as they departed with face was still cloaked in darkness, holding the stool Ryd had been tied to. Gripping the legs, they used it like a battering ram.

"What are you doing?!" Ryd shouted, shielding his face with his arm.

But instead of shattering, the circular glass popped easily from its pane as gobs of molasses-like smoke and lapping flames popped around the lip of the deck, through the open porthole, above where Ryd stood.

The figure said, "Now," and shoved him.

"But," Ryd began as he toppled awkwardly from the porthole into stunningly cool water.

He clawed and thrashed in panic, coughing and spitting. Meanwhile, the hooded figure gracefully dove behind him in such perfect form that barely a splash was made at all.

Ryd gasped for air. "I can't. I can't..." he cried as his head bobbed up and down. "Swim," he croaked then bobbed again under the smooth surface of the muddy river. His heart seized with anxiety as he imagined himself dying. *This is really it*, he thought.

"Be still!" his savoir commanded, but still Ryd kicked furiously. "Still!"

The voice was piercingly frustrated and shrill. Ryd, snapped from his frenzy momentarily flailed to turn in the water so he could see his rescuer.

The black hood fell away to reveal a woman soaked from the plunge. Her thick crimped hair floated in the water at her shoulders and her sepia skin glowed in the moonlight. River water dropped from her sharp nose. She untied her cloak's toggle, letting the weighty, waterlogged fabric sink to the river's muddy depths.

"You're a…" Ryd coughed, sputtering in surprise, still bobbing for his life.

"What'd you think I was?" the woman retorted. She kicked expertly over to his side and threw her arms around him from behind. She floated on her back, attempting to force Ryd to as well as he bucked and flailed. "Calm!" she screamed into his ear. Her strong grip on his chest and fluttering heartbeat behind his back convinced him to be still, despite the opaque water, dark night and nearby barge ablaze. "Or we both die," she said firmly.

Ryd instantly relaxed and gave himself over to be rescued. The woman kicked rhythmically towards the sloped shore. It was thick marshland with reedy grass, ambiently lit from the nearby barge blaze. The woman stood once the water was shallow enough leaving Ryd on his own.

Ryd started to buck the moment she let go of him. He was terrified.

"Stand up," she said as she rolled her eyes, slogging through river mud slowly. "You may not swim but your legs are not broken."

Ryd struggled to stand then ran his fingers through his hair. He blew his nose loudly, clearing bloodied mucus from his nostrils straight into the river.

The woman sneered at him from atop the bank with her hands on her hips.

"Are you through? We must go. We mustn't stay here long."

Her words were noticeably over-annunciated.

Ryd studied her in the moonlight. The woman's dripping wet tunic and trousers clung tight to her long legs, slender frame, and ample chest. Her sharp nipples pointed through the gauzy black fabric. Ryd knew he shouldn't stare, but he couldn't stop himself.

The woman squeezed her mane of crimped hair. She shut her eyes briefly as water poured from it onto the bank, after which her curls pulled into tight ringlets. Crickets chirped and frogs ribbited loudly all around them in brilliant, boisterous concert. The fire aboard the barge lit the night sky a deep, smoky red. It looked as if the whole sky was angry.

Then something slithered past Ryd's calf. He jumped and sprinted from the water, splashing loudly in his wake.

"For the Horned sake!" the woman cried, throwing one hand up in the air.

"Something touched my leg!" Ryd shouted.

The woman glared at him with deep brown eyes, unresponsive, one hand still on her popped hip.

"I... I'm sorry," Ryd fumbled. He paused then glanced down sheepishly. "I..." he paused again and glanced up, meeting her stern, burning stare. "Thank you for saving me."

"You're welcome," she said hotly.

Ryd squeezed water out of his tunic. "Who *are* you?" he asked.

He wasn't sure if he was more impressed or intimidated by her. He'd never met such a daring woman in all his life.

"It isn't safe here," she said in a silvery hush. She turned. "Come with me."

"Tell me your name first."

He noted her height as he followed her. She was taller than he.

"You aren't in a position to make demands."

"Please?"

"No," she said firmly. She stopped. "Come," she added, glancing back at him, then again down their path - a narrow trail cutting through the spikey grass parallel to the water towards Littlebell.

"I can't just go with you..."

"What choice do you have?"

She's right, he thought woefully.

Softening, the woman seemed to note Ryd's emotion and

reached out her hand.

"Come with me."

Her presence was overwhelming. As if under a spell, he furrowed his heavy brow and slightly nodded. Ryd took her hand.

"Where to?" he said dutifully.

The woman silently turned without replying.

"This is where I started," Ryd said under his breath. He glanced back and forth. "I was here."

Ryd followed the mystery woman down the bank of the river and around the perimeter of the Occident. The Missi's water was calm in the still hours of night apart from the commotion on the smoking barge. The uproar drew a small crowd to watch a flurry of phlegmy-accented men frantically shovelling buckets of water onto the flames. High-pitched wails pierced the night as unmoving bodies floated lazily away from the scene of the disaster or sprawled the bank with mouths and eyes agape, staring up at the stunning slivered moon.

Now, Ryd trailed her through the buzzing Occident around high-stacked stalls with heavy tarps separating the alleyways.

The atmosphere was far different from earlier. It was louder and rowdier in the black of night. Ryd noted many not wearing the typical patterned Littlebell fashions, most particularly, a pack of hulking Baneswood men, taller and broader than Ryd had ever seen, with their fire-colored hair strangely knotted at the top of their heads, or in dreads down their backs. These men all had overgrown beards and carried spears. All wore leather trousers and boots with no shirts. All bore rippled muscles and collars of fur around their necks and copper bands at their wrists. One woman was with them and she was dressed similarly, with her hair in two long braids instead of knotted on her head. The crowd instinctually parted for them as they passed by. Oddly to Ryd, nearly all these men sported dark tattoos with depictions of grand battles, fearsome beasts, and women. He was fascinated by their markings, as tattoos were forbidden in Westerviolet.

Then Ryd's jaw nearly dropped at another group of passers-by. High natives from Hellswater. Ethereal visions with diamond shaped faces and mahogany eyes. Four women and two men, the females huge breasted, all with hair so blonde it nearly appeared white. All wore thin hammered metal bands at their necks with delicate gems inlayed, male or female. The women's lips were stained blue. Pale gossamer cloaks floated in the group's wake atop fitted jumpsuits. They looked to Ryd like nature sprites of legend.

Two other women with knitted shawls and draped jewel-tone gowns more similar in style to what Ryd had seen the Lady Brochet wear on occasion passed by after that. Natives from Animus Rock. These women had dark hair blunt-cropped to their chins, oiled back, with eyes black-lined, and gilded piercings all up their ears. They chattered loudly as they walked arm and arm, sauntering through the rowdy ruckus as if on a Spring meadow stroll.

There were also several groups of men and women crouched over games of shell beads, throwing coins down rapidly, cheering or booing depending on if they were winning or losing. Ryd was briefly fascinated, despite his overwhelm. Gambling too was banned in Westerviolet.

Finally, Ryd and his rescuer exited the marketplace with the flaming barge at their backs. In their immediate path was a cozy tavern. The same that Ryd saw as he was beaten by Brutt.

"Here?" the woman asked.

Ryd nodded. "That alleyway there. I was here."

The woman eyed Ryd up and down, studying him. He felt he was being examined from the inside out. Finally, she blinked and sighed. Seemingly satisfied, she wordlessly gestured Ryd towards the front door of the tavern's structure. This building was built as the rest of the buildings in Littlebell were, with cod. Hay and sand mixed with mud from the river, stacked layer after layer and allowed to dry into walls.

The cress that was found everywhere in Littlebell curled up

and over the face of this building, spilling across the thatched roof like a purple creature engulfing the building whole. Firelight poured from the front windows over top planter boxes filled with white moon flowers. At this late hour, the lacy petals woke in graceful bouquet, dousing the immediate surroundings with an intoxicatingly exotic, tranquil scent. A single scarlet candle flickered in the front window, illuminating the bottom pane.

"We're here," she said over her shoulder. She pushed the black door open with a whine.

Ryd's heart thumped loudly in his chest.

They entered the quaint establishment with worn tables and square stools dotted with Littlebell patrons, apart from two foreign guards with burgundy cloaks and griffin emblazoned armor, seated in a far corner. The mood was repressed and anxious. The Littlebell citizens glanced warily to where the King's soldiers sat, one gnawing on a roast leg of fowl, the other slurping ale. A musician plucked at a rundle – common in Littlebell - an oblong, carved wooden instrument Ryd had never seen in the opposite corner. It produced a tinny, strumming melody. The fireplace roasted fatty fish and fowl on a blackened spit, juices dripping and sizzling on the wood ablaze. Char scented the air. An aging woman in a faded gown, once brilliantly sunbloom patterned, topped with a sullied white apron, wiped down empty wooden tables with a cloth. The woman's thick greying braid hung impressively down her spine and swayed like a pendulum as she worked. An old man with wide nose, almond eyes and square jaw in a humble, yet pristine scarlet tunic stood behind the bar. He eyed them closely.

The man in scarlet placed both hands on the bar top slowly. Ryd's companion strode over. Ryd skipped to follow closely behind, nervously studying the scene.

"Catch anything today?"

The woman replied casually, "Not a day goes by that I don't wish I'd caught more."

The bartender glanced briefly to the side of the room with

the Bellamine guards. Noting they weren't paying attention, slugging ale and laughing loudly, he nodded curtly to her and went for the exit. Ryd noticed a flash from a dagger peeking beneath the flap of the man's tunic as he turned, fastened to his hip. *Illegal*, Ryd thought.

His heart skipped a beat.

"Was that a code?" Ryd whispered to the woman's back, following her as she ducked behind the bar after she too glanced to the Bellamine guards to make sure they weren't watching. The door led out to the backside of the tavern. Warm air hung stagnant between them in the claustrophobic alley scented with earthy silt, moon flowers, and charred barge.

"This way," the man urged before ducking into a small doorway hidden in the spikey purple greenery overtaking the rear of the building. Ryd wouldn't have noticed it had he not known it was there. The woman followed the older man as he ducked beneath the leaves, then through the frame.

Ryd looked up at the glistening stars briefly. He thought of Col. He took a deep breath, then followed them in. He realized quickly it was an entryway leading down several switchbacks of smaller staircases. The three of them were finally emptied into a larger area with a deeper, larger, steeper staircase overgrown with thick moss. A pathway carved into the underground overgrowth on the stairway revealing ancient metalworking beneath. Ryd peered down into the engulfing darkness at the bottom of the larger staircase suspiciously.

His father had of course told him stories about the dens beneath Littlebell, but he'd believed them to be myths. Until now.

"Where are we?" he asked warily once they'd made it to the start of the second staircase, voice echoing about the cavernous chamber. "What is this?" he asked, gesturing at the stalactites and stalagmites clinging to both ceiling and ground.

The young woman ignored his question and instead lit a torch, illuminating the room from wall to wall. The mossy faces were dripping and glistening. "Hold on when you walk," she commanded. "Or you'll fall."

The older man glanced sympathetically to Ryd after noticing his fretful, bewildered brow.

"It will be alright," he said warmly. "I heard what you did for Ed's brother." He patted Ryd on the back once. "You deserve a hero's thanks."

"What is this place?"

"They'll explain once you're in," the man answered, deep voice washing over Ryd like slow-moving sap. Something about this man innately calmed him. Maybe it was that he reminded him of his father. "Go before these burn off and you're in the dark," he added, handing him the roaring torch.

"You aren't coming?" Ryd asked quickly, taking the torch.

"I have a bar to tend," the man replied kindly. "I will be down later." He went back up the staircase.

The woman turned the other way, already headed down into the strange cave's mossy depths.

"What's your name?" Ryd nearly shouted at the old man's back.

The man turned from part-way up, warm red eyes crinkling in a smile.

"Odion. You?"

"Ryd."

"Good to greet you, Ryd," Odion said, gesturing in the customary Littlebell greeting.

Ryd's puzzled expression revealed his nativity.

"Let's go," the young woman commanded sharply, breaking Ryd from his lull.

Ryd sighed. He turned and rubbed the back of his neck with one hand. He held the hot torch in the other and began a timid decent down the slick stairs, cool on his bare feet. They dropped sharply for several minutes into the stairwell's belly. Torchlight flickered off slick stalactites trickling with water. Echoing drips were the only sound apart from careful footfalls.

Ryd clung to the mossy railing for what felt like an eternity until they finally reached the base.

Then, the pathway flattened out in a long, completely overgrown corridor. Heavy dark moss clung to every inch of the floor, walls, and ceiling. It appeared dark as the stairway at first, until the tiniest floral blooms opened upon sensing light. Miniature yellow buds exploded from the butter moss as Ryd and his rescuer's torchlights passed through the corridor, flashing in a halo around them as they walked. The flowers opened and closed with the passing flames, a cascading wave of the gentle yellowed blooms. Ryd had never seen anything like it. Eventually, the pair reached the walkway's end, split into two doors, highlighted in rings of the buttery flowers now as they hovered in front of them with the torch.

"We are here," the woman said as she looked to the right door. It was newly constructed split-wood painted burgundy, perched in a mossy, ancient frame.

"Where's here?"

"You're in the Dens," she said. "This is Ashkeep."

His father's stories had been rooted in truth after all, Ryd thought. He racked his memory for clues but came up wanting. All he remembered was that the dens were used during the wars to hide refugees. There were dozens of them all over the city, all with different hidden entrances and depths. Nothing more.

"Okay," Ryd said. "What's Ashkeep?"

The young woman narrowed her eyes, as if internally laughing at him.

"You like my misery, is that it? You have no idea the day I've had."

Her playful smirk fell to a brooding sneer. "Yes, and mine has been flowers, thanks for asking."

She spun in a rush.

"Wait!" he cried. "Don't be angry."

She spun back, brown eyes glaring. "Who said I was angry?"

"Fine." Ryd sighed again. "Fine."

The young woman glanced Ryd up and down then chucked softly to herself. She shook her head.

"Go on," she gestured at the burgundy door.

Was she really going to leave him alone without any knowledge as to where he was? Could this be a trap? Ryd's heart flipped in his chest. He was not made for adventures like this.

"Really?" he asked.

"What more do you whine for?"

Ryd was completely overwhelmed. A big part of him wished he'd never left Westerviolet at all. Despite his missing brother.

"You aren't going to tell me what Ashkeep is?"

"Get inside or you'll miss sup."

Sup did sound good. "But…"

"Just go. I've had enough of you!" she shouted.

The outburst startled Ryd, forcing him to take a step back, as if he'd been physically pushed. He'd never been spoken to by a woman that way. He didn't realize women could speak so forcefully.

"If you hadn't saved Karl, I wouldn't bother with you at all," she added, waving hand in the air like she was swatting an irritating fly.

"Wait, but…"

"I will deal with you later."

The woman darted through the twin door on the left, slamming it behind her with a crash before Ryd could follow or see what was inside.

Ryd shook his head as he turned to the door on the right. He raised his hand to knock first, then removed it, feeling foolish, then he reminded himself of Col. He must find his brother. The mere chance that Col was behind the burgundy door outweighed the adrenaline pumping through his veins and the nervous thoughts bouncing around in his mind. He wiped new beads of sweat from his brow and the bridge of his nose. He took a deep breath that filled the crevices of his lungs with stagnant, mossy air.

Then, Ryd pushed the door open with a creak, despite his cowardice. He walked forward into the unknown. He saw Col's face in his mind.

WESTERVIOLET LORD'S STUDY

C ommander Budic scaled Westerviolet's back staircase then walked the length of the hall adorned with portraits of the Brochets past, hurrying as much as he could with stiff leg, repeating what he was about to say to the Lord over and over in his mind. He was drenched in sweat when he reached the Lord's Study. He adjusted his armor, removed his smooth helmet and wiped his forehead as he entered.

"Oh good," Tomas said, glancing up from the elder desk. "You're in time."

"My Lord?"

Tomas stood from his seat. "I just was heading down."

Budic shifted his weight while holding his helmet behind himself with both hands. The cool metal provided a slight reprieve to the castle's sweltering heat, despite the open window. He swallowed hard before he spoke.

"My Lord, I have news."

"Come, come," Tomas said, gesturing at Budic to follow him as he shuffled across the room.

"My Lord," Budic said, visibly worried. "It is important."

Tomas paid no heed at all to his Commander as he approached the gaping unlit fireplace, constructed from the exact same green stones that made up the castle herself. Tomas was accustomed to Budic's overactive concern and disregarded it when it suited him. He placed a wrinkled hand against the rock, almost able to· feel the pulse from the ancient times witnessed by these very stones. "Do you know how long this castle has stood?"

"My Lord? There is an urgent..."

Tomas interrupted slowly. "Do you know?"

"A long time," Budic said dutifully, despite the pressing message he had to share. "Hundreds, maybe thousands of years. No one knows for certain when it was built, Lord."

"That's right," Tomas said, shaking one finger towards him. "And how long has Brochet reigned?"

Budic frowned. He was not sure where Tomas was going with this line of questions. He was anxious to share news of Aslf.

"Longer than that, my Lord."

"It takes time to be great, Budic," Tomas said distantly as he studied slight variations in the massive stones with his eyes.

Budic balked internally at the use of his given name by the Lord—quite rare.

"Like my blood," Tomas went on, "or this castle and her secrets."

His hand passed over stone after stone, pocks and natural ripples catching on his papery old skin before resting on an oblong rock at the right of the chimney. The same that normally sat on the elderdesk.

"Most things are fleeting," he went on, eyes focused on the stone, "but Brochet blood, and this castle, are eternal."

Tomas pressed the oblong rock hard. Instantly, the fireplace churned as if the stones were climbing from their mortar. Budic, startled by the sound, jumped back. The whole structure moved in a slow scrape to reveal a dark tunnel and a dim spiral staircase. He had witnessed the Lord open the door to the Lair before, but it amazed him every time.

"My Lord," Budic said, eyes darting. He was unable to hold the news any longer. "It was murder!" he yelled loudly just as Tomas began towards Westerviolet Lair's shadowy depths.

Tomas stopped. He turned to face Budic in a rush, meeting his Commander's mournful gaze for the first time in their exchange.

"Who?" he barked.

"My nephew." Budic's red eyes locked intensely on Tomas's hazel. "Guardsman Aslf."

"Hard to believe," Tomas scoffed. He was annoyed at the

interruption, teetering at the edge of the Lair's spiral staircase. He was anxious to continue his latest studies. The lair had just received its latest batch of newly impregnated maidens.

"There's evidence," Budic said.

"What evidence? Quickly," Tomas beckoned him to hurry with a hand gesture, "there's work to do."

"Aye," Budic cleared his throat. "The boy was struck."

"How do you know?"

"Bruising to the head," Budic told him. "Showed up later. Hudde discovered it."

"I see," Tomas said slowly, squinting his eyes, considering how much he trusted the Guildsman Hudde's word. That man was as sour as a lemon. But also, clever. "What else?"

"The boy held the weapon in his right but favoured the left," Budic said. "My Second was convinced by the girl who discovered him that the boy had not the strength in his right to make a wound as deep as he did." He paused. "It was a set up," Budic finally said gravely. "Someone wanted it to look like it was by his own hand." He paused again. "There's been a murder in Westerviolet."

"Preposterous," Tomas said dismissively as he left his position at the stop of the Lair's stairs to rest in a straight-backed emerald chair with embroidered snakes in the cloth, carven snakes for arms and feet, antique and faded from years of use. Tomas leaned backwards, narrowing his eyes as he thought. "Unless," he finally said, mind's wheels almost visibly turning.

"Unless?" Budic took an eager step, anxious to hear. He hoped Tomas followed his own train of thought.

"Aslf discovered a culprit in misdeed and was silenced for it," Tomas said surely, turning his head to study Budic's reaction to the idea. "Why else would one put a useful boy down?"

"I have a theory for you to consider, my Lord," Budic said. He knew the weight of his accusation, but not it's truth. He'd spent all night coming to the conclusion, then all morning deciding if he ought to tell the Lord what he suspected. But it was the only scenario that made sense. "My men can't find the

Stablemaster."

"The same sent to Croft? The only one who returned, with all else slain?!" Tomas bellowed as he forcefully stood. "I'm just now hearing this!?"

"I told you it was urgent."

Tomas waved his hand flippantly. "What is his name? You know what, I do not care." He shut his eyes tight, then rubbed his temple. "Just find him."

"I've sent men to patrol the Narrows. And the way up to Croft as well as into the Hills, but no sign."

"Why would he betray Brochet?"

"Do you suspect he discovered his brother's fate?"

"Nonsense," Tomas said, then paused. "How?"

"Why else would he go through all the trouble?" Budic asked. "And why punish Aslf?"

"Some men need no reason for violence. It is the way of the Kingdom."

"Aye, nothing truer."

"What do we know about him?"

"That's why it's worrisome," Budic said.

"Out with it!"

"Burkhart was his father."

"I see," Tomas said as he thought, pacing to the long rectangular windows above the stable yard. He looked down with a serious glare as he searched his memory. Tomas had nearly forgotten how Burkart was acquired, it was so long ago.

Budic went on, raising his voice to carry across the massive study. "I know where he came from. What we did to," he paused, "obtain him." Budic had done his best to suppress his memories of that horrid time, so, recollection was difficult. He swallowed hard. "I was low rank then, but I went on the raid."

"You did, didn't you?" Tomas side eyed him. "So, the boy has ties to Littlebell. What of it?"

"My Lord," Budic said, leading Tomas to the same realization he'd come to. "What if he's of the Rebellion?"

"Preposterous!"

"But my Lord," Budic said, "if the ploy is to distract with

chaos from within, what better than to corrupt our own and cause a ruckus that will divert attention from the true enemy." Not wanting to appear out of line, he added, "With respect."

Tomas paced in youthful long strides, white cloak flapping in his wake. "Say it's true," he said. "How do you say it happened? How did they corrupt him?"

"I'm thinking as I say this, but, what if while at Croft they got his ear?" Budic offered, not having just thought of it at all. "What if they knew of his father's story somehow and won him? What if they convinced him to murder Clemmo and his men and my nephew as well, all in the name of the Rebellion? It falls in line."

Tomas furrowed his bushy brow as he accepted Budic's theories loosely. "So, say it's true. Where has he gone now?"

"My guess is Littlebell. Or Croft. Maybe Animus."

"Have you found anything else?"

"Not much," Budic said, still gripping his helmet behind his back with both hands with all his might. "I've investigated all the Guardsmen and castle workers. The only thing is, well..." he paused.

"What?" Tomas looked at him. He frowned. "What is it?"

"Digory is missing."

Tomas rolled his eyes as he moved from his place against the windows, back to the gaping Lair's entryway. "Sybil," he said bluntly.

"You believe she sent him somewhere?"

"No, I believe she took him with her to the Rock," Tomas grumbled. "I'd call her a cursed defix if she wasn't my blood."

"We don't know he's gone with her," Budic said, concerned by Tomas's hubris. "What if he's the villain?"

"Couldn't be," Tomas said flippantly. "He'll appear when she does."

"The only ones I haven't spoken to yet are Sybil and the little Lady."

"Never mind that. They won't know anything."

"Aye, my Lord," Budic said dutifully, still protesting internally.

As Tomas shuffled closer to the fireplace he added, "And get the word out that I want this," he paused, "what is his name?"

"Ryd."

"Ryd's head."

"His head? My Lord..."

"A greater sum if he's brought alive then."

Budic lowered his head in a slight bow, grateful for the boy's reprieve. Burkhart was a good friend, rest his soul, and he owed man's memory this much.

"I'd like us to speak to him first, my Lord," Budic asked carefully, knowing he was pressing his fortune with the Lord's pleasant mood. "to ensure the boy's guilt."

"Hmm," Tomas dismissed with a flick of his wrist. "He's guilty. Bring him alive," he said resolutely, clearing his throat in a hacking cough, "so he can be of use." He gestured into the depths of the Lair.

Budic swallowed hard. "Aye."

"You've never liked the Lair," Tomas said bluntly.

Budic was taken aback. He nearly stuttered, having trouble holding Tomas's piercing gaze.

"W...why do you say that?"

"No, you hate it. Despise it. I can feel it. Radiating off you like a stink."

"My Lord?"

"Do you know why I like you, Budic?"

Budic shook his head, 'no'.

"You're smart. You know your place. You do your part. If the Kingdom was made of earthblood like you, things may be different. But alas," Tomas said wistfully, turning to the Lair's dark depths, "it is not."

ANIMUS ROCK VILLAS

S ybil lay wide-awake despite the cool breeze and silent calm. She was restless, fiddling with the loose strap of her sleep gown. She'd rolled around in a fit, awake for hours, jerking her feet between tangled, humid sheets, staring impatiently at fine cracks in the plaster on the ceiling, waiting for sunrise.

Anxiety was an old friend of Sybil's. During the day she kept busy and its voice was muffled, but at night, it screamed, gripping her heart and squeezing. Hard. She felt it in her chest the most, like hands pressing down on her. She worried if she were to sleep too long, she'd never wake up. As a child she's confided to her father how it felt. He asked her what was making her feel that way and she couldn't explain. It was everything. Tomas rolled his eyes and laughed at her. That was the last she'd spoken of it. To anyone.

When she couldn't take it anymore, Sybil kicked the pale green quilt and white cotton linens to the foot of her cherry-wood bed. She placed her bare feet to the wide-plank floor.

Insomnia was a friend of Sybil's too. She was accustomed to not sleeping. She often found distraction in wondering around the castle's quiet halls in the depths of night, like a ghost haunting Westerviolet.

This night, Sybil thought to explore the unfamiliar Thorne Villa. She walked the galley hallway illuminated by the glinting moon past billowy curtains. Her feet felt the polished black wood beneath them. She paused in front of an oversized entry. It was unlike the other standard doors in the Villa. This one was carved in stems, branches, and sharp pointed thorns. The door's handle was a massive jewel bloom cast in copper. It was far too tempting not to investigate. Sybil ran her pale fingers across the dark-stained wood of the door to match the floor, pausing briefly to test the carved thorns. She touched one with her finger and immediately winced. She brought the pinprick wound with a bead of blood to her mouth. She didn't realize how sharp it was. Sybil pushed the door open with her other hand as she sucked on her tiny wound, careful this time to avoid any thorns. It opened with silent ease to reveal a grand chamber with high ceilings, rich tapestries, gauzy curtains, and a massive four-poster cherry wood bed, larger and grander than in the guest chambers, with an expensive-looking black, grey and pale-green quilt.

This was more like it.

Sybil smiled to herself. She twirled in a delicate dance as she entered the chamber then sauntered about as if she were the Lady of the villa, make-believing the finery was hers to command. She spun and leapt across the floor, red skirts of her sleep gown flowing like blood in water. Then, she collapsed backwards onto the ornate quilt with a melancholy sigh, fabric cut in delicate half-moon shapes, arranged in an intricate floral collage. She ran her hands across the careful stitches and shut her eyes tightly.

She would be elder one day, she thought to herself. She'd reopen the Brochet Villa and decorate it as she pleased. Although Thorne's tastes suited her refined sensibilities for the time being.

She glanced around the chamber curiously and noticed a carved cabinet at the opposite side of the bed. Then, Sybil crawled across the pale green quilt in the near-darkness and opened it to discover a glass decanter with red-tinted liquid inside. *Animus wine*, she thought happily. Sybil uncorked the vessel with a loud pop while mischievously smiling. She smelled the pungent liquid and gagged.

A rich voice broke the unearthly hour's silence.

"Next time, ask if you are thirsty."

Sybil gasped. She turned in fright and nearly dropped the decanter. A tall, lanky figure filled up the doorframe. The man nearly blended with the shadows. If it hadn't been for the candle he held, he would have. Sybil only saw dark skin, the outline of his refined nose, and narrow eyes in shining prasine green.

"Montague?" Sybil clenched the decanter in front of herself like a shield. The cabinet next to his bed lay suspiciously open.

"Monty," he clarified, taking a confident step further into the chamber. His chamber.

Sybil shifted her weight, angling slightly away, eyes locked as she studied her accuser.

Montague Thorne had cheek-length hair, black like a raven and wavy in dark ringlets, a mole on his forehead, and deep smile-lines by his eyes. His face was pointed to match his nose and he had ample lips and long Thorne fingers. He wore a thin-cloth, pale green cloak over a white low-v neck tunic. Fine clothing, but too casual and intimate for Sybil's taste.

Monty was more beautiful than he was handsome. He was the opposite of her true love, Rosen-dead now for half a decade. Rosen, the only man she had ever laid with, was muscled and strong, almost as if he were of Dale blood, carved out of stone, with a brooding stare and quiet ways. Unlike Monty, with his willowy frame and knowing smirk. Sybil disliked him immediately.

He took leisurely, long strides towards her as he pointed at the decanter.

"What is that you have there?"

"I couldn't sleep," Sybil said defensively.

"You're quite bold, aren't you?" Monty laughed, properly amused by this petite woman's rage. It radiated off her like warmth from a blaze.

"How long were you watching me?"

"I caught the performance," Monty said, not hiding his amusement at all.

"You aren't supposed to be home."

"That excuses thievery?"

"Do not tease your honored guest."

"Who?"

Sybil shouted, "Me!" with her cheeks burning hot.

"Who says you're honored?"

Sybil's distinct eyebrows rose quickly. She'd had men hung for far less.

But Monty was known for his wit. It was part of why Sybil's father, Tomas, grew a liking to him. Monty was clever. He liked to tease, especially women. "Too far?" He extended his hand in the shadow-filled room. "Let me make peace. Welcome."

She refused to give him her hand.

"Why did you sneak up on me?"

"It's my chamber," he said, as one would speak to a child. "My villa."

"But..."

"For all I knew, you were a thief. You're fortunate I didn't take off your head and ask questions later. Truce?" he asked warmly. "We can drink to it." He pointed at the container that Sybil still held.

"Well..." Sybil started, knuckles now snow-white from her tight grip.

"Well, what? Did you have something else you were doing?" Monty said with a brilliantly white smile. "Come, let's sit on the balcony."

Sybil relented despite her burning pride and followed Monty into the darkness under the stars, clutching the wine tightly in front of her. Instantly the pair was engulfed in a serenade of crickets and an embrace of warm air. Moonlight reflected like a shiny coin off the Missi below.

All about them were dozens of plants all native to Graceview's realm including lattice covered in graveshade ivy that sparkled in the moonlight and purportedly was best utilized in tea to ease grief, planters full of vireila blossoms used in the most expensive of perfumes, and large bushes of eidolic roses–each bloom containing a faint echo of its gardener's emotion. Sybil felt awe mixed with contempt as she passed by them.

Monty lit a standing candelabra. It dimly illuminated the foreground. He gestured for Sybil to sit in a recliner topped with velvet pillows. The sky above was mostly clear, starry with blackened streaks of clouds desperately trying to hide the moon. Monty disappeared inside briefly and returned with two green glass goblets intricately etched with jewel blooms and thorns. Sybil handed him the decanter. He poured.

"I didn't figure you partook," Monty said, half-impressed, turning to glance at Sybil as he handed her a glass, topped to the brim. "You never can tell."

"Doesn't everyone?"

Sybil nonchalantly took a sip then coughed violently as the unfamiliar liquid burned the back of her throat. It wasn't Animus wine. Not at all.

Monty burst into deep-bellied laugher. "That, pet, is more than ale."

"What did you give me?!" she screamed as she wiped her mouth with the back of her hand, then checked her nightgown for spittle. "You poisoned me!"

"Yes," Monty replied simply.

Sybil's deep-set eyes narrowed.

"Is there no mad honey in Westerviolet?" Monty asked casually, taking a sip, feeling her eyes pierce him as he sighed with pleasure. "I suppose there wouldn't be. Pity to live in such a conservative realm. You miss out on so much."

"This is…" Sybil paused, eyes widening, "mad honey?"

She shook her head in disbelief.

"There's none left."

She eyed the viscus red-brown liquid before taking another more cautious sip, this time only barely grazing her lips with the tainted ale.

"There wasn't."

"So, there is now?"

"Now, you must keep this between you and me. Can I trust you, Sybil?"

"Of course," she said as she quickly lowered her voice, leaning forward and putting a hand on his. She locked his eyes and squeezed his hand with hers slightly. "Of course," she repeated sincerely, knowing how much of a lie that was.

"It's back," Monty said.

He dropped her hands then took a thirsty sip, nearly finishing his glass. After, he refreshed it with a pour. She hung on his words, still leaning towards him, waiting for more. She frowned when he didn't respond.

"That's it?" She slumped backwards in the crisp iron seat, unimpressed. "What's back? Mad honey?"

Monty nodded, silken ringlets jumping beside his prasine eye. "The lines reopened."

"How, without Duskfang?"

"It is no longer Calvanese."

Sybil lifted her glass. "Then where did you get this?"

"I have ways."

"Who is it now? I cannot believe it would be your kin. Then, Basil Graves, or maybe the Guild? I can't imagine either would be interested…"

"No," Monty interrupted, holding the crystal glass from the bottom with his palm. He partly gestured to her with that pinkie, jostling the dark liquid back and forth.

"Then, who?"

"Minney."

"No!" Sybil squealed, nearly chuckling. "You lie."

"It's true," Monty said. "The honey hails from Littlebell."

His confidence shook her, and her commanding tone wavered. "They've discovered how to make it?"

"I know not," Monty said.

Sybil noticed a slight twitch in the man's eye. And, besides, she could simply sense it. He was lying.

"Prihim is supposed to be unflappable," Sybil said, wheels turning. "How is he behind it?"

"He may not know of it. I have a feeling he," Monty paused, then said with a smile, "is distracted."

He took another sip.

Sybil took a long sip herself. "I like this," she said to the glass. "Once you get past the burning. It's… nice,"

She traced the deep etchings with the point of her slightly wounded finger. All her cares felt fuzzier the more she consumed, as if she'd stepped into a protective haze. It was as if she was dreaming. Nothing was real. Nothing could harm her. She was invincible. She took another sip.

Monty raised his glass towards Sybil and winked at her, pupils hugely dilated. Instead of green, he almost appeared to have black eyes.

"Oh!" Sybil leaned forward earnestly. She loved gossip. "What do you mean distracted? With Council?"

"No, the Council is business as usual. I'm talking about his *personal* affairs."

"What's *that* mean?"

Between Monty's charisma and the drug, Sybil was fully entranced.

"Primin Minney is fucking Galla Morfit."

"What!" Sybil replied in a squeak, looking down briefly with a grin, and then back to him. She squinted her eyes. "Really?"

"Yes, really."

Sybil smiled wide. This type of drama fuelled her, particularly since it involved Galla, Rupert Morfit's twin sister. Sybil disliked the woman from their days back at Academy, so many years ago. She was something of a rival. The opposite of Sybil in every conceivable way.

"Aren't they married?"

"Indeed," Monty agreed, matching Sybil's grin. "To good natives. Other than each other, mind you. There are children too."

"Is this knowledge common? Am I the last to know?"

Monty shrugged. "Not uncommon. I tell you because they both sit on Council and might as well be one vote."

"Interesting," Sybil said slowly. Distrust seeped in. "Why help me with Council?"

"Your father."

Sybil expected more details yet didn't press, although a twitch of her eyebrow indicated she wanted to. She changed the subject. "Who else should I be concerned with?"

"Let's see. There's Ogo."

"Ogo Regnard? What about him? He was older than me at

Academy. All I know of him is that he's all nerves and hates his father."

"Word is that he should be here at Animus Rock in preparation for this session, but no one's seen him."

"Is that so?"

Sybil wiggled her glass. Monty leaned forward to refresh her drink. Firebugs danced in flashing loops through the swampy reeds along both sides of the Missi's riverbed. Crickets sang. Frogs ribbited. Shouts occasionally came from barges on the Missi. The night-time air was fully alive.

"What's his plot?

Monty chuckled at Sybil's naiveite as he set the decanter down on a bent iron table. "Have you heard of what's brewing?"

Sybil leaned a bit and dropped her voice to a coy rasp. "You get right to the dirt, don't you Montague? No wonder father fancies you."

"Monty," he corrected flatly. "It's the honey."

Sybil replied to his original question, "I have not heard."

"That surprises me for a daughter of Brochet."

"What does that mean?"

Monty's eyes sparkled. "I presumed he raised you to know these things before someone like me tells you."

"What is it then?"

"They call themselves the Rebellion. Or the New Rebellion, or something." He took a sip. "Asking for trouble, if you ask me. Which mind you, no one did."

"You are funny, Montague."

"Monty," he said firmly.

Sybil took a long, lustful sip. Dark stains appeared at the corners of her lips. "Why are they asking for trouble?"

"They poke the beast then cry in pain when bit," he said and sighed. "For once, can't there be another way?"

"Avoid war?" Sybil shook her head and her dark blanket of hair brushed her breasts. "For as long as there has been time there has been war. There is no other way. To live is to fight."

"I do not accept that, Sybil Brochet."

"Is that so, Montague Thorne?"

"For the Horned sake, it's Monty!" he yelled at her, bewitched by her addictive beauty, the veil of ale and a third unnamed element he couldn't place. He held back a smile.

"Oh, no." She shook her head, combing the hair with her hand before twirling a strand between her fingers mindlessly aside her breast as she spoke. "Don't tell me that you worship that horrid thing."

She and her father often looked down upon any Vanguards stupid enough to adhere to the Faith of the Horned. It was an earthblood belief system. A doltish one at that.

"Be careful with your pretty tongue, pet. I may not consider you a blasphemer, but many within these walls would. They love their goddess."

"It's for the weak minded," Sybil said dismissively. "Not for Vanguards."

"Are you sure?"

"Yes," Sybil spat confidently. Her deep-set, black eyes were as widely dilated and gleaming as Monty's. A rustling breeze caught her hair and jostled it about her face as she took a long sip from the green-tinted crystal glass, feeling Monty's eyes on her the whole time. The attention fuelled her. She lowered the glass, placing it down with a resolute clink.

"I am the goddess I worship."

He chuckled at her and slightly raised his glass. "That, I believe," he said in delight tinged with admiration.

Power oozed off her.

She nestled into her chair, contented with his praise, rubbing one hand over her arm, chilled with bumps from the breeze.

"Are you sure you don't say that because your father hates it?" Monty baited.

"Father banned those foolish earthblood beliefs, yes," Sybil said.

She took a long, burning sip of the mad honey ale. She gratefully accepted more of the haze. She hadn't realized how burdened her mind had been until her cares were lifted from it. Her chest was light. She felt free.

"Oh," Monty said quietly.

"What is your meaning?" Sybil asked threateningly.

She ignored her vision tunnelling as well as her chest flushing. This mad honey was quite powerful.

He squinted at her. "You really don't know?"

"Montague." Sybil sat forward. "Tell me what?"

"Mo..." he started, then shifted his eyes. "You know what, never mind," he sighed. "You know of Tomas's sister? Your aunt, the late Farrah Brochet?"

"She died before I was born," Sybil said. "Father told me my hair is thick like hers and we have the same laugh, but that's all I know of her."

"I see."

"What is it?"

"Do I have a story for you," he said. "Your aunt Farrah was a fanatic."

"A fanatic? Lies," Sybil shook her head, frowning like a cloud about to thunder. "She was a great woman."

"Perhaps," Monty offered, "but also, a very religious one."

"Farrah Brochet believed in," Sybil asked with surprise, "the Horned Woman?"

"Not just believed in her," Monty said. "She converted others. I was just a boy, but I remember it was quite the scandal at the time. A good, oldblood Vanguard no less, succumbing to the opiate of the," he paused, "*earthblood.*"

"Is that why Tomas hates the Faith?" Sybil asked. "Because his sister believed?"

"Not only that," Monty said, refilling his drink, decanter now far less than half-full.

"What, then? My father is a reasonable man." Monty eyed her knowingly. "What?" she laughed. "He's a bit intense at times but..."

"Intense is a good word for it."

"So, why then?" Sybil asked, ignoring his sarcasm. "Why is the Faith banned? Why did I know nothing of my aunt's beliefs?"

"Have you heard of the Pilgrimage?"

"Oh, everyone has," she said dismissively, thinking of the yearly trek all true believers took to Glassy Stream, to pay homage to their goddess. She took a sip.

"Farrah Brochet went in 4021."

"No!" Sybil gasped. "Father must have been outraged. Why did he allow it?"

"He didn't know," Monty told her. "She went without permission."

"Of course. Wait, 4021?"

"Yes."

"Isn't that the year she died?"

"It is."

"She died on that pilgrimage?"

He shook his head 'no'.

"Montague, what is it?"

"Are you sure you wish to know?"

Sybil's black eyes glared. "Tell me," she demanded.

Monty took a deep breath, then sighed. Although he enjoyed the power he held in this conversation very much. He hadn't been sure what to expect from his mentor Tomas's daughter. The fact that he commanded her attention so easily boosted his ego tremendously. He didn't care that painful information he was about to impart would likely wound her. Monty never minded causing pain. He rather enjoyed it, as long as the attention was on him.

"She never returned from that Pilgrimage," he told Sybil. "After a year of searching for her, she was declared dead. Your father took it out on the Faith, exiling or burning every believer left in Westerviolet. He banned mention of any of it ever again."

Sybil distantly gazed over Monty's shoulder. "I thought it was to control them," she said softly.

"Who am I to presume Tomas's reasons for doing what he did?" Monty asked rhetorically, studying Sybil's reaction. For the briefest moment her facade dropped. Sybil looked scared and small. He softened. "I only tell you what happened," he said gently.

Sybil snapped from her lull, iron bars of her mind clinking back into place. "What I want to know is, how did my father ever befriend an earthblood-lover like you?"

Monty grinned. "What now?" He took another sip.

"You've told me about my family," Sybil said, bending her knees, pulling them beneath herself and crossing them under her sleep gown. The deep red fabric glinted in the moonlight. "What about your family? What about you?"

"Me?" he asked. "I'm a simple Thorne."

"Nothing about Thorne is simple."

"Touché," said Monty, chuckling. "Ustin is my father," he offered her. "Our branch lives at Animus Rock."

"Why not Graceview?"

"We've been here since Humfra sent Valentin to Animus. He married Gravesblood. That's what caused the first Regnard split, by the way."

Sybil rolled her eyes. "You act like I don't already know," she said, unimpressed. "How does that have anything to do with a newblood Thorne?"

"It has everything to do with me," Monty retorted with placating cadence. "Valentin Graves was my great-grandfather. His daughter Yette married Miles Thorne, and my father Ustin is their youngest son. He moved to Animus, and now here I am too."

"Why aren't you in the Brotherhood, then? You're practically a Graves."

"I am a Graves, in part anyway," he said. "But my bloodline is absent of dead blood."

"I thought Humfra forced Harrye to have deadblood children in secret."

"He did, as punishment for marrying Avice Dale and fathering Valentin," Monty replied, nodding once. "That's why they banished Valentin from Anstout. Sent him to Animus Rock." He paused, then spoke with a bit of pride in his voice, "Valentin was pure Vanguard."

"I see," Sybil said slowly, trying to decide if she believed him as she took another sip.

"I was born and raised here at Animus. It's where I got to know Tomas, since he spent a great deal of time on Council," Monty told her. "Your father and mine formed an alliance years ago. That's why you and I sit here today."

"What about politics?"

"What about it?"

"You have an earthblood mother."

"What does that matter?"

"Aren't you New?"

"New and Old are just names," Monty said, smiling, chuckling. "I'm my own way."

"I like that," Sybil said. "Cheers, to that. To our own way." She held out her drink.

"May your blood reign forever," he said, clinking his glass with hers.

"Here, here," she smiled.

Then, the pair sipped mad honey and looked up at the stars.

Hours passed and the moon hung low in the sky. The decanter was nearly empty. Monty and Sybil lounged opposite each other in drugged, drunken bliss.

"Be ready for Cuthbert, the old bag."

Sybil turned to her side, revealing the curve of her hip and waist. "Who?"

"Cornelius's brother," Monty said, eyelids low drooping. "Norland."

"Ah, that's right." Sybil nodded more slowly than usual. "Why?"

"He's bitter that his brother leads and grouchy that the traditional Old he loves so much is a thing of the past. Hates Animus too and won't shut up about it. He causes trouble at every turn."

"What if I agree with him?" Sybil said hotly with half a smile on her high cheek boned face.

"I'd expect you to be smart, not call Galla an earthblood bitch right to her face in front of everyone."

Sybil giggled. She wished she could have witnessed that for herself. "Ouch," she said.

"Right." Monty felt a hollow stab of sympathy for his friend, although he enjoyed Sybil's attention more. She was more fun. "It doesn't do much for the Old's cause to have him. He's a... challenge."

"Got it," Sybil said. "What of Ivor?" She knew little about that branch of the Thorne family, although she'd heard he had oldblood ways. "What role does the Magistrate play?"

"My cousin is tricky," Monty said, wholly entranced with Sybil, the late hour and mad honey ale. Though the night-time hours were in half of Monty's blood, he did not have red eyes and he was raised Vanguard, to be awake during the day. "Ivor and I are both Thorne but we come from different worlds. He was raised at Graceview. My uncle is basically Cornelius Norland's brother," he said. "He's his brother-in-law, but they are close like blood. This puts Ivor and Hadrian quite close too," Monty said, tone deep with meaning. He shifted his hair out of his eyes. "And, they are. Ivor tends to favor Hadrian's beliefs and I fear he's bordering on radical. He calls me soft."

He shrugged and glanced to the side briefly before sipping the last drops of ale out of his glass goblet.

"But can he interfere with the Council?"

"Don't you remember your lessons on Animus Government?"

"I'm sure you will refresh me," Sybil said playfully, batting her black eyes.

"Per the law, he technically can't," Monty said. The crickets' hum dimmed slightly as even they took rest in this unholy hour. Monty pontificated on, gesturing in authority with one hand, empty green glass tight in the other, glinting just like his eyes. "The Magistrate tries the guilty," he said. "The Magistrate gives sentences. The Magistrate, however, has no say in making new laws or voting on policy change or taxes or anything to do with running the Kingdom."

"Why not?" Sybil asked, always analyzing. She remembered

her lessons but wanted to hear how Montague viewed it. She imagined the innerworkings of Council were far different than how they appeared on the surface. All things were that way.

"To prevent one branch from having all the power. Council makes the laws with the King," Monty said simply. "Magistrate enforces."

"I see," Sybil replied, digesting what he'd just said. "Why did you say 'technically'?"

Monty leaned backwards with a squeak of his iron chair. "Nothing gets by you."

Sybil smiled. In her drunken, drugged state, she was deeply attracted to this charming man. Her earlier judgement of him lifted. Sybil shifted to the side and the thin nightgown strap slipped from her shoulder to rest on her arm. Consciously or not, she wanted to be seen as desirable.

Monty eyed the strap as Sybil watched, before continuing. "I say technically because the Magistrate is permitted to provide advice to the Council. Naturally, their opinions carry heavy weight."

Sybil leaned forward on crossed arms. "Why?"

"Council is always looking for future favors," Monty said. "You must understand how valuable control over one of the Magistrate votes is."

"You're saying that members of the Council vote the way that the Magistrate wants, so that when it comes time for a hearing, that Magistrate member votes the way the Council members want?" Sybil asked rhetorically, laughing to herself briefly. "Quite corrupt."

"You almost sound impressed."

"Oh, I am," Sybil grinned. "This Kingdom amazes me," she added, nearly slurring her words, eyes shining from ale. "We're in the capital of the most enlightened and... refined Kingdom in all the lands, and yet the elite deal in shadows."

Monty turned to face her, scooting forward with much effort in the sloped iron chair. He leaned forward to rest his elbows on his knees. "My dear, we are the elite," he said, before a twisted smirk curled across his pretty cheeks.

Sybil lowered her bare feet to the cool balcony floor. "Oh, I know," she said lightly, weaving her web carefully. "It is so nice to have someone to talk to," she added, scooting forward a bit, taking his dark hand into hers. "I enjoy your company, Montague."

"And I, yours Sybil," he said warmly, faint lines crinkling aside his eyes as he softly smiled. "You're so beautiful," he said in a breathy whisper. The closer he leaned towards her, the more he felt himself consumed by her dark glare. "More so than even your mother."

Sybil was hit with a burst of desire and slowly brought Monty's hand to her mouth, kissing one finger with soft lips, then the next. She hadn't planned it this way. She wasn't sure what she was doing. She wasn't thinking, which was a first for Sybil. She just couldn't stop herself. The allure of the power she felt over him was too great. She needed more.

He raised an eyebrow, nearly too stunned at first to speak and too pleased to say anything for fear of awakening the beauty to her senses. Why would Tomas's oldblood daughter associate in this way with a mixed blood like him? It spoke to her unhinged nature. Despite the influence of mad honey blurring his thoughts, he realized that she was one to be wary of. To act this way proved her dangerous. But he filed those thoughts away.

"What are you doing?" he asked; puzzled, pleased, and amused all at once. "Would your father approve?"

Sybil stopped kissing his hand but still held it near her face. Monty felt her soft breath on his fingers. She dropped her tone to a hateful whisper, like a hissing snake about to strike. "If you mention him tonight again, I'm leaving," she said.

Monty bowed his head. "Carry on, Lady," he grinned.

At that Sybil thrust forward. She braced herself on Monty's lean thigh, pressing her lips against him. She kissed him slowly. She allowed herself to fall back into the nearly forgotten fire inside of her, almost lost after Rosen died. Monty wrapped long arms around her and traced the bones on her shoulder with his fingertips, kissing the porcelain skin down the crease of her neck. How long had it been since a man held her that way? Touched her that way? Other than Digory, who did not count. The haze of the mad honey made it that much more enjoyable. Like she was dreaming. This couldn't be real. She would never do this. And yet, she was.

Sybil melted into Monty beneath twinkling stars and the slivered moon.

In the background, the sun began to peak over the horizon in a deep red line.

Sybil awoke with a pain in her skull like she'd been kicked by a horse.

Groaning, she rolled over to feel soft sheets against her cheek. She peeled open her eyes. Beside her was the indent in the mattress where a warm body had been. She ran her hand over the quilted bedspread and smelled the pillows as jumbled memories flooded back to her in a rush. She brought a hand quickly to her throbbing temple. Her hair cascaded down over her shoulders frizzed and un-combed. Her lip stain was smeared. Her red silken night gown lay in a small puddle at the wake of the balcony, in line of the bed.

Sybil took a deep breath then sighed. She slapped her cheek once, then the other before throwing the fine sheets off. She walked naked through the chamber with her head high. She glanced about. She didn't see Monty.

As with all uncomfortable things she had said or done, Sybil decided not to feel shame or even think about what happened the night before. Her mind was unbelievably complex. Her ability to compartmentalize was unparalleled. She could push thoughts away with ease. It's part of what made her so dangerous.

Sybil returned to her own chamber to refresh herself as if nothing had happened at all. She splashed water on her face and violet oil behind her ears. It did little to distract from her head's throbbing, but she brushed that aside in her mind too. She put a deep purple berrybalm on her lips and white powder on her already pale cheeks. As always, she left her eyes unlined. She braided her hair, knotting it on a high bun on her head, then inserted several clear diamond-tipped pins in a nod to traditional oldblood style. In pre-Plague times, all the Brochet women wore them, so the legends said, and she felt as if she was better for doing so herself. Closer to the gods of legend in some tangible way.

She put on a white and grey day-gown with long gathered sleeves, a high neck, draped Animus Rock fashion skirts with a slit on the right side leading all the way up to her thigh. She then donned knee-high Baneswood boots and the necklace with the long silver chain and green-gem Brochet emblem pendant. It hung in an indent against the flowing fabric between her breasts. She felt a surge of inexplicable power when she put it on.

After assessing herself, Sybil went downstairs to discover an empty villa. Room after room of crisp furniture in dark wood or iron with gauzy white drapery was empty. Finally, Sybil wandered out to the back porch and a burst of light from the early sun stabbed her between the eyes. She shielded her face with a slender hand as she stepped onto the veranda.

Monty sat there with Rose and another guest around a table topped with plates of fruits and nuts and cheeses. The sky was pale from the early light with only thin cloud cover left over from the dawn. In the middle of the table was a bouquet of spiky purplecress with curling tendrils.

"How good of you to join us," Monty said to Sybil. "You look lovely."

Sybil nodded her head slightly. "Thank you," she said. "I had a good night's rest."

She bit her lip and glanced down.

Monty tried not to smile.

Sybil looked up, hair pins glistening in the early sun as she glanced from the stranger back to her host. "Who is your guest?" she asked pointedly. The man's skin was lighter than

Monty's, but much darker still than her own. He had wide-set, deep brown eyes and blonde hair in tight curls. He was slight and wore a pale-yellow cloak secured with a broach in the shape of a bell, as well as a polite expression.

"This is Juste," Monty said. "He is… a friend of mine."

"Juste Minney." The young man smiled to reveal a wide gap between his front two teeth. The man raised his hand and contorted it in a strange way, then shook it wildly.

Sybil cooled. A Minney at her table. It was unthinkable. "What is *he* doing here, Montague?"

She did not return the heathen gesture and crossed her arms instead. Earthblood greetings were off-putting. Although taught at Upper, she'd never taken the time to learn them.

Monty frowned.

"Why is he here with my daughter?" Sybil demanded, looking furiously from the Minney to Rose's questioning face.

Rose was eating a piece of candied lemon, petting Ellie, dutifully by her side.

"Answer me."

"Oh," Juste said, leaning back in his chair as if physically intimidated by the tiny woman. "I don't mean to…"

Monty put his hand up. "Quiet," he said. "You did nothing."

"He is intruding Montague."

"This is my villa, pet."

"And I am your resident guest," Sybil said with resolve. "I am your priority."

Seeing the cold fire burning in her eyes, Monty knew Sybil was set on making a scene. "Come with me," he said to her in forced whisper, standing abruptly from his seat. He stormed to her side.

"Rose, wait for me please. Don't speak to him," Sybil said over her shoulder as Monty firmly grabbed her arm, leading her into the Villa. Rose nodded and looked down at the half-eaten fruit on her plate. She didn't understand what was wrong with the gap-toothed man. He was pleasant, she thought. He'd even brought flowers.

Honking river loons competed with the pleasant chirping of

delicate songbirds in the air all around.

"What the curses was that?" Monty fumed at Sybil once they were alone. He towered over her, pressing her up against a wall.

"What was what?"

"What do you mean, *what*? You insulted my," Monty paused, eyes shifting briefly, "... friend."

"Why do you keep saying it like that? What is he doing here so early?"

"That is none of your business," Monty said flatly. His nostrils flared. "I'm losing patience."

Sybil studied Monty's eyes; any hint of warmth she'd felt towards him a few hours before was wholly gone. "Why didn't you wake me up when you left bed," Sybil lowered her voice to a seductive whisper, "after last night?"

Monty raised a condescending eyebrow. "What did you think that was?" He chuckled. "My pet, we had mad honey last night."

Sybil felt like chilled water hit her in the face, but she refused to accept what she knew was true.

"Don't lie to me. You wanted it."

"I did or I didn't, it makes no difference," Monty said, recoiling from her both physically and in his soul. "It happened," he added, shrugging.

She was beautiful, Monty thought, but he knew better than to entangle himself in such a way with the daughter of Tomas Brochet. Particularly if she was stupid enough to entangle herself with the likes of him. She would get them both killed.

Sybil felt the blood freeze in her veins. "So, that's it? After all that and we're what?"

"I have known you less than one day, Lady," Monty said. "We are acquaintances who have known each other for less than one day."

"Don't treat me like a child."

"I will so long as you act like one."

Sybil frowned. She was now repulsed by him. But she always got her way.

"There will be nothing between us, then?" she asked

hopefully.

Monty put his hand on her shoulder. "Pet, don't be so pitiful. I'm not a man who can be tied down. It's nothing personal. You should try some of my oldblood cousins." Sybil was still, sharp eyebrows raising slowly, angelic visage stunned. She had never been betrayed in such a way before. "Do you understand?" Monty asked her slowly. "This is my fault, really. I should have stopped you."

Sybil winced. "Yes, of course," she said with detachment. "How silly of me," she added, looking away, adjusting a pin in her hair.

"You aren't angry?"

Sybil breathed in and out deeply. "Not at all," she said, exhaling into a reaching, flashing smile, hating him inside. Already plotting his demise. Far too deep for him to see. "We are allies who shared a drink or two, nothing more."

Monty exhaled, fully relieved. "I'm so glad you agree," he said honestly, pleasantly surprised. "You mean a great deal to me you realize..."

Sybil interrupted, "Yes, yes of course," by flipping her hands in front of him. "Now, let's go enjoy the company. I'll play nice," she smiled coyly, biting her lip in one last effort to be desired.

"You do that," Monty said, patting her on the shoulder as a man would an obedient dog. He turned and walked back to the balcony.

Once he was gone, the smile dropped from Sybil's face as if it had never been there at all.

THE VANGUARD SHIP, SPACE

About 2000 years ago…

R eynold returned to his room, head aching. He had to excuse himself from the Thorne girl's examination. He knew he would receive heavy marks for his absence, but he couldn't bear to be near her any longer. Looking at her delicate face and searching, blank eyes did something to him that he could not understand. He hated now that he fed on her. He was infected. The soft, sweet nature of her soul was winding around his wretched one. He felt like garbage.

He laid on his bed and shut his eyes, hoping sleep would take him. Instead, the pounding in his head grew. He found himself out of his own body, in a place completely foreign to him. He had only read about such places on his tablet, in history lessons. But nothing could have prepared him for how beautiful and awe-inspiring it was to see such a vision, what felt like, in person.

He saw trees. Grass. Sunflowers. Sky. He was on Earth, he realized, and everything was not dead. It was brilliantly green and blue and yellow and alive. He took a breath, tasting the air in his lungs. He tilted his head and felt hot sunshine on his face. Tears welled in his eyes, awash in confusion and joy. He reached forward to touch a leaf, but it dematerialized in his hand like ash. The sky dimmed and the sun cooled and the vibrant colors faded.

"No!" he cried, tears falling down his cheeks where he lay in his small cell in the spaceship. "Please, no! Let me go back!" But the vision fled from him like shadows in the light.

Decades passed. Reynold grew into middle age, but he never forgot the vision he had. The older he grew, the more it ate at him, gnawing away at the soul he had built from so many others. Dymphna's goodness had corrupted him and the vision her powers cursed him with reverberated in his mind constantly. In the sterile Graves laboratory testing specimens, he would find his mind drifting back to Earth. To the greenery and blue sky. The sunflowers in the distance. He pined to smell fresh, new air, not recycled. He yearned to touch the leaf in his fingers; not have it crumple into dust. He kept his obsession hidden, still feigning his loyalty with the Mission to align with the others of his bloodline, and the other Vanguards, but internally, he spiralled.

Reynold, preoccupied with his vision, attempted to recreate it in secret. Over and over, he tried different conditions and scenarios, first laying on his cot in his cell, then in all other locations he could think of. He submerged himself in water. He put himself in the freezer. He even, in an act of desperation, considered going out into the airlock and opening the doors. He thought, maybe if he were dead, he could return to Earth, to the vision, if only for a moment. *No*, he would think pointedly to himself every time the idea came to mind, he would not settle for a mere moment. He needed to live in that green, lush world.

While before the incident with Dymphna, Reynold had several companions and was active socially, afterwards, he recoiled. He spent most of his time working, experimenting, studying and trying to get back to the vision that overturned his entire life. He had only one friend. One confidant. Drusana Brochet's daughter, Junia. She was about his age and reclusive as he became. They bonded over their mutual love of solitude. She was very beautiful, as Brochets were, and despite her quiet ways, undeniable. She fell for the sharply handsome, yet sullen Reynold, and eventually, in a quiet ceremony, the two wed.

A wedding between Brochet and Graves caused a commotion throughout the ranks of Vanguards. Typically, Vanguards of each bloodline used scientific, medical techniques like IVF, cloning and gene editing to breed. It was rare in that time on the Vanguard that children were born naturally. Typically, the only time that Vanguards from different bloodlines wed, it was with the goal of creating a child with unpredictable powers. This practice had never been attempted by Brochet and Graves.

Junia was the only one that Reynold told about his vision. Years into their marriage, after it was clear Junia could not have children, he brought it up.

"There is more for us than breeding," he said, putting his arm around her in the dimness of their shared cell. Together they looked out at the black blanket of stars.

Junia was quiet. She held her breath, trying not to cry. She was a failure. She had risked everything–the support of her bloodline, her standing amongst the Vanguards, and even her position in the laboratory–because she felt a pull towards motherhood that she could not explain. Vanguards were not a sentimental lot, and she could not put voice to her instinct. But in their younger days, when she told Reynold about her secret desire, for a child of her own, he was shockingly understanding. Warm. Supportive. That was the moment she fell in love with him and decided, at all costs, it was him for her and him alone. And she was hollowly happy with him. But, without a child, she knew she would never be whole.

"Is there?" she said distantly.

"The Earth."

She glanced up at him. "The Earth?"

"It is liveable."

She looked back to space. "Nonsense," she said.

"It's true. I've seen it."

Junia pulled herself out from under Reynold's arm and looked into his sparkling dark eyes. After feeding on the Thorne girl's soul, he never had to feed again, and her light never left him. That was another effect of consuming the soul of a powerful Vanguard. "How?" Junia asked. "I have watched the drone footage. What remains is still badly irradiated. There is no hope of returning for millennia."

Reynold shook his head. "I saw it," he said. "In a vision."

Junia lightly laughed. "You don't have visions."

"I did. Once. Well, twice. A long time ago. When we were young."

"How?" Junia asked in wonderment. "You are a Graves with Graves power."

"It is true," he replied. "The power is not mine."

Junia leaned closer.

"You must swear to never speak of this."

"I swear."

Reynold's chest snagged with guilt. He knew Junia may look at him differently after she knew the truth, but he didn't care. He had to tell her. Regardless of the consequences.

"I fed on the soul of a powerful Vanguard."

"You did what?"

"In my youth," he added quickly. "I..." he hung his head, "I didn't know she was powerful."

"I see," Junia said. Before, she thought that there was something special about Reynold. That he was unlike his brethren. That he didn't need to feed. That, inside of him, unlike the rest of Graves, he was good. She didn't know she had been sensing Dymphna's soul the whole time. "Who?"

"The Thorne with vision."

Junia's eyes widened. "Is *that* what happened to her?"

Reynold ran his hands through his black hair. "I'm what happened to her, yes. And I've spent my whole life coming to terms with it."

"Is she what made you good?"

Reynold nodded slightly.

"And by feeding on her soul, you got her powers as well?"

He nodded again. "I think they only activated once she was nearly dead."

"How interesting," Junia said with detachment.

"You aren't fearful of me?"

Junia half smiled. "No more than before," she said.

Reynold relaxed. So Junia did love him truly, then. "I have her power," he said. "and it allowed me to see the future."

"How do you know it was the future and not the past?"

Reynold frowned. He didn't know. But he felt it. Besides, his bloodline was fairly sure how Dymphna's powers worked. They called it "temporal sight". She could see possible futures. Reynold figured that was the power he had as well. He told Junia as much.

"Then you saw a possible future for Earth?" Junia said, studying Reynold's eyes carefully with hers.

"I did," he replied, "and it's more beautiful than anything you could ever imagine. It makes me sick, Junia. I cannot tell you how many times I've nearly thrown myself from the ship itself just to return to it in death."

"That's preposterous," she said. "It would not work."

"Surely."

"Have you tried recreating the conditions?"

"I have," Reynold said, heart racing with excitement. Speaking with his wife about his hidden passion enlivened him exponentially. "Hundreds of times. I cannot replicate the result."

"Then your science is poor," she said, smirking at him.

"You've always been better than I, dear."

She nodded. "It's really as beautiful as you say?"

"It could be," he said. "Will you help me get there?"

Junia stared deeply into Reynold's eyes. She knew he was asking the near-impossible, but that was what the Vanguard was for. Achieving the impossible.

She smiled.

LITTLEBELL DENS

Present Day

Hazy spirals swirled in the red-tinted room as Digory sank further into the pile of pillows, listening with drugged detachment as Leon and Nis philosophized back and forth. The festivities had faded. Music, shouts and laughs from the common den outside died long ago.

Digory had never felt so separate from himself. While it was unnerving at first, he was soon seduced by mad honey's warm psychotropic effects. Colors swirled and patterns swayed. Mostly, though, he enjoyed how every care or burden he'd hidden in the back of his mind seemed not to disappear completely as they did with ale, but to not matter to him in the slightest anymore. His worries were gone. No longer did Sybil plague him. His deep need to please her, to receive her praise, to belong in her world; gone. His thoughts were soft, like clouds.

For the first time in his life, Digory felt at ease.

"Who would have thought, a boy from nothing would be Lord of the Underground?" Nis asked loudly to no one in particular, smiling to himself. "I think I've done well. I'm no Vanguard but look at all I've got."

He sat back in his seat, hubris over-boiling.

"You and I are destined for far more than our lot in life, brother." Leon leaned towards Nis. "We are ambitious. Not limited by the constraints of," he gestured wildly, "the mind. Or the blood. Or by what we're told we're supposed to be. We see what we want, and we take it." He then chuckled, eyes bloodshot and nearly shut.

Nis nodded once. "Aye," he said. Holding his finger up to indicate 'wait', he took a long drag from the pipe, then blew smoke between his smiling teeth. "It's what sets us apart." He sharply coughed.

Digory's gaze pinged back and forth between the men, but, like them, he wasn't truly there.

"That's it!" Leon pointed at Nis. "That, right there!"

Digory interjected in his deep voice, "What is it that makes you different?"

Nis turned to Digory. "What do you mean? We are different. Better." He leaned forward and shoved the pipe down the table. Leon lit it and took a long hit. He kept the smoke in his lungs before tilting his head up to exhale. To Digory, he looked like a cloudy fountain.

"I see what he is saying," Leon said. "W*hy* are we different than the rest? What makes us capable of things others are not? It can't be blood. I know many who would kill me for the thought, like those Old bastards, but it's true. I share blood with my brother but it's as if we're from different worlds. He blindly fights for 'what is right' when he is wrong. He follows laws without thought. Why will he not listen to reason? What do you think it is?"

"What if," Nis said, "the more you suffer, the stronger you become? I was alone on the street after exile from Grayspindle, and I'm who I am today because of it."

The sharp memory of his mother's face as she cast him out of their village bubbled in the back of his mind briefly and was thankfully drowned by another drag of mad honey. He exhaled the heavy cloud gratefully.

Leon looked at Digory. "What do you think?"

Digory was half lost in a daydream about Westerviolet, seeing himself shoulder to shoulder with Lord Tomas. Whimsical indeed. "What did you say?" he asked from behind his own haze.

"What do you think sets us apart?"

"I think," Digory said, mind moving slowly, "you're more if you want to be."

Nis frowned. "That's not an answer."

Leon rose and handed the pipe to Digory. He took a long

173

drag. To Digory's internal dismay, he was enjoying the consciousness-shrouding reprieve of mad honey greatly. He liked its effects much more than ale. He felt safe and he'd never felt safe - not in his entire life. Digory blew the smoke out straight in front of him in round puff that crept across the floor like red-tinted fog.

"If we decide we are more, then we are. It comes from within us," Digory said. "That's what I believe."

"Aye?" Leon squinted. "What do you suppose gets you there?"

Digory shrugged. He had his opinions, but in this drugged state, his typically charismatic sentiments felt muddled. He opted to stay quiet.

"So, what? Fortune then?" Leon asked. "The Horned Woman?"

Digory burst into laughter, nearly spitting, chuckling loudly as Nis smiled and shook his head. Digory scratched his beard with one hand and with the other, passed the pipe to Nis. He had a lowly opinion of those who ascribed to the Faith, at best.

Leon frowned. "What? I didn't say I believe in her."

"You believe fortune comes from a goddess? There's some ethereal woman with horns who protects those who have faith in her?"

"He has a point," Nis defended. "So many believe."

Digory started to argue but took a break, eyes distant as he paused. Thinking of the Horned Woman, he smelled lavender. Saw a smile in his mind's eyes. But it was difficult to focus under the veil of mad honey. Particularly if smoked. "I forgot what I was going to say," he finally said, then shook his head and smiled. A faint image churned in his mind, but he couldn't quite grasp it. He shoved it aside.

"I'll admit, her word and promises are tempting."

Leon asked, "Like what?"

"I'm not for the rituals, or pilgrimage, or sacrifice, or any of those other religious curses," Nis said harshly, "but I can get on board with the concepts." Nis came from a mill town on the borderlands of Littlebell where it met Wraithswail, deep in the south of the Kingdom. There, it was uncommon to find believers in the Faith of the Horned. Due to influence from Hidden Den primarily, most didn't believe in anything at all.

Nis took the pipe back from Digory and glancing down at it said, "This is heavy shit," to no one in particular.

"You'll turn the Kingdom inside out with it."

Nis glanced at Digory. "You think?"

"What of the Horned Woman's promises?" Leon prodded.

Nis swung head to face Leon, obviously surprised. "You don't know?"

Leon, shrugging, said, "Vanguard," simply, to explain he'd never been encouraged to learn about her. The Horned Woman was the native's goddess. New Vanguards believed in the Teachings. Old Vanguards claimed to believe in the Ancestors, but newblood Vanguards considered that to be an oldblood excuse to do as they pleased.

Nis half smiled and chuckled to himself. "Alright." Digory smirked at the comment as well, knowing how little Vanguards were taught of the Horned Woman at Academy, from Sybil. He himself didn't know much either, as it was forbidden in Westerviolet. Even mention of the goddess or her faith was a crime punishable by death. It was as if she didn't exist. Nis took a sip from his goblet. Digory leaned forward a bit in anticipation.

"I like the core of the belief," Nis said.

"Which is?" Leon asked.

"The defix is us," Nis replied. "We're each horned, you see?"

Digory was confused.

Leon looked to Nis, eyes drooping, trying to follow. "Whatever stops us is our own doing?"

"We are in control of our own destinies, ourselves. Anything we feel is wrong comes from within," Nis explained to them. "If you can look at your own horns, accept that you have them and join the Horned One, you'll evolve and achieve eternal life."

"That is heavy," Leon said.

"You get to live forever?" Digory added offhandedly. "That

was Brochet's aim."

"It was," Leon nodded. "But it's not like that matters. The Old ways are dead." He smiled to himself, imagining all the oldblood fools spinning cruel webs that they'd one day trip into themselves.

"I'd wager it matters to some," Digory said under his breath, thinking briefly of the Lair. All the experiments he caught rumour of. For example, if twins were birthed by a lowborn native, when they were of age, one was tortured to the point of near death and the other kept alive and forced to watch, then their brains dissected and necessary parts extracted to be made into tinctures for various purposes. He'd watched one such procedure once.

Neither Leon nor Nis heard him.

"I look at my horns," Nis said boastfully.

"Aye? How?"

"None of your concern," Nis said. "They're my horns."

Digory snickered. He quite enjoyed this Nis character. He was fascinating. A shell of a man, deeply haunted, propped up by his own ego alone.

"I'm so glad to be surrounded by real company," Leon said as if he was preforming on stage as he widened his doe-eyes. "Open minds that discuss ideas, not just petty laws and politics and gossip. I am so sick of Prihim's world."

He spit on the floor.

"What do you aim to do about it?" Digory said.

"What do you mean? I run Littlebell," Leon said proudly. "I am doing what I wish."

"You run Littlebell under the eye of your grandmother while your brother issues commands from Animus Rock." Digory said, expecting a reaction. "You're little more than his errand boy."

Nis tried to stifle a grin.

Leon was instantly indignant, fuming, just like Digory thought he would be. He'd played right into Digory's hand.

"I am a gift to this world like a Minney should be. An artistic genius! The true muse! While my brother is a poor Morfit copy.

Prihim fooled father. He has Mimi and Vera fooled too, but I know what he is. He disgraces the bloodline. I deserve Littlebell!" Leon shouted, slamming both fists on the table, empty goblets and pipe jumping with the act.

That was the thing about mad honey. It while it stifled anxiety, it also heightened one's emotions, once you were submerged in its depths.

"What's so bad about Prihim?"

"He's opposed to our business."

"It's true," Nis said. "He causes trouble at every turn."

Now, Digory was getting somewhere. Some information that may prove useful. Despite his drugged state, he was still as manipulative as ever.

"What else?"

"He's an idealist," Leon explained. "He believes everyone keeps their promises and follows the law, but I know that's insanity. He's far too trusting of Morfit. I'm sure they'll lead to his downfall. I say Littlebell should keep to herself, but he won't hear me."

"How to you plan to take his Council seat?"

"I don't want his seat."

"That's the only way you control Littlebell. If you speak for her."

At that, Nis's ears perked up. "I think our new friend might be right."

"Prihim would never step down," Leon said defensively. "Besides, he's untouchable."

"No one is untouchable," Digory said.

"What are you insinuating, friend?"

"Nothing," Digory smiled. He met eyes briefly with Leon, sure the man caught his true meaning. Then he turned and changed the subject. "What are your plans, Nis, now that you have a new ware?"

"I've already got lines going up and down the Missi from Wraithswail to Animus Rock with tablets and mad ale," Nis replied, jagged scar pulling across his nose as he spoke. "From there it's trickling both westward and eastward. The mountains have the least supply, and there its most coin, so I send caravans out to the areas where my honey is popular but hard to come by. The barracks of Ravenshroud, the mountain forts of Ironbark and the Baneswood valley slums that can be reached without conflict, to start. Once they are hooked, word will spread. I've heard it's already begun. Soon, my regular lines can sell it for double, maybe even triple the coin."

"Is it going to last forever?" Digory was curious about the honey's source. "Your supply?"

"I'll worry about that. It is mine to command." Then, Nis turned with a growing smile on his face. "I rule the Underground!" he cheered, throwing a fist into the air, like he'd just fully realized it for himself deep down.

"Aye!" Leon mirrored the cheer and gesture. "And I Littlebell." Leon glanced to Digory sunken into a pillow, running his hand over brushed velvet. "What is it that you desire?"

"Me?" Digory looked up, snapped out of his drugged detachment. "Nothing."

"Come on Rune," Nis said as he pushed the pipe towards Leon, who shook his head in refusal.

Nis pushed the pipe to Digory.

He took a drag. "Okay," Digory blew out red-tinted smoke, scented like a meadow of wildflowers and tobacco caught ablaze. "I have a destiny and it lies in the heart of an infuriating woman." He couldn't believe his candor. On a deep, nearly subconscious level he resented how forthcoming this mad honey made him.

"Ah." Nis grinned, leaning backwards, crossing his arms at his chest. "I knew you and I were the same. When I met Yrsa it ruined me."

Leon nodded. "Love will do that."

Nis called him out. "What do you know of love?"

Leon sighed distantly, thinking back to what he had with Longin so many years ago. He didn't allow himself to recall those memories often. Things were much different now. That was another time. Now they were strangers.

"You'd be surprised."

Nis ignored Leon. He looked to Digory. "Tell us of her."

Digory began to refuse but due to mad honey's influence, he quickly relented, putting his hands behind his head, leaning back against the cool bricks. He'd never admit it to himself, but it felt good, although unnervingly human, to connect.

"She's fearsome in a way that makes you hate her and yourself and everyone else in this pitiful world every second you're apart from her."

"Friend," Nis said, "I hate to say it, but I'm not sure that is love..."

But Digory wasn't finished. He continued in deep baritone. "She's fearsome like a forest fire is as it rages or a thunderstorm as it crashes. In a beautiful, awesome way that makes you gasp at her power, and beauty. In a way that makes you bow to her."

"That sounds more like it," Leon said, smiling, pleased with Digory's theatrics. "Does she love you back?"

"She'd never say it," Digory slowly swept his head to meet his wideset eyes with Leon, then Nis, "but aye she does."

"How is *she* your destiny?"

Digory shrugged. "I love her. My life is hers."

"She won't whisper her secrets," Nis murmured with lowered eyebrows.

"What nonsense do you speak now?"

"Duran," Leon said.

Digory still didn't follow. "What?" he asked again, this time tinged with frustration, not enjoying when anyone knew more than he.

"Whisperfield," Leon explained. "That is the saying about Whisperfield. He means women are like that too."

Maybe it was mad honey clouding his memory, but Digory had no idea what the men spoke of. "What?" he asked a third time.

"Duran," Nis interjected. "He means Duran."

"Oh..." Digory paused, embarrassed that he didn't remember himself, racking his brain, only vaguely able to recall the name. "I don't know much about the extinct bloodlines," he finally admitted. Any information he did have eluded him in his present drugged state.

"Whisperfield is their castle," Nis explained. "Was," he added, "and the entrance to Scorpion Rose as the legends claim."

"What do you mean *was*?"

"I forget most natives don't know, Nis. Let me tell him," Leon said. "Whisperfield is in the Eversands. At the edge of it. Dangerous to go there now since it's been abandoned for so long."

"How long?"

"Since the North Plague. When Duran went extinct. None of the other bloodlines could find the entrance, if you can believe that, so the whole realm was abandoned. There are still natives, but they're feral. Barely a part of our Kingdom any longer. Just like those in Winter Garden and Duskfang."

And just like Winter Garden and Duskfang, Whisperfield attracted all kinds with an adventurous spirit, willing to risk the alleged dangers in exchange for the promise of the treasures rumoured to be contained within their walls. Winter Garden's castle was said to contain a hidden room full of charmed Beaumont gems and glass bead jewellery hidden behind cursed doors. Duskfang was said to hold the secret of mad honey but was surrounded by Deadbloods. And Whisperfield allegedly held the secrets of Scorpion Rose. Although, no one could find it.

Digory nodded. "What's Scorpion Rose?"

"It was an Assassins Guild founded by Duran," Leon explained. "Very, very old. Most say they were wiped out since no one's heard anything from them in, like, two hundred years."

"Most say?"

"Of course, there are murmurs that they're still around and active today in the bowels of the Whisperfield mazes."

"Do you believe it?" Digory asked Nis.

"I'd like to. But I doubt it's true."

"What about you, Leon?"

"It's just a ledged," Leon replied surely. "If it was real, I'd know about it. They're extinct like Duran. Pity." He shook his head.

"Why?" Nis asked. He rubbed the corner of his eye and yawned. "Weren't they notoriously Old? Great enemies of your bloodline?"

"Sure, that," Leon said offhandedly, "I'm supposed to hate them, but I would still kill to try Scorpion smoke."

"Oh, that's right!" Nis said excitedly.

"More smoke?" Digory could barely keep up in his present state. "What's that?"

"A specialty of Duran and part of the Scorpion Rose ritual," Leon said. "They made it from scorpion poison. The Eversands is teeming with them. Scorpions, I mean, not Duran." Chuckling, Leon alone enjoyed at his own joke.

Digory was intrigued. "What's it like?"

"Much different than what we have here," Leon said melodramatically, leaning forward, speaking, as always, with his hands. "They say it makes you the opposite of yourself. Think things you'd never think. Do things you'd never do. Frightening stuff if you ask me. I'd try it," he said with a wide dimpled grin.

"Right?" Nis nodded, meeting the Minney's eyes. "Me too."

"Here, here," Leon cheered.

"None for me, thanks," Digory said, sinking backwards into the velvet pillows with a smile.

-

Much later, long after Nis had excused himself and Leon nodded off where he sat, Digory rose from his spot in the pillows.

"I must be going," he said loudly as he hovered over Leon.

Leon awoke in a gasp, rubbing his eyes, yawning deep, ridiculous 16-point crown he'd worn all night finally toppling aside, rolling loudly across the hard floor. "Of course," he said quickly. He stood to say goodbye. As he leaned uncomfortably close, Leon whispered Digory's ear, "You say no one is untouchable?"

Digory's eyes were heavy. His vision clouded as if he wore a buzzing helmet he couldn't take off.

"What?" he asked Leon gruffly.

"Shhh," Leon hushed, leaning closer, deep bags under his eyes from little sleep. He placed a hand on Digory's shoulder. "Quiet. When we spoke of my brother, I said he couldn't be reached. You said no one is untouchable." He met Digory's intense, unblinking, wide-set gaze. "Did you mean it?"

Digory nodded once, flexing his bearded jaw. He understood Leon's insulation instantly.

"If it can be done, see to it. You'll be in my debt." Leon dropped his hand from Digory's shoulder, dark eyes searching Digory's red ones. "You understand?"

"Do you care how it's done?"

Leon winced, trying not to think about it. He turned away, pressing his hand to his temple's rising headache. "Just see that it's done."

"Aye," Digory nodded. He was impressed by this Minney and instantly gained respect for him. To order one's brother dead was powerful play. Minneys were not all what everyone thought.

Leon popped his eyes open eagerly, nearly beaming with glee. "You'll do it? Who would have thought you were more than a pretty face?"

"Not me. I get by on my looks alone."

"You know who Primin is. Where to find him?"

Digory's heavy brow dropped. He glanced to the entryway, then back to Leon.

"Don't speak of it anymore. It will be done."

Leon nodded. "Right, of course." He withdrew a fist-size sachet with a tightly bound drawstring from his pocket. It smelled like tobacco. "Before I forget, Nis wanted me to give you this."

Digory took the sachet from Leon. He turned in his wide palm. "Is this?"

Leon nodded. "You can put it in any pipe. Don't mix with real tobacco unless you'd like to muck up the high."

Digory nodded as he tucked the item deep in the back pocket of his trousers. "Thank you."

"Oh and, Nis said to tell you not to eat the stuff. Whatever you do, do not ingest it. Ever. He said it'll kill you."

"Got it. Smoke, don't eat."

"There you go." Leon smiled with a deep dimple. "When will you be back by this way, new friend?"

"I imagine not before too long."

"It was a high pleasure meeting you, Rune of Baneswood," Leon said sincerely, looking up earnestly to Digory, much larger in height and stature. "I hope to see you again."

"And you, Lord Leon Minney, the true elderclaim of Littlebell."

Leon felt his heart nearly explode from happiness upon hearing those words. Despite his mounting headache, Leon threw arms around Digory in an intimate hug. Digory shrunk from the interaction, cringing internally as he hated to be touched, and patted the much smaller man several times on the back until he released. He inhaled deeply and glanced around the arched-ceiling chamber a final time before turning to walk out the door. Before passing under the tapestry into the main den he paused and glanced back over his shoulder briefly.

"Do you need this tunic back?"

"No, you keep it." Leon added with a smirk, "Prihim won't miss it."

Digory nodded. The irony that he was wearing the man's shirt that he was planning to kill wasn't lost on him.

He pushed aside the tapestry. He walked through the dishevelled and empty main den, stepping over sleeping bodies, up the staircase and into jarring early morning light. Then, Digory paused. He took a deep breath of warm, damp air before finding his way back to the white and black vase sign.

ANIMUS ROCK CASTLE

S ybil clutched a small hand-written book in the pockets of her skirts as she hurriedly ascended the Animus Rock castle steps. She'd taken it from the forbidden East Tower back in Westerviolet, saving it for this exact purpose. She had time alone. Rose was about to begin her lessons for the day and Monty was off at market. Her friends, Faye and Aftea, planned to meet her in Eden when the sun was highest in the sky in order to gossip. But that gave Sybil ample time. The sun was just then beginning to shine brightly. The market was just opening. Life in Animus Rock was just beginning to bustle. It would be hours before her friends looked for her. Before Rose was done her lessons and needed her mother.

Sybil revelled in alone time, despite requiring attention desperately. It was another part of her paradoxical personality.

She entered the gaping entryway of the largest, grandest Vanguard castle of all, feeling the pulse of time descend around her. How many Ancestors had walked through those very same doors? Why, she just stepped over the place where The Boy King was murdered, ending the Blood Wars. Every bit of this castle was steeped in Vanguard history. She clutched the book in her skirts. Her heart pounded with excitement.

Given what Sybil had discovered in Westerviolet, she was now convinced that she had been wrong. Power was no myth. Curses were no legend. She realized, to her delight, back in Westerviolet, that the Kingdom had only forgotten it's birthright. The Vanguards had knowingly or otherwise hidden their power from memory. Brochet had stuffed all evidence of the power of ancient times in the East Tower, then forbade entry. But what about the Bellamines? The reigning Kings of the entire Vanguard Kingdom since the beginning? Surely they too were hiding something.

The book Sybil clutched was similar to others she found in the East Tower. It was a series of detailed maps and notes, speaking to hidden passageways, staircases and chambers within the Animus Rock castle. She'd flipped through it once she reached the villas and one page in particular garnered her interest. It was the map of a Ninth Tower.

Animus Rock famously had eight towers, as everyone Kingdom-wide knew. The view from the top of the Eighth was said to be the most beautiful in the lands, and the secrets it held were said to be equally stunning. Since she was a girl, Sybil had dreamed of that view and those secrets. Even in adulthood. It's what kept her going after Rosen died. It's what spurred her interest in returning to Animus Rock. It's what sent Digory on his mission to deliver a letter to Hector Graves, spurred by the pressure put on her by her father Lord Tomas.

But a Ninth Tower? The idea was unthinkable. And yet, there it was, perfectly designed, even taller and grander than the Eighth, with notes and annotations for how to reach it. She entered the castle, passing through the main halls, past the large Throne Room that doubled as a ballroom on the equinoxes and solstice, past the halls for mess and other various gatherings. She passed the stairs leading down into the First and the gaping, blackened mouth where the Second Tower used to be. She glanced at the entrance to the Third Tower briefly, wondering how Rose's lessons were going. She hurried past the Fourth Tower, thinking of the impending Council session briefly as well. Then past the massive Fifth Tower, mostly empty, reserved for Vanguard Day celebrations and the Sixth Tower, empty too, apart from memorabilia displayed from across the Kingdom, functioning like a museum of sorts. Finally, the entrance to the Seventh Tower, where the royal family resided. The entrance to the Eighth was within that tower. She'd never seen it. She wasn't allowed inside.

She continued to walk. She went around corners and down several corridors. There wasn't anyone in this far section of the castle, so she did not have to conceal the small book. She opened it. Inside, there were various writings atop the drawn maps, as if added over many years, if not decades or centuries, in varying penmanship and ink. She found the page titled,

Ninth Tower in scrolling script. The map led one past

all of the other towers, to a dead end at the far reaches of the castle.

Sybil approached it. A note read,

Removed from official plans. Still accessible.

Below that, a later note read,

Entryway non-contiguous.

Sybil stood in front of the stone wall, frowning. She'd seen the Lair open before. She knew that Westerviolet had secrets that she couldn't possibly understand. Why would Animus Rock be any different?

She felt all over the stone, searching for a hidden entryway. For a rock in the wall that had any give or was slightly out of place. She looked behind the white painted sconces with burgundy candles and on the stone floor. She rapped on the wall with her knuckles, still, nothing happened.

"Lady Brochet," a voice snapped her from her puzzlement. She spun, thrusting the small book into her skirt pocket. It was a high native from Animus. She didn't bother learning their names. "May I escort you to Eden? Are you lost?"

"Why, yes," Sybil said, smile dazzling. "Silly me. I have not been here in years! Can you imagine my embarrassment," she said, taking the young woman's arm in hers. "Walk me there, will you, sweet?"

The young high native blushed, then went to tell all of her friends afterwards how she walked arm in arm with a Brochet. Surely, no one believed her.

LITTLEBELL CASTLE

About 100 years ago…

His black eyes burned like pieces of coal aflame. He'd had a lot of time to reflect as of late and decided to be a different man. A better man. To be remembered by history as good, instead of evil like his blood name. Like his grandfather.

"Please," Bin Norland appealed Sia Minney, "let me be a proper Vanguard husband for your daughter."

Sia's thin plucked eyebrows rose high and she straightened her back, nearly like a cat hissing when angered. To her, this was the highest insult. "I will never allow it. Never," she repeated in a low hush. "It is not our people's way," she added with a proud glint in her eye.

Bin took a deep breath then sighed. He had already broken his elder's command and his pact with Brochet. He had already betrayed everything he stood for, everything he was raised to be, just to save the girl. Marrying Lilli was the only way to rescue her. How couldn't Sia see that? It was either that or he was no better than Lucien and Amos themselves.

"I will provide a good home for her," Bin said, heavy brow raising, flexing his block jaw. His scratched at the base of his wavy black hair, beginning to turn white at each temple. "She will be well protected at Ravenshroud."

"Humph," Sia snorted, flaring her nostrils as she glided to stand aside a very tall mirror in a gilded frame. She studied her own reflection with a curiously raised brow, so svelte she nearly appeared underfed with slight hips and a graceful gait. When she moved Sia looked like she was gliding. Displeased with the Norland's appearance and further insulted by his proposal, she turned to face him in a pout, heavy braid swishing against her back. "I said no, *Norland*."

Bin began to anger, feeling a burning bloodlust encouraged in himself early on bubbling in the back of his throat. "Can you not see I do this for her?" He squinted his raven eyes and lowered his deep voice to a whisper. "I love her."

"Ha!" Sia laughed and threw her head back. "Love, please. You do not love," she said down her short nose. Her red eyes flashed. "You cannot love. Oldblood, you are no match for my lovely Lilli."

Bin flexed his jaw. "It is what she wishes as well," he said, remembering the girl's warm words the last they met. The caress of her skin against his, however brief. He knew she felt the same about him. Besides, anything to spare her the fate that awaited if he followed Lucien's commands and brought the girl to his Lair.

"Impossible," Sia denounced, crossing her flowing robed arms. The floral embroidery buckled in deep loops and lines to match her frown. "My Lilli would never." She paused then glanced to the setting sun outside, illuminating the nearby square window of the Littlebell castle. "You must go now."

"But Lady," Bin said, stumbling, feeling his world bursting in two. "She is all I have, I beg you. I must rescue the girl."

"Rescue?" Sia asked, frowning deeper still. The light outside reflected off her honeycomb braid. "What would the girl need rescue from?"

Bin began to answer Sia, began to tell her about Brochet's plans, then raised his brow and sighed. "Nothing particularly, Lady," he said, lowering his eyes to study the top of his boots briefly, then back up to meet hers. He squinted. "I am simply saying that I love her and wish no harm to befall her." He'd never spoken truer words, he thought to himself, a bit proud despite the horrendous repercussions awaiting him, especially now that he had no blue-eye when he was to return to Ravenshroud. Still, Bin was glad he'd risked it all. Besides, he wasn't done trying. Not yet.

Sia nodded with a disbelieving look in her eye. "Surely, Norland. Whatever you say. Are you through now?" she added without giving him time at all to reflect.

Bin was jostled from his trance instantly. "Aye," he said, nodding as he turned his raven head. Then he bowed low and deep to Sia, in a traditional fashion that nearly made her blush it was so outdated and formal. "I thank you for your audience, my Lady," he added with shocking diction and breeding.

"I... why..." Sia trailed off, then cleared her throat. She steadied herself inwardly and reminded herself of who she was, and further, who *that* man was. "Goodbye," she said in a cool even tone, eyes tracing Bin's forlorn expression with slight confusion on his way out.

He really did appear love struck, Sia thought to herself, then brushed all concern with the Norland aside as she enjoyed the last gorgeous moments of the sunset over the horizon. She had surely made the right decision for her bloodline.

Lilli heard a rustling in her woods unlike any she was familiar with. It didn't sound like the berrydeer or the ruby foxes and certainly not like any type of bird. It was certainly footsteps she heard, followed, to her surprise, by the precise slice of a dagger through flesh. She'd heard that sound before, which is how she knew exactly what it was.

She crouched on instinct with her back against her favorite tree - a tulip poplar with an enormous trunk and reaching roots that created a lovely place for her to sit and look at the forest and think. Then, she frantically ran her hands across the ground until she landed on a heavy jagged rock. Lilli clung to the rock and huddled against her tree, listening to careful footsteps slowly surrounding her.

"Lilli Minney!" Bin Norland's deep voice rang out through the woods, sending birds flying from their peaceful perches. "I am here to rescue you!"

At that declaration Lilli instantly lowered her guard. She remembered the dopey hulking man from the Animus garden maze. He may bare a fearsome blood name and his kin may have done horrible things, but she knew that he was harmless. Holding the heavy rock down slightly she stood up and shouted, "Who's there?" already knowing full well who it was. Part of her wanted him to think she had other suiters who may feel the need to rescue her in her woods. She wasn't sure what was so alluring about this strange pale man. She did not fear him. Not one bit.

"Lady Lilli," the voice said again, wavering slightly, confidence obviously stung. "It is I, Bin Norland," the man said, trying to sound heroic but to Lilli, it was just awkward. She half-smiled in consolation and offered him a hand. She noticed a handful of Warmen hanging back in the shadows, lifeless eyes locked forward, wide bodies keeping watch over the perimeter. She knew the Morfit guard she'd insisted to her mother she did not need was the one who had been slaughtered. She knew mother would care, but she didn't at all.

Death didn't bother Lilli the way it did other people.

"Bin Norland," Lilli repeated with a growing smile, standing fully from where she'd been crouched, dropping the rock. It landed with a softened thud into a heavy clump of emerald moss. "It's about time you visited me," she added cheekily.

"Lady," he said, blushing, feeling like he was an Academy boy again, "it is not safe here."

"Where is it safe?" she asked playfully, stepping away to flit in and out of the surrounding small saplings like a restless butterfly. She paid no heed to the bedraggled Warmen hovering in the trees' shadows.

Bin eyed her with longing. "Lady," he said again, feeling the pressure of his newly formed enemies pulsing at his back. Lucien would find out any moment now - he always seemed to know what was happening in the Kingdom first - and they had to escape before he did. How could Bin tell her he'd been plotting her capture, spurred by her brother, since her birth? He couldn't bear to. Instead, he half-lied. "Lady, Brochet is after you. They aim to drag you to Lucien's Lair before you're deigned elderclaim in ceremony. Lady," he added, taking a step towards her, yearning to hold her tightly in his arms, "you're truly not safe here." He cleared his throat. "Allow me to marry you." He widened his dark eyes earnestly. "Provide for you, protect you at Ravenshroud."

Lilli was nearly punched breathless by the weight of her new circumstances. "What of my mother?" she said instantly, knowing Sia Minney would never allow such an arrangement.

"I've spoken to her and she refuses," Bin said honestly.

"You could have easily tried to lie to me," Lilli said. "Why didn't you? If what you seek is for me to follow you?"

Bin shrugged. "You are smarter than that, Lady."

At that compliment, Lilli brightened. She'd already decided to go with Bin Norland if for no reason other than it was to be an adventure, but given his high assessment of her, she was all the more delighted about it. She took several bounding steps through the leafy forest and landed at Bin's feet. She offered her hand to him, then rose her head and nose ever so slightly, just like she'd seen the queen do once.

Bin raised his eyebrows. "What are you doing?" he asked in a grunt.

Trying not to giggle, Lilli shook her hand, letting the fingers flop a bit as if it was dead to her, until he did something about it. She gestured with a raised eyebrow twice towards her hand, then made a slight pursing motion with her lips.

Bin brightened realizing she wanted him to kiss it and happily took her dainty fingers into his clumsy ones. How could he ever be so fortunate? His world exploded in happiness as he placed his lips gently on the top of her hand. "Does this mean yes?" he asked timidly.

She nodded, then broke into a smile warm enough to melt even the iciest corners of Bin Norland's once-frozen heart.

ANIMUS ROCK'S THIRD TOWER

Present Day

It rained over Animus for days and days. It felt like the sun would never shine again.

Today, heavy drops fell from the sky spattering the steps into the Third Tower. Children ran through the Lessonroom door with dripping hair and water spots all over their smocks. Rotrude welcomed them. They settled in their seats. Rain rapped loudly against the Lessonroom's windowpanes in nearly horizontal sheets.

Today, she was to cover the extinct bloodlines.

"There were sixteen Vanguard bloodlines to start," Rotrude began, feeding off the palpable excitement in the room. "Four are lost. Three were taken by the North Plague of 3833, as discussed in a previous lesson and the fourth disappeared in a cloak of mystery," she added with a showy inflection. The children giggled in anticipation. Rotrude revelled in her attentive audience, warming internally. She loved to feel her true purpose, that she was making a difference in the Kingdom. "The stories about the old bloodlines are usually a favorite. Oh, where to begin!"

She glanced about the room at eager faces and gem beads glistening despite the dim light, taking mental assessment of all she had to cover, before continuing.

"If you remember, in 3800 – over two hundred years ago– the Nomads burned Animus Rock's Library. Also known as the Second Tower," she said. "At that time, Vilma Calvanese was the elder of the Calvanese bloodline. Calvanese were different from all the other bloodlines in one remarkable way. They were *matriarchal.*"

The Calvanese bloodline was said to have sprung from an original female god who was particularly strong willed and brilliant, of the same rank as Bellamine, Brochet and Graves. Prior to the Plague, they were a powerhouse of the Kingdom, with strings even more tightly wound around each realm than Thorne and powers more impressive than Beaumont. By all remaining historical accounts, Calvanese women were in full control. However, in the shadow of the Plague, under King Danil's reign, their greatness was hidden from record. All remaining knowledge of them and the powers they possessed, apart from the secret of mad honey, were kept by Hidden Den. All but erased from the Kingdom's collective memory.

One of the twins raised his hand high above his head and waved it back and forth wildly. Rotrude pointed to him.

"Yes, Lord Warn?"

She wasn't quite sure which twin was which, still after having already taught them once before. They were exact copies of one another. They acted alike, too.

"What's that mean?" the boy blurted eagerly.

"It means their society was run by women." Rotrude tucked her white oiled hair behind her particularly small ears. The boy and his brother snickered. "I know, this is very different from your bloodline. Or Norland. Or Graves. But for the Calvanese it was law," she explained, speaking with her hands, Third Tower robe sleeves billowing. "Unlike other Vanguards, Calvanese didn't consider children and marriage to be synonymous. They oftentimes had children with multiple Vanguards about the Kingdom to mix the blood. This behavior was frowned upon by the New bloodlines, but the Old saw it as sensible. The practice was freely accepted."

Rose had heard of the Calvanese bloodline from her mother. She leaned forward in anticipation. It excited her to know that at one point in history, women essentially ruled the Kingdom. She'd frequently wished that she'd been born during that time. She was afraid of her grandfather. If things were like they were during the Calvanese's time, her mother would rule instead. This daydream pleased her greatly because if her mother could rule, so could she.

Malla raised her hand. Unlike Rose, she'd never been given any schooling on Calvanese, or any other extinct bloodline. The Demos way was to look forward, not to the past.

"Yes, Malla?"

"What did they look like?"

"They were exotically beautiful with olive skin and swirling, hypnotizing, hazel eyes. They also had curly black hair and wide hips and bumped noses," Rotrude said wistfully. "There's a painting of Vilma outside the Council Hall if you're interested," she added, remembering the impactful artwork, shuttering at how it had been censored, irritated she wasn't permitted to point that out to the children.

Calvanese women typically worn large skirts and open vests, leaving their breasts out. A fact which the modern powers had buried.

Avina slowly raised her hand.

"Do you have a question, Avina?"

"Yes," she said softly, deep brown eyes meeting Rotrude's red. "What did they do?"

"Do? The Calvanese had a great amount of power from trade," Rotrude told her. "Their main export was Mad Honey."

Malla shouted, "What's that?"

"Remember to raise your hand, Malla." Malla sank backwards with pouting lips. "To explain Mad Honey, I must explain Duskfang."

Rotrude paced the front of the Lesson room, large sandaled feet kicking out beneath her robes.

"Duskfang is the Calvanese castle, built directly into the deep caves and caverns of the southern Cursed Hills," she said. "These caves are infested with small dire bats from which Calvanese gets their emblem."

Several hands rose in the air, waving to be called on. Rotrude pointed at Tiphanie.

Tiphanie's ruddy face scrunched. "If they made honey then why isn't their emblem a honey bee?"

Rotrude was unable to look directly at Tiphanie for fear her deep-set hatred of Regnard could be felt.

"It was a bat instead of a bee because it was the bat that led them to the bees, and protected their caverns from intruders," she explained, pausing her pacing by the tall windowpane under torrential rains' assault. The rain rapped loudly against the glass, like arrows assaulting a curtain wall. "Some legends claim that the bats are bewitched by a curse from the Calvanese to act on their command, to this day."

All the children listened, entranced.

Rotrude assessed the listening faces, placing her large palm up against the window's glass. She felt it cool beneath her skin. She watched rain race in drops down the opposite face. She had on good authority that the bats were indeed cursed, from Hidden Den's exploratory expeditions to the caverns in the wake of the Plague. They acted wildly and their bites conveyed an unnamed disease said to be worse than Dread, that made victims laugh manically until they died. It was also said that the Guild lost many valuable members to Duskfang's depths during that time. She wasn't permitted to share that fact. Although she didn't always agree with the direction from Hidden Den to hide pieces of the Vanguard Kingdom and its's history from the Vanguard children, Rotrude held her oath to the Guild above all else.

"Duskfang is a feat of architecture, just as all the other Vanguard castles are. It was built with straight lines of black brick jutting up from the ground in stark contrast to the natural curves of the cave. The castle reaches a staggering forty-two stories high at the tallest point. It is named Dusk Keep." She brought her hand away from the glass, wondering to herself if it was as dramatic as the records claimed. She longed to see Duskfang castle in person. She heard it was hard not to gasp upon entry. To see the infamous Calvanese bats circling Dusk Keep, screeching at all hours. The sound was said to be maddening to anyone not explicitly welcomed by Calvanese blood. But there was no proof of those claims and Rotrude's superiors deemed it best to keep such information from young Vanguard minds. Wouldn't want them getting too curious and trying to find out for themselves.

"There is a large hole in the top of the cavern that lets in light and sun. This allows a giant flowering Rhododendron to grow," she explained, leaving her perch by the window.

She paced back across the center of the Lessonroom.

"Calvanese kept rows and rows and rows of honeybees that fed on the rhododendron's magenta flowers. Something about that flower from that bush and those particular bees in that cave created the most in-demand commodity that the Kingdom had ever seen. Mad honey."

Rotrude's heavy footfalls were cut by loud pattering of rain.

"Mad Honey is a deep auburn color with a reddish tint. It can be ingested directly or mixed into a beverage. Hundreds of years ago mad ale was very popular at court. Many in the Kingdom were opposed because of the negative side effects of the drug–fatal when not used correctly. Addictive in most cases. Some said it drove those prone to it into madness with prolonged use. Many claim that's where it got its name. Others postulate that the Plague and following Blood Wars were in part caused by the madness of the honey. That the Vanguards at the time were not thinking clearly. Regardless, Calvanese used their wiles and the popularity in combination with the addictiveness of mad honey to convince the King that Mad Honey was to be legal and taxable for trade as long as dealt by Calvanese." Rotrude took a breath. "So, to answer your questions both Avina and Malla, Calvanese produced mad honey and in the years before the Plague. And they were an economic powerhouse."

Lightning cracked outside and lit up the black sky.

"Vilma Calvanese was the elder of the bloodline during the Nomad Conflict and when the North Plague hit. She had two daughters named Nicoletta and Dilette, both renowned beauties," Rotrude continued. "Their father is unknown. I've mentioned the eldest daughter Nicoletta before," she reminded the class. "She allegedly seduced Bernarus Beaumont away from his wife and children to father three daughters with her at Duskfang in a scandal that shook the Kingdom."

The dark wind whipped a tree branch thick with early autumn leaves hard against the windowpane in a crash, causing the children to jump. Leaves spun in the rainy air.

"And then there was her sister, Dilette Calvanese. She was married to Henrik Warn." Rotrude paced to the far book-lined wall. "He was the elder of Ironbark as well as eldest brother to the only surviving warn, Erik Warn. Henrik was the last Old Warn."

Rotrude's eyes lingered on the Warn twins momentarily, wondering which ancestors they would become like. They were so young yet.

"Dilette's marriage to Henrik was a strategic move to unite the Old in the east and the west," she continued. "This Old alliance in coordination with Ravenshroud, Lyonshall, Westerviolet, and Anstout had the New realms at the time surrounded. But, like we discussed in our last lesson," Rotrude said sombrely, "the North Plague killed all Calvanese, hundreds of them that there were, as well as almost all the Warns along with nearly the rest of the Vanguards, and Kingdom. After this, the Old lost total control. This led to the political climate for social unrest, rebellion, and the start of the Blood Wars." She looked from face to face after the weighty monologue. "Do you have any questions?" she asked. "No?" she pressed.

No hands raised, so she went on.

"Calvanese culturally had children very young, and many of them. They were historical very fertile."

Evia Norland raised her hand slowly. Rotrude called on her. "How many?"

"At the time of the Plague, Dilette was thirty-two years old with six children and four grandchildren," Rotrude said. "Little Igino Warn, Dilette's youngest son, and Veriana Calvanese, her youngest granddaughter, were both less than two years old. Both perished along with the rest of their families," she said gravely. Rotrude swallowed hard. She tried not to think of babies dying from Dread. How confused and scared they must have been, particularly as children tended to survive longer than adults before succumbing. Likely, the children had to watch their mothers die and then suffer and die alone. Possibly for days before they succumbed themselves. She couldn't imagine a more tragic fate.

Evia sat up a bit straighter in her seat, nodding with cool green eyes. She adjusted the band around her forehead with aubergine gem inlayed. She'd already written the Calvanese bloodline off in her mind, based off what her father told her. It was an unruly bloodline, full of insanity. Such as all women were.

"The Calvanese had untraditional views about most things including marriage as well as naming their children," Rotrude continued to explain. "Male children were given the blood father's Vanguard name, but all female children, regardless of parentage, were named Calvanese. To a Calvanese woman, men were secondary. Instead, these women were focused on their commerce, their studies, and their power over the men in the Kingdom." She wanted to explain more, about the legends of their powers, about their curses and control over the defixes, but Hidden Den forbade it, so she bit her tongue.

The lighting outside began to subside as the storm moved away although thunder still rumbled faintly in the background, like a growling dog. The rain dwindled to a misty drizzle as the sky brightened.

"The Calvanese legacy is one of success, in terms of profitable Vanguard bloodlines," Rotrude said, pacing. "While it's true the aim of the original Calvanese Vanguards has been lost to time, the modern research of the bloodline went into the depths of the mind. This resulted in the *alleged* powers to bestow blessings and curses."

Rose raised her hand carefully.

"Rose?"

"What kinds of curses?" she asked with a piercing glare unmatched to her soft voice.

Her mother didn't tell her about that. The concept was entrancing. She had to know more.

"It's unclear as there are no records," Rotrude lied, as she'd been instructed to do.

Rose could tell and it piqued her interest even more.

"What we know is from oral history," Rotrude explained.

She stepped backwards a few paces, crossing her arms as she leaned against the front wall.

"They experimented on the Duskfang natives who passed tales of the horrors on through generations."

That much was true, Rotrude thought.

"Calvanese funded these ventures with the profits from the mad honey," she said. She was fully seeped in romantic admiration for the lost bloodline, and it showed. Despite their Old ways and the horrors they caused, she was able to look past all of that by telling herself that it was a different time. If they had survived to the modern day, they would have certainly realized the error of their ways and turned New. Even if that certainly would never have been the case.

"Calvanese's color was dark red, or pink, magenta really, the color of the rhododendrons, and their motto was *mulier est hominis confusio*. It means, '*women is man's ruin*.'"

The girls in the Lessonroom giggled. Jire and Jole Warn rolled their eyes.

"After Calvanese was gone and the mad honey circulation dried up, many went to Duskfang in search of it."

She pushed off her rest at the wall, pacing to hover over the front row of students.

"Unfortunately, none found it. Instead, all either disappeared or returned and horribly cursed," Rotrude told them, thinking back to her studies. Many of the victims were kept contained in the belly of Hidden Den, for research purposes. Many lost their ability to see or hear. Some had hair turn all white, or others grew tails. But the most chilling cases were those who saw and heard things that were not there. The general fact that curses were enacted was permitted to be shared, to deter any of the modern Vanguard children from wanting to go exploring themselves. Although the details were to remain secret as with most knowledge the Guild held.

"I will go into detail when you're in Upper Academy, if you

wish," Rotrude lied again. "You're too young now. It's rather gruesome. But these phenomena led to the common belief about the Kingdom in the legends of the Calvanese curses. Numerous superstitions arose to protect those about the Kingdom from the omnipotent curses of the Calvanese, in fact, in the years following their extinction."

Lucette Busk timidly raised her hand.

Rotrude turned her head to the far side of the room, surprised to hear the Busk speak, usually so quiet.

"Lucette?"

"Like what?" she asked softly.

"You mean what superstitions?"

"Yes," Lucette said in a breathy whisper, shoulders slouched as if she was trying to disappear.

She wondered in quiet moments if she herself was cursed. To her, it certainly felt like it.

"I'm sure you heard of many of them," Rotrude said gently. "You just don't know where they originated. Take, for example, to cross one's fingers."

The children nodded in recognition. It was a common gesture, typically reserved for merchants and costermongers.

"This protects from unwanted Calvanese curses during a business transaction, they say," Rotrude said exemplifying the motion crossing her fore finger and middle on her left hand. "You see it today. In many realms this is considered good luck while closing a deal. It is here at Animus Rock."

The children collectively murmured in understanding. Rose could sense that the Lessonmaster was not revealing the whole tale. She resolved to ask her mother about it.

Avina appeared deep in thought before shooting her hand into the air.

Rotrude called on her.

"Does it really work?"

"Alas, no one knows the secrets of the Calvanese curses or the superstitions to combat them, as no one knows the secrets of Duskfang and Mad Honey," Rotrude told her, lying again. "With Calvanese gone, we likely never will."

Malla began to speak, then caught herself and raised her hand urgently. Rotrude, pleased by the effort and endeared by her excitement, nodded in the striking girl's direction.

"Why not?" Malla asked.

"On top of the curses, there are current reports that Duskfang is overrun by deadbloods. The territory is forbidden to enter. It's forever unreachable and lost to history, just like the great Calvanese bloodline."

"Forbidden?"

"Yes," Rotrude said pointedly, raising her white eyebrows high. "It is law. Anywhere with deadbloods is off limits. Can't have another outbreak of Dread Death."

Malla nodded. She'd heard from her father how bad it was. Why she was to have nothing to do with the Nomad traders that frequented Hellswater, although she thought their young men were particularly cute. "Yes, Lessonmaster," she said.

Outside, the storm broke. Warm sunlight sparkled through the thick-paned windows dotted with drops of rainwater. Steam rose ominously from every stone on the castle. Light cut through the haze.

Rotrude paced the center isle of the Lessonroom, sweeping her head from left to right.

Rose sat to the right side nearest the windows. She gazed over her shoulder outside, watching the misty fog rise. She contemplated how bizarre it was for a whole bloodline to be gone–how many people's stories and lives were lost. She felt drawn to the Calvanese story and desperately wanted to know more. She decided she would ask her grandfather, if her mother didn't know. Grandfather knew everything, Rose thought.

Evia sat directly in front of Rose trying to imagine what it would be like for women to be in charge. What a ridiculous idea! Women were hardly better than dogs, except for herself, of course.

Lucette Busk slouched in a seat behind Rose staring furiously at her desk, feeling silly for having spoken up. She burned from the slight bit of attention cast at her moments before and did her best to fade into the shadows on the side of the Lessonroom.

In the back sat the twins, Jire and Jole with jovial looks on their blush cheeks, not thinking about much of anything. Just as most Warn Vanguard men were said to be, they preferred action to thinking.

Malla Demos was front and center in the room next to Avina Minney, and behind them was Tiphanie. From the left glared the trio of nearly identical frosty Thornes.

"Onto the next lesson," Rotrude told them all. She continued to pace.

"Long-sworn allies of Dale, bloodline Horne, occupied Hunter Post at the sparser edge of the Baneswood forest until extinction from the Plague. Horne kept to themselves and intermarried with their natives, occasionally marrying brothers or cousins, and some alliance-driven marriages to the Dales to the West, and seductions by the Calvanese to the South. Not much is known of the culture internal to the bloodline itself, especially prior to the Nomad conflict. Horne was notoriously exclusive and private. They wrote almost nothing down. They only had one book but it doesn't have a name because it was their only one. Today, it's referred to by outsiders as the Horned Book. To members of the Faith, it has no name."

Evia's hand shot up.

"Yes, Evia?"

"What's the Faith?"

Malla snickered and looked to Avina. Meeting her eyes elicited a small smile. Evia responded in scowling frown.

"The Faith of the Horned," Rotrude told Evia, "Is rooted in the beliefs of bloodline Horne."

Her pale green eyes widened. "You mean, it's a *religion*?"

Malla met eyes again with Avina. This time she got her to break into a wide smile until both girls giggled like windchimes. Tiphanie smiled too, leaning close to Malla and Avina to participate. Both newblood girls ignored her.

"Yes, you can call it a religion," Rotrude said, ignoring the newblood girls' snickering. "That is what the Faith has become. Horne originally developed an intense belief system around the guidance of the Horned Woman. She is a deity they saw as their own bloodline's savoir," she explained for the Norland's benefit, although it felt silly to. She couldn't imagine never having heard of the Faith. The Faith's beliefs are what kept her sane during her childhood of captivity. "These beliefs were kept to their realm until after the Plague when word spread of many natives who were spared or saved by the Horned Women when they prayed to her in Horne's realm. This sparked the pilgrimages to Glassy Stream, on the border of Hunter Post and Baneswood, and later the creation of the Glass Temple. There are several adjunct temples in other new realms, as well. Littlebell and Croft Hold in particular."

There was a rumor that Horneblood had indeed survived the Plague but used the disease to disappear completely into the thick of their realm's wild mountain forests, to be completely left alone by the other Vanguards. However, this rumour was fully unproven.

Evia rose her hand again more deliberately this time, staring at Malla and Avina in spite despite their laughing and condescending glances.

"Evia?"

"Who's the Horned Woman?" she asked while glaring meanly at Malla and Avina.

Malla glared meanly back as Avina cowered and glanced away.

"As I said before, the Horned Woman was the Horne bloodline's deity; the goddess they believed in and worshiped. The belief in the Horned Woman began with Emihir Horne," Rotrude told Evia as the newblood children and Thorne girls, in full knowledge already of the Faith of the Horned, half listened on.

Only Rose paid attention sharply, for like Evia, it was all information she was hearing for the first time.

"Emihir was a first-generation Ancestor. That means she was born in the Kingdom after the Landing," Rotrude said. "Her father Enil was one of the Landers who founded Creed Point approximately a thousand years ago."

The Thorne girls nodded knowingly. The others looked confused, vaguely recalling the narrative, if at all. They were listening closely now, too. Details of ancient Vanguard history were notoriously hard to come by. Most only knew of the Landing because of the yearly celebration, at the first sighting of yelloweeds. It was a Kingdom-wide holiday full of song, fasting, and homage, celebrated piously in Old realms and begrudgingly in New ones.

"Many argue what happened to her is a result of years of experimentation gone awry. Others argue it was a true spiritual awakening." Rotrude paced. "Emihir claimed she dreamed that a woman with two horns atop her head shared the secrets to life with her. She said the woman preached that she had the keys to happiness and eternal life. Emihir wrote everything down. This became the book. The Horned Book." Rotrude looked from child to child before continuing. "Most paintings and statues of the Horned Woman use the likeness of Emihir Horne in memory of her contribution, because she never described what the woman looked like. Only that she had horns atop her head."

Rose raised her hand. Her doll-like face was pensive-set.

"Yes, Rose?"

"What did the Horned Woman tell her?"

"The Horned Woman first described to Emihir where to find a natural spring that was blessed with magical waters as a reward if she chose to believe in her and share her message," Rotrude replied. "She told Emihir she'd lead her people to unlock the secrets of the power of the land. According to legend, the natural spring was where the Horned Woman said it would be, after which the Horne people began to worship her, praying for her to unlock magic for them. Many have gone to the spring in search of some of that magic. Many devout believers are convinced Glassy Stream is the source."

Several hands were in the air now. Rotrude called on Tiphanie.

"What power?" she squawked. "What kind of power?"

"I can't tell you," Rotrude said to the pale girl with cheeks red flushed. "I don't know if she unlocked power for the Horne bloodline, or anyone. There is no proof of any tangible impact," she lied, "although many stories of people who were healed after bathing in Glassy Stream." That much is true, Rotrude thought. "The Horned Woman did change a lot of people's lives. Many today pray to her for peace and calm. There is an endless amount to teach you of the Faith of the Horned itself," she said, pausing at the front of the Lessonroom, revelling in warm sunbeams streaming in through the windowpanes, glinting brightly off her white, well-oiled hair and long-hanging ear pendants. "I'm sure some have heard a great deal from your parents or peers in your realms, and others know nothing at all." She glanced at Evia. "This, however, is all you'll be learning about the Horned Woman and the Faith here."

The Lessonroom moaned. Malla raised her hand and Rotrude pointed at her. "But why," Malla whined. "Father says it's true." She remembered his lively tales about his experiences with the Faith. The one, in particular, of an old, old man who said he gave the waters of Glassy Stream to his puppy to drink, back when he himself was a child. The puppy, although decades old, was still tiny and playful and didn't appear to have aged a day. This, however, was highly taboo. The Glassy Stream waters were for bathing only–forbidden to drink. "Why won't you teach us?"

Rose turned to address Malla directly. "It's really true?" she asked with widening black eyes.

"Father and Grandmother say it is. They say she's real."

"Children, quiet," Rotrude chided with a frown. "No talking amongst yourselves. According to an ancient law that no one has bothered to remove from the records, I'm not permitted to teach you about it here in detail." That was at least partially true.

"But, why!" Malla whined louder.

"Malla, enough!" Malla recoiled in her seat and Rotrude took a deep breath. "Vanguards are logical," she said firmly.

"There's no space for the unreal. That is the Council ruling backed up by the Guild, therefore, the Academy isn't permitted to go into further detail about any," she paused, eyes darting, "beliefs. It's not just the Faith. We don't instruct about the Teachings or the Ancestors either. We teach you the difference between good and bad; between right and wrong, but we do not differentiate between belief systems. And we do not speculate about power. Not here."

That statement didn't sit well with Rose. She placed her hand into the air carefully.

"Rose?"

"How can there be good and bad?"

Rotrude sighed, turning away from the girl dismissively. "Don't cause trouble."

"I'm not," Rose said forcefully. "Tell me how," she said as a command, not a question.

Rotrude turned back. She was hit by Rose's black eyes. The Brochet girl's otherworldly stare fully unnerved her. All the hair on her neck stood up. She felt as if her mind was turned inside out.

"Some things are just wrong," she answered with finality, looking away.

"Like what?"

"Like..." Rotrude paused and turned back. "...like murder," she said. "It is strictly forbidden throughout the Kingdom and the punishment is death."

"That doesn't make sense."

Surprised, the other children hushed amongst themselves, murmuring about what the dark-eyed girl could mean.

Rotrude froze in her tracks. "How does it not?"

"There are executions. I passed one with Mother, just the other day. A boy not much older than me. I saw him dangling there, the whites of his eyes red to match the rest before the color drained out. Mother said it was blood. His mouth was open. His neck was bent as much as my arm," she demonstrated.

The Newblood girls, Avina and Malla, disgusted, glanced

away. The Thorne girls, the eldest in particular, leaned forward.

"Mother said that he was caught stealing a horse and that the King ordered the execution."

"Then it was good and right to end his life," Rotrude said. "Even if he was just a child."

Rose frowned. "Killing is not wrong if ordered by the King?" she said in her small voice.

Rotrude was struck. "It's... it's..." she stuttered, pale cheeks hot. "It just is," she finally said, flustered. "If everyone agrees that something is wrong, then it is." She took a triumphant deep breath, feeling a rock in her stomach over the thought of a child hung for such a small crime that he likely didn't even commit. "Enough of this," she added, storming away from Rose, Third Tower robes flapping angrily.

The children looked from Rose to Rotrude as if watching the Baneswood Games.

Rose wondered if this Lessonmaster was a dolt for not seeing her meaning, however, she feigned innocence. "But I thought you said a long time ago it was good to experiment on natives," she said in a questioning tone, "but now you say it is bad and wrong." She stared with penetrating intensity at Rotrude. The words impaled the principled woman like spears.

Rotrude instinctually backed away. "It was," she paused, "a different time then. We're more civilized now," she added. "Enough of this," she barked through a frown.

"But how can anything always be good or always be bad? You just said it can change." Rose was audibly frustrated, not understanding at all. It irritated her when things didn't make sense.

"That's all I'll say on the topic."

Rotrude was internally furious at this girl for her obviously manipulative, troublemaker ways. She made her final judgement about the Brochet girl in that moment. "We are moving on."

Rose huffed. She still didn't understand and began to conceptualize Rotrude as someone who spoke a lot without having really anything to say. She fell into a pout. The other children were quiet and a bit stunned by Rose's deep questions, faces illuminated from bright light flooding in after the storm.

"Moving on," Rotrude said lightly.

She'd learned long ago how to handle troublemakers in her Lessonroom—ignore them.

"Bloodline Horne was considered savages by the Old. Some thought that they were traitors to the Vanguard cause and to the Kingdom itself; something neither Old nor New. There were rumours that Horne executed their most prized sons and daughters as human sacrifices as well as cannibalized for ritual, and as tortured for pleasure, but no one knows for sure. They were woods-dwelling people as their city Hunter Post is deep in the wilderness. Their only interaction with others outside their realm was through the Dales."

Tiphanie raised her hand.

"Yes, Tiphanie?"

"What'd they look like?"

"Horne intermarried with Hunter Post natives, so their complexions were swarthy and hair was brown and coarse. They were short and stocky woodsmen, known historically as great hunters. Although unlike the Dale spear hunters, Hornes were trappers—a profession later absorbed by Baneswood. Both men and women had broad shoulders, flat faces and big mouths. They were famous for their tattoos—also adopted by Baneswood later. Men and women alike commonly went bare-chested and wore skirts of tanned leather with leather strapped sandals and gloves. It's said that Horne strove to be a just society, giving men and women equal rights within their realm and allowing women equal weight in key decision making. All living Horne as well as their realm natives had a vote at what they called the Fire Poke, which was only resorted to when there is a grave matter to be decided upon. That's some of the little information we do have. They were notoriously distrustful of strangers and were known to kill trespassers in their woods," Rotrude said, crossing her arms in front of her chest. "But as I said, that's all anyone really knows about them. Any questions?"

A few hands shot up.

"Avina?"

"Were they rich like the Calvane- Calavav…"

"Calvanese," Rotrude said. "No, they were not. Not rich in coin, anyway. Horne was self-sustaining and only traded with Dale on rare occasions with meats or furs or other items that they had to barter with. There were known for something else, though."

The children leaned forward, listening closely.

"Horne was known for their connection to animals. Dogs in particular. They bred them for companionship and developed unexplainable connections with the beasts until eventually producing what today is called the 'horned hound' - a loyal and lovable animal with an exorbitant amount of soft fur, light brown with white and black markings, especially around the left eye, now inextricably linked to the Faith of the Horned. After the bloodline and most in Hunter Post went extinct, the dogs were seen after by natives and bloodline Dale, until the practice was adopted by many in the Baneswood realm. Today, both Baneswood and Hunter Post have a prevalence of natives and Dales alike that keep horned hounds as beloved pets. They are nearly worshiped."

At that, the three Thorne girls scrunched up their faces in tandem, trying to process why someone would ever want to do such a thing. Dogs were no better than vermin within Graceview, as in Westerviolet. At the same time Rose smiled, reminded of Ellie.

"Some pockets of the Faith have absorbed dogs into their religious practice, taking the Horne preoccupation with them as evidence to the dogs' importance. After the Plague killed every single living Horne, Hunter Post was absorbed by Dale. It's now a satellite of Baneswood. Glassy Stream cuts the border between Baneswood and Hunter Post. The Glass Temple is there in honor of the Horned Woman, the final stop of the Pilgrimage of the Faith of the Horned. It's a massively impressive structure built atop pre-Landing ruins." Rotrude looked around the high-ceiling castle Lessonroom.

"Questions?"

Birds chirped loudly on the windowsill just awoken after the storm.

"What did they do to the natives?" Avina asked quietly, unable to let go of the sullied Vanguard past. It pained her to consider the crimes her ancestors and their allies may have committed. "In the beginning," she added even softer.

Rotrude spoke gently. "The aim of bloodline Horne was to conquer consciousness, in addition to their affinity for animals. Early tests were with astral projection, lucid dreaming, and near-death experiences." But what did children know of those things, Rotrude thought quickly. "It all means going somewhere in your mind," she clarified. "This was done with various poultices and tonics, as well as musical tones." As the children nodded, she went on. "Those were the types of experiments that natives and Vanguards of their realm alike underwent. Coupled with the experiences of later generations, this methodology transformed their society into one of the most influential and ground-breaking religions ever seen. Many great minds at Hidden Den speculate those from Hunter Post are more apt to believe in the Horned Woman because of their altered bloodlines after centuries of these types of procedures. One theory states that only those with the correct blood can interact with her. This may explain the connection to dogs as well."

Rotrude paused.

"What else of Horne?" she asked out loud. "Ah, well," she answered herself, "Redvers Horne, born in 3740, was an old, proud man at the time the Plague hit. Too proud to take his family somewhere for shelter when news it of the spread came. He reportedly died, along with his two sons, Luthais and Cathal, and daughter Clara, all by his sister and wife, Lucretia Horne. Luthais, Redvers's son, was married to Viola Demos and they had four children, and five grandchildren. All died in the plague. Redvers's son Cathal married Elornora Calvanese and had two children named Ugo and Veriana. That family too died from the North Plague."

She looked around the room to assess drooping eyes and slouched bodies in the straight-backed seats. "Would you like a quick break? Or should I continue?"

"What's next?" Malla asked.

Rotrude smiled slightly at the girl's enthusiasm, although it was wearisome. "Duran. The assassins," she added dramatically.

"I want to hear that!"

"Me too," Rose chimed in.

The Warn twins groaned, having already endured the lesson last session, but Malla and Rose exchanged glances in acknowledgement of their shared interest in history, particularly dark and shadowy. The look was exceedingly brief. As soon as they made eye contact, each girl looked away.

"Alright. The ladies have spoken," Rotrude said warmly. She was pleasantly surprised to see a newblood and oldblood agree on something. "Let's get to it. Not too much longer," she said to the bored, groaning twins.

"Blood Duran was a bloodline of spies, assassins, and thieves that partook in games and riddles. Their castle, Whisperfield, is a huge maze on the edge of the Eversands, making it nearly impossible to attack and easy to slip in and out of undetected. There are a network of tunnels, secret entrances, and hidden walkways into the castle and around the property," Rotrude said. "Duran was rumoured to have a huge storage of treasure stolen or swindled from throughout the realms, as well as the secret to Scorpion smoke."

In times of old, when the Old reigned uncontested, the Kingdom was far more treacherous, Rotrude thought briefly. She couldn't imagine the noble men and women of the most powerful bloodlines acting in the ways that the Vanguards did centuries before. Little did Rotrude know, in the modern day, even her most beloved Newblood Vanguards were just as devious, if not far worse.

Unrelenting sunlight burnt away the fog and illuminated the lands sprawling in the wake of Animus Rock Castle. Only a few stories up, the windows from the Lessonroom gave a view of the entrance to Eden and some of the Commons, but not much more. While the other children listened intently with eyes focused on Rotrude, Lucette alone stared out the window. She watched a murder of ravens cut across the sky, wishing she could fly away with them.

A rainbow appeared between clouds.

"Bloodline Duran descended from a god obsessed with pushing the mind further and further," Rotrude explained. "Jasmine Duran was manic in her pursuit, at the expense of reason, legend says. Duran descendants evolved to have extraordinary perceptive and processing abilities due to her experiments, sometimes at the sake of sanity. They were exceptionally smart, fast, and agile," she said. "But also exceptionally unhinged."

Rotrude rested her side and hip on her desk and half sat on it before continuing the lesson.

"Duranblood complexions were typically light. They were short and slight, but nimble. They blinked far less than most and had an intense, unnerving stare, similar to the stare Gravesbloods tend to have, although their eyes were not grey. Durans had dark crescent shaped eyes and black pin-straight hair that both men and women grew long to down their backs. Depending on their rank, they would braid their hair differently."

"Like mine?" Avina asked.

"No, not like yours Avina," she said warmly, noting the girl's impressive braid; a symbol of breeding, beauty and status in Littlebell. "Duran braids had connection with different ranks in Scorpion Rose. They were not wide like Littlebell's. They were thinner, and oftentimes in designs across the skull."

Several raised hands. Rotrude pointed to Malla.

"What's that?" Malla asked. "Scorpion Rose."

"Duran founded Scorpion Rose," Rotrude told her. "It was a Guild of Assassins only reached through Whisperfield and only spoken about in whispers. They were known to recruit through the Kingdom by scouting children and snatching them when they showed promise. Like Calvanese, the inner workings of Duran and Scorpion Rose are unknown and died with them. It's assumed that no members of Scorpion Rose survived the Plague because there has been no activity observed from them in over two hundred years."

She paused, feeling the children internally pleading for more information, but even she herself, with her in depth knowledge of the Kingdom that she learned at Hidden Den, didn't have any to give.

"Any other questions?"

Rose interjected without raising her hand. "What if they're in hiding?"

Rotrude chuckled, turning to face her. "They could be, I suppose," she said. "But it's unlikely in over two hundred years not one brand has been found."

"Brand?" Malla asked loudly.

"Ah, yes," Rotrude nodded, turning to look at her, realizing she hadn't fully explained, engrossed in the lesson, forgetting to discipline them. "Scorpion Rose was famous for marking victims with a small brand of a scorpion holding a rose. A very literal emblem."

Evia raised her hand dutifully despite others beginning to shout out questions. Grateful for the obedience, Rotrude called on her.

The blonde asked, "Were they Old?"

"Yes, very much so," Rotrude confirmed, gilded ear pendants clanking. "They offered services to the highest bidder and far favoured the aims of the bloodlines intent on experimentation and degradation of natives," she said. "They committed some of the greatest atrocities known to history."

Many hands raised. Rotrude called on one of the twins, for she couldn't tell the difference.

"Like what?" Jole asked. "Yeah!" Jire echoed.

It seemed their interest had picked back up. Rotrude smiled.

"Lionel Duran, born in 3790, was an elite member of Scorpion Rose," she said. "Reolus Graves, born in 3780, contracted him to assassinate Reggient Minney, on the day of his daughter's wedding to Cassyon Beaumont no less."

Avina interjected loudly, "Why?" doe-eyes wide with horror.

"For two main reasons. Reolus Graves was privy to August Norland's plan to kidnap Auina Beaumont from Littlebell on the wedding day. Remember we learned about that already." Children nodded. "In the chaos caused by a murder, the act was thought to be easier to execute and would help in creating a diversion," she said. "The second reason; Reggient Minney was Reolus Graves' greatest opposition on Council. They were due to vote on a major fortress project in days' time. If it had not been for the North Plague, the face of the kingdom would be gravely different today."

"What happened?" Jole asked.

Rotrude almost chided him for not waiting to be called on but was too deep into her story to pause, and glad to have his interest at all. "Lionel Duran completed the murder of Reggient with the help of one other," she said. "With the assistance of Adam Morfit, who betrayed his best friend Reggient Minney, because Lionel threatened his family. Adam Morfit told Lionel Duran where Reggient Minney would be, and Lionel murdered Reggient per the plan. Reggient Minney's body was found with his throat slit moments before the wedding started."

A few children audibly gasped. The Thorne girls, notably quiet this lesson, seemed the least surprised by the horrors. Malla looked angry aside Avina who looked like she might faint. Rose just seemed curious and Evia, a bit proud. Lucette still looked out the window, lost in her own daydream, only half listening.

Rotrude continued.

"The atrocity caused an uproar," she told them, "but not long after, the symptoms of North Plague began. Lionel Duran reportedly escaped Littlebell before succumbing to Dread death, although he was infected. He unknowingly brought the disease back to Whisperfield where the entire bloodline perished."

Proper punishment, Rotrude thought.

"Even with Duran gone and the Old changed forever," she

said, "the memory of what the Old did to the Minney bloodline left an impression. The story travelled all the way down the Missi to the Guild at Wraithswail where Alden Morfit heard how his father Adam betrayed his own people and the Minneys. It was there in Wraithswail where Alden met Reggient's son, Miles Minney, and swore from then on that he would protect him and all their descendants to follow. That was the solidifying of the Morfit and Minney alliance."

The children murmured in acknowledgment of another piece of the Vanguard puzzle.

"The Duran brothers, Brenon and Lionel, were 40 and 41 years respectively during the Plague," Rotrude explained, speaking with her hands, resting her hip against her desk. "Both died, as well as all their descendants. Brenon Duran married Ceana Horne and they had four children: Armand, Wildred, Porthos, and Jeanette. Wildried Duran married Deodata Calvanese and had two children, Achille Duran and Rosa Calvanese, both babies when Plague hit. Lionel Duran married Cicely Graves, born in 3781, sister to Reolus Graves and aunt of Balthasar, the only Gravesblood who did survive the Plague. Cicely and Lionel had one son, Ewen, born in 3802, who married Heulwen Warn, and they had four children: Anges, Rosalind, Llwellyn, and Montague. All died."

Rotrude could tell her words hung over the young children with weighty influence.

"Alright," she finally said with a smile and a sigh. "We're on to the last one. And look, the sun is out, and the birds are chirping," she added, gesturing to the illuminated windowpanes. "We'll be done before long and you will be free to enjoy your afternoon."

The sun shone in bright streams through the high windows lining the right side of the room. Rotrude stood at the front, bright light casting her hard features in shadow.

"Beaumont is the most recently extinct bloodline," Rotrude told them excitedly, new energy bubbling with the tale of the most mysterious one. Her favorite, apart from Calvanese, to study and learn about personally.

She first explained about their castle and realm, both bearing the same name: Winter Garden. How, similar to Eden's maze with its unnatural climates, Winter Garden's castle and city weather was perpetually cold and snowy regardless of the season. The cool grey castle reached high into the snow clouds and was surrounded by an arabesque of flowers: frost flowers, goldenglow, pepper lilac and pink trillium mostly, that bloomed beautifully about the grounds and were frequented by snowy white butterflies, impossibly. The natives of Winter Garden were known for their woven wares, hats and baskets mostly, as well as their glass bead jewellery, and those, along with trading the more desirable natives as slaves, were their primary sources of income.

"Lost around the time of the Uprising," she went on, "in 3988, not even a century ago, much more recently than the previous three," she said, "Beaumont blood descends from the lead god, long before our history began. His name was Alabaster Beaumont. He is your savior, the god who founded the Vanguard. He's the reason why you all are here. His descendants, the Ancestors, continued his life's work, searching to unlock the potential of the human mind and body. After generations of work, intermarrying, and testing on themselves, Beaumonts were finally successful in creating a child with abilities. According to the records that survived from before the Plague, that was Bernarus Beaumont."

Rotrude wanted so badly to elaborate, to explain to these children that power was not extinct at all and that each of them likely had innate abilities too, that had been long suppressed one way or another, but was strictly forbidden. To do so would mean imprisonment in the First Tower, if not death. She held her tongue.

Tiphanie raised her hand quickly.

"Yes, Tiphanie?"

"You mean someone actually had power?! Real power?!" she squealed, brash voice echoing about the high-ceiling hall. The other children cringed with every word. "Grandfather told me that was a myth the Old made up so the natives would obey them."

"Not a myth," Rotrude replied curtly, eyeing the Regnard girl with unavoidable malice. "There are good eyewitness accounts of his abilities. Bernarus was not shy with his gifts and would flaunt them at parties." She studied the children. "Many say Bernarus was a product of bad blood. That he had a tainted mind. Some say he drank too much mad honey. Others say he was simply a fool."

Rotrude noted the eldest Thorne, Orosia, whisper something to each of her sisters, after which each nodded slightly. She wondered what the girl said while continuing to explain.

"The Beaumont family was the right hand of the royal Bellamines and had protection of the crown, despite jealousy, accusations of dark powers, and dissenters to what they were doing," Rotrude said. "After years of inbreeding and experimentation, this bloodline's pale white skin, high cavernous cheekbones, and black hair were exaggerated, producing some children that were near translucent with dark eyes and veins snaking beneath the thinnest skin on their arms, and face. Bernarus Beamount's hair lost pigment and turned white in two streaks at his temple. This feature was nicknamed the 'mark of madness'."

The children listened intently with wide eyes.

"Beaumonts were thin with toned elongated limbs and strong features. They were prone to varying degrees of lunacy and several ancient, legendary Beaumonts prior to Bernarus were lost to suicide. This further pointed to Bernarus's instability. By early 3799 the Beaumont family had grown so powerful that they had undeniable control within the Kingdom. Despite warnings of discontent in the North and urges of Demos and Morfit to open trade lines with the Nomads, King Abner the Unready - remember him - refused on the advisement of his friend Bernarus Beaumont alone. This led to the Nomad attack on Animus rock in 3800, that we covered already."

Malla raised her hand.

"Yes?" Rotrude called on her.

"It was all Beaumont's fault, then," she said.

"Nothing is ever so simple," Rotrude warned the girl a bit too harshly, because she was getting tired. Malla sank backwards a bit. "And if it were the case, they paid dearly for it," she added a bit more warmly. "The North Plague of 3833 killed all living Beaumonts except brother and sister Vlad and Isa Beaumont, mentioned in the last Plague lesson. They married in hopes of having another child with the same blood powers as their father did. Unfortunately, that did not happen. They did have two children, but neither were born with a hint of power. The children's names were Bert Beaumont, born in 3835, and Lucia Beaumont, born in 3837. The pair married each other in 3855 and had five children; Temi, Elanua, Vanel, Aly, and Alla."

Rotrude paced loudly up and down one of the isles.

"Aly eventually became Queen," she said, "when she was wed to Danil Bellamine. Remember his name later, for many argue he alone caused the Blood Wars. Aly's legacy was tarnished with his. Temi and Elauna Beaumont married but had no children. The pair was murdered during the Blood Wars at the Battle of Winter Garden, in 3880."

"What about the Blood Wars!?" one of the Warn twins interjected. "Yeah!" the other shouted. "Let's hear about that!"

"Boys!" Rotrude chided firmly, to which they both shrunk. "That will be next lesson. One at a time," she explained. The boys rolled their hooded eyes as they groaned. "Vanil Beaumont was married to his sister Alla, and, after surviving the Battle of Winter Garden, the pair fled to Animus Rock. There they received sanctuary from their sister Aly because Alla was pregnant. There, over three years, the pair had two children, named Alaya born in 3880 and Emvin born in 3883. Neither child reportedly inherited any of their ancestor Bernarus' powers. Alaya and Emvin - sister and brother - were married and had three children named Cellene, Giraud, and Kelissine after the conclusion of the Blood Wars. Through Cellene and Giraud's marriage, generations later, their great-great-grand daughter Eraine Beaumont and her cousin (and their other grandchild) Edman Beaumont married and had five sons. The Five Beaumonts, they were called at the time. These boys all reportedly had the Beaumont white-pale translucent skin, prominent features, and black eyes. They were known for their intellect, ambition and military prowess. Remember them later, because the Five Beaumonts were critical during the Uprising. Tragically, all died."

For the first time all lesson, Orosia raised a slender hand carefully into the air. "How do you know they all died?"

Taken aback, Rotrude paused. "We know, Orosia, let me finish" she scolded. At the dismissive response, Orosia's already chilly visage steeled even more. Rotrude felt an inexplicable chill fall about her shoulders like an icy cape. She shrugged it off. "The eldest of Uraine Beaumont and Edman Beaumont's five sons' names was Hudson Beaumont, born in 3966," Rotrude said. "He was the only one of the boys who married, to Josiane Thorne. They had one daughter named Sofana Beaumont. She is known historically as the last Beaumont."

Orosia raised her hand once more. "Yes?" Rotrude called on her again, pressing air hard against her throat in frustration, unable to hide it after the long lesson. She was ready to be done.

"What happened to her?"

All the other children swung heads to Rotrude, even the Warn twins, listening closely.

"I said, let me finish," Rotrude hissed through a clenched-teeth half-smile. "Sofana Beaumont was three years old when she was murdered with her parents at Winter Garden, in 3988. Many say it's one of the key events that prompted the New realms to come together against the Old again, sparking the Uprising, which began two years later, in 3990."

BANESWOOD BORDERLANDS

The light was low. It was the perfect time for hunting. Red eyes were weakest at the liminal times of day, right before the sun rose and just after it set. But Rhain saw clearly.

He stood in between tall hardwood trees at the cusp of Baneswood Forest, wider than the trunks himself, one with the shadows. His passing prey did not notice him at all.

He breathed slowly. He waited patiently. Rhain, if nothing else, was calculating. Calculating, until it was time to strike. That was when his rage took over.

His vision dripped and his head pounded. It had been far too long since his last hunt, because his uncle Sampson just wouldn't let him be. He couldn't slip away from Hunter Post unnoticed. This irritated Rhain. But only slightly. That was how it was for Rhain—he didn't feel much of anything apart from irritation, disgust, and rage.

Rhain's prey moved slowly, completely unaware that it was being watched. Rhain studied its movements. It was not going to be a hard takedown. Not at all.

He had been stalking this prey for weeks. Watching its movements. It's daily and nightly routine. Where it got its water. When it ate its food. What times of day it was alone.

He picked this prey because it was a large specimen. Rhain enjoyed a challenge, and it had been months since he'd found one. Even longer since he battled against his brethren in the Games. He briefly thought of the wide arena, filled with cheering and jeering, spattered with years of blood. The red hallucinations pulsing through his vision got brighter.

He had to strike soon. He couldn't control it much longer.

Birds all around squawked loudly, pulsing in clouds as they returned to the trees from the nearby valleys and fields. Rhain watched them swooping across the flat grey sky, dimming with each passing moment, like angry swarms, all moving together. *Like the earthblood,* Rhain thought, *and Vanguards alike.* He hated all of them. Every one.

Rhain didn't bring much with him when he was hunting. A knife to process the kill and a large canvas to tie up the carcass in, to transport the meat later. That was all. He didn't like to bring much with him. He didn't like to be weighed down.

He sighed, ache in his head blinding, waiting for his prey to be still. *Why won't it stop moving,* Rhain thought. The dripping red in his vision, like blood pouring down a windowpane, increased. He could barely see.

There was a time when he didn't hunt. Back when he competed in the Games, when he perpetually won, he didn't have to. Bloodsport satisfied his cravings. The cravings that he inherited from his father. The cravings that nearly tore him apart from the inside out after his accident, when he could not move, when he could not fight. That was a fate worse than the First. Worse than even death.

After the accident, Rhain attempted to return to the Ancestors many, many times. He made a tea from nighthorn flower and he spread the berries on bread. Nothing happened. He tied a rope around his neck and a high chandelier of Hunter Post's castle and stepped off a chair, but his neck was too muscled, and he was too heavy–the chandelier fell from the ceiling. He held a dagger to his throat nightly, even after his leg healed enough to walk, daring himself to press harder, willing himself to feel the sweet release of pain, and death, but something held him back. He was not sure what. Maybe it was the thought of blood. There was nothing else for him.

The light was nearly gone. The birds above Rhain had nearly stopped squawking. *Why won't it stop cursed moving,* Rhain thought again, watching his prey scurry back and forth. He was almost out of time.

Finally, his chosen prey was still. Rhain narrowed his eyes. It was time to strike.

Rhain emerged from the treeline like a shadow come alive and hobbled slowly towards his prey.

It didn't see him coming until the very last moment.

"Good to greet you," the large, muscled native said, turning quickly, squinting his eyes to see in the dim light.

Rhain punched the man in the face, square in the jaw, knocking him backwards considerably. The man swung back in an attack, clumsily, as he was caught unawares, but Rhain was quick. Much faster than he appeared to be. He moved and then let out a barrage of punches so angry they had the fury of all the Ancestors behind them. The brutal attack was so uncalled for and so insane that the borderland native had tears in his eyes.

"Please," he managed to croak between punches. "Why?"

But Rhain kept punching, harder and harder until his own knuckles bled from hitting bone. He punched until the man stopped gargling.

LITTLEBELL DENS

The door opened smoothly. To Ryd's surprise, not a head turned in the overcrowded den when he entered.

There were dozens of round tables with splintered wood surfaces and heavy artisan-carved wood seats. Nearly fifty bodies filled the tight room. The majority were children. Every face was a different shade or hue, with wide eyes or slanted cheek bones or upturned noses, spanning the spectrum of humanity. Ryd hadn't seen such diversity! Not until now. While features distinguished between them at first, it was their adornments, makeup, and clothing that pushed the Ryd's imagination over the top. Many wore adornments on parts of their faces he had never seen done before. Several children sported the thick Littlebell braids. Others, the customary thinner braids also popular in Westerviolet. But there were also some with hair flattened down against their head with a thick oil that stank of fish, likely from Hellswater, or pulled at the very top of their heads in intricate knots, likely from Baneswood. Some had clanking piercings, likely from Animus Rock, and others thick black eyeliner, likely from Croft Hold. Some had scars covering their bodies, likely from Iron Bark, and others had bright white hair, likely from Lyonshall. Some wore robes with boots while other skirts with bodices, capes, and sandals. Some had furs with leather and still others wore gauzy cotton pants that fell around their thin legs, like drapes. A gaggle of small boys with black curly hair and drooping eyes wore undertrousers with nothing else at all. They were likely from Ravenshroud.

Ryd frantically scanned the den from left to right for Collen, but he didn't see him.

At the end of the long den, with sawdust floor covered floor and mossy brick walls, sat a table of adults. An owl in scarlet red was painted on the brick behind them. The seat at the head of the table was empty and at the rest sat four men and one woman drinking from iron goblets, chatting back and forth. Utensils sat on the table tops unused.

Apparently, sup had yet not been served.

"Who are you?" an unfriendly grunt demanded.

A man not much older than Ryd sat at the right of the empty seat at the table, course black hair cut close to his head and chiselled face clean-shaven. The intimidating man had a rough horizontal scar down the length of his cheek by his ear. He hardly had a neck, it was so wide, and his head connected straight to bulky shoulders, with budging traps and muscles spanning his back and spine. Ryd could tell his form was obviously for function and strength, not show, and he was intimidated immediately. The man wore massive leather armor, obviously old and used, inlayed with dark feathers, worn over a black tunic with scarlet red trousers and brown leather boots. He leaned backwards in a relaxed stretch, teetering it on two legs instead of four. The hefty furniture pitifully creaked under his weight as he drank from a heavy goblet with his feet up on the empty chair.

To annunciate the question, the colossal man squinted red eyes at Ryd.

The previously rowdy room filled with chatter and laughter turned in an immediate hush at the sound of the huge man's voice. Soon, one by one, the children noticed Ryd's presence. Excited whispers rose in a crescendo until everyone nearly yelled with glee at the visitor.

A striking woman stood from her seat at the table.

"Children! Do not fuss," she said with warm command. The excited gaggle instantly quieted at the sound of her voice. She gestured with open hands, buckling her bell-shaped sleeves. "Let us welcome our guest!" she said warmly.

The red-eyed woman was tall with drooping eyes. Ryd had never seen anyone like her, not even around the muddled den. Extraordinarily, she had light skin with enormous dark brown markings covering her hands, arms and neck, as if she'd been spattered with ink. Her dark hair was spattered light the same. Or was she dark with light markings? Either way, the woman's square face on one side was pale cream, while on the other, it was dark brown.

The children dutifully obeyed the woman's command, settling back into their seats at the round tables dotting the den.

The woman nodded curtly once, curly hair bouncing, satisfied with the children's obedience. She turned to face Ryd and tucked her hair behind her ears. "Welcome," she said with a smile, faint lines crinkling beside her red eyes. "Come." She gestured with a bell-sleeve. Her ensemble moved with her as she gestured to Ryd to come closer.

"This is the hero who saved Ed's boy?" a second man asked, pale blond hair flattened to his head with rank oil. "It must be," he said to himself. This man was much slighter than the first and wore a brown poncho secured with an owl brooch. His skin tone was a sallow green tan and his eyes, upturned.

"He was not what I was expecting. Is he what you were expecting, Longin?" The man in the poncho turned his head to ask a tall man with a sneer and wavy hair parted the side, hanging down over one red eye.

Ryd listened carefully. Why were they talking about him like he wasn't right there?

"He's older than I expected," Longin replied.

"We are so glad to greet you," the final man at the table said eagerly with a toothy, crooked smile. He had round cheeks and an ample frame, with straight honey blonde hair and huge red eyes. He looked a bit like a suckling pig, Ryd thought. He was not used to seeing natives of that size, even high ones, as Westerviolet rationed everything. Although he had become more accustomed to fleshy natives as he walked the Littlebell streets. The portly man wore a scarlet cape secured with an owl brooch over his otherwise nondescript clothing.

"The cards told me that the moon would bring good fortune," he said surely, glancing to the others at the table.

"Hmph," the large man grunted before taking a long swig.

He set his goblet down then peeked gently beneath his tunic. Ryd was confused by the gesture until he heard chirping and saw a tiny beak, then a flash of black feathers. Zolios, for all his gruff ways, loved animals. It was his pet bird, Tilen. Lately he went everywhere with him.

"You shouldn't be so blasphemous, Zoilos," the pale blond man teased. "Even a failed Warman like you hasn't seen everything. Isn't that right, Jelany?"

"That's right," Jelany, the portly man, replied assuredly.

"Excuse them," the woman told Ryd with an eye roll. "Please take a seat." She gestured and two small children dragged a heavy chair over to the table. The pale blond man shifted his weight to scoot his chair to make room, scraping loudly against the floor.

"You couldn't have stood?"

"Waste of time," the pale blond man replied with a placating smile.

"This is Drakon," the woman introduced him with a sigh as Ryd took the seat aside him. "Odion should join us if he is done in time. You've met him, I assume?"

"The bartender, right?" Ryd said carefully.

The table laughed.

"Yes," the woman said, smiling. "The bartender."

Ryd didn't understand what was so funny. His cheeks burnt hot.

"This is Zoilos," the woman gently offered. "He looks much meaner than he is, I assure you."

"Zoilos," the man with no neck grunted. Tilen's chirps could be faintly heard from his breast.

Ryd nodded.

After pacing around the table, the exotic woman stood behind the portly man who sat to Ryd's right.

"This is Jelany," she said placing her hands familiarly on his shoulders.

"Good to greet you," said Jelany pleasantly.

"I'm Longin," the tall man said before the woman could introduce him. His raspy voice cut the den.

"Yes, right." The woman rolled her eyes as she half glanced to him. "And I am Plusia," she said, taking her seat at the round table once more. "That brings us to the most important question." Plusia paused dramatically, drooping red eyes studying Ryd's deeply.

"What question?" Ryd asked, unconsciously leaning as far back in his chair as he could. He felt a jolt of adrenaline when her attention turned to him. All around them, the sounds of the children awaiting sup grew louder.

"Who are *you*?" she asked bluntly.

Every head at the table swung to him to stare.

He swallowed hard. "I'm Ryd," he said, while glancing from face to face.

"Is... that it?" She frowned. "You aren't here to join us?"

"Join you?!" Ryd exclaimed. "To join you I'd have to know who you are."

At that Zoilos threw his feet to the ground with a stomp. He banged his goblet to the table, sloshing liquid all over. He removed a bone dagger from his sheath and held it towards Ryd across the round table. Drakon, the pale blond sat ready to pounce with his hand hovering over his own bone dagger. The others, Plusia, Longin, and Jelany, drew back from the table instinctually, apprehensive of the unfolding scene.

Zolios's hulking frame teetered over the round table. "Start talking," he commanded slowly.

"Wait!" Ryd cried.

"No one finds us by accident, mate," Drakon said, gesturing his head at Zoilos. "You'd better start talking. He doesn't seem too happy with you."

Ryd looked from Drakon to Zoilos. "I was brought here!"

The children all around didn't seem to notice the confrontation, still joking and laughing loudly while awaiting sup. There were a multitude of accents bouncing off the subterranean den's cool damp walls.

"Who are you?" Zoilos growled slowly, brow lowered ominously until his blood red eyes were barely visible slits.

"I've been shot at and insulted then beaten and tied up and

nearly burned and drowned," Ryd said woefully, on the verge of a breakdown. "The past few days have been torture. And I know torture. All I want is to find my brother! He's run away."

With mention of his lost brother, all eased back. The intensity dissipated instantly.

"Why didn't you say so?" Plusia asked with a grateful sigh, exchanging glances with her companions. "See, everyone," she said warmly to Zoilos in particular, although all listened closely. "Nothing to fear. Put away your weapons."

Reluctantly, Zoilos sheathed his dagger. He lowered to sit, unblinking threateningly. He didn't take his eyes off Ryd the whole time. Drakon, conversely, casually removed his hand from his hip and leaned back in his chair until crossing his arms at his chest. The mood returned to the pleasant state it previously was in.

Ryd bit his lip hard. He felt completely overwhelmed and looked for anyone to meet his gaze. "Where am I?" he pleaded to no one in particular.

"Here, have some of this, mate," Drakon said with a kind smile. He pushed Ryd a goblet.

Ryd sighed loudly as he glanced upwards at the ancient, overgrown ceiling.

"Not a drinker?"

"After the day I've had, why the curses not?"

He took a long, lustful sip of the burning ale. Instantly, Ryd felt the warmth in his chest and welcomed the sense of false calm.

"That's the spirit," Drakon said loudly, clapping him on the back. Ryd coughed and sputtered.

"What is this?" Ryd asked, coughing again.

"Fire ale," Drakon said proudly. "The finest."

Zoilos shook his head, snickered, and took a long, unflinching drink.

"How's it different from regular ale?" Ryd asked.

He looked down into the goblet to study the prismatic liquid.

"We make it ourselves," Drakon told him.

"Tell us, good hero, of how you saved the boy," Jelany asked

Ryd with child-like eyes.

"The boy? What boy?" Before anyone could respond, Ryd said, "Oh, you mean the one I thought was Col? That feels like so long ago."

Plusia leaned forward. "Who's Col?"

"My brother Collen." Ryd's throat pricked as he said the name, seeing his brother's endearing smile full of crooked teeth in his mind's eye. "That's when I saw the boy. I thought it was Col, but it wasn't. A huge man was attacking him," Ryd held his hands out to show how large Brutt was, "and I pushed him aside. Before I knew it, I was knocked out cold." He lowered his hands into his lap. "Did the boy escape?"

"Aye," Zoilos grunted with a slight nod. He reached into his tunic again to pet Tilen.

"Good."

"Yes, you saved him," Plusia gushed warmly. "That's why we call you a hero." She met Ryd's eyes. "You are."

Ryd thought of how he only saved the boy by accident, then tried to flee in fear. "I'm no hero," he said. "I pushed a man down." He knew deep in his heart that he was a coward.

"You pushed down one of the worst men this side of the Missi," Jelany replied, eyes wide. "Not to mention, leader of the Fellowship in Littlebell. If you aren't a hero, no one is!"

"Here, here!" the table cheered, slamming their fists in unison.

"Wait," Ryd said. "The man said that in the alley. The Fellowship. What is that?"

"How have you not heard of the Fisherman's Fellowship?" Drakon was shocked. "What realm are you from?"

The Fisherman's Fellowship supplied fresh catches up and down the Missi and were widely known for their brother-like comradery, brutality, and opportunistic ways.

"Baneswood," Ryd responded quickly.

"Are you sure? You look like you're from here," Jelany said pleasantly.

"What is the Fisherman's Fellowship?"

"A horde of crusty men with the Old's thumbs far up their

asses," Drakon spat.

Plusia added, "It was a brave thing that you did. No doubting that."

"Who did I save?"

"Karl," Jelany said happily. Ryd turned to look at him. "Ed's little brother," he clarified. "Once Karl told Ed what had happened, you had to be rescued."

"Who is Ed?"

"Our leader," Jelany said.

"When do I meet him?"

Drakon, Jelany, and Longin exchanged glances as Plusia warmly smiled and Zoilos shook his head. Ryd eyed them cautiously and began to speak but was interrupted by the loud ding of a bell.

It was time for sup.

The room burst into a jubilee as a wide boy with a gummy smile pushed a cart from table to table filled with clay pots of varying heights. Ryd craned his neck to watch the process that began at the outskirts of the den. The children handed their bowls to the boy and told him what they wanted, and he filled the bowls accordingly with a wooden ladle that he mixed between pots. Immediately, the den wafted with notably foreign spices mixed with sun-ripened, rotting meat.

To Ryd, who never ate flesh—it was reserved for Vanguards and Guardsmen within Westerviolet—it smelled terrible.

Ryd watched as some children were given porridge made with oats from Croft Hold, fish broth stew from Hellswater, and others a spiced ground meat dish called cured mutton, a staple in Baneswood that he had never heard of. The boy had to take three trips back and forth from the kitchen to refill until finally, he reached the table where Ryd sat. Although Ryd hadn't had a proper meal in days and his stomach ached, when asked what he wanted, he hesitated.

"He's of Baneswood," Plusia said.

The serving boy nodded and took Ryd's bowl and filled it with the strange meat before setting it in front him with a thud. The others quickly dove into their meals while Ryd eyed

Drakon's bowl of porridge hungrily, poking at his own bowl of spiced meat. He wished he hadn't hesitated.

"Not a fan of cured mutton?" Drakon observed in a glance.

"Never had it," Ryd said flatly, looking down at the intimidating rank dish.

"Never had cured mutton in Baneswood?" Drakon raised an eyebrow. "Isn't it from there?"

"I'm... I'm from the borderlands."

Zoilos was halfway finished his own bowl of it already. "It is good," he grunted while chewing, dark meat and juices covering his mouth and teeth.

The smell was more than Ryd could bear. "I'm not hungry." He pushed the bowl away.

Drakon observed and laughed. "Don't let that slob ruin it for you." He nodded in Zoilos's direction. "If you've had the day you've said you've had, you should eat."

Plusia agreed. "He's right. Sup would do you good."

Ryd agreed with the logic. He pulled the bowl of mutton closer again. It was true, sup would do him good. He took a deep breath and went for a timid bite of his meal. The heavy, unfamiliar spices poorly masked the ripe bite of meat begun to turn. Gagging, Ryd did his best to ignore a wriggling maggot as he swallowed.

"Better?" Plusia asked.

Ryd forced a smile, feeling dark pieces of meat stuck between his teeth. "Thank you," he said truthfully to all of them, looking at Plusia in particular. "To be honest, I haven't really eaten in days."

"You poor thing," she said.

Ryd glanced around the den again, impressed by the children's obedience without guards or threats. "What is this place?" he asked. "I still don't know."

"This, mate, is the heart of the city." Drakon showily gestured one hand at the cavernous den littered with tables and children, ceiling fully green with overgrowth, walls slick mossy bricks. "Of the Kingdom," he added.

"Aye, we save lives," Jelany added proudly with a chin-jiggling nod.

"You've found the Free Boys, Ryd," Plusia said.

"The Free... Boys? But, you're a woman? And all grown?"

"It's just a name really."

"What are you?"

Drakon responded. "Founded by the mistreated orphans of the Fellowship."

"We fight," Zoilos said.

"For peace," Plusia added.

"That doesn't make sense," Ryd said.

"I agree," Longin said sharply.

"Quiet," Zoilos said. "No more of your lies," he growled towards the slender man.

Smirking, Longin shifted his asymmetrical hair out of his eye briefly as he sat back in his chair.

Ryd could feel the tension between Longin and the other members of the Free Boys, but he didn't dare bring attention to it with questions. He was grateful to be accepted amongst them peacefully.

"If it weren't for the alliance with Leon, we wouldn't be here," Plusia chided Longin. "And you would have nowhere to run. Don't cause trouble just because you're sore. Be grateful."

"If it wasn't for Leon I...I..," Longin countered, eyes darting, tan face reddening defensively, "I wouldn't need to be here."

"But you are," Plusia retorted, losing patience. "And if it wasn't for Leon, there would be no Ashkeep. Meaning, there would be no safety for the Free Boys. The alliance, however controversial, is necessary."

Grumbling, crossing arms at his chest, Longin fell silent again.

Ryd had no idea what they were talking about. "The alliance with who?"

"Leon," Drakon said.

The name sounded familiar. Where had Ryd heard it? "Who?" he asked again.

"Minney," Drakon replied, scraping the edges of his bowl,

hungrily finishing the last of his porridge. Instantly Ryd remembered who Leon Minney was. Vera's unkind brother. He hated him without a second thought.

Ryd's curiosity bested him. "What's his problem with Leon?"

Longin interjected harshly. "My problem? He's dragging the Kingdom into the sewers." He gestured around. "Literally."

"Be honest," Plusia said. Her annoyance was clear despite the natural warmth of her tone. "Your problem is that Leon bested you."

Longin held a piercing gaze with Plusia while pushing his rank unfinished bowl of fish stew away from himself slowly. *That bitch doesn't know the half of it*, he thought angrily, remembering each lie Leon told. He finished his drink and set his goblet down violently. Then, he pushed his chair away from the table with a loud scrape before walking away. A child in a threadbare green dress with leather sandals ran over, scooped up his empty bowl, and ran off.

"What's wrong with him?" Ryd asked once Longin had gone.

Although most at the table finished their meals, Ryd still poked at his bowl of meat, taking slow bites with trepidation until finally giving up. It was too disgusting. He pushed the bowl away.

"He's got his trousers in a knot," Drakon said, handing his bowl to the child in green, returned to collect more of the table's empty ones. "Don't mind him."

"Probably mad sickness," Jelany added with fearful inflection. "I hear if not treated properly, it can last for eternity. On the Horned."

Then, the kind bartender from the tavern entered the den. He paced the length of the room, taking a seat next to Ryd, dragged there by a pair of children. Odion carried with him a bowl of fish soup. Ryd scrunched his nose as the turned scent hit his nostrils, although it was slightly more pleasant than the meat.

"Mad sickness?" the older man asked having overhead the conversation as he walked in. "Don't tell me you're on it now Jelany," he said with parental anger, frowning while he adjusted himself in the chair.

"No! No, Horned knows it's not me!" Jelany cried. "Longin."

"Ah, I see," Odion said, relaxing. "Should I speak to him again?"

"He's on edge, blaming what happened on Leon again," Plusia said. "Your guidance would be appreciated."

Ryd wondered what had happened. What Leon had done. Why Longin held such a wrathful grudge.

Odion nodded. "After I've eaten." He took a bite. "I see you've met our hero," he said through a side glance while chewing.

"Stop calling me that." Hot blood rushed to Ryd's cheeks. He looked down. "I didn't do anything."

"Yes, you did," Drakon said warmly. "You saved one of us. That makes you one of us."

"Will Ed be joining us here? Should we wait?" Plusia asked Odion as he hungrily slurped at the soup directly from the bowl. He shook his head 'no' with a full mouth. "Is everything alright?"

Odion finished chewing, licking fatty broth from his lips before speaking. "Finishing up with Luzia."

Plusia visibly relaxed. "Ah, why didn't you say so?"

At the mention of a female name, remembering the ordeal on the barge, Ryd perked up. "Is that who saved me?"

Drakon nodded. "Aye, she went to assist."

"And that barge is the..." Ryd paused at the unfamiliar term "...Fisherman's Fellowship?"

"Their headquarters in Littlebell, that's right," Drakon confirmed. "Was," he added with a smile.

Laughter erupted around the table. "Here, here!" they cheered together, beating the table again with their fists. Of all the evils within the Kingdom, the Fisherman's Fellowship was particularly hated, particularly by the Free Boys. They were something of a nemesis.

"You say you look for your brother?" Drakon asked.

"Yes! Yes, my brother. Of course," Ryd said eagerly, ashamed he'd nearly forgotten to ask about Col. "Where could he be? I don't see him here."

"I'm afraid this is the whole flock," Drakon replied sadly. "If you don't see him here mate, he's not here."

"Well hold on," Jelany said. "Can you describe him?"

"He's about this tall," Ryd held up his hand to forehead height as he was sitting, "with skin the color of mine and almond shaped eyes, and a wide nose like mine too," he added, pointing at his own handsome face. "His hair was very short the last I saw him, and curled, but it would be growing longer now." His chest felt a pang, realizing how long it had been since he'd seen his only remaining kin. "He looks like me, just smaller, with crooked teeth. His name is Collen but everyone calls him Col."

"Did you all catch that?" Odion looked at each around the table. All nodded back at him. "If he's here, we will find him. You have my word."

"We'll look," Zoilos grunted.

"Thank you so much."

Odion burped and pushed his empty bowl away. The green-garbed child dutifully bused his bowl away like she'd done all the others.

"Are you finished eating, dear?" Plusia asked Ryd.

"Yes," he said, feeling his stomach still growling. "Not that hungry," he added sheepishly.

Plusia eyed his nearly full bowl and shrugged. "So be it. Shall we go?"

"Let's," Jelany said warmly.

"Go where?" Ryd asked no one in particular.

"To the common den," Drakon said, scooting his seat back with in an ear-scratching scrape.

Ryd's nerves knotted in his stomach. Or was it just hunger pangs? He had never been more unsure of himself in his life. He felt like his entire world had been dumped on the floor and trampled on, and now he was left sifting through dirt to find the shattered pieces.

He walked with his new companions down a series of long hallways with dirty sawdust floors, damp brick walls and mossy ceilings until they reached another room. This one was far wider than it was long with a lower ceiling, more dimly lit with benches and chairs strewn around. Children ran and laughed and played all about. The walls here were brilliantly colored from years of children's graffiti in an overwhelming mural wrapping the room's perimeter, in red tones mostly, with paints made from dried vegetables and river mud. In the furthest corner was a large shelf with various boxes and drawers. Children scattered about pulling items from the shelves, shells and husk dolls mostly, chasing each other back and forth, and scribbling over the exposed parts of the mossy walls with pieces of dried clay. Ryd followed the adults past the joyful chaos into a small room off to the side.

In the side room were worn plush chairs and a wide leather sofa with a colorful hand-woven rug underfoot, in stark contrast to the dilapidated walls, ceiling and sawdust floor. There was a squat table in the middle topped with an assortment of scarlet candles of varying heights. Wax melted directly onto the table. On the walls were countless pieces of parchment, each depicting a visage of a wanted criminal. Each person in the room besides Ryd and had their likeness on the wall. Odion's likeness was the oldest of the bunch, yellowed and fading, depicting a much younger man. From the likeness shown, he was hardly recognizable. It was how he was able to tend the Red Tavern's bar each night.

Ryd took a seat on the far side of the couch, eyeing Odion's First paper. Drakon sat beside him. Odion sat in the chair directly to his right as the others sat across from him.

A young girl with a knot of black hair high on her head and a mole on her chin entered the room holding a tray of short clay cups.

"Thank you Uillia," Plusia said as she set the drinks on the table.

Ryd took one when he was handed. After eyeing it first, he

gave the cup a quick sniff, then sipped in line with the rest. The fire ale scorched his throat, but he welcomed the detached peace it brought his mind. Uillia nodded awkwardly before scurrying from the room.

"So Baneswood, is it?" Drakon asked. "We've not had one come from Baneswood in quite a long time. They seem pretty happy in Baneswood. What's your realm like? Fashions changing?" He eyed Ryd's sorry beige tunic and trousers unchanged from Westerviolet, dingy and ruined from days of travel, plus the ordeal on the river.

Ryd's stomach clenched at the thought of being found out. "These aren't mine," he blurted instinctually.

"Not yours?" Odion asked.

"Aye," Ryd said, nodding, building the story in his mind. "I was attacked by raiders," he said, intentionally not mentioning Digory, "and they stripped me of my furs." They did wear furs in Baneswood, right? That sounded right to Ryd.

"Hill's Shadow?" Jelany asked him from a chair across the room. Ryd nodded.

"That does not explain why you wear those rags." Drakon's tone challenged him to respond.

"A farmer took pity on me and gave them to me," Ryd lied. "Where are you from?" he countered desperately to get the focus off himself. He hated lying.

"Me?" Drakon asked rhetorically as he scratched his triangle jaw. "Hell," he said finally. Ryd laughed at the term – from a tale used to scare Westerviolet children – but Drakon stared at him seriously.

"Wait, you're true," Ryd noted his expression. "Where?"

"Hellswater, mate."

"Hellswater?"

"Aye, all the way up the ass crack of the Missi where it meets the Rysp Lakes." Drakon took a sip from his clay cup. The others lost interest in Drakon's story as they'd heard it many times before and began to chat amongst themselves.

Ryd said, "Sounds far."

"Very."

"If it's so far, brought you here?"

"It's a long story."

"I have time."

"As you wish." Drakon shifted his weight back into the worn seat, then began. "Like I said, I'm from Hellswater. My father was a high native, ranked within the Fellowship and raised me to be one of them. My whole life I grew up to their code."

"What's the Fellowship like?" Ryd asked, wishing now he'd listened more when Digory droned on about the Kingdom. Digory probably knew what the Fisherman's Fellowship was, Ryd thought. He briefly wondered how his travel companion fared.

"The Fisherman's Fellowship started innocently enough," Drakon explained, crossing one leg over the other, sipping from his cup. "Years ago, I mean a long time ago, far before even my father was born, all fishermen banded together. First in Hellswater, then it spread down the Missi to Animus and The Confines, then to Littlebell and finally Wraithswail way south. The stories from the old days are full of hope. Father told me how the Fellowship was once the sanctuary for all natives in the Kingdom. The Fisherman's Fellowship ran orphanages in secret and even worked with Morfit and Demos during the Blood Wars to bring natives to safety."

"They sound like good guys." Ryd scratched the back of his neck. He eyed the rest of the First papers plastered across the small den's walls.

Odion interjected, heart heavy, "They used to be."

"What happened?" Ryd asked.

"They turned during the Uprising. Began taking coin from the Old and sabotaging the New," Drakon said. "Many claim the Fellowship's treachery is why the New lost."

"That's awful," Ryd said gravely. He glanced down, ashamed of his connection to Westerviolet and the role Brochet undoubtedly played.

"That wasn't the worst of it."

Ryd looked up. "What then?"

"Remember the orphanages?" Ryd nodded. "The Fellowship

sold children to the Old," Drakon said. "I hear to Graves and Brochet in particular."

Ryd's stomach dropped in disgust.

"I know," Drakon replied, noting his face. "Unconscionable. I felt the same way. It's why I'm here."

"Why?"

"When I found out I left," Drakon said, with a hint of spite. "Turns out I wasn't the only one to have the same idea."

"Why's that?"

"Hate for the Fellowship is what founded the Free boys."

"He's right," Odion said.

"You were in the Fellowship?"

"Nay," Odion said, shaking his head. "I was sold to the Fellowship by Brochet as a boy, but I escaped."

At the mention of Brochet, the hair on Ryd's neck stood up, but he ignored it. "You founded the Free boys?" he asked in growing awe.

"Not by myself." Odion's forehead deep wrinkled and his red eyes twinkled in the lacking light. "But, yes."

"He's humble," Drakon added quickly. "We owe our lives to him. He sacrificed so much."

"Why aren't you the leader?" Ryd asked.

Odion shrugged. "It doesn't suit me."

"You ran away from Hellswater then joined the Free boys?" Ryd asked Drakon, repeating his story.

"That's right, mate," Drakon confirmed in a nod. "Once I learned the whole truth. Not going back, ever."

"Why the First Papers?" Ryd pointed at Drakon's likeness sketched and pinned to the adjacent wall. "Is it illegal for natives to leave Hellswater?"

"Nay," Drakon said. "That is the case for Plusia, and that one over there," he pointed at Zoilos in heated debate with Jelany over the best way to roast fowl across the room. "They're wanted for leaving."

"What about you, then?"

Drakon took a long drink, flexing his triangle jaw, then sighed. "It's a high price to pay for freedom."

"That's not an answer."

Odion interjected. "I think that's all the answer you'll get out of him. He's not even told me what he's done. But whatever it is, Demos wants him badly for it."

"You aren't here to save the children." Ryd's face clouded as the truth of the situation became clear. "You're in hiding," he said, glancing at the walls covered in First Papers. "What did you do?"

Drakon laughed. "Now you're onto us."

"But…"

"We all are," Odion interrupted. "Every one of us is hiding."

"I thought the Free Boys took in New natives only," Ryd said, thinking back to what Digory told him and what the Morfit guard at the gates had said.

"That's what you're supposed to think," Drakon said. "It wouldn't make a good hiding place to announce its location."

Ryd turned to Odion. "What did you have to sacrifice?"

"What now?" Odion hadn't heard the question. He was distracted by Zoilos and Jelany's lively debate.

"He said that you sacrificed so much and that he owes you his life," Ryd asked pointedly, gesturing back at Drakon while staring at Odion, tiring of being on the outside. "What did you do?"

Odion leaned back and fell deep into thought. It was like Ryd had slapped him.

"It's okay if you don't want to go into it." Drakon said gently.

"It's fine," Odion said wearily. "I'll tell him."

Ryd wondered what memory could shake such a stoic soul. "What is it?"

Odion brought his hand to his temple. He shut his eyes, rubbing his head as he spoke.

"I was sold to the Fellowship as a boy to be transferred to the Omen, I overheard," he explained, terror palpable as if it happened to him yesterday. "I escaped to Littlebell, but Brochet didn't forget about me. Years passed. I'd grown and married Alice. I had a son," he said, voice cracking. He stared at the short clay cups on the table without taking one. "I thought I'd found freedom, but they found me. Finally. Brochet found me and my family. They wrenched Alice screaming from my arms," he said hollowly, reliving it as he spoke about it.

His eyes were that of a haunted man. Ryd's heart wept for him.

"They bound and gagged me and her and our boy as well. They took us down the Narrow. After a skirmish I escaped, but my wife and son were gone, taken with the *snake* Brochet's men. That was when I returned to Littlebell. I dedicated my life to saving others as I couldn't save my family. I knew they were already gone." He flexed his jaw. "Our world is dark," he added under his breath.

Ryd grunted.

"What is it, son?"

"It's nothing."

"You can speak it to me," Odion said, studying the young man's darting eyes.

"Just something my father used to say," Ryd said offhandedly, then paused, swallowing a painful stab of emotion.

"Tell us," Drakon urged.

"Our world is dark," Ryd replied, "but that wasn't the whole phrase. My father used to speak it to me during our worst times to bring me and my brother comfort."

Odion urgently sat forward in his chair and his red eyes shot open wide. "What was the whole phrase?"

"What's going on, Odion? Is everything alright?" Plusia asked him.

"But it is still beautiful."

"Odion?" Plusia asked with confusion. "Is everything alright?"

"Say it again!" Odion commanded. His eyes widened unnaturally as if they were about to budge out of his head. A vein pulsed on his forehead.

"What's happening?" Jelany looked up. Zoilos noticed the intensity in Odion's voice too and stared back and forth between Odion and Ryd, waiting for a response, prepared for a fight.

"But it is still beautiful," Ryd repeated.

Odion nearly shouted, lips curling into a smile. "The whole thing now!"

"Our world is dark, but it is still beautiful," Odion and Ryd said in unison.

Drakon looked from face to face. "What just happened?"

"Tell me," Odion eagerly asked Ryd, eyes flashing, ignoring the others, "did your father have any markings?"

"Markings?" Ryd asked. "No, I don't think..." he said, pausing as he thought. "Well, he did have one. A birthmark on his hand. I have the same one." Ryd held his hand forward to reveal a small, dark mole on the back of it.

Odion said under his breath, "I can't believe it."

"I don't under..." Ryd said carefully, putting the pieces together slowly, before pausing in shock. Odion stared intently with the widest grin Ryd had ever seen as he held his own hand out. It too had a small, dark mole on the back of it.

"Wait," Ryd exclaimed, sitting forward. "Are you my..."

"I don't know how it is possible, but it must be," Odion replied, nodding with tears shining in the corners of his eyes. "The more I look at you, you look just like my boy." His voice cracked, "I can see my dear Alice in you too. Tell me, where is your father? Oh, pray your grandmother is alive? My beautiful Alice!" the older man said excitedly. He looked like he might weep tears of joy.

"I'm sorry," Ryd said quietly. "It's... only me."

"I see," Odion said with obvious disappointment, adjusting his tunic, sniffling once. "Did you know them? Tell me." He wiped a tear then met Ryd's eyes eagerly, speaking with his hands, "please".

"Father spoke of Littlebell often," Ryd told him. "He said he'd heard stories of it. Looking back, it was strange because he knew nothing else of other realms. He never mentioned I had..." Ryd hesitated as the concept was so foreign it seemed impossible, "...grandparents."

"What of your mother?"

"I don't... I mean," he caught himself. "She died," Ryd guessed plainly.

Odion furrowed his brow. "How did my son get to Baneswood?"

"He never told me anything about his past," Ryd replied, hoping that was enough. Odion didn't press.

"What was he like?" Odion asked wistfully instead, eyes glinting joy. "My son," he said whimsically. "What kind of man did he grow to be? I lost him when he was just a boy. He was so smart. Laughed so easily. Called me 'Papa' and would scream in delight when I poked his nose. He was no more than three years."

"He was a patient man. An honourable one," Ryd said to start. "The stablemaster."

"Aye? Baneswood Stablemaster? Good to hear, a strong position," Odion said proudly, eyes distant, lost in memory. A lone tear trailed down his cheek. "How did he die?" he narrowed his eyes.

"My father was haunted," Ryd added, unsure how to explain. He decided to be blunt. "He turned to drink."

Odion sighed. "It pains me that my defix followed even him so far from my side."

"But you aren't drinking."

"Odion doesn't drink," Drakon interjected. "Hasn't since I've known him."

"I used to," Odion said, swallowing hard. "Why I lost them that day. I was drunk then. The last day ale touched my lips."

Ryd sombrely nodded, picture coming clearer now.

"Did he live a good life in Baneswood?" Odion asked hopefully. "He was happy?"

"Aye," Ryd said, not able to meet the old man's eyes.

"My dreams have come true."

"This must be a sign from Her!" Jelany grinned wide.

"Give it a rest," Zoilos growled at him. "They are busy."

"A sign?" Ryd asked. "From who?"

"The Horned Woman, of course!" Jelany said.

"Of course."

"I would be worried about if you didn't know, mate," Drakon said in half-jest. "You're her neighbour or something, is that it? Isn't Glassy Stream right there?"

Ryd laughed nervously, remembering that Digory had mentioned that place too, not having the faintest idea of where it was. "Of course, I know. Yes, it is."

"Call yourself fortunate to hail from Baneswood," Drakon told him surely, running a hand over his hair, taking a sip from his clay cup with the other. "You were born with a chance, unlike some of them."

"I'll drink to that," Zoilos grunted.

Young Uillia re-entered the room. "Will you tell us a story?" she asked Plusia. "They're asking," she added, pointing to the common den.

Plusia smiled warmly, glad to be a mother to all as she could not bear children of her own. "Surely," she told the child. "I will be right back," she said, then exited hand in hand with the slight girl.

"Like her," Drakon said, lowering his voice a bit once Plusia left. "Count yourself lucky you avoided her lot."

"Where's she from?"

"Anstout," Drakon said. "North, where it's much colder."

"I've heard of it," Ryd told him, flexing his jaw. He tried to ignore the spike of adrenaline he felt thinking about entering the realm. If he ever did get back to Digory.

"I'm sure you've noticed her skin," Drakon added, referencing Plusia's mixed hue. "It's why they wanted her."

"What do you mean? Who wanted her?"

"Graves."

"What for?"

"I don't care that the King swears they don't. I believe Plusia," Drakon said, meeting Zoilos's eyes. Zoilos nodded surely.

Ryd wasn't following. "Don't what?"

"Experiment," Jelany said.

"What he said," Drakon agreed, pointing at Jelany, nodding.

"What's she say? Plusia I mean," Ryd asked.

"That Graves tested all the children in her village and took her and a few others then killed the rest," Drakon told him, normally mischievous eyes glassed in reverence. "They kept her in the Anstout First until she was a maiden, subjecting her to Horned-knows-what. She fell in love with a prisoner. Killed him and made her watch. All for their tests."

"Oh," Ryd said, unsure how to respond. He was familiar with Vanguard cruelty. Their ways didn't shock him. He'd heard of far worse.

"Yeah," Drakon agreed, taking a thoughtful sip from his clay cup before continuing. "She doesn't talk about what they did to her, though. No details, anyway. Or how she escaped. I don't think it was pretty."

Ryd reflected on this, glancing up to Plusia's First Paper on the wall; square jaw and distinctive speckled skin apparent. "Anstout isn't friendly to natives?"

"I hope you're joking, mate," Drakon said as Zoilos chucked from across the room.

"Why would anyone live there?"

"They are born there. And they aren't permitted to leave."

"If caught, they're cut down," Zolios added in a grunt.

Ryd inhaled deeply then exhaled slowly. *Like Westerviolet*, he thought. *Great.* "I was afraid you'd say that."

"What now?" Drakon asked, raising a brow.

"I owe a debt to," Ryd said, pausing briefly, thinking how he could explain, "a friend." He pulsed his jaw.

Odion asked him, "What debt, son?"

"He helped me reach Littlebell in the search for my brother and in exchange, I'm accompanying him," Ryd explained.

"To Anstout?" Drakon asked with wide eyes. "You *are* brave. I wouldn't tell Plusia if I were you. Unless you want her to convince you not to go, herself."

"I've been assured we have safe passage."

"If you say so," Drakon said sceptically, taking a sip.

"When you return, I want you to join us," Odion said warmly, red eyes glistening, cheeks wet with happy tears. "Join me as my blood. I believe you are my lost grandson. Please, let me have back the years I've lost yearning for family."

Ryd was taken aback, not having considered what he was going to do after finding Col. "I will," he said finally.

Odion reached over to where Ryd sat and grabbed his forearm and squeezed, in typical Free Boys fashion. "It's good to have you here," he smiled, "grandson."

Ryd smiled happily at his long-lost grandfather, overwhelmed yet overjoyed, as the woman who saved him from the Fellowship entered, accompanied by a fleshy girl of the same height.

"How did training go, ladies?" Drakon asked carelessly over his shoulder as they strode into the room. Ryd's rescuer wore a red shift that clung to her breasts and waist before extending down to her calves, with a long black cloak secured with a rose brooch; an emblem Ryd had never seen.

"She's learning fast," the mystery rescuer remarked proudly, glancing to her weightier companion in a matching black cloak. "Much more advanced than I was at her age."

"Mate, meet Ed," Drakon said to Ryd, gesturing to the pair of women.

"Where?"

The room burst into laughter.

"I was waiting for this to happen," Jelany said with a wide smile.

Drakon patted Ryd on the knee. "You've done it now, mate."

"What? Her?!" he exclaimed, looking to the striking woman who pulled him from the river. "*She* is your leader?"

"Don't look so surprised," Ed spat. "My name is Edwessa. Ed, you see? Men…" She shook her curly hair dismissively before sitting in a chair aside Jelany, who handed her a cup of fire ale. She took an unflinching sip before setting it down with a hard thud. The larger young woman took a seat in the adjacent chair. She was several shades darker than Edwessa with tight thin braids that snaked all over her head and met at a point at the base of her neck, converging into a tight bun. She had ample hips and full cheeks and she kept her eyes down when introduced to Ryd.

"This is my apprentice, Luzia," Edwessa said.

"It's good to greet you," Luzia said quietly, only slightly raising her eyes.

"You too," Ryd replied, glancing back to Edwessa. "Apprentice in what?"

"I take it you've met everyone."

"I think so, if this is everyone," Ryd said.

"What do you think of Ashkeep?"

"It's… nice."

Drakon and Zoilos exchanged smirking glances.

"Nice?" Edwessa's brow furrowed. "Nice? I save your life, and your call your sanctuary *nice*?"

"*Nice* knowing you," Drakon whispered to him.

"That's not what I meant," Ryd huffed.

"It's what you said," Edwessa retorted.

"But, I really do think it's nice!" Ryd replied defensively. "I'm sorry," he added, sighing, "it's been a long day. Moon, really."

"And again," she screeched, "about the day you've had, when I rescued you!"

"Are you insane?" Ryd couldn't predict the rise and fall of this woman's mood. He'd never met one like her. It infuriated him. "What is wrong with you!"

Drakon and Zoilos winced.

The anger dropped from Edwessa's face instantly. "Be gone by sunrise," she said with eerie calm.

"What?" Ryd paused, taken aback. "I didn't mean it, I…"

"What choice do you have?" she said sharply, glaring at him with a deep brown glare before turning, then gracefully floating across the room to the door.

Edwessa paused before exiting. "Luzia, you may stay if you wish," she said to her larger companion.

The girl leapt from her seat to be at Edwessa's side. "I'd rather stay with you, Ed," she said softly. Gently smiling, Edwessa nodded once. The pair was almost out of the door into the main common den when Ryd spoke again.

"Wait, I can come back, right?" Ryd asked loudly at the

women's backs.

Edwessa stopped. Without turning to face him she said sternly, "Go, and do not come back." Her voice echoed with chilly command. "Not to Ashkeep in Littlebell. Not as long as I lead." With that, she left the room.

Drakon broke the silence Edwessa left in her wake. "What flowers would you like on your pyre, mate?"

"Is she serious?"

"Afraid so," Odion said, sighing, leaning back in his seat. He crossed his arms stoically at his chest.

"But, you founded this place," Ryd looked to his new-found grandfather. "Don't you have any power?"

Odion's heavy brow crunched in wrinkled lines. "I'll talk to her, but you can't stay now," he said. "Maybe when you come back, after that delivery you mention. Perhaps she'll change her mind. She's knows not that you are my blood. That will sway her opinion. I am sure of it."

Ryd sighed from the back of his throat. "What is wrong with her? Why is she so insane?"

"Stop calling her that, boy, if you like your head attached to your neck," Zoilos growled protectively.

"She's not crazy. She's Vanguard," Drakon told Ryd plainly.

"You lie!" Ryd was shocked. "She's one of them?"

"One surprise after the next for you," Jelany remarked.

"How did that happen?" Ryd asked. "What's her story?"

Drakon offered, "She's a Minney."

"A Minney? Is that the connection to Leo?"

"Leon," Drakon said. "And yes. He's her distant cousin through some great grandparent, or something. The story goes, way back, years ago, one of her Minney ancestors betrayed the rest of them. That branch of the family lives with Busk."

"How did Edwessa end up here?"

"Edwessa and Karl," Jelany added.

"Karl is a Minney too?"

"They escaped," Drakon told him, nodding. "They're hunted like the rest of us," he gestured to the walls plastered with First Papers.

"What happened?"

"Edwessa's grandfather was plotting to give Karl to the Omen," Drakon said. A chill descended Ryd's spine at the thought, "so she ran off with him. They came here to Littlebell to seek refuge with Lady Lalia, but she turned Edwessa away."

"Then we found her," Odion added.

"Aye," Drakon agreed. "She remade the Free Boys into what we are today."

"Here, here!" they chanted.

"How?" Ryd asked. Granted, she was skilled and fearless, but he didn't understand the group's unflinching loyalty to Ed.

"Laila and Primin were of no help to her," Drakon explained. "They do not sanction the Free Boys, in fact the opposite, but Leon sees us differently. Edwessa approached her long-lost cousin. She proposed an alliance with him and more importantly, the Bees. This is why she leads us. The alliance."

"Bees?"

"Nickname for Nis's gang."

Ryd really wasn't following. "I have never heard of such a thing."

Zoilos grunted, "Do you live under a stone, boy?"

"They sell mad honey," Jelany added pleasantly.

"Mad honey?"

"Aye, it's back, controlled by the Bees now," Drakon explained. "They ran the dens under Littlebell until Edwessa formed the alliance. Now we share," he said. "You must not get out much," he added. "I thought all knew of the Bees. They certainly distribute in Baneswood."

"I... I do not partake," Ryd said.

"She found us a real home," Jelany added with a beaming smile.

"What does Leon want in return?"

"When the time comes, for the Free Boys to recognize him as the man of Littlebell over his father and brother," Drakon said. "Then, we will no longer need live in the shadows."

"Lord Prihim is Leon's biggest worry," Jelany added. "It's not like Lord Giacomo is a threat to his elderclaim anymore."

"What happened to him?"

"He ran the Littlebell Theatre," Drakon said. "Put on glorious performances, in the Red North anyway. He was quite renowned for his Minney artistic talents like the best of them are. Except Lord Prihim, that is. Charming and witty. Lord Primin isn't. In fact, he was quite the embarrassment to his father, the rumors say, so they never saw eye to eye. But Leon was gifted like Giacomo and his father's favorite. It drew a divide through the family that pushed Primin out of Littlebell and towards his Animus Rock studies."

Ryd nodded.

"This is where Longin comes into play," Drakon went on. "You remember the tall mate from supper? The one with the rod up his ass?" Ryd nodded again. "He was a performer. I've heard he was best mates with Leon, in fact. It's Leon who got the guy hooked on mad honey then refused him. It's Leon who he blames for all his troubles."

Ryd understood more of the man's anger towards Leon Minney earlier. "What happened to Longin?"

"This was before Edwessa came," Jelany stepped in as Drakon was taking a sip of fire ale. "Longin was in line for the same role as Leon. Days before announcing the lead for his next production, Giacomo fell while preforming *Native's Revenge*. He was crippled. Hasn't woken up since."

"It was Longin?" Ryd asked widening his eyes.

"Most thought it was he who dropped the rope, because he would have benefited from the man's demise, but there was no proof," Drakon said. "Leon, being a Vanguard, caused a stir and nearly ran Longin from town with spears and torches. Even though he was never sent to the First, all Littlebell believes that Longin did it. He can't work anymore. He can barely show his face. After time begging on the street, he found his way to us."

"It's why he threw a fit earlier," Jelany said.

"Right," Zoilos agreed.

"Why?"

"He was driven from his life by Leon, then Edwessa came

and laid beside the guy," Drakon explained. "I feel for him."

"She…" Ryd trailed off, "…with her family?"

"No, no," Jelany assured, shaking his head, laughing. His chuckle was contagious and soon the room joined in. "It's a saying. It's a thing people say." He laughed more as Ryd frowned.

"Interested in women? That your game, boy?" Zoilos poked with a deep grunt. "To cunt." He raised his clay cup.

"Must you?" Jelany asked pointedly. Followers of the Faith didn't use such crass language.

"What? Are you one of Leon's boys?" Zoilos poked.

"Son," Odion cautioned. "We are friends here. Be kind."

Zoilos lowered his eyes and sheepishly shifted his weight. "Aye."

"I believe in love, that's all," Jelany defended himself. "It's in my cards."

"I'm sure it is," Drakon said, raising an eyebrow. "Not for me."

"No love for you, brother?" Jelany asked.

"I don't deserve it."

"What of the outer edges of the abandoned realms? The smaller villages? No one would find you there. It's what I dream of," Jelany said wistfully. "Why can't you have that too?"

"Not in my cards, mate," Drakon dismissed. "I promise you that."

Giving up on Drakon, Jelany looked to Ryd. "What about you?"

"Me?" His heart leapt whenever the room's attention turned fully to him.

"You, boy," Zoilos urged. "Is there cunt in your life?"

Jelany rolled his eyes again.

"Nay," Ryd said. He felt his cheeks get hot. He looked away.

"A handsome man like you without a woman?" Drakon asked sarcastically, looking Ryd up and down. "No surprise Edwessa was furious with you."

"Why?" Ryd asked, supremely confused but Drakon only

shook his head and smirked.

Jelany leaned forward, and in a whisper said, "Ed likes, well, expects... attention. Especially from a good-looking stranger like you. You're not the first she's rescued. Let's just say that."

"Don't fall for it," Drakon added smartly. "That woman is a defix herself, all due respect, surely. And it seems you haven't. Are you sure you don't have another? Edwessa is fierce but she is a beauty, and Vanguard no less. Must be quite the woman to keep your mind somewhere else."

"I met a girl," Ryd admitted, looking from man to man in the room. "I mean, woman. I mean," he paused, losing himself in the newly poignant memories from just a few days ago. "She's the most beautiful woman I've ever seen in my entire life with honey curls and a laugh like running water she makes me feel like maybe this Kingdom isn't completely full of shit."

"Wow," Drakon said slowly.

"To love!" Jelany raised his glass high, toothy smile flashing.

Ryd followed suit. Then Odion, and Zoilos. Finally, reluctantly Drakon.

"Here, here," Odion said, then set his glass down without drinking.

Jelany finished his as the others took a sip.

Ryd said, "To love," half-heartedly.

He took a sip, then coughed.

ANIMUS ROCK VILLAS

R ose sat in her appointed bedchamber in the Thorne villa. Westerviolet never quite felt like home, but at least it was familiar. Within the Thorne villa, she felt out of place, like she was intruding wherever she went. She'd walk out of her chamber and accidently disturb the native servants going about their duties, and it mortified her. How they scrambled to apologize and leapt out of her way. How they bowed so low, their heads nearly touched the floor. Maids and cooks and gardeners. The Thorne Villa had so many gardeners.

The low natives of Westerviolet were more well-hidden. Rose rarely saw them, and if she did, they did not look her in the eye nor speak. But at the Thorne Villa she was constantly confronted with their scared, wide-eyed stares and shaking hands as she approached. She felt sorry for them. She didn't like any of it.

So, Rose mostly kept to her chamber while at the villa, apart when it was time to eat. The chamber was smaller than hers in the castle, but she'd brought her sketching coal, and she had a view of the Missi and the brilliant Animus sunrises over it. Plus, she had Ellie by her side. Rose would sit most days that she didn't have to go to the Third Tower, sketching what she saw with Ellie at her feet. It was a welcome reprieve from her sketches of the countless people screaming at her, without eyes, in her sleep.

It had gotten worse of late. Ever since she fell from Westerviolet castle, before Col died, her dreams had multiplied in duration and magnitude. There were more people now. Their screams were louder. It was as if they were all trying to tell her something, all at once.

It would be maddening for most, but Rose, in a twisted way, found it comforting. The eyeless people were a constant in her life. Ever since she could remember, she'd dreamed about at least one or two of them. As she grew, there were more. Until now, at the very cusp of puberty, she saw hundreds. Maybe thousands. Or more.

LYONSHALL

"How can you stand him?" Ben asked Wolfgar pointedly. His words echoed behind the pointed nose guard and diamond eyes of his iron helmet. He was proud of the young Norland for gaining position amongst the most cut-throat of Gravesblood, but would never admit it outright, as that wasn't the Omen way.

Bennjam, who the men called 'Ben', had sickly tan skin and sunken red eyes, always appearing underfed no matter how much he ate, marking him as an Omen native instantly. He wore a black cloak secured with the Brotherhood emblem brooch. The Brotherhood's legendary spiked helmet, sharpened points catching sun on the polished tips, sat over his matted hair. On his hip was the Brotherhood standard dagger with black-polished glass blade and bone hilt etched with hundreds of fine lines; one per kill. He also wore standard Brotherhood straight sword, common in form. Just one glance at his fearsome armor was enough to send all who encountered him in the other direction. Echo's Omen Brothers were not to be trifled with.

"I've heard Quentin smells like eggs gone rotten and... and..." Ben said, then sucked on his teeth.

"Dead cat," Rex spat.

Ben laughed and pointed at the interjecting man behind him with bravado.

The group, apart from Wolfgar Norland, all laughed.

The convoy had been traveling for days, down the gentle slopes of the edges of the Cursed Hills, through wide valleys lush with overgrown mountain weeds and full of fire deer.

Although Wolfgar was the highest ranking among them, he was also the youngest and often felt left out of the older brothers' sarcastic repartee. He couldn't wait to arrive at Lyonshall and be rid of them, to start his likely precarious journey to act as a spy for Echo's Omen within the belly of Animus Rock. He sighed with relief when he realized they were nearing the Scarlet Forest.

The convoy passed one of the maples on the outskirts of the legendary woods. The whole tree burned red as they rode by. The deep-setting sun backlit the red-leafed tree as if it were on fire.

"I don't have a choice," Wolfgar said.

The weight of this latest mission lay heavy upon his shoulders. He half turned, jostling his hair in front of one close-set eye despite the heavy horned helmet. His cheeks flushed from the low-hanging sunlight.

"He'd have both your heads if he heard you, you know."

Ben blinked and grunted sincerely. "Aye," he said.

After passing the lone scarlet tree, the convoy crossed a flat expanse of grasses and burdock plants. The lanky weeds were tipped in seeds, fluffy and cotton-white to carry in the wind. It was warm for the men in their heavy Brotherhood attire and all welcomed the crisp breeze that flew down from a nearby cloud-capped mountainside, through the tall plants and grass in the meadow.

Each gust of wind threw countless seeds into the air. The seeds drifted up and then sluggishly down around them like miniature snowflakes, sticking stubbornly to their sweaty faces, dark chainmail and helmets' many horns. It was like hot, late-summer snow.

Behind Wolfgar and Ben rode three other Brothers. All five men in the convoy comically swatted at the air, thick with the white seeds.

Ben felt a large fluffy seed stick to his goatee. "Why do you ride with us?" he asked Wolfgar slowly as he plucked the seed out, examining it closely before flicking it away.

Ben turned towards Wolfgar as he attempted to toss the fluff away again, but it stuck stubbornly to the tips of his gloves. He shook his hand in the air several times before giving up and wiping his fingers on his horse's tawny flank. By then, though, he had already accumulated much more of the static-clung fluff because the meadow was wide and blanketed with these cursed weeds. Ben glanced around in futility. The Scarlet Forest loomed in the coming foreground, not too far off. He resigned to deal with the seeds until after they'd passed through the meadow.

The others behind him continued to swat and paw at the assault of fluff, chainmail clinking as they spat curses in futility behind Ben and Wolfgar.

To the First with this! one of them cried. The others chuckled in goading laughter.

"Ben," Wolfgar barked, blinking aggressively then awkwardly as a fluffy seed caught on his tawny eyelash, ruining the stoic impression he attempted to make. "I don't owe you an explanation," he said, fluff seed stuck in his eye. "I am your superior."

"Ha," Ben said. He cleared his throat, then spit at the weeds. "You are indeed."

Wolfgar frowned at Ben's playful tone as he picked the seed out of his eye.

The three Brotherhood members behind them paused their flailing to snicker at Ben's remark, but Wolfgar didn't turn. Instead, he shifted in his saddle atop a black stallion with white diamond over its right eye that no one had ever bothered to name. He straightened his back and puffed his chest, doing the best he could to ignore an itch from a new seeded piece of fluff caught on his neck. He wouldn't be made a fool of again.

"The fellows be wanting to know," Ben said as he swatted the seeded air.

"Know what?"

"Your..." Ben dropped his tone, "legitimacy as the Key. Have you..." he chose his words with great care, "consummated your participation?"

Wolfgar met his question with a sharp glare.

When a Vanguard became Key, he was presumably introduced to the deep secrets of the Omen. Including how procreation with Deadbloods was possible. Many in the Brotherhood assumed there were Deadblood women held as slaves.

"How does it work?" Ben prodded.

He, like all the Omen Brothers, was infinitely curious about the inner workings of the elite members. Despite the knowledge being forbidden, of course.

At this, all the men but Wolfgar laughed. Until Rex inhaled a fluffed seed with a choking cough, and all turned to laugh at him.

Horseshoes clipped against Bleak Path's solid rocks, moss-laden for the most part, some as long as a man's leg. Stones so heavy, local legends spoke of how they were laid by Vanguard powers long ago. Impressively, the path was carefully constructed through every mountain ridge the group scaled or meadow they passed through since the journey crossed into the Regnard realm.

If Lyonshall had a prime strength, it was surely her infrastructure.

Soon, the flaming forest of red maple trees rose up before them, draping the next hill and surrounding valleys. Bleak Path cut directly through it. This undulating landscape was dotted with clumps of basswood trees with massive sepia trunks and golden, heart-shaped leaves, glittering amongst this scarlet forest like piles of coins on fire.

The convoy suffered through the last of the fluff. The seeds floated upwards on drafts of cool air, churning, then tumbling in an early autumn blizzard. White fluff drifted to the forest floor slowly and mixed with the fell leaves on the ground in rust and mustard hues. Orange sunlight poked through plush clouds, high and full in the West, casting ribbons through the forest. It was a mystical, ethereal-feeling scene.

Wolfgar coughed then spit into the last of towering weeds. A chill descended about them, as if while sleeping someone pulled off the sheet.

The convoy clopped into the Scarlet Forest. All blinked in reverence as if entering a temple, in silent awe of the natural beauty. It truly felt otherworldly here. There was a legend that said each tree sprung from the site where a babe was slain and the trees still contained the souls of the victims, therefore locals largely avoided it, or passed through it with reverence and caution. And indeed, at the bases of many of the trees were small trinkets, carvings and even husk dolls, to pay homage to the trapped spirits. Wolfgar barely glanced at them. He didn't believe in such things. But he could appreciate the striking beauty of the forest at sunset.

The inferno-tipped maple trunks looked black without direct light, like charred like skeletons ablaze, dancing together in the swirling breeze with red leaves aflame.

The thick road of mossy stones was lined on either side with red trees, and every so often clumps of yellow-tone ones. An owl hooted. Light from the setting sun tried to poke through the fire red leaves, jumping across the men's shoulders in tiny spots and lines.

"I am the Norland Key," Wolfgar answered Ben, voice falsely deep. "I hold the title." He removed his helmet to pick off errant fluff. "I have nothing to prove." He swatted at gnats buzzing by his square-jawed face. His chainmail jostled and horseshoes clopped beneath him.

A squirrelly man with a slack jaw behind him prodded. "Aye, but did you earn it?"

"Curse you, Ugo," Wolfgar said under his breath. "I didn't ask for this." He sighed, then took a deep breath and put the fearsome, sharp-horned helmet back on his head. He buckled the fitted strap under his freshly shaven chin.

"I heard," Ben said, feeling a bit sorry for his mentee, "from one of the old Brothers that most can't take it."

"Even after passin' Assessment?" Ugo croaked from behind.

"Aye," Ben barked half backward over his shoulder, amber stallion neighing in protest as he accidentally jerked the reigns. "My apologies, fellow," he whispered to the beast. Ben leaned forward and patted his solid horse's wide neck. He had a soft spot for animals, although he didn't let the others know that.

The owl's hoots faded into the distance, absorbed by the warm inferno of trees in their wake.

"And?" Wolfgar half turned, voice metallic through the helmet. "Speak plainly Ben." He knew the man's words were about him.

"Aye," Ben relented with wide-raised eyebrows. As he shifted back and forth from the natural step of his horse, he popped his neck to the left, and then the right, with bone-crunching snaps. *Crack. Crack.* Wolfgar cringed. He hated the sound of cracking bones. "What if you're not fit," Ben said cautiously, "blood-wise?" He shifted, chainmail jostling. Clinking. "Has there ever been a Norland Key to survive?" The men behind hung in anticipation.

"How dare you!?" Wolfgar shouted with immature bravado. He swung his head and scant light sparkled off his horned helmet. He knew he had to make a point of this to be respected by the men at all. Quentin and Basil had killed Brothers for less. His hand fell to his dagger on left hip. The three Brothers behind cheered, jeering at Ben, laughing at the young Wolfgar's reaction.

"Don't let him send ye ta the Wing," Rex scratched.

"You are trying," Ben said low and deep, calmly, ignoring Rex's heckling. His aura was so peaceful it bridled Wolfgar, carefully easing him back to a casual seat atop his diamond-headed steed. "I will give you that," Ben added, gristly voice tranquil. "I meant no disrespect, just that we cannot help our own blood, is all." He paused. "You are Norland. Not Gravesblood."

"And you are earthblood."

Ben nodded and popped the knuckle in his left thumb, *Crack.* And then the right. *Crack.* Wolfgar's spine crawled, yet he kept eyes unblinking as the shoes of all five horses clopped loudly beneath them, reverberating with piercing, intensity against the thick path stones and textured bark of the passing trees. He was struck. How dare Ben suggest his blood anything less than ideal for the position of Key? Was this not his birthright?

Inherited from his brother, but still, his birthright, nonetheless.

"You didn't ask for this," Ben agreed, feeling sorry for the lad. "You can't help the sins of your brother. My own was a murdering thief." His voice caught with contempt. He remembered the look in his brother's eye as the man lost his head for his crimes. Long ago, back when he was just a boy. Ben had watched on, unflinchingly. It was in that moment, in fact, that a young Basil Graves had spotted him and recruited him for the Omen. It was then that he left his home and his life changed forever. "It didn't stop me from making something of myself, as you can too."

"Aye," Wolfgar conceded. "But," he heaved his shoulders in a steadying sigh, "I don't care who you are to me. Never insult my blood again, Ben." He shifted his gem-green eyes to study the red ones of the older, sallow-complexioned man. The three Brothers behind murmured.

Ben stoically nodded. He took a breath as if he was going to say something, then didn't. He swallowed loud, popping the knuckle in his pinkie finger instead. *Crack.*

Wolfgar cringed.

As the sun drooped, light leaked through close-grown trees and fire-kissed leaves while a beckoning birdsong rang out above them. One strong at first, then two three and four until the trees above them came alive. Wolfgar glanced up. He saw birds with grey beaks and slender bodies dancing and bobbing in flight. Nearly half of these fowl were rose-red, blending in perfectly with the fire-colored maple leaves. The other half were golden yellow, the same as the clumps of basswood trees. The birds chirped in deep-throated, melodies as they dove from thick, reaching branches, swooping from tree to tree, catching small insects, glinting blue beetles, mid-flight. He wondered what they were called.

"How's it being the youngest in the Spire?" Ben's gruff voice cut the harmonious bird song. "The youngest Key ever?"

Wolfgar shrugged. "Like I said, I didn't ask for this." He thought of Davide. He missed his older brother.

Ben interrupted, "Enough," with a sharper tone than necessary. The three following companions, chattering before amongst themselves, fell silent again, leaning forward ears first. "He fell for Basil's spawn, the fool." Ben stroked the scraggly hair on his chin with his gloved hand. "That was his fault, his path," he said, eyes narrowing within his helmet, "not yours."

Ben wished Wolfgar could understand that Davide's death had been his own fault, alone. It was not Wolfgar's burden to carry. Though this was the first the pair had spoken of it.

The maples lining Bleak Path on either side formed a bloody canopy with their overhung branches, touching over the long reach from side to side. The sun inched lower to their left, threateningly, as less and less light escaped to them through the trees. It was getting cold and dark.

Ben's words pricked Wolfgar. "What is your meaning?"

"I mean," Ben said, clearing his throat, "Davide's duty was to himself. And he failed."

"No, no," Wolfgar shook his head, blond strands glistening beneath his blackened helmet. "You say he fell for her?" Wolfgar's voice wavered, unsure. "You mean, he loved her?"

"Aye," Ben said with a chuckle. *Everyone knew he fucked her*, Ben thought. The feat was discussed with awe, in fact, as Maud Graves was as notoriously lovely as she was notoriously difficult.

Harmonious sunset crickets erupted all about the convoy in an intimidating, screeching serenade. Wolfgar stared ahead of himself wordlessly, chewing on his lip and picking at pulled leather on the saddle with his thumbnail.

"What did you think happened?" Ben half glanced to Wolfgar once, then double-glanced when he saw the young man's pained expression. The question had upset him greatly. "Better question," he asked more softly, "what'd they tell you?"

"Basil told me that Davide," Wolfgar paused and set his jaw, "raped her." The words caught in the back of his throat with a raw crack. "He told me my brother was cursed and true death was the only way to cleanse him. I didn't believe it, but Quentin confirmed it. Said he heard it from Maud, herself." Wolfgar's strong jaw pulsed. He felt like he might cry. Ben glanced to study Wolfgar's profile, then shook his head in disgust. "He didn't?" Wolfgar questioned the gesture. "Quentin lied?"

Ben held his finger up to Wolfgar briefly, looking behind him to address the companions. "Do you remember Maud, and Davide? The one put down a moon ago."

Wolfgar silently winced.

Rex smacked his thin wrinkled lips, squinting in mocking thought for an instant, then quickly said, "Aye."

Instantly, Ugo chuckled at the bad joke in an uncomfortable bark of a laugh. Wolfgar's thumb dug into the leather of his saddle as he listened, internally fuming. He painfully missed his brother. He was already silently plotting revenge for what Quentin did.

"They were fucking," the third man, Ogil, skinny with lean limbs, croaked. Like the others, he wore the dark metal horn-spiked helmet with polished pointed tips that sparkled in the final moments of daylight.

"See," Ben said, turning back to Wolfgar. "Ogil remembers."

"I don't care if," Wolfgar paused and half looked over his shoulder, "Ogil remembers. I need to know what is true. If what you say..." he trailed off, narrow eyes focusing. "It would change everything."

"Aye," Ben said. "The truth is often that way."

Wolfgar raised his head wearily.. Everything he'd built his life upon was seemingly a lie. He cleared his throat and almost said something but didn't. He scratched at his neck and finally pulled out the itchy, matted and sweaty piece of fluff from the meadow before and tossed it vindictively into the woods. The sad seed dropped to the forest floor silently.

Wolfgar finally spoke. "What about Maud?"

"What about her?"

"Basil told me she was sullied from Davide. That he," Wolfgar swallowed hard, "raped her." He pictured the striking woman's white-grey eyes and mischievous smile. "Why she was taken to the Wing." Ben shook his head 'no', and Wolfgar's piercing eyes widened. "His own daughter," he said in a whisper as the monstrous reality sunk in. His breath condensed on the chilled iron of his helmet's nose guard.

"Aye," Rex offered in a scratchy bark behind him. "That's Basil, for ya."

The group, apart from Wolfgar, all laughed.

The sun threatened to fall behind the mountain's shadow. Brilliant orange rays beamed through vivid red leaves in final concert before night. When the light did finally drop behind the craggy, squat, snow-capped mountain in the west, an icy gust whipped about them as if the woods itself missed the warmth and was in protest. The expansive Scarlet Forest dropped into dark shadow as the sky burned violet high above. In the near distance, the hooded canopy of red trees parted.

The group could see a half-circle of dim light at the end of their bloody tunnel.

"Tell us," Ben changed the subject as he popped both thumbs. *Crack, crack.* "Why Lyonshall?"

Wolfgar swung his head. "Quentin didn't brief you?"

Rex interjected from behind with a scratchy shout. "He told us you would."

Wolfgar took a deep breath and sighed. He shook his head, smirking with annoyance.

"Brainsick Quentin at it again?" Ben said.

Wolfgar snorted into a smile. "We're going to Lyonshall to check on it," he told Ben with a jaded tone. He was lost in a tumult of thoughts. Remorse for having believed the lies about his brother. And ideas of how to seek revenge.

"Check on it? What in the First does that mean?"

"There's a rebellion brewing in the New, Basil says," Wolfgar sighed, fully distracted by the news of Davide. "There's concern it's taken Lyonshall. We're to investigate."

Blanketing fog arose around them just as they exited the bloody canopy. They spilled into a lush, low-grown valley dotted with huge boulders and rocks. The screech of crickets here was particularly deafening.

"We could be walking right into a trap," Ben said, glancing to and fro across the grey-cast meadow.

"Riding, but yes." Wolfgar retorted smartly with half of a smile. As he studied Ben's worried brow, though, he added unsurely, "It should be fine." The goofy grin dropped entirely from Wolfgar's face.

Ben shook his head as they rode the declining path into the deep fog.

"Splendid," he said, smiling ironically, squinting. Despite his evolved vision, Ben was barely able to see anything at all in this magic light of dusk. The same with dawn. He could see perfectly in day or night, but when the light was in between, they were nearly blind. All natives were that way.

This sloped meadow was covered in short-grown rockroses. Rock roses were flowering growths that bloomed directly from stone. They had no roots or soil, or apparent need for water. They should not exist, but they did anyway.

Rock roses were said to appear where human intent lingered, in places of vows, or judgements made, or executions carried out. The stone was said to remember pressure, and the rock roses responded to it. Their powered petals were used by Regnards of old to create ink specifically intended to sign treaties or oaths.

The rock roses' pointed leaves were darker on one side than the other and their short-lived golden blooms were already wilting brown in a day. All about the convoy wafted morose decaying floral notes, as if the whole valley was a blooming morgue.

"Keep your eyes open for rosebears," Ben warned when he noticed the rockroses. Rosebears loved them and were plentiful in Lyonshall's mountains. It's where the bloodline got their emblem from. The Regnards of old were said to have tamed them and used them as other bloodlines used horses. But there was no proof that the legends were true. Apart from the massive Rosebear tooth necklace the elder traditionally wore, of course.

The convoy passed through the rockrose meadow to scale the next crest then they rounded a sharp bend. The low valley disappeared behind them into the engulfing blackness of dwindling twilight as they scaled the mountain face. The sun was gone but the memory of it remained in sapphire streaks along the western sky.

Far ahead, rising through the heavy fog, was the backlit monstrosity of Lyonshall. It's five red-stone towers looked like blood-stained fingers rising threateningly from the mountain on the northwest ridge, like the mountain itself had a hand clawing up through it.

"Looks alright to me," Ogil chimed pleasantly, eying the massive fortress with widening eyes. None in the convoy had travelled to Lyonshall before. It was rare Brotherhood members left Echo's Omen's realm. The excitement the Brothers' collectively felt was palpable.

The crickets' symphony all around them droned as Wolfgar groaned to himself. He kept his eyes on the path ahead.

The ancient Vanguards constructed Lyonshall Castle on an isolated outcropping nestled into hard mountain-rock above this wide valley of rare rockroses. It's five pentagonal towers surrounded a gigantic copper dome. A mighty curtain wall encapsulated the compound despite her precarious elevated location. A misty, pastel-green mountain lake shared the outcropping with the castle and was rumoured to have healing powers, yet it was strictly forbidden to swim in or drank from, except by the elder of Lyonshall, so the rumor could never be tested. Her curtain wall bisected the foggy waters and a dazzling, glinting waterfall cascaded from the western mountain's cliff. Water flew from the mountain's rocky precipice in a torrential churning pour until pooling in a small river at the base. Black-trunked scarlet trees identical to those in the forest before were planted all about the lake and engulfed the north-western portion of the castle's grounds.

All five of the castle's pentagonal towers jutted from a rounded, fortified base constructed of modest red rocks marbled black in tiny streaking lines that looked like frenzied lightening on close inspection. Each tower and post along the mighty curtain wall were topped with a blood-red triangular flag bearing the Regnard roaring rosebear emblem.

Bleak Path led them upwards towards the castle, cutting directly through solid stone, revealing layers of pressed rock in greys, blacks, and browns from the weight of time. The mountain's solid rock faces grew upwards on each side of the convoy, high reaching above them, only wide enough for two men to ride abreast comfortably through the narrow gap. The men fell in line behind one another with a thin sliver of blackening dusk visible straight up as they scaled the climb. The rocky walls did not have deep etchings where tools carved the pathway, chisel by chisel, in ancient times. It was unknown how the pass was created. Although every so often, marks from spears or sword-falls were apparent, evidence from long-ago wars. Moisture leaked from the face and tender moss grow in lush, vibrant patches. Rex and Ugo glanced around warily. Ogil, who had fallen behind the others and now rode at the back of the caravan alone, shuttered and placed his left hand instinctually to his dagger. The only faint light filtered in through the crevice from emerging stars above.

Ben leaned closer to Wolfgar and spoke barely above a whisper. "I know you can do this," he said. "It's what we've trained for." He met eyes briefly with his young mentee, down-turned red gaze glinting. "I follow you, my Lord," he added with reverence..

Wolfgar smiled in a boyish grin. "Thanks Ben," he said with clear gratitude then shifted forward again in the saddle, goofy smile falling slowly from his face. He puffed chest a bit further and set his brow. He fell into a contemplative lull, preparing himself for what was about to come.

Lyonshall was built deceptively high on the mountain she sat on. It took much longer to scale than it seemed like it should. The convoy trekked until the sharp inclined walls flattened out in a gravelly courtyard leading up to dozens of stone buildings with sharp pointed rooves, arched doorways, and no windows. Nearby, a gaping entry to a cavernous mine shaft. Dozens of broad-shouldered, square-torso workers in once-burgundy red jumpsuits, now rubbed black from soot and rubble, filtered in and out of the mine wheeling carts full of various minerals.

Nearly all were barely out of childhood and male or appeared to be, with very short ash-white hair regardless of age. Almost all had a top lip bigger than bottom, upturned noses, and extremely small ears. All had dead expressions on their faces.

It was night now, pitch black outside, and the Lyonshall miners toiled without any direct light. Their cart wheels creaked and bare feet crunched against rock. Illumination did come from Lyonshall, though, in the form of enormous fiery torches lining the last leg of Bleak Path up the slight mountain incline. The torches cast jumping, shadowy light across the workers and the incoming convoy.

"Is that it?!" Rex interjected, like nails against glass. "Those Reddie bastards complain 'bout a cursed paradise!"

"That's the precious mine, you fool," Ben half turned. "Look there." He pointed into the distance. Now that they were nearly at the top of this mountain they could see into the next valley. Down there was a dark metropolis of workhouses, dormitories and processing plants all centred around a series of mines as far as the eyes could reach along the mirroring meadow. Lyonshall's city. Hundreds of thousands of souls pulsed in black dots, exactly like ants.

Rex didn't respond. He swallowed in a solemn gulp, nodding once with a clink of his shifting helmet. Humbled, he lowered his head and allowed his black and white spotted horse carry him the rest of the way, following the others with slow, tired steps up the stone road.

When the convoy approached the curtain wall they felt hot fire against their cheeks. The crickets' hum died down with only one now and then chirping on and off. Icy and unforgiving wind whipped about them causing black cloaks to billow out behind the men with horn-tipped helmets atop their steeds. Lyonshall's red painted front gate creaked wordlessly open for them as they approached.

Wolfgar glanced to Ben then steeled eyes forward. "We go in," he said, moving first as leader into the daunting five-towered fortress.

Ben smiled to himself with pride. The boy may yet become a

man. "You heard him," he grunted stoically at other men while keeping feelings hidden, trotting through the Red Gate into the gaping mouth of Lyonshall.

The others exchanged wary glances, then followed Ben dutifully inside.

Lord Lachlan Regnard, Lyonshall elderclaim, held his hand out in front of himself, first palm out then palm in to examine his yellow fingernails. His fur-lined burgundy cloak flapped against his thin wrists.

"Xoana's boy, eh?"

His quaking voice reeked unpleasant accusation as he dropped his hand into his lap. He'd never been very keen on his youngest, ugliest daughter, although she worshiped him. The old man studied Wolfgar behind shaded spectacles from a slouched position in the elevated seat. He was fading in his old age, as most of the Kingdom's elders were, and was exceedingly moody as well as notoriously paranoid. His surly disposition wafted from him like a vile stench.

Wolfgar stood in the shadow of Lyonshall's extravagant throne carved from one breathtakingly huge red gem. It towered high in enormous, glittering, near-clear terminations pointed at the ceiling. Although only dim oil fixtures lit the massive hall, the Red Throne inexplicably glowed.

A stained-glass window spanned the wall above the throne from the crystal terminations to the vaulted roof, depicting a fearsome rosebear wearing the Regnard banner with ferocious teeth and sharpened claws tearing apart a native man. The beast ripped innards from the body with its claws and teeth in gruesome detail. Wolfgar studied the impressive glass, unlit and lifeless in the dead of night.

Red Plumes stood in formation along each side of the rectangular hall behind massive pillars in front of finely crafted ceiling-height tapestries lining the walls.

"Yes, Lord Lachlan." Wolfgar shifted his weight but not his eyes away from the stained-glass. It was legendary throughout the Kingdom. A masterpiece. "I am Wolfgar Norland," he said confidently, tone echoing loudly about the massive hall.

"I thought Basil put you down?" Lachlan asked slowly. He eyed the boy's strong jaw with thinly veiled jealousy. Oh, how he'd always dreamed of looking like a proper oldblood. A proper Vanguard. How he'd yearned to be accepted as one of them. He hated the boy instantly for being everything he was not.

Wolfgar swallowed hard. "That was my brother."

Lachlan removed his spectacles to get a closer look at the boy, revealing bright red eyes to match his throne. His next words tumbled from his thin lips already tinged with suspicion.

"Why are you here?"

Long grey hairs of Lachlan's eyebrows bobbed as he furrowed his brow. He wore a heavy cloak, in his bloodline for centuries, burnt burgundy red on the outside lined in plush rosebear fur, bunched tightly all around his sinewy neck, and too loose at the sleeves. A bone necklace with dozens of rosebear teeth hung across the chest of his thigh-grazing red tunic, secured with a wide black belt high on his pouched waist, embroidered with shining black thread. He had tight grey trousers to complete the ensemble, puckering and loose against thin legs, tucked into ankle-high shiny black boots with pointed toes. A traditional look that had long since fallen out of fashion. But Lachlan hadn't been to Animus Rock for so long that he didn't know. He thought he looked wonderful.

"There have been reports of trouble here at Lyonshall," Wolfgar said carefully, despite his nerves. "The Omen is an ally, Lord Lachlan. Basil sent us to check on you."

Ben winced from his position behind the young Key.

"Check on me?!" Lachlan shouted, tiny flecks of spittle spraying from his mouth. "As if I am a child," he muttered, more to himself this time, shifting his jaw, shoving his lower out further than his upper, buckling it in a sickening pop.

Crack. Wolfgar cringed. "Gravesblood never gives me due," Lachlan whined on. He shook his fist. The tooth necklace clanked loudly. "Not once! Even after I ended the cursed Uprising myself! Ungrateful scum. I don't trust one of them. Not one!"

As Lachlan shouted, the scant light illuminated his pale, pasty skin and coarse blonde hair. It was greyed and patchy in his old age, yet untrimmed and lengthy where it could grow with long unruly tufts clinging to the sides. In comparison, the top of his head was shiny bald. His eyebrows were light and barely visible, yet scarily long and swept back to pass the corners of his red eyes. His features were expectedly Vanguard apart from his eyes, with Regnard upturned nose and weak chin. Lachlan's world-weary skin was papery, wrinkled, and pallid. His fingernails were markedly long, especially on his pinkies and thumbs.

He was hideously ugly.

"That isn't it, my Lord."

"What, then?"

"We have a great deal of respect for you. For your strength, and the legacy of Regnard and the storied castle of Lyonshall," Wolfgar gestured around, heart thumping in his chest. "For your courage."

"You didn't get your oratory skills from your mother," Lachlan said dryly, clearing his throat of phlegm with a snort. "She was never quite so eloquent." He thought briefly of his stubborn, yet fiercely loyal daughter. The only one of his spawn who had not disappointed him. And yet, she looked so much like him, he hated her.

"My Lord, I speak truth. Basil admires you," Wolfgar lied quickly.

His companions from the Brotherhood shifted nervously back and forth behind him. He could feel it.

Ben eyed Wolfgar's closely as he whispered under his breath, "I hope you know what you're doing, Key," to which Wolfgar shot him a half-backwards glare.

The legendary Regnard forces, the Red Plumes, stood at

attention all throughout the colossal throne hall. They looked like statues they were so dutifully still. The walls behind them were alive with the flickering light upon black striped stones and red-tone tapestries. Wolfgar noted the Red Plumes briefly, intrigued by the mythical lore surrounding them and their ostentatious adornments. He'd listened wide-eyed to the stories about them since he was a small child.

They bore pristine, mirrored silver armor from head to toe with matching silver metal helmets tapered to a rounded point at the crown, tipped in a long, looping red feather plumes in dazzling red, from where they got their name. The finely crafted helmets' faceguards folded forward during assault to block the eyes, leaving only tiny viewing slits, but now, at this peaceful hour, all the Red Plumes' helmets were at ease, tacked back, folded up then back over the top of the head, to give the men a better view and less intimidating countenance. They stood in formation at both ends of the chamber, congregating around the red crystal throne and the high-arched, black-column lined entry to the Throne room from the castle's central copper-domed round hall at the far end. Everything about them was still. Even their faces were blank.

"The *dead* admire Lachlan the Mighty? I'll say, it is about time," Lachlan grumbled before standing like a stone statue creaked to life, slowly moving toward his grandson. "They are Brotherhood?" Lachlan gestured with a shaking hand to Ben and the others, quite obviously wearing Brotherhood attire. His bone necklace rattled against his skeletal chest.

"Aye. I speak for them," Wolfgar said. "Good men."

"No such thing," Lachlan said with a half-smile. He coughed again and his necklace jangled loudly. Then, Lachlan fell into a fit of hacking before clearing his throat and, with much effort, righting himself.

"When's the last time you spoke to your son?"

Lachlan looked up. "Ogo?" His son was everything he'd hoped for in a boy - strapping, pale, green-eyed. But sadly, his mind was New. "Lost cause," he said with a wrinkled nose. "Sent him away." He shuffled forward across the dark stone floors, slowly.

Wolfgar removed his helmet. His handsome, boyish face was dirt-streaked and sweaty, and his piercing eyes were determined as he planned his next words cautiously. "Have you gotten word from him at all?"

"Nay," Lachlan grumbled. His pointed boots scuffed softly as he lugged his feet with limping, listless gait and the train of his impressive fur-lined cloak dragged idly behind him on the floor.

"Why not?"

"I have no desire," Lachlan croaked slowly. "It offends me to look at him. I'd cut him down if he weren't my blood."

Wolfgar felt Ben's apprehension growing without having to look at him. He ignored it. "Why?" he asked.

Lachlan's face reddened. "The boy's a traitor. He votes New. Can you imagine the betrayal? He's just as my father was. It's my nightmare become real. He does it to trifle with me and get attention. Ogo just wants attention," he barked, sickly visage curling into a disgusted frown. "Always has."

"He only votes New to undermine you?"

"Aye," Lachlan replied quickly, red eyes questioning Wolfgar's gem green.

Wolfgar blinked once. The old man reminded him of a withered old tree, knotted and dying – reaching - too far from the light. "Could he want more?" he asked.

Lachlan narrowed his gaze. "He plans to rise up against me? His own blood?" He paused, long-bushy brows dancing, red eyes wild and sceptical. "He would not *dare* do that to me. He has newblood ideas but, but, he is my blood and he is loyal to me," Lachlan croaked, spittle sticking in a string between his thin, dry lips. "He is my boy." He'd always imagined having a son, teaching him how to gut a fish, how to polish his sword, or how to give a proper Vanguard greeting. Although he'd never admit it outright, Lachlan still had hope that Ogo would come around and be the son he had always dreamed of. He toyed with a particularly curved, sharp tooth at his necklace's point, picking at it with long fingernails as he pontificated.

"Ogo respects me and my place as elder of Lyonshall. He knows why I do this. It's bigger than he can understand. It's the Vanguard aims we were born for!"

At that Lachlan raised a mangled hand and erupted in a cheer, to which the Red Plumes together stomped their feet twice, creating a lurching echo as if thunder had cracked within the hall. Then Lachlan lowered from his cheer painfully, wincing loudly as he buckled forward. He rubbed his lower back and groaned. An attendant emerged from the shadows in a pristine red, tight-fitting suit with her white-grey hair pulled in one long simple braid down her back. She hurried to Lachlan's side and clung to his arm to steady him, but he shoved her away.

As in Westerviolet, only the most beautiful of natives were chosen to be castle maidens.

"Can't you see I'm fine," he croaked angrily at her, cheeks blushing to match the tapestries. He slowly righted himself with his face scrunched in scorn. The lovely white-haired attendant scurried back into the shadows.

"Aye," Wolfgar nodded at Lachlan's fervour after glancing curiously at the fleeting woman. "But, my Lord… What if you're wrong?"

Lachlan slowly hobbled towards Wolfgar. "What did you say, eh? How dare you insult the Lord of this realm, your elder and blood!" His blood-specked eyes glowered red like his throne even behind his spectacles as he inched up to Wolfgar's face. At the outburst, Wolfgar's Brotherhood companions, including Ben, stepped back several paces into a wide, black column's shadow. Wolfgar was left to bear the brunt of the notoriously unstable Lachlan Regnard's wrath alone.

The vast differences between the two men were clear as they stood face to face in the near center of the dimly lit hall. They looked nothing alike despite the relationship of grandfather to grandson. Wolfgar had thick blond hair that parted to one side in comparison to Lachlan's coarse untameable balding curls. Wolfgar's skin had honey undertones, while Lachlan's was pallid with shades of sickly green. Wolfgar had a strong, masculine jaw, while Lachlan's was drooping and slack.

Wolfgar had piercing green eyes while Lachlan's were dull, squinted and red. Wolfgar was taller than the old man and broader. He looked down at him.

"My Lord," Wolfgar said firmly. He met Lachlan's indignant gaze with calm and poise, "I am here on duty. It would be treason to back away, to not ask you this," he said, bringing his hand cautiously to dagger hilt. "I would betray my Brotherhood and the alliance with Regnard. Worse, to defy my mission would be to betray our relationship. Our blood."

"Aye?" Lachlan absorbed his grandson's fervour. "Join me." Lachlan rested one boney hand on Wolfgar's shoulder with unexpected familiarity. His long fingernails caught on the fabric of Wolfgar's cloak.

Alas, before Lachlan could say another word, he was interrupted by a sickening crash.

A flaming boulder barrelled through the stained glass above Lachlan's patchy balding head. Wolfgar impulsively tackled Lachlan, tossing his helmet aside with a metallic scrape across the floor. Lachlan's spectacles fell. Wolfgar shielded the old man from glass shrapnel with his heavy Brotherhood cape as ancient multi-coloured shards of every size rained down about the hall. The beautifully morbid stained glass of Lyonshall was gone.

"Guards!" Lachlan's old voice cracked pitifully. He again screamed louder, "GUARDS!" from underneath Wolfgar. The Red Plumes were already running from numerous side rooms and hidden spaces to join the others in formation. They encircled their Lord, enclosing him in a half-ring of silver armor and swords facing towards the arched entryway to the Throne Hall. Their backs were to the shattered glass window.

Lyonshall had never been breached before. One could feel the surprised panic reverberating about the hall, despite the steeled and resolute jaws of the Red Plumes. Wolfgar's heart pounded in his chest as he felt his elderly kin's skeletal frame beneath him, shuttering in fury and doubt.

In the back of his awareness, Wolfgar noticed a faint tone begin to play. The tone crept around the standing army. It seemed to infect each Red Plume, one by one. Each soldier's posture slouched and their eyes began to open up wide, as if they'd just awoken from a long dream, all of them together, at once.

Then, sickening thuds and screams erupted as a shower of fire-tipped arrows rained down through the shattered space where the stained glass had been above the Red Throne. Men shouted and cried, scattering as they were skewered with heavy arrows from behind. The arrows were unbelievably able to pierce the storied Red Plumes' impenetrable armor. Instantly, the men fell out of their tight formation despite Lachlan's commands. Soon the room erupted in a frantic panic. All hurried to escape the flaming onslaught, clamouring past Lachlan and Wolfgar through the high-arched doorway. On the other end of the round copper courtyard was the exit herself; a massive red door reaching the height of five men. The only way out of Lyonshall's castle, or in.

"Stand firm you fools!" Lachlan cried to his troops at the top of his lungs. "Stand firm!" The Red Plumes ignored his screams, or couldn't hear him, for they were screaming themselves. Arrows skewered most and others were simply on fire; many with their red plumes ablaze. It was unnerving to see the legendary troops panic and fall. It was like watching a god bleed.

"That is our last defense!" Lachlan sputtered. He was in shock at the men's impossible betrayal, clutching his side. He pulled himself across the chilled marble floor despite Wolfgar pulling him back. Never in all his years had he seen a Red Plume disobey. Not once! *They would throw themselves from a cliff if commanded*, he thought. He watched his soldiers clamouring towards the main gate's enormous door. "They will soon be over the wall, you fools! Curses!" Lachlan growled at his men. "The gate is all that is left! We must not fall into their trap! It's the only way in! Don't you see!?" He wailed pitifully from the ground, not able to comprehend why the men broke ranks. Such disobedience should be impossible. It was impossible. And yet... "Do not do as they wish! Do not open the gate!"

One, then two bodies dropped heavily on Wolfgar's back, flailing, pierced with deadly arrows. Both fell silent within seconds. The dead weight lay heavy on the young man, especially while pulling Lachlan back and dodging stampeding footfalls. It took a moment for Wolfgar to realize it was his companions Ogil and Ugo who had fallen upon him, laying with mouths agape and eyes half-open amidst the countless, bloodied, fallen Red Plumes with their silver armor pierced by blackened arrows. Men either writhed in agony or laid silently in pools of blood.

Wolfgar wanted to mourn for his Brothers. But there was no time. Still, guilt nagged at him for leaving their daggers behind.

Lachlan continued to desperately scream. His soldiers took no heed. Dozens of them opened the front gate. It creaked open slowly with a morbid groan to Lachlan's dismay. He watched from the chaotic Throne Hall. Panicked Red Plumes and white-haired maidens alike rushed past each other in a frenzy towards the door, pushing and shoving to escape the flurry of arrows at their backs. Many screamed in agony as they were trampled on the ground, trapped in the stampede. Wolfgar had never witnessed a more horrible scene. And he had been privy to a decade of Brotherhood dealings.

"Stop! Stop!" Lachlan wailed. He reached towards the chaos and Wolfgar pulled him back, watching shadows dance to cries of the dying. He swallowed hard and ground his jaw. Although he was well accustomed to death, he never got used to it. It sat poorly with him each time.

The draped red tapestries lining the Throne Hall between each massive black column caught fire with the first arrows. Now, colossal flames lapped up to the vaulted red and black stone ceiling. Flaming arrows littered the walls. Embers floated down like glowing rain. Wolfgar's nose pricked at the scent of singed hair and flesh. The floor was sprinkled in colored shards from the destroyed stained glass. The enormous, still flaming boulder lay atop the shards in the near center of the hall. A cool evening breeze rushed into the hot room from the gaping opening above the Red Throne as everything burned; lapping flames lit up Lachlan's upturned nose, dark-circled eyes, and gaunt cheeks with ghastly detail.

"You've lost them, my Lord," Wolfgar said.

He scanned the bedlam for Ben, hoping he hadn't fallen.

Hot tears leaked freely down Lachlan's wrinkled cheeks. "It does not end this way," he said, bone necklace jangling as he wiped a tear from his face proudly. "It does not," he growled louder. "Not like this."

Lachlan steeled in anger.

Wolfgar met his grandfather's panic-stricken red eyes. "My Lord," he said gently over the din, "it is lost."

"No!" Lachlan shouted and pushed Wolfgar with all his feeble might. This time, out of frustration and exhaustion, Wolfgar let the old man go. The warm, dead bodies of his Brothers rolled lazily aside. "My life is not for nothing!" Lachlan wobbled upright. "It does not end this way!" He put one hand on one knee, and then the other and with much effort brought himself to stand.

"My Lord," Wolfgar said, "we must try to escape." He realized their chances of survival were slim, especially in light of the betrayal of the Red Plumes, as he glanced around the ruined castle. But he still had to try.

"There is no escape," Lachlan said. He bravely held his polished ceremonial sword out towards the open entryway.

"My Lord there is always…"

"Not once they finish opening that gate there isn't," Lachlan interrupted without taking eyes off the massive red door, visible through the center of the castle. "The only way in, or out."

Wanting to protest but not knowing what to say, Wolfgar stepped back. He heard the red door clank fully open at the far end of the castle. He still didn't see Ben.

Morfit troops flowed in like water through a burst dam. They had golden armor, single spiked helmets, and matching cowl-neck capes. Most bore curved gold-tone swords with varying colored tassels and jewels on the hilt. Others had bows and arrows. These golden troops used their curved weapons to expertly cut down the Red Plumes and white-haired natives alike. The Red Plumes didn't even fight. It was if they didn't know how. Bodies fell left and right as the gilded invaders stormed into the throne hall. They fought with sweeping and jumping motions, boots crunching over red glass.

"Stand firm!" Lachlan shouted. He paced like a mad man. He screeched at the soldiers and was ignored, although one did bump into him while running. Blood-curdling screams echoed throughout the castle as the attackers cut everyone down. The strange tone still buzzed in the background. This horrifying frenzy swarmed beneath the central copper dome, right outside the black-stone columns marking entry to the throne hall.

"Stand firm!" Lachlan repeated, voice cracking. Another tear dropped down his cheek. "I command it, as elder of Lyonshall!" Yet his men continued to flurry about like a hive doused in smoke.

The flames lapping the hall's tapestries roared louder, illuminating the space in fearsome red shadows, casting an orange glow over the terrible onslaught. Then, the flaming arrows stopped.

A throaty chuckle cascaded over the massacred throne room.

Lachlan rose to meet the intruder indignantly. "Face me as a man!" he bellowed, ceremonial sword trembling in his outstretched hands. "Show yourself!"

The foreign troops marched into the Throne Hall like spilled gold and quickly surrounded the remaining Red Plumes, corralling them with their backs to the Red Throne. Wolfgar smartly unfastened his Brotherhood cape and armor quickly as well. He also dropped his sword. He tucked his dagger far beneath his undertunic as he followed the others, blending into the group backed up against the throne.

"You!" Lachlan shouted. He shakily pointed his sword at the intruder. It was Ogo. His son. A middle years man with a permanent sneer. He wore strange, silver-hammered armor, emblazoned with the emblem of a rockrose. The soldiers in gold parted as the man in silver walked towards Lachlan, lifting his long legs high to step slowly over crumpled bodies. "You!?"

Lachlan shouted again, shaking his head in disbelief. His tears flowed freely now. "Why?" He sounded very small.

"Don't embarrass yourself," Ogo said dismissively, biting his thumb nail, other hand on his curved sword's hilt. This man appeared to be far more of a Thorne than a Regnard, although in his veins flowed both bloodlines' blood.

"What is that, Ogo?" Lachlan asked angrily, pointing his sword at his son's chest. "Traitor!"

"It's Regnard's new emblem," Ogo replied snidely. "You are through, old man. The Old and her tired ways are a thing of the past. It is time for the rockrose to overtake the rosebear. You have corrupted our name for too long. I will not, cannot stand for it any longer!"

"Corrupted? No…" Lachlan's eyes darted, "I elevated it! My grandfather sullied everything. I… I brought us back to helm! Put Lyonshall back on her true path."

"True path," Ogo scoffed with a half laugh, walking forward, boots crunching through glass. "Old man, there is no true path. Look around you. Watch your Lyonshall burn. There is nothing in this world except what we make of it, ourselves."

"Blasphemy!" Lachlan shouted. His thin lips curling in disdain, red eyes on fire to match the hall. "We are what the old gods made us! How can you not see that everything we owe is to the Ancestors' aims? Our duty, nay, birth right, is to follow the Vanguard work!"

Ogo shook his head. "You are so blind. Can't you see how power and greed have corrupted you?" He brought a hand to his temple. "The Vanguard is a lie."

"Watch your tongue."

"Think," Ogo countered. "I know what it is I've been told, what the Vanguard traditions are, cursed First we celebrate the Landing each year, but what proof is there of the Landing? Of the old gods? Of Vanguard power? To me it seems like a story to put few above many, nothing more."

Lachlan gasped. "Blasphemy!" he screamed. "I have seen the ship, itself. The Vanguard. Near Creed Point. She exists!"

"Aye," Ogo said glibly, nodding, blonde hair glinting in the firelight. "But you believe man flew to the stars in her?"

"Son," Lachlan said, voice trembling, "have you lost mind!? We... we are Vanguard. There is nothing else. You must look at the bigger view, my boy. It's more than just you, or I. Our legacy is our cause!" he cried.

"I pity you, Lachlan." Ogo walked closer, illuminated by the flaming tapestries in a brilliant display. Shadows danced across the man's striking features as he approached his hunched, ugly father. "You are trapped by the past. By a lie! What is real is what is now. Our legacy is what we do, right now. Your legacy is one of despair."

"You don't know what you speak of. You are a child!"

"I speak truth," Ogo countered, face clouding. He was no child and wanted to slap his stupid father for suggesting such. *It is he who is the child*, Ogo thought. "If not for you, the Kingdom would be more evolved by a century, or more. The people would be free! Instead, you set us back before the Blood Wars." His voice dripped malice while he paced back and forth. "You kept me here, at this fortress, this prison. You tried to corrupt me." He thought back to his boyhood years, before he was sent to Animus Rock for Academy. How he was taught to blindly hate, without purpose. Taught that the natives were less than Vanguards, hardly better than beasts. How his birthright was some kind of ridiculous yet elusive blood power. He cringed, remembering his previous mindset, before he truly saw the reality of the Kingdom. "I was trapped. I knew nothing of the way the Kingdom really was."

"How can you say that about your blood home? I kept you safe here! I protected you!"

"You imprisoned me here to control me."

"The lunatics at the Rock corrupted you," Lachlan muttered. "It is their fault you betray me."

"They opened my eyes!" Ogo shouted, losing all feigned calm. Despite all his studies, he could not shed his Regnard temper. In that way, he was still his father's son. "Opened my eyes to your betrayal," he added in spite. His long strides jostled his black chainmail with a resolute clink at each step.

"They taught me what you did." He bit at his thumb nail again. He tasted blood but couldn't stop. It was a habit he couldn't help.

Lachlan's long-haired eyebrows parted defensively. "For the greater good! Our cause is more than the lives of *earthblood.*"

Ogo's striking visage darkened. "Do not call them that," he said, pointing a quick-bitten finger with such aggression that his hair jostled out of place. "You speak of my blood. Your own blood!" Ogo screamed.

"It doesn't matter. That is what you can't see. It's bigger than us."

Ogo shook his head. "You are insane." He smiled manically. "I don't know why I gave you a chance to speak. Foolish me, thinking you would see it my way. I should have known."

"What do you expect?" Lachlan's old voice echoed amidst dying cries and the rumbling flames engulfing the hall. "You burn your blood home down. The greatest Vanguard castle of all."

Ogo scathed back, "This was never my home," with shadows pooling beneath his eyes, as if he was possessed by a defix. "I am ashamed of you," he said evenly. "You are no father of mine."

"Ogo," Lachlan pleaded. His eyes glassed from the blow. He stepped forward, voice softening, inwardly surprised at how his son's words slashed him. He felt like his heart was shattered like the storied stained glass littering the floor. "Do not speak that way. It's not too late, never! We can rebuild. You can join me. Together, we will pursue the aims we were destined to. The birth right of our blood! You don't have to continue down this path of..."

Ogo looked away. "Stop," he said.

Lachlan took a wobbling, hopeful step. "Together we can do it all, my boy."

"Enough!" Ogo shouted, eyes shining. "It's too late for that."

"Why?" Lachlan took another step. "I've lost everything." He looked around at his grand castle on fire. "Must I lose you, too?"

"You lost me long ago."

"Son..."

Ogo cried with all the breath in his lungs, "When you murdered mother!"

Wolfgar listened on closely, careful not to be noticed. Even he, from his sheltered upbringing at Echo's Omen, knew Lachlan's story. How the Uprising ended. And the horror of what happened to Lilwen when Lachlan surrendered their daughter to Wallace.

"Is that what this is about?" Lachlan lowered his heavy sword in trembling hands slightly. "You know I never laid a hand on her," he said. "I loved her," he added hollowly. And he had, in his own way.

Mind already made up, Ogo wasn't listening. He smelled blood. "You drove her to it!"

"I had no choice!" Lachlan countered pitifully. "Wallace is the reason I'm here, you're here. I couldn't refuse. I had no choice!"

"That is where you're wrong," Ogo said. He stepped to his father until he was a sword's distance away. "There is always a choice."

"Son," Lachlan pleaded. "It is not too late," he said, half-meaning it, holding his sword up once more in terribly shaking hands.

Ogo swung and knocked Lachlan's weapon away with a long-stride step and expert motion. It fell with a clank, sliding across the dark stone floor until thudding into a charred body.

"Son, please." Lachlan's gaze darted as he put his hands up and backed away.

"Don't call me that," Ogo said, vision pulsing from anger. "I am not your son." He lifted his sword and stepped forward, reminding himself of his plans. How everything hinged on this. All about him the fire burned hot. Sweat beaded on his brow and temple. His cheeks flushed red. Anger thrashed in his chest. Anger he'd held deep inside since childhood, dealing with his father's outbursts, hiding in fear from his unpredictable ways.

Lachlan cowered, trembling, unable to accept his impending fate. "It's the way it's always been! I had no choice. Son, please!"

Wolfgar watched with wide eyes with his back against the Red Throne in the cluster of Red Plumes prisoners cornered by the golden soldiers. He desperately wanted to step in. To save his grandfather. His own blood, no matter how wretched it may be. He decided against it at the last moment, choosing to follow his mission instead.

Wolfgar watched Ogo lift the heavy sword in his hands then shout in a guttural yell as he swung it down, swiftly into where Lachlan's wrinkled neck met his shoulder beside his ostentatious rosebear cape. Lachlan instantly crumpled. His old skin exploded in a gush of bright blood.

Ogo was quickly drenched in it, dripping from his eyebrows, nose, and lips.

Then, Ogo spit blood at the corpse.

"I said, don't call me that."

He ran one hand through his flaxen hair spattered red while holding the still dripping sword in his other. He'd thought his father's death would bring his soul peace, but the anger thrashing in his chest grew stronger.

The fire crackled and roared. Moans and cries were quieting down. The golden troops systematically executed the dying in the background. Oscar Morfit, son of Rupert, a young man much shorter than Ogo with black-lined brown eyes approached him from the side.

"What of the prisoners, my Lord?" he asked quietly, gaze locked on the remaining Red Plumes with their backs against the Red Throne. The terror in the Red Plume's eyes unnerved him. They were said to be unflappable.

Wolfgar was hidden in their midst.

"Burn them," Ogo said, "with the rest of it."

"But my Lord..."

"Don't question me," Ogo replied without taking eyes off Lachlan. "Do as you are told," he added harshly, still studying his father's body sprawled sadly on the ground. "This was what he deserved, Oscar. You see that, don't you?"

"Yes, my Lord," Oscar agreed unconvincingly. His father had sent him to be Ogo's ward to toughen him up. He cared that he made his father proud, although the grisly scene turned his stomach. But that was no consequence. Morfit was a proud name and he wouldn't sully it by disrespecting his position. He nodded, swallowing hard, small knot of hair on the top of his head bouncing while he stared unblinkingly at Lachlan's body.

Ogo softened at Oscar's horrified expression. "Sometimes justice is ugly," he added more gently. "This is what had to be done."

Oscar swallowed hard. "Yes, my Lord."

"You see that I had to do it?" Ogo casually wiped his blade on a nearby fallen man's cloak. "I had no choice. You see that, don't you?"

"Yes, my Lord." Oscar nodded as Ogo re-sheathed his weapon. "You have taken back your bloodline and realm, my Lord. You should be proud, my Lord." His tone lacked enthusiasm.

"That's right, I am. I am proud! Wait until your father hears." Ogo was in constant competition with the respected Rupert Morfit. It had been that way since Academy. Rupert was many years younger but still always bested him, at everything. "Let's see how smug and righteous he is then! If I have a say, the Kingdom will remember Regnard as a great saviour, not a filthy villain." He spat again.

"My Lord, should I have someone see to the," Oscar eyed dead Lachlan and his dim eyes, "body?"

"Hmm," Ogo paused, looking down his long nose. Lachlan's head hinged at a grotesque angle from the gash in his neck, cutting clear through to his white clavicle bone. Blood stained his rosebear cape. "No. Leave him there. Let him burn."

"But, my Lord," Oscar squeaked with frown, "he's your father. He is Vanguard. This is your bloodline's castle," he added in a reverent hush. "One of the greatest castles the ancient Vanguards ever built. A testament to history. You can't just..."

"I can do as I please. I am elderclaim now. Let it burn."

Without another word, Oscar dutifully lowered his head as he went to relay the command to the golden troops' Honor Defender. A man of high rank to execute the deed.

Ogo was pleased. He smiled to himself. He felt triumph after so many years of oppression under his foolish father. Ogo turned to leave the flaming Throne hall after a final sweep with his eyes. Golden forces parted as he passed. All filtered out behind him one by one until only the Red Plumes were left trapped in the room on fire.

Then, Ogo's men barred the heavily fortified door behind them.

The hall erupted in a second wave of panic. Men ran to every corner of the room, scraping for an exit, although they knew full well the only way in and out of the massive castle was through the front gate. They were trapped.

Wolfgar knew the situation was dire. Arrow pierced and sword slain bodies littered the floor as the room grew hotter and hotter from lapping flames on either side, jumping out from the scorched tapestries. He scanned the panic again for Rex and Ben but they were nowhere to be found in the chaos. Following honed instincts, Wolfgar turned and begin to climb. He knew up and out would be his only escape, if he could scale the Throne and leap into the night.

Dozens clamoured over each other, with clanking shouts and angry wails, to scale the face with the same idea as he. Luckily, not only was Wolfgar he a better climber from practice at Ravenshroud as a child years ago, for the realm is littered in trees and there was very little else to do as a child, but he wore leather gloves and no chainmail whereas the rest of the Red Plumes had heavy silver armor with no gloves at all, only gauntlets. Wolfgar fended off several panicked men and pulled away others already climbing, hands horribly bloodied from the rock face, to make room for himself. He fought his way up towards a cool breeze flowing through the gigantic opening above the throne, leading into the star-filled night. The jagged points were enough for Wolfgar to grab hold of with his hands and to use as foot holds for his boots. He watched men fall with cries and sickly thuds back below when they failed. Finally, he alone reached the lip of the broken window.

Wolfgar carefully cleared away broken glass with a gloved hand until there was enough space for him to rest briefly on the opening's lip and look back inside to reflect. He lifted himself up over the edge. He sat, studying the hordes of dying men. Dying was nothing new for Wolfgar to witness but he couldn't help but be surprised. He'd learned how the Red Plumes were specially enhanced, for superior tactical skills, making their performance unparalleled in battle, even to his own bloodline's Warmen. He knew their armor was protected and impenetrable, or so he had believed until this very night. *What could pierce the Regnard silver?* he wondered to himself as he turned to investigate how far he had to jump, and if he could survive.

Cool evening air rushed by him from outside as he peered over the lip. There was nothing but grass below. A series of scarlet trees clustered in the distance, edging the pale green lake. It glinted in the moonlight, reflecting the stars above. Wolfgar's neck began to sweat as flames lapped at his back. Before he could think twice his instincts drove him to throw himself from the lip. Wolfgar landed in a roll. He miraculously stood, bruised and shaken with bloodied hands despite his leather gloves, but otherwise unharmed. He looked back at angry flames pouring from Lyonshall with ribbons of fire curling to the roof. Even the blood-red flags atop the five towers were ablaze.

After one last wistful glance at the ruined castle, Wolfgar escaped alone into the evening.

Wails and screams filled the cool air behind him.

THE CONFINES

R yd waited impatiently for Digory under the white and black vase sign at sunrise as they'd agreed to do. His head was foggy with memories from the evening before sullied with too much unfamiliar ale and not enough sleep. He rubbed his eyes, yawning again as he watched the day merchants wheel carts to their daily haunts and night merchants leave their nightly posts to rest for the morn. He was beginning to get accustomed to Littlebell's raucous pulse.

Would this be his home someday? Until he'd met Odion, he'd not given any thought to where he would end up once he found his brother. But now that he had been united with his long-lost grandfather, he allowed himself to drift into soft daydreams of working side by side Odion and Collin at the Red Tavern. Serving ale to Bellamine troops and tangerine-lipped maids. Helping take care of the children in Ashkeep beneath it. These ideas brought a smile to his face.

Over his shoulder, birds fought over trash stuck between the cobblestones, squawking and pecking angrily. The sun rose low, hidden behind the sprawling Littlebell buildings. Artisan Alley was unexpectedly chilly. Ryd's head pounded as he shivered where he stood in shadow. A red and blue striped flag flapped loudly above his head, snapping him out of his daydream, as if to intentionally annoy him, not helping his considerable headache at all.

Where is he? Ryd thought angrily. He rubbed one of his bare arms for warmth, wondering what they were going to do about their imprisoned horses.

"Aye!"

Ryd glanced up and saw Digory sauntering to him with a grin on his sharp-jawed face.

"Unbelievable."

"I see you made it through the night," Digory said, squinting his bloodshot eyes. "How'd it go with…" He gestured with his hand, newly acquired tunic's finely embroidered sleeve buckling.

"I didn't find Col," Ryd said sadly. He raised an eyebrow at Digory's expensive new garb. "Where'd you get that?"

Digory noticed the pooling bruises beneath Ryd's eyes and his slightly swollen bottom lip. "What happened to you?"

"It's a long story," Ryd said. He sniffed the air once. "Are you drunk? It is but morn." He frowned. "How are you drunk?"

"Not drunk," Digory said.

"What then?"

He smiled slightly. "I had quite the time."

"Clearly."

The sun peaked over the lip of the city and cast Digory's sharp features half in shadow. "Where is the beast?" he asked.

"This way." Ryd moved in the direction of the stable. He shut his eyes to appreciate warm sunlight on his face. They walked through the crowd beginning to bustle in this period of transition between night and day. "You don't have coin, do you?"

"You told the stable you'd pay?"

"Aye, a cranky stout man."

Digory shot Ryd a sideways glare. "Dolt," he spat. He inhaled deeply then he rubbed his beard and yawned. He stretched and smoothed his hair.

Impatiently, Ryd waited at his side. "Are you through?"

"Why are you going at such a speed? Do you have a plan to free the steed? No? That's what I thought."

"There's more," Ryd said.

"What more?"

"Mable and Chester are there."

"Who the curses are Mable and Chester?"

Ryd sighed. "The horses from Westerviolet."

Digory turned to him, brightening. "Ay! The Ancestors may

favor us after all."

"Why? I told you," Ryd said, "they're in the stable. And Treave did not seem the type to give away for free."

"Treave?"

"Grumpy stablemaster," Ryd added, skipping to walk at Digory's slightly faster paced side.

"Where'd he get them from?"

"He said he found them."

"Aye."

They approached the dirt path leading directly to the stables off the side of the yellow stone Littlebell castle.

"Aye what?"

"You said it was this way?" Ryd nodded. Digory immediately started off down the path to the stable.

"Wait!" Ryd shouted at Digory's back, "What is your plan!?"

"Who said I had a plan?" Digory said without turning back, still intoxicated from both ale and mad honey, casually walking to the stable still. "I thought you did."

"Slow down," Ryd whispered harshly, skipping to follow him, doubling his pace to catch up with the longer legged Digory. "You're drunk. Wait!"

"Do you want your beasts or don't you?"

"You smell like a tavern."

"I will take that as a yes. Get out of my way. I'll get your cursed horses."

"No!" Ryd's heart beat anxiously. "Digory, what are you going to do?"

"I'm going to get your horses."

Ryd paused in the stable's wake. He was wide-eyed and speechless as he watched Digory enter. The wooden stable door closed behind him.

After a series of uneasy moments for Ryd, Digory strolled out of the stable with Mable and Chester in tow, groomed and fitted with finely crafted Littlebell saddles.

"How did you…?" Ryd asked with surprise, happiness, and confusion as Digory handed him Mable's reigns. He'd raised that horse from a foal and cared for her almost as much as his own kin. He was more than delighted to see her.

"You are welcome," Digory said with a nod. "I'll take the one I had before. He suits me fine." He mounted the brown horse, Chester, who whinnied with annoyance.

Ryd rubbed the back of his neck, pricking with sweat in the mounting heat. He felt pangs of guilt for the fate he'd led the stablemaster to, no matter how ornery he was. Ryd asked the question, although he already knew the answer.

"Did you hurt him?"

"Who?"

"Treave."

"Who?" Digory asked again, this time more impatiently.

Ryd patted Mable's neck gently for comfort. "The stablemaster," he said meekly.

Digory narrowed his eyes. "Don't ask questions you don't want the answer to."

Ryd swallowed hard as he thrust himself atop Mable.

"It's either the Missi or Archer Passage," Digory said, looking towards the water in the near distance through a break in buildings.

Images of Brutt and the flaming barge were fresh in Ryd's mind. "The Passage," he quickly said.

"Not a fan of water?"

"We have the horses."

"Aye," Digory laughed, scratching his beard with one hand. "They will fit on a barge."

"Is it much faster by water?"

"Nay."

"Then why by barge?

"Not faster, but safer journey to be sure," Digory said. "We'll need to work for passage with the Fellowship, but that can be arranged."

At mention of the Fellowship, Ryd shook his head adamantly. "No, no barge."

"No barge?"

"No," Ryd said. "I... can't swim," he added quickly.

Digory chuckled, half believing it. "Why am I not surprised?"

Ryd shrugged.

Digory sighed against the back of his throat again. "Really, no Missi?"

Ryd nodded with pleading eyes.

"So be it," Digory said, to which Ryd let out a grateful sigh. "The Passage it is. Shall we go?"

"Don't look so smug," Ryd said, studying Digory's expression.

Digory smirked to himself as the pair trotted to exit Littlebell. "Who can't swim?"

Days passed. By now, the pair was far along Archer Passage– a marshy, windy road mirroring the Missi along the eastern bank until it forked at the Confines, giving the option to cross the water at Grim Pass and head northwest to Anstout, or continue up the coastline through Baneswood and Croft Hold, on towards Hellswater northeast. The path was wide enough for three to ride abreast. There was tall, seeded grass stretching flat out as far as could be seen to the east on their right side, and marshy wetlands to their left in the west. The sky seemed to go on for creeds, dotted in plush white clouds that cast dark shadows on the mainly flat countryside below. Gnats and shiny green beetles buzzed loudly in the shifting grass, jostled by gusts of warm wind.

"I discovered something at the Apothecary in Littlebell," Digory said, rubbing sweat from his brow with a grey embroidered sleeve. The sun was high in the sky and beat down relentlessly. "Aren't you going to ask what it was?"

"No."

"You aren't curious?"

"No," Ryd said curtly, avoiding Digory eyes. He was distracted, beating himself up over not doing enough to find Col. He vividly remembered the last time he saw his brother. How forlorn he'd been over their father's death. How distant and cold he'd been to the boy. It ate at him from the inside.

"You haven't loosened up?"

"No."

"Fine," Digory baited a final time, looking forward now to the flat stretch of damp path ahead. "You don't care how I miraculously healed?"

Ryd turned, broken from his self-pitying trance. "What?" he asked quickly, flashing to thoughts of Vera.

Digory smirked. "Now you're curious?"

"Just tell me," Ryd said angrily.

"I met Minney."

"Oh?"

"Their elder Laila saw to my wound," Digory said. Ryd was immediately intrigued. "She said it looked it had been healing for weeks. How could that be?"

"What's Laila Minney like?" Ryd asked eagerly. "She works in the Apothecary herself!?" A Vanguard amongst the people, so freely accessible. The concept was shocking.

"Really? That is what you care about? The Minney. Not that I'm a cursed god?"

"You aren't a god, Digory."

"Then explain how that happened? Explain how I healed like I did?"

"I can't."

"No? The bare you kissed had nothing to do with it?"

Ryd swung his head. "What did you say?"

"Ah now I have your attention?"

"Digory," Ryd growled. "What do you know?"

Digory grinned. "You moral ones are so simple. I wasn't sure there was a woman. I could have dreamed the cursed thing. I felt stranger than if I was dreaming." Ryd sighed, rubbing one temple while clutching reigns in the other. "So, who was the bare?"

"Don't call her that."

"Fine," Digory relented with a smug half smile, "but now you must tell me. Was it she who healed me?"

"I don't know," Ryd said. "My head hurts. Leave me be."

"You're a bad liar," Digory said, speaking with one hand as

he hypothesized, the other clutching the reigns loosely. "Who could she be, in a hidden cottage so close to the castle?"

"Don't."

"From what I remember, it was small," Digory said to himself mostly, completely ignoring Ryd's warning. "She lived there alone. So, why would a beauty like that live hidden on the outskirts of the castle, completely alone?"

"Leave it alone."

Spiny frogs ribbited loudly, interrupted every so often by honking river loons and squawking cranes dotting this marshy shoreline. Mable and Chester's horseshoes sank into damp soil of Archer Passage with slapping clops. Why it was cut so close to the river, one could only guess. It was assumed this path was so ancient that the Missi was different when it was constructed, but now in the present day, the road was a soggy mess. Most, if able, avoided it. Most took the Missi.

"It would be silly if she were *earthblood*." Ryd cringed at the hateful term, digging his thumb into the leather of the reigns. "No point in that. No, she is surely Vanguard. Could it be, the elusive Vera Minney? Blue-eye Minney beauty disappeared years ago?" He looked at Ryd with a grin.

"Stop, Digory. Please," Ryd's voice tinged. "I promised her."

"Oh, and you have fallen for her! This is something," he grinned wider. "Am I right?"

"How do you know about them?"

"Who?"

"The Minneys."

"I met Leon Minney," Digory said. "Spent the evening with him, in fact."

"Digory stop," Ryd replied, thinking it in jest, "I've had enough."

"It's true," he retorted seriously. "We met at Littlebell's Apothecary. His grandmother, the elder Laila Minney runs it, can you imagine that? The elder of a bloodline, mopping up blood! The jokes about Littlebell compose themselves."

"You did really meet Leon Minney?"

"Aye," Digory said with a nod. "I went with him to

Littlebell's theatre, if you can believe that too."

"Isn't he," Ryd paused in search for a word. He'd caught the innuendo spoken about the man in Ashkeep.

"Into men's asses?"

Ryd flinched. The predilection was wholly forbidden in Westerviolet. Punishable by death. "Is he?"

"Very much so," Digory said nonchalantly. "But how would you know that if you know nothing of Vanguards?"

"Wait..." Ryd turned, puzzled. "Are you?"

Digory laughed loudly. "Our preoccupations last evening were not sexual. Not at all."

Ryd rolled his eyes. "Drink."

"Not drink," Digory said. "Well, yes drink. But that was not all."

"I'm tired of riddles. I told you," Ryd groaned, speaking the truth, "my head hurts."

"Did you partake in drink last night?" Ryd side eyed him. "You did! Friend, you surprise me."

"I'm not your friend."

"What'd you drink to give you ache, this late in the day?"

"They called it fire ale."

"Ah."

"What?"

"Fire ale," Digory said. "It's the worst."

"Why?"

"Earthblood way of saying–I made it myself," Digory explained with one hand, still holding the reigns loosely in the other. "A poor man's booze, not fit for swine much less humans, but some drink it all the same. What heathens gave that swill to you?"

Ryd shrugged. "Long story."

"I'm intrigued."

"I'm tired."

"Humor me."

Ryd relented. "The tavern," he half lied, "by the Occident."

"Aye? A tavern serves that? Littlebell is not what I thought she was."

For an instant Ryd wanted to explain his adventures but stopped himself. He was painfully aware of how he couldn't trust Digory and how alone in the world he truly was. Instead of elaborating he simply said, "Aye."

"What brought you there?"

"Looking for Collen."

"Who?"

Ryd's dark face clouded. "My brother."

"Oh right." Digory swallowed imperceptivity hard. He changed the subject effortlessly. "What of those Free Boys the gilded guard told us about?"

Ryd coughed once. "Never found them," he said.

Digory studied Ryd, wondering how someone could be so terrible at lying. "Seems I had all of our fortune," he said, letting Ryd think he'd been fooled. "So, you gave up and went to the tavern to drink alone? And you say you aren't your father."

"Funny."

"Uh oh," Digory said under his breath, pulling backwards on Chester's reigns. They came to an abrupt halt.

Ryd followed his lead with a wide frown.

"What now?" He patted Mable to calm her. She neighed and whinnied while her horseshoes sank into the muck of the passage as the pair slowed their pace.

Digory gestured with his head down the path. "Not good."

"If it's another one of your…"

"No," Digory interrupted. "Look up the road."

Ryd popped up his head and strained his eyes. Ahead was cluster of guards with dark brown shields and light brown capes with crudely hammered armor. They carried shields with a brown, black, and white emblem of the sunrise over a river. They stood, hulking, yet hunched, like mounds of shit on the path ahead.

"This is what I meant when I said the Missi was safer," Digory explained, calculating the risk expertly as he had trained to do. His eyes danced across the horizon. "That's Busk."

"What's Busk?"

"You really don't?" Digory sighed loudly. He turned to look directly at Ryd, red wide-set eyes burning angrily. "How do you know *nothing*?"

"What?" Ryd replied with high eyebrows. "Vanguard?"

"Yes, their army. We must be in their realm now."

"What do they want with us?"

"The whole Confines realm is basically a big bare house," Digory said, full of disgust mixed with a bit of awe, "and a gambler's box and fighting pit."

"Really?"

"Yes, really," Digory mocked. Ryd frowned deeper. "The Confines sits in the marshland across the river from Animus Rock." He gestured into the distance. Animus Rock castle's eight reaching towers could be faintly made out across the flat skyline. "It's where all scum trickles from Animus, Croft, all the other realms really. The Confines began as a penal colony for the first Vanguards, that's what Sybil told me. Since then, Busk has made a livelihood of earthblood baser instincts, capitalizing off them, you see. If you have enough coin, you can do anything there. Those are the stories, anyway. Sybil hasn't been," Digory trailed off.

"So, you've only heard the stories."

"Right."

"What do they want with us?"

Both men slowed their horses to a barely moving trot.

"My guess?" Digory glanced at Ryd, then back to the brown-clad warriors in the near distance, like piles of dung arranged in a line. "We're unwilling recruits for the Arena."

That didn't sound good to Ryd at all. "What's that?"

"The Dark Arena." Digory checked the placement of his dagger, still hidden beneath his borrowed tunic.

Ryd had no idea how to begin to calculate their odds of surviving. His voice trembled. "W... what's that?"

"Depends how you look at it. To Vanguards, it's a sport. To earthblood, execution..." Digory rolled his sleeves up.

Ryd's heart dropped. "Execution?!"

"Oh yes," Digory nodded, nearly smirking, crossing his

muscled arms at his chest atop the chestnut steed. "I can't believe you don't know. They make them, I mean us, fight each other."

That's..." Ryd trailed off. His hand dropped to Mable's neck to rub her hot fur, "that's awful!" The animal's coat was fleetingly comforting against his skin. He revelled in the steady beat of her heart.

"Indeed," Digory said. He didn't seem phased at all. In fact, the man's chilly calm was deeply unnerving.

"How does it work?"

"Winners live to fight again and again," Digory explained with one hand as he pulled the reigns to slow in another. "Losers are put down. There's no escape from it. Once you're in the Arena, you don't leave."

Ryd couldn't believe it. And they said Westerviolet was supposed to be bad. "The Council can't stand for it!"

"You would think, but it is very legal," Digory told him. "There is one condition."

"What condition?"

"All participants must be convicted prisoners, or volunteers," Digory said over the hum of the frogs and horseshoes slogging through river mud. "It's been that way since the Blood Council."

"Why volunteer to be slaughtered?" Ryd looked nervously to the Busk guards ahead. "For their amusement?"

Digory nodded. *That's exactly it*, he thought to himself, wondering how anyone could be so naive. "At first, Busk blackmailed or threatened many into it," he said. "Then, they stopped caring, and the rest of the Kingdom did too. Now they just capture earthblood most times because it's easier than waiting for criminals, I suppose. The other realms turn a blind eye. I've heard usually they target travellers on Archer's Passage and force them to fight until they die," Digory gestured around him. "So, us."

"Why here?"

"I'd say because travellers oftentimes disappear anyway. Raiders, dread wolves, disease. No proof it was Busk. They won't be missed."

Ryd intently studied Digory's bearded profile, strong jaw flexing and eyes narrowing, marking his practical thoughts. He had a regal look about him when he was serious. "What do we do?" he asked his hardened companion.

Digory was as honest as he'd been in a long while. "I'm not sure," he said with his eyes locked ahead. Although he knew when the time came to fight, he would know exactly what to do. It was always that way with him.

Ryd loudly sighed.

"Do not make sudden moves!" a nasally declaration rang out over the swamp. Three Busk guards, referred to as Pawns, stood shoulder to shoulder across the path ahead with their captain, Pawn Leader, mounted atop a brilliant while stallion behind. All wore dingy, threadbare cloaks with hoods and brass buttons to secure beneath brown leather helmets stitched with sinew. The Busk armor was molded leather with tarnished brass fastenings, varying greatly from Pawn to Pawn, likely more homemade than uniform. Boots too varied from one to the next. They looked a bit like children who raided their father's closet, as everything they wore was ill-fitting. Each of the men on the ground held rectangular wooden shields painted haphazardly with the sunset over the Missi. All men had particularly large and flat foreheads, as if their heads had been squeezed or stretched.

The tallest man standing on the far left shouted at them. "You are in violation of the Confines law!"

"Here we go," Digory said under his breath as he and Ryd approached the blockade side by side atop their horses. "What law, my good Lords?" he said confidently with a smile. He noted the men's crudely fashioned armor and weapons, hoping they indicated poor training too. He slightly bowed his head.

"Do not question us, *earthblood*."

"I'm sorry, but," Digory looked from Pawn to Pawn, "isn't that what you are, too?"

"Quiet!" the tallest, and first to speak shouted. "By order of Elder Ralph, you are under arrest!"

"What have we done?" Ryd asked innocently.

"I said, quiet *earthblood*," the Pawn with the underbite spat back.

"You hate yourself for doing the Vanguard dirty work, don't you?" Digory mocked. "My Lord."

"Seize them!" the man atop the white stallion commanded loudly.

"Really?!" Ryd shouted at Digory as two of the Busk pawns charged on foot. "Are you trying to kill us?!"

But everything was going according to his newly formed plan. Digory had otherworldly instincts when it came to fighting. Ignoring Ryd, Digory pulled his hidden dagger and flung it at the tall man. The legendary green blade toppled hilt over point, miraculously striking him in the only gap between his ill-fitting armor, right at his throat. The pawn clutched his neck and dropped his weapon, eyes horrified, coughing blood, then fell to his knees.

As the second Busk pawn fast approached, incensed over the fate of his fallen companion, Digory gracefully dismounted.

"Are you insane!?" Ryd yelled at him, tugging on Mable's reigns.

Without looking back Digory shouted, "Get it!" He chided himself for his rash actions internally, not quite sure why he acted so impulsively, but would never admit it to Ryd.

Ryd was totally overwhelmed with thinking he might die and had no idea what Digory was talking about. "Get what?!"

"My crossbow!" Digory shouted. He was angry at himself for not being ready with it to start. He slowed his pace slightly, lowering his shoulders, eyes focused on the incoming Pawn like a predator about to strike while at the same time jerking his dagger from the fallen man's neck. When the weapon's cool hilt touched Digory's skin he felt its familiar surge of power. His dagger somehow made time feel slow, as if he was trapped in a dream. While it fascinated him early in his training, now, Digory had grown accustomed to his dagger's odd *feeling* to where he no longer thought about it and simply benefited from its effects.

Basically, it allowed him to do things faster than everyone else.

"What did you say?!" Ryd yelled louder, even though he half-caught what Digory said. He had started towards Chester to search for the crossbow.

Meanwhile, the second Busk pawn barrelled forward in an overzealous, sloppy form until Digory stepped away at the last moment. The guard toppled to the marshy ground. Digory followed the flailing man, face splattered in wet muck, in three long strides then kicked him down as he crawled across the path towards his dropped sword.

"Get him! And the other one!" their leader squealed at the remaining two solders; voice raised above loudly gusting wind through the marshy grass at their sides.

Ryd pulled back on Mable's reigns. She whinnied loudly. "We have to go!"

Ignoring Ryd's whines and the Pawn Leader's cries, the morbidly focused Digory leapt forward and grabbed the fallen sword. He gripped it expertly despite its unfamiliarity. This was his element. He never felt more alive than when he was fighting. Amid shouting protests from the other Pawns and their leader, with a practiced gesture, he plunged the crude weapon into the back of the fallen pawn's neck in a sticky red eruption.

Digory shouted at Ryd again, "My crossbow!" His face was splattered with the fallen pawn's blood dripping from his beard.

"I can't get it!" Ryd yelled, leaning comically far out of his own saddle to reach Chester's, just a bit out of reach. He grasped hopelessly for the fastenings.

Useless, Digory thought to himself as he stood just in time to clash swords with the next two pawns over both freshly fallen bodies of their comrades, crumpled and bloody atop threadbare brown cloaks, now soaked from the wet mud. These pawns were slow and clumsy just like the last with characteristic underbites in varying degrees of severity and deep bags under beady beet-red eyes. An unfortunate looking bunch. Digory moved with swift precision even with the borrowed, crude, unbalanced weapon. He made a mockery of them easily, dancing around these Busk pawns' lazy footsteps and slow reactions effortlessly while their leader helplessly watched on.

The remaining Busk soldier on the white stallion, the Pawn Leader, in great contrast to his unkept appearance and crudely hammered armor, shouted commands every so often that were drowned out by the metallic ringing of swords clashing against shields. As Pawn Leader, he was responsible for the outcome of this mission. From the looks of it, he was close to returning empty handed. Watching his Pawns fall, the leader decided he had no choice but to ensure the mission not a total failure. He charged the remaining man by himself.

When Ryd saw the guard atop the stallion charging him, his heart dropped into his throat. "Digory!" he cried.

Seriously? Digory thought, unable to believe a grown man had so little pride. "The cursed crossbow!" he shouted.

"I can't!" Ryd shouted back. "It's stuck!"

Digory sighed angrily as he countered a heavy overhead strike with a loud clank, then leapt over another sweeping blow. Swords clashed as mosquitos swirled in the oppressive air. The two Busk attackers were gasping and sweating, slowing down in the muggy heat, while Digory was iron-focused and spry.

"Digory!"

"Shoot him!"

But it was far too late, for Ryd hadn't managed to free the crossbow in time. Instead, in his panic, Ryd spurred Mable off perpendicular to the Passage. Naturally, Chester followed his companion dutifully in galloping pursuit, chestnut flank flashing against the bobbing grass of the horizon as the blockade leader atop the white stallion chased them.

"CURSES!" Digory shouted as Ryd and the horses, with his long-range weapon and all their provisions, disappeared into the tall grass. The Busk Pawn leader took off after them.

Another flashing sword fall snapped Digory from his griping, bringing him back into the stinging reality of the present.

Digory instinctually brought his weapon up to block, then countered left against the brown and white shield with a thudding clank, then right against the weapon with a clash, then dropped and spun to the pawn's dizzied dismay. Finally, he leapt upwards in an explosive rush. With his final lurch, Digory plunged the borrowed sword in and up the one of the pawn's leather-clad sides. When he withdrew the blade, it made a sucking pop and a gush of blood mixed with clear liquid poured out as the pawn crumpled to the marshy floor.

The remaining pawn let out a guttural battle cry at the sight of his fallen companion. He charged at Digory in fury.

Digory smiled. He was pleased that he'd sparked the man's passion because it meant he'd die easily. He held his position, wondering if this Pawn would fall for the same ploy as his companion. The incensed man charged with murder in his eyes and sword swung high above his head until he was inches away. Though, right before the sword's tip pierced him, Digory stepped aside and slammed the broadside of his weapon square in the man's back to propel him forward. As planned, the man toppled to his face. Panicked, the fallen Pawn scrambled to stand. Digory kicked him down with a boot placed in the center of his spine. The Pawn crawled frantically, bulbous fingers clawing at the muddy earth and feet kicking pathetically as Digory trailed him slowly.

The Pawn pitifully tried to stand again and once more, Digory kicked him down.

The man sniffled. "Please, please! Spare me!" He wailed to the swamp. "Please!"

"Ugh." Digory swatted at buzzing mosquitos and gnats. "The least you could do is face me as a man."

The squat man wailed, trying to stand and run a third time. Tears pooled in the corners of his eyes.

Digory shook his head before kicking the Pawn harder than the last times with a loud thud. The defeated man collapsed face first into the marshy path's floor.

"Coward," Digory growled. He was annoyed that the fight was over so quickly. He wanted to take out his frustration for losing his crossbow. But the man lay still in the dirt, apart from the spasms of sobbing. Digory kicked him mercilessly in the ribs with a crack. The Pawn rolled over to look Digory in the eye while coughing and painfully hacking, holding his side tenderly. Mucus ran down his face, and his cheeks were wet with tears. His nose was horribly broken and bloodied.

Digory moved slowly. He held his sword to the man's soft neck, resting the tip deep into the folds of his flesh. He wore a sneer as if he was inspecting turned meat. "I have questions," he said, eyes unfeeling and unblinking. "Answer me, and you are free," he said. "Understand?"

"Y..y…y..yes," the man nodded furiously, chin jiggling beneath his underbitten jaw.

"Why did you stop us?"

"You b..b…broke B…busk law."

"Wrong," Digory said loudly. He pushed the sword's tip slightly deeper into tan flesh, starting a dark trickle of blood.

"Ow!" the man cried, squinting eyes full of tears. He sniffled over and over. It sounded a bit like a snorting hog.

This was tedious work and Digory tired of it. He wanted to be on his way since now he had a new task before heading onto Anstout. Recovering Ryd. "I'll try again," he said, looming over the man cowering like a rodent in a trap. "Why did you stop us?"

The pawn sniffled. He cracked immediately. "We below," he admitted. "Elder don't like when we below."

"Below what?"

"Quota," the man said with teary red eyes.

"For what?" Digory asked, then answered his own question. "The Dark Arena?"

The Pawn nodded. "Some of them go."

"Some?" Digory squinted, pushing on the sword.

The man's eyes widened as his neck throbbed. "I don't know what he does with all of them," he whimpered. "Please, Lord. Please!"

"But most are taken to the Arena?" Digory urged. The sniffling man nodded. "Who is he?" Digory went on, narrowing his eyes. "You said Elder. You mean the elder, Lord Ralph Busk?"

"Aye."

"The man on the white horse," Digory said looking over his shoulder. "He's your Leader?"

"P... pp... please, I have children..."

"Shut up," Digory said. "Who is he?"

"He... he... he be Leader," the man nodded. "P... pawn Leader."

Digory nodded once. The Busk Vanguards were known to treat Pawns as if they were disposable. This man would not be missed. He'd heard about the way the Busk Pawns worked; ruthless, bloodthirsty and disloyal to the core. He'd known under light torture alone the Pawn would crack instantly, like he just did. "When he catches my companion," Digory asked, "where will he take him? To the Confines city?"

The sniffling man nodded furiously. "Prison," he said with a hallowed tone.

"Where is that?"

"Under the A...a... arena," the man sobbed. "P... p... please spare me! I am Onolo. I have family. I am good! I fight hard! I fight for you! P... please, L... lord! Please sp... p.... pare me!"

Digory didn't know about a prison beneath the Dark Arena, although he wasn't surprised there was one.

"Thank you," he offered the Pawn as he slid the sword deep into his dark fleshy throat without a second thought.

Then, Digory withdrew the weapon still pondering this new facet of the puzzle, the Dark Prison, as Onolo, his unhappy dying victim, lay in the marshy mosquito-filled muck, gurgling blood.

The terrain of Archers Passage shifted from grassy marshland to a downright swamp in the blink of an eye. Tall grass gave way to much shorter and thicker grasses than before, with thinner and darker leaves, barely reaching Digory's knees. This gave him an unobstructed view of the Missi.

Digory had no choice but to follow the path towards the Confines. He hoped fortune would quicken once he got there, going on foot without steeds or provisions. He took with him only one of the fallen Busk Guard's swords and sheath to carry it with, tacking it to his waist and practicing wearing it as if he'd been trained in its use, as to not draw attention once he reached the city. The Busk sword was unbalanced and crude although of familiar proportions. Digory wielded it expertly.

He cavalierly assumed the laws were indeed slack in the Confines as he had heard, and no one would bat an eye at his weapon.

The closer Digory got to the city, the more the passage moistened. It was exceedingly difficult for him to trudge this last creed. Heavy muck stuck to his already weighty boots. It didn't help his mood either that the biting insects worsened considerably in the wake of dusk, frenzying around his sweaty head drawing lumpy red welts on the exposed skin of his neck and wrists. He itched them mercilessly. The sun sank low over the western bank of the Missi casting the hazy clouds deep orange over the endlessly flat skyline. He squinted and shielded his eyes.

Up ahead, the stark contrast between the Animus Rock and the Confines cities sitting across the river from each other was quite the sight. Even the cynical Digory paused to absorb the juxtaposition.

Rising ominously from the far bank of the Missi, Animus Rock towered over everything in its wake. Digory gazed at the precise monstrosity with her eight sky-piercing towers and massive curtain wall in awe. The dramatic sunset perfectly backlit the architecture as Digory approached, illuminating the outline brilliantly, so picturesque that exact image was likely already captured on an expensive tapestry somewhere, he figured to himself.

A wide barge floated lazily past Digory towards the looming cities providing a focal point of contrast between the massive fortress on the western bank and the shoddy ghetto he approached in its shadow to the east.

In stark comparison to the Vanguard's capital city, the Confines spiralled haphazardly from the opposite bank in one cluster of sloppy buildings after the next. It was mostly hovels and shacks built without any apparent planning at all. The city encircled a short wall protecting a wart of a castle. This city was pathetically undersized compared to Animus. Particularly, the wall was nothing like the looming Animus Rock wall, and unlike Animus Rock, only protected the castle itself. Unlike the countless posts along the Animus Rock wall across the river, the Confines wall had one lookout point–a lone tower at the head of the wall facing Animus Rock across the water.

The Confines castle was unimaginative if not downright ugly, obviously constructed for function not style. It boasted a simple six story square brown keep with thin rectangular slits for windows. Neglect was evident from every angle. The castle was losing stonework and siding, crumbling left and right. Ugly, although she stood strong.

Unlike Littlebell, there were no gates at the entrance to the Confines. There wasn't even an entrance. Instead, one moment Digory was surrounded by marshlands and then low-down buildings rose about him the next. Not one appeared sturdily constructed, rather, pieced together from driftwood, scavenged parts, and thatched reeds. Also, unlike Littlebell and her laid stone cobblestones, the road Digory followed was unpaved. Muck, rocks, and dirt filled the path as the length of Archer Passage had been. The main funnel into the city was particularly off-putting, lined with heaps of garbage and excrement tossed carelessly from the windows of tenants above. It smelled awful. Dead bodies lay rotting in various stages of decay, some seemingly tossed there, and others collapsed from illness or overdone drugs before reaching the city. Digory couldn't help but bring a wrist to his nose at the immediate stench, sneering with a sharp raised brow while he passed by.

He wondered how this filth was permitted at all. He thought someone should burn the whole place to the ground.

Digory passed through the narrow lanes of mismatched shops selling forbidden, nefarious wares. There were stalls selling illegal dread wolf fangs, hollow candles and even allegedly legitimate Vanguard teeth, scavenged from the burn sites of old wars.

One dark robed costermonger with his hood obscuring his face said, to Digory, in a hush, "Take this," he held out a vial of incandescent liquid, "and you will see your fate, I swear it."

"What is it?" Digory asked.

The man's voice lowered still. "Veilroot powder, smuggled from the Vanguard tree itself combined with my own proprietary blend of course."

"Of course," Digory said, slipping away into the hardened crowd.

He swept his head back and forth. He was on alert yet amused as he observed men and women alike stumbling up and down the filthy path, many with flasks of ale or hazed eyes, filtering in and out of various establishments. The majority were dressed in humble dark robes masking whatever their choice of fashion was underneath. It was apparent no one wanted to be seen in the Confines. Digory had been right too about his weapons. Many others bore daggers or even spears. No one batted an eye at his stolen sword.

The light was feeble as dusk descended over the city. The setting sun painted the haphazard roadways in a grey-tone glow.

Angry shouts poured from a nearby establishment. A woman was flung headfirst through the open doorframe. She landed on her face in the dirty mud. Digory watched her peel her head out of the filth, spit, hack, then pitifully heave yellowed bile.

Digory paced over. She figured this unfortunate girl may know the city and be of some use.

"Rough day?" His gaze was sympathetic. He offered the young woman a hand.

She took it. The girl's grip was far stronger than Digory expected and left grime in his palm that he quickly wiped away on his trouser flank. He noted her unfamiliar clothing and strange tattoo around her neck—a black line the thickness of a thumb about the circumference—despite her thick layer of mud.

"How could you tell?" Her sarcasm tinged heavy with anger.

Digory pulled the muddy young woman upright then studied her more carefully as she tried to compose herself. The poor girl wore wrinkled, now-muddied trousers stuck tight to her wide legs and a once-white, now brown blouse secured with a braided black leather cord that clung limply to her rounded shoulders and square waist beneath an intricately sewn vest. At her hip was a rusted dagger, poorly hidden, sticking out from her back like a misshapen lump. She was very short. Looking down at her, Digory noticed the woman's mud-matted hair was in fact tied behind her head with a length of string, yet so unruly, it appeared loose all the same.

He flashed a smile and looked her straight in the eye. "I'm Digory," he said.

"Lysistrate Edna," the young woman said confidently. She took several steps backwards so she could get a better look at Digory without craning her neck. She stood up extremely straight, glaring defiantly.

Digory half smiled. He crossed his arms. "What now?" For a reason he couldn't place, Digory was immediately curious about this filthy, ugly woman. Despite her circumstances, she still had pride.

"My name is Lysistrate Edna," she said, softening slightly. A glob of muck dropped from her eyebrow to her cheek.

"Lystr…" Digory began.

She sighed loudly then took a few bounding steps to him until she was just a pace away. She had to bend her neck drastically to meet his gaze. "Lys for short," she added, looking up with pale red, heavily hooded eyes. "It is a proud name," she added under her breath, muttering to herself, "where I am from."

Digory nodded his head to greet her. "Lys," he said.

The poor girl had a long-hooked nose, a small head for her heavily muscled frame and a needy countenance. Despite her muscled statue, she somehow still seemed meek, insecure and small. Her nails were bitten to the quick and grimy like the rest of her odd outfit; long ago orange-dyed trousers and frayed vest over a muddied white tunic. Digory didn't recognize where the style may be from. Surely a realm he had never been to before. She was certainly homely, although the layer of filth didn't help her looks either.

Digory pointed to her neck. "What's that?"

Lys's eyes widened as her hand jumped to the black line around her throat. It was then Digory noted the young woman's hands were deeply scarred, with symmetrical patterns and lines. She must be from Ironbark.

"I still forget it's there sometimes," she admitted sadly, glancing away.

Digory's interest roared. Who was this strange woman? She couldn't be who he thought she was, could she?

"What is it?" he asked her with unabashed curiosity.

With dusk, the Confines saw a similar shift of energy that was seen in Littlebell. Daytime establishments closed and nighttime sellers came out of the woodwork, carrying giant satchels and packs on their backs, most of them headed towards their nightly haunts at intersections and path corners. Unlike Littlebell's city, where you could find anything legal for purchase, the Confines city was reserved for illicit items. One merchant arrived carrying a variety vials and potions, hollering how his tonics banished defixes, attracted coin made dreams come true. Another dealt in counterfeit coins for barter, melted down from the edgings of true coins, repressed by hand.

Digory noted a third merchant with an unusually tall cart covered with a thick blanket. His eyes lingered, wondering what its purpose was, when a weathered man with white-blonde beard, diamond tattoo over his eye and patterned scars gave a few coins in exchange for a blonde child not older than age ten, pulled from the cart. The man was a diamond trader from Lyonshall.

Fascinating, Digory thought, realizing that these men sold children as slaves.

Although Littlebell had her problems, she was nothing

compared to the Confines. It was overrun with crime, drug abuse and poverty, rampantly evident at every turn no matter where in the city you went. The Confines was so notoriously dangerous that natives very rarely lived within the city proper themselves and instead situated their families in Sweet Hill–a cozy village a few creeds to the east–travelling to and from the chaos daily or nightly to earn coin, then returning home.

Digory watched the flurry of activity out of the corner of his eye, aware of just how dangerous the Confines was and his own vulnerability at this time of day. It was difficult to see clearly at dusk.

"The collar," Lys said simply. She gripped her throat as if the mark was a physical chain.

"What is it?"

"Deserter's mark."

"Warman?" Digory asked, realizing his folly once he said it, for there were no women at all permitted in Ravenshroud's forces. Everyone knew that.

Lys put a hand to her hip. "Do I look like a man?"

"Hard to say under all that shit."

Lys half smiled. "Not Warman."

"Busk, then?"

"Nay," she said, shaking her head. "Warn."

A shield dame, Digory thought, realizing he'd as right. He had never been to Ironbark nor contested their forces but held high regard for the Warn Mercenaries storied dedication, kinship, and brutality. And, they were notorious for their scars. That explained her hands, then.

"I've never met a shield dame," Digory said, "Are you any good?"

"If I was, I wouldn't have this," she said and touched her neck, then sighed.

Digory looked down at the short, ugly girl and almost felt sorry for her. "How did you find yourself here, covered in shit?"

"That is a long story."

"Then, tell me, why were you thrown from there?"

"I'm out of coin."

Digory's eyebrows raised high. "You gamble?"

Lys clouded. "Why are you surprised? Can I not be two things you don't expect?"

"I like things I don't expect."

"Save your trouble, I've not sunk that low."

"What is your meaning?"

"Are you not trying to buy me?"

Digory laughed deep and loud from his belly for a good moment as Lys's face burned.

"Stop laughing at me," she said with a frown.

"I'm sorry but buy you!? You could not pay me all the coin in the kingdom to take you to bed, girl."

Lys looked away. "You don't have to be cruel," she said quietly.

"Ahh," Digory rubbed his beard. "Buy you! Imagine." He chuckled again as his burning fire-red eyes studied her impishly.

"Forget it," Lys dismissed, cooling like metal. "What do you want then?"

"Why does everyone think I want something?"

Lys looked at Digory. "You seem like you're up to something," she finally said. "And you aren't from here."

Digory's adrenaline spiked. "How can you tell?"

"Your shirt."

"You can tell from my shirt?"

"Look at the seeming, and stitching. There, on the hem," she pointed, noticing the minute detailing on the cuffed edges despite the dusk light. "That's a beautiful tunic. There's no way it's from here."

Curses, Digory thought to himself as he realized his folly. He shoved his sleeves to his wrists to hide the embroidery. "How do you know?"

"My mother is a seamstress. I was raised in the craft."

"You are right," Digory said carefully, knowing a lie would be fruitless. "I am not from here."

"I assume you're here to bed a woman," Lys said. "That's the only reason Littlebell men journey this way." She paused, narrowing her eyes, shifting her weight. "Yet you command a Pawn guard's sword, so surely you are not of Littlebell." She paused again, analyzing Digory in more detail, looking for more clues to who he was. "Your eyes are red, but you are not a Littlebell hue. You have so much hair. And you are so tall. Who are you?" she asked slowly.

Digory deflected back to her. "Why are you here if you're of Ironbark?"

"You don't want to know," she said with pain in her eyes.

"But I'm curious about you," Digory said forcefully. He held her eye contact for a bit too long, drawing her in to where Lys felt compelled to answer even though she didn't want to. He had used this ability many times, to bed Westerviolet's more daring biomaidens mostly, although to lay with a Guardsman was strictly forbidden. If discovered, punishable by death. Or worse. It still worked every time. Digory could cause a lot of damage with his eyes. He was undeniable.

"My father died," Lys said while studying her feet. "When I was just a girl."

"How?"

"Training accident," she said sombrely. "The last time I saw him was that morning when fed the fowl. He told me I was the most beautiful girl in the world. That's the last thing he said to me."

This irritated Digory, for he wished only to hear how her fortune fell. He had no sympathy for lost kin as he had none of his own. "Pity," he said.

Lys squeezed her thick hair and shit water dripped from it. She gagged, then continued. "After that, we had to leave our farm. Mother took my sisters and I to live outside of Cavernous Creek, in the shadow of the Bones, where we worked in the seamshop. There I met Antonis. I was nearly a woman. He came from Greenfrost with the latest recruits. He's shorter than you with copper hair, but with a beard like yours, only longer. And closer set eyes."

So, nothing like me at all, Digory thought. "Sounds as a dream."

"Don't," Lys said with a frown that threatened tears. "We fell in love," she said. Digory realized he'd read her right. She sounded like every maiden he'd lured to bed, or to the cellar, or to Pinewood; stupid and naïve, just far less lovely to look at. "He told me how we'd nuptiae. He told me how he'd come back for me once they sent him away. He told me to wait for him, but I had to be near him. I knew we were meant to be together. I knew if I could only prove it to him, he would see in time."

Based off the reckless look in her eye and the desperate whine of her tone, Digory could already tell what she was going to say. "You didn't," he said.

"I did," she nodded slowly, shutting her eyes. She exhaled, obviously ashamed. "I followed him to Camp Ironbark."

Digory snickered. "How *does* a seamstress become a shield dame?"

"You sound like my sisters," Lys said. She looked like a wilted flower, despite her strong frame. "They always called me puny and small, but that's what kept me going." She looked up with a renewed ardour. "They were wrong. My love for Antonis was all the strength I needed. I knew if I was stronger and better, if I could fight by his side, he would be reminded of his love for me. And I would make my father proud. I would take his place among the ranks, as he was never blessed with blood sons."

Digory sighed. "Women," he said while smiling, until noting her wilted form. "Alright," he prodded faux-sympathetically. "What happened next?" He'd heard this much of her story. Why not the rest?

Lys fiddled with her mud caked hair, separating the waves and un-matting the knots. She avoided Digory's eyes and spoke much quieter now. "When I got there, he was different," she said. "He laughed at me, like you are laughing now."

"And yet you stayed?"

"I knew he loved me," she spat, glaring at him with narrowing eyes. "I am right for him. He was supposed see in time. If I was good enough, nothing else would matter. If I was better, maybe he would love me again."

Digory hardly knew what to think of Lys. Ironbark training was said to be beyond brutal. It was inhumane. The lengths the mercenaries of Ironbark's realm went to ensure their fighters were the best were beyond any other in the Kingdom, save the Guardsmen. For Lys to even survive training was an admirable feat.

Weary from travel he leaned his shoulder against the driftwood wall again. He crossed his arms. "How did that work out for you? Did you get your fine Lord? Or at the very least, did you get to fight at his side?"

"He deserted for love."

"You *did* get him?" Digory was taken aback. "Really?"

"No," she said sadly.

"What then?"

"He bedded daughter of our Commander," she said. "The pair wasn't permitted to nuptiae, so they ran off to Littlebell."

"Wait..." Digory pushed himself off the wall to stand straight. "You didn't..."

"I did," she said painfully, shutting her eyes tight. She sighed. "I know, I know I shouldn't have," she said quickly, obviously not believing that, "but he is wrong about her."

"You deserted for him? You actually followed him to Littlebell? After surviving training, you still threw it all away?" Digory grinned wide. He nearly laughed. "Incredible."

"I was trying to protect him from that bare," she muttered, then shut her eyes and sighed. "When I found him in route to Littlebell he rejected me. Laughed at me again and told me I was a dolt." She paused as if she wasn't fully there with Digory, instead trapped back in the past hearing Antonis say the words. Digory wished briefly he could meet this man called Antonis, to understand why a woman completely transformed her life, then betrayed it to be by his side. He would never understand women. He watched Lys's stretched expression crack the drying mud on her face.

"Not hours later, a patrol from Ironbark passed through looking for us," she explained. "I honourably confronted them to face my crimes, but Antonis and Esmelsa ran away."

Now Digory had to bite his lip not to laugh, completely amused by the tale. But he held his tongue for he wanted to hear more. He could tell the girl still had *some* pride, so he best not push her if he wanted her to continue.

"After the tattoo," she grabbed her neck, "they beat me," she shut her eyes, "and had their way with me," she added softly, "then left me for dead."

What else did she expect? Digory thought. *She's fortunate to be alive.* "How did you end up here?"

"I had my sights on Animus," she explained, glancing to the towering shadow of the city across the river. "To start a new life." She paused, then added woefully. "I never made it."

"Why not?"

"Lost a wager on the barge so I had to jump ship before we docked. Now, I'm on the run from the Fellowship. This is the only place they don't care to look for me. No one cares to look for anyone here. I've been kicked from nearly everywhere in this forsaken city too," she added, gazing up and down the dim city street briefly. Above, the dusk sky burned dark, shimmering blue like a gemstone. "I've got nothing," Lys said. "What about you?"

"I'm not sure I can top that," Digory said. "I'm here for my friend."

"Few have friends here."

"I can imagine," Digory glanced about, "but it's true. Prisoner of Busk."

Lys made a face.

"What?"

"Your friend is dead."

Digory frowned. "If he's not, where is he?"

She chuckled dismissively and rolled her eyes. "He probably is."

"If not?"

"Dark prison."

"Sounds menacing," he said sarcastically, wondering if there was connection to the fabled Dark Arena.

"It's under the arena," she told him, confirming his

suspicions instantly. It was the place the Busk spoke of.

"Could you take me to it?"

She crossed her arms and pinched her brow. "Why?"

"To get him out."

It was Lys's turn to laugh. She threw her head back, shaking it side to side with mud and shit flecking from her hair. Her chuckle reminded Digory of a chirping bird. A loud, annoying one that wakes you up just before it's time for post. "I told you, he's already dead," she said more firmly this time once her laugh subsided. "No one comes out of the dark prison once they go in."

"How does it work?"

Lys made a gesture with her hands as if lowering a bucket into a well. "Men dropped down into the basement prison through holes in the ceiling alone."

"No door in or out?"

She shook her head. "To the dark prison? Nay."

"Interesting," Digory said under his breath. "What else?"

"It sits under the Dark Arena," Lys explained. "It's where the fighters are kept. I've heard many men die down there before ever reaching the arena, the conditions are so horrid."

Digory knew that's where Ryd had to be. "Take me there," he said forcefully.

"He must be some friend for you to go there in search of him," Lys said. "If we arrive to see his body hung from the rafters, don't blame me. You were warned."

Digory internally winced. He felt an unfamiliar emotion towards Ryd. A twisted sense of loyalty. He swallowed it like bile. "So, you will take me?"

"What's in it for me?"

"What do you want?"

She sighed as he'd called her bluff. "That's a good question," she said rhetorically then paused. She brought her hand to her neck, deep in thought. "Curse it," Lys finally said. "All I want is something new. Something more than ale and debt. Aye," she said getting more used to the idea with every word she spoke. It didn't hurt that Digory was alluringly attractive, and mysterious. And the first to ever listen to anything she had to say. That in and of itself was a welcome blessing. She hadn't realized how lonely she'd been. It was nice to have company.

"I'll help you. Take you to the Dark Arena, but no more than the first floor."

"Have you not been further inside?"

Lys widened her already bulbous eyes. "I have… but it's bad, even for the Confines," she said cryptically. She seemed genuinely shaken. "I'll just say that."

Digory didn't press because he had a task at hand. "Lead the way, dirty Lady," he said, then patted Lys on the behind. Muck spattered everywhere, including across the fine grey tunic he wore. Noting the mess, he sighed.

"A shame to sully such a handsome tunic." Lys clearly enjoyed the attention from him, hiding a snicker at his folly. "And worse still."

"What?" Digory spat.

She eyed him. "You'll be a target in that."

He wanted to tell her she was wrong but realized instantly she was right.

"Fine," Digory said dryly as he pulled the embroidered tunic off and over his head to reveal tight skin, honed biceps, and etched abdominals. He was also riddled with scars. Then, he gestured at Lys with the tunic crumpled in his hand held outward. "After you," he said, before following her into the rising night.

The Dark Arena was a hexagonal building of mismatched wood at the center of an enormous, chaotic intersection. Six streets converged in a giant jumble of shouting and shoving and yelling with the Dark Arena at its center. Battered, bloody bodies in varying levels of decay hung from each of the six sides of the exterior of the building. Ravens squawked loudly, pecking at the remains.

A towering doorway led to loud chaos inside. There were

four stories, each sporting a wide balcony teeming with bodies. Each balcony's railing was lined with outward facing, tilted mirrored glass to reflect to the horde of onlookers on the ground floor what went on in the depths of the arena.

A square pit was cut directly down into the center of the floor. The ground was sand dyed dark brown from old blood and splattered fresh with new. Every wall of the square pit was lined with thick, iron bars with terror-filled prison inmates, forced to watch the other prisoners fight until they themselves were pulled from the prison at random to participate.

Digory's nose pricked at the metallic scent of blood. Instantly he noted that the crowd seemed as violent as the fighters. He felt grateful he had both his dagger and the commandeered sword. He had been concerned he'd a target carrying a weapon so obviously, even if he seemed familiar with it, but relaxed quickly noting nearly every patron illegally had some type of personal dagger, axe, or spear. Digory fit right in.

The whole Dark Arena was one massive entity of swarming bodies. The entire place whirred in visceral excitement as many gulped ales while others whelped guttural cries. Tobacco smoke billowed. The crowd contested amongst themselves, drawing excessive blood that spattered across everyone nearby. Everyone pushed and shoved in the throbbing chaos, waiting for the festivities to begin, vying to avoid encroaching on the lip of the arena's inverted center stage. Anyone unlucky enough to be knocked down into the arena was forced to fight. Bets were screamed left and right at men in hooded red robes holding large pieces of parchment walking inexplicably through the riot unscathed.

On one of the four sides of the square fighting pit was a platform with two intricately carved chairs with plush cushions. This elevated stage was encapsulated by iron bars and only accessible by a key-locked iron gate-door, to keep out the savage audience. It was known as the Vanguard cage.

In the largest most central chair, an older man sat wrapped in a light brown leather cape with well-crafted yet worn seams and a high neck with a metal buckle at the side of the collar.

He was so bald that even in the scarce light his hairless head shone. He was shrunken and pale with watery green eyes and a noticeable underbite. A Busk through and through. Slouched comfortably to the side of his seat, Busk elder, Lord Ralph Busk wore a surly expression while he chewed on his lip. He studied the din before him disapprovingly.

The man on Ralph Busk's right wore a darker leather cloak of similar fashion, but his collar had long leather straps that lay braided down his chest instead of a buckled or toggled, indictive of his new blood. This man had caramel skin, bright green eyes and jet-black curls that receded at each temple. He was slender, with long crossed legs. Compared to the elder man his skin was very, very dark. Edwarde Minney squinted critically, tapping his high laced boot impatiently against the floor. His rodent-like eyes leapt back and forth.

"Busk?" Digory asked Lys as he eyed the men on stage before them. The pair stood warily to the side of the chaos as Digory hurriedly scanned for Ryd. He didn't see him.

"Aye, one of them," Lys said. "The one there, shrivelled with a head like an ass cheek," she clarified with venom. "That's Lord Busk."

"Tell me how you really feel."

"I'm not kidding. He's," she paused in search of a strong enough word. "evil."

Digory pointed at the other. "Who is he, then?"

"What?" Lys craned to hear over the shouting and brawling crowd.

Digory pointed emphatically. "Him!"

All around them, bodies shoved.

"Lord Edwarde Minney," she yelled back.

A gong reverberated about the closed vaulted ceiling. Lys and Digory hushed and looked towards the platform. The entire arena quieted to an excited rumble.

"Bring them in," the slumped old man hissed. He tapped his heavy ring twice against the arm of the wooden chair with a crack and the room erupted in loud cheers. The brown clad Busk Pawns led, carried, and dragged four men into the foreground.

Digory stood tall to see over the churn.

"These boys are fresh, my Lord," a guard barked up at the stage. "Not yet thrown to the dark." The guard grinned to reveal brown-yellow teeth. The front two were missing entirely.

"Good," Ralph Busk purred, then turned his head to Edwarde Minney.

The younger man with dark curled hair uncrossed his legs slowly and stood.

"You belong to the Arena now," Edwarde began, deep voice booming. He lived for this, when the crowd was his. He could feel his body pulsing with adrenaline. *They will all hail my name, someday,* he thought. His worn cape cascaded in folds around him as he stared at the four horribly whipped and beaten men, gesturing to each side with both hands, palms face up. "This is your Kingdom. Your future. Your temple! And you *will* anoint these dark sands with your blood!"

The rowdy onlookers all about Digory and Lys flew into an unabashed uproar. Many tossed rotten cheese, warm ale, and muck from the ground at the prisoners. These four men stood side-by-side with heads down. The arena's odor, while rank to start, fouled considerably.

"You are in for a treat," Edwarde bellowed. He spoke with a wide faux-warm smile, like a Wiley Demos costermonger. "Before you, four unsullied men. Men never thrown into the darkness. Untested! Unproven!"

"What happens if you win?" Digory asked Lys amidst Edwarde Minney's speech.

"You fight again," she said simply, not taking her eyes off the stage.

"What if you never lose? Can a prisoner win freedom?"

Lys laughed. She shook her head, 'no'.

"All four will die, that is true. Which first? Last? Tell the Viccouri. Make your mark on this forsaken world!" Impatient patrons began to murmur, then talk freely, until the whole arena hummed with muttering excitement. "Place your bets. Is today the day that you become richer than a Thorne? Find out! Place a bet!" Edward gesticulated with bravado. To his side, Ralph Busk picked at his lip with long fingernails, observing the ruckus from his elevated platform, unsmiling behind its iron bars.

"What's a Viccouri?" Digory yelled in Lys's ear.

"You mean who," Lys corrected. "They are," she said, pointing at the men in red robes.

"What are they?"

"They report to the high Viccouro."

That's not helpful, Digory thought to himself, getting frustrated. "What's he do?"

"Keeps the bets," she explained. "Pays them out after it's over."

Digory nodded. He wanted to know more but was distracted by more pressing matters. Ryd. He did, however, notice men and women alike fumbling over one another to get to the men in red robes spread throughout the arena. Surprisingly, no one laid a hand on them despite the violent chaos. The Viccouri moved effortlessly through the crowd as many jumped out of their path.

"How do they pass through this First freely?"

"It's a high crime to touch them. To do so gets you a trip straight down." He stomped to indicate the prison below their feet.

"Got it."

"The second gong nears!" Edward bellowed. "Is today the day that you rise from the shit? Is today the day you take what is yours?!"

The crowd cheered and screamed, pulsing in a rhythmic harmony that mimicked a beating heart.

"What have these men done, you ask? Why are they worthy of the Arena and the salvation it brings?"

"What's he mean?" Digory asked Lys over the pontificating. She yelled over the din. "What?!"

"He said *salvation.*"

"Some think that the Dark Arena is some kind of temple. A

religion. To die here means to live forev…"

"There he is!" Digory interrupted with an excited shout.

"Which?"

"The one second to the end. Blond with the wide nose. There! He just lifted his head."

Ryd stood before the feral crowd, in line with the other three Busk prisoners.

"…he was found with the bare's flesh in his mouth, blood and spittle from her flayed chest strewn about and intestines in his lowly hands," Edwarde said dramatically as he pointed at Ryd.

The crowd gasped and booed.

"The most gruesome crime ever witnessed! The most horrifying deed I have ever heard done in all my years! But, is he violent enough to best the rapist," Edwarde pointed to the second man, seemingly of Nomad blood with thin, eye-lidless eyes, "or this wretched thief?" he gestured at the first in line, likely a Regnard native with child's face, square build, and mop of white-blonde hair.

"Your friend is the cannibal?"

"Yes! Well, no," Digory said to Lys, still focused on Ryd. He was pitifully naked like the other prisoners, standing with head hung and his body was covered in dark welts.

Lys frowned. "What do you mean?"

"That's him," Digory said, "but he didn't do those things."

"What did he do?"

"Nothing! Well, he ran. He was stupid enough to run. If he'd listened, we wouldn't be in this mess, but no, don't listen to Digory."

"What are you talking about?" Lys yelled over the cheering. "I can't hear you!"

"Nothing," Digory said. "That's him," he yelled loudly in her ear.

Lys nodded. "I'd say your peace now. If you wish, can leave before it begins."

Digory scanned the chaos. He analysed each inch of the arena before falling back to Ryd. "What? No, no, we're getting him out," he said as he pieced together a plan.

Lys laughed playfully. "You're mad."

Digory winked, set his jaw, then shoved his way through the crowd towards the Vanguard cage despite Lys's cries from behind to stop. As he approached, he felt the raised wax Brochet emblem atop the letter from Sybil in his pocket with his pointer finger. At the last moment, he slipped Primin Minney's tunic back over his head.

He really did have a plan.

Edwarde pointed at the last prisoner before him, near Ryd's height, with a bird-like nose and braided black hair. A native of the Ravenshroud realm. "Here we have a true fighter, one of the chosen themselves! We have a seeker of eternity, and pursuer of the glorious unknown. Cheer for your true champion, no matter where he..."

"Lord Ralph Busk!" Digory yelled up at the shrunken man on the platform, interrupting Edwarde's passion with deep, commanding baritone. Ralph Busk turned slowly in his chair as if disrupted by a barking mutt. The raucous crowd hushed considerably.

"Guards!" Edwarde shouted, pointing at Digory. "Throw him in!"

"Wait." Ralph raised a shaking hand at Edwarde. "What does he want?"

"My Lord," Edwarde lowered his voice, "he has interrupted the ceremony..."

"Quiet," Ralph grumbled. Edwarde shrunk backwards, stung. "Look at his clothing, you fool. *Vanguard.*" The man keenly observed Digory's fine borrowed tunic. For all his flaws, he always paid attention to detail. Ralph shifted his attention to Digory. "What do you want, earthblood?" he hissed.

The crowd hummed in confusion and frustration, antsy with anticipation for the event.

Edwarde frowned.

"I am a messenger from the Elder Brochet, true Vanguard son, just as you are!" Digory said confidently, loud voice ringing up every one of the arena's four floors. "Here, is the emblem." He lifted the wrinkled, folded parchment, holding the palm-size wax emblem clearly depicting the intertwined Brochet snake faced towards Ralph and Edwarde.

Both men strained to see.

"What does the snake want with Busk?" Ralph barked. "The last time I saw him, he told me his stones smelled better than my realm."

Digory bit his lip not to smile. "It says Lord Tomas apologizes!" He shook the letter. "He invites you to meet at Westerviolet."

"Pass it here." Ralph grabbed at the air with his wrinkled hand. "I want to read his words for myself."

"You have something of his," Digory went on, gesticulating wildly as he spoke with one hand, sneakily lowering the letter back to his side and slipping it back into his pocket again with his other.

Ralph's old voice groaned. "Speak plainly, earthblood."

"The cannibal. From Westerviolet. Tomas commanded me to bring him back for punishment."

"Who?"

"That one, right there." Digory pointed at Ryd, second from the end with tattered skin and purpled bruises. Ryd's blood-shot eyes blinked slow. Digory nodded slightly. *Trust me, I'll get you out*, he thought. He hoped Ryd could understand.

"Is this true?" Ralph questioned Edwarde. "Do we have one of the old snake's? Where'd you find that one?"

"I... I assure you, my Lord." Edwarde's eyes darted back and forth faster than usual. "He hails from the Confines as you decreed."

"You assure me? Where did you find him?"

"My Lord…"

Ralph sighed with frustration. "Check his brand," he commanded.

The guards closest to Ryd turned his body aggressively to get a better view of the skin on his hip, then nodded to Ralph to confirm there was indeed an ouroboros emblem branded there.

Ralph exhaled slowly against the back of his throat in a

dissatisfied hiss. Edwarde took a timid step. He wanted to defend himself or explain, but Ralph ignored him totally and focused on Digory instead.

"Tomas sent you to my steps for the cannibal? Why?"

"I know not, my Lord," Digory bowed his head. "I am but a humble messenger," he added, looking hopefully up towards the stage.

With each moment passed the arena's crowd grew increasingly impatient, smelling blood, as Ralph and Edwarde fell into confidence, whispering so low only they could hear, determining Digory's fate.

"My Lord," Edwarde appealed Ralph. "If the messenger is who he said he is, this is a high insult."

"He is who he says he is," Ralph retorted as one chide would a child. "You saw the emblem. His clothing."

Edwarde ran a hand over his curled black hair. "You must not yield to Tomas Brochet," he said in grave seriousness as he met Ralph's watery eyes. *This old man has no pride*, he thought. *No wonder the Kingdom laughs at Busk.*

"Yield? He comes asking for peace. Brochet finally comes crawling to Busk, the way it always should be."

Edwarde sat back down and leaned towards Ralph. "That's what he wants you to think. For centuries Busk has been taken advantage of, but no more!"

"You forget your place," Ralph growled at Edwarde. "You are not my son, nor are you my blood. You're a dirty mongrel barely able to call yourself Vanguard. You certainly are no Busk," he added cruelly. Gutted internally, Edwarde shrunk. "You know nothing of our ways, our culture, our creed. You're a Minney, and the worst kind. In your veins flows the blood of traitors. I married you to my daughter and this is how you repay me? You even failed your children! My grandchildren. Useless," Ralph hissed.

"That was not my fault," Edwarde spat back, seeing Edwessa and Karl's faces flash in his mind's eye.

Outraged, Ralph slapped him hard with the back of his ringed hand, breaking the skin of Edwarde's cheek. Blood trickled and dripped from his jaw as the crowd gasped and cheered at the unexpected violence.

Digory was pleased, for his plan was working.

At the change in volume and mood, Ralph snapped out of Edwarde's confidence. "Enough!" he shouted at the crowd, gazing up at level after level of thrashing bodies. He turned to Digory. "I accept," he said. "Tell Tomas I accept his offer. I want to know what the old snake is up to."

"Thank you, thank you!" Digory shouted up at the Vanguard cage. "Brochet thanks you!"

Ralph dismissed Digory with a flip of his hand. "Edwarde, tell them to free the cannibal."

"But, my Lo…"

"Do it. Or you take his place."

Edwarde nodded curtly. He adjusted his cloak as he gracefully stood, preparing himself to preside over the ceremony once more. The wide, theatrical smile returned to his surly face. At least that much of him was true to his Minney blood. His stage presence.

Digory turned and walked towards the prisoners.

"Release the cannibal!" Edwarde commanded. His eyes darted. "He has failed the arena. His fate rests in the hands of Brochet now."

"Boooo," echoed the crowd. Another round of tossed garbage and shit began. Digory ducked, blocking his face with his forearm.

The guards obeyed Ralph's command and unshackled Ryd's hands and feet. After touching the raw flesh at his wrists briefly, Ryd instinctually cupped his hands in front of his exposed nudity. A wave of relief washed over Digory as Ryd was freed, but before Digory could catch Ryd's eye again, Edwarde began to speak.

"The Arena must have her fill! For every one lost, one is gained!" Edward shouted. He pointed at Digory. "Throw him in!"

"Wait, woah. Wait! I must deliver the man back to Lord Brochet!" Digory cried as he threw both hands up, realizing instantly how dire this situation was. He hadn't planned for this.

"I'll see to it he's delivered," Edwarde countered with a terrible grin. "No reason you must be the one to do it," he said ominously, then glanced briefly to Ralph for approval. Ralph Busk shrugged. Taking that as permission, Edwarde commanded the guards, "Seize him!"

Four bumbling Busk guards approached Digory from each side. His back was against the sheer drop into the arena cut out below. He stepped slowly backwards with his hands up in peace despite having both a dagger and sword as the cheers from onlookers grew in volume and rung in his ears. Digory baited his attackers slowly. The guards held their swords and shields at the ready, urging him back until he was one step from toppling in.

From the corner of his eye, Digory watched as Ryd was tossed away from the arena into the dark street outside, naked. Grateful, he internally smiled.

Then, a guard lunged at Digory, attempting to startle him into falling backwards. Instead, with inexplicable reflexes and agility Digory leaped from its path, leaving the guard to woefully topple into the open arena's fighting pit with a crash. In the same instant, in one movement, Digory tore the expensive grey tunic over his head and wrapped it over and over in his hand. Then, timed perfectly, as the next guard lunged he moved aside and lunged himself with the wrapped-up tunic, grabbing the incoming sword's blade. Digory used the guard's own momentum to flick the sword up into the air, flipping over its hilt three times until it landed in the center of the man's skull with a deadly thud.

The guard quickly crumpled. Stunned silence reverberated through the audience.

The other guards paused in shock as Digory pulled the sword from the fallen guard's head. The movement exploded blood and brains across his bare chest. The onlooking crowd went berserk. This is what they were here for. Digory grinned with teeth white against his red-spattered face while holding the blood-soaked weapon in his left hand, unsheathing his other borrowed sword with his right. A large part of him lived for times like this. It was the only thing he really knew how to do. What he was good at. What he was built for.

In that moment, Digory was a ghastly defix to behold, grinning wide, deadly and ready to pounce with dual bladed weapons. His favorite way to fight.

"Guards!" Edwarde shouted, tone wavering nervously as he looked around. "More guards!" he cried anxiously, watching Digory make fools of the next three men to attack him, fluttering between the incoming in a flurry of leaps, jukes, and aggressive spinning attacks. Reinforcements were having trouble navigating the buzzing ruckus to reach the fighting, trapped behind the crowd's pulsing. Digory's reflexes were indescribably fast and allowed him to analyse complex situations instantly, knowing instinctually how to respond. He'd been this way for as long as he could remember. If he were to touch his glass dagger, this ability would only amplify.

"Get him!" Edwarde screamed.

The decibel in the room reached painful levels from the hooting and shrieking and booing directed at Digory as he cut his way through the Busk forces tasked with protecting the Dark Arena. One guard lunged at Digory from behind and was stopped by a rusty dagger in his chest, flung from a distance. Digory glanced around quickly to note his savior. He nodded in thanks when he saw Lys smiling at him from across the way.

"And her!" Edwarde pointed at Lys across the room. She dropped to the ground. The guards lost sight of her. "Eternal inferno, GET THEM!" he screeched, completely losing control, veins popping from his neck. "You are a cursed DOLT, old man," Edwarde turned to shout at Ralph, then haphazardly at passing guards. "Get them! What are you doing? Stab him, you cursed mud-eating cunt!" He kicked at his prison's cool bars.

"Edwarde," Ralph Busk commanded stoically, "quiet."

But Edwarde screeched as if he'd lost touch with his mind. "Get them, get them!"

"Edwarde!" Ralph shouted. He went unheard.

Edward spun into a frenzy in their enclosed platform, shouting commands at the guards, rattling the cage, watching helplessly as Digory bested the men, clinging to the bars with both hands.

Digory flew from attacking guard to guard in a rainstorm of blood, slicing throats and severing limbs easily with his pair of swords. Only once did a Busk Pawn's sword cut him - in a gash across his forearm - but it didn't slow him. Not in the least

Although he considered it fun to fight this way, like the storied sweep fighters did, Digory was nostalgic for his crossbow and wondered how he would recover it once he finished cutting his way through all the Busk men. Just as he thought he'd bested all of them, more brown-clad guards hurried in to counter him. Soon, Digory's biggest issue was stepping and tripping on already fallen bodies or clipping members of the encroaching audience with his flashing swords. The crowd had lost all semblance of order and furiously yowled in rounds of excitement at Digory's expert display, until a new sound arose in the background.

Screams unlike before erupted.

He almost didn't notice them at first. Not cheers, but cries and pleas for help staccatoed the roaring shouts at Digory's performance. He smelled the smoke before he saw it—black clouds creeping under the edge of one side of the hexagonal building and small red flames lapping at baseboards. The crowd on that side of the arena rushed to escape, quickly stampeding towards the only way in and out, on the opposite side of the building.

Within seconds, the flames reached the floor of the second level. Soon, thousands of bodies on the balconies of the wooden building shoved and pushed and fought to get down. They were trapped. No longer concerned with ceremony, order, or Digory's spectacle, most ran or leapt towards the door. Several bodies fell or were pushed over the balcony railings, toppling the vaulted distance into the sea of pulsing screaming people below with bone-crushing cracks. One unlucky man fell from the fourth and hit some of the mirrored glass on his way down with a brilliant chiming crash and a shatter of blood before landing with a thump, killing several below. Countless shouts and wails came from the floor where many were trampled. Bodies jumped and hung from one railing to the next down to escape higher floors.

Soon, the whole building was consumed with churning smoke and smelled of charred wood, burnt hair, and seared flesh. Screams filled the air as bodies succumbed to the flames. The second floor collapsed with a groaning crash and a burst of orange sparks on one side of the arena, engulfing many into the inferno. Flames climbed the walls to the third and fourth floors trapping thousands. Ash floated through the singed air.

"Guards!" Edwarde Minney screamed, panicked, rattling the gate on his cage. He coughed as the black smoke filled his lungs. "GUARDS!" he cried louder as his beady, darting eyes bulged out of his head.

Flames crawled slowly towards the wooden Vanguard platform. Huge embers of wood fell from the rafters and crashed in explosions of sparks. Beneath the arena, the unfortunate souls of the dark prison wailed in their make-shift oven, literally baking in the pit beneath the stage.

Amidst the pandemonium, Ralph Busk smirked. He glanced around and chuckled to himself, realizing the poetry in his own demise, looking at the building now emblazoned with flames. What a fitting end. Just as predicted. And fully deserved. He smiled. He would be with the Ancestors soon. Slow at first, he shook his shining bald head, then laughed, and laughed. He coughed from the smoke, then laughed more.

"You've gone mad!" Edwarde shouted at him. "We are trapped!" he cried.

"I won't be found clawing at the bars of my cage, like an animal," Ralph hissed at Edwarde. "Not like you," he added. "You never did have any pride."

Soon, the Dark Arena filled to the brim with angry, blood-curdling screams. The most desperate shouts rose from the prison below as wild arms flailed out from the bars on each side of the sunken, square prison and the men and women inside baked alive. Thick smoke churned and searing flames consumed the building.

Then, the roof gave way with a roaring crash.

The Dark Arena collapsed into itself in a brilliantly horrific blaze, consuming everything inside, like an imploding star.

Digory crawled on his hands and knees through dead bodies and debris, coughing, wretching to get smoke from his lungs, slowly moving away from the burning structure that had already started to catch the surrounding buildings ablaze. He'd ditched the swords long ago and clutched his dagger, blindly crawling through the chaotic panic of Confines natives screaming, crying, and desperately trying to douse the flames. When he was far enough out of the smoke to properly breathe, he rolled onto his back and sighed.

To his own amusement, he was alive.

As he laid there, he felt a tingling sensation but did not realize that it was caused by the gash on his arm healing itself.

He rubbed dust from his eyes as he gazed up at the cloudy starless sky flickering with shadows from the burning city. Anxiously, Digory felt in his pocket for Sybil's letter. He relaxed when the wrinkled parchment met his fingertips. He nearly panicked again at the thought he'd lost his dagger, before realizing he clutched it in his hand, so tightly he drew blood. He re-sheathed the weapon. He sighed, laying his head back in the mucky path. He coughed again and shut his eyes. Then, he was poked in the ribs with a big toe.

Digory peeled his eyes open. He realized quickly that he was face to face with unapologetic nudity.

Ryd's.

"Oh, put some pants on," Digory said, pushing his tired body to stand. "Did you do this?" He gestured with his thumb at the flame-engulfed building, thrilled his companion was alive, doing his best to hide it.

Ryd nodded, huge purple welts beneath his eyes and Mable and Chester in tow. "I lit it on fire," he said, "and I found the horses." He smiled wearily.

Digory's satchel was still tacked to Chester. His crossbow presumably inside. He was relieved at the sight.

"You saved my life, again," Digory said slowly, "when I've repeatedly told you not to. He was unable to comprehend it. He furrowed his brow and studied Ryd's serious expression with intense, fire-red eyes. "Why?"

"You saved mine."

ANIMUS ROCK VILLAS

"I am amazed at the smoke," Sybil observed casually from Thorne villa's fourth story veranda.

Today she wore an emerald blouse with thin, billowed sleeves gathered at her wrists tucked into a white skirt. While at Animus, she tended to favor more Animus Rock-friendly fashions. More draping than her typically chosen, tightly tailored attire, although still characteristically oldblood. "So much, even after they've long doused the flames. Look how high, still." She pointed into the sky, watching thick black columns of smoke rise from the charred skeleton of where the Confines had been.

Monty and Sybil, just like the rest of Animus Rock, spent the morning gossiping back and forth about what could have caused such a horrible fire.

"A blaze that big takes longer than a day to go out," Monty replied. "That was no small building. The place was massive, and full of shit. No wonder it lit like a cow pie."

Sybil wrinkled her nose. Her dark eyes were locked on the scene across the river.

The sunken Busk skyline had a black blemish where the Dark Arena once stood. It wafted huge, black clouds still more than a day after the incident, raining white and grey embers down around the land nearby, hence, the entire Confines swamp was covered in a layer of ash. Even from the villas across the river the piles of charred bodies could be seen, lying, waiting to be counted then burned just as the city had.

Sybil studied the gruesome scene with morbid curiosity as she pulled her knitted shawl tighter around her thin shoulders.

"Good riddance to that place," she said. "Father told me how vile it was. It was full of sin. It's no wonder it burned to the ground."

Monty took a sip from the glass he held. He shook his head.

Sybil disliked the way his eyes taunted her, like a bully, not a lover. "You do not agree?"

"You never went there yourself, did you?"

"I... No, I did not." Sybil turned her head and lifted her chin proudly. "Not suitable for a Brochet."

Monty took another sip. "I see."

"Stop that." Sybil furrowed her brow. "What?"

Monty smiled. "Stop what?"

Sybil crossed her arms in front of herself and pulled the shawl tighter.

"Not all men feared that place. Some men worshiped it," Monty added cryptically.

"You're kidding."

"It's true. To some it was the ultimate calling. They used the word *salvation.*"

"To be beaten to death? Not the salvation I crave."

"You don't strike me as the type to seek salvation at all."

Sybil narrowed her black eyes to slits. "What's that supposed to mean."

"I figured you know what is true like I do," Monty said carelessly.

"What is that?"

"We're all damned."

Sybil rose her eyebrow and lifted her glass. "May your blood reign forever," she said approvingly with a clink of his.

"I'll admit it's tempting," Monty continued. "The promises of the arena. The glory of the fight, the kill."

"Keep talking like that and they won't believe you're New, Montague."

Monty's green eyes glared. "How many times must I tell you I hate it when you..."

Sybil interrupted in her typical flighty, feminine tone. "So, are old Ralph and his pet dead, then?"

"One would think," he said, then paused with a smirk. "The old man is very dead I hear. Charred to the bone. They knew it was him because he still sat in the elder chair, in the Vanguard cage, heavy ring nearly melted around his finger."

Sybil frowned. "Why didn't he escape?" She knew from her father that Ralph Busk certainly had no honor. Why did he stay, if not for that?

"Oh," Monty said as he raised his eyebrows, realizing Sybil didn't know about the Vanguard cage, "you've not been." Although not proud of it, Monty frequented the Confines a handful of times in his younger, more adventurous years.

"Montague tell me."

"We Vanguards have a close view of the fighting," he explained with one hand. He took a sip with the other. "In an iron cage locked by one of the Busk guards long before the Arena fills and unlocked long after the festivities end, so no one can touch us. I assume no one unlocked the cage for them. They were trapped as the Dark Arena burnt down around them."

At the thought of old Ralph Busk going down in painful flames, Sybil smiled wide.

Monty smiled back, enchanted by her sharp beauty, for Sybil was striking like a lightning storm was. Her presence was awesome and held a strange power over all who beheld her, drawing them in, twisting their image of her. It was hard to look away from her. Despite this, Monty believed he understood Sybil clearly beneath the gilded façade and was fascinated by her malice. It intrigued him. She was so much different from the others. She was unlike anyone he'd ever known.

"You are sick, woman. You know that?"

"You can't blame me. He was horrid." She met Monty's eyes. "It was a fitting end. The things he did. I know it was just earthblood, but I can't bear think of those little girls and boys just…"

"Then don't think about it," Monty said firmly, not liking to think about the taboo practice the Confines realm held to be commonplace himself either. Although Monty never witnessed the abuse of children himself. He didn't frequent the fourth story of the arena. "The man is dead."

A pall fell across the pair as each drifted into unpleasant thoughts, remembering the stories they'd heard since childhood of the *bad* Elder Busk, watching the sun try to poke out from behind the sky's false black clouds coming from the city across the river. It was nearing midday, yet it was far cooler than to had been the previous days, likely because the fire had drowned out the sun. Fortunately, wind gusted from the West. The terrible smoke was pushed away from Animus Rock.

Sybil finally broke the silence. "What of Edwarde?"

"That is the surprise," Monty said. "Alive."

"Alive!" Sybil smiled incredulously. "In the cage too?"

Monty nodded once, adjusting black wavy hair from one eye. "Miraculous."

"I'm not sure I'd wish to be alive if I were him."

Sybil pursed her lips. She hated indirectness. "His condition that poor?"

"Worse," Monty told her as he pushed up the sleeves of his burgundy and gold embroidered tunic. "Nearly all of the skin from his body is gone. All his hair, and most of his face. I hear he cannot walk either and yet still is causing problems."

"What has the traitor Minney done now?"

"He won't hand over the castle," Monty explained. "Commanded the guards who saved him from the rubble to lock it down. He's basically taken over the Confines for himself. Terje is locked out of his birth right. The man went insane, I think."

"How exciting," Sybil said, a glint in her eye. "What happens next?"

"They say Terje whined to Rupert and I hear he plans to back the man's claim to the Confines. They've sent word to Edwarde that the Morfit army will lay siege to the castle if Edwarde doesn't surrender."

"He would be a fool not to."

Sybil took a slow sip of the throat-stinging beverage, revelling in the chest-warming sensation and lightness it brought behind her eyes. She'd grown accustomed to, maybe even fond of mad honey, although she'd rather die before admitting it.

"You'd be surprised what a man will do when he's got nothing left to lose," Monty said.

"What of his children?"

"Well, pet, you know two ran off."

"I didn't know that," Sybil said tersely. "I've been gone from Animus for some time, Montague."

He sighed, crossing svelte legs, then explained. "The eldest ran off with the youngest after Ralph went to hand them over to Basil." He took a quick sip from his etched glass. "Missing now," he added.

"Can't say I blame them."

"That leaves the middle daughter," Monty said, "and no one knows much of her. I've met the frail girl once, but I fear her father did nothing to protect her from her grandfather and his," Monty paused, "predilections."

"Poor thing," Sybil said quietly.

Monty nodded in agreement. "If she lives, she is damaged, trapped inside the Confines castle with her charred father. Most assume she's dead," he said. "Edwarde will likely burn the place down with her and himself inside before he surrenders. If she lives, she's dead inside already."

Sybil furrowed her brow. She sipped her drink, admiring the billowing smoke. "If you don't think about it too much, it's really beautiful."

Monty looked at her, half smiled, then shook his head.

"Who do you think did this?" Sybil herself didn't have the faintest idea. That was rare.

"Obvious," Monty said with bravado. Sybil leaned in, pulling her shawl a bit tighter. "A plot by Ogo and Rupert to seat Ralph's son Terje at the head of Busk, and in doing so, gain control of the Busk army for the Rebellion."

"Why wouldn't Terje himself be behind it?"

"Terje couldn't harm a beetle," Monty said dismissively. "The man has no clout. Might as well be a Minney. I say from knowing him he would not concoct a plan that would harm so many, no matter how much he disagrees with the way his father runs his bloodline's realm. He's a coward. He's told me himself that his father would die soon enough, after which he would remake the city. He was in no rush. He wouldn't burn it down."

"Ogo does seem the likely culprit," Sybil conceded, yet she wasn't fully convinced. Something wasn't right. "Still, untimely with a Council session so near. Why draw such attention? If it were proven to be him, he'd hang for it."

"To prove a point, maybe? Even the score? Strike fear into the Old?" Monty speculated. "I don't know. What I do know is, Hector will fume. He was already our opposition. Now I'm sure he'll cause problems for us thinking Ogo is behind this."

Sybil wasn't following. "Cause problems how? Who is 'us'?"

"Mad Honey," Monty said disparagingly, raising his etched green glass. "Keep up pet," he added with a wink.

Sybil returned a wide smile while her heart iced over, then melted into a fiery burn. She hated Montague more with each passing moment. But she ensured he'd never be able to tell, of course.

"Galla leads the crusade against it. I expect nothing less from her. She never did know how to have any fun."

"You told me the honey comes from Littlebell," Sybil said, wondering if he was trying to trick her. "Isn't Prihim behind it?"

"I also told you that Galla Morfit and Prihim Minney are fucking. What do you think?"

"Ah, so he supports her, and opposes the honey. It comes from elsewhere in Littlebell."

"It seems."

"How will you vote when it comes to it?"

"It is a pleasure just as ale and should be taxed as such."

"Your opinion has nothing to do with your involvement?"

"What do you mean, involvement? I have connections. Nothing more."

Sybil's tone chilled. "Your gap-toothed friend, then?"

Monty's face clouded. "His name is Juste and I will not

tolerate you throwing another tantrum like a child. You are beautiful, but that kind of behaviour is unbecoming. Unacceptable too."

Sybil frowned. "I had forgotten his name," she said cooly. "I mean to say that the honey is from Littlebell, Juste is a Minney, and you yourself are in possession of mad honey after being in his company. You seem to know quite a bit about the subject. I am connecting stars, Montague."

"Don't bother your pretty head with it." He shook his chin to adjust black hair out of his eye. *Nothing slips past this woman*, he thought, nearly impressed. "I enjoy it, as you did the other night." She didn't have to know how intimately connected to the mad honey trade he did happen to be. Or the specifics of his relationship with Juste Minney.

"I wondered when we'd speak of it again," Sybil said with a coy smile. She lowered her voice. "I can't stop thinking about you." Although she already despised the man, Sybil knew how to use a situation to her own advantage. Or so she thought.

Monty softly smiled. "You are so beautiful. I'll admit that over and over Sybil, but no," he said with finality. He shifted his legs to cross away from her and took a resolute sip, finished his glass fully, and placed it empty on the side table with a clink.

Sybil's stomach dropped. "Why not?" she tried to ask casually but knew she sounded shrill.

"Sybil," he sighed, "you're too much."

She sunk back in her chair with a pinched frown. *Maybe you're not enough*, she thought.

"Don't pout, my dear," Monty said with a chuckle, refilling his glass. "You should thank me for the truth."

"Oh, what good is the truth?" Sybil asked rhetorically, twirling a strand of dark hair escaped from her high head knot stuck today with green gems. "Nothing in this world is true. My own mother taught me that."

"Taught you what?"

"Why, to lie."

Monty lowered his brow. "To lie?"

"Like, when I told you last eve that your hair did not look

oiled when in fact, it did," she said with the widest smile she could, and a glint in her black eyes.

"Very clever," he said. He shook his head. "Nearly charming," he murmured under his breath.

"What was that?"

"Nothing," he smirked, "nothing at all. Stay away from me, you enchantress." He lifted his glass to her.

"You say that like you mean it," Sybil said playfully, slightly sticking out her bottom lip.

"That's because I do."

She frowned.

"You're mad, dear," Monty explained. "Don't feel bad, the best of us are," he added with a wink, nodding to his empty glass. "Not to mention, you're Tomas's daughter. And Old. You have basically told me you hate everything my mother was. Why would I ever want anything to do with you? Why have a conversation with you much less get within the grasp of that sweet venomous cunt between your legs that nearly snared me the other night?"

Sybil stared ahead of herself elegantly, unblinking in silence.

"Nothing?"

She slowly turned her head to lock Monty's eyes, seething wrath beneath her sharp beauty. "You insult me and now you'd like me to speak? Is this what you ask if all your guests, or do I receive unique treatment?"

Monty ran his fingers though his shiny black hair. "I will leave you to yourself then Lady," he said abruptly, standing in such a rush it nearly made Sybil jump from her chair.

"Montague, wait. I didn't mean to anger you," Sybil said softly, internally pleased he was angered. It meant she could more easily control him.

"Anger me." Monty turned, half-smiling, nearly incredulous. "There is your madness, Sybil. Right there," he said, ironically furious she'd sparked his temper. "You think everything is about you. You think you're why I did anything at all. It's not all about you!" he shouted at her.

"You sound angry to me," she cooly replied, delighted he'd

lost his temper. Her great grandfather Lucien always said that the first to lose their head lost the war. "I've had enough for tonight anyway." She rose to stand.

"Now you are leaving me here?" Monty asked her, half-amused and half-indignant.

"I am," Sybil said with a coy, victorious smile.

"Brilliant," Monty replied. "I can enjoy the rest of this then."

He sat back down, grabbed the decanter, and refilled his glass.

Sybil's eyes widened then narrowed and she opened her mouth to speak, then closed it. She wasn't sure if he'd bested her or not, but didn't like how she felt, as if she was sulking inside while he basked in the evening, victorious. Monty watched her through the corner of his eye and smiled. She turned away from him in a huff of white fabric bustling and swishing around her thighs as she stormed back through the billowy curtains and down the hall to her appointed chamber.

A notoriously light sleeper if she got any at all, Sybil awoke to a flurry of footsteps. She listened as a group made their way up the stairs and around the hallway, past her own room, and what sounded like down the hall to Monty's bedchamber. She listened longer, watching delicate curtains flutter from gusts of wind until the scuffles of footsteps and whispering died.

Curious, Sybil rose from her bed silently. She slipped her night robe around her shoulders, tying the silken tassels to secure it at her hip.

Sybil stepped down the hallway on the balls of her feet and paused with each creak and groan of the old building. The only light came from shadows cast off the bright half-moon outside of the floor to ceiling windows to her left. She leaned close to Monty's door and still heard nothing. Under the doorframe were the soft shadows of candlelight. Sybil held her breath, and pushed the heavy door in slightly, just enough to peek inside.

Sybil brought her hands to her mouth and gasped silently at

what she saw. Nudity. Bodies gyrating. Unspeakable things. Then, she backed out of the doorframe and disappeared down the hall without being seen.

WESTERVIOLET LORD'S STUDY

About 100 years ago…

The Busk boys were just trying to make a name for themselves after the betrayal of their father. The corruption of their father. How were they supposed to be accepted with half-tainted blood? Instead of even trying to take a Vanguard wife, he succumbed to a native, from their home realm of the Confines, no less. Florian and Arcadius Busk were ashamed of their mother and birthright for as long as they could remember. They fantasized about the storied days in the wake of the plague when their ancestor Garvan Busk worked hand in hand with Graves to rebuild the Kingdom. They were proud boys, in a sense, yet ignoble in another, always scraping and cheating to try and come out on top and clean in the end.

Although nearly thirty years each, neither had married. Both were awaiting the death of their father, to ensure they could pursue a proper Vanguard marriage instead of a more political one within the realm. Neither Florian nor Arcadius Busk cared for the small-minded games that the Confines High Natives and political leaders played, not like their father. No, the boys had their eyes set across the river. They had their eyes set on Animus Rock, on getting as close to the King as they possibly could.

Given their ambitious sensibilities, Florian and Arcadius latched onto Lucien Graves. Given the latest information they'd come across, the boys thought they had a way into his inner circle. They boldly called a meeting with Lord Lucien Brochet, Westerviolet elderclaim.

The three men stood in the Westerviolet Lord's Study, Lucien behind the elderdesk with hands resting against the massive face while Florian and Arcadius took turns fiddling with different backs of chairs or pacing around the room.

Lucien scowled at their lack of poise and breeding. "What is it?" he barked at them then flexed his strong, cleanshaven jaw. His time was too valuable to be wasted by Busk.

Both Busk boys slightly jumped, used to their own father's heavy hand. "My Lord," Florian took the lead as eldest, stepping up dutifully to face the feared Lucien head to head. "I bring word."

Lucien barely met the man's eye then looked back down, apparently studying a very important parchment resting on his desk between his hands. "We have use of the Missive," Lucien said dismissively. "What use do I have of *your* word?"

"My Lord," Arcadius Busk interjected for his brother, thinking him sometimes too soft spoken to get the point across correctly. "Your man has betrayed you," he said bluntly. The words cut through the air like a spear. Florian winced.

"What." Lucien shot his head up and hissed like a statement, not a question, eyes narrowing into laser focus. He slowly rose from his hunched position over the desk, elongated form towering over the slightly slouched Busks. They instinctively cowered. "Come closer to me," he said, eyeing Arcadius. "You," he barked louder.

Florian nodded at his brother to approach, assuming to disobey was worse than compliance. Arcadius returned the nod and dutifully walked to face Lord Lucien Brochet.

He was terrifying in name and reputation alone. In person, the man seemed jovial and friendly, even charming. It was hard for those who met Lucien for the first time to understand how he had the reputation he did.

After a while though, it always became clear.

Lucien stared Arcadius up and down, narrowing his eyes and widening them as if studying an animal in a cage. Then he reached out his right hand with fingers slightly pointing towards Arcadius. He glanced to look at his brother Florian. "Remember this next time you think to disrespect me," he said, beginning to squeeze his fingers, "in my blood home."

As Lucien constricted his grip, Arcadius inexplicably began to wheeze and sputter.

"What are you doing to him?" Florian looked at Lucien, wide-eyed in panic. It was unbelievable. Power. True visceral Vanguard power. The stuff of legends. "My Lord," he squeaked. Lucien didn't respond. "My Lord," he said, louder this time, taking a step towards the man.

"Do not approach me!" Lucien bellowed in Florian's direction, still clutching the air, Arcadius still coughing and sputtering for breath. The poor young Busk man's sallow skin began to turn a sad shade of purple and his eyes started to bulge out of his head. A vessel burst in one and the whole socket filled with blood. Then, Arcadius's wheezing stopped, and he just gulped for air silently, just like a fish cast to the bank.

"Please," Florian wailed, collapsing to his knees, listening in horror as his brother crumpled and spasmed on the floor of the Westerviolet Lord's study.

But Lucien didn't release his invisible grip on the man's neck until he'd stopped moving entirely.

Florian sat for a long while on the floor of cool stone in complete shock, not believing that his beloved brother was dead. He couldn't be. They were meant to be old men together. The boys were not a full year apart in age and acted more like twins than brothers, having done everything together since they were very small. His heart cracked in two, yet Florian knew this was his one chance to ally with Brochet forever, something both he and his brother had always dreamed of. He knew he had to do justice to his brother's memory. And he knew whatever he did, he could not cry. He flexed his jaw and righted himself, standing over his younger brother's warm body.

Lucien Brochet smiled at the clever Busk's reaction. He was pleasantly surprised. This young man may be useful after all.

Lucien already knew his one-time companion Bin Norland had betrayed him. He'd already begun the arrangements to secure the situation ended in Brochet's favor, however, as he was standing in front of the Busk elderclaim, he realized that there might be another way.

The next day the entire Busk Brown Guard marched on Littlebell in Bin Norland's name and sacked the castle, making it quite clear that they did so only because Sia spurned Bin.

Afterwards, Sia Minney was convinced that Bin Norland kidnapped her daughter Lilli against her will.

And the Littlebell clock tower burned.

ANSTOUT

Present Day

Ryd turned to Digory. His mind had been racing for creeds.

"What is this Graves elder supposed to be like?"

Mable whinnied loudly beneath him, shaking her head and flailing her tawny braided mane.

"Woah, girl," Ryd said gently. He patted her neck. "Woah."

The pair, miraculously atop Mable and Chester respectively despite their ordeal in the Confines, trekked the long path through the ancient Black Hills in the North. Cool gusts of wind travelled down from the tall hills in the near distance. The vegetation, after parting from the Missi River, turned spikey and sparse.

"He's not the one we're meant to give this to," Digory said, patting his trouser pocket twice. Now, he wore a black leather coat that fell long to his ankles with a high collar that buckled at one side. On his head, a pointed, moulded hat in black leather with blue stitching and a shimmering green feather in the band. The ploom listed rhythmically with regular gusts of wind. It was a Wraithswail bagon, just like Sybil had told him to wear. The hat was a bit blackened from smoke, but otherwise, fine.

The bagon caught Ryd's eye. "I can't believe you got that," he said.

"What? This?" Digory placed fingers on the brim and tipped the hat.

"You look like you should be on the arm of Leon wearing that ridiculous thing." He paused, then grumbled. "I can't believe you traded that fine tunic for it either. Should have gotten better provisions."

"You shouldn't joke of one's preferences," Digory said

piously. Ryd rolled his eyes. "And besides," he continued, "you don't know what you're talking about. Once again." Digory adjusted the brim.

"Oh, please. What's that mean?"

Digory side eyed him. He shook his head.

"What?"

"You'll see."

Ryd sighed and looked forward. He studied the rocky, harsh terrain around them. The sky was steel grey awash with white, wispy clouds that fell like a sheer sheet over the land and blanked out the sunlight. Everything cast in a pale, unearthly glow. Ryd couldn't take it. He had to know what he was getting into.

"What's he like?"

"Which one?" Digory said. "The real elder who is steps from the pyre, or Hector?

"Both."

Pointed spruce trees dotted the landscape of grey, white, and black rock jutting up from the ground into towering black mountain peaks capped with snow. Bushes with drooping leaves and round, white-flowing spittle, crowded up to the bases amidst time-knotted brambles, massive slate-grey ferns, and upwards growing, vertical bulbs of frothy foamflowers. An ear-tearing caw rang out throughout the peaks as a wide shadow flew across the land—a hawk with a wingspan nearly that of a man. Hawks were rampant throughout Anstout. Ryd watched the bird's shadow trail across the scape ahead of them.

"Hjalmar Graves is very old," Digory said," but even so hasn't been the elder for long."

"Why not?"

"His father. Haulfrun. Lived forever. Nearly, anyway. Wouldn't die. Know anything about him?"

Ryd shook his head.

"Wretched guy, they say," Digory told him. "Infamous. Legendary."

"Why?"

"Some argue he alone started the Uprising."

"Really?"

"I wish I was good enough to make this shit up," Digory replied with a flashing smile. "It's true."

"What does this have to do with Hjalmar Graves?"

"It has everything to do with him," Digory said. He scratched his beard with one hand while holding the reigns with the other. "Hjalmar fell deeply in love, apparently. When he was young. With Demosblood."

"Love? Demos?" Ryd asked slowly with growing recognition. "Aren't they New?"

Digory pointed a finger. "There you go. You can imagine how the son of a deadblood raised at Echo's Omen reacted when he found out that his eldest son and heir to his blood seat had run off to Hellswater with an earthblood, essentially."

Ryd frowned. He stared ahead at the undulating path. He wasn't sure he wanted to know, but curiosity bested him. The more he learned of the Kingdom around him, the more he craved knowledge. It was almost as if a long-worn frost was lifting from his mind. One he'd never known was there before.

"What'd he do?" Ryd asked grimly.

"Not only did Haulfrun Graves storm Hellswater and burn the place nearly to the ground to find his son, but he also took the Demos girl too," Digory said, as if impressed, because he was. "It makes it so much worse that she was said to be gorgeous with huge melons for breasts and puffy lips that could swallow a man whole. What a waste."

"Digory, don't talk about her like that," Ryd warned, glaring daggers. "She's dead. It's disrespectful."

"What? It's what they said about her," Digory raised his eyebrows defensively. "No wonder Hjalmar couldn't resist. I'm only a messenger."

Ryd sighed, not wanting to spur Digory on. But he wanted to know. "What then?"

Digory met Ryd's questioning red eyes. "Haulfrun forced Hjalmar to kill Anna Demos. Murdered her with a dagger, Brotherhood execution style."

Ryd winced. "That doesn't sound good."

"Here," Digory gestured with his right hand against the side of his chest, "between your fourth and fifth rib. All Brotherhood have a tattoo to mark the spot. It's the fastest way to the heart. To stab someone there is to ensure a quick death. An honourable death."

Ryd shook his head, thinking that nothing about the Brotherhood could possibly be honorable.

"The whole ordeal with Anna Demos ruined Hjalmar," Digory went on, horseshoes clopping loudly beneath him, "and then his father lived on as elder for another fifty years or something ridiculous. He only just died. Haulfrun's ways were cemented as the norm for Graves and their realm. Why, in fact, he made his son follow the family," he paused, "tradition."

Ryd turned his head to look at Digory. "What tradition?"

"Both Hector and Herman Graves are half dead."

Ryd sighed, remembering Digory's fascination with deadbloods. "Ah. Right."

"Anyway," Digory continued, "word is that Hjalmar resents the Old for everything that was done to him. They say he's softening in his later years. Ironically, his younger brother Dorian was all about their father's beliefs and the Old. Haulfrun gave Dorian and his descendants Echo's Omen but kept Anstout for Hjalmar. A mistake," he added.

"How?"

"Tomas thinks Hjalmar goes soft," Digory explained. "He's sympathetic to the New. His favorite lives at Animus, married to the King's sister, living the life of a pampered pet. Hjalmar has eased up on the earthblood in his realm—he's producing less in the mines—and he's allegedly halted his experiments."

Ryd frowned, remembering the story Drakon told him of Plusia. "I thought experiments were illegal."

Digory shrugged. Legality was moot to the likes of Gravesblood. As it was to Brochet.

"That's good, right?" Ryd looked to Digory hopefully. "That Graves has stopped, I mean."

"Depends," Digory said. "For the ones who live in that realm, sure, it's a delight. But if you ask Sybil, it's a travesty."

"Right," Ryd sighed. "They enjoy it when the people suffer."

"The trick is," Digory said, "they don't see them as people. Us, I mean."

"What do you mean?"

"I mean," he said, breathing in the thin mountain air through flared nostrils, "notice how they always call us 'earthblood', or mongrels, or spit at our breeding? It makes it easier to treat us as dogs and still consider themselves righteous."

"You're saying Vanguards are only so cruel because they pretend we aren't people?"

"Not pretend, believe. And belief makes anything real."

"Where do you come up with this, Digory?"

"I make it up as I go along."

Ryd looked at him. "That hat is really ridiculous," he said, then winced as Mable leapt over a fallen log in the path.

"What happened to you?" Digory turned, surprised by his concern and anger at whoever hurt his companion. What a strange emotion. He quickly shrugged it aside. "You still haven't said. What did Busk do?"

Ryd was quiet for a while. Birds squawked nearby. Wind whipped fell leaves. "I wouldn't wish it on anyone," he said quietly.

"It's alright if you don't remember."

"I remember every detail," Ryd said quickly, then sighed. "It's all I can see when I close my eyes."

"Now you must tell me."

Digory was sickly curious and deeply relieved he was still his horrible self, despite his momentary lapse of empathy before. He sat up a little straighter atop Chester, listening intently. He was glad the rotten soul that he knew himself to be was back.

"I don't know where I was," Ryd said, voice distant and hollow, as if he was lost in a dream. "Everything was dim once they removed my blind. There were figures wearing round spectacles. I've... I've never seen anything like them."

"What did they do to you?" Digory asked in a gruff whisper.

"They hung me up and they beat me," Ryd said hollowly. "They whipped me, more and more until I finally cried out and begged them to stop. A man entered and stuck me in my neck. Then, he left. After that I hung from a chain by my hands for, I don't know how long, until two more returned." The memory was so painfully poignant, Ryd felt he was reliving it with each word. "They unchained me then brought me to that filthy fighting pit."

"The Dark Arena."

"Right," Ryd said. "Then I saw you there in that awful crowd. How did you find me?"

"I met a woman. Ugly thing," Digory told him. "Shield dame, in fact, if you can believe that." Ryd was impressed. He'd heard of them from children's tales. Fiercer than the men of Ironbark, it was said. "She knew a thing or two about the streets of that town," Digory went on. "She helped me find the arena, in fact." He paused. "I owe a bit of my escape to her."

"Where is she?" Ryd asked eagerly, instantly thinking they'd have a useful companion. He hushed when he realized the likely truth. "Fallen in the flames?"

"I," Digory hesitated. "I don't know."

Ryd turned in genuine disgust. "What? You mean… you didn't even look for her? After she saved you? Digory…"

"I know, I know," Digory said quite honestly, throwing his head back. He ran a hand over his hair and scratched his beard. "I should have, shouldn't I?" He paused. He looked at Ryd. "Oh well. She's probably dead."

Ryd smiled, glancing to Digory and his blaze attitude, thinking how nice it must be to have no soul. He looked back to the path. He shook his head.

Digory noticed Ryd's judgement. "What?"

"And here I thought you changed."

"Dangerous assumption, friend."

Ryd pulled Mable to a halt. "Is this serious?" he said, glaring ahead. His eyes snaked the intimidating staircase cut in the mountain's stone ahead of them. "This can't be serious."

"Very," Digory said flatly. "First, you're afraid of water. Now heights. What next?"

He pulled Chester to a halt, too.

In front of them rose a tall staircase carved directly into the granite. It looped around sharp bends, up crumbling ridges, and over a valley littered with razor-like boulders. The pass widened and narrowed at random without a guard or railing, even at the most sheer overhangs. It was high from the cavern floor and at the mercy of windy gusts. A shoddy wooden structure with old hay and a trough filled half with moss and needles, and half with water, sat at the bottom of the staircase. It seemed Anstout's castle had not had outside visitors in quite a long time.

A hammered sign was tacked directly into the rockface next to the makeshift stable. At the top, a smiling skull over two crossed bones with the phrase '*Mors Mihi Lucrum*'. Beneath the Graves crest, the words carved deep and bold: **Beware to all, friend or foe, who ascend the Black Stairs.**

"Unnecessarily ominous if you ask me," Digory said. "It doesn't look that bad." Wind whipped around craggy peaks with angry whistles, as if the mountain disagreed with him.

Ryd's heart plummeted into his stomach. "Sure," he said.

"You must learn to trust," Digory chided with half a smile, ostentatious feather plume bucking in the wind.

Ryd tied up their horses in the sad stable. "Against the odds we found them just to leave them once more," Ryd sighed. "I'll be back soon for you both," he whispered and nuzzled his nose into Chester's neck as he patted Mable's flank, although with a glance up at the Black Stairs, he wasn't so sure that was true. These were his only true companions in the whole Kingdom. Now more than ever, he loved them dearly. It hurt him to part from them.

"Really?" Digory asked with a chuckle.

"They're not just dumb beasts, you know," Ryd said. "They understand."

"Right, course."

"Don't believe me all you want but it's true. Dogs more so. Cats. All animals really."

Digory sighed.

"All that trouble to find them after the Arena. I'm going to care for them, Digory."

"Are you done?"

"Fine let's go," Ryd said with another reluctant sigh, tearing his eyes away from his trusted companions.

He followed Digory up the deadly staircase to Castle Anstout.

The castle rose from the highest peak for creeds. It was true to its reputation, intimidating as it was impressive, gigantic towers jutting up from the craggy skyline. Ryd swallowed hard as he realized how huge the structure must be if it already looked so large from the bottom of the stairs.

The higher up they went, the narrower the path got. It started rather wide. Ryd felt mostly comfortable with it, but the higher they climbed, the more the side of the mountain seemed to drop off. Also, where before there was lush coverage from the spikey forest, the higher they went in elevation, fewer evergreens dotted the mountain.

Ryd could see the other mountains surrounding this one once the trees were out of the way. He studied apartment-like homes built directly into the opposing rock faces of each one. Rag-wrapped individuals climbed in and out, using long ladders and steps of stone. The people filtered into long lines, then in and out of nearby mine shafts. Ryd looked away and painfully sighed.

Overhead, tawny hawks glided around the highest points of the peaks, like guards patrolling the sky.

Digory, uninterested in the earthblood of Anstout, was enamoured by the grand shadow-like castle, built with the same stone from the surrounding mountains, cut into oversized blocks of speckled granite. The oldest and tallest part of the castle sat on a high piled motte. It was a monster of a round tower with a pointed roof and alternating square and round windows, allowing strategic view of the mountains and valleys all around. From there, eight other rounded towers of matching architecture but varying heights and ages were strewn around the base and the bailey. The grounds were covered in low-trimmed grass and neat shrubbery that ran all the way to the edge of the flat valley atop the mountain. Past the edge was an unforgiving drop to the true valley below. There was no need for a wall or moat to protect the intimidating fortress, for the location was deterrent enough. The extent of the fortification apart from sheer, craggy drop of the mountain's face was a modest, practical gate house acting as the entry point for all travellers who dared climb up the treacherous stairs.

It was unbelievable to consider the manpower it would take to build such a monstrosity. Digory couldn't imagine. It seemed impossible, yet there Anstout stood.

In the midst of their ascent, a cool rain began to fall from the blanket of soft grey clouds. A dewy mist was cast across the evergreens, slicking the granite stairs beneath their feet.

"Watch your step," Digory said. "And don't look down."

"You should have said that first," Ryd replied angrily, already staring with wide eyes down over the edge of the cliff. He pushed a few rocks with his boot. They toppled down the side of the mountain. Ryd listened but never heard the stones hit the valley floor, instead they tumbled for what sounded like forever until fading away into the foggy canyon below. It looked like they were climbing into the clouds. Ryd couldn't see the valley's lush blanket of spruce trees anymore. His heart seized in his chest.

Ridge after bend arose before them as the pair scaled the winding, carved stone staircase awash with fresh rain, winds whipping cold against their damp clothing, hands, and faces.

"We won't make it," Ryd said, breathing hard. He walked several paces behind Digory, hands gripping the adjacent wall.

"We will," Digory barked without glancing back, one hand steadying himself on the left rock face, the other clinging to his ridiculous cap. "Keep up."

"You're going too fast."

"Come on. We're nearly there."

"They'll probably kill us once we walk through the gate," Ryd said miserably, nearly clinging to the rock face wall. He took one timid step after the next.

"They won't," Digory turned his head to Ryd.

"Don't look back at me! Curses, you'll fall!"

Digory laughed. "Worry about yourself." He said, still holding his hat with his hand. The whipping winds and rain increased and the green plume hung moist and limp against the brim of the hat despite the gale. "We're nearly there. I told you. Look, just past that pass."

Ryd's eyes widened at the impossible gap marked by a detached bridge of rocks, like stones through a pond. One had to step from each stone to the next to reach the other side. "Oh great, just that pass."

"Quit it. You will be fine. Truly, you'll fall if you keep talking like that."

Ryd stopped. "You're really going to cross it? That? Really?"

They came to a flat outcropping that led up to the threatening path. One misstep would be certain death from the plummet to the sharp rocks hidden beneath cloud cover below.

"It's called Dead man's pass, and yes I am," Digory replied, remembering the stories he'd heard about Anstout. About how many men had succumbed to the Black Stairs–to Dead Man's pass–before ever reaching the castle. It was said that Gravesblood of old fed on the souls of the fallen. But native who was able to reach the castle was awarded their freedom. That was the myth, anyway. "So are you."

"I should have known it was called that. Of course it's called that."

Digory ignored him.

"This can't be the only way."

"It is."

"The rain, and wind!" Ryd cried. "Look how high up we are. There!" He pointed to the ledge.

Digory turned to cross alone. "Suit yourself."

"Wait, what?" Ryd's voice nearly squeaked and he internally cringed at how he sounded, but his fear overtook his pride. "You'll leave me? Here? We're nowhere."

"Rather than listen to you complain, yes, I would," he shouted back over his shoulder.

Ryd frowned, nearly about to turn around.

Digory raised his eyebrows. He rubbed his beard with his

hand. He turned back to Ryd. "Come on. Anstout is right there," he said with reassurance. He wouldn't admit it to himself, but Digory was growing fond of Ryd. He'd hate to abandon him now after all they'd been through. "Let's just get this over with."

Ryd sighed loud. He looked up at the looming castle. "I can't believe I'm doing this."

"That's the spirit," Digory said warmly. He turned to the castle then stepped onto the first stone.

"No wonder no one attacks this place," Ryd muttered.

The wind whipped about them. Rain stung their cheeks.

Ryd trembled in terror, leaping from stone to stone. With each footfall, he imagined himself slipping and falling. He tried desperately not to look down, attempting to focus on Digory's back, to no avail.

"Digory," Ryd called out shakily. He was frozen in horror, barely halfway across the pass.

Digory just stepped safely onto the other side. "Curses, what is it?" He turned and exhaled in expected, yet thankful relief for crossing safely himself.

"Digory! I can't do it!" Ryd teetered where he stood, looking down, then at the next stone in line. It was particularly small compared to the rest, and at a bit of an angle. If he could make this leap, he would likely make it fine to the other side. But only if he could make this leap.

Digory laughed. "Oh, you can! Friend, if I can, you certainly should be able." He gestured around. "Look, the weather is not even that horrid."

Then, if on command, the already churning skies opened in fury, drenching the pair. A bolt of lightning cut the sky behind them.

"You can make it I say! Trust me," Digory shouted over the downpour, "you can make it!"

Ryd took a resolute breath, seeing his brother's face in his mind's eye. Everything he did now was to eventually find Collen. He reminded himself of that and discovered renewed strength. He exhaled slowly and glanced to Digory.

"You have this, stablemaster," Digory said. He was surprised at the nervous knot in his stomach for Ryd's well-being. He almost hoped Ryd would fall, just to punish himself for caring.

Ryd thought that was the nicest Digory had ever been to him. Between that and the thought of his brother, he gathered the gumption to move. He began to scoot towards the edge of the rather large stone he currently perched upon. His body was nearly numb from the icy rain and he could hardly feel his feet. But he knew he must do this.

He took a leap to the next, smaller step.

As soon as Ryd's foot planted, he slipped. He felt it in the pit of his stomach that he'd miscalculated. He'd failed.

Digory saw Ryd falling and reached out towards him with his hand, for no reason other than he felt like he should. And screamed, with everything in his lungs, for no reason other than he felt like it should be done. He didn't think, he just did. And at the same moment, the sky opened up again in a blinding crack as violet lightning cut the dark clouds all around him. His heart felt as if it snapped in two when he imagined the man who he'd spent all this time with, who had saved his life, was about to plummet to his demise. He hated himself for caring but barely cared about that anymore. He crumpled in sadness.

Ryd wasn't sure what happened, but he landed on the next smaller step as he'd planned to do. It was as if an invisible gust of wind rushed from behind him and propped him up. He looked up to see Digory collapsed, hands on his face. Was he crying?"

"Digory, Digory I made it!" Ryd shouted with glee. He easily hopped the following steps with his newfound confidence. He was quickly at Digory's side.

"What, you did? You did!" Digory leapt up, tossing the waterlogged Wraithswail fashion onto the muddy rocks at his side. He ran and hugged him. "Aye, you did!"

"I… I don't know how," Ryd said, "but I made it!"

"Aye," Digory smiled. "You did." He put his hand on Ryd's shoulder. "Let's get going." He turned towards the hulking gate house ahead. Thunder rumbled low all around them.

Both Digory and Ryd were drenched from the cold, unrelenting weather. Both men shivered. Water dripped from Digory's short hair and beard. Rain clung to Ryd's course curls and from the bridge of his wide nose. Side by side they approached. Ryd was shaking from adrenaline. He couldn't understand how Digory seemed so calm.

Guards with black hooded capes and darkened chainmail stood at the ready in front of the stark, rectangular gate house with long spears in hand.

"Here we go," Digory said under his breath.

"State your business," one barked like an underfed attack dog.

After a short exchange and a flash of the tattered, yet somehow intact Brochet emblem on Sybil's letter, Digory convinced one of the Graves guards, a tall yet slender man with black hair, splotched skin and hollow eyes, to escort them to Anstout Elder Hjalmar Graves–son of the infamous Haulfrun, the first Vanguard with dead blood.

"I thought we had to talk to Hector," Ryd whispered to Digory. They followed closely behind the black cape.

"We do," Digory whispered back. His eyes swept the tidy interior of Anstout's arching gatehouse, leading them into the grassy bailey surrounded by narrow grey stone buildings with drastically angled rooves. He noted a smith and a black-painted building with a keyhole shaped door that he figured was the Apothecary. "He shouldn't be far," he whispered as they scaled the steep steps into the Anstout castle herself. They entered the bastion behind the black-clad, spear-toting guard. "The trick will be getting him alone."

"How do we do that?" Ryd asked quietly.

He was quickly thrust into unabashed awe of the castle's grand architecture. It had impossibly high vaulted ceilings and walls of enormous stone blocks unlike anything he'd ever seen, grander in size than the green stones of Westerviolet.

Doorways were huge and arched. The floor was small cut blocks of black stone in geometric patterns, arranged like tiles lined with greyish grout. Ryd was fully impressed, although he didn't have anything to compare it to. Anstout was the first castle he'd ever been inside.

His awe gave way quickly, the further they walked. Ryd was confused, frustrated, and terrified of what was to befall them after the rumors he'd heard.

They followed the Graves guard through the main hall of the castle, turning right down a high arched corridor, then left. Every so often the pair passed a pack of guards in formation, walking with eyes straight and feet in rhythmic step, holding spears to the ready at their side. Apart from that, the castle was totally empty.

"Here," the guard barked, arriving at a tall yet otherwise nondescript wooden door. "Vanguard blood elder, Hjalmar Graves," he said with forced formality, pushing it open with a creak.

Black curtains draped partially open in front of square windows dotting the un-plastered stone walls. The floor was of the same tiled stone and bare as well, just as the rest of the castle. Everything felt crisp and cool. Sterile. Lifeless. Like eyes without light in them. Candlelight flickered from round tables, illuminating tiny glimmering specks naturally embedded in the stone. The entire room sparkled.

Two men sat together at a round table. A pale woman with a large forehead and a dead expression sat with straight-back against the far wall in a wooden chair. She stared ahead at nothing, unmoving. Ryd felt sorry for her instantly. She looked very much like she'd rather be dead.

Digory, no time for sympathy, ignored the woman instantly. He listened closely instead to the men at the table, emblazoned in conversation, unaware of the interruption.

"You will do as commanded," an old voice creaked slowly from the mouth of a proud-looking man with pink-white face and faded yellow hair. "As your brother has done."

"He's a fool," a younger growled, followed by the screeching squawk of a fearsome hawk perched on his broad shoulder. The hawk's golden feathers glinted in the candlelight. "He and the King. Together they nearly make a man." His voice grated like a bolder rolling from a mountain face and was equally powerful.

"You won't speak that way," the older man chided the younger, deep etched lines beside his eyes. "You forget your duty."

"You are the one who forgets," the younger said slowly. He paused and narrowed his icy gaze. "If only grandfather were here…." He trailed off. It was obviously a threat.

"No more!" the old man bellowed firmly, slamming a fist on the table. Candles jumped.

"My Lords," the guard interrupted them.

The younger man slowly turned his head to face the interruption as if irritated by a pest. A chill ran up Ryd's spine when he caught the man's piercing eyes briefly. He felt like he'd been dunked in ice. He knew exactly who that must be. "What do you disturb us with?"

"Lord Hector. They bring word from Brochet," the guard announced, tone buckling slightly from nerves. Apparently even his own guards were terrified of him, Ryd thought. The guard lowered his head and stepped back, allowing line of sight to Digory and Ryd.

Hector Graves frowned. He studied them with his unnervingly pale eyes set deep into sullen skin pulled tight over high cheekbones. He toyed with a small cloth satchel in one hand and glared at Digory and Ryd, intense and unblinking, with shoulders squared to them. He had an elongated neck, hands, and fingers. Something about him was just *off*. Digory noted the man's practical riding pants, unexpected so far west of the Missi.

The fearsome hawk with hooked beak and brilliant beige, cream, and golden-brown feathers glared at them from its perch on Hector's wide-shouldered coat lined with braided black and brown leather strips for the sharp talons to rest on.

Ryd frowned curiously at the wriggling and squeaking cloth

bag in Hector's slender hand.

Without breaking eye contact with the pair of men, Hector pulled a delicate mouse out of the satchel by its tail. He held the poor white creature up to watch it squirm in terror. Ryd's stomach dropped and Digory nearly smirked, impressed by Hector's chilly calm. Emotionless, Hector Graves lifted the fearful mouse to the hawk. It squeaked a final time as its spine snapped with a small crunch and it was ripped in two by a razor-sharp beak. Bloody pieces of flesh and intestine fell across Hector's coat as the bird ate. He didn't flinch.

"Brochet?" Hector asked with a hint of surprise. "Tomas?"

"Finally making good on his promises I hope," the Anstout elder Hjalmar barked dismissively from his seat. Hector, Digory, and Ryd all turned to look at him, sitting with a straight back, fists clenched tight on the round wooden table. He didn't look anything like one would think Gravesblood would look like.

Hjalmar Graves's skin was much brighter than his son's with warm pink undertones instead of grey. Instead of ice grey, his eyes were a sparkling green and his full head of hair was once-blonde and now streaked white. He had the characteristic Graves widow's peak. He obviously too inherited more of his mother's Thorne blood than his namesake, Graves. Hjalmar bore the same striking high cheekbones, etched jaw, and intense stare as Hector (it was obvious they were kin by the shape of their face and eyes) but his jaw was clean-shaven. Unlike the younger man with few wrinkles, Hjalmar had deep creases around his eyes and heavy bags under them too. The old man's skin was thin and draped over sagging muscles. He looked like wrinkled parchment.

"Aye," Digory nodded, addressing the elder. "He wants to discuss it." He glanced at Hector.

"That doesn't sound like Tomas," Hjalmar said slowly. "Not at all. I assume he sent communication. Hand it here," he commanded.

"No letter," Digory replied quickly, trying to figure out how to bypass the elder as Sybil commanded. Ryd looked at him in shock.

"My Lord," the guard who led them there interjected.

"What is it?" Hjalmar replied.

"He lies," he said with a sick smile, glancing back to Digory briefly, then to Hjalmar once more. "He flashed the emblem to be let through the gate."

"Thanks." Digory said dryly. The black cape mockingly blinked at Digory as he was excused to depart.

"Who are you?" Hjalmar questioned Digory more seriously, voice tinged with suspicion as the spiteful guard slammed the door behind him with a clank. "Why are you here?"

Hector stood, revealing his impressive height. The hawk still on his shoulder screeched loudly again. Ryd jumped backwards, startled. Digory set his jaw.

"Hand it to me," Hector interrupted with bone-chilling calm without breaking eye contact with Digory.

Ryd looked nervously back and forth between the two men.

Digory held the intimidating man's gaze, unblinking his fire-filled eyes with his nerves steeled. He was not afraid of Hector. "As you wish," Digory replied after a pregnant pause, as if the glare was a contest and when no clear winner could be declared, he stepped forward. He handed the sad, crumpled parchment to Hector with the warped Brochet emblem pressed into the wax.

Digory was fully relieved to be rid of the thing, overjoyed he'd actually delivered it as promised. He kept his word to Sybil. Now for the repercussions.

Hector placed the writhing satchel of rodents on the table and took the letter. He carefully flipped it over in his large, long fingered hands.

Digory stepped backwards in line with Ryd, holding his soggy hat behind his back. Both men dripped water all over the tile-like stone floor.

Hector studied the letter from top to bottom before even breaking the seal. He felt over the wax with his thumb, and investigated the edges of it, and even smelled it before looking at his father and nodding.

Hjalmar nodded back. "Open it. Read it for me, will you? These old eyes are not what they used to be."

Digory shifted his weight again. This could get interesting. He held his hat with both hands. He glanced down and studied the water dripping on the floor, pooling like a lake atop the small tiles.

Ryd looked back and forth between Hector assessing the letter and Hjalmar watching him do it.

"Yes, father," Hector said slowly, breaking the wax seal easily with the sharp nail on his thumb. The parchment ripped a bit when he did with a quiet tear that cut the bated silence in the room. Hector held the note out before him, up to flickering candlelight, squinting his grey eyes into analytical slits as his pupils gazed through the contents, line by line. Everyone watched him.

"Well," Hjalmar urged. "What does it say?" He cracked the knuckles of his right hand against the table with a sickening echo.

Ryd jumped a little bit, terrified, pretty sure they were going to be tossed from the cliff he'd just barely survived climbing. He'd fail his brother and die pathetically alone.

"It says," Hector paused as his eyes danced back and forth, Digory holding his breath, "exactly what the earthblood said it does." Digory exhaled loudly through his nostrils, flexing his jaw, trying hard not to smile, for he could see it in Hector's eye; he was lying. Whatever Sybil wrote was making Hector Graves lie.

"And that is?"

"Tomas wants to see you," he responded automatically, so sincerely Digory believed it himself. He was fully impressed by the man's frozen composure. The world seemed to cave in around Hector Graves, as if he was bewitched with a powerful force that drew in everyone's attention to him. No wonder the Kingdom bowed to his wishes. His presence was chillingly intoxicating. He paused briefly before continuing. "Asks that you travel to Animus Rock with me for the fall equinox," Hector's eyes scanned the document. "You are correct. It's about the pact and the girl."

"I knew it," a smile broke across old Hjalmar's face, completely believing the tale. "Yet I'm an old man. Too old to travel the distance. Tomas knows this. Can he not come to Anstout?"

"It seems he can't," Hector said with finality. He lowered the letter. He held it tight in his hand, and it crunched at his knuckles. The hawk on his shoulder screeched again. The terrible note echoed about the hall.

Millie Busk, Hector's wife, silent until now, let out a horrified squeal and jumped in her chair as she was startled by the bird's call. She cast her eyes down and brought her hands to her mouth. Hector swung his head to her. He snorted a laugh, the first emotion he'd shown thus far, then went back to facing the men. The poor woman shuddered. Then she cowered against her wooden chair as if she was hoping she could disappear into it. Ryd's heart bled for her.

"Then there is but one choice," Hjalmar said. "It's clear. You must go in my stead. Speak to Tomas for me. Let's see Brochet make good on their word."

"Absolutely father," Hector said, bowing his head slightly, smoothing his sharp greying beard with his hand. "As you command," he said as he rose. "You, and you," Hector addressed Digory and Ryd as if he was chiding dogs. "You are Tomas's earthblood? Of Westerviolet?"

Digory nodded.

Hector looked at Ryd. Ryd nodded. "You are valuable, then. You will accompany me," he said as a command, not a question.

"Accompany you?"

"Tomas permits you to talk back like that?" He fished another small squeaking mouse from the black bag he held. He fed it to the hawk with a squeak and bloody crunch of small bones.

"Of course, my Lord," Digory said, bowing dramatically. He realized why so many feared this man.

"Do not hurt him, Hector," Hjalmar warned his son in

gravely tone. "He is Tomas's. You know the law."

"Father, you do not need lecture me of the importance of allies."

"I caution not to harm the man. Or the other. They claim Brochet. That is a command."

Hector glared under his heavy brows. "Yes, father," he said simply. "I would never suggest otherwise."

Ryd looked from Digory to Hector again.

"We leave for the Rock at dawn," Hector said to them. "As," he paused, glancing to Digory, "Tomas requests," he added with a sharp glint in his eye. Digory thought he caught the briefest glance from the hawk at the same time, but that had to be coincidence, he assured himself.

"Good boy." Hjalmar sat back. "Perhaps he plans to join you on your quest for reform."

Digory automatically smirked. At his response, Hjalmar paused, obviously stung, then spoke cautiously, as if not to offend one of Tomas Brochet's high-ranking men. "Have you not heard of Hector's campaign for tolerance?" Hjalmar said, indignation palpable beneath his political poise. "Tell him of your work, son," he urged Hector.

Digory was visibly amused. It seemed Hector had painted his father a false picture of the state of the Kingdom indeed. "Yes, Lord Hector," he said mockingly, glancing to the willowy man. "I implore you."

Hector's glare held. "It is you who should be so glad for my tolerance," he told Digory.

"My son understands that the only way for Graves to survive is to compromise. To come to an accord, as it were. Isn't that right, son?"

"Yes, father."

"Good boy."

"Dawn," Hector said ominously as he looked from Ryd to Digory. He stared for several seconds, blinked slowly, then turned from the room. He walked the length of the hall, past the pair and out through the door they entered, gliding by them with long, inhuman strides. Hector's fearsome bird leapt from his shoulder, and, after a few loud flaps soared behind him.

Hector stopped to give instructions to the guard on the way out. Digory and Ryd could faintly overhear.

"Get those earthborn away from the old man," he growled. "No one speaks to him. And once he's in his chambers," Hector added, "lock him in there."

The guard hesitated.

"Go," Hector barked louder, wrath dripping from the command.

"All is well, son?" Hjalmar shouted from the distance of the hall when he heard Hector's commanding echo.

Hector didn't answer. Instead, pressing resentment and bubbling hatred for his loon of a father down in his throat, he steeled himself and hurried away. It was all he could do not to gouge the man's eyes out where he sat.

Digory and Ryd listened as his heavy footsteps bounded away down the hall.

Digory and Ryd were kept chained to a grate near an outbuilding in the middle of the chilly bailey for the whole night, after they were each given one ladle of water and a crisp of bread. Generous by Anstout standards.

At first light they were kicked awake by heavy boots.

"Get up," Hector looked down at them over his sharply manicured beard, squinting icy eyes. His wide-shadowed hawk soared in circles overhead. "This way," he added. Ryd scrambled to stand as a guard unlocked his chains. He rubbed his wrists. Digory rose more slowly with the same practiced hubris he always exuded, studying the legendary feared Hector Graves in the flesh.

On this misting morning, Hector strode away, then half looked back over his shoulder at Digory.

"Nice hat," he said knowingly, eyeing the sadly tattered headpiece Digory clung to.

With half a smile Digory tipped it to him. The feathery plume

was waterlogged from the rain the night before and the leather brim was wet and soggy, covered in dirt and mud from outside.

Hector laughed loud like a crack of thunder and shook his head once as he walked away.

Ryd, freezing and terrified, was now confused as well.

"I don't get it," he whispered.

"He said he liked my hat," Digory replied flatly.

Hector's laugh stopped instantly and he barked, "Quiet."

He was amused by the brashness of Tomas's tall earthblood. He had never been looked at that way by a lesser man—without an ounce of fear. There was a fire in his soul. Although Digory's bravado amused him, he did not want him to forget his place.

Ryd jumped and Digory snickered as they followed Hector through the mountain top courtyard, expecting to scale the mountain face. Instead, they were led into Anstout's impressive castle again. Hector took them into the main hall, through a narrow corridor, and then down a dizzying spiral staircase. They fell into silence apart from the heavy fall of footsteps through the castle's underbelly.

"I thought we were leaving," Digory said.

"Quiet," Hector growled.

They descended into the pitch black. The shiny damp walls transitioned from cut blocks to undisturbed rock, staircase obviously carved directly into the mountain's hard stone at this depth, lined with velvety moss on every moist wall face. After a while, the steps became cruder and started to feel particularly slick beneath their feet. Ryd wondered what dungeon Hector was leading them to. He planned his last moments, woefully mourning his fate and failure, never having found Col. Digory, conversely, followed Hector with extreme curiosity, but no fear at all. He knew that whatever Sybil had written would keep them safe. For all of her insanity, Digory trusted her implicitly. Finally, the group reached the bottom of the staircase. It opened into a wide cave. Oddly, despite their native eyes, both Digory and Ryd were unexpectedly blind in the darkness of this cavern. Shockingly, Hector moved forward as if he could see perfectly and disappeared without a word.

In the darkness, they could hear disembodied moans, cries and the occasional scream. They were in Anstout's First.

"Hey!" Ryd yelled out. He was unnerved by the darkness. "Where do we go?" His voice made a muffled echo. He jumped at the sound from high nerves. His terror of not being able to see was overwhelming. This was a first, for sure.

"Rope," Hector said.

"What did he say?" Ryd asked Digory softly.

Digory kicked his feet across small rocks covered in cave moss to discover a rope.

"Here. I think I've got something."

Unlike Ryd, Digory was not afraid. Only intrigued. He wondered if the mountain Anstout castle was built upon had some sort of magical properties. He wondered if that's why Graves chose this mountain top as he lifted the rope with one hand and felt around for Ryd with the other. He accidently smacked him in the face.

"Sorry," Digory said insincerely. "Can't see you. Here, come over here." He pulled Ryd towards him. "Grab this." Digory handed him the soggy rope.

Ryd clung to it, terrified, following Digory and Hector's footsteps in the stones ahead of him, trying to ignore the pleading cries all around him. Soon, the sounds of the dungeon faded behind them. It was like something out of a terrible dream.

"Here," Hector stopped abruptly. Ryd bumped into Digory's back and jumped in fright before realizing who it was. At that, Digory shoved him away in annoyance outwardly, although deep down felt a pang of sympathy for the man's fear. The emotion was so foreign, he immediately brushed it aside.

Meanwhile, Hector moved something. Rock rubbed against rock. Then, magically, the stones ahead shifted as light blasted into the space through a circular opening. Both Ryd and Digory shielded their eyes. Once they'd accustomed to the brightness it was clear they were standing in a mossy, stalagmite-laden cave. Ryd marvelled at the natural beauty of the cavern. It reminded him of the Free Boy's Ashkeep and he thought briefly about Odion, Edwessa, and the rest of them, hoping they were doing okay. A large stone rolled from the exit of the cave with a grinding scrape. Brighter, early-morning sunlight streamed in.

Hector had brought them to the base of the castle's mountain. Their path spilled them into a sloping, lazy meadow facing east. They were blasted with the orange rays of the rising sun; overly impressive as it skirted the lip of an oriental mountain and brightened the whole sky.

Ryd was instantly flooded with relief when he realized Hector was true to his word and wasn't trapping them in the dungeon. Then he was hit with another pang of anxiety. Mable, Chester! They had been too long without proper oats or water and were surely lonely, he thought woefully.

"We left our horses," Ryd said abruptly, almost shouting at Hector despite his fear of the man. "At the bottom of the Black Stairs."

Hector continued walking through low-growing foliage tipped in lacy petals without giving a response. Widow's Breath. Crushing them was said to cause one to hallucinate the voices of the dead. Digory noticed how Hector seemed to step around the blooms so perfectly he barely disturbed one, so Digory too began to avoid crushing them. On a whim he stooped to pluck one flower and snuck it deep into his trouser pocket. If he ever made it back to Westerviolet he intended to ask Hudde what it was.

"My Lord?" Ryd said, crunching mindlessly over the delicate lilac flowers.

"Horses?"

"Aye," Ryd said, nodding violently, "good Westerviolet steeds. Valuable."

Still not crushing the lilac flowers, headed towards a modest stable in the foreground surrounded by a handful of native hovels, Hector grunted, "So be it. We will go around for Tomas's."

Ryd was elated. "Thank you, my Lord," he said. He jogged

after the willowy man with skeletal broad shoulders and lanky gait. Hector didn't respond.

Hector retrieved his stallion from the stable, then led Digory and Ryd towards Mable and Chester. They travelled quite a distance around the base of the mountain, until Digory finally broke the silence.

"You lie to your father about Council," Digory said bluntly at Hector's back. "Why?"

"For the same purpose I lied about the contents of that letter," Hector said without turning on his steed.

They paced a sloping dirt path around the mountainside.

"What purpose is that?"

"Control," Hector said.

"What did it say?" Digory asked. "The letter."

Hector stopped abruptly, pulling his stallion's reigns in a protesting neigh, turning so swiftly it startled Ryd and he nearly fell backwards. Digory stood his ground easily, amused he'd gotten a response.

"Do you intend to ask; do I know it is from Sybil, not Tomas?" Hector clarified with unblinking, icy eyes on Digory's fiery ones.

"What did she write?"

Hector's tone-tinged annoyance but his eyes betrayed him. This man really did not fear him in the slightest, Hector noted, studying Digory curiously. Not one bit - he could feel it. There was something different about him. His soul was unlike any he had smelled before. How odd.

"Why do you still speak?" he spat at the earthborn to quiet him.

His hawk cawed loudly overhead as if in agreement.

Ryd hid his smile as he studied Digory's deep frown.

CROFT HOLD

Affter the disaster at Lyonshall, Wolfgar kept to the woods, evading all major roadways and towns despite it doubling his travel time. He was weary and shaken after the ordeal, but it was worth it to him to ensure no more conflict on his passage. He got his bearings from the stars like had Ben taught him to do and headed south and west, towards Animus Rock.

Wolfgar walked for days through mist-filled forests, wide valleys of tall grass and tilled farmland. He ate roots and the occasional bird he was able to snare. Every so often he passed by modest villages nestled into the rolling landscape, populated with round-faced natives with mostly chin-length, coal-black hair. They seemed like hardworking people, always in their fields or filtering in and out of mills, rarely resting or smiling. For as good as they had it, Croft Hold natives seemed to be a surly bunch.

While traveling, Wolfgar stole a nondescript tunic hanging to dry next to a fallow field of sunblooms. He left his Brotherhood attire in a bundle under a nearby log and adjusted his dagger, hidden on his ankle. He was weary, hungry, and his hands hurt something horrible, still aching from the deep cuts left after he scaled the red crystal throne. It seemed Lyonshall's lake did not boast healing powers after all.

It was early afternoon when Wolfgar reached the crest of a sunny hill carpeted in delicate poke flowers, tiny stems supporting huge, dainty blooms in yellows, whites and creams. A wide valley lay before him. He shielded his pale eyes from the bright light and stepped into better view.

The stories were true. *Croft Hold's bridge must be the grandest in all the lands*, Wolfgar thought as he studied the magnificent structure with her gilded masonry and sturdy arched frame, secured by huge pillars rooted deep into the lake, gilded too. The bridge ostentatiously shone in the sunny bright light of the valley. Many valley natives frequently complained, stating the testament to the engineering talent and wealth of Croft Hold was a flamboyant monstrosity, but, to outsiders, the bridge was a sight to behold. It was legendary throughout the Kingdom, said to have been built not long after the Landing. Wolfgar had only heard of it from his mother's bad-mouthing and was pleasantly surprised. Growing up at Ravenshroud, he wasn't accustomed to such finery. He quite liked it.

Squinting, Wolfgar further studied Croft Hold. The castle was as impressive as the bridge, just differently so. It sat atop a man-made island surrounded by an ethereal blue lake. Each valley in sight of the dewy water was either neat rows of harvested farmland or clusters of homes cut right into the hills, with expert thatched awnings. An impressive road that transitioned from dirt and rocks to laid cobblestone snaked from the right-hand of the scene. Another road of dirt winded around the back of the lake and met the golden gilded bridge, where it blindingly glistened in the afternoon sunlight.

Croft Hold's bold castle jutted up from the valley floor in two, three-sided towers with triangular windows sprouted from the diamond-shaped black stone keep. At the southside was an ornately structured, impressive gatehouse with a heavy wood and iron drawbridge to connect the Golden Bridge to the grounds. The castle was constructed from jet black stone, in stark contrast to the gilded bridge leading to it. A low wall of the same black stone wound the perimeter of the island, hugging thatched outbuildings and the bailey.

Black swans alike glided throughout the pale lake like dark gems against a silken garment, matching the dark tone of the castle. Frogs serenaded loudly from the bank, even in the middle of the day. Crickets melodiously hummed.

Satisfied with the layout, planning to avoid confrontation by keeping a wide birth, Wolfgar turned his back on the castle. He cut down a hillside through an overgrown thicket, parallel to the impressive cobblestone road. He turned away from the cobblestones when he reached the bottom of the hill, veering off into a forest of mangled oak trees.

Orange beams cut through the trees, backlighting the glossy leaves like stained glass. The whole forest glowed. Wolfgar marvelled at the natural beauty of these woods. He swept his head back and forth slowly, impressed by the huge trunks and imposingly reaching branches that reminded him of an old man's hands. These trees were different than the reaching poplar ones of Ravenshroud he was accustomed to. He was quite fond of those trees. As a boy, he used to believe they would speak to him. He told them all his worries. They made him feel at ease.

His boots crunched over brown fallen leaves, muffled by a heavy layer of green moss.

A small voice chirped down at him. "Who are you?"

Wolfgar stopped. "Who said that?" He looked from side to side.

"Up here."

Wolfgar looked up to his left.

"No, over here!"

He swung his head up to the right. In a particularly snarled tree's branches hung a gangly girl. She had wide-set green eyes and coal-black hair all the way down to her waist. Notably, she had tan skin, a square jaw and an intimidatingly intense stare. The girl bravely dropped a shocking distance to the forest floor without hesitation, landing on both her feet and hands like a cat before pouncing upwards after the momentum of her fall. She stood and brushed herself off.

"Who are you?" she asked forcefully, looking up at Wolfgar indignantly.

"Me?" Wolfgar asked with a smile. "Who are you, little one?"

"Do not call me little! You do not know who I am!" Her tiny voice bellowed as she removed a thin curved blade from a miniature sheath at her waist and held it towards him.

Wolfgar replied calmly as he raised his hands. *This child is surely Vanguard*, he thought. "And you don't know who I am." Then, he added, "I wouldn't threaten someone before I knew their name," with a glint in his eye.

The brash girl hesitated. "You sneak through my woods and your skin is light," she said accusingly, then paused. "I... I thought you were oldblood coming to steal me."

Wolfgar chuckled at the girl's aptitude, wondering what this exotic-looking child's bloodline was. "Who told you that?"

"They're after me because of my blood," she said solemnly. "Don't you know who I am?"

Wolfgar shook his head. This seemed to bother her. "Do not worry your pretty face," he said gently. "I'm not here for you."

She put her gilded blade away slowly. "Then why are you here?"

"Thank you," he nodded towards her sheathed weapon and lowered his hands. "I am a survivor of the Fall of Lyonshall."

"The fall?" she said. "What happened? Who are you?" she asked more forcefully, face clouding. Her hand hovered over her tiny weapon.

"There was an attack," Wolfgar said. "Lord Ogo Regnard took Lyonshall. I was there to witness it."

"Tell me who you are," the little girl demanded, eyes darting back and forth. She crossed her arms tightly atop a silken, intricately embroidered gold jumper, torn and dirt-stained, over grey cotton trousers and muddy, scuffed black booties. She was obviously very wealthy as well as equally rambunctious.

"If I do, will you tell me who you are? You must be Vanguard as I am."

"You are Vanguard!? Who are you? What are you doing in my woods?! You are so pale," she paused. "Are you from the Brotherhood?" she asked warily, eyes widening, backing away slowly.

"No!" he held his bloody hands up again. "No, I am not!" he lied loudly. "I was a prisoner!"

"A prisoner?" she stopped, obviously curious. A gust of wind rustled brown leaves at her feet.

Wolfgar had practiced his answer silently for days. "I'm

undocumented," he said convincingly.

"Really?" the wide-eyed girl asked him. "You mean you're not in the Tree?"

"Y...yes," he said with growing confidence when she accepted his answer without question. "You're right, I'm not in the Tree."

"What's your name?"

"Jude," Wolfgar said quickly.

"Where did you come from?"

"I told you little one," Wolfgar said teasingly, "Lyonshall." The young girl half-smiled at Wolfgar's playful tone. He never found trouble bonding with anyone, adult or child. He had a way with words, always knowing what to say. It had been that way since his earliest memories. He was likable. Fortune followed him. He always figured it was due to his Thorne blood inherited from both grandmothers. "I was trapped until Ogo came and," Wolfgar paused, "liberated me."

The girl brightened. "They are looking for you too! We are the same," she said with a wide smile.

"Yes," Wolfgar said. "Now, I told you who I am. You tell me who you are."

The little girl accepted his logic and approached him with confident steps over crunching leaves and twigs. The knarled oak branches swayed overhead in the breeze. "My name is Gilbrete. Gilbrete Morfit."

"Aren't you too light to be a Morfit?"

Her brow furrowed. "It isn't nice to assume things, uncle says."

"That wasn't nice, you're right," Wolfgar conceded contritely on the outside, amused inwardly. "But it's true that you are nearly oldblood pale. Odd you bare the Morfit name."

The little girl's face turned violet. "It's not my fault I have *their* blood," she huffed bitterly. "I want to look like Oscar and Ola, but I can't. It's not mother's fault. She escaped. We're not like they are."

"Like who are?"

Gilbrete's words dripped hatred. "Norland," she said.

"Norland?" Wolfgar asked with surprise. "Norland" Could this be Brynmor's lost mongrel grandchild? Wolfgar knew that Norland family tale well. Every Norlandblood did.

That would make this child his blood cousin.

"Mother is a Norland, silly," the girl said. "They hurt her. Father and Uncle saved her from them. They've protected her here. I was born here. Uncle tells me that the Norlands want to take me and hurt me. I must always be on the lookout for spies."

"That is smart," Wolfgar said. This *is* Brynmor's lost granddaughter, he thought. "Your uncle is smart."

Gilbrete Morfit nodded smugly. "I know."

Wolfgar studied the prideful child. He was not surprised at all that she shared his blood, based off how she acted and looked. Norlands were notoriously bold. And she had a block chin with shining green eyes.

"Could you take me to your father and uncle?" Wolfgar asked, disobeying his commands to head straight to Animus Rock out of curiosity, and instinct. He told himself it was to garner more information for Basil, but deep down, he simply wanted to learn more about the Kingdom. About Morfitbloods - his enemies - who he'd heard so much about but never met. "I think they would be interested in what happened at Lyonshall," he added truthfully.

Gilbrete paused. She studied Wolfgar's wounds from Lyonshall and his strong flexing jaw.

"If you're a friend of the New then you're a friend of mine."

"In the name of the King I am."

She tucked her thick hair behind both ears then said, "Yes I will take you."

Wolfgar smiled. He dropped to his knee atop leaves and met her eyes. "Thank you, child," he said warmly.

She beamed at his attention. "You're welcome," she said politely, glancing away shyly, for he was very handsome. Wolfgar stood. "What was it like at Lyonshall? Mother told me if I wasn't careful Old Lachlan may scoop me up and eat me!"

Wolfgar laughed and shook his head. His straw hair shone in

the light cutting through the still-green oak leaves. "You don't have to worry about that, little girl. The man is dead."

"Good," she said firmly. "One less bad man in the world."

"One less bad man," he echoed.

The phrase was harder for Wolfgar to say than he thought it should be. It tasted like blood on his tongue.

After trekking through a good bit of woods and across a wide meadow, Gilbrete led Wolfgar over the Golden Bridge, then finally into the black stone keep. She walked him hand-in-hand past questioning looks from the round-faced natives all around. The people of Croft Hold were a stoic, hearty lot who valued hard work and tradition over frivolities. They wore practical clothes and didn't seem to wear any adornments at all, paint or jewellery, apart from heavy black lining around the eyes, male or female. The Croft natives stared at Wolfgar's strangely pale skin with wonder and distrust, but to Wolfgar's welcome surprise, no one stopped or questioned them.

On his way inside, Wolfgar assessed the neat, orderly surroundings filled with clean patrons in dull, drab tunics or gowns secured with patterned belts, busily going about their days with stone expressions on their faces. The stereotypes Wolfgar had heard about them seemed to hold true - that they were diligent and uptight.

The streets were swept and tidy apart from occasional squealing hogs and frolicking, laughing children. Foreign merchants and traders sold wares directly outside of the castle, lining the path on both sides before crossing over the bridge into the castle proper. Orange furs, salted meats and fishes, as well as various spices were available for purchase there.

Inside the curtain wall, however, were just the wares of the Morfit lands. Harvested crops already milled such as grain or oats, tobacco, and the products of processing including specialty ales like moonfren bitters (said to cause prophetic dreams), oils like smokeleaf (used for lamps) or frostmint (used to make candy), sauces like nightfire sauce (extremely spicy) or ambervine syrup (usually drizzled over oats), and juices like eclipse brew (made from black currants and charcoal, said to cleanse the blood of madness) lined many stands. There were outfitters for fine, albeit drab clothing and glistening specialty-made weapons. The weapons shop stood empty. It was only frequented by Vanguards.

One particularly showy shop was outfitted in sparkling stones, where locals traded and gambled with the sought-after gem beads that were thought to carry with them charms, curses, and other various powers. Another directly beside it carried varieties of mushrooms including rare dream caps (said to help one control dreams).

Wolfgar's eyes widened as Croft Hold's structure loomed before him. The towering brute of a castle intimidated even the hardened Omen Brother. He craned his neck to study the competing towers in mirrored black stone jutting from the diamond-shaped keep. On approach, he noted the massive blocks used to build the structure, twice the height of a man and four times as wide, reminding him of his blood home Ravenshroud, although she was built from different hued rocks.

Instead of black, Ravenshroud's castle stones were burgundy purple.

Once inside the structure, Croft Hold's castle opened as if a beast had swallowed them whole. The vaulted ceiling of the keep came to a point topped with a glistening clear stone that must be enormous to appear so huge from far below. Directly below the gem, embedded in the marbled floor was an enormous fire pit atop a wide column. There were countless dark-dressed citizens with blunt cropped hair and dark lined eyes buzzing and flowing in circular motion around the unusual temple-like torch in the center of the grand hall. Despite the hubbub, it was surprisingly quiet.

Croft Hold natives typically did not speak unless they had something vitally important to say.

Gilbrete continued leading Wolfgar through the castle by

hand. They navigated a series of hallways and stairwells with stark walls and clean swept floors, lit every few paces with wooden torches. Wolfgar grew more and more wary of his decision to enter with every step. By the time the small girl stopped, Wolfgar was fully convinced he'd made a mistake, feeling how trapped he really was so deep into Croft Hold's castle. He wasn't sure he could find his way out alone even if he tried. Finally, Gilbrete dropped Wolfgar's hand. He swallowed hard, silently. Then, the girl pushed through a door in near copy of the giant drawbridge at the helm of the grand castle.

A fire burned at the end of a thin window-less hall.

"Father," she commanded as she strode into the dimly lit room, tiny voice cutting the smoky air.

Wolfgar trailed closely behind.

Two men sat in high-backed chairs in patterns of gold and white that sparkled in the jumping firelight. Wolfgar began analysing them instantly, and although they shared similar features, they couldn't be more different.

The man on the right sat with a straight back and held a curved pipe and let out puffs of heavy tobacco smoke. He gave off an air of respectability and command. The man had a round face, thin lips, and short hair oiled flat to his head. He had muscled forearms sticking out from his silken golden tunic and his belt housing two jewelled, curved weapons in in ornate sheaths. *Vanguard AND a sweep fighter*, Wolfgar thought to himself, impressed, realizing instantly who that man must be. The sweep fighters were an elite branch of the Morfit military, specially trained in a dance-like fighting style, focused in jumping then sweeping with dual-handed curved blades. Where the style got its name.

Comparatively, while likely Vanguard, the man on the left was surely no fighter, Wolfgar thought. It was obvious from his posture alone. The man slouched in his chair and clutched a goblet encrusted with red jewels, wearing a pink tunic with gold and green and turquoise embroidery with blue jewels sewn into the collar. Like a Spring garden exploded all over him. Overly ostentatious, Wolfgar thought, particularly compared to the rest of the realm's drab countenance. This man seemed pathetic. He looked nearly identical to the other man, except was a bit leaner and far softer and his black-lined eyes were bright red, not brown. His hair was not oiled and his curls stuck out from his head like springs. He also had the beginnings of a second chin.

"Gilbrete," Glenn Morfit - the man with the goblet - jumped up. He looked to his brother nervously. "What are you doing?! Why would you disturb..."

"Let her speak," Rupert Morfit boomed. Smoke blew from his nostrils as he spoke.

"Yes, brother." Glenn said dutifully and collapsed to a seat, pink shirt glistening. He took a long sip from the silver jewelled goblet with shaking hands.

"Uncle Rupert," Gilbrete stomped confidently forward. She cast a disapproving look towards Glenn. "Father," she said, "this is Jude."

"Jude," Rupert said slowly. He eyed Wolfgar up and down.

Behind them, a fireplace roared with flames from top to bottom, backlighting both men in their glistening high-backed chairs to the point it was nearly impossible to make out the details of their features. Wolfgar caught what he could between dancing shadows.

"Jude, who?"

"He is Vanguard, father," Gilbrete assured.

"Will you allow the man to speak for himself?"

"Yes, uncle," she stepped back and lowered her head.

"Brother are you sure this is a good id..."

"Glenn," Rupert turned to the man with the silver goblet with a stormy brow, "do not question me."

Glenn Morfit took another shaky sip and lowered his head. "Yes, brother."

"Speak, Vanguard," Rupert commanded Wolfgar, exhaling thick smoke through his flared nostrils.

Wolfgar stepped forward and said, "The girl is right. I am Vanguard. A bastard. A prisoner."

"Bastard? Who?"

He hesitated.

"Who, young man?" Rupert's tone warned.

"Wallace Thorne."

At the powerful man's mention, tension in the room bristled. "Explain."

"I am his bastard," Wolfgar said. "I was left with Lachlan Regnard, at Lyonshall, as his ward. I was trapped there, my Lord," he added. "I only escaped when Lyonshall fell."

Glenn leapt from his chair again, sloshing his drink across his brother. "Lyonshall has fallen!"

With a deep frown impressed into his jowls, Rupert wiped the liquid from his face and brow, smudging his dark lined eyes. He studied his sullied tunic. He sighed. "Brother, calm yourself or you will leave," he said with finality.

Every move Rupert made and word he said was deliberate. Like how a statue would act if it came alive.

Glenn lowered his head. "Yes, brother," he sat down. He looked at his empty goblet woefully, tipping it into his mouth for a last drop.

"Tell more, Jude," Rupert said carefully, turning his piercing gaze back to Wolfgar. "Lyonshall has fallen? How?"

"Ogo," Wolfgar said simply, nerves steeling despite his apprehension. He stood with back straight and strong square jaw flexed. This man's presence alone made him sweat. His power was palpable.

Rupert narrowed his round eyes. "Speak plainly."

Glenn watched on, clutching his goblet, fussing with the gemstones, desperately trying to catch the eye of one of the dark robed attendants huddled off to the side of the chamber. Wolfgar glanced at the man briefly, wondering if they purposefully denied him a drink just to toy with him. Finally, one attendant, a woman with black-greying hair, appeared to take pity on Glenn and dutifully shuffled over to the thirsty man with a wooden pitcher. She refilled his goblet to the brim. Glenn looked pleased.

"My Lord," Wolfgar told Rupert honestly, still smelling the

searing flesh, "he burned Lyonshall down. I only nearly escaped."

Rupert didn't seem surprised. "What has he done with Lachlan?" he asked calmly.

Wolfgar swallowed hard, taken aback by the man's reaction. "Cut down," he said gravely. His verdant eyes were locked on Rupert's mud brown. "Left him there to burn. The Red Plumes too. All of them. They never had a chance. It was a massacre," Wolfgar said solemnly. He added quickly, "I am grateful for my freedom from the tyrant Lachlan, but we lost a lot of," he paused, "good men." He looked down and swallowed hard again.

"You believe this man, Gilberte?"

"I do, uncle," she said surely, nodding. "He is kind. He could have hurt me where he found me in the forest but instead, he wanted to be safe here from the Old like us. And remember what you say about helping those in need. It is only just, and fair to give when we are fit to give."

"But brother, he is so pale," Glenn interjected, leaning forward, indignant look in his eye. "What if this is a trick?! What if this is a ruse by the Bro..."

"Enough, Glenn," Rupert glanced dismissively. "Look at him. He's just escaped a great battle, like what he describes happened at Lyonshall. Why else would he come from there? Why would he come to our door for aid? Hold up your hands, Jude."

Wolfgar held his hands towards them. They were maimed and bloody.

"A lot of trouble to go through as a spy," Rupert added, gesturing to the injuries.

Glen narrowed his eyes suspiciously at Wolfgar. "Why is he muscled as if practiced in sword?"

"Mines," Wolfgar barked quickly.

"There. You see?" Rupert gestured at Glenn.

"But..."

Rupert ignored his brother as he always did. As everyone did. Instead, he addressed Wolfgar again.

"The enemy of my enemy is my friend," he said after a contemplative pause, genuinely convinced, deciding it did him and his bloodline more good to keep this stranger closer than otherwise. "It's decided. You are a friend of Morfit, Jude, bastard of Thorne. You'll sup with us this evening," he added, not as an invitation, but expectation.

Everything Rupert said was that way. If he wanted it done, it was already done.

"Then, what is it that you wish?"

"I wish to continue on to Animus Rock," Wolfgar replied. "Being part of my birth right and all," he added, hoping that would be something an undocumented Vanguard would say.

"Be careful there," Rupert said before puffing twice on his pipe. Heavy smoke poured from his mouth and nose. "Up and down are not the same there as they are here."

"What is your meaning?"

"It changes us Vanguards to live with the others," Rupert replied. "To mix between bloodlines. That's part of why we Morfits have kept our blood pure and only strengthened ourselves with the blood of our native brethren. Not all see it as I do, like my wife," he said tersely, "but she serves her purpose there at Animus as I do here. Everything for a purpose," he said firmly.

"Aye," Wolfgar nodded, honestly agreeing with the sentiment, wondering how much truth there was in rumor. He'd heard many things about Rupert Morfit - that he was dull, cowardly and weak. But meeting the man now, Wolfgar wasn't sure what to believe.

Rupert cringed. "Let's work on your language while we're here, shall we? No 'aye'. It is vulgar. 'Yes'," he corrected formally.

"Yes," Wolfgar rolled the unfamiliar letters over his tongue. He thought of how Davide would tease him if he were here right now. Knives stabbed his throat when he remembered his true brother was gone for good. He took a deep breath. He glanced away.

"Good," Rupert nodded, satisfied. "Gilbrete," he said

commandingly. He looked to the serious green-eyed girl. "Take our new friend to the guest chambers."

"Yes, uncle."

"You are a guest of the Morfits of the storied Croft Hold," Rupert said to Wolfgar, voice booming. "We are at your disposal. We live to serve others. Whatever you need, just ask."

"I can't thank you enough," Wolfgar said. "I had no idea you would be so," he paused, "nice."

"What did you think we would be like, Jude?" Rupert asked evenly, an amused twinkle in his brown eye.

"I," he paused again. "I don't know."

"Not everyone is evil in this world," Rupert said kindly. "I'm sure you've heard all things about us, living with the miser Lachlan. But there is good left out there. Here, we will prove that to you. My people are a hardworking, honest people. A just people. You can trust us. You will not befall unkindness while in my realm, that I assure you."

"I don't know what to say," he started, then swallowed. "Just, well, thank you."

"Anything for a New Vanguard brother," Rupert warmly replied. "Come," he added, gesturing to Wolfgar to take a seat, "tell us more about your time at Lyonshall."

It was night.

Wolfgar fully felt out of place. The spacious square hall lined with windows, filled with glass furniture, was nothing like he'd ever seen. It was far more ostentatious than anything he had experienced before. Above the arched doorframe of the hall was the Morfit emblem; the lady of justice, carved into shiny black stone. He studied the carving from his seat at the glass table.

He'd spent all afternoon lying to Rupert, recounting his life in the Lyonshall minds, and he was exhausted in every way. Now, even though no one questioned him, he was still overwhelmed. Everything from the tables and chairs down to the utensils and plates was made of clear glass in clean, straight lines. Intricately woven carpets in reds and oranges and yellows lined the hard-stone floor. A glass chandelier with countless dripping candles hung low from the rafters. Scenic tapestries of foreign jungles with unfamiliar flora and fauna hung from the four the walls, each so large once could not look at the entirety at once. Wolfgar eyed the one across from him curiously, wondering what the furry beast with sharp teeth and spots was called.

"To our guest," A stunning woman with white skin and unusually long, flat blonde hair lifted her glass. "May your blood reign forever."

"Here, here," the others chimed in.

Wolfgar lifted his glass in turn and took a sip in unison.

"Rupert tells me that you've been a prisoner of Regnard. Is that right?"

"Yes, Lady, that's right."

"Unbelievable," she said and shook her head. "Yet I know the feeling."

"Aye?" Wolfgar asked with a raised brow, thinking he knew who this woman must be. He adjusted his hair out of his eye. Rupert stared pointedly at Wolfgar, until Wolfgar picked up on his meaning. "I mean, yes?" he corrected himself.

"Oh Rupert, don't torture him," the woman said in a flighty tone. "After what he's been through, must you correct his language?"

"It is never too late to polish."

"Let him talk like he wishes," Glenn chimed in from the far end of the table, holding a leg of a roasted fowl in his hand. He spit pieces of unchewed food as he spoke.

The striking woman glared at him. "Did we ask your opinion?" she asked sharply, devoid of warmth totally, completely opposite to how she addressed Rupert. She wore a golden choker with a round, fist-sided gem at her throat that caught candlelight as she spoke.

"No, Severine," Glenn said woefully. He sank in his chair.

So, this is Severine Norland, my kin, Wolfgar thought. "I don't mind," he interjected. "The corrections, I mean. Wouldn't want to stand out at Animus," he added, true to his character Jude, he hoped.

"I hate to tell you," Rupert said, "but that will happen no matter what you do."

"Why?"

Rupert smiled, shaking his head as he ran one palm over his dark slicked back hair. "Look at you."

Severine snickered into her hand.

Wolfgar, true to his heritage, with his pale skin and piercing green eyes, looked Oldblood through and through. Because of that, most would assume his motivations before he opened his mouth and said a word.

"I thought you're not supposed to judge others off of their looks," Wolfgar said.

"That's what we tell the children," Severine replied lightly, voice like clinking chimes, "but it is unavoidable."

"Right, of course," Wolfgar said into a bite of food. He chewed the strange dish apprehensively at first, then with growing enthusiasm. It was fire deer meat rubbed in expensive silverthyme imported from Graceview that Wolfgar hadn't tasted before, laid atop a bed of sautéed roots. It was good. For someone who was mainly given eggs and porridge to eat, it was very good.

"It's not your fault you've got Thorne eyes or oldblood skin," Rupert said, "but others will treat you like it is."

"Like your sister," Severine added with a sneer, green eyes sparkling cruelly. "She can preach tolerance and acceptance all she wants, but Galla is a bigot and," she paused, slightly smiling, "a bitch."

"Severine," Rupert scolded.

"What? It's true!"

Rupert stifled a smile. He always had a soft spot for his twin, despite her fanatical ways. Galla was principled. A lover of truth. And she was not afraid to push for what she believed was right. No matter who stood in her way.

"Galla is passionate," he defended. "And she has helped so

many. Don't be so quick to judge her."

"Please." Severine rolled her eyes. "If it weren't for you, she would have delivered me back to Cornelius herself. I'm a liability. Rupert, she hates me and the girl. You're a fool to deny that."

Rupert calmly looked to the intense woman. "Are you finished?"

Severine glared at him. Wolfgar studied her strong jaw, pallid skin nearly lighter than his own, and black-lined eyes.

"You mustn't be so hard on Galla, dear," Glenn told Severine warmly, turning his body to face her, speaking with goblet in hand. "She loves you like a sister." His Animus wine sloshed around as he gestured. Wolfgar watched the dark liquid oscillate back and forth in the glass, nearly spilling on Severine's dress with bunched seaming underneath her breast, decorated in thin golden lines, each time he moved. Glenn didn't seem to notice.

Severine's legs were crossed at her thin ankles, away from Glenn. She ignored him.

"It's favouritism Rupert," Severine continued to whine. "She's as dark as night so the people think she's good! I'm pale so I'm *evil*." She shook her head with frustration, delicate brow pinched, small nose scrunched. "That woman is awful. She's the biggest hypocrite I know. Here I am - a truly decent Vanguard - but the natives still shutter in sight of me because of my skin. Don't even get me started on my poor daughter and what she must endure." She paused, turning to Wolfgar. "You understand."

He swallowed and nodded.

"Enough feeling sorry for yourself," Rupert said dryly. "Stop pointing the finger until you yourself are perfect."

Severine revealed a shockingly white, warm smile. "Are you saying I'm not perfect, Rupert?"

"I think you're perfect, my love," Glenn slurred from down the table.

"How nice," Severine said flippantly to him without breaking eye-contact with his brother. Wolfgar could feel the tension and it was clear to him that there was more to Rupert and Severine's relationship than they would likely admit outright. "Tell us," she turned to Wolfgar slowly, "what happened at Lyonshall?"

"Ogo took it," Wolfgar replied through chewing.

Severine laughed like a clinking chime. She held eye contact with Wolfgar for a moment longer than was comfortable for him. He looked away and blushed. It wasn't often he was in the presence of a beautiful woman. Well, any woman. Even if that woman was his own blood. "We know Ogo took it, silly," Severine said, flipping her long, limp hair over her shoulder. "Tell us how."

"With a trebuchet I believe and flaming arrows Lady. Arrows that pierced the Red Plumes armor," Wolfgar said, swallowing his bite. "Used boulders to overtake the wall. One shattered the Lyonshall glass. Don't know how he did it."

"No!" she gasped. Rupert and Glenn looked at her quickly. "Oh, I know it was an evil image, but it was history," Severine defended in a pout. "I'd heard stories of the glorious colored glass of Lyonshall," she added wistfully. "Mother told me stories. I've always wished to see it."

"Well, Lady, it's gone now," Wolfgar said flatly.

"Pity," she sighed, glancing down. "That was it, then?" she asked, popping her head up, new life breathed into her questioning. "A few flaming rocks took the grand fortress down?"

"Not quite," Wolfgar said slowly. "Lachlan could have held Lyonshall, if not for the betrayal of his men."

"Betrayal?" Severine urged.

Glenn too hung on Wolfgar's every word from the far end of the table, leaning forward on both elbows. Conversely, Rupert listened with his typical straight back, seemingly unaffected by the tale.

"They ran," Wolfgar said, still not comprehending what had happened. *How* it happened. "Lachlan commanded the Red Plumes stand firm, but instead, once their armor was pierced, they ran, letting in Ogo's forces." He paused. "Then Ogo slaughtered everyone."

"Ah, cowards." Severine said lightly.

Rupert nodded. Wolfgar was taken aback as the man's lack of surprise.

"There were Morfit troops with him," Wolfgar added gently, not sure if that fact was inflammatory.

But Rupert replied a simple "Yes," as if he'd expected it all along. Silence cascaded over the room, segmented by the cracking fire when he didn't offer any explanation.

"Did you know Ogo was going to attack Lyonshall?"

Glenn looked to Rupert with wide eyes. "Did you, brother?"

Rupert glanced from Wolfgar to Glenn slowly, finishing chewing a bite of food. "Everything is going according to plan," he said.

Glenn smiled, satisfied, and took another hulking bite from his drumstick. "Rupert always knows what he's doing," he said proudly through chewing.

Wolfgar looked down to study his meal.

"If I were you, I'd be worried Galla would curse it all up."

"Severine," Rupert raised an eyebrow. "Language."

"You shouldn't be so blind to your sister's tricks," the icy blonde warned. "She enforces the laws by day and breaks them by night. Why, I've heard rumor that her twins' father may even be…"

"Severine," Rupert interrupted her harshly. "This is no place to discuss our bloodline," he paused, "details. Not in front of a guest," he added, gesturing to Wolfgar, eyes commanding her to be quiet.

"Hm," Severine sighed. "As you wish, Rupert," she said dutifully, biting her lip. "You're probably right." She paused. "Can't have the whole Kingdom calling the honourable council member Galla Morfit a *bare*."

"Severine," Rupert growled. "You press my patience."

"And you mine," she furrowed her intense brow at him. "I'm done anyway," she said sharply, pushing herself away from the table. The glass chair caught on the rug beneath it. She struggled to push the chair back and Wolfgar jumped from his seat to help her.

"At least *he* has some Vanguard honor," she said hotly. "Thank you," Severine looked at Wolfgar.

"Don't leave, my love," Glenn pleaded Severine, then hiccupped from wine.

She rolled her eyes at him, then looked to Rupert.

"If you expect me to ask you to stay, I will not."

Severine frowned. Turning in a huff, she rushed from the hall. Her silken dress floated like a heavy fog behind her.

Once she was gone, Rupert looked at Wolfgar. "Don't hold that outburst against her," he said. "She's been through a lot."

"I do not judge."

"It's hard for her to stand in between worlds," Rupert continued. "She's seen the horror of the Old realms first hand. She knows what ours stands to lose if we fall. It's real already for her. She's lived it."

Wolfgar flexed his jaw, wondering what Rupert meant. "Who's Galla and why does Severine have a problem with her?" he asked instead. "It almost sounds like she's…"

Rupert finished his sentence. "Jealous? You picked up on that too, did you?"

"What's going on?"

"Galla's brilliant, but," Rupert paused, "she's a lot. Considers herself a crusader for the downtrodden. She's a hero in Croft for all the laws she's championed. The people adore her."

"I see," Wolfgar said. "Why doesn't Severine like her?"

"She was the only one to oppose Severine's sanctuary here," Rupert told him. "After she escaped Ravenshroud, Galla tried to send her back. Even after Severine explained to Galla what her uncle and cousin were like, Galla fought to send her back to Ravenshroud. Severine has never forgiven her."

"You can't blame her," Glenn said. Wolfgar had almost forgotten until this moment the man was there. "Galla didn't give her a chance. She hates her just for her skin."

"Yes, yes," Rupert waved his hand in dismissal of his brother.

No one ever took Glenn seriously. Glenn didn't even take himself seriously.

"Why did she call Galla a hypocrite?"

"The rumors," Glenn said.

"Brother," Rupert warned.

"What rumors?" Wolfgar pressed, exceedingly curious, particularly about the Vanguard world he'd been kept from, until now.

"My sister likes to enforce laws, but," Rupert paused, "acts as if they don't apply to her."

"Which laws?"

"It doesn't matter." Rupert puffed his pipe, thinking of Prihim, the lovestruck idiot. "She is a champion of the Rebellion in the best way. Regardless of her vices, she would not betray us."

At the word "rebellion" Wolfgar's ears perked up, realizing his curiosity may pay off after all, leading him to valuable information for Elder Basil before even reaching Animus. "Rebellion? What are your aims?" Wolfgar asked him.

"Why so many questions?" Glenn shot back, distrusting gaze on his face.

"Brother, leave it."

"But…"

"I would be shocked if he had no questions," Rupert interrupted Glenn. "He likely knows little of the world, being trapped in Lyonshall with the old miser Lachlan all this time, isn't that right?"

Wolfgar nodded, wide-eyed, wondering if he looked innocent enough. It seemed to be working.

"Our aims?" Rupert asked rhetorically. "Simple really. Freedom. Freedom and justice."

"Freedom?"

"Yes," Rupert replied as if it was obvious. "To liberate the people from the oppression of thoughtless, purposeless tradition."

"You mean the Old?"

Rupert nodded. "Precisely. It's nonsensical to pursue a way of life simply because others did it that way before you. It's a testament to the madness inherent in their blood. The madness

Morfit avoids by cutting ours. If nothing else, the existence of the Vanguard curse is proof it's unnatural."

"But, what of the mission of the Vanguard?" Wolfgar asked, wondering how any Vanguard could deny the Landing. He added quickly, "Lord Lachlan spoke of it."

"You are as brainwashed as Severine was when I met her," Rupert laughed. Glenn frowned and took a long sip.

"What do you mean?" Wolfgar asked.

"The Old has it wrong. The ultimate aims of the old were not their individual short-sighted ideals, like Brochet's aim to control life or Graves, the dolts, trying to conquer the Deads."

"It wasn't?"

"No, no," Rupert said surely. "Those were merely," he paused, "guidelines. The ultimate aim of the gods of legend, of Alabaster Beaumont himself, was simply to evolve."

"Evolve? But isn't that what the Old believes?"

Rupert's face clouded. "The Old is trapped in the prison they built for themselves. They are blind because they refuse to open their eyes to the larger picture that as long as we cling to the past, frightened of the future, we will never grow. And without growing we will never achieve the potential of what human beings are meant to be. Alabaster Beaumont, god or not, had to have known that he could not conceptualize the extent of human evolution. We have reached the point in history where the old Vanguard ways can take us no further. It is now that we take what has been learned and move forward to unexplored territory of humanity. In order to truly evolve, we must let go of what we want to become, to see what we really can be."

Wolfgar frowned. Rupert's sentiment bothered him. He didn't know why.

"What troubles you about that, Jude?"

"Without aim or purpose, how do we ensure anything is achieved at all?"

"It's a question you must answer for yourself."

"What do you believe?"

"I believe lack of direction does not necessarily mean lack of purpose."

Wolfgar squinted his narrow-spaced eyes.

"You strike me as the type with the capacity to understand," Rupert added, responding to his expression. "Others raised in the Old, I fear, are unable," he said. "The ones at the top are the most horrendously afflicted with this lack of concept. It is terrifying." Rupert finished his drink in a gulping sip. He briefly thought of Lachlan Regnard. Then of Tomas Brochet, the snake. And course, the obstinate Hector Graves.

Glenn listened on, nodding wholeheartedly, obviously enamoured with his older brother, believing every word he said.

"Like who?" Wolfgar prodded.

"Hector," Rupert said instantly, tone dripping distain. "You hear the man speak and it's as if he walked right off the Vanguard ship. As if he was present for the Landing, itself! His beliefs are shocking. He has absolutely no grasp of the importance of natives. The wealth of value they bring. All he can see is the furtherment of his bloodline. If it does not benefit Graves, Hector isn't interested." Rupert's voice cracked for the first time with a spike of sadness, tinged with anger. "I don't know how to make him care about anything."

"But Hector isn't elder, is he?" Wolfgar asked, already knowing full well the situation with Graves. He wanted to know how much Rupert knew.

"He isn't," Glenn offered.

"No," Rupert corrected, "but he speaks for Graves, nonetheless. He's on Council. Everyone knows he disregards ancient Hjalmar's command. It is only a matter of time before the old man dies and he rightfully holds elderclaim."

"What about Herman?" Glenn asked Rupert. "I like him. Will Hector listen to him? You should hear how the people adore him. It doesn't hurt that he's married to a celebrity, either."

"Yes, Verity is striking and fashionable," Rupert conceded. "But more importantly, the King listens to his sister. It's no wonder Herman Graves is Humphry's closest advisor. Unfortunately, Hector doesn't listen to Herman. Hector doesn't listen to anyone."

Wolfgar was trying to follow. He'd not been sent to Academy intentionally. Basil had insisted he and his brothers receive their full education at Echo's Omen when their father signed them away. He was Vanguard but knew little to nothing of his birthright. "Hector Graves's brother is married to the King's sister?" he asked.

"He is," Rupert said, nodding once.

"But Herman Graves is New, not Old," Glenn added confidently.

Wolfgar looked at Rupert. He nodded again. "Glenn's right. Herman advises in favour of the New. It's said it's driven quite a rift within Graves, but I remain cautious. Bloodline ties are usually impenetrable. It wouldn't surprise me if Herman sways back to his blood beliefs eventually. Time will tell."

Wolfgar nodded. The fire crackled. "Will you go to Animus Rock for fall Council?" he asked Rupert.

"I will shortly," Rupert nodded, puffing on his pipe again. "In my position, it is important that I'm aware."

"What's your position?"

"Why, he's First Magistrate," Glenn said proudly.

"Congratulations, my Lord," Wolfgar said dutifully.

Rupert half smiled and waved his hand, pale brown tunic buckling at his sleeves. "I've had the position for years and years now. Came with my blood."

Wolfgar's curiosity was unending. "Is it difficult to vote? To have that power?"

"It can be," Rupert admitted.

"What was the hardest thing you've done?"

Rupert paused and thought for a moment. "I once sent a friend's father to the gallows."

"Who?"

"Gilberth Minney," he replied. "As a child, his son Edwarde and I were close friends at Animus, for a short time, if you can believe that, until we learned of the great divide between our fathers, of course. When I grew and joined the Magistrate, I sat on the trial raised for his father."

"Gilberth Minney was sent to the First, then?"

"Yes," Rupert said stoically. "He'd turned on us during the Uprising in an act that led to the loss of countless lives. The man deserved to pay for betraying Littlebell and the rest of the New."

Wolfgar nodded carefully. He didn't know how to feel. It was bizarre experiencing the other side of the coin.

"Here, here!" Glenn raised his glass.

Wolfgar popped up his head, struck with a poignant thought. "When you overtake the Old," he asked, "what happens to those Vanguards and their realms?"

"That's where justice comes in," Rupert said. "It's a new world," he added with a cruel smirk.

Wolfgar knew exactly what he intended to do, yet still he asked. "But, my Lord..."

"That should answer your question."

"But..."

"Don't concern yourself with it, Jude," Rupert said warmly, exhaling smoke from his nostrils like an angry kiln. "I can imagine how difficult it must be to leave an Old realm and learn that there is a better way. The Old realms and Old Vanguards have had their time of glory." He paused for emphasis. "It is their time to fall."

Wolfgar met Rupert's eyes. He nodded solemnly.

That night, long after sup ended and the conversation dwindled, Wolfgar went to the bed he'd been allotted. Despite it being far finer than anything he'd ever slept in before, he knew he couldn't stay there.

He left a quick note, scribbled on a scrap of parchment he found:

"Thank you for your kindness. I must be going. May we meet again. — Jude"

Then, he waited until every light in the courtyard had gone out. He listened for every servant and household pet to retire for the evening. Then, he neatly made the golden embroidered sheets on the hulking wooden bed in the guest chamber. He breathed deep and looked about the ostentatious room before stealing into the cool castle corridor. He ducked down spiral stairs.

Finally, Wolfgar escaped into the crisp, mist-filled autumn evening aroar with crickets and frogs about the jewel-toned lake.

He was so overwhelmed by his circumstances that he forgot about his hands. They no longer hurt. Beneath the bandages that the Croft Hold attendants had given him, if he had bothered to check, he would have realized that they magically healed. Perhaps Lyonshall's lake was still potent after all.

ECHO'S OMEN SPIRE

The Spire was uncharacteristically dim for daytime. It relied on sunlight to fill its vast expanse and for a few moments at midday, each day, it grew eerily dark. The fire jutting up through the thick table in the center of the room burned low. Shadows danced on the men's serious faces.

"Remind me," Basil said, "how many do we have this year?"

"Seventy-five."

"Good," Basil replied slowly. "And unworthy?"

Quentin swallowed.

"How many?"

Quentin exhaled, wishing the results of the testing had been different. Wishing that more men had tested grey. He could lie, of course. He could tell his father that more were worthy of the blessings of the Brotherhood, however, when it came to the ceremony, when the unworthy would surely die, his lie would be uncovered.

"Three thousand and two." He added, "father."

Xavier leaned forward. The old armchair squeaked with the shift of weight. "Brother, there is not space."

Basil, seated at the head of the table, waved his hand dismissively. "Be rid of the rest. They are little use to us."

"Father," Quentin started, "with the impending war Hector warns of, shouldn't we take all we can?"

"You are not suggesting what I think you are," Basil soured. He rubbed his temple with his hand.

But Quentin still pressed. He knew his father was stubborn and attached to the old ways, yet times were changing. Quentin feared Basil's hubris could lead to the Brotherhood's downfall. He didn't understand why the men chosen must test grey at all. "Three thousand and two men is a lot of men. They all passed training. We need every one," he said. "Now, more than ever."

Basil turned his head towards his son, challenging him with narrowing eyes. "Why?"

"Busk fell," Quentin said with a hint of a smile. He was please he knew something before his father.

Basil spun angrily. "Xavier," he growled. "What happened? How do I not know?"

Xavier leaned back. "I aimed to discuss it after the plans for the ceremony were secured."

Basil glared at him. "Discuss it now."

Xavier swallowed in a gulp, then exhaled air heavily through flared nostrils before responding to his unstable brother. "The Dark Arena burned to the ground," he said. "Ralph Busk is dead. The Missive just arrived with the news."

"Hector assured us that Ralph was an ally, to be trusted," Basil shouted. "The sick bastard, fucked everything, even in death!" He slammed his fists on the table.

Quentin saw an opportunity and took it. "This wouldn't have happened if you were Graves elderclaim," he said bitingly. "Great Grandfather Haulfrun was a fool," he added in a mutter under his breath.

"Watch your tongue!"

"Your Great Grandfather had a penchant for tradition," Xavier explained. "There was no other way."

"If Hjalmar or his cunt newblood-loving son are behind any of this, they will burn!" Basil leapt from his chair and hammered his fists again, knuckles first, into the table so hard his skin bled.

"There may be hope yet," Xavier assured calmly. He was trying to quell his brother. He had always been water to his flames.

"How?" Basil turned, then buckled, wincing in pain. His hand leapt to his temple again and rubbed it furiously, streaking himself with blood.

"Father..."

Basil held up a hand, "I'm fine," he grunted, forcing down the numbing pain. "Explain, brother," he pointed to Xavier.

Then he righted himself, smoothing his thin hair.

"Edwarde holds the Confines, still."

The sun fell enough in the sky to cast warm streaks of sunlight into the wide room. Clouds were cast burgundy. Basil's white-blind eye glistened in the light as he grinned to show long teeth.

His face brightened. "That little bastard!" Basil squawked. "The old Busk's pet may save us all."

"Well," Xavier started, "he is badly burned. He was in the Dark Arena when it fell to the ground, as Ralph was."

"A shame," Basil said insincerely. "Say," he paused, calmly lowering again to sit. "Ours frequented the Arena. Did we lose any?"

"Better question," Xavier replied sadly, "is how many."

"Pity," Basil sighed, irritated at the inconvenience, ambivalent to the lost lives.

"How many?" Quentin asked.

"Too many," Xavier said. "Thirty-three."

"Who?"

"Most of the fifth Norland key division," Xavier said gravely.

Quentin snickered. Xavier frowned. Basil side-eyed his son with his good eye.

"Why do you disrespect them?" Xavier was stern. "They were good men."

The angle of sunlight into the Spire cast a dusky glow across the angular noses and jaws of these Graves brethren. Quentin's beady ash eyes dropped into shadow as he leaned back and crossed his arms.

"They were sloppy," he said with scorn. "No wonder his men diddled little boys on the fourth."

"We don't know they were on the fourth," Xavier countered firmly, always assuming the best. "Perhaps the third...."

"You're both wrong," Basil interjected loudly. "I'm sure they were on the ground to be near the blood and the coin. You can get your cock wet elsewhere. Our men are smarter than that. And," he added, "very much dead now. Let us move on."

"All the more reason to accept more than seventy-five this

evening, father," Quentin said eagerly.

"No," Basil replied with resounding finality. "If they did not test grey, then no."

Quentin boiled as he sunk backwards in his seat, pulling his arms tighter around himself unconsciously. "Why not?"

"I said, no."

"Speaking of Wolfgar," Xavier leaned forward. "We haven't heard from him."

"Give him time," Basil said.

"What do you see in him?" Quentin whined. "He is just like his traitorous brother. I see it in his eyes!"

"Quentin," Basil growled with palpable disdain.

Quentin pricked at his father's tone. "If you listened to me about Davide it wouldn't have come to what it did. My sister's belly wouldn't swell larger each day with a bastard Norland while his child brother galivants about the land spreading the Brotherhood's secrets to the King knows who."

Basil's voice deepened. "Quentin."

"You should stop, nephew," Xavier said softly.

"Wolfgar is no Brother," Quentin went on, unrelenting. He pushed his chair back aggressively from the table and stood in a rush, sensing this was a chance to be heard. "He repeats the words, but he does not believe. I tell you; he will not die for us!"

"QUENTIN!"

Quentin jumped backwards. The reaction was engrained in him from countless years of Basil's heavy-handed discipline. His earliest memory was his father's mean sneer as he told him to pick the switch he was to be beaten with. Quentin hadn't chosen a thin enough one, so Basil chose one himself. That beating drew blood and left scars that Quentin still had to this day. He was three years old.

"One more word and I will consider *you* the traitor, to speak that way of the Brotherhood's elite," Basil warned his son. "Do not think you are special. The Brotherhood spans Vanguards, you fool. I am ashamed to call you my son when you speak that way. A disgrace," he shook his head. "You've made this worse," he added, glaring angrily, rubbing his head now with both hands.

"Father," Quentin moved sympathetically towards Basil.

"Don't," Basil growled.

Quentin froze as if stabbed with an icy dagger. He looked down.

Xavier shook his head and sighed.

Outside of the Spire, the sun beat down brutally. The trees blanking the surrounding mountains were changing color in a patchwork of reds, yellows and browns, dotted with deep emerald evergreens and caps of snow.

Today, in the Echo's Omen courtyard, there was little wind.

Four young Brothers stood in a huddle. Across the grounds was a horde of men at the base of the Spire, naked and chained to a long wooden fence. Recruits after assessment, not yet initiated.

"Why didn't we have to do that?" a little boy with a mop of thick black hair and grey-pale skin asked.

"Don't be stupid, Alec," a taller boy with matching features and steel grey eyes said. He had black wisps of wiry hair growing at his upper lip and at the tip of his chin.

"Shut up Aron," the smaller one spat back.

The bickering boys were Quentin's sons, Aron and Alec Graves. Their companions were Wolfgar's youngest brothers. They all wore dark tunics with black chainmail armor overtop, stamped with the Brotherhood emblem. They wore spiked helmets as well, secured with buckles under their chins. Each had a straight-blade sword at the hip and a black glass dagger with bone hilt on the thigh. Each wore high, thick-sole black boots. Their heavy cloaks were crumpled in a pile in the dust behind them. Regardless, their faces were flushed and sweaty. Their hair was matted to their necks and foreheads.

"It's because we're Vanguard," the stocky Norland said. He was older than the dark-haired children, nearly a man, with a wider neck, muscled chest, and calloused hands. He had pasty white skin. His blonde hair was sheared close to his round head, highlighting his clean-shaven square jaw and pale-green slits for eyes. Edouard, one of Wolfgar's younger brothers. Full of brutality and rage. As Norland as they came.

"Why does that matter?" the smallest and youngest, Alec Graves asked.

"We're all that's left. Why should we prove we are worthy? No," Edouard shook his head. A wide vein bulged on his neck whenever he spoke. "Those blood heathens must prove to us that they won't go earthblood and slit our throats in the name of some cunt of a goddess in the middle of the night."

Bertrand Norland stood behind Edouard. He was Wolfgar's youngest brother - a hulking boy with short brown hair and a pimpled face. He chuckled low and deep a handful of times at the comment, then fell back into intimidating silence. It was rare Bertrand spoke. Usually, Edouard talked for him.

"Bertrand agrees," the Edouard said.

At his side, Bertrand grunted.

"There," Aron glared at his smaller copy. "Now go. Leave us and play, or something, like children do."

"I'm not a child!" Alec cried.

"Well, you sound like one," Edouard said. "Maybe they *should* send you through assessment. Can't have crying Minneys on the force."

"I'm not a Minney! Stop it!"

But Edouard Norland smiled cruelly, enjoying taunting the youngest Gravesblood. Edouard's younger brother Bertrand chuckled low. His wide, rounded shoulders rose and fell as he laughed. Aron looked up at the older boys and began to laugh at his younger brother's misery. Edouard laughed for a moment too.

Alec frowned, looked down, and kicked dirt with his child's boot.

"At least my brother isn't a traitor," the little boy said under his breath. "Not like yours," he added, glancing to the side at the Norland boys.

Edouard's smile fell. "What was that?"

Aron snickered and looked away.

"Nothing," Alec said, smiling.

"Say what you will about Davide." Edouard lowered to a threatening whisper. "But he was no deserter, not like Rik."

Rik Graves, Quentin's brother and the boys' uncle, had disappeared years before. Most assumed he was dead, while others gossiped about the chance that he had deserted and betrayed the Brotherhood. Although there was no proof of misdeed. He was on a supply run along the Deadline had vanished completely.

"Don't talk about him," Aron stepped up angrily to Edouard.

Alec added with a boy's squeak, "Uncle didn't desert!"

Edouard crossed his muscled arms in front of his chest and looked down at the Graves boys in challenge. "Where is he, then?"

"Grandfather Basil says he's with the deadbloods," Alec said knowingly.

As the boys were bickering over where Rik Graves had disappeared to so many years ago, a man stumbled into the foreground. He had caked blood all over his face and wore a singed Brotherhood uniform. He limped towards them as if he'd travelled a long distance on foot.

It was Ben.

"Where is the elder!?" Benjamin cried pitifully, voice cracking as he hadn't had proper water in days. "Where is Elder Basil!?" he shouted again, then said, "water, please," with a croak and tripped. He fell on his face in a cloud of dust.

Ben lay unmoving. The boys scurried over to his side.

"Get him water!" Edouard commanded, vein in his young neck building. Without hesitation Alec jumped and ran to water for the fallen Brother.

Edouard shouted at Aron. "Go get your grandfather!"

Like his brother, Aron followed Edouard's command unquestioningly and sprinted as fast as he could across the grounds, into the castle, and up the dizzying staircase. He panted hard and his boots clacked against the cool stone as he ascended the Spire, floor by floor.

Finally, when it felt like his young legs would fall off and his lungs might burst, Aron reached the landing. His father, grand uncle, and grandfather sat in deep discussion around the fire table.

"Father!" Aron screamed as he skidded into the room. He stopped to gulp air and put his hands on his knees to rest, then stood again.

"Aron, where is your cape?!" Quentin shouted.

Aron's eyes opened wide. "What? No, I must tell grandfather, there's a…"

"Do not talk back!" Quentin said angrily, making a point of the interruption to show Basil he was a firm father. "You are out of uniform. A disgrace to our name."

"But, father," the boy pleaded. "I have to tell…."

"No!" Quentin shouted. He look a bounding step towards his son, skeletal frame towering. "You do not come in here and interrupt us, no matter how important it is."

"Yes, father. But this…"

"What did I say?" Quentin cut Aron off again, feeling Basil's gaze on him.

"There will be no talking back…"

"Oh, will you let the boy speak?" Basil said dismissively, rolling his eyes at his son. "Don't bully the child. What is it, Aron? Here, come to your grandfather," he said softly and gestured to him. "Sit right here, next to me."

Stung, Quentin returned to his seat and sat down slowly. Basil had never been so soft towards him. Not once. He leaned backwards, placed his long-fingered hands delicately in his lap, and fumed silently.

"Grandfather, there isn't time," Aron replied with wide eyes, still breathing heavily, grey face sweaty and splotchy. He held Basil's intense stare.

"Alright then," Basil said with amusement. He had a soft spot for his grandchildren. "Out with it."

"It's Ben," Aron told him. "He's back!"

"Why didn't you say that?" Quentin scoffed at him.

"Back!" Basil exclaimed. "Wolfgar?"

"No Wolfgar, just Ben," Aron said, shaking his head. "Covered in blood," He panted. "Alone."

"Where is he?" Xavier asked.

"In the courtyard. Came through the gate, then fell."

Basil pushed his chair back with a scrape and stood. "We must speak to him."

"Father, has Regnard betrayed us?" Quentin asked with concern.

Basil, tired of his son's antics, waved his hand at Quentin to dismiss him.

Basil looked at Aron. "You say he's in the courtyard?"

"Yes, Grandfather. With the Norlands."

Basil studied Ben's sweaty, pallid visage lying in the courtyard dirt. "Does he live?"

"Aye," Edouard nodded. "Barely."

Basil, Xavier, Quentin, and Edouard stood around the body as Bertrand hovered behind and Alec and Aron peered through their legs.

"Has he said anything?" Xavier asked.

He was both deeply concerned for the man's life and gravely worried about what his condition indicated for the future of the Brotherhood.

"Nonsense mostly," Edouard replied. "Babbling on about arrows and fire. Deserting Red Plumes, can you believe that? He must have eaten dreamcap." He wiped sweat from his forehead, then against the cloth of his dark pant leg. "He's gone mad."

Basil crouched down next to where Ben's half-conscious head rested. "Man needs encouragement," Basil barked. "More water." He gestured to Aron.

Aron carried over a wooden pail and ladle. Basil snatched the ladle from his hand and poured the liquid directly on Ben's face, into his eyes and nose and mouth until the man sputtered and coughed. His tired red eyes squinted open.

"Where is my Key?"

Ben's eyes widened. He pushed himself upright with a grunt.

He'd never been addressed by the elder directly, particularly so informally. He looked from Basil's face to the ladle of water in his hand. Thirst spiked in his throat.

"Elder," Ben croaked and reached.

"What happened at Lyonshall? Where is Wolfgar?" Basil prodded as he pulled the water away from Ben's pleading grasp. The men and boys watched on, standing in a circle around the fallen Brother, casting their shadows down.

"Ogo Regnard, my Lord," Ben said pitifully. "Please," he pointed at the pail. "Water," he croaked again.

Basil was unmoved. He inched closer to Ben's pain laden face. "Ogo holds Lyonshall?" Basil's blind white eye glinted in the sunlight. "He did this to you?"

Ben's lips were cracking lines of blood and his eyes could barely open. "Attacked," he muttered. "As we met with," he coughed, "Elder," he paused again, coughing in a pitiful hack, "Lachlan," he finally added.

"What of Lachlan?" Xavier asked pointedly.

Ben shifted his eyes to meet Xavier's briefly. "Dead," he said.

Basil handed Ben a full ladle of dirty, lukewarm water from the wooden pale for his cooperation. Ben gratefully slurped it down.

"Dead how?" Basil asked slowly, still crouched next to the dying man.

His head was aching, pounding in the bright sunlight, but he paid it no mind.

"I told you," Ben said sharply, in pain, losing patience. "Ogo."

"Ogo killed his father," Basil said as both statement and question, angry for Ogo's treason and in fear of what that meant for the Brotherhood Kingdom-wide. "You saw this? With your own eyes?"

Ben wearily nodded.

"What of Wolfgar?" Xavier asked. His voice tinged. "Fallen?"

The circle of bodies around Ben tightened as all leaned closer to hear his answer. Quentin's eyes shut, wishing it to be true.

Ben took a moment to respond, attempting to shift himself

upright despite crushed ribs and a deep gash in his side. He glanced from Xavier to Basil, then to Quentin, resting his gaze finally with the Norland boys, Edouard and Bertrand.

"I don't know," he said.

"You don't know?!" Basil shouted. He stood, resting his long fingers and palms on his shaking knees to creak upright. "One flaxen hair on Wolfgar Norland's head is worth more than your life! He is Vanguard, you infernal curse! You exist to serve and you have failed your very mission! Failed!" he screamed.

"Father," Quentin stepped forward. "You knew this could happen. We knew there was the potential for trouble there."

"Remove that smug smile from your wretched face before I do it myself."

"My Lord," Ben pleaded up at Basil from his seat in the dirt, shielding his eyes from the high angled afternoon sun despite the sharp pain in his wound when he moved. "I did what I could. I stood, to protect him!"

"You're lying," Xavier said simply.

Ben was taken aback. He turned to Xavier slowly, meeting the man's eyes behind his long-ago broken nose.

"You didn't know what happened to him," Xavier added astutely, utilizing his Guildsman skills. "If you'd attempted to protect him, you would know whether he escaped or perished. You would have said that first. Instead, you said you didn't know."

"I am tired," Ben looked from man to man anxiously. "I forgot," he widened his eyes, fear bubbling in his chest. He sensed his impending doom. "I tried to protect him, but we were separated. There were so many men. So many bodies. That's why I don't know."

"Hmm," Basil eyed him, shielding painful sunlight with the back of his hand. "What more can you tell us of Lachlan and Ogo?"

Ben pushed himself upright further with a painful grunt. "Lachlan cried like an infant," he said, squinting, "Ogo nearly chopped him in two."

"Cut his head off?" Edwourd asked with a morbid half-smile.

"Nay," Ben said, shaking his head once. "Swung downwards with a heavy straight blade, and struck the old man here," he pointed to his clavicle, midway between his shoulder and his neck. "Blood was everywhere," he said. "The other Vanguard didn't seem to like it as much as Ogo did," he added.

This sparked Xavier's attention. "Other Vanguard?"

"Darker, and shorter," Ben told him. "Thin. Young. Dark lined eyes. A boy."

Basil stopped his fuming tizzy to bark out a thought. "Rupert's son," he said angrily.

"Do you think it is, brother?"

"Surely," Basil nearly shouted back. "It falls in line with the web that is being weaved before our very eyes, and still, we are impotent to rebuke it!" He broke from the interrogation circle again, pacing in wide arcs around the surrounding courtyard.

Quentin asked Xavier, "What's he mean?"

"The New Rebellion," Xavier said softly. "If Oscar Morfit is Ogo's ward, it means Rupert sanctioned the attack on Lyonshall, which is nothing less than an act of war."

"What do we do?"

"We must write Hector," Xavier said calmly.

Basil stormed back to the huddle. "Execute him."

Ben threw his hands up. "Elder, my... my Lord!" he cried sadly, knowing that the Brotherhood he loved so dearly was about to betray him. His instincts screamed at him to run, to try and flee, but he'd sworn an oath. He'd given the Omen his life long ago.

"Father," Quentin's eyes darted, frantically trying to think of a way to save Ben. That man was more of a father to him than Basil ever had been. "He is a good man, he is a solid..."

"Since you are so invested," Basil said to Quentin with a cruel gleam in his good eye, "you do it."

"But," Quentin skipped forward closer to Basil, "father, he is Key Trainer. How will we replace such a talented asset? Please!"

Basil held up his hand to stop his son's whining. As he did the wind picked up the tail of his long black cloak, lifting it behind him like a living shadow. "Say a word more and you join him. No Brother speaks that way to the Elder," he paused, lowering his tone, speaking slower as he repeated himself. "No Brother."

"Yes, Fath... Elder," Quentin said. Defeated, he lowered his head.

Benjamin put his hands onto the ground beside each hip. He listened to the wind whip faintly in the distance around newly turning autumn leaves. He felt rocky dirt on his palms. He stared out ahead of himself with a glossy gaze. He dug fingertips into the earth. As the Vanguards around him bickered with each other, he shut his eyes and tilted his chin up, soaking his last moments of life in. The wind blew cool against his cheeks. He was grateful for everything he'd accomplished. Everything he'd contributed, to the Brotherhood and to the Kingdom, herself. All the boys he'd made men. Ben, with eyes still closed and face tilted upright, smiled.

"Now!" Basil shouted at Quentin. "Did you not hear me?"

Basil's latest tantrum broke poor Ben's solitude, thrusting him into fear-eyed panic. His chest began to rise and fall quickly as his breaths frenzied, internalizing his impending fate from his seat in the dirt.

"You know the custom," Basil nodded to his son. "See to it."

Quentin swallowed hard. He pointed at Edouard. "Remove his emblem and hold him up." Quentin said with a low mumble, unable to meet Ben's eyes when he said it. He flexed his sharply angled jaw.

"Aye," Edouard nodded. He looked to his brother Bertrand. "A hand, will you big guy?"

"Hm," Bertrand grunted.

Green eyes sparkling, Bertrand and Edouard together crouched next to Ben and strap by strap, unfastened his Brotherhood armor. Then, the Norlands lifted him upright.

Ben's weathered body was pale with fear and awash with sweat. His chest rose and fell in panicked succession. His wounds leaked puss and blood. His eyes darted from Vanguard to Vanguard.

The naked earthblood men chained to the posts on the other side of the grounds noticed what was happening and started to make noise. Some clapped slowly, and others hooted. Some stood and craned to see. One or two shouted curses. One sole man yelled aloud a Horned prayer.

The wind stopped blowing and the air hung hot and stale and still again, as if nature herself was holding her breath.

Quentin stood a few paces in front of Edouard and Bertrand who held the smaller, darker man upright. Ben was badly bruised, cut, and burned, visibly in much pain. If it were not for the Norland boys, he would not be able to stand on his own.

Quentin looked Ben up and down. He felt knives in the back of his throat and the threat of hot emotion right behind his eyes. He knew he would just as soon be dead if he were to cry or show any feeling at all, so he bit at the inside of his own lip until it bled to distract himself.

"What are you waiting for?" Basil grunted. He rubbed both temples with his hands as he winced, black robe sleeves billowing with each movement.

"Father..." Quentin started.

"The cursed sun!" Basil shooed Quentin with one hand while still rubbing his temple with his other. How his head ached! "Hurry it up. Then I can go back into the blessed dark."

"Yes, yes," Quentin sighed. He removed his dagger from his thigh. He flipped it in his hand. He approached Ben. "Do you have anything left to say?" he asked him. Quentin met Ben's fear-wide red eyes with his iron-grey ones.

Ben started to speak with a heavy crack of emotion. "I only wish to..."

"Do it already," Basil spat, shielding his face from the light completely with the wing of his cape.

Ben frowned. One tear fell from the corner of his eye. He held gaze with Quentin and nodded.

Quentin put one hand on Ben's shoulder and held his dagger tight. He took a breath. He aimed for Ben's side. On Ben's flesh between his rib bones was a scrolling tattoo in dark-black ink. Quentin drove his dagger into the space marked by the tattoo, just as he had done many times before. He aimed the dagger in and up, through rib bones, to the left slightly, and directly pierced Ben's beating heart. Ben cried out as his new wound poured blood. He writhed and contorted but the Norland boys held him tight. Quentin pulled the dagger out by twisting it, breaking the suction of his chest cavity, jerking the weapon downwards. It made a quiet pop. This brought a second gush of warm, bright red blood.

Before Ben even stopped writhing, the Norland boys dropped him with a thump into a pool of bloodied dirt in the Echo's Omen courtyard.

HUNTER POST

Blood pulsed in Rhain's vision each time his uncle spoke. He needed an escape, a release. But he couldn't have that until he finished this conversation. Although stalwart like a statue on the outside, inside, he was screaming. Raging. He needed to relieve the pressure he felt building in the back of his skull. He needed to cause pain. He needed blood.

"Good work today."

Rhain's uncle Sampson was a simple man. A man that was satisfied by trapping and a warm meal every evening. He was past his prime with brilliant red hair streaked with the tell-tale white and grey of age, pulled tight with a string at the nape of his neck.

Rhain had similar features yet was much younger, with hair deep red. His thick wavy locks were pulled into a tight Baneswood knot. Both men had bushy, long beards. Both also had heavy, caveman-like brows, that lowered as they eyed each other in the dim-lit hall. The looked like Dales through and through. The younger man was heavily muscled while the older was hunched, thin, and shrivelled. The older man's eyes were deep brown, and his skin was the same. The younger man's skin was pale and his eyes shone grey.

The younger man expressionlessly grunted.

"I mean it, Rhain," his uncle said sincerely, leaning closer. His tone was warm. He cared. "I don't know what I'd do without you. Do you know how much coin it would take to replace you?"

Rhain half turned his head to hide his crooked smile. He shrugged humbly. "I take things apart."

Sampson Dale couldn't believe the boy's modesty. "Son, you fix complicated traps like they're nothing." He added with wide parted brows, "it would take a creed of men to do what you do alone."

Rhain leaned back in his chair. It made a protesting groan at the young man's weight. *I'm not stupid like most are*, he thought. He grunted.

"It's been a strong take this year," Sampson changed the subject.

"Could have been better," Rhain grunted, unblinking. He stared ahead with his heavy brow furrowed. Underneath his beard were high cheekbones and a strong jaw.

Sampson studied his nephew's hard expression. "I know you don't want to be here. I know you don't want to talk to me. But son, it is the best thing for you. It's," he paused and scrunched his forehead, unable to imagine the pain he'd gone through. "It's all I can do, is try to understand. That's the only way I can help you. But you must talk to me, Rhain."

Rhain glared ahead. His grey eyes that changed hue with his mood bored a hole in the opposing wall. Each irritating word his uncle spoke was like a small dagger in his mind.

"I can't imagine what it was like. I mean," Sampson paused, "I…" he stuttered, imagining the boy bearing the brunt of Baddon's harsh ways. "I wasn't there. I'm not your father."

"I know," Rhain said deeply. "You're not."

Sampson jumped in his chair, blinking furiously. Rhain, comparatively, did not look away. He didn't even flinch. He almost seemed pleased.

"What is it you want to ask me, Sampson?" Rhain threatened as he leaned forward, bringing his hulking fame to hover over the table.

The old man leaned backwards. "I told you, I want to help you," he said. His eyes darted. His heart thumped. It was like he was caught in a snare. "I can't help you unless you talk to me."

Rhain leaned back in his chair. He grunted. *There's no helping the damned*, he thought.

Sampson exhaled. "Son," he said. "You can trust me. I'm not like your father. I'm not Baddon. It's why I convinced him to let you leave and come tend the Post here with me."

"Father discarded me," Rhain said with chilling detachment. "I'm useless to him now."

"That... that isn't true! Listen here, your father cares about you, in... in his own way."

"My father has never cared for a thing," Rhain said distantly, *"except maybe blood,"* he thought to himself.

The earliest memory Rhain had of his father was when Baddon tied a young native girl up with a rope by her hands, flayed her in front of him, and then forced him to clean up afterwards. Rhain was five.

"He cares for value and use, that is all." The young man spoke with unexpected diction and refined inflection, especially given his gruff countenance. It hinted to his unbelievable intellect.

"He's a hard man to know," Sampson conceded. "But you're still his son. Still a Dale of the great Baneswood."

"No more," Rhain grunted.

Sampson thought he'd misheard the boy. Dales were a proud people. It was unthinkable that a Dale, particularly the son of the elder, even the second, would rebuke his blood so.

"What?" he asked with widening eyes.

"I'm dead to him," Rhain said cooly. "After the accident, my value is gone."

"It's not true." Sampson was shaken by his nephew's lack of emotion. "I just told you. Your mind. You're," he paused, "a genius. Fit for the Guild even. Or more! Work directly with the King!"

Rhain grunted. To him, words meant nothing. Function was all that mattered. He crossed his expansive forearms in front of himself. "I can't fight. Not in the Games. No more. I'm useless."

"Rhain," Sampson's voice cracked. He mourned for his nephew. The closest thing he'd ever had to a son. He'd never been given such a blessing. His wife died young and he didn't have the heart to find another, as she was the love of his life.

He'd taken solace in his dogs and work. When Rhain was injured, he took him in, to spare the young man his father's inevitable wrath.

"There's more to life than competing."

Pure anger clouded Rhain's face. "There wasn't until this happened." He patted his leg, with ankle to knee in a wooden brace, tight with leather and sinew.

Sampson frowned. "I am sorry, but you must find a way to live past it."

Rhain glared at him. His little patience was nearly gone. "What is it you want, old man?"

"I told you. I want to help you."

"You said that. But what is it you really want?"

"Nothing!" Sampson nearly jumped, fidgeting, eyes darting beneath Rhain's chilling gaze. "I... I told you. I want to help."

Rhain glared at him carefully. He could smell the lie on him. "Uncle?"

Sampson sighed. He smoothed his greying copper hair once then set his jaw. "Are you still going to Animus?"

Statuesque Rhain didn't show any reaction at all. "I am," he grunted.

Sampson sighed again, louder.

"What?" Rhain's voice deepened. He despised half-talk. "Speak your mind, old man."

Sampson was tired. He loved his nephew and wanted to protect the troubled boy, but he was afraid of him. He paused again, wondering how he could ask his question delicately. He knew he must be blunt. He couldn't ignore the slamming doors in the evening and missing tools any longer. The rumors from the natives of a monster on the loose. Reports of missing people and mutilated bodies. "Where do you go?"

Rhain was expressionless. The pair sat suspended in uncomfortable silence with only the flickering candle between them before Sampson spoke again.

"Son, you disappear," he said more forcefully this time. "You'll be gone sometimes for days, weeks. Don't pretend that I don't know."

He expected some kind of defence or outburst, but Rhain only grunted.

Sampson was getting frustrated. It carried in his tone. He leaned forward again, placing both hands flat on the table.

"Rhain," he tried again, "where do you go?"

"That's not what you really want to ask me, is it?"

"No, but..."

Rhain glared with dead eyes.

"Fine," Sampson conceded. "I'm... I'm worried you'll... hurt someone," he said timidly. Sampson's voice shook as he leaned backwards as far as he could in his chair, as if trying to avoid Rhain's potential wake of destruction. He was known to destroy things when provoked.

"If you go to the Rock. I... I don't trust you, son." He repeated with gentle tone, "I'm worried you'll hurt someone there, Rhain."

Rhain blinked twice and neglected to respond for several bated, uncomfortable seconds. He finally said, while crossing his massive arms slowly at his hulking chest, "I won't."

"That's it? Nothing to convince me?"

Rhain's patience fully dwindled. He began to see red, literally, in his sight. Dripping red hallucinations pulsed in his vision like blood pouring down a windowpane. He'd never told anyone this happened to him but knew for himself what it meant. The old man shouldn't push him so. What happened next was not pleasant.

"No," he grunted.

"I... I won't let you leave!" Sampson cried, voice tinny and panicked. "Not unless you swear you will not harm anyone," he added, tired bags under his eyes illuminated by candlelight. "Not while at the Capital."

Rhain stood slowly, crooked smiling, titanic shoulders casting a wide shadow over his elderly kin. "You won't," he paused," let me?" Rhain stepped forward once, then twice. On his left footfall he visibly winced, briefly, although he never lost momentum. This man was familiar with pain.

"Son," Sampson pleaded instantly, but Rhain was swifter

than he appeared. He rushed around the length of the table and violently thrusted the old man back while still seated. He held Sampson by the tunic with both hands.

Then, he lifted the old man from his chair, like a child lifts a doll.

"Son, please," Sampson begged. His voice cracked and his thin legs flailed beneath him. A wide, dark spot pooled on the dingy, matted carpet floor. He had relieved himself from fear.

Revolted, Rhain powerfully shoved Sampson up against the wall, so hard it shook and knocked one of the large, snarling heads mounted there from its position. The dread wolf trophy crashed next to them and the jaw popped loose and skipped across the carpet. Rhain leaned closer to Sampson, still holding him up above the ground, while Sampson kicked and bucked.

"Please," he wailed, but Rhain was unflinching. Sampson's gaze pleaded with his nephew, but the boy's calm, cool eyes were glazed over. There was no getting through to him. Sampson wasn't sure the boy had a soul at all.

Rhain leaned in, so close that his breath condensed hot and stale against Sampson's old, wrinkled cheek. He lifted the frail man off the wall. Then he thrust him back to it with such force that it knocked the wind from his lungs. He coughed in a hack. Spittle caught in his moustache and beard.

"Please!" Sampson pitifully wailed. He was terrified. He feared death itself.

But Rhain dropped his uncle and stepped back, disgusted by his kin's embarrassing pleas. He looked down and crossed his wide forearms at his chest.

"I am going to the Rock."

ANIMUS ROCK

Gusting wind whipped and howled in the marbled grey afternoon as the Animus Rock fortress wall loomed before Wolfgar. He studied the structure, feeling the breeze bite his nose. Its massive stones were rain weathered. Creeping tendrils snaked through cracks and crevices. The eight majestic towers of the castle jutted up in the background through the sheer grey clouds. Ravens twirled around them.

It was quite the sight.

He'd never been to Animus Rock before but had known what to expect from tapestries he'd seen and stories he'd heard. And his father always told him and his siblings about what it was like there. How one could feel power dripping from every crevice of it. History leaking from the walls. Still, it was difficult not to be impressed.

Wolfgar walked in partial awe down North Pass—a dirt and pebbled road cut through a sloping meadow of low-growing wolf-joy. Along the perimeter of the wall, points of arrows rested ready, hidden and ominously aimed at all incoming. A cluster of guards on foot waited at the base of the wall.

Wolfgar eyed them curiously.

All wore burgundy red capes and huddled around each other, joking and laughing. Tall red shields painted with white griffins rested in their background against the wall. The lackadaisical men eyed the sparse trickle of travellers who entered the Capital through this quiet gate.

Bellamine Guards, Wolfgar thought. They used to be a well-known force, greatly respected throughout the Kingdom, however under King Humphry's leadership, they floundered. Wolfgar slowed his pace to fall in-line behind a man with a cart piled with red and white root vegetables. A Morfit native. The only other passer-by.

"Ay," a slouched guard grunted. "You!" he stood up straight, puffing his chest at Wolfgar.

This guard who spotted him was nearly indistinguishable from the others, with a matching shaven head, no facial hair, and crimson eyes. The only way to tell him apart was his varied skin tone and ostentatious unibrow. He furrowed it and frowned when Wolfgar continued walking with his eyes turned away and head down.

Unibrow stomped forward. "I say ay!"

"What is it?" a slighter guard with a hooked nose shouted.

"He eyes not right!" Unibrow yelled to the Hooked nose. "He color too!"

Wolfgar heard the guards' shouting and stopped, heaving his shoulders in a sigh. Even in the overcast light his pale skin shone. He turned his incriminating green eyes towards the guards. He hadn't quite thought this through.

"See!" Unibrow pointed at Wolfgar. "Come here."

Wolfgar dutifully approached the blockade, stomach knotting, hand hovering over his only weapon; his dagger, hidden beneath his borrowed tunic inside his trousers. He clenched his jaw.

The man riding the vegetable cart shook the reigns of his mule vigorously. He looked over his shoulder at the Bellamine guards with concern until he was safely through the gate and away from conflict.

Watching the man flee, Wolfgar shook his head. He thought to himself that earthblood are all the same. No honor. Just as he was taught.

"Aye," Hook Nose said slowly. He squinted one of his deep-set red eyes circled with black bags. "Green? Only Vanguards 'ave green!"

"I told ya," Unibrow said proudly.

Wolfgar stopped in front of them. He was tired. Exhausted, actually. And he still wore the beige tunic that he stole with the nondescript brotherhood trousers and boots from when he left

Echo's Omen. He didn't take with him the clothes the Morfits offered him. They were too ostentatious. They didn't seem proper. His cut and burnt hands had however been tended to by the Morfits, and his palms were wrapped in thick beige cloths.

"Call the Captain," Hook Nose commanded Unibrow.

Unibrow dutifully jogged off and spoke to a man on a brown mare. He trotted over. Wolfgar thought this man was obviously the Captain given his elevated armor. His dark brown hair was plaited into hundreds of tiny braids, pulled back into one wide ponytail with a length of leather. A style only permitted by high ranking Bellamine officers. The rest of the forces had their heads shaved.

"Who are you?" the Captain asked Wolfgar.

"Jude Thorne," Wolfgar said plainly. He felt practiced by now, having survived Croft Hold undetected. His disguise was a good one.

"Vanguard?"

"I am," Wolfgar nodded.

"There is no 'Jude Thorne'. I know the bloodlines." The Captain said sceptically, urging his steed closer. The brown mare whinnied and bucked her head slightly. He seemed smarter than the others. And prouder. "I'll ask you again," he lowered his tone. "Who are you?"

"I'm a bastard," Wolfgar said with honest eyes. "My Lord," he lowered his head.

"Captain," Unibrow barked.

"Captain," he repeated dutifully.

"A bastard? Thorne bastard?"

"Aye," Wolfgar nodded, looking up at the Captain. "A ward of Regnard since birth."

Hook Nose chirped, "Whose bastard?"

Wolfgar answered without a beat. "Wallace," he said. "Thorne." He pulsed his jaw in anticipation of the response.

At that, all the guards who had been eves dropping from afar, gathered around. "Hm" the Captain put his hand to his clean-shaven chin. "Why are you here? Did you escape? Or did Lord

Lachlan have change of heart?" Several of the listening guards snickered at mention of Lachlan Regnard.

"Ah, course. You don't know.".

"Know what?" the Captain barked, confident tone faltering slightly.

Wolfgar understood on a deep level he should speak true. The Bellamine guards would appreciate nothing less. He'd heard the rumors of how brutal they could be if you interacted with them poorly. Or irritated them at all. They were known to be bored and unruly. The slightest provocation typically elicited a disproportionately intense response.

"Lyonshall fell. Lachlan is dead. Ogo is elder now," he said.

"Can't be," Unibrow interjected loudly. "No man bests the Red Plumes."

Wolfgar knowingly shook his head. "Morfit. With Ogo."

"You're telling me the shiny Morfits and the pretty boy Ogo took down Regnard?" Hook Nose stepped in. "The man never left Animus," he added with a smile. "Untested in battle. Couldn't harm a beetle." A chuckle mumbled through the grouped men.

Animus Rock citizens particularly knew all there was to know about the most powerful Vanguards especially, following their marriages and disagreements and fashions with a close eye. To the natives of Animus Rock, Vanguards were celebrities, and the most exciting topic to gossip about.

"Aye, but it's true," Wolfgar said. He looked to the Captain. "I saw it all. In the chaos I," he paused, "escaped."

"Hm," the Captain rubbed his chin, considering the tale as the other guards whispered amongst themselves. Wolfgar patiently awaited his fate. The brown mare shifted her footing and jostled the Captain in place, clinking his armor as he deliberated. Wolfgar took shallow breaths. He dug his fingernails into his palms through his meagre bandages behind his back, to distract himself from how loud his heart was thumping.

"He's an undocumented Vanguard," the Captain concluded finally, "so we must bring him to Humphry."

"Aye, Captain," the men aped in cacophony.

Wolfgar breathed a silent sigh of relief. Just as Basil had instructed. He'd be delivered to the King.

"Should we bathe him or give him fresh clothes?" Unibrow asked.

. The other men glared at him. "What? He's going for the King. He be smelling like a horse's ass."

The group burst into a chuckle. Wolfgar smelled his own arm pit, then shrugged. "You think this is bad?" He grinned warmly.

The Captain smiled. "Leave him as he is. Makes his story believable."

"Aye," Unibrow nodded. "Call an audience?"

"We won't need to," the Captain replied as he glanced up at the sun glowing from behind white clouds. "Not if we go now. We should find him in the Throne Hall. He should still be there."

Wolfgar wondered silently what he'd gotten himself into now.

"King Humphry."

Wolfgar followed the guards in burgundy cloaks into the city, though blocks of grid-like city streets, directly to the looming Eighth Tower itself. He'd been awe-struck by the infestation of natives living lives only deserving of Vanguards. Their expensive jewel-tone garments. Women with clinking chimes hanging from their earlobes in silver and gold. Men with modest colored tunics and dark capes, mostly with metal side toggles. Children in colorful smocks running amuck, *like packs of wild dogs,* he thought. To his surprise, the earthblood here kept themselves well. Similar to the inhabitants of Croft Hold, only varying in garments and skin tone. It even seemed hair styling, for women at least, shared fashion with Croft. Nearly all women had cropped hair right beneath their chins. And most had it oiled back.

Now, Wolfgar stood behind the Captain as he addressed the King.

The Animus Rock throne room was round lined with massive smooth white columns and topped with a copper dome. The floor was tiled shimmery pale yellow green, like a low growing meadow of gemmy floral blooms blowing in warm gusts of wind, glinting from the sun. Except, unlike a natural meadow, in this room there were no windows. Instead, huge flaming torches sat in front of each column. The only light in the hall came from them.

Humphry Bellamine, an unimposing man with sloped shoulders and large ears, sat reclined atop a black rock throne. Wolfgar disliked him immediately, although he couldn't put his finger on why. He was momentarily entranced by the enormous throne the man sat atop. It was carved in entirety from one monstrous block of tourmaline, with thick armrests and a high reaching back in a triangular shape, ending in a severe, sharp point at the top. Two particularly large torches spit arching red and orange flames on either side of it. The Bellamine Griffin was tiled into the section of wall high above the throne in deep reds and burgundy. The emblems of the other bloodlines were tiled between the other columns. There were sixteen murals total, all glaring down at Wolfgar.

He faced the King.

"Approach," King Humphry beckoned with a finger from his slouched seat. Wolfgar kept a cool countenance despite the knot in his stomach. If anyone were to find out his secret, it would be worse than the First for him. He stoically looked to the throne to study the Vanguard King, Humphry Bellamine.

The young man wore a black metal band encrusted with eight glistening red stones, marking him as King. While Vanguard women, particularly in the past, wore diadems and gem bands, men did not. The crown marked Humphry as King immediately.

If it had not been for the crown, and his position in the lofty throne, Wolfgar would not have known the man he stood before was of any note. Humphry had a long, bored-looking face and close-set red eyes. His chin was soft. His ears were large, as Bellamine bloods' tended to be. He tapped one shiny, polished boot impatiently against the glistening floor. He looked nothing like a King.

"Your Eminence," the Captain said. He bowed his head. The other guards did the same.

Wolfgar looked from one to the other, then lowered his head too as the Queen caught his eye.

To the King's right sat a pale woman of striking allure. So pale, Wolfgar wondered if she was Vanguard herself, although that would be impossible. Her waist-length hair was oiled and tucked behind her ears. Around her brow, atop her hair was a black band with a sole red gem in the center of her forehead, matching the King's, only smaller. Traditional adornment for the Queen. She had razor high cheekbones and monolid red eyes that rolled whenever Humphry spoke.

"Queen Gracea," the Captain nodded. She blinked back at him silently.

"What is it, Rolf?" King Humphry whined. "I'm sick of listening to the stupid, ungrateful citizens complain all day. I don't have the time to sit and listen to whining, you know? I am King, you know? I have much more important matters to attend to."

"Of course, your Eminence," Captain Rolf said, lowering his head again. "But this is critical," he glanced up. "It is deserving of the King's attention."

Humphry sighed loudly from the back of his throat. From his side the Queen shot a disapproving gaze. Humphry noticed and sighed again, rolling his eyes. "So be it," he said, flitting his hand like he was shoeing a fly. "I'll allow it." Before Rolf had a chance to speak, Humphry shouted, "On with it!" rather impatiently.

Wolfgar was taken aback. It was as if he was watching a spoiled child pretend to be King. No wonder his kin and brethren at Echo's Omen had little respect for him.

Rolf, practiced in dealings with the King, wasn't shaken. "We've discovered an undocumented Vanguard," he said.

The King sat forward in his chair. "Undocumented? How? Impossible!" The Queen crossed her legs, obviously listening, although still unimpressed.

Two others, a man and a woman sat in observation on one sloping side of the throne room, near where the King's personal Bellamine guards stood. At Rolf's announcement the man, Herman Graves, with dark middle-parted hair and icy pale skin, leapt from his chair.

Rolf said, "Here," grabbing Wolfgar by the shoulder. He shoved him towards the King and Queen.

Wolfgar stumbled into the foreground. His markedly Vanguard features were clear in the dim torchlight.

"Found him trying to enter through the Onyx. Says he's a bastard. Thorne."

"Thorne?" Herman interjected.

Wolfgar swung his head to study him. He hadn't paid much attention to anyone in the chamber besides the King and Queen up until now.

He'd heard of Herman Graves all too often. Herman, the soft younger brother of Hector, was nearly as derided as Humphry was among the high ranking Norlands and members of the Brotherhood. He was thought to be weak and inconsequential. A bother. However, standing in the presence of the man, he was far different than Wolfgar had expected.

Hector reeked of Gravesblood. He had a short forehead, hollow cheeks, and a pointed jaw. He was tall, almost too tall, with elongated legs, neck and arms. His eyes matched his skin in icy pale grey. Although unlike Hector, Herman felt different. He wasn't cold. Warmth poured from him, as well as composure and compassion. Wolfgar was impressed immediately.

"Shut up Herman," Humphry said, like the brat he was.

"He says that he was a ward of..." Rolf began, but Humphry interrupted him.

"You too," the King said flatly. "Speak boy," he commanded, although Wolfgar was nearly the same age as he. "Who are you?"

"My name is Jude," Wolfgar said. With each telling he felt himself slipping further and further into Jude's skin.

"Yes, yes, I don't care," Humphry said, biting on the sleeve of his fine tunic. "Who you are makes no difference. What blood?"

"He told you," Wolfgar said, "Thorne."

The King frowned.

Rolf cleared his throat loudly. Then, when Wolfgar didn't take the hint, the Captain stepped forward and nudged the young Vanguard in the back.

Wolfgar turned and said under his breath, "What?"

"Your Eminence," Rolf whispered to him.

"Your Eminence," Wolfgar said loudly. He couldn't believe that's what they were required to call that sorry excuse for a man, much less their King. He now fully understood why Basil and the others hated him so.

"Continue," Humphry said.

"I was a ward of Lachlan's," Wolfgar paused, narrowing his close-set green eyes, "your Eminence," he added with a sigh.

Herman Graves took bounding steps across the chamber to hover at the Tourmaline Thone's side. "Was?" he asked. He was gravely concerned, hovering to the left of the King.

"Let him finish, darling," Verity Bellamine, the King's sister, sitting off to the side, said in a fluttering song. "Here, come back to me," she gestured lightly with her hand. "Don't want to make Humfy grumpy."

Herman grinned. "You are so right, Verity, my love."

Wolfgar had heard about Verity Bellamine. Everyone had. In person, she was as striking as the rumors told.

Verity Bellamine had dark skin to match her brother and like the King her bottom lip was bigger than her top, but unlike the King, she wore a dark purple lip stain. She had large ears, pierced from lobe to cartilage with hanging, shiny silver metal embedded with clear, black, and red gems. A style she was known for and made famous Kingdom wide, at least in New realms. Her dark brown, straight, shoulder-length hair was well-oiled flat and tucked behind her ornamented ears. She had deep-set brown eyes with the top lined black. Her resting face, although stunning, perpetually appeared like she was smelling something foul, except when she smiled. Around Verity's wrists were countless clinking, jewelled bangles in every color.

She was adorned like a gift sheep, Wolfgar thought, about to be slaughtered.

"Sister!" King Humphry shouted. He leaned forward in the throne, face turning violet. "I will not tolerate your..."

"Oh, lighten up Humfy."

Herman Graves, soothed by his wife's voice, calmly went back to his seat at her side. Verity held his hand. The pair intertwined their fingers.

"Let the new Vanguard finish, won't you? I'm dying to hear," Verity said, then glanced to her younger brother. "Aren't you?"

King Humphry sat back, crossed his arms tight, and fumed. Meanwhile Queen Gracea bore a slight smile at his unhappiness. Wolfgar was amused at the dynamics in the hall. He silently noted the interactions, to report back to the Omen later, of course.

"Well?" the King asked angrily, eying Wolfgar impatiently.

Captain Rolf cleared his throat loudly again and turned to glare at Wolfgar, intending him to respond.

Wolfgar took the hint. "Lyonshall fell. Lachlan is dead. Ogo's Regnard's elder now," he recited.

Verity gasped.

"Serves him right," Humphry said hotly. "Pompous fool never listened. Did as he pleased. He was a dolt I say."

"How did it happen?" Herman asked loudly.

"It was a massacre," Wolfgar said. "Every Red Plume slaughtered. The castle burned."

Verity threw her hands to her mouth. Herman furrowed his brow and shook his head. Humphry looked sideways at his sister, chuckling at her outburst. Queen Gracea, from her lofty seat aside the King's Tourmaline throne, appeared indifferent. She was from the North, only doing her duty, and cared little for Vanguard Kingdom happenings. Most said she cared for very little at all. She rarely even spoke.

"You say Ogo holds Lyonshall now? He is Regnard elder?" Herman said, obviously concerned. "If you say all Red Plumes were slaughtered, if such a thing can be true, then what army did he command? Lachlan held the Regnard army. Ogo has no men."

"Not all," Wolfgar replied, shaking his head once. "There were some in silver armor with the mark of a rockrose."

"Ogo has men you say? From where?"

Wolfgar nodded, then shrugged.

"He's converting Lyonshall border natives then. It must be," Herman said astutely, mostly to himself. "Where does he get the coin, I wonder," he thought out loud. "I assume he had help?"

Wolfgar nodded again. "Morfit," he said. At that, Herman Graves's eyes widened slowly. He looked to Verity and she met his gaze. She squeezed his hand.

Humphry clapped his hands twice. "Enough, enough," he said. "This is boring. I don't care about that old man and his doltish realm. I want to leave." He threw his head back pitifully. "Is it time for sup yet?" he whined.

"But, your Eminence," Herman pleaded, tucking his hair behind both ears, "this could indicate grave danger for Bellamine. Their alliance is more than just theory now. They've attacked a realm. Broken our laws. And somehow, they possess a power we do not yet understand, if they are able to fell the Red Plumes. What's stopping them from moving on Animus, herself? What if one of them is after your throne? Humphry, friend," he paused. He lowered his voice. "It is a declaration of war."

"Nonsense," Humphry dismissed with another flit of his wrist. "Family dispute is all that is. It's between Ogo and Lachlan." he laughed loudly at the thought of the dead man, alone. "Or it was." His cackles reverberated off the rounded walls and copper dome of the hall.

"Humphry," Herman said softly. "We must tell the Council." It was the King's duty to announce such a monumental occurrence and lead the discussion on how to handle it

Kingdom wide. To neglect to do so was worthy of punishment.

"I said, enough!" Humphry shouted, cruel laughing smile crashing down like a boulder from a mountain. "Now…" He said, drooping eyes looking angrily to Wolfgar. "Finish telling us who you are. I tire of this."

"Oh, do tell us," Verity said lightly. Her presence was magnanimous. All instinctually turned to her when her deep, melodious voice spoke. "I told you, I'm just *dying*." She leaned forward with eyes widening.

Humphry looked at his sister. "Stop saying it like that Veri. It's bad fortune."

"Oh, you and your superstitions Humfy," she cooed. The twenty years King furrowed his brow. He hated when his big sister teased him. Huffing, he faced Wolfgar again. The young Norland stood with wide eyes in witness of the intimate royal dynamics.

King Humphry pointed at Wolfgar. "You will act like you didn't hear that."

"Hear what?"

"Are you stupid? Hear that I was… Oh, wait, you were doing as I commanded," a smile broke across the silly King's long face. "Of course, I knew that."

Wolfgar bowed his head slightly, "Of course, your Eminence." He guessed that the King was not much older than himself, around Davide's age before he died, but acted like a young child. Wolfgar couldn't believe it.

"Now, clever new Vanguard," King Humphry said as if it was a challenge. "Explain so we can be done with this!"

"I was given to Lachlan as ward," Wolfgar began. He flexed his jaw. "I don't know anything but Lyonshall."

"By whom?" Verity chimed in. The men's heads swung towards her. "Who gave you to Lachlan?"

Wolfgar swallowed hard and dry, feeling a lump in his throat. He craved the cold mountain water he was accustomed to. The air hung hot and still in this hall. Wolfgar felt the glinting tiled images of the competing Vanguard emblems shining down at him from every angle. He knew everyone's eyes in the room were on him. He looked from face to face. He repeated the only Thorne name he knew, as he had at Croft Hold, as he had been commanded to. "Wallace Thorne," he said, then secretly bit the inside of his cheek.

"Ha!" King Humphry laughed. "The pious old coot. Finally!" he shook his head in glee.

"What is your meaning?" Wolfgar asked brazenly, speaking out of turn, driven by curiosity.

"You know nothing of your alleged father?" Herman interjected with surprise. "Only his name?"

"Aye," Wolfgar nodded, blond hair glinting in the torchlight.

"Humphry can't stand Wallace," Verity said. "He always teased Humfy when he was young, isn't that right?"

King Humphry grunted indignantly.

"Your Eminence," Herman interjected, standing again from his seat. "It is not wise to be hasty. Are we sure he speaks truth?"

"My love," Verity turned her body to face Herman, tilting her ebony face towards him. "Why do you question your King?"

Herman was caught off guard like the wind got knocked out of him. "I... I.." he stuttered and looked at her, surprised his wife didn't take his side.

"Good, sister," Humphry praised, smiling wide. "She's right. Don't question me. But I like you. I will indulge you."

Herman sank back to a seat next to Verity, defeated and still seriously concerned. She took his hand into hers and patted it gently. "Thank you, my King," Herman said half-heartedly.

"Look at the boy," Humphry gestured to Wolfgar. "He is muscled. Put to hard labor in the Lyonshall mines, yes?"

Wolfgar stared blankly before realizing the question was for him. "Yes... yes," he assured quickly.

"And his eyes, see that? Of course, the Thorne shade of green!"

Herman squinted, "Maybe, but your Eminence..."

The King interrupted, "Finally, and most obviously, his sickly white Thorne skin, just like that old, stupid bastard Wallace." Humphry paused and eyed his subjects proudly, Bellamine griffin's talons fierce in shimmery tiles behind his head above the throne. "There, you see, I have solved this riddle. He must speak truth."

"At least check him for a brand," Herman said.

"I do not have one," Wolfgar interjected quickly, "my Lord."

"Yes, and why would he? Doltish thought, my Second," Humphry said, then laughed. "Since he is Vanguard, his skin would not take one, even if applied!"

"Besides," Verity said lovingly to the deflated Herman, "it makes perfect sense. You know as well as I do that it was Wallace who really drove this Kingdom into the dirt. This whole storm that my poor brother must deal with daily is his fault. He was not just a bully then. He still is! He should not be permitted to hide behind his father's shadow. Wallace is to blame for it all. He is rubbish. This boy proves that," she said with finality, gesturing to Wolfgar.

"But how?" Herman asked. "Excuse me," he dropped Verity's hand and shifted backwards. She frowned and turned her nose up at him, crossing her arms at her chest. "The Wallace I know would rather a thousand deaths before this tie to a native-born child."

"My darling," Verity tisked sceptically, raising an arched eyebrow. "You underestimate the man. You have such a pure soul, so unlike your brethren."

"Speak plainly," Herman said with a crisp frown.

The King watched the couple bicker with amusement, leaning towards where they sat in the hall with an elbow on the throne's crystal armrest and his chin resting on his hand. He loved drama.

"All the more reason for him to hide the result of his sin, in the one place he thought no one could find it. The Lyonshall mines," Verity said hotly.

"Then why not kill him? I'm sorry," Herman looked at Wolfgar, "for everything you have been through, truly," then he looked back to Verity, "but why not be rid of the nuisance and then have nothing to fear?"

"Who cares," Humphry whined. "I'm bored. He is Wallace

Thorne's bastard because your King commanded so. Why not accept what is apparent?"

"It is too easy," Herman squinted his eyes again. "Why would he speak so well? Rough, but practiced. Why do we not simply examine him for any markings? What if he hails from a vault? The Brotherhood itself perhaps! I wouldn't put this past my brother..."

"You are paranoid, husband," Verity smiled, interrupting casually. "Isn't he, brother?" She looked at Humphry.

Humphry laughed. Gracea to his right yawned. Wolfgar shifted his weight from right to left foot. Humphry continued and stared at the young man. "Now, what to do with you. What to do with you," he said.

"Send him to Monty," Verity suggested blithely. "After all, he is Wallace's nephew. They're cousins!" She clapped. "Oh, how lovely. A Thorne reunion!"

Humphry sat back in his throne and chuckled. "I like that. So be it." Humphry dismissed with a wave of his hand and limp wrist. "He goes to Monty."

"But, your Eminence, what if..." Herman started.

But King Humphry interrupted. "Stop it. He claims he's Thorne. Now he's Thorne's problem."

Wolfgar knocked three times on the high arched door of the last yellow-stone villa in the row.

He stood in the crisp fall air with slowly setting afternoon sun warm on his face. River loons honked over the Missi. Carts jostled over cobblestones and children laughed somewhere out of sight, nearby. With every sound his body tensed, preparing for an attack as he'd been trained to do for so many years. He couldn't comprehend how the earthblood walked freely, without weapons or armor. How did they believe they were safe here? How could anyone think anywhere was safe?

Wolfgar was lost in thought until an ethereally pale woman

pushed open the heavy door.

Her thick hair was pulled into a clean knot on the top of her head, pinned with green gemstones. She wore a black, long sleeved, deep V-neck blouse tucked into a dark green skirt, tight on her impossibly small waist, flowing down to her calves. Around her neck, resting between her breasts, sparkled an encapsulating green gemstone pendant circled in the Brochet ouroboros.

She reminded Wolfgar of a cat, with her pointed, detached gaze.

"Who are you?" the woman spat.

He looked up in surprise. "I was going to ask you the same thing."

Sybil Brochet pinched her nose with her fingers, turning her head away from this man's stench as she spoke. "Are you sure you have the correct villa?" *Who is he?* Sybil thought. He was pleasant to look at, with a boy-like charm, but smelled terrible.

"No," Wolfgar said bluntly, shifting his eyes once. The chill this woman gave off was daunting. "I'm looking for Monty. They told me to ask for him. Thorne."

"Yes, yes. This is Montague's villa," she said. "But," she added with half scepticism, half curiosity, "I don't know you."

Sybil furrowed her eyebrows to highlight her only wrinkle; a deep line bisecting her forehead between her eyebrows from thought. She studied the visitor. He was young, barely a man, but weathered and muscled as someone far older, with wide shoulders and veins snaking up his forearms. He wore earthblood clothes. His flaxen hair was oily and dirty and matted to his head. He had long stubble all over his strong, square jaw. His sparking, near-set green eyes were weary.

"Can I come in?"

"Tell me who you are."

Wolfgar loudly sighed. "They say I'm Monty's cousin."

"Who says?"

"The King, and others."

"How would you not know?"

"It's," he paused, "a long story. Can I come in?"

"Hm, the King you say?" Sybil was quiet. She put her hand to her chin and looked Wolfgar up and down. "No, you can't."

"I can't come in?" Wolfgar asked in disbelief. "Really?"

"You can go around."

"I don't understand."

"I won't have you traipsing through this elevated villa stinking like you do," she said, looking up at Wolfgar standing in the arched doorframe. "You'll go around back. I'll have the earthblood throw some water on you. I'm not sure any of Montague's clothing will fit you, but I'll see what I can find. Once you're civilized again, we can speak as civilized Vanguards do." She looked him up and down again. "You are certainly not civilized right now."

Wolfgar stared with wide eyes at the intimidating, small woman. He had never met anyone like her.

"Y... yes, my Lady," he replied, actually frightened for the first time yet on his journey. He bowed his head slightly.

Wolfgar sat at a table with Sybil on the first level veranda in a squat chair.

He had been stripped naked then doused in bucket after bucket of chilled brown water from the Missi by two elderly earthblood men, attendants of the Villa, until the thick layer of grime on his skin fell away. He ran his fingers through his hair to squeeze out the ash, and dried blood, and dirt. He scrubbed sweat and musk from his crotch. He shaved his jaw with the ever-sharp blade of his own dagger.

Then, Wolfgar was given a soft blue tunic and pressed grey trousers by two giggling earthblood girls who nearly tossed the garments at him then whispered down the hall of his rough beauty as they scurried away. He shrugged, not understanding dames at all, for he had never lain with a woman, as he threw the tunic over his head. It was very tight to his frame. His muscular back, shoulders, and arms bulged against the expensive fabric. The trousers were tight as well, and far too long. Wolfgar rolled the cuffs at the bottom. Finally, clean shaven with wet hair and barefoot in the unfamiliar, expensive attire, Wolfgar wandered around the expansive villa with dark floors and billowing gossamer curtains, until he found Sybil.

She was beyond the open doors with white curtains bucking in the breeze, sitting with a black shawl wrapped around her thin shoulders. Sybil looked out at out at the boats and barges floating lazily up and down the river, brow furrowed, lost in thought.

"Now, that's better," Sybil said with a smile when she noticed him. "You are nearly presentable."

"Thank you, Lady."

"It's your turn.".

"My turn?" Wolfgar lowered himself to sit. His hair dripped on his shirt leaving dark blue marks down his rounded shoulders. "To do what?"

"I let you in. I cleaned you up. Clothed you," Sybil said, looking him up and down. *He's certainly beautiful*, she thought. Statuesque features, as if carved from alabaster. "I've done more than my share," she went on out loud. "Tell me who you are."

Sybil took pitcher and filled a goblet with Animus wine spiked with mad honey. In the sunlight, against the yellow of the glass, the red drink shone bright orange. She filled a second goblet. She passed one of them to Wolfgar.

"What's this?" he asked eying it sceptically.

"Something to help you think," she replied. "Drink it," Sybil commanded sweetly.

Not wanting to offend her, Wolfgar took a long sip. He coughed once, then stoically finished the rest of the goblet in a gulp.

Sybil was visibly amused and a little impressed. "Thirsty?"

Wolfgar shrugged, unshaken by the sensation of burning knives going down his throat. He'd tasted far worse. "What is it? I've not had anything like it."

"Impressive," she remarked with slightly widening eyes. "Some can't keep mad honey down when they've not had it before."

"Mad," he furrowed his heavy brow, "honey?" He'd heard the tales but was far too young to have ever seen any in the flesh, much less taste it.

"Yes," Sybil said. "Now tell me who you are."

"But..." He still didn't know who *she* was.

"No." Sybil was firm. She took his goblet and poured another for him. She handed it back forcefully.

Wolfgar sighed, already tired of the tale he'd been instructed to tell. "I'm Jude Thorne."

"There is no Jude Thorne."

"That's it though."

Sybil frowned. "What's it?"

"I'm undocumented."

"An undocumented Vanguard? There hasn't been one in hundreds of years." Sybil leaned forward, pulling her shawl tighter in anticipation. "How did it happen? Which Thorne is your kin?"

"Wallace," Wolfgar recited.

Sybil raised her eyebrows high. "Really?" she asked, taken aback. Wallace Thorne, an ally of Brochet, was nothing if not calculating. He did everything by the book. He would be the last Vanguard she'd guess would have an undocumented child.

"You seem surprised."

"Why wouldn't Wallace document you?" Sybil retorted sharply, black eyes darting, studying his green ones. "Why keep you a secret? Who is your mother?"

Wolfgar leaned back in his seat. "Don't know."

"Ah, earthblood? Really? Must be Nomad, for you are so pale. Hm," she studied him again, eyes boring holes through his flesh. "That's why they sent you here, to the other son of an earthblood Thorne's front porch," Sybil smartly surmised.

"Monty Thorne is half?"

Sybil nodded. "No one bothered to hide him. Opposite."

"Really."

"Oh yes," Sybil told Wolfgar, nodding, pulling her shawl with one hand, holding her mad honey goblet in the other. In the time she'd been at Animus, it had gotten cooler, leaves had begun to fall, and she'd grown very accustomed to having a goblet of mad honey with her at all times. She glanced over the riverbank and noted charred ruins of the slovenly city across the Missi. The Confines was in tatters and now occupied by countless Bellamine guards, buzzing around the ugly wart of a castle. Sybil briefly wondered about Edwarde's fate in the back of her mind as she spoke. "Nearly runs Animus Rock in the shadows, as Thorne always does."

"Who is Monty's father?"

"Wallace's brother, Ustin."

Wolfgar nodded.

Sybil glanced back to the strapping lad. He was too pretty for his own good, she thought. Even better, he seemed not to realize it at all. He was young, though. Sybil didn't have a use for him. He was still a child. "Where were you all this time?"

"Lyonshall."

She sat back in her chair with a pleased half smile, languidly swirling the ale in her glass. "That makes sense," she said.

Wolfgar tipped his goblet far back, beginning to enjoy the burning liquid's symptomatic lull. "What?" he asked her with a hint of confusion after he'd finished his goblet.

"Lyonshall, Lachlan, Wallace," she said sharply.

"I'm not following."

"I thought you were Vanguard," she said impatiently, noting his glass was empty. She refilled it quickly.

"Not raised as one, Lady."

"Everyone knows the real story," Sybil said. "Even my daughter could repeat it back to you."

"What story?"

Sybil sighed. "It was Wallace who spurred young Lachlan to betray his father, and the New, and sent Lyonshall back to the Old ways after the Uprising. Lachlan Regnard and Wallace Thorne are allies. Wallace Thorne is married to Lachlan's daughter."

"But, the Lady Elder of Lyonshall was Thorne," Wolfgar began, trying to follow the connection. He'd never been properly educated in the Ancestors or the Teachings nor did he attend Academy, so he hadn't memorized the Vanguard Tree. The late Echo's Omen elder Dorian ensured no Brotherhood members were warped by the rotting New brains of modern Vanguards, banning all from attending Academy. Wolfgar was always curious, though, and retained knowledge from his mother mostly before he'd been sent to train with the Brotherhood as a boy.

"It's true," Sybil said.

"That means that..." Wolfgar trailed off, then made a face.

"Yes, Wallace married his niece," Sybil said, slightly amused at his naïve disgust. "It's no wonder amid all of that scandal he hid your existence. It's a pity he didn't do a better job, for his sake." She sipped her drink, then sighed with a smile.

"What do you mean?"

The marbled sky darkened from the setting sun above them as fowl honked louder on the Missi.

"It's gloriously illegal to do what he's done, to neglect to document a Vanguard son," Sybil said, beaming, a cool breeze rustling fine wisps of hair fallen from her high-head knot. "He'll be sent to the Magistrate, surely. Maybe the First, if fortune holds."

What?" Wolfgar's heart dropped. He didn't know he could get another Vanguard sent away, tortured, perhaps killed. Not that killing bothered him, if the man deserved it. But it was the principle of the thing. "What... what if Lachlan lied to me?" he asked with a crack. He felt empathy bubbling in his stomach like bile.

"What now?"

Wolfgar realized his situation was precarious and best stick to his story, despite the impacts it might have on the Kingdom. "What if Wallace denies it?" He wondered if Basil, Xavier, and Quentin knew what could happen and led Wolfgar into this. He realized they surely did. They seemed to dislike the man greatly.

Sybil laughed. "Oh, don't worry about old Wallace Thorne. I am sure it's no lie."

"Is there no way to," he paused, "test?" What would happen if he was discovered? He could only hope he wasn't.

"None," Sybil said simply, not knowing herself that there was an old test for bloodlines that had been largely lost to time. "The man is scum and has it coming," she gestured with the goblet as she spoke, dark liquid sloshing back and forth towards the lip of the yellow glass, threatening to spill. Sybil didn't seem to notice. "The King has been waiting for an excuse to ruin him," she said. "It was only a matter of time. They won't test you. Your word is enough."

Wolfgar nodded once. "I caught that from the King."

"What did you think of him?" she asked casually.

"King Humphry? He's," Wolfgar paused, "rotten."

Sybil laughed.

"Why is he like that?" Wolfgar asked innocently, like the young man he was beneath the teachings and beatings of the Brotherhood. "I imagined the King to be more like, I don't know, a *king*."

Sybil smiled wide, high cheekbones pulling apart to reveal a flashing white smile behind cherry tinted lips. "That is what kings are like, my sweet," Sybil said. "My great grandfather taught me that once." Her heart pricked, as it was one of her only clear memories of the man. She was so young when he died. "Kings are just people. Like people, there are good kings and bad kings, but very rarely great ones."

"He didn't care when I told him Lyonshall fell."

"Lyonshall fell?" Sybil said with surprise. She took a sip. She pulled her shawl, coal black eyes wide and distant.

"Oh, right, yes. It did. I've told the story so many times I forget what I've said to who."

"Whom."

"What?" Wolfgar looked up.

"The correct grammar is 'whom', not 'who'."

Wolfgar didn't know what grammar meant. "Oh," he said flatly.

Sybil pursed her lips at him. "What about Lachlan?"

"Dead."

"Father will be so pleased." Sybil smiled. "Was this Rupert's doing? He is a pain but at least he was of some use if we owe him thanks for this favor."

Wolfgar figured his persona *Jude* wouldn't know the man. And he was keeping his trip through Croft Hold secret. "Rupert?"

"Morfit," Sybil clarified. "Gold Capes."

Wolfgar nodded strongly. "Aye, in part."

"In part?"

"Lord Ogo led the attack," Wolfgar said. "In Lyonshall's Throne Hall." He pointed at the Eighth tower. "They told me he was Lachlan's son."

"Oh."

"Oh?"

"That isn't good."

"Why?"

She snapped back to the present. Sybil met Wolfgar's eyes. "It's what happened during the Uprising," she said, "but in reverse. The son betrays the father. You'd think they would learn by now." She shook her head. "You don't see that sort of thing happening at Westerviolet, do you?" she asked rhetorically. "No of course not." She took a long, pensive sip from her yellowed glass goblet.

Before he could consider whether his character Jude was aware of her bloodline's name he asked, "You are Brochet?"

"I am," she confirmed. "Sybil."

"Good to greet you," he replied with a confident, boyish smile. He'd heard about her yet hadn't expected her to be so beautiful. Nor so cold. Like a sculpture of ice.

She half smiled at him, thinking he looked like a man until he grinned, then he just looked like a large boy. "You too, Jude," she said warmly. She felt affection for him, like she should protect him, although the idea was silly. A man his size needed no protecting. The wind jostled a long wisp of Sybil's hair from her tight bun and it curled down loose to frame her heart-shaped face. She quickly tucked it behind her ear.

Wolfgar gulped his drink to finish it again. He burped. Sybil crinkled her nose.

"The King really had the idea to send you here? Even that surprises me."

"Well, actually it was a woman."

"Woman? Not the white queen?"

"Who?"

"Gracea," Sybil said with an upturned nose.

"A friend of yours?"

"In a sense," Sybil replied. "Why not be friends with the Queen?"

"Humphry's Queen? The pale woman?" Wolfgar remembered the bored blonde on Humphry's right. "No, not her."

"Who, then?"

"His sister?" Wolfgar said unsurely. "Her name was..." he paused, scrunching his brow. "Something with a V?"

"Ah," Sybil sipped her drink.

"Is she the King's sister?"

"Yes," Sybil said, jealousy dripping from her tongue despite her pleasant smile. "Verity. Verity Bellamine. An icon, really. Have you seen all the fools who hack up their ears and douse their hair with that awful-stinking oil just to be like her? Many whisper that she really speaks for Humphry, but he'll cut off the head of anyone who dare say that to his face."

"She surely speaks for him," Wolfgar said, cheeks flushed. He spoke with more candour now and his eyes glassed as he felt the mad honey bubbling warm in his breast.

"Really?"

"Oh yes." Wolfgar nodded, sipping his drink eagerly. "She ran the whole thing. Bossed the Graves man around too."

Sybil balked as if she'd caught her toe on a board. "I thought you were raised at Lyonshall? Know nothing of Vanguards?" she questioned pointedly.

Instantly recovering as if on instinct Wolfgar replied, "I know Graves has grey skin and eyes and that man did." He wasn't sure how he responded so quickly, knowing exactly what to say. He figured it was the mad honey talking. Pleased with the mental escape, Wolfgar didn't ask about any of mad honey's other effects.

"Fair," Sybil relaxed. "That's Herman, youngest son of the elder and a bleeding-heart New. He's married to Verity. She has him the in the palm of her hand. Many tried to say that he seduced her or drugged her with some strange Anstout potion somehow, to force her to fall in love with him, but the second you see them together you know the truth that he'll do anything she says. No one could believe the princess could be in love with a Graves. Years ago, it was a huge scandal," Sybil paused and took another sip, "but now everyone has mostly gotten used to it. Herman has proven to be nothing like his kin. They say he really does love her, despite the superstition."

Wolfgar leaned forward, knowing what she meant, quickly remembering the part he played. "What superstition?" he asked, scrunching his brow as Jude.

"You don't know what they say?"

"No."

"Dead blood can't love," she said in singsong.

Wolfgar chuckled.

"You do agree that he loves her from what you saw?"

"He did everything she commanded, like you say."

Sybil sat back in her chair, smiled to herself, then frowned.

"What are you thinking about?" he asked her, fully enchanted by Sybil's sharp beauty as was everyone was who met her.

"Hm?" she looked over to him, as if broken from a trance. "Nothing, nothing," she dismissed quickly. "What else did you think about Verity?"

"She's very fair, in an odd way."

Sybil coughed on her drink in laughter. "Go on," she said, clearly pleased. "Why odd?"

Wolfgar was plied with ale and mad honey and very candid now. "She's not *that* beautiful, but, there's just something about her. You just," he paused," want to look at her. To be near her. She's," he thought, "undeniable."

Sybil sighed.

"What? Did I say the wrong thing?"

"Men are obsessed with that woman," she said curtly. She pulled her shawl tighter.

"Are you jealous?" Wolfgar asked, already knowing she was.

"Of course not," Sybil said angrily. She picked up her glass, took a long gulp to finish it, and set it down with a clink on the table. "Why would you say that?"

"Just a question." He changed the subject. "She doesn't look of what I think of when I think Bellamine," Wolfgar said.

"Why not?"

"I don't know," he replied honestly. "I always heard Bellamine was oldblood and oldblood is pale."

Sybil shook her head. "No, no, there have been earthblood queens for years. Hasn't been a proper Vanguard queen in centuries," she added, thinking to herself that she intended to change that.

"But Gracea nearly looks like you."

Sybil waved her hand. "Gracea is Nomad," she said simply. "Seems the far North ones are light like us. Has nothing to do with the skin's hue. It's all in the eyes. Did you notice hers?"

"Red?"

"Exactly," Sybil said. "She is nothing like us."

"Did the King inherit anything from his Vanguard blood?"

"Not like Verity did. Unfortunately, she is smart and daring, while he is childish and impatient," Sybil said. "Her and the King are dark like earthblood, but both do have the Bellamine ears as their forefathers did."

"That's it then, their ears?"

Sybil shrugged then said, "Verity's eyes are brown as well."

"If Verity is the smart one, why does she not wear the crown?"

Sybil took a long sip. "Oh Jude, it was all part of the plan."

"What plan?"

"I'm not even supposed to know this. Do you need a refill?'

Wolfgar looked to his goblet. He shrugged. "Sure," he said, deeply enjoying the oblivious sense of calm he felt from the ale. He wasn't permitted such pleasures at the Omen. Sybil filled it to the brim. "What plan?"

"Well, naturally you know of King Nycholas don't you?"

"No," Wolfgar said honestly, genuinely confused. "Who?"

Sybil sighed. "I almost forgot you…" she trailed off, "never mind. He was the traditional old king who fuelled the whole political mess leading to the Uprising. He was also Humphry's grandfather. We spent days and days learning about him in Academy it felt like. He was the last great Vanguard king, father claims." Wolfgar listened intently. "King Nycholas led a brutal campaign, winning battles left and right, until he grew bold and himself charged on the front lines at the battle of Winter Garden."

"The King? On the front lines? Really?" Wolfgar nearly laughed at the absurdity.

"His allies, the Beaumonts, were under siege. It's said he fell into a fit and refused counsel. He wouldn't take no for an answer. He demanded that he be present to protect them."

"He died there?"

Sybil nodded. "It was obviously a huge win for the New realms and toppled the momentum of the war entirely."

"Obviously," Wolfgar repeated, nodding. He took a long, lustful sip. He smiled and shut his eyes. He leaned back in his chair. The cool, autumn wind blew about him.

Sybil went on. "This placed his only son, Giaired, on the throne. He was extremely moderate. Father despised him," she added. "He tried to end the war right there by writing up some document, trying to be like infamous Ueli and the Blood Council," Sybil chuckled. "Poor man."

"What happened?"

"Do you want to know what they told the people or what I think?"

"Both."

"The official story is his heart failed him," Sybil said. "That the new King Giaired crumpled in his study, barely two decades into life and not a week into being king."

"What do you think?"

"Nighthorn," Sybil said.

"Your reason?"

"His death placed the spoiled, untrained and malleable Humphry on the throne," she said. "He was just a child, not yet ten years, so Cornelius Norland stepped in as ward of the boy, as elder of Norland and leader of the Warman and all, it was only natural. No one had the force to rebuke him." She didn't mention it was under Tomas's surveillance, and direct counsel as well, as was nearly every happening Kingdon-wide. "Then, Cornelius essentially raised Humphry. That's why the King is what he is today and the Kingdom spirals into madness. It's insanity," Sybil said, smiling, shaking her head.

"You almost seem pleased."

"It's quite beautiful when you see it all from above. Grotesque, but harmonious, nonetheless. Like a dance."

"I like you," Wolfgar said, slurring words slightly, vision fuzzy from ale, mind fuzzy from honey. He sipped his goblet. Basil would like her too, he thought.

"Oh?" Sybil paused. "You like me?"

"Now, I don't know a lot of women, Lady," he said frankly, "but yes."

"Why?" Sybil, still smiling, leaning forward slightly, feeding off the flattery.

Wolfgar sat forward in his chair and the borrowed tunic he wore ripped from seam to seam down the back. He looked up at Sybil, mortified he'd ruined such a fine garment. His mother would have threatened to kill him for that.

Sybil giggled, tickled by the boyish reaction. "Oh, it's fine," she assured. "Really. Monty has more coin than Humphry himself. He's a Thorne. He can afford a new shirt for his cousin."

Wolfgar relaxed slightly, "Of course," he said. "But I am sorry."

"I've already forgotten about it."

Wolfgar smiled gratefully back.

He pulled the tattered tunic off over his back. With every movement his young muscles rippled. Sybil watched as the low hanging sun reflected off his freshly oiled skin.

Then she noticed an unnatural black mark on his ribs.

"What's that?" she asked bluntly. Wolfgar froze and his heart dropped his chest. She pointed at the scrolled black letting. "That," she repeated. But she already knew what it was.

The wind picked up and whistled between them. Goosebumps covered Wolfgar's pale body.

"I… I don't know what you're talking about," he shifted in his chair, swallowing dry, moving to cover the marking with his arm.

Sybil sighed. "Now you must tell me. What is that? What does it mean?"

Before Sybil finished, a nondescript maiden dutifully delivered another shirt to Wolfgar. This one, deep green, nearly matched the tone of Sybil's skirt. It had more give than the silken one. When he pulled this new tunic over his head it suctioned tight to him. The soft velvet felt foreign on his calloused skin. He rubbed his hand on his sleeve over and over.

"Well?" Sybil asked.

"It seems the tables have turned," a hearty voice boomed into the foreground. "Do I throw a tantrum when you sup with a handsome guest? No. Surely not."

"He's here," Sybil said softly to Wolfgar, locking eyes with him for a bit too long. Wolfgar looked away and down. Sybil continued staring at him, grinning.

"Montague!" she said with pageantry, breaking her gaze from the boyishly handsome stranger. "Where have you been? You're an awful host, to deny your very own family your presence."

"My… family?" Monty strode into the light on the veranda. He flashed his brilliant white teeth. "The resemblance is shocking."

"Very funny," Sybil said. She placed her hand on Wolfgar's bulging forearm and felt the protruding veins fast-pumping blood beneath his hot skin. Monty seemed put out by the gesture. "This, Montague, is your long-lost cousin."

"You're kidding." He took a seat between the two of them. "I have to hear this."

"It's serious Montague, he's undocumented. Wallace's."

"Really?" Monty leaned back in his chair. He gestured to the nearly empty pitcher. "You're sure this isn't the ale talking?"

"Oh Montague," Sybil batted her cavernous eyes. She squeezed Wolfgar's forearm again. She uncrossed her legs then re-crossed them to face him. Wolfgar accidently saw down her blouse and his cheeks instantly blushed scarlet. He looked away quickly, but not before he was wondering what the crease of her chest's skin felt like. Monty watched this and smirked.

"Who are you supposed to be?" he looked Wolfgar up and down. "Gotten comfortable already here, I see. Why don't you help yourself to my boots, or perhaps a cloak too? You seem to have everything else."

"I gave him those things," Sybil said with a stormy frown. "Don't taunt him. If you blame anyone, it is me."

"Pour me one, will you?"

Sybil poured Monty a glass and handed it to him.

"Have I corrupted you, dear Sybil?" he asked. "Drinking before sundown?"

Sybil squeezed Wolfgar's arm harder. He looked at her, but she didn't take her glare off Monty. "Not at all, Montague," she said cooly. "I'm just welcoming the guest. Your guest. Now, it's your turn. Welcome your cousin."

"Cousin?"

"Aye," Wolfgar said.

Monty took a sip. He coughed four times, patted his chest with his fist, then took another, longer sip. "Explain," he said.

Wolfgar scratched behind his ear. His hair had dried slicked back in a wavy flow. He adjusted the uncomfortably tight-fitting pants and took a deep breath.

"Wallace Thorne gave me to Lachlan Regnard as ward," he recited. "Ogo Regnard burnt Lyonshall to the ground and that's why I'm here. The guards spotted me and took me to the King. He sent me to you."

Monty looked at Sybil. "Is this what he told you, too?"

"It is."

"Pardon us, one moment, will you?" Monty asked Wolfgar.

"S... sure," Wolfgar said, then hiccupped. He swished the

dark liquid back and forth, watching orange shadows cast on the table from the yellow glass.

Monty gestured to the door inside with his own goblet. "Sybil, please?"

She huffed, but obeyed, sitting her drink down too hard, splashing it from side to side. "Fine." Sybil followed Monty out beyond the gauzy white curtains, down the corridor and out of earshot.

"What?" she leaned away from him, crossing her arms tightly beneath her black shawl.

Monty's eyes twinkled like dewy leaves. "He's lying," he said.

"How do you know?"

"He doesn't have any native blood."

Sybil scrunched her brow. She'd suspected that too but wanted to hear what Montague thought. "If not, then what?"

"He's either from the Wing, or some hidden Brotherhood experiment alike," Monty said, resting a long-fingered hand on the wall to lean against it. "Does he have any tattoos?"

"Tattoos?" Sybil asked, knowing full well he referred to the black mark on the Jude's side. "How should I know?" she lied, pulled her shawl tighter.

"He is adorable in an unrefined kind of way, I will give you that," Monty said, "but don't allow that to cloud your judgement. There's something wrong here. I can feel it."

"Humphry says he's your kin," Sybil countered. "I'm sure he will try Wallace for it. You know he'll jump at chance."

"The King is convinced he is Thorne?" A wave of surprise washed over Monty. He sighed loudly, lowering his hand from the wall, shaking his head. "Then it seems at least for now that I am stuck with him."

"So, it seems," Sybil said with a smirk.

"I tell you, he is trouble." Monty met her eyes intensely. "Stay away from him, Sybil."

"Is the great Montague Thorne *jealous*?"

"Woman, I mean it. This is serious," he lowered his tone further, pulling her closer to him. "It's fine if he's who he says, but if he isn't," he faded away, then steeled. "I'm not jealous," he assured. Sybil took in breath full of his scent, a heavy cologne in notes of exotic spices. She folded her arms.

Monty gazed lustfully at the crease of cleavage beneath Sybil's blouse.

Noticing this, Sybil outwardly frowned and adjusted her shirt, inwardly rejoicing at the power shift, then wiggled her shoulders to shake off his grip. "Who he is makes no difference," she said. "It doesn't change that he's a guest of this villa, sent here by your King. If you won't entertain him, I have no choice but to. It's only proper." She bit her lip and looked up at him with wide eyes. "Come and enjoy the evening with us, or don't." At that she let go of her blouse, allowing the fabric to buckle loosely again beneath her black shawl. Her breasts nearly tumbled out once more.

"Sybil, wait," Monty started, but she had already turned.

She walked away from him, heeled boots clacking with fast footsteps down the long, echoing hall.

Monty couldn't see it, but she wore a wide grin.

THE VANGUARD SHIP, SPACE

About 2000 years ago…

Reynold and Junia began full-time experiments to replicate Reynold's visions and came up wanting. Finally, Junia suggested something Reynold always knew he should do, but resisted.

"Your vision occurred directly after you were in the presence of the Thorne girl," Junia said, one evening in their bed. "That is what we must do next."

"We cannot," Reynold said.

"We must," Junia said, "if there is any hope of achieving our aims.

Reynold sighed, tracing the bone of Junia's collar with his long finger. He kissed her head. She was right.

The next day they went to the bowels of the Graves laboratory. They were senior scientists at that point and no eyebrows raised when they requested access to that particular specimen. Throughout the bloodlines, the senior scientists were permitted to experiment as they pleased, so long as they appropriately documented their findings. And, of course, adhered to the Code.

They entered the examining room. Dymphna lay still, eyes open and searching just like the last time Reynold saw her, but she had aged significantly. Her hair was unkempt and so long, it nearly touched the pristine metal floor. Her face was remarkably wrinkle-free. She was attached to monitors and a feeding tube. The droning beeping was enough to drive Reynold insane, apart from the guilt weighing on his heart.

"I've never seen her," Junia said curiously, "but I've heard my parents discuss her. Especially when I was young. There was such high hope that she would help us further the Mission as the first Thorne with sight did. Such disappointment when, after her first vision, she provided no more. I'm surprised they've kept her living, to be honest."

Reynold furrowed his brow. He approached Dymphna. Junia mirrored his movements on the other side of the bed where she lay. They looked down at her together.

"Do you feel anything? See anything?" Junia asked her husband.

He shook his head. "No."

"Try touching her, like this." Junia stroked Dymphna's cheek.

The invalid sat up violently, nearly striking Reynold.

"The child with blue eyes," she said in a cracked, hoarse whisper.

Reynold and Junia looked at each other in amazement.

"The child with blue eyes will change all," she said. "She must be protected. She must be protected. She must be protected. She will come and come again if she is not protected. She is your only hope."

Then Dymphna lay back as violently as she'd sat up, crashing back into her bed so hard she likely injured herself. Her eyes stayed open, searching back and forth.

"How interesting," Junia said, looking at Reynold. "It's like I jolted her to life, briefly. Although I did not try to use power."

"Can you?"

"You know it doesn't work that way for Brochets," she said. "Our power is passive."

"It wasn't this time."

Junia nodded. "I have an idea now," she said. "Come with me."

They went to an empty examining room after recording Dymphna's vision in their notes, past cells and cells of screaming and crying specimens of all bloodlines.

"Lay on the bed," Junia said. Reynold obeyed.

"I don't see what you're going to do," he told his wife. "You touch me often and never has it sparked a vision."

She smirked at him. "Tell me what you see," she said and grazed his temple as she had Dymphna's.

Reynold was thrust into blackness and emerged in bright sunshine, but there was no greenery. The wind whipped harshly. The air was cold.

ANIMUS ROCK

Present Day

The low-creeping wolf-joy blanketing the valley leading up to the Animus Rock Castle fallowed. The tiny, bell-shaped yellow and white blooms faded muted greys and fell from their browning stems. The sky was brilliantly light blue, *like Vera's eyes*, Ryd thought wistfully, painted white with rippled clouds. The air was cool and stale.

Hector Graves rode atop a black stallion with a shiny coat, well-brushed mane, and braided tail. His bird of prey gilded above him, matching his trot's speed. Behind, Digory and Ryd sat atop Chester and Mable respectively. They hung back from Hector and allowed a substantial distance to grow between them. The group had been on the road for several days. They'd first cut through black granite mountains lined with reaching spruce trees, then travelled south, in parallel to the Missi.

Now, days into their journey, Animus Rock rose before them on the horizon. The brown Missi flowed on their far left. To the right, past the fallow valley, was flat tilled farmland as far as they could see.

Ryd leaned forward to pat Mabel's neck. "Good girl. Almost there." He looked ahead at Hector. "What do you think is wrong with him?"

Their horses clopped against the hard-packed dirt. Hector's hawk cawed overhead.

"He has dead blood."

"Besides that."

Digory shifted his eyes from the hawk's shadow pacing them in their journey to Ryd. "Have you ever thought that it's just that he's Vanguard? Considers himself above us?"

"Maybe," Ryd took a pregnant pause. "But there's something

different about him."

"Oh, what then?" Digory asked, amused. "Tell me what your theory is."

"How do you know I have one?"

"Because you're the type of man to need everything to make sense," Digory said, studying the dead stems of the valley flowers. "You spend your time defining things by how the Kingdom tells you they should be, not how you see them." He looked back to Ryd. "You can't see the truth."

"What truth?"

Digory met Ryd's questioning gaze. "Nothing makes any cursed sense."

"What in the Kingdom are you talking about?"

Digory sighed as images of blood pouring from the stable boy's chest flashed in his mind. "I'm just tired," he said. "We've been at this for-cursed-ever."

"Don't whine," Ryd replied hopefully. "Look, that has to be Animus!" he pointed ahead. Eight grey stone towers rose high on the skyline.

Digory recognized this view of the horizon from Westerviolet's East Wing tapestries. "So, it seems."

"Don't act like you aren't excited," Ryd looked to Digory briefly, then turned his head towards the eight towers again, remembering the stories his father told him from boyhood. "I've always dreamed of the Capital."

"You sound like a child," Digory chuckled, eyes on the hawk, circling in the air over prey in the nearby meadow. "Men don't have time for dreams."

Ryd frowned, tired of Digory's abuse. "What's your problem?"

"Oh, come on."

"Why do you do that?"

"Do what?"

Ryd started to speak then paused, eyes darting back and forth, studying Digory's wideset flaming glare. "Nothing, never mind."

The pair fell into a bated silence. They watched Hector's

hawk dive with terrifying speed into the wilting meadow until pulling upwards at the last moment with a large rodent writhing in its beak.

Digory broke the silence. "What is your theory, then?"

Ryd exhaled loudly from the back of his throat and threw his head backwards to glance up at the sky. He revelled in the hot sunbeams on his face. "My theory about what, Digory?"

"About our new friend up there," Digory gestured ahead. Hector was far ahead on the path, out of earshot, watching his pet hunt.

"What about him?"

"You said something isn't right about him." Digory preferred banter to silent time with his thoughts. "What do you think it is?"

Ryd sighed. "It's got to be the dead blood. Right?"

"You're right. It has to be," Digory agreed with a nod. "And I was just toying with you. I agree, there is something wrong with that man."

"Yes," Ryd exclaimed, feeling vindicated, "thank you!"

The massive curtain wall towered as they neared. There was nothing but expansive meadow on this north-eastern part of the land, making the height of the wall starkly dramatic, particularly with the huge shadow it cast. The young men rode without speaking, listening to the sounds of nature for several minutes.

Digory broke the lull. "Tell me where you really went in Littlebell."

Ryd's heart dropped to his stomach. He hated lying and kept his eyes locked forward. "I told you already."

Digory smirked as he studied Ryd's stubborn profile. "Aye, but you lied."

Ryd swung his head to Digory. "No, I didn't."

"You did."

"How do you know?"

"No respectful establishment would serve fire ale," Digory pointed out. "I know that if the Morfit at the front gate told us where to find those free things or wherever your brother was supposed to be, they couldn't be that hard to find. I think you found them and you're protecting something."

Ryd frowned. He studied Hector's shiny stallion ahead. He would like to care for such a magnificent beast.

"Like the girl," Digory said. "Vera, is it? You're protecting her too?"

"I told you I don't want to talk about her."

"I already know about her," Digory countered. "Why not?"

"Digory, stop."

"Come on."

Ryd inhaled through flared nostrils then exhaled very slowly. "Fine." He rubbed the back of his neck with his off hand. "I'll tell you. If you tell me something."

"I'm listening."

"What are Leon and Mimi like?" At Digory's expression, Ryd clarified, "Minney."

"Mimi?" Digory chuckled. "Is that what the girl called the elder Minney? I was right! She *is* the lost blue-eye!"

Ryd turned to him angrily. "Shhh," he said, then his anger quickly fell to thinly hidden panic. His voice cracked and he looked towards to Hector, then back at Digory with wide eyes. "He can't hear. He can't know. Why, if anything happened to her, I don't know what I'd do."

Digory relaxed in his saddle. "As you wish."

"Digory, I'm serious."

"Yes, yes," Digory said dismissively.

Ryd couldn't let it go. He had to protect Vera. "Do I have your word?"

Digory felt a painful pressure in his chest like he'd been kicked by a horse but ignored it and turned to Ryd. "My word," he said sincerely, locking Ryd's eyes before turning forward again.

Ryd relaxed a bit.

Digory glanced sideways. "You know you're sitting on a pile of coin, right?"

Ryd spun his head. "What did you say?"

"I'm sure even the righteous New would seriously pay to find her whereabouts," he went on baiting, scratching his beard in need of a trim. "She's priceless."

"Digory, no," Ryd said in a hush. "I... I think I," he paused. "Forget it."

"No, tell me," Digory commanded. "You what?"

"I love her."

"How could you love her? You don't know her."

"We talked for hours," Ryd defended proudly. "As you lie near death, I may add."

Digory started to chuckle, then devolved into full laughter.

Ryd frowned and stared at him. "You owe her your life, you know," he said, but Digory kept laughing. "What? What is so funny?"

"I can't believe I didn't see it until now," Digory said, finally calming a bit, wiping laughing tears from one eye. "But it must be true, since you act like a boy thrown into a bare house." He paused. "You've never been with a woman, have you?"

Ryd's cheeks exploded. "I... well...I..."

"Oh, it's alright," Digory offered mockingly. "Don't feel bad. I understand perfectly," he added, glancing to Ryd's forlorn expression. "I'm ensnared, too."

Ryd perked up. "Sybil?"

Digory sighed. "Aye," he said, tone wistful, "I've loved her for as long as I can remember."

Ryd was shocked at his candor. "Truly?"

"Yes," Digory nodded, meeting Ryd's gaze, inwardly surprised at how good it felt to confide. He'd never spoken of Sybil to another soul before, except for her brief mention to Leon and Nis, although he'd held back her name and lofty title, of course. "It's true. I..." he paused. He cleared his throat. "She's all I have."

"Why?"

"Orphan."

Ryd looked at Digory for what felt like a long time. The man made a lot more sense to him now. "I'm sorry," he finally said.

"For what?" Digory asked carelessly, knowing full well why Ryd was sorry. He glanced back to Hector. His hawk had returned to him and perched on his branch-like shoulder, ripping a rodent's flesh into writhing bloody threads.

Ryd studied Digory's sharp jawline even under unkept beard and high cheekbones. "You..." he paused. "You don't have anyone."

"It is my lot," Digory shrugged. He'd come to terms with his fate long ago. "What of you, then? Kin superior to mine?"

Ryd sighed. "My father was a decent man. He did his best for us, considering. And little Collen is such a good boy. He's all I have. I have to find him."

"Right." Digory ground his jaw. "Why 'considering'?"

"Hm?" Ryd tried to think of a good lie. He couldn't trust Digory with the Free Boys secrets, could he? "Oh... I..."

Digory's intense gaze burned a hole through Ryd. "What happened to your father?"

Ryd frowned. "Why do you care so much?"

Digory shrugged again. "Then don't tell me."

"It's not that I don't want to tell you, Digory. It's just that..."

"You don't trust me, I get it," he said, taking the words from Ryd's mouth. "I rescue you from death and you still don't trust me. Rings true," he said angrily. He wasn't even sure why it bothered him so much. If he were Ryd, he wouldn't trust himself. He didn't even trust himself.

"Hey, no, wait," Ryd said. He'd thought Digory to be impenetrable, but it appeared he had hurt the man's feelings. "You yourself have told me not to..."

"No, no," Digory said. "Forget it."

"Now you're acting like Hector," Ryd teased, trying to get a rise out of him, but Digory didn't respond. Instead, he ground his jaw silently. "Come on," Ryd said. "I was kidding." Digory didn't respond. "You care that I trust you?" Ryd asked finally. "Really?"

"Forget it."

"Fine," Ryd sighed loud. "I trust you. I trust you, alright?" Digory's scowl brightened and he half smiled, turning to look at Ryd. Ryd, heart thumping out of his chest, knowing it was a bad idea, took a breath, then said, "I met my grandfather in

Littlebell."

"You... what?" Digory's tone was instantly curious. "*How?*"

"He was an orphan of the Fellowship, sold to Brochet as a child, but he escaped Westerviolet. He took refuge in Littlebell," Ryd said, thinking back to his time in Ashkeep, remembering Odion's kind eyes. "Years later he had a family when the Lord's guards found them. He escaped, but his family was ripped away. After failed attempts to recover them, he gave up and stayed in Littlebell. That's where he founded the Free boys, so anyone else who lost their families would have a home."

"Wow." Digory bounced on his horse's saddle as he digested the information. "You believe it?" he asked.

Ryd nodded, thinking back to Odion's knowledge of his father's birthmark, the one that matched his own. He looked down at his palm.

"But your father never told you this?" Digory remembered tales of the Littlebell raid from his early childhood. He'd listened to the Guardsmen bragging about how many they took. "Just the man in Littlebell?"

"He recognized my birth mark. Said father had the same one," Ryd defended. He clenched his fist. "He also knew things he shouldn't know. Things my father used to say. The man must be my blood. I'm sure father wouldn't speak of it for fear that harm would fall on Col or I."

"Why he drank?"

Ryd nodded sombrely.

Digory mulled over the information. "Your Grandfather founded the Free Boys? I thought they were strict about no Old realm earthblood."

"He said that's what we're supposed to think. That's how the refugees are kept safe."

"Clever," Digory said slowly. "Where did you find these Free Boys?"

"Where the gold cape said, by the Market," Ryd replied. "Their hideout is hidden underneath a tavern. They call it the dens."

"Really," Digory said slowly. "They're hiding in there?"

"From Prihim and Lalia Minney," Ryd said, confirming with a nod. "They told me they have an arrangement with Leon Minney to use part of the dens."

"So Prihim doesn't know of their existence?"

"He does, but doesn't know where they are," Ryd said. "Doesn't know they're in the dens anyway. He doesn't agree with what they're doing and thinks it's dangerous for Littlebell to harbour refugees. They told me Leon has it out for his brother and Ed took advantage of that."

Digory frowned. "Ed?"

"Edwessa."

"Who?"

"Vanguard, if you believe it," Ryd told Digory. "The daughter of Edwarde Minney," he said with upwards inflection. "I don't know who that is, but someone said something about him and Busk."

Digory burst into loud laughter again, unable to open his eyes or breathe the fit was so strong.

Ryd scowled. "What is it this time?"

Still chuckling, wide smile flashing, he turned to Ryd. "You burnt that cursed man down, friend."

Ryd's almond eyes flew wide open. "What!?" he cried. "What do you mean?" he asked, already knowing what Digory was going to say.

"Who did you think sat in the Vanguard cage at the Dark Arena?" He paused for dramatic effect, then said, "Edwarde Minney."

"Oh no," Ryd whispered.

"So now you have two Vanguard girlfriends?" Digory teased. "I am impressed, I have to say."

"What?" Ryd interrupted. "Ed? No. She's, she's...she saved my life." His head throbbed with guilt. "I can't believe I killed her father."

"Relax," Digory said offhandedly, "From what I hear, the man had it coming."

"You must promise to keep this all a secret too Digory." Ryd looked at him. "Please, you must. You must! I will owe you everything."

The stable boy's last dying cry echoed in his mind. "No, no don't say that..." he trailed off, then paused. "You have my word. I won't say anything."

Ryd was touched by the hint of Digory's warmth. "I didn't like you at first, but you've grown on me," Ryd said kindly. "I am indebted to you, truly. Thank you for being a friend." He sighed with relief. "Once I find Col, I'll go back to Odion in Littlebell. He's invited us to live there with them. I intend to marry Vera too." He looked at Digory sincerely. "You are welcome to join us."

"Ryd," Digory said softly, knot in his stomach. He knew he had to tell him. It had gone too far.

"I swore to her that I would come back for her, and no matter what it took I would find a way to make Mimi agree to the union, or we would run away together," he gushed candidly. "She said that she would help me raise Col as her own."

"Ryd," Digory repeated, voice hollow.

But Ryd wasn't hearing him, lost in his happy daydream. "I will help Odion and Ed and the others grow the Free Boys, with Collen by my side."

"Ryd," Digory said a bit louder.

Ryd quickly turned his head like a man snapped awake. "What is it?"

"I have to tell you something."

"Tell me something? About what?"

Hector stopped on the path ahead. "Hurry up heathens!" he shouted back at them. "Gallop, now!"

Ryd and Digory exchanged a quick glance then spurred their horses meet up with Hector.

"Good," the grey-skinned man nodded. "Follow more closely," he began trotting again. "Do not embarrass me," he said over his shoulder. "The gate approaches."

"Why was it so empty?" Ryd whispered to Digory. "Nothing like Littlebell's entry, or even the Confines."

They'd just passed through the Onyx Gate at the Northeastern point of the city. Now, they silently trailed Hector Graves as he trotted with purpose in the direction of the Vanguard Villas on the top of a ridge, out of the shadow of the wall, overlooking the brown Missi.

The city here was uniformly clean with swept cobblestones, polished oil street lanterns, and shined windows. Row after row were neat, mixed stone buildings, three stories in height, with modest porches decorated with pots of red flowering garnet vine mixed with blood flowers. The male citizens wore long tunics that buckled on the side, with high buttoned necks and tapered trousers tucked into leather boots of varying styles. They walked like clucking roosters with their chests puffed out. None carried weapons. Women wore long, draping gowns gathered at the bust, in silken jewel tones, with fur or cloth shawls around their shoulders. Many had piercings from lobe to cartilage. Children, boy or girl, wore grey, smock-like frocks with simple trousers and booties. Nearly all citizens, male or female, had slicked down, oiled hair. The women seemed to favor black lined eyes and blunt cropped bobs, appearing to Ryd like well-dressed raccoons.

"We're in the North of the city," Digory replied. "Onyx is closest to the Villas."

"That doesn't make any sense to me."

Digory sighed, turning his head to his under-educated companion. "At Animus Rock, the North is for the wealthy and the South is, well, not." The sound of horseshoes knocking against cobblestones filled the air. "The Villas are for the Vanguards. Only very rich and Vanguard enter through there, except for the occasional merchant with the correct approvals," he gestured back over his shoulder at the Onyx Gate. The trickle of costermongers who followed them each had a red Bellamine symbol painted on their prospective cart. "Usually, Old blood Vanguards enter that way, given the placement. As you can imagine, doesn't see a lot of traffic.

There aren't that many of them."

Ryd nodded.

They followed Hector right, then left through the city grid for several square, uniform blocks, bringing them to the foot of the yellow-stone buildings. Up close, these structures were expertly crafted with fine carven detailing at the helm of each door frame.

"Each bloodline has one?" Ryd asked.

Digory nodded.

From the highest veranda of the last villa in the row came a cry. A shrill voice shouted down, "Why, if it isn't Hector Graves!"

Digory's heart jumped.

Hector pulled his stallion to stop. He looked up. Ryd and Digory followed suit.

"A dagger and thorns?" Ryd whispered to Digory.

"What?" Digory asked without turning his head, searching for where the voice came from. He knew exactly who that was.

"There," Ryd pointed to the doorframe. "The emblem."

Digory squinted. "Thorne," he said.

"Wait right there!" the feminine voice commanded. "Don't move one bit! I'll be right down!"

"I can't believe it," Digory said under his breath and shook his head, smiling wide.

"What?" Ryd asked. "Wait..." he made the connection, "Is that?"

"Sybil," Digory said. Her name tasted like blood on his tongue.

They waited in the chilly shadow of the wall behind Hector until Sybil Brochet burst through the high-arched door of the Thorne villa.

"Why Hector Graves himself, I thought that was you," she said with a wide smile. "Come," she offered her hand.

Sybil wore a dark grey blouse with a high neck, tucked into a black flowing skirt with a slit to her thigh. She looked like a thunderstorm come alive. As she almost always did, Sybil wore the green gem ouroboros pendant around her neck.

She glanced for an instant to meet eyes with Digory, blinked, then looked back at Hector as all three men dismounted and tied the steeds out front.

"Why didn't she say anything to us?" Ryd whispered to Digory. "Did she not recognize you? Does she not know it's you?"

"Just go inside," he whispered back. "She knows."

They followed Hector into the high-ceiling villa after Sybil. Ryd glanced around in unabashed awe at the splendour and finery while Digory was lock-jawed with eyes set on her.

"Why are you here?" Hector asked. "Not at your Villa? Why stay with…" He paused and grasped a gauzy-white curtain, lifted it and sneered. "*This* blood?"

"Follow me up here, will you?" Sybil gestured towards dark-stained wooden stairs. "It is a beautiful afternoon. Will be quite the sunset, don't you think?"

Hector grunted, nodding, not caring for pleasantries or the sunset. Yet, he knew he had a part to play. "After you, Lady," he said, then paused halfway up, turning slowly to address Digory and Ryd. Each had a foot on the staircase. "Why are you following us? Did she invite you as well?"

"Oh, I'd like them to come, if you don't mind, my Lord," Sybil said casually from the top of the stairs. "If there is word from Father, of course."

Irritated, Hector bowed his head slightly. Sunlight reflected off the sheen of his sharply trimmed beard. "Surely," he said.

Ryd looked at Digory. Digory nodded. They followed Sybil and Hector up the stairs.

"You ask why I'm here. Our Villa lies dormant, I'm afraid," Sybil said as they ascended. "As you know, Father has given you proxy at Council for the past few years now, save a solstice here and there. In his declining age, it is too much for him to travel. He made the decision to save our coin and not bother with upkeep. Although, when I am elder, it will be restored to its former glory."

"Thorne because?"

"Montague occupies it," she replied. "Ustin and father are old allies. Rose and I stay with him."

"Ah, yes," Hector brightened slightly. "The girl."

Sybil pursed her lips. "Almost there, this way," she gestured around the bend at the top of the stairway landing, leading the group out onto the fourth story veranda. In an iron chair topped with plush pillows sat a pale, block-jawed blonde man in an exceptionally tight white tunic. Hector froze when he saw him.

"What is this?" he asked slowly, eying the man he recognized as Wolfgar Norland, so far from Echo's Omen. Wolfgar jumped in his chair when he saw Hector.

"My Lord," he opened his eyes wide, then bowed his head. When Sybil glanced away, Wolfgar blinked quickly at Hector. Hector blinked slowly, once.

"It's really quite the treat," Sybil said. She walked behind Wolfgar and placed her dainty fingers on his muscled shoulders. From where he hovered in the doorframe, Digory's hands balled into tight, pale-knuckled fists. "He's an undocumented Vanguard! Isn't that exciting?"

"How curious," Hector said slowly, stepping forward with long strides. His face showed no emotion. His grey eyes stared ahead, unblinking, as if carved from stone. "Bloodline?"

"That is why he is here," Sybil said. "Humphry says he's Thorne. Wallace, his father."

Hector smirked. "Very curious indeed. He will hang for this?"

"Wallace?" Sybil said. "The King has been waiting for an excuse. No doubt," she nodded, a cruel gleam in her eye. Wolfgar swallowed hard and looked away. "His name is Jude Thorne," Sybil squeezed the muscles around his neck. "Jude, this is Hector Graves. He's a very important man, you see."

Wolfgar shook Sybil's hands off, stood, and bowed his head towards Hector. "My Lord."

Eyeing Wolfgar carefully, still unblinking, Hector addressed Sybil as she lowered to a seat. "How do we know he is who he says?"

Sybil shrugged flippantly. "The King commands it is so."

"I see."

"The young man harboured at Lyonshall by Lachlan," she said. Sybil adjusted the plush pillows beneath her until her face brightened. "Oh, I nearly forgot. That is another piece of news."

Still standing, glaring down at Wolfgar, Hector asked, "What more news?"

"Lyonshall has fallen, to Ogo no less."

At that, Hector shifted his gaze to Sybil. "Rupert?"

"Yes," she said. "Surprised?"

"No." He paused, then asked overly slowly, "You are sure?"

"It's what he told me, isn't that right?"

Hector stared at Wolfgar. "What did you see?"

Despite the intense pressure of addressing Hector Graves, Wolfgar stood firm. He'd only met Hector once, in passing while at the Omen, but he knew how to deal with men like him regardless. The same way he dealt with the wild dogs that roamed the perimeter of the barracks. Show no fear. Even if you were terrified. "The Morfit forces were there, but Ogo had his own army too. They burned Lyonshall. Killed Lachlan."

"You saw this?"

"Aye, my Lord," Wolfgar nodded, locking eyes truthfully.

Hector was stoic, furrowing his brows and slitting his eyes in focus. Wolfgar bowed his head slightly, then recoiled to sit, glancing behind Hector at the earthblood men lurking in the doorframe, listening to their conversation. He eyed the tall one's indignant stare and smirked, then looked away. Digory noticed this and frowned.

"We have much to discuss, Lady Sybil," Hector said slowly.

She nodded. "We do."

"What you write is true?"

She nodded again, smiling sweetly. "Sit?" She gestured towards a matching chair to the one Wolfgar was in.

"No."

"No? Oh, Hector. You refuse my hospitality?"

"I do," Hector blinked once. "I have your letter."

Sybil's smile fell a bit. "I see."

"Our discussion can wait."

Sybil bowed her head low. "As you wish, my Lord."

"Do you mock me?" Hector asked, not angry, instead fully curious about Sybil's strange patterns. She was unpredictable; unlike any other woman he had met Kingdom-wide. It was almost as if she altered her personality to suit her company. Like she didn't truly exist at all. How curious, he thought.

Sybil half-smiled and her black eyes glistened. "Only a little," she said.

"You are bold, woman."

Sybil squared her shoulders to him. "Lord Graves, you have no idea."

Digory and Ryd silently observed. Wolfgar sat back in his chair, trying to stay out of it, wary of Hector, still listening the best he could. His eyes were cast down and he fiddled with his ill-fitting, shrunken tunic, like a boy outgrown his clothes.

Hector turned his head slowly to the Norland, distracted by his fidgeting. "What are you wearing?" he asked, each word deliberate. Basil would surely flay him if he caught him dressed that way, Hector thought.

"The tailor hasn't come with clothes, my Lord. I... I...," he paused. "I borrowed these."

For the first time since Ryd and Digory had been by his side, Hector showed emotion, chuckling at the idea of Basil's nonsensical fury. It had been far too long since he'd seen his loon for an Uncle. He preferred the man's insanity to his father's ignorance, surely. At least Basil didn't shrink from a fight. Wolfgar's cheeks turned scarlet and Digory smirked at him in the shadows. Despite the crisp air, Ryd's forehead beaded in sweat. He shifted his weight back and forth from foot to foot, thoughts panicked, heart beating loudly in his chest.

"We will continue this tomorrow," Hector said suddenly, stopping his chuckle as quickly as it began. What an odd man, Sybil thought to herself. "Excuse me, Lady," he added with utmost formality. Hector Graves bowed low to the slight woman. "I will retire for the eve."

"Of course, my Lord," Sybil said sweetly, leaping from her seat, gliding over to his side. "I'm sure you are exhausted. How rude of me. Of course, rest," she cooed. As Sybil rushed to him her skirt opened in a slit with each stride. Her pale thigh flashed. All four men's eyes shot to her warm, exposed skin.

She pretended not to notice.

"I don't trust him," Digory growled angrily. "She isn't safe. Not there." He turned his head to Ryd. "Not while *he's* there."

"You heard them." They followed Hector towards the sixth Villa in the row, nearly at the middle. Above the arched doorway was an engraved emblem of a smiling skull with crossed bones underneath. The Gravesblood Villa. "The King said it," Ryd defended Jude Thorne's story naïvely. "Don't you think he knows?"

"I do not," Digory shook his head. "From what the Brochets say, titles don't mean anything. The King is a dolt. The way he talks, Tomas himself runs the Kingdom."

Ryd rolled his eyes. "I'm sure they checked."

"Checked what?"

Ryd paused. "I…I don't know." He paused again. "Isn't there some place you can check who's Vanguard?"

"Only the documented ones," Digory replied. "If he was never documented in the Tree, there's no way to know."

"Oh."

"Even if he tells the truth, we know nothing of the man," Digory went on as a gaggle of smock-wearing children ran past, giggling. "He could be a rapist, or murderer!" he shouted. A few of the children looked back in confusion at Digory's outburst, then continued happily on.

"Digory," Ryd stopped walking. "Here, come here," he said placing his hand on the man's shoulder. Digory balked at the intimate gesture. "I know you care about her, but she will be fine." Digory made a face and wiggled his shoulders to knock

Ryd's hand away.

"Stop talking like that, will you? You remind me of Leon," he smirked. "Trying to touch me so."

"Very funny," Ryd sighed. "I was just trying to help you." He paused. "Forget it."

"Already have, boy. Already have." Digory scratched his beard and took a deep breath. He exhaled loudly. "It's fine. I'm fine."

"You seem fine."

"Shut up," Hector barked over his shoulder at them. "You chatter like women."

The pair exchanged a glance then fell into silence, following him up the Graves Villa's front stairs, through the high arched doorway.

The décor was so different from Thorne's Villa that, at first, it felt like another world. The interior floor was brushed flat concrete, stained with marbled black, covered in a reflective sealant and appeared to move and flow like molten metal with changes in light. Heavy, blanket-like curtains hung in unornamented, pleated fashion, straight down to block out all light. Metal orb lanterns poked with tiny holes filled with flickering candles hung from the lofty ceiling of the first level. The walls were all painted black. Flames roared in a towering fireplace. Furniture was practical in straight lines, without ornamentation, in iron or wood stained dark. It felt like walking into a moonless, stary night.

Above the fireplace, an ancient, yellowed piece of parchment was preserved behind glass. One symbol, unfamiliar to both Ryd and Digory, was written on it in dark, scrolled ink:

"What's that mean?" Ryd whispered.

"I don't know," Digory whispered back.

Hector paused in the foyer, obviously perturbed, glaring at

the pair pointedly. When neither responded he barked, "Around back," loudly, making Ryd jump.

"What did you command?" Digory looked up slowly, almost like a challenge. Hector sighed loudly and frowned. "I don't know what you intend," Digory added, "my Lord," with a mocking bite. Ryd winced.

Hector disregarded the man's insubordination, considering him equal to an annoying pest. Not worth expending energy on. "Earthblood entrance in back," he said with detachment, remembering these pests were Tomas's so he wasn't to exterminate them. Hector looked from Digory to Ryd, yet neither responded and silence hung heavy in the dark villa with swirled black floor. "Go!" he finally barked and Ryd jumped again. Digory, without reaction, spun where he stood and retreated to the exit. He didn't fear Hector Graves.

"I'm going to tell her it isn't safe," Digory said with eyes straight ahead, boots clacking against cool cobblestones.

"Wait, what!?" Ryd skipped after him, squinting from the painfully bright, early afternoon sun. "Don't do that. Don't go back there. Digory!" Despite Ryd's protests, Digory walked double-speed back to the Villa at the end of the row. "Come on. We're both lucky to be alive. Don't press it. Hector thinks we're some kind of collateral. He wouldn't be happy if we went back there without him."

"Curse Hector," Digory growled with disgust before spitting on the cobblestones.

Ryd sighed loudly and skipped to keep up, "Wait!" but it was too late, for Digory had reached the stairs to the Thorne Villa. He double stepped up them and in seconds rapped loudly on the door. Ryd paced in a circle, thoughts panicked, imagining how horrible the depths of the First must be. Preparing himself for death, itself. "You shouldn't be doing that," he said. "I can't believe you," he added, wide-eyed.

"Relax," Digory said over his shoulder as the villa door creaked open, Sybil's svelte frame in backlit. She looked up at Digory with a blank expression. He stared down at her with a half-smile on his face.

"Well?" she asked sharply. "What is it?" She crossed her arms.

Digory broke into a full smile. "Still as wretched as ever, I see."

"You shouldn't be here," she said in a hush, leaning away from him. "I hope you don't expect me to let you in," she added, noting his unkept appearance, pulling her shawl tighter.

"I did it, my Lady," he said eagerly, stepping forward, ignoring her. "Delivered the letter to Hector, and not his father. It was difficult, but..."

"Do you expect some kind of reward, is that it?"

"Sybil, no, I just..."

"You just, what?" she interrupted again, black eyes sparkling. "You missed me, didn't you, silly man?"

Digory recoiled. "Stop it woman."

"Do not speak to me that way," she glanced over Digory's shoulder at Ryd, standing at the foot of the staircase with head down, "especially not in front of him."

Digory rolled his eyes. "Oh, who gives a curse, it's just Ryd."

"Oh, he has a name?" Sybil raised a brow. "You say that like I care."

"Sybil, I have things to tell you."

"It can't be now," she said waving her hand at him. "There's company." At his stormy expression, Sybil smiled. "That's right, you saw, but you were not introduced. It wouldn't really be proper. Couldn't have anyone begin to suspect. Besides. He's Vanguard. He's above you."

"Of course," Digory said dryly, thinking back to the block-headed man. "He's part of what I wanted to talk to you about."

"Who?" she asked, glancing inside the Thorne villa briefly, then back to Digory. "Jude?"

"Yes," Digory said, "if that is *really* his name."

"Oh, you're being ridiculous."

"Sybil, I have an eye for these things," he replied sternly. "He's lying. And Hector knows him. I saw it."

"Hm, you don't hide it well Digory, but I know why you say this."

Digory frowned. "What?" he asked, hands on hips.

"You are jealous!" she exclaimed happily. "You are, I see it in those earthblood eyes of yours."

"Sybil, please," Digory said, trying to get through to her, fire red eyes intensely studying her perfect features. "We must speak."

"Hm," she adjusted wisps of hair out of her face, avoiding his eyes. "Is there anything else?"

Digory pushed towards her. He grabbed her by both arms with calloused hands. He leaned in near to her cheek, soft beard brushing up against her skin. "When can I see you again?" he asked her in a breathy whisper. She shut her eyes.

"Digory, stop it," she said quietly.

He felt her small body tremble in his arms. "You don't sound like you mean that."

Ryd looked up at the interaction nervously. He began to interject, then stopped and sulked into the shadows cast by the reaching yellow-stone town homes.

"I mean it, Digory," Sybil said unconvincingly. Her chest rose and fell in lust. "Let go."

He ignored her and pushed her up against the doorframe. "I know what you are, woman," he said into her ear, breath hot on her white cheek. "You have all these men fooled, but I see you Sybil," he added, pausing for effect. "I'll let go if you tell me when," he grazed his lips against her neck, up to her earlobe. "When can I see you again?"

"Digory," Sybil breathed.

"Tell me," he whispered.

"I said stop!" she shouted, shoving him away with all the force she had. Digory fell back in surprise and toppled down the front steps, landing hard on his rear on the cobblestones. Sybil pulled her shawl tight around her shoulders, huffed, then slammed the Thorne villa door behind her.

Ryd emerged from the shadows and offered a hand.

"Don't say anything," Digory mumbled.

"I wasn't going to," Ryd said with raised eyebrows, helping him stand.

————=)(=————

Shadows flickered against black-paint walls. A letter lay upon a stark table in the Graves Villa's second-floor study.

Brother in Death,

I write you upon hearing the news, and if fortune holds the missive will reach you before Session next.

The wretch Lachlan has fallen! Lyonshall burned! Your warnings have come to pass. Cousin, dire times fall upon us imminently if we do not right this.

You know as I do – the Lyonshall lines are lifeblood.

It is you, yourself, who advises not to rely on Tomas, however I fear we have no choice. (For your knowledge I reached to Brochet, although have not shared news of Lyonshall, yet.)

Regnard, Busk. Who next to fall to the scourge of the earthblood? You were right, cousin. War is imminent. They grow impatient, but as always, I humbly await my blood elder's command.

Know that we've sent one of ours into your midst there. He's my eyes and ears. He is loyal to us over his kin, that I assure you. You can trust him.

You will know when you see him.

Elder B

Hector stood in front of black curtains half parted looking up at the reaching Animus castle towers. He held the wrinkled parchment covered in Basil's characteristic scribble as he stared out across the city. He narrowed his eyes.

"Curious," he said out loud, with a smirk, to himself. "Curious."

ANIMUS ROCK'S FOURTH TOWER

Herman was concerned. He knew Hector all too well and the man had been quiet on Council for too long. Like a predator patiently stalking prey. As he waited for the Vanguards and high nobles alike to filter into the massive glimmering space, Herman played the potential scenarios over in his mind. How he would quell his brother's characteristic outbursts, if it came to that. How he would keep the session moving, for tradition's sake. Tradition and balance were of the upmost importance to Herman Graves. Aside from his family, that was all he cared about.

The Council Hall sat on the highest floor of the southmost Animus Castle building, the Fourth Tower. This ornate chamber had no windows but was capped in a clear glass to illuminate the would-be dark chambers from top to bottom naturally as the sun drifted from East to West through the sky.

It was very similar to the Throne Room. Each face of the hexadecanol hall was muraled with shimmery tiles in swirling, competing designs, each themed for one of the sixteen original Vanguard bloodlines. In front of each emblem was a thick, wooden desk paired with a high, straight-back chair painted to match the respective emblem.

At the end of the hall adjacent to the entryway was a mural of a fearsome griffin with sharpened talons dripping blood in pale and burgundy reds. The Bellamine emblem. King Humphry slouched in his chair in front of it, and Herman Graves sat at his right hand. Queen Gracea and Verity were side by side in burgundy chairs against the wall, behind them.

The room was dark, and abuzz in a cacophony of voices

awaiting commencement.

There was a matte black obelisk in the center of the hall, pointing straight up to the dome, surrounded by a darker circle with black notches. The sacred dial. After the sun broke a certain height in the sky, peeking over the edge of the dome, it filled the shadow-filled room with light, illuminating the blood emblem murals in a shimmering spectacle. The sunbeams dropped onto the black obelisk and cast a shadow down. There were five notches total.

The shadow fell onto the first notch.

A hush fell as the sun illuminated the hall. All took their seats, except one.

Herman Graves stood from his seat and tucked his hair behind his ears with both hands. He cleared his throat.

"This is the 221st AP Fall Equinox Council," Herman said, voice booming. "Welcome, especially to those who have travelled far. We gather here, as we always do four times each year, to honor our birth right, to decide what is best for our Vanguard Kingdom, together." He glanced to his brother, Hector.

Across the room beneath the daunting Graves emblem, Hector stared, unblinking and expressionless, his hawk resting causally on his willowy shoulder.

"I remind you, no interjections. No outbursts," Herman warned, eyes resting on Hector again. Hector blinked once but otherwise didn't respond. "You'll each speak in turn. We are civilized." A mumble echoed about the crowd. "Silence! You know the bylaws," he reminded loudly.

Of the other fifteen sections, the four extinct bloodline's sections had more chairs than the others. Per tradition, onlookers, high-natives and non-Council member Vanguards wishing to watch the proceedings sat in those defunct sections to observe.

Faye, the wife of Rupert Morfit, sat in the ancient Calvanese's section, in front of a burnt-orange, magenta, and black mural of a bat. She was a sickly pale woman, given her Regnard ancestry, with dull, flat hair to her shoulders, fashionably oiled and tucked behind her ears, with an upturned nose and black-lined green eyes. She wore a golden robe expertly draped around her soft midsection and expansive chest, secured with an opal brooch at her bust. She also wore a pink gem band on her neck. Her husband sat directly by her side. Rupert wore a matching embroidered coat with a dagger at his hip. His legs were crossed away from her. He puffed on his pipe with a wary expression.

Next to them was Simon Minney, darker than Rupert with deep set brown eyes. He wore a pale-yellow tunic with gold buckles and a high neck collar, tied with a braided leather cord.

The next section was void of Vanguards entirely. Only a sprinkling of high natives, the merchant's union leaders mostly, sat beneath Duran's emblem, a mural of a scorpion with pinchers open, ready to snap, tiled in dark golds, tans, and yellow.

Then, there was the Horne emblem depicting a half-clad woman with flowing black hair and pointed horns, smiling knowingly, eyes intensely focused, appearing to follow you no matter where you walked in the hall. A depiction of the Horned Woman, or Emihir Honrne herself, depending on who you asked. The artwork was tiled primarily in black, grey, and pale green. In it sat a young man with expansive shoulders, long red beard, and deep red hair pulled atop his head in a neat bun. From the Horne bloodline's section, Rhain Dale observed, expressionless with slitted grey eyes. He had arrived at the Rock the day prior. He sat back in his chair with deeply scarred arms crossed in front of him.

"Roll call," Herman bellowed. "Vanguard Council, announce yourselves," he bowed his head, "as is tradition."

King Humphry sat forward with a sigh. All the duties that came with his lofty position irritated him. He often wasn't sure why he bothered being King at all. It was so tiresome. "Bloodline Bellamine," he said begrudgingly, then slumped back in his chair. He was already bored of the wearisome formalities.

Next to the Bellamine griffin was a mural of a stylized sunset over a snaking brown river. Busk. A pale, ugly man with an oblong head, receding chin, and close-together brown eyes sat in front of it. He was middle years. His brow beaded in sweat. His eyes darted nervously, like a trapped hare's.

"T... t... Terje Busk," the man said with a shaking voice, gripping his hands together in his lap under the table. Anonymous chuckles filled the air. "I... I mean, B... Bloodline Busk." His cheeks blushed violet. This was his first time on Council, in the wake of his father's recent death. Terje crossed his arms tight in front of his chest tight, hating castle politics, wishing to return to his garden.

Herman nodded kindly, then gestured for the next in queue to continue.

Sybil sat in front of the Brochet emblem mural, the ouroboros. It was a snake with its tail in its mouth, tiled in emerald greens atop an iron grey and black background. She wore her green-gem pendant over a long black gown that skimmed tight to her slight frame, showing off her miniature waist and wide hips. The dress was long to her ankles, only exposing the pointed toe of her shined black boots and high to her neck, with sleeves to the bones of her wrists. Her hair was parted in the middle and left long and flowing to frame her face. It fell scandalously down all about her shoulders all the way to her waist in bouncy, thick dark curls. Her eyes were unlined. She wore a deep red stain on her lips.

Sybil had intended to be disarming and, judging by the looks she got from the others in the hall, she'd accomplished it. The men eyed her with longing and the women with scorn. She was pleased.

"Bloodline Brochet," she said.

The next to speak after Sybil was Cronog Dale, heir to elderclaim after his father Baddon. He had characteristic Dale hair tied in an intricate Baneswood knot on the top front of his head, pale skin, and brown eyes. He bore high cheekbones, deep wrinkles, and a strong jaw covered in a neatly cropped beard. Not unlike Hector Graves's beard, as if he'd mimicked the man's style. On Cronog's sloped shoulders lay a massive coat of layered orange pelts, showcasing his rank.

"Bloodline Dale," Cronog Dale grunted. Behind him was a mural of the skull of a deer and it's sixteen-point antlers in bone white, over tiled browns and forest greens. From where he sat under the Horne emblem, Rhain Dale observed his older brother, silently scowling. He wished to rip the man's throat out of his neck. He would, someday. Just not yet.

The next mural was tiled in turquoises, light blues, and seafoam greens, churning in swirling patterns to match the Rysp lakes. Over that background was the Demos emblem, the outline of a mythical siren in shimmery black tiles.

It was Archer Demos's turn. He had green-tan skin, ice-white hair and a heart-melting smile. "Archer here," he said with a toothy grin on his diamond shaped face. Herman cleared his throat loudly and frowned. "Bloodline, I mean," he corrected cavalierly, eyes flashing, leaning in his turquoise painted seat. "Demos," he added, kicking the chair back, putting heavily calloused bare feet onto the table. Demosblood notoriously didn't wear shoes.

Herman wordlessly nodded from across the room, then shifted his eyes slowly to the next section in line. He met eyes with his brother.

"Bloodline Graves," Hector said slowly. After he spoke, his hawk screeched, as if on command. He sat with a straight back with feet planted firmly on the floor. Hector revelled in the Council tradition yet despised Herman's current pull over it. Although, he was determined to further his own plans regardless of his little brother's mettling.

Herman nodded at Hector slightly, then shifted his eyes to the next in line.

In front of Littlebell's wall-size emblem of a bell in yellow and white and gold tiles sat a man with a furrowed brow and deep creases beside his brown eyes. He looked as if he carried the worries of the world with him. Prihim Minney. His wavy brown hair was cropped short to his head all over, thinning at the back and top despite his relatively young age. His top lip was larger than his bottom and he was lanky, but tall with wide shoulders. He wore an intricately embroidered grey tunic and simple grey pants with a braided belt. He was boyishly handsome, with a dimple in his right cheek when he spoke.

"Bloodline Minney," Prihim Minney said.

"Bloodline Morfit," a woman with a shrill timbre said after that, without any prompting from Herman. A flutter of scoffs and visible eyerolls bubbled about the hall, briefly.

Galla Morfit had a stern glare, rounded face, and straight black hair to her jawline, oiled back slick and tucked behind her ears, accentuating her widow's peak and strong brow, for a woman. She wore an ostentatious gold robe, customary for Morfit Vanguard women, that was tucked at the bustline and looped around her neck. Galla's deep-set red eyes were lined heavy in smudged black. She sat with sturdy legs crossed, and arms crossed as well, tapping her foot either nervously or impatiently, it was impossible to tell. Behind her, a glaring visage of the Morfit Woman of Justice in gilded tiles. Galla and the emblem bore the same expression.

At Herman's urging, the ancient Norland man at the next desk began to speak, then fell to hacking coughs. Behind him was Ravenshroud's mural of two bone-white skulls in profile, facing one another atop a dusky, deep purple background. He wore a black cape over black robes secured with a tight black belt with a jagged dagger tucked within it, around his expansive midsection that jiggled as he hacked.

"Bloodline Norland," Cuthbert Norland finally grumbled once he'd settled himself, rubbing his greying yellow moustache and goatee.

The next seat and section lay vacant of Vanguards. It's mural, a rosebear ripping apart a native, tiled mainly in vivid red, sparkled like flecks of blood in the light.

"Regnard absent," Herman announced loudly. "Next!"

Monty sat in his bloodline's section; a mural of a dagger wrapped in a greenish thorned vine. "Bloodline Thorne," he said loudly.

After Thorne, there were two more murals, both sections unoccupied by Vanguards. The first depicted a howling wolf in silvers, blacks, and browns. The second, the extinct Beaumont emblem of a tiled fist holding a bolt of lightning in golds, grays, and reds. A gaggle of well-dressed onlookers clustered in each.

"Warn is absent as well," Herman noted, wondering briefly where Kensa Warn was, eyes grazing across the wolf emblem's section. It wasn't like her, or Warnblood in general to miss Council without appointing proxy. He noted this as odd and planned to send a missive to see about their status shortly. "Thank you all," he added, eyes glancing around the hall, bowing his head again. "Now, we begin." The room mumbled again. "Silence!" Herman shouted from his place by the King's side. The shadow cast by the obelisk on the floor inched slowly towards the next marking. "Let us commence," Herman went on, eying the time. "Open counsel first, until final mark, then vote on old business." He glanced about the hall. "Who to start?"

Council proceedings could be tedious, but Vanguards were nothing if not traditional. This day was a typical Council session, on the surface, although for those who knew of happenings from around the Kingdom, the excitement was palpable. The Confines was recently burned to the ground. Lyonshall as well. Regnard and Warn absent from Council proceedings. Anyone paying attention was on the edge of their seat. Anyone paying attention knew that the Kingdom was on the brink of war.

Hector stood quickly. "I."

Galla Morfit jumped as well, but Hector spoke first. Herman pointed at his brother. Galla sulked back into her seat with a scowl.

Hector pushed his chair back from the desk then strolled into the center of the chamber, right onto the circle in the shadow of the obelisk. He paced around it with his head tilted up towards the onlooking Vanguard brethren, shadows cast off the angles of his cheeks and jaw. His bird of prey stay perched on his shoulder, only occasionally flapping impressive, golden wings for balance as Hector paced.

"We are under siege," he said ominously to wary glances in the audience. "Everything our legendary ancestors stood for, everything we have today, is in jeopardy." The arabesque of tiles about the hall cast fantastical shadows across Hector's sharp face. "Everything our forefathers did, and sacrificed, for us, could be for nothing." He paused for impact. He had a very deep voice and was quite the orator. He could feel the entire chamber collectively on the edge of their seat. "The Vanguard existence is threatened." Hector paced slowly, heavy boot-steps echoing about the floor. "War looms on our horizon," he paused again, glancing from each entranced face to the next. "War looms on our horizon if we are callous, and unthinking, and emotional. War will come, that I assure you," he said with a frown, "if each of you, right now, do not act."

Hector stopped pacing in front of the King, glaring up at the slouched, bored man with chilling poise and calm. The King furrowed his brow when he noticed Hector's intense stare and pushed himself upright in his blood-colored chair.

"Stop looking at me like that," he said like a child. "Herman," he turned his head quickly, scrunching his face, "make him stop looking at me like that."

"Your Eminence," Herman said softly, feeling his brother's glare hot on them. The King squirmed in his chair and frowned.

"Enough, will you?" he spat at Hector, then turned his head. "Deal with him, Herman. Make him stop," Humphry whined but before Herman could respond, Hector spun, jarring his bird from his shoulder.

The amber-feathered beast screeched loudly, flapping up into the high reaches of the hall's dome as Hector paced with clacking footsteps back to the Graves bloodline seat. "Of course, your Eminence," he boomed as he strode away, returning to stand behind his desk. "Does this better suit you, your Eminence?" Hector drew out the words as he spoke them.

"Y... yes, it does," Humphry crossed his arms, then his legs right over left, tapping his foot in the air, trying to appear that he wasn't as flustered as he really was. Still arms crossed and nose tipped high, he wiggled a few of his fingers. "Carry on."

Herman winced. He knew his brother had little respect for the Animus government and this embarrassing display wasn't helping. If he couldn't right the mood of the room soon, Hector would make a mockery of this Council session. He was sure of it.

At Humphry's go-ahead, Hector nodded, placing each of his expansive pale hands on the table, resting his broad, yet slim frame down on it. He downcast his brow, glaring up under his dark eyebrows in a piercing stare. His hawk screeched again from where it circled in the dome's highest point. The sound cut through the air and reverberated off the walls. Many jumped in their seats.

"War," Hector growled like a rumbling storm's thunder.

Galla leapt from her chair, golden robes glistening in the nearly overhead sunlight. "The Old spreads fear, just as they've always done!" she chirped.

"Galla Morfit," Herman warned.

"Herman, this is a charade. You know as well as I do," she said. "An embarrassment that you entertain." She pointed at Hector emphatically. "He is evil! Unconscionable! Why, why, he is absolutely deplorable I say!"

"Galla, enough," Herman said firmly, although he agreed with her. "He has the right to speak. You know the law."

Hector's lips curled into a smirk from his place beneath the skull and crossbones emblem as Herman scolded Galla. The grim colors, angle of the sun, and dark garb made him appear one with the shadows. As if the emblem behind him was more alive than he.

Galla, with chin held high, huffed in her seat. As she glared at Hector she smoothed her oiled hair, wishing she could punch that awful man. He met her gaze, raised an unimpressed brow, then turned to scan the rest in the room. Galla kept her eyes locked on him as he continued to speak, seething hatred, arms crossed tightly in front of herself.

"She wants you to ignore me," he warned the others loudly,

"because she herself is close to the source of the poison that is seeping into our Kingdom, into our realms, and killing us. She wants it to get in!" he shouted to many questioning faces and disapproving shouts. Representatives of the Fisherman's Fellowship cheered. Leaders of the Costermonger's Union booed. Galla gasped. Rupert Morfit sat forward in his chair.

"Brother," Herman said, wondering what Hector was up to. "That is quite the accusation." He lowered his tone threateningly, locking eyes with him. "Near your point," he warned.

Hector stood completely, long arms dropping to his sides. "I will speak true," he said, smoothing his pointed beard with a gloved hand. "Lyonshall has fallen," he boomed, pausing for dramatic effect, grey eyes sweeping, "to the traitor, Ogo!" He pointed to the vacant section tiled with a terrifying rosebear.

The room devolved into an uproar at Hector's bold claim, until Herman yelled, "Settle, settle! One at a time!" and all quieted in a hush.

"I am not finished, *my Lord.*"

"Hector," Herman sighed, but Hector ignored him and spoke louder.

"Regnard has burned from within!" Hector's command was so believable, he had everyone's ears. "Ogo, the traitor, has betrayed his father. Murdered him in cold blood! Pushed to it, by the madness of the New!" More gasps. The various Vanguards about the hall exchanged worried glances and mumbled whispers, while all natives present, whether servant or guest, shifted nervously in place.

"Hector," Herman stood and leaned forward. "Stop," he commanded. "Your point is clear!"

"What's worse," Hector went on, fully ignoring his brother and the discontent bubbling in the hall, feeding off the energy, "is that he had every justification to come to the crown, to you, King Humphry," Hector looked directly at the immature ruler again, then away to the crowd, "and beg that you back his claim as elder. Each one of us would have voted against the wretch Lachlan," Hector picked up momentum, "and Ogo could have taken the seat without blood. Instead," he paused, and stroked his beard, feigning confusion, "he attacked in secret ambush. Why would he do such a thing? Unless, perhaps, to take control of the Kingdom for himself!" He pointed at the Regnard emblem's section, filled with empty chairs.

"Where do you get your information!? How could Ogo accomplish this all, with no army of his own?" Prihim Minney, the balding man in grey, shouted, spurred to action by Hector's pageantry and his own curiosity. "This cannot be true if it comes from the lips of Graves," he said, dripping distain. He waved his hand in the air, dismissing Hector entirely.

"Prihim," Herman warned the Minney. Galla Morfit glanced at Prihim with a look of concern, then quickly spun her head back forward, steeling her gaze. Sybil was wide-eyed in observation and noted the Morfit woman's action silently. Monty was right. *They are certainly fucking*, she thought.

"Why, even the King knows that Lyonshall falls!" Hector gestured to Humphry. "He can tell you himself, is that not correct?"

Humphry sat up in his chair. "Me!?"

Herman placed a gentle hand on his forearm. "My King, I warned you that..." but, Humphry stood up.

"No!" Humphry shouted. Herman ran both hands though his hair and sighed. He sat back. "What do you mean, I know?!" King Humphry challenged Hector Graves.

"Do you deny it, my Lord?" Hector toyed.

Verity and Gracea looked at each other, exchanging a silent glance, waiting for the King's response.

"I... I..." Humphry faltered.

"Hector lies!" Galla cried, tired of tradition, unable to hold back from screaming the truth.

But Hector ignored her and continued. "Because, of course, you all know the law. As King and Vanguard leader, you are required to alert all the realms of discontent within. As is law." Hector's voice boomed, echoing about the dome, "it is our Vanguard blood right to vote on what to do with traitors. It is illegal to attack a blood castle, to kill an elder. To know of it, but fail to report it, your Eminence, is treason itself." As Hector let his heavy words settle, Galla quickly shot a look at Prihim. Prihim missed her gaze. Sybil blinked as she observed this silently.

Feeling responsible, knowing this could end in disaster, Herman intervened. "Thank you for announcing it for the King, my Lord," he shouted at his brother. "You have done your Kingdom a great service!" he added with overt formality. Hector recognised Herman's intent instantly and was pleasantly impressed, albeit irritated, at his brother's quick thinking. He had aimed to take the Throne for himself. Herman's quick thinking smoothly thwarted him.

"What? He... He..." Humphry started to object, but Herman grabbed his old friend's wrist tight under the table. Although over a decade older than Humphry, Herman was fond of him, took it upon himself to care for him, and considered him like a brother, for his true brother was all but lost to him.

"Trust me," Herman whispered low, locking eyes with his King. "Hector is dangerous, just," he said under his breath nearly into Humphry's ear, "let me handle it." Humphry tensed and glared Herman. Herman slowly blinked at him and squeezed his forearm harder. He didn't break eye contact.

"Your Eminence," Hector boomed from the opposite side of the hall. His elegant bird had returned to his shoulder's perch and cleaned herself systemically as he spoke, adjusting and pecking at her under-feathers with practiced precision. "How do you answer my charges?"

Humphry blinked at Herman, nodded, then relaxed back in his chair. Realizing the King had taken his advice, Herman stood with his chest puffed out to address his brother. "He thanks you for your announcement, as proxy, of course."

"Of course," Hector said slowly, lips curling into a sickening grin. He half bowed his head towards the spoiled brat Humphry. *Herman bests me this time*, he thought, *but there is always next.*

"The deadblood is right!" Cuthbert, the rotund, grey-blonde man grunted loudly from beneath the Norland crest. The outburst threw him into a hacking cough for a second. He sneezed, blew his nose long and phlegmy into his hand, then wiped it across the side of his stomach in a long mucus streak before speaking.

"It is our law! We must vote on the traitor as we did with Lachlan before," Cuthbert Norland said, still leaning back as if enjoying a fool's display. "You young mongrel bloods don't know what it was like before, when the true Vanguards lived. There was decency and loyalty. True honor, justice! The pursuit of our birth right and the glory of our blood. The good times before this *New* insanity! To think! To consider the child Ogo anything other than a traitor for the sin he has acted against his bloodline. The horror." He shook his head, chin jiggling. A cluster of dark armoured men hovering behind him grunted approvingly.

Galla upturned her nose in disgust. *Those inbred oldbloods are the worst*, she thought. *Not worth the space they occupy.*

Hector nodded his head, "Here, here good Cuthbert." Sated by praise, Cuthbert Norland bared his yellow teeth that remained in a smug smile.

Prihim felt helpless as he glanced around the hall. He knew how these oldblood bullies worked. He wasn't sure what Hector and Cuthbert were up to, but he suspected it wouldn't be good for the New. Besides, he was worried about Galla. She was a target. And despite all his urgings and warnings, she refused to soften herself. "I want to know who assisted him," he shouted, aiming to take the heat off his secret lover. "He couldn't have done it alone," he added pointedly, assuming Ogo had conspired with the Old for help. Hector half smiled as he watched Galla glance nervously at Rupert. *Prihim doesn't know*, Hector thought.

"It should be an issue of the realm, left to the realm," Cronog Dale offered.

"Cronog, it is larger than that," Hector warned him.

"Why must it be?" Cronog stood from his seat, pelt coat flapping behind his thin thighs. "Why should I care what happens in their realm? It is their business. Leave Baneswood to herself. Lyonshall can do as she pleases," he said to a series of approving mumbles from his red-pelt clad Baneswood natives in tow, standing in a row behind their Vanguard, tattoo-covered chests bared.

"We are nothing but the sum of our realms," Hector said to him.

"Cronog is right," Galla's tinny voice cut the air. "Who are we to intrude? This is not the Uprising, when Lachlan's betrayal changed the face of the Kingdom! These are times of peace. We should not encourage violence by enacting more violence. We are a civilized people. Our world calls for a new, evolved way of being. Not an old, outdated, stale one."

Monty Thorne studied the crowd. Like Prihim, he'd warned Galla time and time again not to fight the old agenda so publicly because it's what Hector wants, *but she never listens*, he thought.

"Do you all hear?" Hector smirked as if he felt deeply insulted, spinning his head around the hall, nearly overhead sunlight flickering off his precisely trimmed beard's sheen, grey eyes flashing like light caught in ice. "Hypocrite, I say," he pointed at Galla aggressively. "We are all one, except when the item in question fits the Morfit agenda!"

"I'm with Galla!" Archer Demos raised his hand into the hair excitedly, defending the native's champion. "Hellswater votes for peace." But Hector Graves was undeterred.

He lifted his hands, palms outward. "Vanguards, I warn you, it's not so simple," Hector said slowly, as if explaining a complex problem to a child. "The only way to ensure peace is to follow our laws. To stay true to our birth right. We cannot chase fancies and think ourselves sane. Without order and structure, there is chaos. You all know chaos is the root of all evil. Think, if Ogo is not punished, what is to stop your eldest son from chopping you in two someday with a broadsword if the whim strikes him? Nothing. Nothing at all!"

Faye Regnard's hand leapt to her mouth as she gagged at the image. Rupert Morfit looked to his wife and subtly rolled his eyes before turning his gaze back to the greater hall.

"How can we accuse the man if he does not stand here to be accused?" Galla shouted into the circle. "Why, all the bloodlines aren't represented. Your Eminence," she addressed the King. "Hector is just spreading fear. He's blowing things out of proportion. Probably trying to take the Kingdom for himself! Ogo handled a dispute with his father, nothing more. Don't let Hector twist this as he does. You know the serpent that he is!"

"Ogo murdered another Vanguard," Cuthbert barked, raising his bushy yellowed eyebrows. "The punishment is death."

"Galla's right!" Prihim interjected, a slave to love. "To decide anything now, without all of the facts, is premature!"

"Vanguards," Hector said cooly, calmly, and nearly expressionless, "the New fanatics prove my point."

"Fanatics!" Galla screamed in outrage. "Fanatics! Why, he tortures everything that breathes and yet I am the fanatic!" She shook her finger dramatically towards the King, then to Hector, "You must do something about him! About them!" She gestured from Hector, to Cuthbert, to Humphry.

"My King," Hector shouted loudly, "without our laws, all we are is emotion, and look where that gets you." He gestured to Galla.

"Hector!"

"Galla," Prihim warned her softly.

"Oh, shut up," Galla spat, fully irritated at his naivety. Didn't he know she could fight her own battles?

"Galla, enough," Herman said. "Calm yourself or you'll be removed."

Monty and Sybil met eyes from opposite sides of the hall. Sybil half smiled, wondering if he picked up on the same dynamics she did, hoping they could commiserate later, but Monty looked away. Sybil's face steeled and she white-knuckle knotted her hands in the dark fabric in her lap. He was no ally, she reminded herself.

After the scolding from Herman, Galla sulked to sit back into her chair. Hector smiled smugly. Herman shook his head and said to himself, "so much for tradition. This has gone to shit."

He sighed under his breath.

King Humphry overheard and chuckled. "You need to lighten up." He glanced about the room, with all eyes awaiting direction. "Alright," he clapped loudly twice, sound echoing about the high-ceiling dome. "What's next?"

"Your Eminence," Herman said, tucking hair behind his ears with both hands, "we haven't finished deliberating on Ogo."

"Oh, just send him to the Magistrate," Humphry said flippantly. "It's what we always do, so let's cut to the quick of it. Let them decide," he waved his hand impatiently. "I'm hungry. What is for sup?"

"There is so much more of this issue to explore!" Prihim interjected on Galla's behalf, before she had a chance to. He looked at her eagerly for a glance of praise but was met with a scowl. Hurt, he sank backwards.

"Quiet!" King Humphry yelled at him.

"Your Eminence, why not a vote here? If tied go to Magistrate?" Herman replied, trying to reason with the most unreasonable person he'd ever met, other than his brother. He glanced at the time on the floor. The shadow was halfway to the third mark. So much spent already. "Let us try to do things properly, your Eminence," Herman said, bowing his head. He felt like the only one who took tradition seriously.

"Hm, oh alright fine," Humphry relented. "Do it quickly, will you?" He patted his belly. "Sup."

Wondering how fortune put him in this unholy position, Herman said in a loud, clear voice, "Call to vote first item of the fall solstice Council, 221 AP. Voting on the fate of Ogo Regnard, of Bloodline Regnard, accused of being a traitor to his bloodline, realm, and kingdom, for which the punishment is death. We will begin with Bloodline Busk."

All looked to the nervous man under the brown sun and river emblem. There was an awkward silence until Herman cleared his throat loudly.

Finally, Terje Busk spoke with a wavering voice, "V... vanguard." He couldn't send a man to the First, no matter how traitorous. It just wasn't in his nature.

"Bloodline Brochet?" Herman prompted next.

"Traitor," Sybil said quickly, loudly, and cooly. The decision was a simple one to her. As Hector said, Ogo broke the Kingdom's laws and should suffer accordingly.

"Bloodline Dale?"

"Vanguard," Cronog grunted from under his red beard, staying out of it like Dale typically did.

Herman looked next to the white-haired man with his heart-melting smile. "Bloodline Demos?"

"I say Vanguard!" Archer said, characteristically grinning, voting New as his bloodline always did. He didn't even have to think about it.

"Bloodline Graves?"

"Traitor," Hector said slowly.

"Bloodline Minney?"

Prihim cleared his throat. He said, "Vanguard."

"Bloodline Morfit?"

"For the Kingdom's sake, Vanguard!"

"Bloodline Norland?"

"Traitor!" Cuthbert said enthusiastically. He banged his fist on the desk.

"And Bloodline Thorne?" Herman looked at Monty.

Monty paused, bright green eyes surveying the hall briefly. "Traitor," he finally said to a confused murmur. Sybil tried again to lock his eyes, pleased he voted her way, wondering what his reasons were for, but he avoided her gaze. She frowned in an obvious pout, hoping he would notice.

"And I obviously say the man's a traitor," Humphry declared loudly. "Attacking his own blood castle that way. Why, sure he should be punished. So, what are the results? Hang the man and be done with it," he told his Second casually.

Herman, imagining Ogo's hearty laugh and endearing stories, swallowed hard. "I'm afraid you were right, your Eminence."

"What do you say?"

"We're tied," Herman sighed. "The decision will have to go to the Magistrate," he said wearily. "You were right, my King."

"Ha!" Humphry laughed, pointing at Herman, very pleased.

"Course I am right. I am King, you dolt."

Herman half bowed his head. "Of course, your Eminence."

Monty stifled another chuckle under his hand. Sybil tried to catch his eye but he avoided hers a third time. Then, out of curiosity she looked at Hector and to her surprise he was staring right at her. She met his gaze and smiled slightly, feeling an inexplicable draw to him. He was a force of nature just as she knew herself to be. She wondered if he felt the same way about her. Hector nodded to her in a slight bow of his head as if to acknowledge her thought and answer "yes, I do".

Meanwhile, shadow on the floor passed by the next notch.

"It must be downhill from here," King Humphry observed lightly, eyes on the clock.

"Your Eminence," Herman cautioned.

"My Lord," Galla shouted, "If I may."

"Wait your turn," Herman frowned at her. He turned back to the King. He lowered his voice. "While we discuss Ogo, we should deliberate on Edwarde as well."

"Hm?" The King was already distracted.

"Yes, your Eminence, listen," Herman said in a more hushed voice. "As your Second I advise you, let's follow the law on this one, especially since..." he paused, knowing how close Humphry was to ruin, understanding his brother's ways, "just trust me."

Humphry sighed loudly. He looked impatiently at Herman. "On with it."

"Yes, yes," Herman tucked his hair behind his ears again and stood. "A second announcement comes from the King," he told the hall. "Many of you are aware the Dark Arena has burned and Edwarde Minney has taken the Confines." Grumbles fluttered about. "Past that, the latest is he has refused communication. We must decide on course of action. What to do with Edwarde." The room erupted in mumbles. "Quiet!" Herman shouted a bit louder than normal, fully frustrated with the lack of process. "Who will speak to a solution?"

Prihim interjected, "Did Edwarde burn the arena himself?"

"How do we know it wasn't you, *earthblood*, or the bitch there trying to shove the undeserving son into the seat? No, no, the boy Edwarde holds the castle, it's his," Cuthbert grunted. "Good for him. Give him the Confines!"

"Never!" Galla shouted, "Terje, say something! It is your birth right! It is your home!"

"I... I haven't been there in years." Terje looked nervously back and forth from each speaker. "Animus is my home."

"Terje!" Galla shouted. "Stand up for yourself."

"There, you see, the boy doesn't even want it," Cuthbert gestured a pudgy hand to the eldest Busk heir.

"He didn't say that," Galla defended indignantly. "He is shy!"

"Always championing the dolts who can't protect themselves," Cuthbert chuckled. "Stupid cunt."

Galla gasped loudly. "That is unacceptable!" she swung her head, pleading with indignant eyes at Herman Graves.

"What, Galla?" he looked back at her impatiently. "I cannot stop the man from saying words."

Monty snickered silently, eyes darting back and forth from Herman to Galla, despite his pity and affection for the woman. Sybil glared at Monty, steeling further towards him.

"Why should we treat the traitor Edwarde Minney any differently than the true heir Ogo?" Galla asked. "I call a vote on the fate of Edwarde. If we must stick to tradition, then I say we stick to tradition," she said forcefully, glaring at Hector with a half-smile, thinking she bested him at his own game. He frowned.

"Edwarde is not Busk blood, so it is not the same," Hector said loudly and slowly.

Humphry pointed at Hector. "He has a point."

"That makes it worse!" Galla cried. "Then we should show no mercy."

"But, he is a man experienced at the helm of a realm, having lived side by side with old Ralph," Hector argued. "What does this hysterical woman suggest? That we put the inexperienced, terrified boy into the throne of the Confines? The one who admits he wants nothing of it?" he asked rhetorically, pointing at the obviously terrified Terje, then threw his head back and laughed. Cuthbert Norland joined in. Sybil smirked, then downcast her eyes and grinned.

"Hermann!" Galla whined loudly.

"Galla, enough."

"No!" she shouted, tired of the men having all the say. "I want you to call a vote," she commanded. "Treat the traitor Minney as he should be treated." She paused, then glanced from Herman to Hector, locking eyes with Herman. "I don't care that he's your brother!" she screamed, face violet, red eyes about to pop out of her head.

"Galla!" Herman bellowed, more for her sake than his own.

Humphry frowned. "A vote it is, if it'll make you shut up." He looked at Herman. "Take the votes, will you? As long as she shuts up!" He rubbed his temples.

Herman nodded and sighed. "Call to vote second item of the fall solstice Council, 221 AP. Voting on the fate of Edwarde Minney, of Bloodline Minney, accused of being a traitor to his bloodline, realm, and kingdom, for which the punishment is death. Bloodline Busk?"

Terje knew how he must vote, although it wrenched his gut to say the words. "T… traitor," Terje said woefully, gaze glassed, lowering his head. It pained him to condemn even his enemy. There was no malice in him.

Next, Herman looked to the ouroboros emblem. "Bloodline Brochet?" Hector glared at Sybil, as if communicating with her without words. She thought with brow furrowed, eyes studying the desk in front of her.

"Bloodline Brochet?" Herman repeated a bit louder.

At Herman's urging, she popped her head up. "Vanguard," Sybil said, dark eyes framed by long eyelashes. She batted them sweetly. Galla gasped aloud in shock. Sybil glanced in her direction. The women met eyes. Galla glowered in hatred. Sybil smiled at her pleasantly. They had never gotten along. As children, the pair was in constant competition. Now, in adulthood, things were no different.

"Bloodline Dale?" Herman asked.

"Vanguard," Cronog barked. "As I said, leave the realms to their own business."

"Bloodline Demos?"

"Why, Edwarde is a traitor!" Archer exclaimed. Even he couldn't get behind such little honor. Besides, as always, siding New for Demos was easy, done without thought.

Herman asked his brother the same question. "Bloodline Graves?" He already knew what the answer would be.

"Vanguard," Hector said as his hawk cawed loudly, making everyone jump.

"Bloodline Minney?" Herman asked.

"Traitor," Prihim said.

"Bloodline Morfit?"

"Traitor!" Galla shouted.

"Bloodline Norland?"

"Boy's a Vanguard through and through," Cuthbert said, chuckling to himself as if he was pleased or amused. Maybe both. "To the First with his wretched soul!" Galla rolled her eyes in disgust and Hector slightly nodded in approval.

By now, Herman was tired. He took a deep breath and carefully sighed as his eyes fell upon the last Vanguard Council member present. "Bloodline Thorne?" he asked towards the section with the thorned dagger emblem.

"Traitor," Monty said simply, one stretched leg crossed over the other. Sybil eyed him curiously. Was this always Throne's play, vote down the middle, neither siding fully New nor Old?

"It's your turn, my King," Herman looked at Humphry.

"Hm, I say give the man the Confines. He's earned it, hasn't he? Dealing with the old Busk for so long," Humphry said. "Vanguard".

"Hmm," Herman frowned, looking down at his notes.

"What is it?" the King asked.

"Tie again," Herman said wearily. "Edwarde's fate will be sent to the Magistrate, too."

"What are we even here for?" Humphry whined.

The shadow neared the fourth mark on the floor.

Herman rubbed both of his temples and sighed loudly,

realizing they'd promptly run out of time if he didn't keep them on pace. He wondered how the whole Kingdom ran before his involvement. Then, Herman composed himself and said, "Your Eminence, we are nearly through. There's enough time for another topic, then open session will close, and we will vote on the remaining business from last time."

"What business?"

"The weapons policy."

"Let's just do that then and be done with today."

"Humphry," Herman said in a weary timbre, "We must announce the undocumented Vanguard and rule on Wallace. Why, Hector could use that against you as well if he discovers it, which he is bound to shortly. It is such a small Kingdom." Herman lowered his voice, shifting a big closer to the King in confidence. "Why, my brother knew of Lyonshall! *How*? The man has sources. The man has ways…" Herman cryptically trailed off, then paused. "I know to be wary of him because he is my blood," he finally said. "I know what he's capable of. And oh, is Hector ambitious." He paused. "Besides, Galla obviously has business to bring up. We must give her a voice, lest this rebellion fester further. They are willing to work with us, and you, if you'll listen… You have to…"

"Are you though?" King Humphry turned his head. I don't *have* to do anything, Humphry stubbornly thought.

Herman's mouth hung agape, shocked at how little Humphry appreciated him. "I… yes, your Eminence. I think I am."

"We can't hear you!" Archer Demos shouted up at them with hands cupped around his mouth. Svelte Hellswater high natives in glimmering blue garments congregated behind Archer, nodding and mumbling approvingly.

Herman looked up. "The King has commanded we move to the final vote," he said stoically. "We deliberate on native weapons."

"But, no!" Galla cried. "We have to discuss the…"

Herman growled in uncharacteristic anger, "Galla!" The harsh woman was taken aback. She frowned, then slumped into her seat. She'd never felt more unappreciated.

Sybil raised her hand silently into the air. Herman nodded. "Why native weapons? My impression was they aren't permitted." She smiled wide and warm. "I apologize; this is the first Council session that I represent Brochet." Sybil dutifully nodded her head to the king. "I am very honoured."

"Tomas's daughter," Herman said, nodding in recognition. She bore a slight resemblance to the man, particularly when she smiled. Her allure was undeniable. "Welcome. Listen as I am about to recap for the benefit of all since it has been a while since we've discussed the topic. It's the only outstanding from last session. You haven't missed much."

Sybil smiled sweetly again, batted her eyes, and nodded. Galla scowled as she watched from her seat across the hall.

"As you all know, Vanguard law prohibits natives from owning weapons unless enrolled in military force. An exception has been made for Baneswood, if natives hunt or trap, only with their customary spears alone." Many mumbles of "yes" and heads nodded. Herman continued. "Hellswater, Lyonshall, Ironbark, and Croft argued equality. Galla and Ogo championed removal of law." He rifled through the notes on the parchments strewn across the desk in front of him and paced the page with his pointer finger as he read. "Arguments were made that the natives have the right to protect themselves against wildlife or raiders, and to leave them defenceless is cruel. Most natives are no threat and it would improve their lives tremendously. As a counterpoint, Monty argued in the name of Thorne and Graceview, that time should be spent cleaning up the realms first, before this vote is taken. Why give them weapons if there was another way? The natives wouldn't need weapons if the realms were safer, he argued. Anstout and Ravenshroud vehemently opposed the proposal in full, stating that the natives in their realms cannot be trusted with weapons to protect themselves and it is our Vanguard birth right to protect them because we know what is best for them. Cronog spoke for Baneswood, claiming it unjust to apply the same rulings Kingdom wide. He called for the decision to fall to each realm individually."

Sybil sighed. *Of course he did*, she thought.

Herman paused and took a breath. "Given Ogo's recent transgressions and the pending Magistrate vote, Regnard's vote will be left out," he said finally. "As will Warn, in Kensa's absence," he added, noting this down on his parchment.

"Herman!" Galla cried. "That isn't fair! The proposal was Ogo's idea! We cannot vote without him! Nor Kensa!"

"Galla, it is our law," Herman countered, grey eyes burning white-hot irritation at her. "Neither are here and neither designated a proxy. That means they gave up their vote." He tucked his hair behind his ears. "One more outburst and you'll be removed." He paused and narrowed his eyes. "Do not test me."

Fully offended, Galla leaned back and stuck her bottom lip as she frowned. Herman ignored her. He couldn't worry about Galla's tantrum. He was far more concerned about what his brother was up to.

"Call to vote on a weapons policy for the Kingdom," Herman addressed the hall, mimicking the same hopeful tone he had when he started the assembly, despite his frustration with the whole process. "Given the discussion from last session," he explained, "you'll have three options. Vote for removal of the law and equality for the natives to own weapons. Vote to keep the law. Vote to turn the decision over to the realms." He paused between each choice, letting them settle over all listening like a heavy layer of dust. Finally, when all were still, emblem-tiled walls flickering in the sunlight all around him, Herman went on. "We will begin where we always do." He turned his body slightly and looked to Terje. "Bloodline Busk?"

"He can't speak for Busk!" Cuthbert shouted.

Herman held his hand up to the old fat man. "He holds elderclaim, and until the Magistrate rules otherwise, he will be treated as such."

"My Lord," Cuthbert nodded, full of disdain.

"Bloodline Busk?" Herman asked again.

"Remove it," Terje said in a small voice. Cuthbert grumbled

loudly and threw up his hands. Terje balked in his chair and said under his breath, "I'm sorry," as he looked down.

"Bloodline Brochet?"

"Keep it," Sybil said with poise.

"Bloodline Dale?"

"Realm's problem," Cronog barked.

"Bloodline Demos?"

"Remove the law, I say," Archer smiled.

"Bloodline Graves?"

"Keep the law."

"Bloodline Minney?"

"Equality all the way," Prihim said. "Remove it."

"Bloodline Morfit?"

Galla smiled at Prihim then nodded and said, "Equality."

"Bloodline Norland?"

"Are you all mad?" Cuthbert barked. "If we don't keep the law, they'll slit your throats while you sleep! Keep the cursed thing!"

"Bloodline Thorne?"

"Let the realms decide," Monty replied.

"King Humphry for Bloodline Bellamine?" Herman looked to the King, tired of this, wishing it to be over.

"I don't care," Humphry said.

Your Eminence," Herman pleaded. "The votes are close. You must deliberate."

"Make it the realm's problem, he said dismissively, stomach growling, bored expression on his face. "Are we through?" Herman furrowed his brow. "What?" the King prodded.

"Removing the law got the most votes," Herman said slowly, trying to meet the King's eyes, hoping he knew that that meant Kingdom-wide, "your Eminence."

Galla leapt out of her chair and clapped. "A victory for the New!"

"Now just wait," Humphry said loudly, frowning, holding a hand up to her. "I said, it's the realms' problem."

"Unless all Vanguard bloodlines are represented, the King cannot overrule a vote," Galla retorted hotly, putting one obstinate hand on her wide-popped hip.

"You heard me," King Humphry's eyes narrowed to analytical slits and he stared at the dark-skinned woman. "Curse the law. Your King has spoken. Leave it up to the realms."

"Yes, your Eminence," Galla said through gritted teeth.

Herman swallowed hard and looked down.

"I want to rip out that man's pompous throat as he sleeps, the bastard," Galla fumed through panting breaths into Prihim's lanky chest, hidden in the fourth tower's shadow-filled forgotten wing. Some of the only moments they had together were in these halls, after Council sessions, when the rest of the Vanguards milled about Eden, talking politics.

They'd never had a problem keeping their liaisons secret when using these abandoned corridors, until now, all because Sybil took wrong turn after the Council meeting adjourned.

She'd gotten lost, which wasn't like her. Typically, Sybil knew exactly where she was going, always, although lately, she felt generally uneasy. And she didn't have the small book she found in the forbidden East Tower of Westerviolet with her. Her inability to charm Montague coupled with her lack of proper Elderclaim designation was gnawing at her, and in her preoccupation, she had made a wrong turn. *What I get for losing my head*, she thought as she paced the identical corridors of this section of the castle, with high walls in ceiling to floor grey stone and scrolling white iron candelabras with fat white and red candles, looking for an exit, when she heard something. Sybil stopped when she could make out whispers beyond a bend. She crept closer, curiosity besting her quickly, dark fabric gown camouflaged with the shadows. She listened.

"Hush. Calm yourself, woman. If anyone were to hear you…"

Was that Prihim? Sybil couldn't tell, but it must be. Sybil

inched closer. She peered around the corner.

She saw it was indeed Prihim with his hands intimately clasped to Galla's fleshy shoulders. He looked down at her in wide-eyed compassion and full-hearted concern. He gripped her so tightly that his fingers left indents into her skin, as if she'd take off into the sky or explode if he let go.

The dark woman's chest rose and fell as she glared ahead in seething fury. "It infuriates me Prim! How?" She spun her head. "How can everyone sit back and allow horrid men to dictate our lives?"

"My love," Prihim pulled her tense body closer to his. Her golden robes glistened in the dim candlelight, contrast against his bland grey tunic. "What is right will prevail. The truth will come to light. The others will stop pretending."

"You are naive," Galla's scowl broke for the first time and she sighed. She looked up at him. She brought her hand to his boyish cheek, falling to a jowl with age. "It is why I love you."

"Trust me," Prihim whispered, "we'll seat Terje and then the New will control the Confines, giving us the entire center of the Kingdom. We'll figure out what's happened at Lyonshall and get Ogo under control. It's clear he's unseated his father, but why so suddenly and without counsel?" He glanced over her shoulder in thought.

Galla pulled his face back to look at her. "Darling," her voice softened, "what's important is that the New has taken a piece of the East, giving us position over Basil's Omen."

"Yes, but is there no chance for peace? Did Ogo have to murder his father?"

"Yes," Galla said dryly. She sounded tired of Prihim's naïve thinking, Sybil thought, indicating she herself was privy to the plan. Which would make sense, because it was backed by her twin brother. "Enough, will you? It's only endearing for so long," she pushed against Prihim's chest. He wouldn't let her go. "Prihim," she glared at him.

"Where do you have to go in such a hurry?"

Sybil tried her hardest not to laugh in amusement at Galla's frustration and bit her lip, smiling from her place in the shadows.

Galla dropped her hands again. "Fine," she said. "Command me just as the other men do."

"Come on," Prihim chuckled. "You need to lighten up."

"I don't need to do anything," Galla frowned. She sounded as if she may cry. "Let me go."

"I was just kidding."

"You treat me like an addendum," Galla half shouted, half whined at him. Her eyes glistened with tears. "Just like all of those stupid men. Cuthbert, Humphry," she spat on the floor. "Oh, and Hector Graves, the worst of them all. He says pretty words and everyone just believes him." Another tear dripped down her cheek. A smear of eye-lining coal ran down her face. Sybil's smile grew. "I just want to help. What is so wrong with that? What's so wrong with me? Why won't they listen!" Another tear fell and Galla collapsed forward like a wilted fern, quietly sobbing into Prihim's arms.

Prihim pulled her close. "Hush, it's alright my love. Shhh," he whispered into her hair. He kissed her forehead gently.

Sybil was enjoying herself far too much and was disappointed when she couldn't hear. Her solution was to inch forward ever so slightly, but alas, her boot scraped against stone. The distinctly human sound echoed loudly.

Galla looked up at Prihim with vulnerable, tear-stained eyes. He shot his head over his right, then his left shoulder like a startled deer until Galla pushed him away and adjusted her robes.

"Who's there!" Prihim shouted deep.

Sybil's heart dropped in giddy excitement as the call echoed loudly at her back. She hadn't felt this alive in years, decades even, when she would sneak through Westerviolet's halls as a small child, listening to her grandfather's secret business dealings. She sprinted down the hall on balls of her feet as quickly and quietly as she could, although her boot falls inevitably echoed loudly. Sybil's breath quickened and her face reddened as she skidded around a bend, then through an archway. It wasn't like her to run, but she refused to be seen.

She ducked quickly into a stairwell and hurriedly descended dizzying floor after floor.

Sybil didn't stop to look back to see if the Morfit or Minney were in pursuit of her. She could feel they were not. She gasped as her breasts painfully jostled from her hurried decent down the spiral stairs and then held them in her hands as she descended the rest of the way. After several floors, Sybil finally reached the ground. She exhaled slowly; sharp nostrils flared and adjusted her tussled hair. Then, before exiting the only door in the unlit stairwell, she paused. She listed but could hear no one. She took a deep breath, confident she had escaped unseen, smoothed her black gown, and walked out the exit.

Once outside, it took a moment to gain her bearings. She leaned against the castle for support until she did. Holding a dainty hand up to her eyes, Sybil realized she stood on the far side of the grounds, in view of the wide staircase where most of the other Council members congregated and discussed the events of the day.

So much to consider, Sybil thought as she righted herself, assessing the group with analytical eyes, like a snake contemplating strike. She took a deep breath, then sauntered over to them with her ever-enticing smile.

ANIMUS ROCK VILLAS

I t was late. All movement in the Northeast part of Animus had died, apart from the patter of rodents' feet as they scurried down dark, narrow alleyways. Rodents were a perpetual problem in Animus Rock's city, even in the northwest where the villas sat, despite the ardent efforts of the King's men to eradicate them. The city simply had too much waste.

Sybil lay on her back with her hands over her covers, mindlessly moving her fingertips back and forth across raised embroidery, listening to the symphony of rats. She couldn't sleep. She stared up at web-like cracks in the plaster above, imagining she was amongst the rodents, not a care in the world other than obtaining a bite of an apple core or mouldy discarded cheese. She would be despised in that form, but she would be free.

She could hear the rats so well because she'd left the window ajar. Sybil enjoyed a cool chamber while sleeping, although it came with such noise. White curtains hung limp in front of the window, barely obscuring brilliant moonbeams. She lay quietly in the dim chamber, ornately decorated but cloaked in shadow.

Sybil lay peacefully, begging her body for sleep until she heard something different than the rodents. A familiar noise, like feet scraping against stone. Her whole body tensed. *This is what I get for spying on Montague*, she thought to herself, until she brushed those considerations aside. She didn't ascribe to the Teachings. *There is no Law*, she thought.

Meanwhile, Digory crept through the window, carefully placing one foot then the other silently onto the floor. The moonlight illuminated the side of his face as he backed in. His dark beard and hair needed trimmed. He wore an eager expression on his handsome, tan, sharp-jawed face. He held a bunch of red blood flowers tight in one fist, with uneven stems and pieces of dirt hanging from the haggard roots.

"Digory, what are you doing?"

He jumped, startled, nearly knocking over a dressing table.

"Shhh," she held her hand up, angry he was being so loud. She wore a thin strapped sleep gown in incandescent, translucent silk. Digory's eyes jumped to her breasts, basically exposed beneath the gauzy garment. She was obviously cold.

"What the curses," he whispered loudly, gaze locked on her chest.

Sybil half smiled. "Did I frighten you?"

"I thought you were sleeping," he said gruffly. "Here," he shoved his fist full of flowers towards her. Soil fell from the stems across the bedspread. "These are for you."

She glared at him, then glanced down briefly. Realizing her nudity, she crossed her arms to hide her chest.

"Digory, you stole those," Sybil said accusingly. "They aren't proper flowers, and look!" she rose her voice slightly, "you are making a mess! Off," she shooed him away from the bed, then used the palm of her hand to wipe the dirt from Digory's flowers off the ornate sheets. She couldn't believe he was here and yet she knew she should have expected it. He loved her like a dog.

Half pleased and half irritated, Sybil threw the covers off herself fully and stood to face him. With the window ajar and the moonlight streaming in, her angelic nightgown lit up in a glow around her. Digory's eyes softened in desire. He stood with his feet and shoulders open to her, with the stolen flowers clutched tightly in his hand.

It's a shame he's earthblood, Sybil thought as she approached him, studying his familiarly handsome features. The closer she got, the tighter he squeezed until the hearty stems snapped and delicate flower petals shook loose, floating down like drops of blood to the dark floor. Sybil's hair was frizzy and unkept from sleep and cascaded down to graze her nipples. He held his breath. Digory's eyes danced from her rounded breasts to her delicate waist to the dark tuft between her wide thighs, beneath the ivory nightgown as she approached him. *This is it*, he thought, wild with desire.

But Sybil went by him instead of to him. Digory turned his head and sniffed the air at her passing. She smirked to herself and removed a delicate black robe from a hook on the wall. As Sybil tied the robe around herself, it sparkled in the light at each crease around the curves of her frame.

Digory rubbed his hand through his beard and sighed. She'd made a fool of him again and he was all too eager for more. Sybil walked back past him to the bed, and he leaned towards her, but she didn't respond. When she sat upon the embroidered sheets, Digory dropped the bent flowers to the floor.

"Hm," she looked to the sad pile of stems and petals.

Digory stomped towards her. "Forget about the mess, will you?" His eyes narrowed intensely. "This is important, woman," he said as he sat next to her forcefully on the bed.

"The flowers nearly fooled me." Sybil turned her head slowly, smoothing her hair. "What do you need?"

"What? No," Digory frowned, scooting closer towards her. He placed a hand on her thigh. She looked down at the gesture but did not rebuke it. Instead, she raised her head slowly to meet Digory's intense red gaze. "No, it's not what I need, my Lady," he said softly. "It's what you need."

"Me?" she smiled wide, and turned her head away, then back, impossibly long hair bouncing about her shoulders. She rubbed her eye with her pointer finger, then stifled a yawn. "Who are you to presume what I need?"

"Sybil," he said intimately. "Not now." He sank into her coal-black gaze. "I need you to listen to me."

She was taken aback by his sincerity and sat upright in the moonlit chamber. She pushed his hand from her thigh and tucked one of her feet under herself, then turned her body to face him on the bed. She took both of his calloused hands into hers. She felt like they were children again, so many years ago.

"Alright," she said with uncharacteristic warmth. "What is it, Dig?"

"I know how to give it to you, my Lady."

She pulled back from him. "Give me what, exactly?"

"What you desire."

"Digory…"

"I told you to listen, woman." He dropped her hands. He scratched his beard again. "I'm about to give you the whole cursed Kingdom," he whispered angrily.

"The whole Kingdom?" her voice fluttered. "Alright, then. I wouldn't mind the whole Kingdom," she said lightly, scooting herself further back upon the embroidered comforters and sheets. It was exactly like when they were children, when he'd sneak into her chamber for them to talk long into the night. She would tell him all about how she dreamed of sitting in the very top of the Eighth Tower someday, crown on her head while he would listen with delight.

Digory sighed. Sybil was as difficult as she was beautiful. "Well," Sybil crossed her arms. "After all that, aren't you going to tell me?"

"I…" Digory started.

"You what?"

He sighed loudly from the back of his throat. "I shouldn't have to beg to tell you this, you know?"

Sybil's pleasant jesting ended abruptly. "I should have screamed when you tumbled through my window," she said. "I should have you hung for trespassing."

"You are impossible, do you know that?"

She locked his eyes. "It's why you love me." His silence confirmed the truth in her statement. They hung in that moment for a finite eternity.

He broke the trance. "What did your letter to Hector say?"

Sybil softened. It again felt like when they were children, playing in the North Tower's halls, when he would finally catch her in their game of tag and demand she tell him what horror was planned for him by Tomas the following day. "Really, Dig?"

"No, listen," Digory said, trying to get through to her. "It matters for what I'm about to tell you. If the letter said what I think it did, then..."

"What do you think it said?"

"I think you made some kind of deal with him behind your father's back," he replied, to which Sybil was silent. But her eyebrow twitched.

"And?"

He'd obviously hit a nerve.

"I don't know what it was, but it can't be good, can it? To be under the rule of that man. Sybil," Digory leaned towards her. "I don't want you owing him anything," he said with tenderness.

"Pssh," Sybil turned her head, upset Digory presumed to tell her anything about her life. She was a woman who could be ruled by no one, she thought, not her father, not Hector Graves and certainly not Digory.

He studied her deeply creased brow. "I know that it makes you nervous, not having a plan."

"How do you know that? That I don't have a plan?"

"Do you?"

"I... I.." she faltered.

Digory stared at her knowingly and she fell silent. "Sybil, you have to trust me. Let me help you," he said softly. "You know that I'd do anything for you," he added in a quiet whisper, placing a wide palm on her leg again where her gown and robe parted.

Every inch of her skin burned with desire the instant he touched her, but she fought it. Besides the fact that he was as a brother to her, he was earthblood, and of low birth. Any way she considered the matter, he was forbidden. "Digory," she breathed.

"I will make you queen," Digory said in a low rumble. Her heart leapt. "That's what you've always wanted, isn't it? Forget your father, Rosen, the Omen, all of it." He glided his fingers up her leg, into the warmth between them.

She gasped quietly. He was right. It was true. "Digory," she whispered.

He brought his lips to her cheek in a polite kiss, and when she did not refuse, he kissed her slowly down her neck, along her collarbone, and to the flesh of her breast thinly veiled by thin fabric. Her heart fluttered and her chest rapidly rose and fell. He looked up at her as she softly moaned. He stared at her in longing.

Then, without warning, Sybil opened one eye. She snapped to. "I can't," she said in a breath. She shoved him away from her, then adjusted her hair. She sat back up.

"Right." He pulled back. He adjusted his pants. He took a deep breath and sighed.

"Well?" she looked at him with crossed arms and flushed cheeks. *Control yourself Sybil*, she thought. He sighed again in longing as he stared at her. "Digory." Her tone snapped him out of his fantasy completely.

"Truly Sybil?"

"Digory!" She commanded in a hushed whisper. "Tell me!"

"First you must promise me something."

"I'm losing the little patience I had for you."

"I want you, Sybil. You know I do," he said, red eyes burning with desire. "I would do anything to have..."

"I will not bare myself out to you, or anyone."

"Impossible woman!" he shouted, standing abruptly, shoving the bedspread backwards in his wake. "Is that what you think this is? Did you even cursed listen to me? I love you, vile, wretched woman." His words flew like knives.

She blinked at him unable to decide if she was amused, enamoured, or annoyed. Possibly all three. Digory was most attractive to her when he was angry, after all. "I heard you," she finally said.

Now Digory was irate. "And?!" he bellowed, frame backlit by the moonlight outside.

"Hush. Rose is sleeping." He nodded and pulled back a bit. "Your love is not magic," Sybil told him. "I do not owe you anything. Loving me does not give you power over me," she said. "Oh, don't be mad," she added as she studied his fuming brow. "Here, come here," she outreached her hand. "You didn't let me finish."

He looked at her like a puppy and quickly returned to her side.

"Give me what I desire."

"You mean..."

"Make me Queen," her eyes darted back and forth, "however you say you can do it, do it. Give me the Kingdom, and you can have," she paused, "what you wish." She wasn't sure if she meant that, but what was the likelihood he could do what he promised? It was a risk worth taking. She'd deal with the repercussions if it came to that someday.

Digory's eyes sparkled. "Don't act like you don't wish it too."

She ignored him. "So, what's the fuss about? You boast bold claims, Dig."

"What if I could give you something Graves would kill for? A stepping stone to the throne."

"Graves kills for sport," she countered. "That means nothing."

"But she is priceless."

Sybil's eyebrow raised. "She?"

Digory nodded.

"Ah, so blood?" Sybil said. "Lost blood?" Digory shook his head, no. "Then what?" Sybil studied Digory's eyes intently. "Wait," she furrowed her brow. "You can't be talking about..." she trailed off. Could he be referring to the infamous Blue Eye?

"I am."

Sybil squealed through a whisper, "But, she is myth!" brightening with excitement.

Digory felt triumph at Sybil's piqued interest. "She's real. I've seen her myself."

"Oh, that can't be," Sybil crossed her other leg under herself like a girl. "I remember father and Basil searching for her when word spread of another blue-eye, but old Laila had even the King himself convinced it was a rumor. Giacomo was drunk and telling tales. I was just a child." Sybil fell into silent thought.

Digory studied her youthful, pensive face.

"Yet Vera Minney is real."

"She is blue-eyed as the rumors claim?"

"Aye."

"I can't believe it," Sybil whispered, gaze distant, remembering her father's stark obsession with the girl. It was all he talked about when she was a child and largely what she would overhear when she was cowering in the dark corridors of Westerviolet, eavesdropping. At the time she had been seethingly jealous of the girl for captivating so much of her grandfather's attention and, although she would never outright admit it, her jealously and therefore hatred of blue-eyes had carried over to adulthood as well. She focused back on Digory. "This is true?"

"On my life, and yours my Lady," Digory bowed his head. "I've met her."

"And you could find her again?" He nodded. Sybil smiled wide. "This is wonderful," she said, grinning, then her smile dropped slightly, "but how it makes me queen, I see not."

"There is more."

"How could you have more?"

"Is that a challenge?"

"Just tell me, will you?"

"I can give you the blue-eye, sure, but I can do more."

"Digory, what?"

"What if I told you I can give you what you need to bring down the New, for good?"

Sybil hesitated at his bold claim. Surely, she wanted to eradicate the New. That was all any Oldblood Vanguard desired. But still, his certainty nagged at her. She wondered what he was up to. "I would tell you I'm listening," she said.

"I have it on reliable accord that Prihim and Leon Minney are at odds," Digory said as he walked towards the window and rested beside it. He glanced outside at the Animus Rock castle's massive shadow reaching up to the stars.

"So? They are brothers. That is nature."

Digory turned to face Sybil. "I've also learned that Leon is the source of this new mad honey."

"Ah, so that's where it comes from. Montague gets it from that gap-toothed child he parades about," she said in a spiteful mumble. After what she'd witnessed the other night, she hated him all the more.

"Who?"

Sybil realized she was thinking out loud. "Never mind. What else?"

"Prihim knows Leon is connected to the source, but so far, protects him from the Council, and Galla. The news is…"

Sybil finished his sentence. "They're having an affair."

"You already know?"

"You underestimate me," Sybil teased. "Galla does not know that Leon is the source of the honey, but Prihim is aware? He hides from his lover and the Kingdom to protect his brother?" Digory nodded. "Fabulous," Sybil said, smiling. "What else?"

"Leon wants Littlebell and the Council seat for himself."

"As most second sons do."

"Yet he is more determined, and drugged," Digory told her. He was obviously desperate for her approval, like an addict to ale. "Not to mention, he has one curse of a god complex."

"You think he wants his brother dead?"

"No."

"No?"

"I do not think. I know he does."

"You know? How?"

"He asked me to do it."

Sybil balked. "To kill Prihim? You're kidding." Digory chuckled, elated at her reaction. "This couldn't be better," she said.

He'd saved the best for last. "It could," he told her.

Sybil was instantly curious. "How?" She watched Digory remove a tightly wrapped satchel from his back pocket. Somehow, it had remained with him, tucked safely away since he left Littlebell. He opened it and pulled a pinch of the dark, organic material from the bag with his pointer finger and thumb. Sybil upturned her nose. "Tobacco?" She'd never liked the stuff. It was a habit of high natives in Westerviolet, not Vanguards.

Digory shook his head, pacing across the chamber to sit beside her on the bed again. "Something new from Littlebell and Leon," he said. "Mad honey to smoke."

Sybil's eyes widened. "Fascinating," she said slowly. She wondered if Montague had heard of it as she reached out to smell it for herself. The scent brought her back to Westerviolet's city, walking through the drab streets with all eyes worshiping her.

He pulled back from her a bit. "That's not all."

"What?" she frowned, snapped from reverie. "What is it Digory?"

"If eaten, it's poison."

"Is anyone else aware? About any of this?"

"Not a soul," Digory said, low and deep.

Sybil grinned. She leaned forward quickly and pecked Digory on the lips for a long second. "My oldest, dearest friend, thank you!" she cried.

Digory tensed at the unexpected affection. By the time he realized that her body was so close, she'd already pulled back. He then noticed he'd been holding his breath. Digory inhaled and exhaled deeply as he watched Sybil rise from the bed adjust her robe.

"What should I do next, my Lady? I could ensure the deed done by morning, if you wish it so."

Sybil paced across the chamber to stand aside the moonlit window. "No," she said, light catching on the curve of her frame. "Wait." She paused again, furrowing her dark brows. "I have an idea."

First light broke over the horizon in a thin red and orange line that pierced the navy dawn sky. The early air was crisp, and damp, and the fog had not burnt off from the night before. An ominous mist hung low about the city with only the eight high towers and the eleven peaks of the Vanguard Villas rising above it. Flocks of honking birds glided overhead with the rising sun at their right and winding Missi beneath them. Sunrise light broke through the mist and, for a few serene moments, illuminated the scene in a warm yellow glow, reminiscent of a burning fire. The opposing clouds were cast bright pink.

"Where is the mongrel, and…" Hector paused, "the undocumented one?"

"Off to the market, to get there for the start of things," Sybil said flippantly, pulling her cape tight in the early morning breeze.

"Jude," Hector said the name under his breath, thinking Basil couldn't have picked a more ridiculous disguise. However, tagging Wallace for the crime was clever, he had to admit.

Hector met Sybil's eyes knowingly, confused by her lack of intimidation and impressed by her implicit understanding. It was rare that anyone could hold his eye for long, yet her gaze did not falter. Hector knew that he exuded intensity. He wore all black. His bird was not with him, she was off hunting, although his coat was fashioned for it with a detailed shoulder. He sat across the table from Sybil with the rising sun at his back. The morning light illuminated his outline, casting his angular face in menacing shadow.

"Of all covers they could have chosen," she said and sighed into a jesting smile.

"Thank you for the invitation," Hector said slowly, changing the subject, nodding to the table's spread. Despite his hard reputation, he was impeccably polite. On the table before them were five round platters of varying sizes bearing coin-size candied lemons, piled pastries, raw berries and cherries, green-spotted leaf cheese with pieces of bread, and salted meats respectively.

"Of course," Sybil slightly bowed her head. "It is our pleasure, isn't that right Rose?" She glanced at Rose, silently watching the interaction, bundled in a woollen cloak, thick dark hair bunched around her small shoulders. The girl bit into a decedent piece of candied lemon and nodded.

"This is her, then?" Hector asked rhetorically as he glanced at Rose's doll-like face and doe eyes listening to their conversation. She would make a perfect specimen, seemingly unaccustomed to pain. He could sense the power brimming in her, just as he felt it in her mother, and the prospect of experimenting with her blood was enticing. Yet, Sybil's plan was interesting. "To see her is to put your request into perspective."

"It is not a request," Sybil said calmly, but firmly. "It is a proposal."

"If I refuse?"

"You won't," Sybil said. She smiled sweetly.

"You are very bold, Lady," Hector said with an unsmiling, unflinching stare. Most would shiver in terror when faced with Hector's direct attention, but Sybil handled it elegantly. She watched him fill a clear glass with water and take long sip. He nearly finished it then set it down with a clank.

"I have heard that before," Sybil said. He leaned closer to her, resting his forearms menacingly on the iron table, lowering his brow to glare at her with the razors he called eyes. "I'm not afraid of you, Hector," she added, unblinking, warm sun illuminating her youthful face.

For the first time this morn, Hector showed a hint of emotion. "Maybe you should be," he said through the faintest smile. It bothered him that he could not unnerve her. What was she?

Young Rose furrowed her brow at the exchange. Like her mother, Rose was not afraid of the Graves man, rather, curious at his unpredictable ways. Sybil glanced at her daughter. "My sweet," she said lovingly, "take the rest to your chamber."

Rose began, "But Mother I just…"

"Rose!" Sybil interrupted shrilly. "Never speak back to me, do you hear?"

"Yes, Mother," Rose hung her head as she pushed her heavy chair with difficulty. She took three more pieces of candied lemon as well as a piece of cheese for Ellie, asleep in her appointed bedchamber.

"Tell our guest goodbye," Sybil commanded.

Rose turned, steeling beneath her pout. "Goodbye," she said to the strange grey man then skipped away clutching the lemons and cheese in her palm.

"The agreement was made long before you, or I," Hector said carefully once Rose had gone. "Who are you to write a few words and change what has been meant to be? Behind your elder's back, no less?"

"I'm offering you an alternative." Sybil leaned forward in her chair. It creaked and she pulled her white cloak tighter around her. The wind whipped cool at the height of the veranda over the river water, biting Sybil's exposed skin.

"An alternative to Brochet blood? I see none worthy."

"Are you sure?" she asked, adjusting herself in her chair, pressing her body in a way that her pale gown particularly hugged her breasts.

What a silly girl, Hector noted as he watched Sybil's peacocking. "You overinflate yourself," he said. "To assume your hand makes up for the promise of a Brochet daughter is foolhardy."

Sybil looked stung by his insult but did her best to remain calm. "Is that not what I am?"

"The accord is for a child," Hector replied. "Unspoiled. For blood, not a wife," he narrowed his eyes. "Payment is long overdue. It should have been you long ago, but not now."

"I could give you one," Sybil said quickly. "A child. And besides," she added, "I am to be Brochet elderclaim."

He took another long sip of water then set his glass down with a clink. "I doubt that," Hector replied. He knew Tomas. The man would find a way to live forever before he handed control of Westerviolet to a dame.

"Is that so?"

He looked her up and down, growing tired of the games, wishing he could handle her as he would earthblood or livestock. "Even if you could give me a male spawn, it is not enough."

"I have something else," Sybil said. "Something more to offer you." Hector stared at her. Sybil was illuminated from the rising sun. She held a hand up to her brow to block the bright light. "Rose is off limits," she said firmly. She squinted her eyes. "It is non-negotiable."

"I see."

"But," Sybil went on before he could say another word, "I have more."

"What more could there be?" Hector said, crossing one long spider-like leg over the other. "No amount of earthblood..."

"No, no," Sybil interrupted. Hector internally cooled with irritation at her chiding. How dare she speak to him in such a way? *I should marry her just to bear claim to hit her across the face.* "Listen, not earthblood," she said. "Instead of Rose, I can give you the blue-eye."

At that, Hector Graves broke into a sickening smile.

"Now you jest," he said through thin lips. "I don't chase tales." He took another sip from his glass. "Anymore," his eye twitched. He'd spent a good amount of his boyhood alongside his Uncle Basil, endlessly searching for the blue-eye. She was the ultimate pursuit, the ultimate treasure, and to finally discover her would solidify his reign over Anstout for sure.

"No jest, no tale. Truth," Sybil met his hungry gaze. "I can deliver the blue-eye to you."

Hector sat forward aggressively in his chair. "Truth?" he asked. Holding back a coy smile, Sybil nodded. "The Minney instead of your daughter, then? Is that all?"

"No."

Hector seemed amused. "No?" he asked, crossing willowy arms at his chest, buckling the fabric of his black cloak.

"That's right."

"What more is there than myth?"

Sybil poured herself a glass of lemon mead from a bulbous pitcher, then scrunched her eyes at the sour tinge as she sipped. She set the glass down carefully and silently back down on the table. Hector watched her patiently.

"I meant what I wrote," Sybil began. "Brochet to Graves is

strategic match. Why, look to history. The Kingdom owes what it is to our bloodlines. If we unite, we will rule all."

Ah, that is what she wishes. To be wed, Hector thought to himself. "Tomas would never stand for it," he told her quickly, not taking his eyes off her enchanting visage. Even he was not fully immune to her wiles. He imagined the fun he might have with her, if she was his. Although, she was small. She appeared frail. She wouldn't last long. He would break her quickly. "The man despises me. You know this."

Sybil frowned. "I alone decide my life."

Hector was intrigued by her spirit. He wasn't technically in want of a wife, although Millie was a husk of a woman. But, even if he was eligible, Brochet had not wed another Vanguard blood since before Plague times. Such a match would not only cause a ruckus amongst his brethren, but it would also send ripples Kingdom-wide. Many would see it as a declaration of war. Particularly the New. He stood and paced to the side of the veranda overlooking the Missi. Activities for the day had long ago begun. Barges and ferries bustled up and down the wide brown river. He watched them with a detached gaze. "What makes you think I need you?" he turned back to her.

"Every man needs a woman."

"Am I not married?"

"She is no wife." Sybil spat. "You need a suitable one."

"I suppose that's you, is it?" Hector smirked. Briefly the light twinkled in his eyes before disappearing like a candle snuffed out. The razors returned. "What else? Say I have no wife. Say I have no tradition? Tell me, why you? So spoiled. Sheltered. Naive." *And she has no idea about me*, he thought.

"I thought that was obvious."

"Pray tell."

Sybil smiled, studying his grey eyes with her black ones. "I will make you King."

Hector Graves's lips curled into a smile slowly from cheek to cheek as he sat adjacent to her. It was as if she said the charmed word and a hidden door popped open in his mind. "Why would you do that?"

"So I can be Queen."

"Is that so?" Hector crossed his arms and leaned back in the iron chair. His face fell inhumanely expressionless again.

"It is mutually advantageous, yes."

"If Sybil Brochet has this power, why bless Hector Graves?"

Sybil half smiled at his inherent sarcasm. "I told you," she explained. "Man and woman. It's the way of nature. I cannot do it alone."

"Do what, exactly?"

"Conquer. Unseat the spoiled child. Change the path for the Kingdom. Not to mention, gain strategic military position both west and east," she added coyly, then sipped her drink.

The wheels of Hector's mind spun. "You speak the words of a traitor."

"I speak the truth, no different than those before us," she told him, knowing Hector cared little for patriotism. "You're aware of this mess with Ogo?"

"Clearly," he said, losing patience, urging her to her point with his tone. He took a long sip of water.

"Do you know of mad honey?"

Hector nodded. "We've been having…" he paused, "issues in Anstout's southern points."

"Issues?"

"Father thinks the earthblood found an old Calvanese caravan and are making a fortune off of it." Sybil shook her head. "What, then?" Hector asked with dwindling patience. "What does Brochet know?"

"I know where it comes from."

"Where?"

"Littlebell."

"Prihim?"

"Does it matter?" Sybil smiled wide and Hector began to grasp her meaning. Perhaps he'd underestimated her. She may be useful indeed. "That is what all will think if word breaks," she added. "That Prihim is to blame."

Hector met Sybil's intense eyes. "In truth, the honey comes from there?" he asked her.

"Distributed from there at least. I know not where it hails. But you see where my point leads?"

He did. A useful idea indeed. Frame Prihim and cripple the New. It would be like dousing a beehive in water. The idea was brilliant. He nodded.

"Something else," Sybil said eagerly. "I have some of a new product. The word is that it's very, very toxic. Worse than Nighthorn." As she searched in her pocket for what Digory had given her, she added in a tantalizing whisper, "Deadly."

A poison? He'd certainly underestimated her. "Is that so?"

"Oh yes," Sybil nodded. "Here," she pulled out the crumpled satchel. "Quite deadly, if ingested instead of smoked, that is."

Hector moved to take the satchel, but Sybil pulled it away.

"Only a Minney should have access to that poison, is what you are saying? Is anyone else aware of this?"

"No," she smiled.

"Good," he said and paused. Then Hector spoke again, slow. "Tell me more."

ANIMUS ROCK

"I think I'm getting through to her, you know," Digory said over his shoulder, stepping over neatly pressed cobblestones.

Ryd sighed. He followed a half pace behind with the Villas at his back.

A group of native teens in wrinkled cloaks passed by them, huddled together, laughing and shoving amongst themselves. A gaggle of young women in flowing garments with jewel-tone shawls, raccoon eyes and oiled hair followed closely. Ryd watched them pass. Although they were like him, in a sense, because they were native, he couldn't feel more different. He'd never had friends. Never been permitted to roam his realm freely. Certainly, there was no jesting and laughing amongst those his age in Westerviolet. He couldn't imagine truly being free. What was it like?

"You understand if we are successful in our mission, she will be mine?"

"Explain it again."

"Here, not that way, this way." Digory changed direction down a side street.

Ryd yawned. "Where are we going? It's the middle of the night. And I'm bred for day."

"It's not that late."

"How do you know where you're going? It isn't safe."

"Don't be a Minney." Digory turned his head to the teens passing by. "Look, young ones are out."

"It is true what they say, then," Ryd watched the boys and girls flirt back and forth. "Here, natives can mate freely? Pick day or night as they choose?"

"Aye," Digory nodded. "The ones who live in the North, anyway."

"What is your meaning?"

"The poor have less options," Digory turned again, this time leading Ryd down a narrower passage with high buildings with square cut windows and narrow, arched doorways. Their footsteps scuffled. A multitude of stars twinkled in the brilliantly clear sky above. Cool autumn night wind rushed by their cheeks. They turned down a winding alley way, then through a tapered road and down another long stretch with identical rows of town homes.

"Surely the wealthy provide for them."

"What makes you think they'd do that?"

"There is plenty," Ryd gestured around at the fine architecture and manicured porches. "If Westerviolet was permitted to live like this, don't you think our people would help one another?"

"Sure, if the blindfold was ripped away, you'd hug your first mate in glee to start, but once your eyes adjusted to the light, and you saw the world for what it was, who you were imprisoned with in the dark would matter little."

"What are you talking about?"

"People are people," Digory replied. "We're just as likely to help one another as we are to hurt. To be any of us is to be…" He paused in search of a word. "Complicated."

They turned a bend that emptied them into a wide courtyard. In the center was a large statue of a strange, winged beast of legend.

"Whatever, Digory," Ryd said, and yawned again, glancing at the sharp teeth on the statue briefly. "It's too late for your nonsense."

"It's early, not late," Digory looked back at Ryd and caught the yawn. He tried to stifle it, covering his mouth with fist. "This way," he turned down another alley, yawning wide. "Stay close."

"Is Hector okay with this?" Ryd whispered loudly at Digory's back.

Digory flexed his jaw. "Is he your Lord now?"

"I bet you don't want to be on the bad side of Graves either."

"Shhh." Digory ducked down another alleyway then out into a stinking road. Ryd rolled his eyes as the scenery shifted from neat porches and swept cobblestones to something grimmer.

The homes and storefronts in this portion of the city were weathered and ill-maintained. Cracked furniture, useless pottery and other junk sat haphazardly thrown in front of most buildings. The cobblestones ran thick with muck, likely shit, and were all coated in a thin layer of dark-tinted water. Tiny insects buzzed in the air. The road, from end to end, smelled heavy of excrement and bile.

"I thought this was the greatest city in all the land?" Ryd said. He was appalled by the squalor. Even Violet Cove wasn't this bad.

"Animus isn't the gem you thought?"

"I mean, look at that." He pointed to the doorframe of an abandoned storefront. A pile of bodies lay dead, rotting in various degrees of decay. Maggots wriggled. A beetle scurried up a corpse's arm and disappeared into its gaping, shrivelled mouth.

"I don't think it was always this way."

Baby's cries came from inside a decrepit structure with half-caved roof and door ajar. A man in Bellamine colors held a glowing brand to the infant's hip. Ryd recognized that scene all too well but hurried by when a skeletal, scantily clad woman with sores around her nose and mouth beckoned to him from the doorframe. Another man sat with a mangy dog in the crux of two adjacent buildings, huddled and coughing in a tattered pelt blanket. The pooch licked his cheek while he scratched its matted fur. They sat in shadow, nearly unmoving, watching Digory and Ryd pass by in the night without a word.

"It's the King's duty," Ryd said in an indigent whisper, heart breaking for the suffering, "to protect the people. His people," he added emphatically. "At least here, in his own walls. I mean..."

Digory interrupted. "He claims he does."

"How could he? Has he not seen what his city's streets look like?"

"The Vanguards act like all is wonderful," Digory said. "That's why the North city natives never do anything to help the rest. The Vanguards have them convinced that everyone is being treated in the way they deserve. As if the ones with more coin or higher status are worthier, and the lesser are destined to a life in…" He gestured around.

"The wealthy just don't come down here? Shut their eyes? Ignore it all? Leave them to suffer?"

"Aye," Digory said. "Claim if they were cleverer, they'd have coin themselves."

Ryd was distraught. "Surely if they knew how bad it was, they would help?"

"They should be thankful they're in a New realm, not Old."

"But this is terrible!" Ryd shouted at no one in particular through the south Animus slums.

Digory shrugged as he stepped over the corpse of a young girl, barely a woman. She looked as if she had just died, like she was sleeping but with eyes open. She had a sprinkling of red freckles to match her auburn hair. Her once red eyes were dim. "At least these people are free."

Ryd felt like he might cry. Every block revealed a different sorrow and he could barely take it. "Something must be done to help them."

Digory stopped and turned. "Stop trying to save the Kingdom. You can't."

"Vera," Ryd whispered, eyes shiny, illuminated by the first-light cast sky. Digory had convinced him to leave the Villas by claiming it was urgent to rescue her. "It's the only reason I came with you tonight. It's the reason I snuck out. It's why I'm here so just tell me now. Why do we go for her?"

"Hector," Digory said quickly, studying Ryd's panicked eyes.

"Hector?"

He forced a sigh. "I've overheard that he learned that your girl exists," Digory lied. "He's starting up the search for her again." He placed a hand on each of Ryd's shoulders. "I've told

Sybil."

"You what!?" Ryd shouted in panicked anger.

"Quiet," Digory hushed. "If anyone heard us..."

"You told Sybil!?" Ryd growled, grabbing Digory's shirt.

Digory bear-hugged his furious companion. A boar-looking man with scraggly beard and pronounced limp paused long enough to glare at the pair, as if disturbed by the outburst, then continued on his way through the dark streets. "Quiet, will you? Trust me!" he hushed in a loud whisper. "We have an accord. An accord!" he shouted again to quell Ryd's furious bucking. "She wants Vera's information on Prihim, nothing more. In exchange, the girl will be given shelter and sanctuary at Westerviolet. Don't worry," he said deeply, "I didn't say anything about the," he faded off, squeezing Ryd's shoulder where the mysterious scar had appeared back in Vera's cottage.

"You want to rescue her?" Ryd wrestled away. "Why would you do that?"

"I told you, I want Sybil," Digory explained. "This puts me in her graces."

Ryd frowned deep. "Can I trust you? Really?" Digory solemnly nodded. Ryd relaxed his shoulders, then sighed. "Alright, alright. Fine. Back to Littlebell then?"

"Aye."

"I'm not going through the Confines," Ryd said.

"The Missi it is, then."

"Is there no other route?"

"You'd think a man could overcome fear of water, to save his love," Digory said.

"No, that's not, it isn't, I... I... mean..."

"What? Out with it. What is your problem?"

Ryd sighed loudly, knowing he'd already told Digory. "I had a bit of a run in with them in Littlebell. I told you."

"Who?"

"The fishermen."

"You mean the Fellowship?"

Ryd nodded. "Ed saved me." He paused. "It's a long story."

"I need more than that if we're forced to take the long way."

"There is another route?" Ryd asked with hope.

Digory scratched his beard. "Aye."

"Then we go that way," Ryd said, terrified of a reunion with Brutt and his companions.

"Give me good reason," Digory countered. "It's only two creed coins each for a hammock and ladle of water and we'd reach your beau in a few days' time, without doing anything at all. Whatever happened with the fishermen couldn't have been that bad."

"What about the other way?"

"The other way takes twice as long."

"That's reasonable."

"One also must cross Wind Valley," Digory added.

"Oh," Ryd said hollowly. He'd heard the legends of a land so rife with Ancestor spirits, some Vanguards were unable to pass through alive, but only in whispers, as those fanciful myths were banned in Westerviolet.

"Yeah. Oh," Digory said with a sarcastic bite.

Ryd looked up at Digory with pleading eyes. "The Fellowship can't find me."

"They'll kill you? Of course." Digory sighed loudly. "Nothing is ever simple." He paused. "Fine. Fine. The Moon Trail it is."

Digory took off walking at double speed.

Ryd skipped after him. "Are... are you sure?"

"Aye." He offered no further details or warmth. Ryd nearly ran, then hovered at Digory's side.

"At least now we can take the horses with us." Digory grunted. Ryd kept pace. "I'm sorry," Ryd said.

"You? Why?"

"I shouldn't have snapped. You're trying to help. I think I'm going through the sickness. Haven't had any tonic since we left Westerviolet." Digory nodded knowingly. Often Guardsmen would act strangely if they'd neglected to take their dose. He slowed a bit. They walked side by side. "You're just fine?" Ryd asked him, glancing upwards, wondering why the oblivion sickness wasn't impacting him as well.

"I've never taken it."

Ryd frowned. The words crashed like a Baneswood gong in his face. "Never? But..." he paused, trailing off, "you have to. We all do."

"Not me," Digory said.

"Why not?" Ryd repeated. "You have to."

Digory shrugged. He turned down a dark alley, and Ryd followed, frowning.

ABOUT THE AUTHOR

E .M. Willett was born to be a writer. It's her calling, apart from motherhood. She also enjoys baking, gardening and reading. She lives on a small farm surrounded by an old oak forest with her husband, young children and dogs where she writes late into the night.

www.ingramcontent.com/pod-product-compliance
Lightning Source LLC
Chambersburg PA
CBHW060240030726
47493CB00024B/1405